David Annand has worked as an editor at *Conde Nast Traveller* and *GQ*. He has written for the *FT*, *TLS*, *Telegraph*, *Literary Review*, the *New Statesman* and *Time Out*. *Peterdown* is his first book.

T0008702

PETERDOWN

DAVID ANNAND

corsair

CORSAIR

First published in the UK in 2021 by Corsair
This paperback edition published in 2022

3 5 7 9 10 8 6 4 2

Copyright © 2021, David Annand

A CIP catalogue record for this book
is available from the British Library.

ISBN: 978-1-4721-5584-9

Typeset by M Rules
Printed and bound in Great Britain by
Clays Ltd, Elcograf S.p.A.

Papers used by Corsair are from well-managed forests
and other responsible sources.

Corsair
An imprint of
Little, Brown Book Group
Carmelite House
50 Victoria Embankment
London EC4Y 0DZ

An Hachette UK Company
www.hachette.co.uk

www.littlebrown.co.uk

In memory of André

Part One

Walk I

The End of the Line: the Broadcastle Underpass to the Yards

Real-time historians of the neoliberal scorched earth, we walk the line, our collective dreams in tatters but our eyes wide open all the time.

Today, the line is a long-dormant railway line – the old Goods Line – which runs north–south right through the centre of Peterdown. It's been twenty years since a train rumbled along these tracks, but it's still the best way to get a bead on the town, divine its *meaning*, its animating spirit, its *thingliness*.

We start on the hard shoulder of the Broadcastle Underpass that takes traffic under the Goods Line. We're doing the whole thing today: the underpass to the Yards. Four miles as the crow flies, a little longer on the track. We scrabble up the grassy verge. Through a hole in the fence. Pick our way through the buddleia, the scattered shrubs brown and bedraggled on this cold February morning, until we reach the track, dew-streaked and ready to go. The ring road loops below us, but we have eyes only for the twin-gauge beneath our feet. The third rail is our sight line, our divining rod. We follow it but never touch it. We know the spark has gone but honour its once mighty power.

More than a hundred years it ran, this line, transporting rolling stock on to the national network. Twenty-four hours a day, it seemed to hum. Chug-a-chug-a-chug-a-chug-a-chug. The soundtrack to our childhood dreams. Our source of pride. Little Peterdown, the single greatest manufacturer of locomotive carriages anywhere in the world.

3

Not that you'd get a train down it now. Not with the silver birch saplings sneaking through the sleepers. The big blooms of brambles. The weeds, everywhere, that we can't name. Half shut your eyes and it could be New York's High Line, only with more anarchic planting. A more relaxed attitude to health and safety.

But it's perfect for walking. The sleepers are even-spaced pacesetters, guarantors of an easy rhythm. And we're in no hurry. We want to savour this, our last chance to walk the line before the defibrillators are applied. For this artery is getting an endarterectomy, the cholesteric flora scraped clear, reinforcing stents inserted; the hope being that the Peterdown lifeblood might flow again.

It was announced just before Christmas, the Goods Line is getting revived, upgraded, made a key part of the new national infrastructure: High Speed+. The plus sign is the evidence of the ambition. The ante has been upped, this is High Speed *Ultra*. HS1 trundles along its under-channel U-bend at a mere 300 kph. Here we're talking serious speed: the route's new Excalibur trains will levitate on magnets, flying along its tracks at near enough 500 kph.

But where will they go, I hear you cry, these trains of the future? Why, to an airport of the future, of course. It's taken decades of wrangling but the nation has finally had the gumption to say, Goodbye, Gatwick! Hasta la vista, Heathrow! And – after eight years, four transport secretaries, three London mayors, and a near-derailment by our old friend Brexit – finally, 'Allo Avalon. A mythical name for a near-mythical airport. A floating island, off the coast of Kent, opened by the Queen on January 1st, exactly one month ago today. Five runways, fifty airlines, five hundred boutiques and an estimated footfall of 500,000 every single day.

But why such haste to get from shiny Avalon to Peterdown, this city of heart failure, of special measures and mismanaged decline? Well, we've only been chosen, haven't we? Picked out of a parade of fellow down-at-heelers, rusty-belters, post-industrialists. We're going to be the regional hub, the splitter station, the knot

4

in a pair of braces, one side pinging up to Edinburgh, the other across to Manchester.

We try to get excited about it. Our modern-day Masters of the Universe are talking two thousand jobs in the short term, many hundreds long term. A much-trumpeted benefit-to-cost ratio of 4:1. But that's not likely to make much of a dent in the savings-to-devastation ratio of closing the train yards in the first place, never officially costed but felt in the folk memory at something like 1:200.

A shortlist of sites for the station is being drawn up. Proximity to the old Goods Line will be key as HS+ will follow its route through Peterdown, once these old tracks have been ripped up and replaced. Soon the boards will be going up, with the diggers following not long after that, which is why we're here today, walking, trying to find some closure before they make modern this remnant of our ever-distant past.

For half a mile we walk, our heads full of how it used be. The constant freight. The epic tonnage. The sound of it. The smell of it. The way the diesel drifted on a still day. Then, slowly, the trees start to open up, the shrubs recede and we're on higher ground. We haul ourselves up on to an old signal box and look west where we can see the ruins of Eastfinche Abbey, reduced by Henry's goons in his great Dissolution down to little more than foundation stones, save for the old south-facing wall with its famed double arch. It stands still, its shadows dramatic in the early morning light. It was the home, they say, of Geoffrie, our maybe mythical monk. The 'aukward abbot', the truth-teller, the trickster in our midst, always hiding in plain sight.

A couple of minutes later, we reach a footbridge over the tracks and hop the fence to gain access to it. The graffiti on the bridge is self-reflexive, rendered freehand. *Vandalism*, it says, simply, in letters three feet high.

Looking west, out across the river and a couple of miles of fields, we see not-so-distant Broadcastle, that newly crowned tech titan with the high-rise cluster at its core. Tonka toy skyscrapers with tokenistic turbines. Pastel panelling, the newly minted cladding already showing its age. The whole thing feels unsure of itself, ill thought-through. Sketchy architecture for an uncertain urbanism.

To live in Peterdown — low-rise, analogue, more broken than brokered — is to hate Broadcastle reactively. A knee-jerk of envy, some say, a spasm of internalised inadequacy. Others imagine it to be fraternal joshing, harmless banter, every insult an oblique expression of brotherly love. But those of us that live it know that it's more profound than mere terrace rivalry. It's a clash of world-views, of ways of being.

They say that back in 1889 strike-breakers from Broadcastle — then the smaller of the two towns, but already pushier, more individualistic — crossed the River Peter and then the picket line. No one will ever know the truth of it but to us Broadcastle will forever be the Scab Lab, a breeding ground for blacklegs. A Petri dish for spivs and rentiers, like property speculator and asset stripper Andrew Kirk. He is the Vale of Peter's starriest CEO, the main man at Moolah PLC, and, as of twelve months ago, owner of our beloved Peterdown United Football Club.

Beyond the hills to the east of us is the Aspire Centre, Peterdown's so-called business park. Kirk has taken advantage of our focus group-friendly accent by building his call centre at the Aspire, turning nearly a thousand of our fellow citizens into telephonic loan sharks, payday pushers, extortionists just inside the law.

Back down on the tracks we push on through a corridor of woodland to the edge of Peterdown. We know we've reached it when the untamed trees give way. Order asserts itself. On either side, the tracks are bounded by a patchwork of garden fences: wood slat, chain-link, ivy-clad.

We're in Ottercliffe, the thirties suburb built to house white-collar workers newly embourgeoised by the boom years of the locomotive. From the track you see the backs of the houses. Red-brick, ornately gabled. But this being Peterdown, not Broadcastle, they're uniform in size. No speculative extensions, no below-ground excavations, no dormers on the roof.

We pick up speed, eager to get to the urban heartlands, the storied centre of the city proper. Before we get there, though, we're forced to leave the track (by a barbed wire fence) as it heads underground, through the quarter-mile Drewdale tunnel. Soon after it was shut in the late eighties, enterprising acid heads threw three-day raves in the Drewdale, taking advantage of its terrifying acoustics and superb sound insulation. These days, it's stalked only by the fabled tunnel rats, a super-breed, said to be untrappable, cannibalistic, carriers of some unspeakable disease.

Up Baxendale Road we go and then left down Ashfield Street, following roughly the route of the tunnel. The tight terraces open on to the Radleigh Road, the Saxon trading route of yore, Peterdown's main thoroughfare.

To our left we can see the Generator. It's a great splat of spun steel. Starchitect-designed. A bit of Bilbao on the M38. Culture-led regeneration, we were told. Another in a long list of leg-ups and handouts and dressings-down. It's an Ideas Store, according to its champions on the council. An Exhibition Space. A Fun Palace. It's a white elephant, says everyone else. A vanity project. A money pit.

We skirt behind Morrisons, through its car park, and take the shortcut down Snakey Path to where the wire fence has been replaced with a run of hardboard panels, each one hammered into place. We look one way and then the other, before we prise back the third board and scamper through.

To our left we can see the tunnel mouth, this end of the Drewdale sealed shut like the other. There are fewer trees this side, though, less space. The old tracks here are grass-covered, litter-strewn. We, evidently, are not the only ones who know that the loose board is a gateway to freedom, a portal between worlds. On prudent tiptoes, we pick through the aftermath of adolescents' ritualising: beer cans, cider bottles, fag butts, spliff ends. The burnt-out remnants of a small fire. There's something touching about these teenage traces, this hedonism on the cheap.

We round the bend and there she is, looming over the trees: the

Chapel. Our place of worship. Capacity of 20,000 and full mostly to the brim (Saturdays at three o'clock, of course, not Sundays at eleven). You can't keep us away, not with Peterdown United Football Club sitting proudly in English football's second tier (after a decade or two rattling around the sport's nether regions, pretty much semi-pro and always flirting with insolvency). The Chapel may look raddled – the sunken seats, the stooped stands, the asbestos pallor – but she still knows how to party. Kirk has talked about a new stadium, out-of-town, all-seater. He used the dread word: modernisation. But the fans are pre-modern; they're tribal, rooted, readying themselves for a fight.

Clouds roll low overhead. We skirt past the Chapel and for half a mile the view either side is residential. Garden after garden. Some neat, some not. Lawns are piebald; leaves lie in drifts, mulching. The patio furniture is upturned, moss-tinged, winter-weary. We are struck by the ubiquity of netted trampolines. They stand there, lifeless, rusting, empty, abandoned butterfly enclosures of long-gone lepidopterists.

Soon, the gardens give way, the trees part and we encounter it as one always should, from below, its looming monumentalism an unarguable affirmation of our impermanence, our insignificance. The Larkspur Hill Housing Estate. Big, brutal and bloody-minded, it was built in 1968 to house the workers of the Yards. To liberate them from the back-to-backs, the slums, the urban shanty. They named it after Johnnie Larkspur, our king of the cut-up and non-linear narrative. The great unread genius of his day (and ours). Not that he ever lived at the estate, of course. He finished his last work – his characteristically prolix and idiosyncratically punctu-ated suicide note – ten years before they started building. Makes sense in a way. Because it's ambitious, the Larkspur. Wilfully diffi-cult. Uncompromising. Complex. Ahead of its time. In all ways just like its namesake. Which has been its problem, really. Because it also inherited his complex relationship with the law, his capacity for self-destruction, that sense of something forever teetering on the brink.

We pass the Larkspur, through its shadow and out again, to begin the final leg towards the end of the line: the Yards. Or what *was* the Yards not that long ago: as recently as the seventies, big orders were still coming in. Locomotives for the expanding networks of Malaysia and Sri Lanka, huge orders for axles and engine parts. And enough maintenance work to keep the Goods Line humming seven days a week.

The wire fence either side of us is overgrown with vegetation so thick it blocks out the light. Today, the only things that hum here are the wasps. By the early eighties the decline had already begun. Orders slowly dried up. Plants closed. Bit by bit the land got sold off. First it was for housing. The government-backed Ridgewater estate ate up two-thirds of the northern sheds. Then Thomas, Evans & Co. shut in 1983. That was the hammer blow: three thousand jobs went overnight. When Allied & Oakshott closed in '86, Tesco took a 100-year lease on the southern sheds. Later that year, the Goods Line was closed – temporarily, they said, but it's been shuttered ever since.

We reach a mass of brambles, a crown of thorns weighing heavy on the tracks. Beyond it are remnants of the Yards – ruins now, overgrown and unloved.

Still, the names associated with this land can rouse the passions still. The Gaskell Foundry, makers of the first locomotives to run anywhere in Asia. Grenadier, masters of the steam-powered engine. Twenty-five thousand employees at its peak. Their *Rampant II*, as fast a train as any in the world in 1878. And the North of England Goods and Locomotives Ltd, with its royal warrant. The Regal Negal, as it was known. Builders of carriages fit for a king.

This is our land of lost content and it cannot come again. They're all gone, Gaskell, Grenadier, the lot of them. They were swallowed up and wound down. Amalgamated and outsourced. Without them, the city is sick, bereft of purpose. But it's not dead, not yet, even if Excalibur is about to plunge through its heart. The future is coming to Peterdown for the first time in a long time. But where will it stop, this ultra-train, and whom will it serve?

1

C olin looked up at the clock. 9.53 p.m. It always astonished him
how quickly the stadium emptied. The game had only ended
fifteen minutes earlier and already it was deserted. Just him and Kevin
Carter from the *Oldham Chronicle* up in the press box and a couple
of ground sweepers going about their work. 9.53 p.m. Twenty-two
minutes until he was supposed to file his copy.

Colin looked over Kevin's shoulder at the document he was working on. He couldn't actually read any of it but it was clear Kevin had
fashioned at least four or five distinct paragraphs. He looked back at
his own screen. So far, he had ten words.

There was a game. Two teams played it. Nobody won.

Which wasn't actually that bad, he thought as he read it back.
Had it been written by one of the great philosophers of the sport –
Camus, say, or Adorno – it might have made it on to a T-shirt.
Might have been quoted, feted, held up as a pithy commentary
on the illusion of progress and the hollowness of victory. But it
hadn't been written by one of the great philosophers of the game.
It had been written by Colin Ryder, sports correspondent for the
Peterdown Evening Post, which meant that its epigrammatic econ-
omy was neither here nor there, all that mattered was that it was
790 words short.

Kevin closed his laptop and pulled his power cable from the socket.
He turned to Colin and nodded. It was a local football correspondent's nod; taciturn, masculine, laced with a kind of browbeaten

solidarity. Colin returned it and watched Kevin as he lumbered down the steps to the exit.

The stadium was quiet, just the sound of brooms scratching on concrete, the scuffle of paper cups as they were swept into piles. Colin looked out on to the pitch. The floodlights were still on, making the grass look unnaturally green. It was like a crime scene when it was empty, the lights forensic and unforgiving. Which was apt, really. Because it was a crime scene of the future, the Chapel. The site of what would be an unforgivable act of cultural barbarism.

Colin closed the document he was working on and opened another, a computer-generated render that he had recently downloaded. It was the kind that architects produce, an artist's impression of a building to come. In this case, an arena; one that was globular, all-seater, out-of-town. The sky behind it was an uninterrupted blue, the concourses teemed with fans, flags flew prettily from poles. Bolted on to the stadium was an on-site hotel, a bowling alley, an arcade of restaurants and an eight-screen cinema. Behind it loomed a giant B&Q and next to that an Ikea. The phrases that leapt from the document were 'leveraged commercial opportunities' and 'maximising revenue streams'. The stadium was sponsored of course, its naming rights allocated before its construction was even confirmed. Each of the rendered arena's external walls was liveried in the sponsor's logo, each letter 100 feet high. The Moolah.com Arena, an 'integrated consumer lifestyle destination'.

Colin looked up across the pitch at the Radleigh Road End. Football had been played on the site since 1876 when the signalmen of the Great Northern Railway had formed Peterdown Athletic, one of the founder clubs of the Northern Counties Trades and Guilds League. The Chapel had been built in 1936 when the club went professional and renamed itself Peterdown United Football Club. There had been patchy modernisation since the thirties: actual toilets, seats installed on two sides, a better roof on the away end, a network of offices under the South Stand, but it was much as it had been for the best part of a century.

The only genuinely new thing about the club was its league

position: with half the season to go they were, given their size and resources, a scarcely credible ninth in the Championship, English football's second tier. With the teams in third to sixth place entering into a playoff for the final promotion spot, elevation to the Premier League was an actual real-life possibility.

Colin looked out at the West Stand clock, the club's insignia etched on its fascia, the minute hand still buckled from the storm in 1992. Promotion this year and the ground would be hosting Manchester United and Liverpool, Arsenal and Chelsea. It had long been the dream of every fan of the club, but just as it might be becoming a reality the club's new owner Andrew Kirk had announced his plan to sell the land and relocate.

'Is the broadband working, Col?'

Colin looked up over his shoulder. It was Terry Robertson, the head groundsman.

'Yeah, Terry, it's fine.'

'That's good, 'cos it weren't earlier.'

'Well, it is now.'

Terry paused, fingering the fat ring of keys in his hand.

'Not the best game, not the worst game.'

'Yeah.'

'If lad ain't fit, he ain't fit. No point playing lad if he ain't fit.'

'Yeah.'

'Anyway, not a cracker but not bad. A couple of goals. Better than none.'

'That's true, Terry.'

'Anyway, I'll be getting on.'

'Right-o.'

'Till the next time.'

Colin shut his eyes and considered the unarguable certainty of this last statement. There would be another home game in nine days. And then another one. And in between them, an away game. And more after that. And then there would be another season. And another. And they would keep coming, relentlessly, until he died. He had been coming to the ground since he was six, got his first season ticket when he was nine. He was thirty-two years old, which meant twenty-five-odd years of uninterrupted support, eight of those as a football correspondent for the *Post*. He did a quick calculation. Three hundred and seventy-six match reports, he had written, including the cup games, the friendlies, the playoff defeats to Leicester. He stared back at his ten words of copy. Finally, it had happened: he had run out of clichés.

* * *

The Geoffrie was a ten-minute walk from the ground. Colin had heard the pub's back room described as 'spartan' but that didn't really capture the desolation. It was like Sparta *after* it had been sacked by the Visigoths, after the pillage, the looting. The walls were bare, the light bulbs hung from the ceiling without shades. The fruit machine, with its flashing lights and constant chirrup, provided the room's only animation and it was bolted to the floor.

After he had bought himself a pint he walked in to join the first meeting of the 'Save the Chapel' campaign, of which he had been appointed media officer. There were about thirty of them in there, sat at the tables, standing in clusters, analysing the game. A few women and a couple of teenagers, but mostly it was middle-aged men.

Rodbortzoon was sitting at a table on the far side of the room. He was on his own, one arm resting on the ample stomach that strained at his T-shirt, the other twiddling at his tight-curled beard. The T-shirt was printed with an image of socialist realist proletarians staring into the middle distance, with a caption underneath them in what Colin thought might be Armenian. It was one of Rodbortzoon's revolving cast of slogan T-shirts, which he was wearing, as always, under his one cream linen jacket. As far as Colin understood it, the intention was to project an image of maverick European intellectual, all sexual combustibility and academic Maoism. In certain parts of the world – Bologna, maybe, or Berkeley – Colin could imagine him getting away with it. With Peterdown as his backdrop, the overall effect was less Baader–Meinhof silver fox, more degenerate garden gnome.

Rodbortzoon taught HND geography at Peterdown's further education college, where his leniently marked course made him a favourite among the town's would-be shampooists and aspirant travel agents looking to meet the college's requirement that they take at least one academic module. After twenty years in the job, there wasn't, he claimed with great pride, a hairdresser's in Peterdown at which he didn't get his beard trimmed for free.

Colin sat down in the chair next to him, tipped his glass in a silent greeting.

'Let me know when you've finished that one,' said Rodbortzoon under his breath as Colin pulled his chair up to the table. 'I have four cans of the lager in my rucksack.'

'For fuck's sake,' said Colin.

'It's the good stuff,' continued Rodbortzoon, 'the stuff you can only get in the Polish shops. The stuff the builders drink in the morning.'

Colin smiled at the comforting security of Rodbortzoon's heavy but unplaceable European accent – the result, he always said without offering any elaboration, of a peripatetic childhood – which, undimmed after twenty years of living in England, still made him sound as if he had a mouthful of wet pebbles.

'Eighty-seven pence a tin and better than the carbonated piss they serve here.'

'One day you're going to get our heads kicked in,' said Colin.

Rodbortzoon shrugged, phlegmatic.

'What did you think of the game?' he said.

'Well,' said Colin. 'Where do you start . . .'

'For me, the problem of United's midfield is a classic example of the soul of the modern footballer under late capitalism. Turner, obviously. But also Connelly. They are always on. Always trying to be involved. Classic presenteeism. Like office drones emailing at midnight. Reply all. Copy in boss. Make sure everyone knows you are working. They have internalised their paymaster's fetishisation of the appearance of dynamism. Even if you have nothing to do make sure it looks like you're working at all times. Run, run, run. Don't think. Just run. Like Duracell bunnies. Never stop. Work, work,

work. There is no time for pause, contemplation. No time to stop and think, for *vision*.'

'They're footballers. Running around isn't a way of appearing to be doing the job, is it? It *is* the job.'

Rodbortzoon wiped the beer from his moustache, scratched the side of his head, rubbed the end of his nose, sniffed.

'Agnelli,' he said. 'Classic capitalist. Head of Fiat. Champion of Fordist division of labour. Owner of Juventus football club. One day he says to his superstar Platini, "I am worried you are smoking." Today, Platini is disgraced, a corrupted bureaucrat. But in those days he was an artist. Cunning like a wolf. He knew how to run of course but only when it mattered. Otherwise he was very relaxed, thoughtful, strolling about the pitch like he was in slippers. He looks at Bonini, the worker bee, who did all the running for Platini, and says to Agnelli, "You only need to worry if *he* starts smoking!" Ha! Football is about *play*. Turner and Connelly always make it look like *work*.'

Colin ignored this, inured as he was to Rodbortzoon's structuralist analyses of Peterdown's marking at set pieces and his anarcho-syndicalist team formations (*I want always 4-4-2. Two self-organising units of four . . .*). He drained his pint, looked around to make sure he couldn't be seen by the landlord, Kenny, or any of his fearsome sons, and then reached into Rodbortzoon's plastic bag, cracked open a tin and filled his empty glass.

'Of course if our boy had been fit, it would have been different. Garry is a player. He knows how to *play*.'

'Yeah, maybe.'

'Still,' said Rodbortzoon. 'One-all against Oldham. It could be worse.'

There was a shuffle and a shushing from the front of the room.

'All right everyone, listen up,' said a voice from the front. It was Brian Winters, chairman of the Peterdown United Football Supporters Club. He stood up. 'I've been waiting for Colin to arrive and now he's here, so let's get on with it.'

Colin held up his hand by way of apology.

'As I'm sure you all know, Kirk's planning to build a new stadium on the wasteland at the old Grangeham forge. The site is eight miles from the city centre in an area that has no public transport and absolutely nothing to do with the history or culture of Peterdown United Football Club.'

The last of the conversations stopped, chairs turned, the room hushed.

'Of course, Kirk is claiming that it's the only financially viable option, but that's not the case and we know it. We've a great bunch of lads in this team and the best young manager outside of the Premier League. We're going places. And as long as we manage the money sensibly we can go places and stay here, if you know what I mean.'

Colin looked up at Brian. He was in his early fifties, but he was weathered, with his pale eyes and hard dark stubble that went right up his cheeks. He had done fifteen years in the Grenadier Guards, and had the quiet authority of a former soldier, that certainty of physical superiority. And yet he was soft with it. Reassuring. Humble. A steady hand, thought Colin. He would have made a brilliant older brother. Although they'd probably have had to have different mums, what with the age gap.

'He's basically selling it to us like it's a choice between staying put and going up. But there's no reason why we can't get into the Prem playing at the Chapel. And if we *did* go up the money from the television deals would dwarf any extra money we'd get from the gate receipts at the new ground. Now, none of us are pretending that Kirk didn't inherit a mess from the last lot but taking on more debt with a stadium move isn't the way out of this. What we need is an owner that invests in the club. We should be building on this generation of players, creating an academy, finding more local talent. We need a vision for the future, not an owner whose principal interest is using the club as a billboard.'

Brian paused and breathed slowly out through his nose.

'It's bad enough having his bloody logo all over our shirts but the thought of him naming the stadium ... It's just too much.'

The expressions of disgust were guttural, from all corners.

'Now, I know he owns the club so it's going to be very difficult to stop him from doing what he wants with it.' Brian stopped, as if by vocalising this he was properly grasping it for the first time. 'But it's too important to too many people for us to go down without a fight. We need to reach out to every fan, and for that we're going to need as much publicity as we can possibly get.'

Mick Claridge stood up, all nineteen stone of him. It was odd seeing him fully clothed. For as long as anyone could remember, he had attended every single Peterdown game, rain or shine, naked to the waist. Colin knew the man's tattoos more intimately than he knew any work of art. There was the club crest, of course, on his chest, just above his heart. The portraits of players past and present on his arms. The letters PUFC, Gothically rendered in an arc across his shoulders. And of course the number ten on his back where it would have been had he been wearing a replica shirt (were there, in fact, a replica top that would fit him). Colin tried to imagine what one of Mick's shirts looked like when he wasn't wearing it. A yurt maybe.

'We'll be all over it on the podcast,' said Mick. 'Getting the message out to the listeners. Letting them know how much we love the club.'

Colin looked at the ceiling and wondered if this was strictly necessary. Mick's hair was dyed green and white and his two daughters were called Paula Ulrika Faye Claridge and Peggy Ursula Frances Claridge. His was the kind of love that got people issued with restraining orders.

'I know that Mick understands the importance of the Chapel,' said Brian, 'as I know all of you do. I think this is a good moment just to remind ourselves of what we've got here and how it's not just us that think it's special, so I'm going to read you the entry about the Chapel in the *Football Away Day Fan's Guide 2018*.

Almost uniquely characterful and soulful, Peterdown United's Chapel stadium stands out from the bland homogeneity that increasingly characterises league football grounds in Britain. With its famous close stands and brilliant acoustics, the design of the ground ratchets up the atmosphere created by its famously passionate home supporters, collectively known as 'The Steam', whose most youthful and vociferous fans cluster together, loud and proud, in the Radleigh Road End. All away fans that value the game's traditions should grasp the opportunity to see their team play at the Chapel, not least for the chance to sample one of their famous mushy chip butties.

'This is a special ground. We've got to keep it that way. I've already spoken to the police and they say as long as we provide a few stewards that will act responsibly and listen to their demands we can march to next Tuesday's game as a protest.'

'So we're meeting in a pub that we would have gone to anyway, to march along a route that we would have used anyway to get to a football match that we would have gone to anyway,' said Rodbortzoon under his breath. 'A very subtle form of protest.'

Ordinarily, this was exactly the kind of observation to which Colin would have assented with one of the characteristic snorts of derision that shot periodically out his nose, neatly punctuating Rodbortzoon's monologuing. But it wasn't often that he was invited to be a part of a group, let alone given an actual titled position within it, and whatever the merits of the critique, he found himself in the unusual position of having some skin in the game.

'I've got an idea how we can give it a bit more oomph,' he said loudly to the room. 'You know the way that Kirk never normally gets involved with anything? Never apologise, never respond. That kind of thing. But that stuff about fifty-eight, that got to him, didn't it?'

Colin paused. A few months earlier it had emerged that the top APR on Moolah's new Payday Price Promise loan was 1,958 per cent. Which would have been bad enough in its own right, but 1958 also happened to be the year of Peterdown's worst industrial accident, the Beagles Yard Fire, in which seventy-two sheet metal workers had died, and the coincidence had made the ten o'clock news. The story would have likely died had Kirk dealt with it quickly, but his refusal to make a statement had kept it alive for three weeks, cementing its place in the public imagination.

'We're away at Darlington on Saturday. But Tuesday night next week, we've got Blackburn at our place, right? Seven forty-five kick-off. Why don't we all turn around at two minutes to eight. 19.58 p.m. All of us, and I mean *everyone in the stadium*, we stand up and turn our backs on the pitch, still and silent.'

The back room of the pub was quiet, all eyes on him.

'It'll be our way of saying to him: first we're taking back the number, then we're taking back the ground and then we're taking back the club.'

'Very nice,' whispered Rodbortzoon, his eyes twinkling. 'Colin Ryder. Situationist prankster. Ha ha! Very nice.'

'I know a lad at Blackburn,' said a voice from the back. 'He's a big character in their away lot. He'll keep them quiet an' all. They know what it's like to be fucked over. They'll be with us.'

'What do we think?' asked Brian.

There was a murmured assent, a glass raised.

'Right,' said Brian, his voice calm, assured. 'I want you all to spread the word. We want as many people marching as possible and we want the whole bloody ground silent at seven fifty-eight. Get on the social media and tell your mates. This is about more than the Chapel. It's about more than football. It's about Peterdown and the people that live here. It's an assault on our way of life. And we're not taking it any more. The resistance starts here.'

2

Howard Roark laughed. He stood naked at the edge of a cliff. The lake lay far below him ...

Ellie closed her copy of *The Fountainhead* and looked out the window of Create:Space's open-plan fifth-floor office. She had no immediate access to a lake, but there was a corporate water feature that might, she supposed, suffice. It sat in the middle of the Landgate Plaza, gurgling mechanically, a polystyrene cup floating on its eddying surface. The Plaza, located as it was in Broadcastle city centre and surrounded on all sides by vertiginous glass office buildings, was not a place where one could reasonably expect cliffs, but there was a flat-roofed Costa Coffee upon which she could stand, she imagined, for a cliff-like perspective on the water below. She sighed and read on.

He looked at the granite. To be cut, he thought, and made into walls. He looked at a tree. To be split and made into rafters ...

Ellie looked at the polyurethane sample strip on the desk next to her. To be cut, she thought, and used to ensure that all the windows satisfy Article 6 of the Energy Efficiency Act, 1995. She looked up at her screen and its CAD render of a Louvre ventilation system. To be installed, she thought, to guarantee the airflow meets the minimum standards as outlined in Approved Document F ...

She put the book face down on her desk. It wasn't easy trying to live up to Rand's vision of the architect as Promethean hero when you worked at Create:Space doing window schedules for an Aldi on the Castleford bypass. If she had stormed into her boss's office and thrown on to his desk a sketch of a constructivist Tesco Metro she wouldn't just be sacked, she would very probably be sectioned.

It was lunchtime and the office was largely empty. A distant phone rang in the far corner, just audible above the collective buzz of the computers. The company occupied floors three to six of the Plaza's Infinity Tower. Sixty-seven employees in all. The vast majority of them working on new supermarkets. The Aldi project was a big one: a single complex with a 24-hour hypermarket, petrol station, two offices and a distribution centre. Her job was to allocate the ironmongery, which meant drawing each individual window, all two hundred and ninety-six of them.

The book jacket photo of Ayn Rand stared up at her. She was a striking woman, all lips and eyebrows and surprisingly on-trend hair. Ellie took in the cool confidence of her strong nose. It took a particular kind of arrogance to describe yourself as the 'most creative thinker alive', but at least it was exuberantly hubristic. At least it faced forward, walked tall.

The lid on her Tupperware was clipped into place to prevent spillage. Ellie unfastened it and used her fork to fluff her couscous and roast vegetables. She was eating *al desko*, as they said. She listlessly picked up the book. It had been given to her by an old friend from university, an acknowledgement of her recent completion of her part threes. She had been a fully qualified architect for two weeks now, a mere nine years behind those of her peers who had managed to reach their twenty-fourth birthdays without getting themselves pregnant.

Feeling listless and snarled up with irritation, she logged on to her Facebook page through her phone. She clicked on the link that took her to her petition page: '*I call on the Department of Digital, Culture, Media and Sport to award Grade II listing to Agosto and Marjorie Blofeld's Larkspur Hill Housing Estate.*' She read down the list of names. One hundred and seventy-three signatories, including six more that morning. Not a terrible start.

The picture at the top of the page was of the estate shot from a nearby hill. It showed the complex of buildings whole, its five distinct sections and the dramatic interplay of concourses and plazas that connected them. You could see the signs of wear, the areas of neglect, but it was surely obvious, just from this one picture, that it was a landmark structure, a building of authentic artistic significance.

Slowly the background babble got louder as her colleagues returned to their desks. Ellie started once more on her lunch. The courgette was charred, coated in rosemary and oil. Unenthusiastically she speared a piece with her fork, wishing she had something hot, a soup or stew to warm her bones.

Someone had left the office copy of the *Architects' Journal* nearby. Against her better judgement she put down the book, picked up the magazine and let the pages fall open at random. It was an interior shot. The room in the photo was stark and cavernous, its vast concrete walls studded with tiny windows, sunlight streaming through them in reverent shafts. If you didn't know what it was you might have imagined it was the basilica of a cathedral built by the adherents of an austere alien faith. Which wasn't bad, when you thought about it, for the baggage reclaim of the new London Avalon airport.

The thing that really frustrated her about the new airport wasn't that it represented a kind of collective eco-suicide, although it obviously did. Nor was it the impact it was having on the paths of the migrating birds, although that was reprehensible too. No, the thing that really pissed her off about it was that it was the best thing built in Britain in her adult lifetime. That and the fact that the alpha male of her year at university, Benjamin Willis, had worked on it.

She turned the page. A single image occupied the centre spread. It was a bird's eye perspective illustrating the symmetry of the vast floating platform, its five runways radiating outwards from the central knot of access roads and waiting bays that circled the terminal. From the sky it looked oddly like a Rorschach blot. She smiled ruefully. Something on to which you could project your desires and fears.

She turned the page again. The money shot. A full-length exterior taken from the coast of the Isle of Grain. The terminal reared out of the sea like a pillar of salt, craggy, monumental, the finest piece of engineering for decades. It was surrounded on all sides by water, the whole thing – runways, terminals, loading bays – constructed on a huge floating deck anchored to the seabed. It had some bewildering technology built into it which allowed it to move in tune with the sea in a way that somehow didn't impact on the planes' GPS systems. As she had opined to anyone who would listen, this ability to accommodate the changing sea level meant that when the air travel it engendered had obliterated Kent and Essex, it would survive for a species of the future to puzzle over, like a floating Ozymandias.

She looked at the images of the train tunnels that ran from the Kent coast under the water to the airport. There was a photo of one of the trains that were already running into St Pancras. They were second-generation bullet trains, a European update on the Japanese original. They had been named Excalibur, and if you squinted they did look a little like swords with their long aerodynamic noses.

The next page was an interior shot. It was inescapably corporate architecture, of course. Home to upscale boutiques, sushi belts, and a champagne bar longer than her street. But it was corporate architecture that had taken flight. You didn't want intimacy at an airport. You didn't want nearness, or warmth. You wanted scale, glass, metal; the technological sublime.

She took a bite of roasted red pepper, single grains of couscous sticking to it like burrs on a sock. It was 1.54 p.m. Six minutes until she had to return to window number 66A (2) and its self-cleaning glass. She logged back on to Facebook and clicked on to Benjamin's page.

The posts were excitable, extensively liked. There were photos of an office space, tired old fittings being stripped back, carpets being pulled up to reveal period floorboards, a close-up of four original Verner Panton chairs bought, apparently, for a song at a car boot sale.

Benjamin was in some of the photos himself, a mask pinching at his nose, his hair full of dust as he happily hacked away at a suspended ceiling. She clicked on a link to his website proper. It was still just a holding page but it had a touch of class to it: clean lines, minimal text, a demure font. *Willis and Carlisle Architects.*

No one had been surprised when he announced that he and Chris

24

Carlisle were striking out on their own. For the last three years he had been the de facto face of the airport design team, his square jaw always at the centre of the ubiquitous magazine profiles of the practice, his unkempt public-schoolboy hair bouncing about artlessly as he explained the airport's intricacies to the fawning hacks on *Newsnight* and *The Culture Show*.

Ellie caught sight of *The Fountainhead* lying on her desk. It had been the great in-joke at university. For a full term Benjamin and his five cronies, all boys of course, had each carried a copy with them everywhere they went, reading faux-earnestly from it in seminars, even submitting as assessed work sketches based on one of Roark's buildings.

She picked up the book, all 753 pages of it. She hadn't read it back then, haughtily certain that Benjamin's relationship to Rand's objectivism was slightly more complex than simple irony. But looking back she conceded that they had been more knowing than she had given them credit for at the time.

And it was good of him to have not only signed her petition but also posted a link to her blog on his page. She clicked on it. *Larkspur Watch*. Her most recent post was a slideshow of six photos of the estate's central structure, Europa House. Constructed from a series of hexagonal modular pods in a patternless, seemingly random way, it was a building that – for all its angularity and techno-futurism – seemed to be emerging organically out of the hill, the first stirrings of a geological evolutionary leap.

She scrolled through the pictures and felt once more a piercing sadness at the state of it. In the last two months alone, three separate flats had had the dreaded blue metal panels bolted over their windows and doors. It made them look like they'd been blindfolded and gagged, prepared for extraordinary rendition. The council claimed that they weren't deliberately emptying it, but there were six thousand people on Peterdown's social housing waiting list, any of whom could have moved into one of those three flats.

'Total failure of a building,' said the voice from over her shoulder. 'Finally getting what's coming to it by the looks of things.'

25

It was Glyn Cook, the office truth-teller. He read mass-market military history and wore his office pass clipped to his belt.

Ellie closed her eyes and breathed calmly through her nose. She opened her eyes. He was still there.

'I can't believe you think that'll ever get listed. I'd blow the bloody thing up tomorrow if it was up to me.'

'That's good to know, Glyn, because I had heard you were in the running to be the next secretary of state.'

Ellie sat at her desk, looking at Glyn's reaction reflected in her screen. He was impassive, eerily still, like a reptile on a branch.

'The only way to sort that estate is to pull it down and start again. It's obvious to anyone. It's just common sense.'

'It's the most architecturally significant building for fifty miles in all directions. Tearing it down would be an act of cultural vandalism on a par with burning a Rothko.'

'That's as may be,' said Glyn, 'but nobody has to live in a Rothko. He can be as "monumentally abrupt" as he likes.'

Monumentally abrupt. He was quoting her, from her blog, the git. Always the contrarian. A wind-up merchant. She could easily imagine him arguing the other side in different company, eager for the back and forth, the feint and jab. She turned to face him.

'But people do have to live in the Larkspur,' continued Glyn, unimpressed in his short-sleeve shirt and tie. 'And buildings need to function. They need to not be damp and cold. Concrete might work in the South of France but not in England. We need buildings that are light, airy. I don't know why we didn't properly embrace the International Style.'

Ellie's brow furrowed disbelievingly.

'It would have been a natural progression from the Deco stuff that works so well in Essex and Dorset. Look at the Isokon. Best building in London. Radical and genuinely formalist. An actual function-led building. The great lie of brutalism is that it's primarily functional.'

Ellie sat in her chair gobsmacked.

'*Glyn,*' she said eventually.

'It all went wrong for Le Corbusier after the Villa Savoye. That was a building with harmony and balance and grace. You lot and your cult of ugliness, I'll never get my head round it.'

'Oh my god, Glyn. I mean, you're wrong on so many fronts. All the damp issues at the Larkspur could be sorted with a bit of cash and you know it. And the Villa Savoye? That's like saying that *Help!* is the best Beatles album. So much that came after it is just obviously superior. The Unités, Notre Dame du Haut ...'

Glyn dismissed her with a wave of his hand and turned to walk back to his desk, his high, proud bottom neatly ensconced in his leisure slacks.

For the next hour she worked, plugging numbers into a spread-sheet, cross-referencing them against the master document, making sure the outcomes corresponded with the render.

Once her eyes could focus no longer she got up and made herself a cup of tea. When she sat down again, she checked her petition to see if she had any new signatures. She didn't. She absentmindedly clicked on the embedded link that took her through to the Larkspur's Wikipedia page. In the fraction of a second it took her eye to scan the shape of the paragraphs she knew. Three new lines had been added. It had happened again.

Frequently voted one of Britain's ugliest buildings the housing estate has become a byword for urban blight with record levels of muggings and gang-related activity. Rumoured to be a no-go area for the local police, the estate's urine-soaked lifts are repeatedly vandalised forcing young mothers on the upper floors to carry their children up dozens of flights of steps. One of the many criticisms of the large concrete blocks, which alienate their inhabitants causing the estate's unusually high level of antisocial behaviour.

This was the third time in three weeks that someone had added a paragraph like this to the listing. The wording had been different every time but it was basically the same mix of half-truths and out-right libel. She looked up the author. Joe1968. A new person. She glared at Glyn accusingly. Was it him? The thought struck her that it might be part of some elaborate, elliptical declaration of a twisted kind of love, the kind of thing stalkers did right before they started breaking in through your bedroom window. No, she realised almost instantly. Glyn took pride in still drawing by hand. This was nothing to do with him. He had barely mastered email.

Above her, the neon lights hummed like a mosquito. Ellie sat up in her chair. This was bigger surely than Glyn Cook and his nylon tie. The Wikipedia edits had started just after the launch of her petition. It couldn't have been a coincidence. Something odd was going on.

She felt her breath quicken. She had made a statement of intent and this was the reaction. She felt newly energised, alert. After eighteen months of drawing window sections at last something was at stake. She placed her empty Tupperware back in her bag. The Larkspur was under attack and it was her job to defend it.

3

Unlike the unremarkable low-rise red-brick buildings that comprised the actual school, the playground at St Kilda's was an unexpected architectural delight. Surrounded on three sides by a low-level fence, its tarmac expanse was dominated by a single metal climbing frame constructed in roughly the shape of an aeroplane, or a giant mythological bird. Two large wings curved simply in austere bent steel. Swings hung from elliptical supports. A slide thrust, tongue-like, from the structure's head. It might not have been at his usual scale but there was, Ellie felt, something undeniably Niemeyer-ish about the whole thing.

It was a blustery morning; dank and grey and English. She was walking through the playground, fresh from dropping off her nine-year-old daughter, Daisy, when she heard a familiar booming voice.

'Oh my god, what are those? Are they Prada?'

Ellie looked down at her trousers, which were grey felt and short in the leg, the hems cut on the gentlest of diagonal angles. They had cost £12 in the sale.

'No, of course they're not, they're from Topshop.'

Janey let her jaw drop in exaggerated outrage. She turned to another mum who was standing with her and said:

'She shops at Top Shop and she looks like she's on a bloody catwalk. I shop there and I look like a fat person in fancy dress. How is *that* fair?'

At all times Janey spoke at least two registers too loud and seemed to be in a state of continual world-reordering amazement. She was the only person Ellie had ever met whom she could imagine being rejected as a presenter of children's television for being too antic.

'Don't be ridiculous,' said Ellie. 'You always look amazing whatever you're wearing.'

Her two-year-old, Alexis, was sitting in the buggy, pawing at the screen of Janey's phone. Ellie bent down and tousled her hair.

'How are the rest of the Riot Squad?' she asked.

As well as Alexis, Janey had a five-year-old, a seven-year-old, and a nine-year-old, Lee, who was in Daisy's class.

'They all slept in with me again last night.'

'All four of them?'

'I can't help it. They're my chicks. I need them in the nest.'

'How much actual sleep did you get?'

'About an hour.'

'I don't know how you function.'

'Two coffees and a Red Bull.'

The other mum snorted in recognition.

Ellie smiled and introduced herself.

'We've never properly met, I'm Ellie.'

'Chanelle.'

'Nice to meet you, Chanelle.'

'You should hear her at Flynn's,' said Janey to Chanelle. 'Epic, she is. Karaoke legend.'

This was a lie. It was Janey who had the voice. A great big talent-show kind of voice. Ellie's was tame by comparison. The second Tuesday of every month they went to Flynn's where, sharing a mic, their eyes invariably closed, almost always three gin and tonics to the good, they sang Bonnie Tyler, Tina Turner, Cyndi Lauper and, towards the end of the night at Janey's drunken insistence and to Ellie's utter horror, Kelly Clarkson.

'Are you coming next Tuesday?'

'I can't. Colin's got a game.'

'Fucking football.'

'My sentiments exactly.'

Over Janey's shoulder, she noticed a group of mothers who had paused for a chat just outside the school gates. In the middle of the group, laughing so hard she was crying, was Yvonne Kington, the leader of Peterdown Council.

'Got to run,' she said. 'Drink next week instead?'

'Deffo,' said Janey. 'Any night but Thursdays. I can never do Thursdays.'

Ellie hurried over to the group by the gates and waited awkwardly while the laughter died down, knowing that what she was about to do directly contravened the unwritten rule when it came to Yvonne, which was that you treated her just like all the other mums. It was her big thing. She didn't play the politician on the school run and you didn't talk shop to her, this was the pact.

'Hi, Yvonne,' she said eventually.

Yvonne stopped laughing, looked at her. She was a small woman, convinced of her own bristling virtue.

'I just wanted to have a quick word.'

'Really? I can feel what kind of word this is going to be.'

'I hate to bother you here but I have emailed your office like ten times. And I've called. Probably half a dozen times.'

'Really?' said Yvonne tersely. 'I never knew. We get thousands of emails. You know how it is.'

She was wearing a red coat belted at the waist. She always wore something red, this was another of her things.

'I'm putting together an application to get Larkspur Hill listed and I'd really love your support.'

A cruel smile curled at the corner of Yvonne's mouth.

'I had heard about this.'

She looked around at her friends.

'I didn't believe it when I first heard it, but it seems some people seriously want to put that dump on a list alongside Buckingham Palace.'

'Well, no, actually. Buckingham Palace is grade one listed. Which of course is a total joke. Even Stalin would have passed on that dreadful lump of kitsch,' Ellie replied unthinkingly, before she remembered that she was trying to be winning. 'But yes. You're right. I want to get it listed. Grade two listed.'

The mothers were uniformly nonplussed. Yvonne looked at each of them before snorting with exaggerated derision, in a way that seemed to arrow in on Ellie's southern accent, her middle-class pretensions, while reminding everyone present that Yvonne was from Peterdown.

'Why?' said Yvonne, all bridle and snap. 'It's a concrete bloody monstrosity. Everybody hates it. Never mind sink estate. It's already sunk. It's a wreck.'

Ellie also understood the power of a good bridle and snap.

'That's quite an admission from the person in charge of our housing policy.'

'Housing policy? What would you know about housing policy? Do you have any idea how much that bloody estate costs to maintain? Good lord, it's an unbelievable drain on our finances. And nobody wants to live there. It sucks all the aspiration out of people. The problems with that place have got nothing to do with housing policy. It's because the building is like a post-apocalyptic bloody car park.'

Ellie was about to launch into her well-rehearsed monologue about the Barbican Centre and how well it had been maintained and how its walkways didn't seem to crush the spirit of the film directors and bankers that lived there, which she would have followed up with the killer observation about the state of the country's Georgian and Victorian housing when it had been left to rot by slum landlords. But she was aware the Buckingham Palace joke had fallen pretty flat and another reference to London would likely only reinforce the differences between them.

'I know it isn't necessarily an easy building to like,' she said softly. 'But it's worth pointing out it was co-designed by Marjorie Blofeld, who was one of the foremost female architects of her generation.'

This solicited a withering look that contained a whole thesis-worth of third wave feminist critique of Ellie's class power and privilege. She could do nothing but blush.

'Look love, it's not going to happen, not while I'm in charge.'

Ellie could feel her cheeks burning, the semi-circle of mums all willing her to leave.

'I'm going to put in an application whether you support it or not.'

'Well I'm sorry, love, it's not yours to get listed.'

'I'm afraid that doesn't actually matter. You don't need to own a building to apply for it to be listed.'

A sour look appeared on Yvonne's face.

'You really think you've got one over on us, don't you?'

Ellie felt tears welling in her eyes. You could be – as half the people in Peterdown seemed to think she was – the personification of entitled self-regard; cold and standoffish and an intellectual snob. And you could complicatedly hate yourself for all these things; your unthinkingness, your ongoing inability to be clubbable, your sisterly failures. But the thing was: you could be all those things and on some topics you could still be right.

And this was one of those and she was. Ellie felt her nostrils flare.

'I really don't,' she said, as she walked off down the street. 'But that's by the by. Sorry to have bothered you, but at least we both know where we stand.'

* * *

The ball was yellow foam, a crater missing from it, like the near-orbit moon of an imagined planet. It stuttered as it rolled, having soaked up standing water. For at least half the boys playing, the ball came up to their knees. But it was no matter. They chased after it like cartoon bees, everyone, save for the two goalkeepers, in hot pursuit.

Colin sat in a swing, watching. It was 3.45 p.m. Collection time.

A shot flashed wide and the ball rolled to his feet. He stood up and kicked it back. The ball lurched, bounced, squelched, and finally stopped at the feet of the four-foot goalkeeper, who smiled in thanks.

Colin smiled back. He had played like this, on the very same ground, when he was a similar age. He had been good then, a key member of the school team. He smiled wistfully. He'd played as a kind of false nine, just ahead of their playmaker, Tom Fenwick. Secondary school had been different, of course. A much bigger place, immeasurably tougher. Both he and Tom had to be content with playing for the thirds.

The ball broke loose. A skinny boy with curly hair was first to it.

He was better than the others, more graceful, more balanced. He took it past one defender, then another. Colin stood up to get a better view. The kid knocked it past the last man and glided round him, leaving just the keeper to beat. The boy dropped his left shoulder and then slalomed brilliantly the other way, running past the ball slightly so he could backheel it through the keeper's legs. Colin watched as it rolled agonisingly into the jumper/post. He recoiled instinctively at the injustice of it and as he did so caught sight of Daisy, who was standing, waiting, behind him.

'I'm still not a boy,' she said.

She had her arms crossed. Her mittens matched her scarf. It had become a thing, recently, this not-being-a-boy thing.

'You've got to stop saying that,' said Colin, dolefully. 'It was funny the first time but now it's just mean.'

'I know it's the big disappointment for you.'

Colin stopped, briefly moved. The idea that there was any chance that she might represent the major disappointment in his life was touching and evidence, possibly, that she wasn't yet fully aware of his actual disappointments, which he wore, he felt, like St Sebastian wore his wounds: openly and for all to see.

It had got steadily colder over the course of the day and the wind was now brisk and penetrating. He took her lunchbox from her and did up one of her buttons.

'Honestly, sweetheart, I never wanted you to be a boy,' he said.

As they walked out the school gates a girl from Daisy's class was waiting while her mum strapped a baby into a car seat.

'Hi, Daisy,' she said as they passed. 'Hi, Daisy's dad.'

'Hi,' said Colin with a meek smile.

He had only really been 'Colin' for his three years at university and his year or so in London. At school, there had been another Colin, Colin Samuels, who had been bigger and better at football, and everyone had called him 'Colin'. Colin had been known mostly as 'Ryder'. Or, almost as frequently, as 'the Gimp'. Occasionally 'the Gimpmeister'. Sometimes 'el Gimperino'. Now and then 'Mr Gimpy Wimpy'.

These days, he was 'Daisy's dad', which, in the grand scheme of things, he grudgingly acknowledged, could have been a lot worse.

They arrived at the traffic lights. The road was clear. Colin went to cross until he felt Daisy tug on his hand: the tug of reproach. He stepped back on to the kerb, waited for the green man. He felt all his parental authority drain from him. In one short aborted step he had bequeathed her the moral high ground. The red man stood firm, reprimandingly still.

He refused to look down at his daughter, aware that she was revelling in this victory, this brilliantly exploited chink in his defences. She had a bridgehead and she knew it. She stared wistfully down the street and said in her quietest voice:

'I'm never going to like football.'

Masterful, and a typical Daisy swerve: exploit any parental transgression with a re-articulation of your victimhood and wait for the concessions to flow. Colin marvelled at her. He would get more change, he imagined, going head to head with the Chinese politburo.

'I don't want you to like football,' he said. 'I mean it hasn't done me much good, has it?'

Daisy looked up at him, all innocence and filial solidarity.

'I like Fresno Kids,' she said earnestly.

'Yes,' said Colin. 'I know you do.'

He looked down at her rucksack. It was covered in key rings. Key rings that were marketed, he often found himself howling incredulously at the moon, at people too young to be in possession of any keys. Each one had suspended from it a plastic doll, lurid nylon hair bursting from its head. Some of them wore vocational outfits: vets, television presenters, nail therapists. The rest of them were princesses.

He felt a momentary sadness. Next year, she would have forgotten them. And then, as an adult, she would look back at photos and see them for what they were: mass-produced rubbish with a cynical marketing plan. She would look back at the photos and be embarrassed that she had fallen for it. That she had cared so much.

The lights changed and they crossed the road. Legitimately now, of course, with Daisy two steps ahead of him, practically pulling him by the hand. Colin thought back to his Panini books, which he first got into at a similar age. He allowed himself to be dragged along, trying to remember the feelings of those long Saturday mornings, he and Eliot Taylor sweeping up the back room of Talacre News. Two packs of stickers each, they got for their work, and they would save them until they got to the park where slowly, reverently, they opened each pack, holding out for the glint of a foil sticker.

Colin turned the corner into Dilston Terrace and found himself overcome by the feeling that if he had a son he might feel some kind of connection with his childhood self. But as it was, he felt utterly sundered from that lad in him, incapable of accessing his boyish enthusiasm and wonder.

'I tell you what,' he said, feeling guilty, 'if you tidy your bedroom when you get home we'll go on the internet and order a pair of Fresno twins.'

The house was on Coopersale Road. The semi-on, they had called it when they had first moved there, because it was semi-detached, obviously, but also because it was semi-serious and semi-temporary: in all ways only halfway there. That was then, of course, nine years ago when there had still been some solidarity between them, some sense that they would soon be moving on.

Colin felt the bite of the wind through his jacket. He looked across the road at the Cauldwells' house with its original sash windows all warped and withered, the glass as thin as paper. He was glad, privately, that their landlord at number nineteen had installed plastic windows, double glazed and tight to the frame. He laughed quietly to himself, trying to imagine the response if he were ever to articulate this opinion openly.

'Can I watch telly?' asked Daisy once they were inside.

He looked at her. She looked at him. The high ground was all hers.

'Sure,' he said.

He followed Daisy into the living room and retrieved the remote control from the high shelf. Ellie's loathing for their PVC windows had little to do with the way they impacted on the exterior of the house – which was, in her opinion, effectively beyond redemption – and more about the way they clashed with the interior that she had created. And it was true, he thought, they didn't exactly sit well with the bespoke plywood walls, the self-designed furniture and the modernist paintings.

But then again, neither, really, did he.

Colin passed his daughter the remote control and briefly considered trying to impose some of the usual prohibitions, but quickly decided against it. He retired to the similarly designed kitchen, where he made himself toast and tea and then sat down at the table with the family laptop. The internet browser had six tabs open. All of them pages from the property site fixerupper.com.

For years, the focus of her attention had been westward: Somerset or Devon. Farmhouses, old rectories. Wrecks in need of love. Colin had been terrified at the thought. What was out there? Yeovil. Plymouth Argyle. For two terrifying weeks she had been fixated with Bath. Colin had had to face the awful prospect that he was going to have to spend his Saturdays watching *rugby*.

He flicked from tab to tab. Recently, her focus had shifted to the London hinterlands. Tottenham. Forest Hill. Crystal Palace.

Colin looked through the particulars, doing mortgage calculations in his head. It was nine years since he had last lived in London, in a huge house on the North Green Road that was big enough to accommodate the whole gang of them that had moved en masse from Leeds to London straight after graduation: Ellie, Patrick, Suzie, Big Tom, Little Tom, Leonie Phillips and him.

Thrown together on the same floor of their halls in their first year of university they had proved to be an enduring unit: the two Toms and their knockabout double act, intense Suzie with her wild moods and terrible love life, lovely Leonie Phillips, Patrick with his cigarette holder and experimental waspishness, and at the centre of it all, Ellie, the lodestar around which they orbited, the rest of them in awe of her singularity, beauty, brilliance.

Looking back, his place in the ecosystem was obvious. He had supplied the authenticity. Colin the neophyte. Northern-ish. Or at least not from the South. Self-deprecating. Nervous. He hadn't appreciated it then but he could see now how exotic he must have been to the rest of them with their good schools and gap years; a boy from Peterdown who had never even been to London, let alone Ljubljana or Lesotho. And his dad was a *postman*. Colin smiled. Well, he works for the Royal Mail, he had always explained to them, but it had never stuck. And it made for a better story, him being a postman's son. Made him – made *them* – more bona fide.

Colin smiled. The North Green Road had certainly been bona fide. Every morning he had picked his way through chicken carcasses and condoms, burnt foil and broken glass, on his way to work in the largely empty old man's pub where he spent his days behind the bar, pulling the occasional pint for one of the few regulars, but mostly at his laptop, writing for blogs, freesheets, in-flight magazines – anyone, basically, that would publish his stuff.

And no one could have accused them of play-acting when it came to the house, either. The draught had blown through it like the winds on the Arctic tundra and it got burgled more frequently than the rubbish was collected, but Colin thought of it fondly still: the fraternity of it, the communal dinners, the thrilling feeling of the whole gang of them making their way in the world.

They had been there for six months when Ellie had finally split up for good with Jean-Gabriel, her long-distance, ludicrous boyfriend. Colin had always been her confidant, the shoulder on which she cried. At first she had been distraught. And then she had been angry. And then self-pitying. And then maudlin. And then needy. And then tactile. And then *really* tactile. He had never been under any illusions. Right from the first time it happened – the house otherwise empty, both of them drunk, the moon full – he had understood that he was a comfort, a milk of magnesia before the next course proper.

It had gone on for three months, their strange sporadic coupling, and had quickly developed its own code: never more than twice a week, always instigated by her, always in his bed, her always off back to her room between him falling asleep and waking up.

Then it happened. The test. The blue line. The sense, she had said, of something inside her, something precious. Some women could, she had said, but she wasn't one of them. And that, as Colin remembered it, was pretty much the full extent of the conversation.

The table top was scattered with toast crumbs. Colin pushed his finger through them. He had accepted it without hesitation – as he would have accepted anything that might have extended their fragile union, that might have embedded him in her life – knowing as he did so that it meant an end to London. Staying in Upper Clapton was impossible: no one wanted a baby as a housemate. They had considered staying in the city, but a one-bedroom flat had been beyond them, let alone the two-bed they would want soon enough.

When it came to it, Peterdown had been pretty much the only option. Cheap as chips, obviously. And somewhere they could expect some support with his mum and dad round the corner, people to whom being a parent at twenty-three didn't constitute some kind of capital crime. Colin took a deep breath and let it out again. He had managed four and a half years away from the place. Not much really in the context of a life.

He pulled that day's *Post* from his bag, folded back the final page, sought out the Championship league table. With fourteen games to go, United were in ninth place, three points off sixth and a place in the playoffs. He shut his eyes. Never again would there be a chance like this. He had spent years in the journalistic wilderness, unfulfilled, unknown, unread. But being the local correspondent for a Premier League team was a wholly different prospect. It meant guest appearances on the radio, opinions solicited ahead of big games, quotes garnered for think pieces. He would come to the attention of the dailies, Sky, the BBC. He would be in demand, eminently employable. He shut his eyes and dared to dream. Peterdown would get promoted and so would he. The big time would beckon. They would move back to London in triumph and Ellie . . .

'Muu-uum,' shouted Daisy, rushing from the sofa as soon as she heard the key in the door. 'Dad didn't wait for the green man.'

Colin stared forlornly at her departing back. The turncoat. Two hours of television *and* a Twix.

'Didn't he?'

'No, but I stopped him.'

He got up hurriedly and started unstacking the dishwasher.

'Here he is, the recalcitrant jaywalker,' said Ellie as she entered the room, Daisy by her side.

'Daisy did really well on her maths test today,' said Colin brightly, a cereal bowl in either hand.

'I did,' she said, running past her mother and back into the hall. 'Let me show you, it's in my bag.'

Ellie fixed him a look, unimpressed.

'I thought we were going to be scrupulous,' she said. 'The accident was only two months ago.'

Colin looked at the floor, the recrimination flooding through him. Juliet Halscomb. Two years below Ellie at St Kilda's. Dragged under an articulated lorry on the corner of Elsmere Street and the Broadcastle Road.

'We were on Jessop Avenue,' he whispered urgently. 'It was totally deserted. There weren't even any *parked* cars.'

Ellie shrugged. Colin had never met anyone who could communicate so much with their shoulders. It was just a simple shift of the collarbone. *You have failed me*, it said. *And your failure is endemic and unending. And there is nothing I can do to change it. All I can do is have my disappointment noted for the record.*

It was a good one, this shrug. He knew it well. There were others. But this was the one he got the most.

'We've run out of rinse aid,' he said.

'I know.'

'It's why the dishes aren't drying properly.'

'I know.'

'I'll get some more.'

'OK, Colin.'

He finished unstacking the dishwasher and sat down at the kitchen table, half-heartedly writing an email. Ellie was preparing to cook, her back to him, her clothes perfect in their simplicity: a grey jumper, jeans, white plimsolls. She pulled a chopping board from a cupboard, placed an onion on it. She had, he always felt when he watched her,

40

an intimate sense of her own body, of its limits but also of its potential for a kind of poetry. The radio was on, classical music. He watched as she piled her hair up on her head and fixed it with a pencil. Her neck was a thing of almost otherworldly perfection, long and lovely, the vertebrae just visible at its base, baby hairs whispering at her hairline. He could never understand the way other men fetishised loose hair. For him, it was hair up that contained the real erotic charge. He looked at her neck, the skin unblemished save for one perfect little mole. From where he was sitting he could see the jut of her jaw. It was extreme, her jaw, beauty at its outer reaches. An evolutionary high-wire act, designed to telegraph its excess.

He returned morosely to the email. She was, as one of his friends had indelicately put it, so far out of his league they were all but playing different sports.

Ellie brought the sharp knife down hard on the onion and felt the tears prick instantly in her eyes. In the background, she could hear Colin folding up his laptop and padding across the kitchen in his stockinged feet. This was the point at which she could set the tone for the rest of the evening by engaging him in conversation: keep him in the kitchen, crack a joke, make everything light and easy. But it had been another epically tedious day at work and she just didn't have it in her. Didn't have the energy to be the one responsible for everyone's mood.

She reached across to get the big casserole dish from where it had been drying on the rack and did her best to ignore the boiler which at some point before her time someone had decided to install above the kitchen sink, a decision that was both acoustically and aesthetically disastrous. She heard its deathly rattle, closed her eyes. If she had been asked to come up with a single object that captured the essential stasis at the centre of her life she would have to think long and hard before she bettered that bloody boiler.

She had ripped out most of the kitchen, remade the interior. But moving a boiler would cost four grand and there was a limit – morally, as well as practically and financially – to the amount of work you could do to a house you didn't own.

'Mum, look what Miss Shaikh gave me.'

It was a wooden New York yellow taxi, the size of a matchbox.

'Miss Shaikh gave you that?'

'I told her about the boxes. And guess what? She went to see the same show as us. She loves Joseph's boxes, too.'

'That's so nice of her,' said Ellie, turning the car over in her fingers. 'It'll look so cool in the box.'

Just before Christmas they had been down to London to see *Cats* when, on a whim, she had taken Daisy to a Joseph Cornell retrospective at the Royal Academy. Two hours later she had to practically pull her out so they didn't miss the start of the show.

'She got this when she was in New York on holiday. She got a whole set of them for her nephew but he never plays with them so she gave me this one.'

The day after they had got back from London they had gone out in search of vintage boxes, the two of them together, on their bikes, calling in at every charity shop in Peterdown. By the end of the day they had found three that were serviceable. A friendly glazier had hand-cut a perfect-sized piece of glass for each one.

Since then, they had been filling the boxes, very slowly and very deliberately. They were still not finished but each box had a name. Ellie's was called 'Dime-Store Alchemy'; Daisy's were 'Welcome to New York' and 'Out of the Woods'.

'Go put it in the drawer with the rest of the stuff, and then come back down,' she said, handing Daisy back the toy, 'we're going to eat in five minutes.'

Once they were all at the table, Ellie removed the lid of their best casserole dish. Father and daughter recognised it instantly as a Tuscan vegetable stew. Colin smiled weakly at Daisy, who returned the smile, similarly underwhelmed. Had Ellie been at yoga or ceramics, or whatever it was she did to get herself out of the house, and he had been cooking dinner – he paused here, cooking wasn't really the right word – had he been *preparing* dinner, the two of them, they knew, would have been eating his speciality: microwaved frankfurter sausages covered in mustard (him) or ketchup (her), rolled in a slice of

42

white bread. They were, Colin liked to think, a stand against something or another, although he was never quite sure what. He served them with a side of prawn cocktail crisps.

Ellie ladled some stew on to Daisy's plate. The colours were muted, tending to the beige. The squash was roasted, the corn pale yellow. The borlotti beans sat smugly in the viscous broth. Daisy picked up her fork with a kind of lethargic surrender.

Colin reached for the ladle and did his best to minimise the amount of Swiss chard on his plate. The whole thing might have been just about redeemable had he been able to grate a shitload of cheese on top but he had finished the cheddar earlier in the week performing a similar rescue job on a three-bean Bolognese.

'Dad's organising a march,' said Daisy as she disassembled the stew on her plate.

'Really?' said Ellie.

'We've started a campaign group,' said Colin. 'We're marching in opposition to Kirk's plans to move the stadium.'

'You're always complaining about what a dump the Chapel is. I thought you'd be happy to see them move.'

'I want them to unblock the toilets,' said Colin, 'not bulldoze the thing to the ground. And the proposed stadium is a total disaster.'

'I saw the plans,' said Ellie.

Daisy's stew was now completely compartmentalised, its constituent elements arranged pie chart-like on her plate. Sensibly, she ate the sweetcorn first.

'We're going to meet at the Geoffrie and then walk through town to the ground. Then we're going to turn our backs on the pitch at two minutes to eight. You know, nineteen fifty-eight. We're going to stand in silence.'

'That's nice.'

'God knows if it will make any difference.'

Having finished the corn Daisy was forcing down a forkful of sweet potato.

'How was your day?' asked Colin.

'Someone has done it again,' said Ellie. 'Changed the Wikipedia

listing for the Larkspur. It's weird. It feels like … I don't know …
Something weird is going on.'

She paused, her fork held in mid-air.

'It's like I've rattled someone. Which seems odd. I mean I've only
got, I don't know, a hundred and fifty signatures.'

Colin poured the last of the wine into Ellie's glass, opened himself a beer.

'And the council are being super-weird about it. They're going
to great lengths to say they're not decanting it, but they've boarded
up three flats in the past month. I don't know, it's odd. The whole
thing is odd.'

After dinner, the three of them retired to their various screens.
Ellie flicked between property websites, bemoaning the iniquities
of the British housing market. Daisy spent Fresno dollars on Fresno
fittings for her online Fresno castle. Colin watched Wolves lose two-
nil to Eintracht Frankfurt in the Europa League.

Just after 9 p.m., Ellie closed her laptop and walked into the living
room. The paper was on the sideboard, folded in half. It was the first
Thursday of the month. The day his sports sketch was published. It
was his chance to stretch his wings, crack some jokes, get a little
florid if he so desired. He had written about the Peterdown mixed-
sex non-competitive softball team. She read the opening paragraph,
smiled, read on.

'Do you know what the most annoying thing about you is?' she
said as she placed the newspaper back on the sideboard.

Colin contemplated this for a second or two but gave up, defeated.
The list of things about him that annoyed her was limitless,
beyond indexing.

'You can actually write,' she said. 'That's the tragedy of it. You can
actually write.'

Colin looked at her, elated. But before he could formulate a
response, Daisy interjected.

'Look,' she said, pointing at the screen. 'Mum's building is
on TV.'

They turned together to look at the television. It was the local news. The reporter was on Baxendale Street, the silhouette of the Larkspur just visible against the night sky.

'Following on from the momentous decision to choose Peterdown as the regional hub station for Britain's first ever bullet train, the government's Infrastructure Tsar, Andrew Eddington, announced earlier this evening a shortlist of three sites, one of which will be chosen for the site of the new station. Top of the list is the notorious Larkspur Hill Housing Estate. Built in 1968, the estate has become a byword for urban decay . . . '

'Oh dear,' said Colin. 'You were right. Looks like something strange *is* going on.'

'I don't fucking believe it,' said Ellie.

'Mum,' said Daisy.

'Also on the list released this evening are the town's mixed-use arts space, the Generator; and the Chapel, the dilapidated home of Peterdown United Football Club . . . '

'What?!' said Colin, nearly spilling his beer.

'Well *that* makes sense,' said Ellie. 'Kirk must have known. He's already planning where you're going to move to.'

'No,' said Colin, blankly.

'I mean, Kirk will be all over it, won't he?' said Ellie, warming to her theme. 'He gets to move the club to Grangeham *and* bank a load of compensation money from the government . . . '

'Hold on a second, the reason they're announcing a shortlist is because there's going to be some debate around it,' said Colin, talking over the news anchor who had moved on to a story about a fatal car crash on the A535. 'You know, public consultation. We've got a campaign group together already. We've got more than fifteen thousand supporters we can call on to get behind us. People *love* the Chapel. Which you can't exactly say for the Larkspur, can you? You're pretty much the only person in the whole town that doesn't hate it.'

Ellie looked shocked and then disappointed.

'Me and the Twentieth Century Society. And the RIBA. And Moshe Safdie, who just after it was built called it the crowning achievement of English modernism.'

She paused for a second.

'And you,' she said. 'You don't hate it, do you?'

Whatever Colin was about to say died on his lips. He looked over at Ellie. There had been something in that *do you?*, something unguarded, something real. He felt a lump rise in his throat.

'No,' he said. 'You know I don't.'

A brief silence followed, until Daisy looked up from her iPad and, with uncharacteristic even-handedness and charity, said:

'They might choose the Generator.'

Colin and Ellie looked at each other. The Generator was four years old and had cost £42 million. It was the council's flagship regeneration project.

'Yes,' they both said softly, in inadvertent harmony. 'They might.'

4

The low winter light was white and hazy over the Beagle Hills, which sat prettily a mile or so to the west of Peterdown town centre. Ellie was at the foot of them, in the car park, leaning against the bonnet of her battered Vauxhall Astra. She took a sip of her tea and looked up. You could see why they were called the Beagles. They were perky little mounds, upright, eager to play. Also, as anyone in the town could tell you, the car park in which she sat was, come dusk, used mostly for dogging.

She wrapped her fingers round the polystyrene cup. It was 8.30 a.m. and she was feeling simultaneously exhausted and oddly energised. The inclusion of the Larkspur on the shortlist had kept her up half the night worrying, but she had got up that morning feeling blearily emboldened. The estate was newly imperilled, but this had brought with it a certain clarity.

'Yeah,' she said into her phone. 'I know, *totally*.'

She was talking to her best friend, Leonie. Their mutual friend, Suzie, had had another falling out, this time with her brother.

'The thing is, I know he can be gauche and everything,' said Leonie, 'but essentially he's a nice guy. She's just fucking impossible at least seventy per cent of the time.'

They had started on the topic of the shortlist and her need to push on with the listing campaign but had quickly moved on to Suzie, as they so often did.

'Why do we talk about Suzie so much?' she asked.

'All groups of friends have at least one person that they talk about all the time.'

47

Ellie let this hang in the air for a second. And then another. And then despite herself she said:

'At least one.'

'Yeah, we talk about you too.'

'But the way we talk about Suzie isn't a good thing. It's like she's a problem we're trying to work out.'

'Yeah, we don't talk about you the way we talk about Suzie.'

Ellie paused and pursed her lips.

'What does that mean?'

'We expect things of you.'

'What does *that* mean? *Why?*'

'Because you're *you*. That's the payoff. You get all the things that make you you. The hair. The legs. The first-class degree. And we get to talk about you.'

Ellie tried to absorb this and found that she couldn't, it just sort of glided over her.

'I don't have the strength to even start imagining how I might unpick all that,' she said.

'Yeah, I wouldn't go there.'

A car pulled up and Ellie watched, waiting to see who would come out. An old man. Not who she was waiting for.

'Change of subject,' she said. 'How are you?'

'You know, actually quite good. I've had an unbroken run of six hours' sleep two nights in a row.'

'Oh god, it's awful isn't it?'

'You really didn't adequately warn me.'

'What could I do? If people knew what it was actually like it would be the end of the species.'

'He is totally darling, though.'

'Oh my god, he is. Send me more pictures.'

Two dogs scrambled from the recently parked car and started jumping at their owner's feet.

'I haven't told you, have I?' said Leonie. 'I've got in with this gang. There's like seven of us that live on these three streets, ours and the two parallel, and all of us had our kids in the same six-month window.'

After years of buying and selling London property, Leonie had cashed in and had decamped with her husband to Brighton where they lived in a four-storey Regency townhouse, two minutes from the sea. When she wasn't on maternity leave, she was a research fellow in the American Studies department at the University of Sussex.

'Ashley is a filmmaker. She makes documentaries for the BBC. Madeleine is a stylist. Elisa wrote a book on women in tech. Naomi is a choreographer. We go to the mum and baby film screening every week.'

Here, Leonie talked about the various films they'd watched, none of which Ellie had seen and at least half of which, to her mind, hadn't even got a cinema release in Peterdown.

'And we've started a book club. I managed to talk them into doing *Dept. of Speculation.*'

'Oh, yeah? How is that?'

'It's great. And they loved it. Next week we're doing Alice Munro and we're meeting up to talk about it at Elisa's and she lives in Embassy Court, the one by the guy who did the Isokon building.'

'Wells Coates.'

'She's on the sixth floor with a sea view. I haven't been yet but she's shown me pictures of the interior. You would melt.'

'God, I miss you,' said Ellie, impulsively.

'Come and see me.'

They said this every time. Once you had changed at Broadcastle and then got the train to London, and then a tube across London, and then another train to Brighton, you were looking at six hours travelling.

'I will.'

She watched a clean bright-black Mercedes pull into the car park.

'Got to go,' she said. 'Speak soon.'

She put her phone in her pocket and righted her hair. The announcement had only made the morning's appointment – arranged the week before, via email – all the more timely.

Ellie stayed where she was as he locked his car, watched him walk across the car park to her. His cashmere coat was camel, its collar popped. His navy wool suit was three-piece with the faintest of white lines running through it. It was a novelty to see a man in Peterdown wearing clothes that actually fitted him.

'Good morning,' he said, a knowing smile on his lips as he extended a leather-gloved hand to her which she took and shook. 'I'm assuming you're Ellie.'

'I am, yes. Thanks for coming.'

'Lovely to meet you. I'm Pankaj.'

He stood there, on his heels, a boyish smile turning up irrepressibly at the corner of his lips. He seemed to try to fight it, but couldn't, and before she knew it he was beaming, a full-wattage smile, all teeth and dimples.

Ellie looked at him askance.

'Sorry,' he said. 'The news that I had arranged to meet a woman I don't know in the Beagle Hills car park caused no end of hilarity in my office.'

'Ha-ha, yes. I hadn't actually made the connection until it was too late.'

'As I was leaving my intern warned me not to put my hazard lights on.'

'Yes,' she said, 'apparently that is good advice.'

Ellie found herself drawn to the tiny hint of grey at his temples. It was just a smudge, but it was oddly attractive on someone as young as he was, only forty or so. Particularly when his hair was so deeply beautifully black everywhere else.

'He seems to be full of occult knowledge, my intern. His name is Aidan. He's nineteen. Half the time I can't work out who is in charge of whom.'

There was, she realised, something ever so slightly camp about him with his bachelor good looks and the cutaway collar on his shirt, but it was more of a theatrical thing than a sexual one, something self-aware and performative. His seemed to be an intelligence that was alert to itself, but in a way that was self-effacing, somehow.

'Don't look,' he said, nodding subtly to his right. 'But I think the woman in that Audi is starting to undress.'

Ellie glanced over at the Audi where a woman deep into her seventies was changing from driving shoes into a pair of wellies, three Jack Russells snapping about at her feet.

'Honestly,' she said. 'These people are just incorrigible.'

She looked at him, smiling disbelievingly at the situation. Here she was in the Beagle Hills car park making jokes about dogging with Pankaj Shastry. Telegenic former human rights barrister. Shadow frontbencher in waiting. The duly elected member for Peterdown Central. Her local MP.

'I think we should get out of this car park before she ropes us into anything sordid.'

'Yes,' said Ellie. 'We don't want you on the front page of tomorrow's *Sun*.'

'No, we do not,' he said, smiling.

'Let's go up here. It's only from the top that you get a true sense of it.'

They started up the hill. He walked with his hands held behind his back.

'So how are you finding Peterdown?' she asked. 'What's it been? Six months?'

'It's great,' he said. 'A place of constant surprises and hidden depths.'

'Not somewhere you knew well before the election, then?'

'No,' he said diplomatically, 'not somewhere I knew well.'

He had been parachuted in, a rising star handpicked by the leadership to fight the first by-election of the parliament, called after old Clive Gough – jig operator, union rep and seven-term parliamentarian – had died walking his dog. The Labour Party central office line had been that it was all about getting top talent out into the regions, and although his selection was eventually ratified by the local party it had been a divisive and difficult process. Far harder indeed than the by-election itself, which he had won at a canter.

'Still, you've timed it well, haven't you? Waltzing in just as we get the station.'

'My task for the next few years is to very humbly bask in the glory and keep quiet about the fact that I have had absolutely fuck all to do with the process from start to finish.'

Ellie smiled. 'So I take it you didn't have much input into the shortlist, either.'

'Not an iota. The eternal plight of the opposition. I only heard about it last night. I haven't even had a chance to form an opinion yet.'

'Looks like I timed this well then.'

'Looks like you did.'

They reached the vantage point. Ellie looked down at the complex of buildings. The first thing that struck you about it was its scale. Its ambition and reach. It was astonishing that something could be so self-evidently singular and yet, somehow, so seamlessly continuous with the environment around it. It was a building totally alive to its context and yet never constrained by it, never hedged, or hemmed.

The winter sun was low, the sky bright. Barely a cloud in the sky. The perfect day to appreciate it.

'I'm sure you went to the Larkspur when you were canvassing but you get a whole new perspective on it from up here,' she said. 'It was the Blofelds' third project and their first in Britain. Unquestionably the most exciting public housing of its time.'

Against the backdrop of the grey concrete she could see a kid on a BMX cycling along one of its open-air decks. She watched him freewheel down a ramp and disappear round a corner. The estate's intricacy was legend, its dramatic interplay of decks and walkways, its playfully unpredictable layout, its authentic consideration of public space.

'The five main sections are all named after one of Jupiter's moons.'

'Of course. Europa House. And Ganymede. Why Jupiter's moons?'

'Johnnie Larkspur. His science fiction book, *Are We Nearly There Yet?*'

'Ah.'

'It's set on Jupiter.'

'Another book to add to the pile. I've done quite well on Arthur Toyle but I have to admit I haven't read much of Johnnie Larkspur.'

'Not all of his books have stood the test of time, but *Parentheses* is amazing. The Blofelds loved him. Agosto wanted the estate to capture the spirit of his writing, that feeling of worlds within worlds. There are so many different routes you could take through the estate and none of them make any more sense than any of the others. He had this vision of it being a place that people would constantly rediscover. You know, never get bored of.'

'I certainly experienced that canvassing!' said Pankaj with a big smile. 'I can't tell you how many times we got lost.'

'Yeah, the walkways between the two towers and Europa are pretty wild.'

'I like the two horizontal bits that seem to come flying out of the hill.'

'Ganymede and Callisto. They're amazing feats of engineering. The echo of two trains powering out of a tunnel is deliberate,' she said. 'And not in a pat way. It was a deeply felt celebration of Peterdown's past but also its future. The town was still banging out thirty per cent of Britain's rolling stock when it was designed. Now of course it looks like a pre-emptive elegy.'

'It's the scale of it that's so impressive.'

'The scale, the hubris, the incredible imaginative leaps. Everything about it was thought through in incredible detail. The window configuration on the two towers is so clever. You feel like you're constantly on the verge of finding the pattern only to be constantly thwarted. It's like it forces you to engage with it like Ruskin would have done, or Pevsner. It demands that you look rather than simply see.'

Ahead of them a man was walking his dog. It was straining at the leash, pulling him into their orbit. As he got closer, Ellie found herself wondering if he had recognised Pankaj. She felt her breath quicken. If he had, who did he think she was? And what did he think of them?

Abruptly, she heard, unbidden (as it always was), the voice of her mother. *Nothing. He thought nothing at all. Because, darling dear, he doesn't realise that he's been cast as a walk-on in* Eleanor Ferguson: The Musical.

Ellie blushed. She had been at it again, *mythifying*. It was her mother's coinage. Another thing she used against her. *Ever since you were eighteen months old I have had a blow-by-blow account of everything*

53

you have ever done or thought. It's like you're writing your own myth. It had been delivered, this assessment, in a jocular*ish* tone of voice – a classic register of her mother's, jocular*ish*, one that left you in a kind of emotional no-man's-land, defenceless.

'There's another great view from down here,' she said, walking ahead of him down a grass verge so that he couldn't see her face. Ellie strode purposefully, irritated at her mother and at her own irritability; Pankaj struggled gamely to keep up.

'If I'd known we were going hiking I'd have worn something more suitable.'

Ellie turned to look at him. He was studiously eyeing every step, assessing each time whether he was on terra firma, keen not to add to the lines of mud already encroaching above the soles of his polished black leather brogues. She was getting a sense of what it was like to be a politician, of the need to be seen to be joining in and at the same time retain your dignity. How tiring to need to constantly balance your desire to keep your expensive clothes clean with the necessity of not coming across too precious about it, to experience every moment as a potential pratfall.

He wasn't doing a bad job.

'There's another path over here,' she said, smiling.

The wind was blustery up on the peak. Pankaj's wool tie flapped over his shoulder like a dog's ear out the car window. They stopped briefly on the tarmac path and looked down the hill.

'Hold that pose,' said Pankaj. He pulled his phone from his pocket. 'Your cape is billowing brilliantly in the wind. And the sun is shining on the estate.'

'What are you doing?'

'The consensus in my largely pre-pubescent office is that I'm not active enough on social media. I have been instructed to take five pictures a day so they can post them on whatever it is they post them on and young people will like me.'

Ellie stood, shocked into stillness. When had a man last taken her photo? She couldn't remember. When had a man who looked like this last taken her photo? She felt a blush creep across her cheeks.

'Oh, they're going to love this,' said Pankaj as he inspected his work. 'Want to see?'

'No,' replied Ellie.

'Well, if you change your mind I'm @shastrymp. I have six thousand two hundred followers. Although Aidan thinks at least a third of them are robots. He's very disappointed by this but I think it will leave me well placed come the singularity.'

Ellie looked at him sideways.

'When everyone will want to be popular with robots.'

'I got it the first time.'

'Yes, I thought you did,' he said, smiling.

Ellie was thrown. She had expected him to be bland, politician-vanilla, everything he said checked and considered. But he seemed surprisingly alive to it, the chosenness of his clothes, the sound of his voice, the absurdity of politicians.

He smiled again and walked a little further down the hill to a bench. She followed and sat down next to him.

'Over there,' she said, pointing. 'Look at the boarded-up windows. The council have six thousand people on the waiting list for social housing and they're boarding up the flats. I don't understand. They say they're not decanting it. But clearly something's going on.'

'I don't have any jurisdiction over these things but I'll certainly ask around, although I should warn you that I don't have the easiest relationship with certain individuals on the council . . .'

'Yvonne?'

Pankaj raised his eyebrows, said nothing.

'She thinks you stole her seat, right?'

He winced.

'I asked her already if she would support the listing.'

'How did that go?'

'That woman is fucking toxic. She did everything she could to humiliate me in front of her friends.'

'If it's any consolation she does that to me every time we meet.'

'Could she know about the station? About where it's going?'

'The *government* don't know where it's going to go. And if they

55

did, do you really think this government would share secrets with a Labour council?' Pankaj laughed. 'They'd sooner tell the Iranians.'

'Standing here looking down at that building and thinking about the very real prospect of it being pulled down, all I can think is: we've already got one station, do we really need another one?'

Pankaj looked at her aghast.

'We have one station that connects only to Broadcastle. Do you have any idea how much *not* being on the mainline costs this town? We're talking about being connected to the most exciting rail link in Europe, possibly in the world. The job estimates are rough at the moment but it's going to create *thousands* of jobs, short-term ones on the build and long-term ones working at the station itself. Good, well-paid, blue-collar jobs. And super-high-speed links can have a massive impact on a town's economy. Markets get opened up by it. Direct foreign investment means jobs. It means growth. Peterdown's economy has flatlined for decades, and only because of the public sector work – take that away and the situation would be terminal. The actual private economy is shrinking year on year. Yes, Ellie, we *need* the station.'

'Fine, the station's coming,' said Ellie, a touch more churlishly than she intended. 'It's a good thing. Of course I want the jobs and everything, but not at any cost. Larkspur Hill is a work of art. If we pull it down people in the future will look back and consider it an act of wanton philistinism. We can't let that happen. The only way to guarantee its survival is to get it listed before the decision is made.'

'Yes, that would work.'

'My only worry is that if the government want to put the station there they're never going to list it.'

'Westminster doesn't work like that. It's a series of fiefdoms run by warlords fighting in slow motion. The listing decision will ultimately be made by the Secretary of State for Digital, Culture, Media and Sport and the location of the station will be chosen by the Infrastructure Tsar. Fortunately for you, they hate each other. If Harvey can be convinced to list the estate, then he would consider hobbling Eddington's shortlist a juicy little extra.'

'It's been done before. Getting it listed saved Preston bus station from demolition.'

Pankaj's phone rang. He reached into his pocket and turned it off without looking at the screen.

'So I assume you're an architect?' he said.

Ellie stamped the mud from the treads of her boots.

'Yes.'

'Which practice?'

'I work for Create:Space in Broadcastle,' she said. 'It's a big corporate firm. Lots of supermarkets, that kind of thing.'

She paused, looked out over the town and thought about leaving it there, but couldn't.

'It's a shit practice,' she said. 'The only things stupider than its name are the buildings it produces.' She paused, breathed, conscious that she didn't want to share any of this with him, but finding herself incapable of stopping. 'But it was a good place to do my part threes. There aren't that many firms around here and the big ones are good when you're a student. Particularly a mature one like I was.'

A crow settled on the grass beside them, scratched around for food. Ellie dug her hands into her pockets, her cheeks burning. He was only forty and had excelled in two careers. She was thirty-three and hadn't even started one.

'I would have done it all earlier of course, but life interrupted for a bit.'

She looked up at him, waiting for the inevitable question, the wheedling out of the details. He held her eye, smiled.

'I'm trusting you not to tell anyone I said this,' he said, pausing for an instant to assess her reaction, 'but I think part of the reason I was parachuted into Peterdown was the colour of my skin. Unfortunately, no one at Central Office was alive to the fact that Peterdown's Asian population is almost entirely comprised of working-class Bangladeshis, a good number of whom have good reason to hate the Brahmin Hindu families like mine who were the architects of Partition.'

He rubbed the end of his nose, sniffed.

'And let's just say that in regards to some members of my family they've got a pretty good case.' He paused, his hands in his lap. 'But it was quite something for my grandparents' generation to have been so prominent in the Congress's inner circle. It allowed them to do some amazing things. And they really did, particularly my great uncle, who commissioned half the buildings in Chandigarh.'

'*What?*'

'Maxwell Fry was a family friend.'

'No way.'

'I like this building, Ellie. I always did.' He looked at her pointedly. 'I just now have a reason to like it a bit more.'

Ellie processed this last sentence with what she knew was a fairly strange lateral movement of the head. She was aware that it had become a tic of hers, a reflexive reaction to a particular kind of compliment, the kind that was direct and discombobulating and not entirely unwanted.

'So,' she said, trying gamely not to blush. 'You'll support the application to get it listed.'

Pankaj smiled. 'Consider me signed up. We can work on it together. It'll be fun. You've got to remember, we're all futurists, us boys from the third world.'

5

The plates at the Rothbury Café were like dustbin lids and still the food came to the edges. Colin was having his favourite: two giant sausages, a thicket of chips, a lake of beans. He cut into one of the sausages and marvelled at its shocking pink interior. It was the food dye, the waitress had once told him, not because it was undercooked. Not that it would matter that much; the sausages were, at best, about twenty per cent meat. Which made them, he hoped, something like eighty per cent bread. If you ate them between two slices of toast, as he sometimes did, it meant your meal was essentially bread on toast. Which may not sound appetising but was just the kind of thing that Ellie would lap up if you told her it was traditional peasant food from Puglia. *Pane di pane.* Bread on toast.

The café was tucked away on the second floor of the Rothbury Market. It had changed little since it opened along with the rest of the market in the fifties; its tables were Formica, its lighting halogen, its condiments vinegary. Had Colin thought about it more deeply he might have found cause to speculate on just why he was drawn so instinctively to places that seemed simply to mark time, stuck doggedly to tired ideas, and so steadfastly resisted improvement, but these were things far from his mind as he sprayed brown sauce on his chips with one hand and with the other logged on, via his laptop, to the most popular of the PUFC message boards. The comments thread under a piece on the stadium's presence on the shortlist was 526 entries long.

He read a dozen or so posts – all of them reassuringly enraged and vehemently pro-Chapel – when his eyes were drawn to an entry by Truther_78, one of the board's most prominent posters. A self-confessed Broadcastle fan, Truther_78 never pretended to be anything other than a provocateur who liked getting drunk and winding up Peterdown supporters, but he had a sharp football mind and Colin was not against borrowing his observations for newspaper articles.

> PUFC in the top three for the first time ever! Bound to finish first! The Chapel is going to be the chosen one for once. Chosen for being such a shithole . . .

He was about to read on when he heard the café door swing shut. He looked up, knowing that it was her. Kerry Harrison. Five feet four inches of lips and hips and heady scent. He felt a familiar full-body flutter. Her black suit jacket was pinched at the waist, the white top underneath it as tight as a swimsuit. Colin drew an unsteady breath as she walked towards him. Her tapered pencil skirt achieved its full constriction two-thirds of the way down her thigh, forcing her to walk in pinched little steps pivoting at the knee. Colin had seen her in one of these skirts before. The feminist in him recognised them as a beyond-parody actualisation of the patriarchy's ability to internalise self-restriction and repression. But on days like this the feminist in him accounted for about ten per cent of his personhood. The unreconstructed rest of him reeled in giddy thrall. He couldn't look away.

'Bloody hell,' said Kerry, sitting down opposite him.

'I know,' said Colin, determinedly maintaining eye contact lest his gaze be drawn down the vertiginous canyon of her neckline.

'It's all we bloody need, isn't it? This bloody station.'

Kerry was Peterdown's operations manager. At just twenty-eight she was the youngest in the league and the only woman. Two things that had not escaped the attention of the nation's tabloid editors, all of whom seemed to have a less conflicted opinion on the merits of her tapering pencil skirts and volumised hair.

Colin watched as she retrieved two phones from her bag and placed them, face up, on the table. At clubs with larger payrolls, hers would have been a largely strategic role, all high-level meetings and cash-flow projections, but at a club like Peterdown she didn't just manage the operations, she executed most of them: she maintained the club's relations with the FA, liaised with the press, talked to fans' groups, administered the surviving outreach programmes, ran the office, answered the phone. Everyone in town knew that she was the beating heart of the club, its soul. None were aware, however, of another similarly significant role: she was also Colin's mole.

'You heard him on the radio this morning?'

'Yeah,' said Colin.

'What a wanker. You should see him, bowling around like he's a big swinging dick.'

Kerry signalled to the waitress, who arrived eventually, placed a tea in front of her with studied, almost comic indifference and withdrew without comment to her position behind the glass counter, her eyes glued squarely to her phone. There was something strangely bracing, Colin had always felt, about this peculiarly British approach to the service industry. He glanced around at the few pensioners occupying the other tables, all of them similarly indifferent to Kerry's presence despite her low-level celebrity. In the eight months since Kirk had taken over the club the café had been the backdrop to a dozen or so of these off-the-record briefings, and they were still to bump into anyone they knew.

Kerry hooked a stray strand of hair behind her ear, pursed her lips in irritation. 'I had to sit in on him doing a press interview this morning. Is there anyone, in the whole of football, more in love with the sound of their own voice?'

She held her mug with both hands, her fingers wrapped round it for warmth.

'You know what pisses me off the most? The way he's been trying to make out that he wants to move because the new stadium will be a better place for women ... and for the disabled ... and for families. I mean obviously I want those things. Christ, it took me long enough to get women's toilets with actual bloody seats on them. But all his chat about inclusiveness is horseshit. You damn well know if the club gets moved out to Grangeham the price of those season tickets is going to double at least, and all those people that can only just afford to come as it is will hardly make a single game.'

'I didn't know he was doing press interviews,' said Colin, his jaw clenched in what he knew from the outset to be a vain attempt to disguise his disappointment.

'It was with the *Sunday Times*. The business editor. Kirk had him bloody purring.'

Colin felt the rejection physically, a deflation in his chest, a contraction of his balls. They seemed to come daily, these confirmations of his irrelevance, his position in the second rank. He did his best to appear unmoved, but it was his fatal flaw, and he knew it, his uncontrollably expressive face.

'He probably thought you'd give him a rough ride,' said Kerry tenderly.

Colin smiled thinly. He had attempted, in their early encounters, a kind of masculine brusqueness that he had imagined might impress her, his approximation of the gnarled virility that he knew she encountered daily in the football world. It quickly transpired that terse dignity and firm handshakes weren't exactly his forte.

'That,' he said balefully, 'or Kirk decided that his time was better spent courting the million people who read the *Sunday Times* rather than the seven thousand who read the *Post*, six and a half thousand of whom only read stories about crime or cats.'

'Oh god,' said Kerry. She paused, bit her lip, proved unable to contain herself. 'Did you see the thing in Monday's paper? The three ginger kittens in the flower pots?'

'That was cute,' conceded Colin.

'The one with the flower in his mouth.'

'Yes, he was lovely. The way he had his paws up ...'

Colin paused. He had tried the hard-but-fair hero but the character didn't fit. Instead, he'd had to make do with a different kind of role: Kerry's sororal subordinate, the unthreatening, unattractive sidekick to her leading lady. He was basically a straight version of the gay best friend. In the Hollywood telling of it he would be the one you were supposed to sympathise with. But also the one you pitied.

'I had this awful thought last night,' he said, keen to move on. 'I was lying in bed and I found myself thinking: has he known about it since the start? About the Chapel being on the shortlist. Is that what Grangeham's about, him trying to steal a march, make sure that it gets chosen?'

'No,' said Kerry confidently. 'He was as surprised as anyone. Don't get me wrong, he's chuffed to bits about being on this shortlist, but he didn't buy the club because he thought he could sell the Chapel to the government.'

A miasma of frying fat hung in the air at the Rothbury, so thick you could feel it as much as smell it. Colin took his glasses off and wiped them.

'He's made a lot of political donations, though, hasn't he? There are photos of him on the internet at a whole load of fundraisers.'

'Really, Col. I'd know if he knew. Honestly, I don't think the *government* knows yet. We've had phone calls from Whitehall and they don't sound like they've made up their minds.' She paused, drummed her long nails on the countertop. 'But let's not split the biscuit: we're in a fix.'

Colin lifted his mug and contemplated the unarguable certainty of this point. Of the three buildings on the shortlist, theirs was the only one with a ready-made replacement and an owner who was unambiguously keen to move.

He felt a familiar sensation of helplessness and humiliation. Fleetingly, he considered the idea that this feeling might be more than a specific reaction to a given situation. That it might in fact be essential, definitive, a kind of distillate of his position in and experience of the world. Mercifully, for his own sake, the usual defence mechanism – the one that stops us seeing our lives in the whole – kicked in just in time.

'Oh fuck it,' said Kerry. 'If I get sacked I get sacked. I'll get another job.'

She pursed her lips.

'I wasn't sure whether to tell you because if it gets out I'm sure they'll know it was me, but ...' She exhaled. 'Something is going on.

I don't know what it is but I know there's more to this than meets the eye. Before the interview that Kirk did this morning he has a meeting with that prick Gus Taylor and Andy Green. They're both, I don't know, managers or whatever, at Land Dominion. Anyway, the guy from the *Times* is early so I go to see if Kirk is done. He hates me disturbing him so I pause at the door and I hear him say: "Of course, this changes everything. We have to keep this on complete lockdown. Anyone gets wind of it and the whole plan is shot."'

'Kirk said that?'

'Yeah.'

'What was he talking about?'

'I don't know.'

'We have to find out.'

'I know.'

'He said "the whole plan is shot"?'

'Yeah.'

'This is how we save the Chapel.'

'And lose me my job.'

'Not necessarily.'

'Yes necessarily, but fucking hell it would be worth it.'

'We need to find out what he was talking about. Like, utmost urgency.'

Kerry stood up, buttoned her jacket.

'I'm on it.'

She sidled out of the booth. Colin turned to watch her as she walked away. Her tights were the kind with a seam along the back, a thin black line that ran from heel to hip. It followed the curve of her calf like a contour on a map, an intimation of her dramatic topography. Colin screwed his eyes shut, stifled the thought. For all his abstract longings about her, he had never fantasized about them actually doing it. He couldn't. For all of Kerry's parabolic perfection, Ellie retained a monopoly on his heart. He had never imagined having sex with Kerry out of loyalty and, when it came down to it, love. That, and the fact that he knew, with some shame, that if he did so he would almost certainly faint.

Six hours later, in the back room of the Geoffrie, Colin found Rodbortzoon at a corner table eating what he recognised to be a large portion of the pub's barbecue chicken wings. The wings were worryingly etiolated, the sauce unctuous and luridly orange. There were twelve of them on the plate, nine of which had been stripped completely of meat like a downed antelope after the hyenas have had their turn.

'What kind of conditions do you imagine those chickens lived in if they can sell a dozen wings at three pounds fifty?' he said, moving Rodbortzoon's plastic bag of books so he could sit down in the chair next to him. 'That's six chickens' worth.'

Rodbortzoon laughed heartily. He was wearing a T-shirt with what appeared to be a picture of Rosa Luxemburg and Rosa Parks wearing berets with their fists raised in the air.

'Your sentimentality about animals would be more affecting if it was mirrored by a similar concern for the oppressed *peoples* of the world,' he said, merrily cracking open a wing. 'But that would require imagination with the capacity to project beyond the Peterdown ring road, which we all know is an effective tourniquet to your curiosity.'

Droplets of the orange sauce hung to the tips of the hairs of his moustache like dew on the morning grass.

'I wasn't actually talking about the animals' welfare. My concern was for yours. That sauce looks like the stuff that gives the Daredevil his powers.'

'Ha! A bargain for three pounds fifty!'

'Yeah, maybe. Although I don't think you're going to develop sonar by eating them, are you? But there is, you know, a pretty good chance that you might go blind.'

'Ha! Ha! Typical reaction of the Anglo-American health and safety control freak. You have such an infantilised attitude towards risk. Your generation is, how the English say, mollycoddled. Ha ha! These really are extra delicious once you get used to the texture.'

He threw a denuded bone on to the pile.

'Anyway,' he continued, 'to business. What did she have for us?'

'Nothing. Or at least nothing yet. She's going to keep her eyes open.'

'So you will have to see her again when she has seen what she is going to see?'

'Yes.'

'Perhaps this time I will come with you.'

'No, that's just never going to happen.'

'You are concerned I would upstage you?'

'Yes,' said Colin dryly. 'That's exactly what it is.'

'I understand.'

'That's good of you.'

'So,' said Rodbortzoon, gesticulating at Colin with a wing in his hand. 'Chapel is obviously no. Larkspur is also no, of course. So it has to be the Generator.'

'Really? You really think they're going to pull that down? They only put it up five years ago. It cost forty-two million.'

'Have you seen the new listings? In March we are to be treated to a two-week run of Grant Nichols's standup tour "Googling My Cock". Not quite De Kooning, Judd, Richard Serra. Not quite the Bilbao of the north. They promise us Shostakovich, Bartok, Pirandello, Brecht. But the building is first and foremost a penis extension. It doesn't work as a concert hall. It doesn't work as a gallery. But it is perfect for "Googling My Cock".'

Rodbortzoon cracked open a wing and nagged at a stubborn bit of meat with his teeth, pulling it cleanly from the bone.

'And for this all the funding was taken from the Bridgeside Theatre Collective and they have stopped touring, and the Vale of Peter Artists Cooperative is closed. These were small things. Local things. But not parochial. The libraries are on their knees. And ... and ... and ... The list goes on. Forty-two million they spend on this centre of the arts and we are left with a city where Flynn's karaoke night is the most culturally significant event of the month. To the Generator, I say, bring on the wrecking ball.'

Rodbortzoon tossed a final spindly bone on to his plate and looked at his greasy, sauce-streaked fingers. He looked for a second like he was considering wiping them on his T-shirt but then got up gingerly, careful not to touch anything, and sloped off to the toilet.

Colin turned his attention to the pub television high in the corner of the room. It was a Premier League match. Second in the table versus third. The camera cut to the two managers on the touchline. They were a study in contrasts: a tracksuited German bouncing around in his baseball cap, kicking every ball; and, opposite him, an impassive Italian, his scarf knotted extravagantly at his neck. In the build-up to the game much had been made of their mutual antipathy but everyone involved knew that their tactical clash was a mere sideshow compared to the battle for ascendancy between the owners: China's pre-eminent construction magnate and the Saudi sovereign wealth fund.

The goalkeeper kicked the ball upfield. Colin watched as the winger trapped the ball and released it to a teammate. Immediately the game settled into its organic pulsing pattern. The passing was slick, geometric, probing. The ball moved from one side of the pitch to the other, its path somehow prefigured, systematised, like a chess computer analysing all the possible moves. Watching it, Colin felt it was impossible not be acutely aware that the players were all the product of elite academies, each one of them the end point of an intense institutional effort: strategic conditioning, disciplined diets, holistic fitness regimes, secret scientific know-how. The score was one-all and the game was being played with such speed and precision and tactical acumen that it ended up being weirdly boring to watch.

'This game,' said Rodbortzoon on his return, 'who cares?'

'Um ... *Everyone*,' said Colin. 'I wouldn't be surprised if there were, I don't know, a hundred million people watching this around the world.'

'Rubbish. No one cares. Not even the fans. These teams, they're not football clubs any more .. It's like movies. The movies are no longer movies. Think of all those Jennifer Aniston vehicles. Romantic comedies. *Soi disant*. They're ninety minutes, on celluloid, etc. etc. They take the *form* of movies. But they are not actually movies. They're simply manifestations of transnational capital as it engineers its own expansion.'

Rodbortzoon paused, picked at his teeth.

'Actually, maybe Jennifer is a bad example. You know, because of the rumours.'

'What rumours?'

'You haven't heard?' He looked about, whispered. 'People say she's an entryist.'

'*What?*'

'You know, a fifth columnist. Sleeper agent. Part of some accelerationist group, keen to speed us to the crisis point.' He sat down, drew in his chair. 'Think about it. You want to accelerate class tension to hasten the social revolution. How do you do it? You make the already immiserated proletariat sit through *He's Just Not That Into You!*'

Rodbortzoon took a hasty pull from his pint, wiped his moustache with the back of his sleeve.

'I mean really think about it. If you wanted to illustrate unambiguously neoliberalism's utter contempt for everything that is meaningful and worthwhile, if you wanted to illustrate that things simply cannot get any worse, that this is the moment when there is nothing to do but to take up arms, wouldn't *Marley & Me* be *exactly* the movie you would make?'

Colin looked at him, mock aghast.

'Is Courtney Cox in on it?' he asked.

'They say that she is the handler,' said Rodbortzoon. He looked immensely pleased by this.

On the other side of the room someone dropped a glass and the smash caught everyone's attention for a second or two.

'Anyway, I digress,' continued Rodbortzoon. 'The point I was making is that these teams are no longer football clubs in the traditional sense of the word. They take the form of football clubs: players, stadiums, etc. etc. But even the fans understand that they are simply moments of transnational capital going about its business. You know, marketing plan for a Middle Eastern theocracy. Vertical integration for a media conglomerate. Whatever, whatever. They are not clubs, just capital.'

'I don't know,' said Colin, looking at the vast crowds packed into the huge stadium, 'they still seem to sell an awful lot of tickets, these non-clubs.'

'Of course! Half is tourists on a package deal. Hotel and drinks included. Straight to the best seats on the Helsinki Express.'

'Yeah, you say that, but there are loads of locals at those games, aren't there?'

'Of course plenty of locals still attend, I know this. They still go. Many thousands of them. They are curious. They are all wanting answers on the same question: how bad can it get? How much can we be patronised and degraded? How far will they go?'

Rodbortzoon was animated now and his tics were coming out, the pulling of his earlobes, the wiping of his nose.

'Hollywood is the master of it. Every year the films get worse – infantilised, stupid, retrograde – but people still go and every one makes more money than the last. The Premier League is the same. They give us cheerleaders and fireworks and a DJ to tell us what to sing. And still we come for more. It's like we're rubbernecking at our own accident! How badly can they treat us? How much will they degrade us, exploit us? How many replica shirts a year? How big a ticket price rise? What will we put up with? Every year we think: I can take a little bit more, a little more pain. We love it. It's maso-chistic. Self-flagellation. Every year, all the fans are secretly thinking to themselves: come on football, take it to its logical conclusion: piss in my face.'

Rodbortzoon delivered this last line at full volume, his arms waving wildly above his head. In any other situation, Colin would have found this mortifying to the point of paralysis, but they were in the back room of the Geoffrie, a place where anything went.

'We don't have cheerleaders,' he said defensively. 'Or a DJ.'

'And that, my friend, is exactly why we're fighting. The Chapel is something else. Twenty-three home games a year and we have twenty-three days of carnival. Not floats and steel bands and all that bullshit. *Real* carnival, back to the original meaning of the word. Every time we congregate there, standing on the Radleigh, singing our songs, dancing our dance, we are more than simply a crowd. We create something. A fleeting paradise. A space beyond. A *utopia*. Where else can you find this kind of gleeful egalitarian chaos? In the Premier League? Forget it! It is long gone. Lower down the divisions there are pockets of resistance, but none as good as the Chapel. We are the plucky little village in Gaul. One of the last redoubts.'

Rodbortzoon was in his groove, up on his feet, pacing.

'It is as close as we have to a populist autonomous zone, a place where, even just for one and a half hours on a Saturday afternoon, the existing order is suspended. For ninety sweet minutes we replace piety with vulgarity. We replace hierarchy with communality. Acquiescence with revelry. Observation with participation.'

He paused and leaned in close to Colin's face.

'We are not fighting for a corporate football club,' he said. 'Me, you and the fragrant Kerry. We are fighting for the carnival. And *that* is why we have to win.'

STEAMING IN: A PODCAST WITH MICK CLARIDGE AND STEVE WANLESS

ORIGINALLY AIRED 7 p.m.
SATURDAY, FEBRUARY 8th

MICK

So. Welcome to *Steaming In*. I'm here. So's Steve.
I'd do my usual intro but I'm not in the mood
for any fancy chat. Not after that. We've had a
shocker. Three-nil. Away at *Darlington*.

STEVE

Not our best outing of the season.

MICK

(voice rising throughout)

I don't want to be critical of Paul Christie.
Lord above, I love the man at least as much as I
love my wife but good god, it's a rain-lashed day
in early February, the pitch is like the Somme
the morning after, the whole game's being played
in the air, and he brings on Gavin Parsons, five
foot seven Gavin Parsons, who can barely get his
head on a pillow let alone a high ball, and he's
wondering why we've shipped three goals in the
second half.

STEVE

First time we've conceded three goals in one half
since 2013.

MICK

We're missing him. There's no doubt about it. Our
Jordan. We're getting a sense of what we are when
he's not there.

STEVE

We've got a tweet in from @steamer_82. He wants to
know what you think about the rumours that Kirk's
been talking to Chelsea about selling them the lad
in the summer.

MICK

. . .

STEVE

. . .

MICK

Do you remember when we sold Gem McBride?

STEVE

The fourth of February 1981. Three weeks to the
day after Andy Cousins had had a full-length
portrait of him tattooed down the inside of
his thigh.

MICK

I cried. I'm not ashamed to admit it. I cried.

STEVE

Not as much as Andy Cousins.

MICK

Selling Garry would be worse.

STEVE

Worse than McBride? I never thought I'd hear
you say that.

MICK

Do you remember the goal Gem scored against
Palace? The one from the corner flag with the
outside of his boot? That was as close as I've
come to a religious experience.

STEVE

That was 77/78. Twenty-seven goals in all
competitions. Thirteen assists. And he barely
broke a sweat.

MICK

I know people like to talk about Gem McBride in
the same breath as Mark E. Smith, Richard Burton,
Dylan Thomas. And I understand why. The genius.
The self-destruction. The crazy teeth. But really
he was the English Elvis.

STEVE

(indulgent chuckle)

MICK

The years he was at Notts County before coming
to us, they were his Sun Studio years. He was
full of promise but he hadn't become himself yet,
hadn't realised the power in those hips. When he
signed for us it was like Elvis signing for RCA. It
all just clicked. For a few years he could do no

wrong. Everything was touched by genius. The hat-trick against Port Vale ... The double nutmeg on Archie Lloyd.

STEVE
That no-look cushioned pass in the quarter-final against Oldham.

MICK
After he left us it was never the same. The money played a part, for sure. Compared to what they get today, Arsenal weren't giving him much but he got a fat signing-on fee and it turned his head. It was like Elvis and Hollywood. All those years he was too busy making films to remember he was the King of rock 'n' roll.

STEVE
He had his moments at Arsenal. The two goals at White Hart Lane. The title tilt in '84. But his heart was never in it.

MICK
By the time Arsenal had had enough and he was shuffling about the pitch at Derby he might as well as have been in a rhinestone jumpsuit.

STEVE
In his biography he claims that he can't remember anything about the 86/87 season. Even scoring that goal from the halfway line. Although he was approaching sixteen stone at that point so you can see why he would choose to shoot if it saved him doing any running.

MICK

When people think of him now they remember that
version of him — fat, drunk, smoking fags — but
those years with us he was the sexiest footballer
in the world. It didn't matter that he had ginger
hair and was missing two teeth. He had such a
swagger about him, such confidence, such flair.
He will always be my favourite player of all time
and the club selling him was one of the darkest
days of my life. But he was born on the Wirral. He
grew up supporting Liverpool. Jordan Garry is a
Larkspur boy, born and bred. Selling him would be
like selling your son.

STEVE

. . .

MICK

. . .

STEVE

We've had another tweet in. We've been copping it
all week on social media. Saying we were too harsh
about the Wigan result. People saying it was a
good game and the best team won.

MICK

These people. They think there's no harm losing
as long as you lose four-three. I just can't
stick it. They're not fans if they feel like that.
They're something else. I don't know what. I don't
even have a word for them. Tourists. They're
day-trippers. They've got no idea. Victory. Is.
Everything.

STEVE

What about being entertained?

MICK

Entertained? *Entertained?* It's not about being
fucking entertained. Entertained is *Avengers*. It's
going up cinema. It's things that don't matter.
Entertained is when you've got no skin in the
game. This is about *far* more than that. This is
about winning and losing. Winning and losing. Us
and them. Always, *us* and *them*. No inch given. We.
Give. No. Quarter.

STEVE

. . .

MICK

Talk to me, Stevie, tell me I'm not going mad.

STEVE

. . .

MICK

I'm shit tired of being plucky. Of being
patronised. No one will look down on us when we
win. No one will call this town shit when we win.
That's all we have to do. That's all that matters.
We have to win and we have to get promoted to
the Premier League. No one will call us shit when
we're in the Premier bloody League.

STEVE

Anyway, back to the game . . .

6

Patrick Summersby had chosen the right spot at the right table to ensure that he was framed perfectly by the symmetrical sweep of the Paradise's famous double staircase. His hair was similarly precise, as was the mannered knot of the cashmere scarf that poked through the parting of his Japanese denim jacket. Colin looked down at his own outfit. A hooded top, T-shirt and jeans that had once been black but were now a kind of piebald grey. He experienced once more the bewildering stew of emotions he always felt when he saw Patrick: affection, resentment, pity, and, of course – overwhelmingly – inadequacy.

'I mean really,' said Patrick dryly, affecting with his hands a kind of fan shape. 'Tell me, honestly, Ellie, can you *ever* have too much chrome?'

'I thought you'd like this place.'

'Like it?' said Patrick. 'Listen to the music. Look at the menu.' He swooned studiedly. 'It's like a portal has transported me back to 1998. There's even a bloke in the toilet handing out paper towels and a spray of CK One ... I come to Peterdown and I feel like I'm sixteen again. I *love* it.'

Patrick's modus operandi was stealth, his operations carried out under the radar. As Colin understood it, Patrick's barbs about the city were a proxy war against him personally. Which was exactly what he didn't need given his already jumpy mood. It was three days since he had seen Kerry and he had heard nothing. In between writing a profile of a phenomenally dull fourteen-year-old tennis prodigy and summoning eight hundred words on United's abject defeat away at

Darlington, he had used his time at the office to embark on what he could only imagine was one of history's most hapless, ineffective attempts at investigative journalism, which had mostly involved him googling 'Andrew Kirk', and then 'Andrew Kirk financial irregularities' and then finally 'investigative journalism techniques', none of which had proved in any way enlightening.

'We could always just go to the Geoffrie,' he said half-heartedly. 'If you wanted, you know, a *pub* pub.'

'Have you tried the wine in the Geoffrie?' said Ellie. 'The choice is red, white or pink. And that's actually what it says on the sign behind the bar: *pink*. Which is just as well really, calling it rosé would be a bloody insult. I've had subtler cartons of Ribena.'

Patrick laughed his high laugh. It was staccato, barking, like it was forced from the back of his throat. The mere sound of it made Ellie smile. She felt a great well of warmth and nostalgia. Patrick picked up a glass and pulled a bottle of wine from a silver bucket filled with ice. He was on his way from London to Glasgow, where he was judging some kind of street food competition and he had come to visit her. In Peterdown.

'It's a Sauvignon Blanc,' he said, pouring her a glass. 'It's actually perfectly drinkable. Which is something to say at £13 a bottle. You go to the Swan these days and half the wines are that for a glass.'

'At the *Swan*?'

'The very same. Well, it's the same building as the Swan. Different owners. Different everything else, too.'

'Christ,' said Colin. 'Even the Swan.'

'The Northie comes of age,' said Patrick. 'It had to happen.'

As far as Colin could tell from Patrick's occasional missives, the recent history of London's North Green Road – which ran from the outer reaches of Hackney up to Waltham Forest – had gone through four phases. There was now, which was, as everyone apparently knew, decidedly after the fact. There was the immediate past – the year or two when the Northie had been at the acme of its international acclaim; its secret supperclubs and basement speakeasies subject to breathless profiles in the *New York Times* – when it had still been a pretty vital place to live. There was just before that, when it was *really* cool – what Patrick liked to think of as *his* time – when things were just starting to happen: the parties in pool halls, the young artists staging group shows in abandoned soap factories, the pervasive sense of something *happening*. And then finally there was the long period before that, when it was just shit.

Colin had lived there then.

And he had gone to the Swan. By which we mean the Swan back when it was shit, too. Despite the warning signs – the broken windows, the tabloid flags, the tattooed dog – Colin had gone to the Swan. We are, after all, talking about a boy with a long rap sheet when it came to misreading signs, a boy utterly naïve to London. The Swan could have had four rotating swastikas in neon lights above the door and Colin wouldn't have clocked what kind of pub it was. And so, yes, Colin had gone to the Swan. He had gone in, got head-butted and left.

'They've completely gutted it,' continued Patrick. 'You'd love it, Fergie. It's the total opposite of shabby chic. I mean, that whole look ... God ... could anything be more *John Lewis*? Anyway, this place has actually been *designed*. It's very clean, very simple. The walls look like they're made of beaten metal. The lighting is brilliant. They've got a couple of Bibendum chairs. In fact, the whole thing is very Eileen Gray.'

'God,' said Ellie. 'I love Eileen Gray.'

'I was on a press trip to the South of France and we visited her place on the Riviera, E1027. What a place. It's covered in these huge lesbo murals by Le Corbusier.'

Colin took the bottle from the ice bucket and poured himself a glass. Out the window and across the road he could he see the television in the Queen's Head. Real Madrid were playing Atletico in the Spanish cup.

'Anyway, the Swan,' continued Patrick, 'which is now called West and Legend, by the way – it doesn't have any Sapphic wall art – but it's still amazing. And they serve natural wine, biodynamic wine, orange wine, all that stuff. Some of it's £20 a glass. In the Swan. The fucking Swan, Colin.'

For the next hour they drank (another bottle of the Sauvignon Blanc) and talked the latest: Leonie's health, Suzie's sobriety (she was better company when she was on the booze, they all reluctantly conceded), Little Tom's astonishing and utterly compromising wealth. The majority of the conversation took as its theme the parlous state of Big Tom's marriage, much of which was news to Colin, who might have been in regular email contact with the man, but knew little about his life beyond his opinions on Aston Villa's back four.

'We've got time for one more,' said Ellie once they had agreed to disagree as to the level of Tom's culpability and, more fundamentally, to what extent a stripper sitting on your lap during a stag do represented a betrayal of trust.

'It's my round,' said Colin, as he stood up to go first to the toilet and then to the bar.

Patrick waited until he was out of earshot. 'So,' he said, 'what's going on?'

'Well,' said Ellie. 'I got my part threes, which is progress, at least.'

'I know you did, darling. I mean have you started applying for jobs? You can hardly move for cranes in London, you'd walk into a job.'

'It's not that simple.'

'I know it's expensive but you can get a flat somewhere to begin with.'

'You don't have kids, Patrick.'

Patrick paused pointedly.

'I know,' he said.

'I didn't mean it like that.'

'I know,' he said. 'And I know you have a kid. But that doesn't exactly make you unique. There *are* breeders in London, you know. Millions of them. And they all seem to be coping.'

Ellie screwed her eyes half-shut. It was at least two days since she had last looked at Rightmove, which by her standards represented Gandhi-like levels of self-denial. Rather than idling away hours on the internet she had been writing to name architects, trying to solicit their support. The lure of London was there of course, but it felt like background noise for the first time in a long time.

Patrick sat back in his chair, drummed his fingers on the table.

'It's not turned out how I expected for us.' He was drunk and maudlin. 'I was so sure we would do things. Tom and Suzie. Leonie. I really thought she would, you know. Christ, even fucking Colin. Our darling little ingénue. Remember what he was like back then? It was like he was drinking in the world.'

Ellie smiled at the sweetness of this, which was rare from Patrick.

'He was always the funniest.'

'He was,' she said.

'Whether he meant it or not.'

Their eyes locked for a second and the look between them contained whole indices of memories and nostalgia and regret.

'You're doing things,' said Ellie softly.

'I write about other people doing things. Which isn't the same. Not that it matters, really. The real tragedy is that you're not doing things, Fergie.'

Ellie paused. It was incumbent on her, she felt, that she nip it in the bud, this version of their collective narrative in which she became a totem for the wider group, her career cast as an opportunity for redemptive deliverance. She needed to be able to make any decisions with a clear mind, chart her own path, not be freighted with too much expectation.

'At the moment I'm here. And I'm doing things. I have a job – it's shit but it's a job – and I'm the only person standing up for this building. And that's important. Everything else can wait.'

Patrick looked at her, sighed.

'I would understand if you were anywhere else, but look at this place. It's so,' here he lowered his voice to a whisper, '*Brexity.*'

'Actually, it was like fifty-three to forty-seven here – pretty much the same as the country as a whole. So it's not that ...'

'Oh, come on, you know what I mean.'

'I mean, there are loads of things you can level against this place, but ...'

'*Ellie.*'

'*Patrick,*' she said, raising her glass. 'It's not often I get a visit from someone I genuinely love, so can we please get on with the purpose of this and get actually properly pissed.'

Patrick relented and met her glass with his just as Colin returned with a fresh bottle, a bowl of olives and some dry-roasted peanuts.

The consumption of this third bottle followed a pattern that Colin recognised from past experience: Patrick and Ellie got increasingly garrulous and uninhibited, he ever more morose and paranoid. His state of mind was not helped by the sudden influx of people to the bar, a significant number of whom had taken the previously empty tables around them and who appeared to be sitting silently, listening to every word they were saying. He sat quietly throughout the entirety of a ten-minute conversation on London house prices, while a woman on the next table stared in uncomprehending and indignant horror at the unlit cigarette that Patrick was holding in his right hand and which appeared to be forever on the verge of coming into concert with the lighter he held in his left hand.

After a long period discussing the extraordinary vitality of some east London neighbourhood that Colin had never visited, Ellie and Patrick started on Peterdown's own imminent development. Loudly and, to Colin's ears, in an accent that seemed to be getting more cartoonishly clipped by the minute, Ellie listed all the buildings in Peterdown she considered worthy of demolition: the Generator (obviously), the Capricorn shopping centre (I mean, with an atom bomb, I would *vaporise* it), the Enterprise Cluster, every building in the Aspire business park and three of the town's newer housing developments. For reasons that he hoped were noble and authentically felt, she didn't include the Chapel on this list but then she determinedly undercut this generosity of spirit by stopping, looking unnecessarily at him and saying:

'And you know what else I'd happily see go? Even though the building itself is a perfectly inoffensive nineteenth-century pub? The Red Lion. Just to spare us another homecoming gig by the fucking Panel Beaters.'

'Oh god, they're from here, aren't they?' said Patrick, who, it transpired, was drunk enough to throw his head back and start shouting:

Colin felt every eye in the house swivel to their table like snipers' sight lines seeking out a target.

'That song has nothing to do with them,' he said in an urgent whisper. 'It's by the Lightning Seeds. And it came out in 1996. You're like twenty-five years out.'

Mercifully, this was enough to stop Patrick, who sat back in his seat with a dismissive wave of the hand.

'The Panel Beaters song is called "The Last of the Street Footballers",' continued Colin. 'It's not a chant. Or an anthem or anything like that. No one sings it on the terraces. It's not that kind of song. It's a song about a local boy and how he learned to play football in the street. He plays for Peterdown. It talks about the Larkspur.'

'It's still shit though,' said Ellie. 'It's music for people who don't like music.'

'Whatever,' said Colin, conscious that it would have been far simpler to just leave it, but emboldened enough by the booze to stand his ground. 'You can hate it. I like it. It's about my life. It's unaffected.'

'And isn't being unaffected just *such* a virtue in pop musicians? I mean, think about Bowie and Roxy Music and Talking Heads ... if only they'd been just a little more *guileless* they might have really caught the public imagination.'

'You don't get it,' said Colin. 'You'll never get it. They all went to art school. They weren't outsiders. The Panel Beaters didn't go to art school. They're the real outsiders.'

He watched unsmilingly as Ellie made great play of banging her glass on the table and hooting derisively.

'You know what your problem is?' he said. 'You want outsider art to be people action painting with their own blood and stuff like that. But the reality is that outsider art is rhyming couplets and watercolours of people's pets. And music like the Panel Beaters.'

'The Panel Beaters aren't outsider art. They barely play anything else on Radio 2!'

'They're from Peterdown,' said Colin, flatly and decisively. 'Any art from Peterdown is outsider art.'

And with that he got up and went for another piss.

When he returned, it was time to leave. Their table at the curry house was booked for 9 p.m. As they walked through the cold streets, Colin found himself smiling irrepressibly at, for once, having had the last word. The evening then took a marked turn for the better when, once they were seated at the window table in the Koh-i-Noor, Patrick made a big fuss of trying to order off menu, something called murgh malai, a dish he claimed was authentic Indian cuisine. It was an argument that seemed entirely lost on the waiter, a man who, judging by his accent, seemed to have been born in Burnley or thereabouts, and succeeded only, as far as Colin could tell, in making Patrick look like a bit of a tit.

'So, Colin,' said Patrick frostily, once the drinks had arrived. 'How's football?'

'It's still going.'

'I was with someone for a bit last year who was into it,' said Patrick as he dipped a poppadum in some mango chutney. 'What a way to spend a Saturday night, watching football on TV. Christ, the game itself is bad enough. Kick kick kick. Run run run. But what I really hated was all the talk. The commentators and the chat. The endless blah blah blah of it.'

'So the bit I do, basically.'

'Well, I didn't really mean it like that but, yeah, I guess so.'

'Yeah, well I'm still churning out the blah blah blah. Although, actually, it all feels a bit more urgent at the moment. If Ellie gets the Larkspur listed, that sorts the problem there. Saving the Chapel is more complicated. We're never going to get the stadium listed and the wanker that owns the club wants to move it out of town. Even if we can convince the government not to put the station there, he could still move us. We've got to ...'

'Wait a sec,' said Patrick, looking first at Colin and then at Ellie, 'so *your* football stadium is on the same shortlist as *your* housing estate?'

'Yes.'

'Ha, ha, ha! Good luck, Colin.'

Instinctively, Ellie and Colin looked at each other and then instantly anywhere but at each other. For a while no one said anything.

Colin understood the power imbalance in their relationship was an observable fact, a known thing that was out there in the world and much remarked upon. He knew it. Ellie knew it. But it was one of the cardinal rules of their relationship that it was a truth that remained unarticulated when they were both present.

Eventually, Patrick gamely saved the situation by moving the conversation on to whether or not he should move to Margate, a topic which managed to sustain them until they paid the bill and left.

Back at the house, after they had paid the babysitter and put her in a cab, Colin poured the last can of lager into three glasses while Ellie pulled her laptop from the bookshelf.

'Come on then, show me the new stuff on your site,' she said, sitting down next to Patrick at the kitchen table.

Patrick took the laptop from her and opened a gallery of his latest images. The first was a close-up of a plate of food. It was pretty, nasturtium-scattered. Patrick flicked right. More food. Some dark green leaves which contrasted pleasingly with the shiny pink seeds of a pomegranate. On it went. Cups of coffee, shot from above, leaf-like shapes patterned in their white foam tops. A vintage cake stand laden with brownies. A café with mismatched vintage cutlery and cookies in countertop jars. Cocktails in receptacles of all kinds: teapots, test tubes, an old-school pewter pot. Ellie watched the images go by. In the London of her imagination – of indeed her memory – everyone wanted to be an artist, a writer, a musician. No one had wanted a street food van.

'You used to do things other than food, didn't you?'

'I still do. I would do more but it's the food that gets all the hits.'

Patrick flicked on to an image of him talking with another man.

'Who's that?'

'That's George Foster. I met him at a coffee festival in Greenwich last week. *Jolt* magazine commissioned me to interview him.'

'Am I supposed to know who he is?'

'He's a big cheese in that world. He's been barista of the year like three times. He invented the half-caf.'

'The what?'

'The half-caf. They mix the beans: half decaf, half regular. It's for when you want a pick-me-up but not the full effect. All the brew-heads love it because they can binge without getting the shakes. It's basically this year's flat white.'

Colin had finished his lager and was rooting through the bottles on top of the fridge, looking for anything that looked drinkable.

'We have flat whites here now,' he said. 'They do them in Greggs.'

'Don't tell me,' said Patrick, 'they're made with small batch Ethiopian and all the milk is single herd.'

'*Single herd?*' said Ellie, sharply and incredulously.

Patrick blushed.

'It means you can trace its origin. I mean it's a bit nerdy, but . . .'

'What, like ancestry.com?' said Colin. 'Do they have *Who Do You Think You Are?* as well?'

'*Moo Do You Think You Are?*' said Ellie, sniggering, drunk.

Patrick blushed furiously.

'I don't even like coffee,' said Colin. He had found a bottle of raki and was sitting at the end of the table with his left hand over his left eye so his right eye could focus on the label, which he was scanning to see if it had a best-before date. 'That's what it is, isn't it? London and all of that. It's just a load of cafés. And I don't like coffee. I like tea. And you can never get a decent cup of tea in cafés. It's better at home.'

Ellie, who ordinarily would have very much liked there to have been a decent London-style café in Peterdown, serving half-cafs if it saw fit, found herself to be newly inclined to tea-drinking. She looked over at Colin warmly. In many ways he was a kind of anti-cook, someone with a startling capacity to make dishes that were less than the sum of their parts, but he was occasionally right about things and he did make an excellent cup of tea.

'Oh, I'd love a brew,' she said.

'Yes,' said Colin, as he pulled the cork from the bottle still in his hand, smelled it, recoiled. 'I don't think we should drink this. I'll put the kettle on.'

Ellie closed Patrick's site and absentmindedly flicked through her bookmarks to the Larkspur's Wikipedia page. Immediately, she could tell it had happened again.

'Oh, for god's sake,' she said. 'This is beyond a joke. Patrick, you're good at the internet. How do I stop these fuckers from changing the page?'

'Pass it here. I did some work for a wine event and part of it involved making a Wikipedia page for them and I ended up getting quite into it. I wrote most of the pages on Nanna Ditzel, and Jacob Jensen and a load of others. I'm basically Wikipedia's main dude on obscure mid-century Danish designers.'

'OK, great. You can make them stop.'

'The whole point of Wikipedia is that anyone can make edits. But if you think it's malicious you can report it. Let's have a look at what we're dealing with.'

Ellie watched as he typed and flicked at the mouse pad with his finger and thumb, followed by a burst of keystrokes.

'This is all one person. He's done the edits using four different avatars but they're all from the same IP address.'

Ellie sat up, suddenly sober.

'Aw, bless him,' said Patrick. 'He has *tried* to cover his tracks. He's used his avatars on other pages to make them look more kosher. His latest avatar is Mike1976 and it's done two other edits. One on Broadcastle City Football Club, another on someone called Ryan Swanage.'

'He was the Broadcastle captain in the eighties,' said Colin as he handed out the teas. 'He's the psychopath's psychopath.'

'It's embarrassingly bad but it must have taken a fair amount of effort. If it was just some kid mucking about you can't imagine they'd go to these lengths to cover it up.'

'So who is it?'

'I can't tell you just from Wikipedia.'

'This is a fucking *conspiracy*,' said Ellie.

'Wait a second,' said Patrick. 'Let's see if he's been really stupid . . . Oh god, he has. He's registered a domain to the same IP. The site was registered in July last year. It hasn't actually been launched yet and there's no contact or address or anything but they must be the people who've been doing the dirty on you.'

'Who are they?'

'Total Solutions PR, it says here. They've got totalsolutionspr.com and .co.uk.'

'Who are they?'

'I don't know,' said Patrick.

7

Usual place. 1pm. Good news!! xo

Colin saved the document he was working on and returned to Kerry's text message, specifically its final sign-off: *xo*. The *x* he was taking to be a kiss, but the *o* as a modifier confused him. Could it, he speculated in a moment of wild optimism, mean a kiss with an open mouth?

Urgently, he opened another tab and googled 'significance of xo at the bottom of a text'. The search generated 833,000 results, all of which pointed to the same thing: *Hugs and kisses*.

Colin sat back in his chair and let out a long steady breath. An *x* on its own at the end of the message signified nothing. It was just a piece of modern punctuation, a digital full stop. But *xo*, surely, was different. Hugs *and* kisses. It was considered, deliberate, laden with meaning.

He slipped his laptop into his bag and grabbed his keys. He walked quickly to the bus stop, his heart racing. *Hugs and kisses.* He would have to have his separately, he thought compulsively. Together would be too much, like eating your main and your pudding at the same time.

The Broadcastle Road was rain-swept, backed up with traffic. Colin sat on the 177 bus, staring out the window. The houses were pebble-dashed, grey under glowering skies. Thirty-six hours had passed since the night out with Patrick and still he was suffering the after-effects. Acute paranoia. Extra-keen self-awareness. The pervasive sense that everything he was invested in was fundamentally, intrinsically wrong.

He pulled his phone from his pocket. He tried to stop himself, but it had become a reflex. He looked down as his thumb skipped across the screen, keying in the letters of her name. There were about thirty different pictures of her on the internet. A head shot from the club website. A couple of her in the stands, in the background at a press conference. Plenty of portraits for newspaper pieces on women in football. One image stood out, though. It was six years old, taken for an article in the *Daily Mail* when she'd got her first job at the club as a callow twenty-two-year-old. She was on the pitch at the Chapel, kneeling on the turf, a ball in one hand. Colin tapped the image so that it grew to fill the screen.

She was wearing that season's home kit: an all-green shirt; white shorts; green and white hooped socks, pulled tight to the knee. He looked uncomfortably at the picture, at her over-primped hair. The way she wore her shorts too high on the waist. Her strangely man-nered way of kneeling. He felt a familiar flush of self-disgust. How many times had he looked at this image? It didn't bear thinking about. His preoccupation with it was just so ... he looked for the words ... it was all just so *Peterdown*.

He stared out the bus window. What was wrong with him? He had a bachelor's degree from Leeds University. A *2:1*. He smarted. And he listened to jazz. Not just *Kind of Blue*. The difficult ones, too. *Sketches of Spain*. That one by John Coltrane. And he read the *London Review of Books*. All right, he had read the *London Review of Books* twice. But he had liked it both times. By the standards of Ottercliffe High he was – and there was simply no other word for it – he was a sophisticate.

The houses stretched out uniformly, thirties semis, old mattresses in two of the front gardens. Colin leaned his head against the glass, shut his eyes. The bus stopped. Colin got off and walked into Rothbury Market. It was a big space, packed tight with stalls. He walked past the rows of anaemic chickens, demurely trussed. Pyramids of meat pies. A barrel of misshapen carrots, twenty pence a pound.

The café was at the back and up the stairs. He paused at the door. Kerry was there already, her back to him. She had taken her jacket off, hung it on her chair. Her hair was up, a single curl falling over her left ear.

He took a deep breath and slid into the seat opposite her.

'So, what have you got for me?'

'Dynamite,' said Kerry, looking either way before bending down and taking an envelope from her bag. She pulled a document from an envelope and placed it on the table in front of him. Her nails were blood-red pools, the varnish tight to the cuticle.

'This was never made public. It's a letter from the council to Kirk in response to an informal enquiry about developing the site. Look at the third paragraph.'

Colin scanned down the page to the third paragraph and read it out loud.

2.2 In principle, the Peterdown Metropolitan Borough Council will not object to the commercial development of the Grangeham site providing the completed development comprises a large scale organisation of genuine cultural or sporting significance to the people of the town.

'Now look at the date. Three months before he bought the club. I remember thinking at the time it was odd that he bought us when it's clear to anyone that he doesn't give a stuff about football. Well now we know. It was buy us or set up the Peterdown Philharmonic. And I doubt you could do that for a quid.'

Colin looked up at Kerry.

'He's not putting up the development to support the stadium,' she said. 'He's putting up the stadium to support the development.'

'If I run this will he know I got it from you?'

'Not if you make it look like you got it from someone on the council.' She stood up, righted her skirt. 'Go stick it up his bollocks.'

8

The first edition of the *Peter Post and Gazetteer* was published in 1888 by owner and editor Archibald Ottercliffe, the anarchist-inclined third son of railway magnate Lord Ottercliffe. It was sixteen pages long and cost one penny. In the 130 years since, the paper has gone through three changes of name and four changes of owner. In 1989, a year after the *Post* had limped to its centenary as a family-owned independent, the increasingly impecunious Ottercliffes offloaded the paper to Trumpet Regional Papers PLC. Trumpet, and its stable of fourteen regional papers, was subsequently bought out by Starbrite Audio to complement their network of local radio stations. In 2004, when Starbrite was dragged down by the post-Napster implosion of its record label, the newspapers were hived off to Gidner Holdings who ran the papers for eighteen months until no amount of cost-cutting could offset the precipitous decline in classified ad sales and the group was split in two. Trinity Mirror picked off the nine still profitable titles, and the others – the *Post* included – were bought in 2015 by the current owners, Sinderby Asset Management.

During the Sinderby years, the *Post* had gone from daily to thrice weekly. It had seen three rounds of redundancies, a wages freeze, and what was described as an 'asset rationalisation' – which included selling the paper's long-standing home, an imposing late-Victorian pile on the banks of the Peter (it was now a Wetherspoons pub), and moving the offices to one of the five corrugated steel buildings that comprise Peterdown's Enterprise Cluster, a commercial park just inside the town's ring road, known locally and not at all affectionately as the Cluster Fuck.

Colin's desk was on the second floor, at the end of a row of four, furthest from the window. It was Wednesday afternoon, two days since he'd seen Kerry. He had used what he had gleaned from her copy of the planning letter as the basis for a piece on the benighted soul of football, placing the plight of Peterdown United in its wider context alongside Manchester United, Newcastle, Wimbledon, great clubs with grand traditions that had been bled dry by exploitative owners.

He had filed the piece already to his editor, Rick Jarvis, and was waiting for comments, but he still had the document open on his screen and was enjoying the shape of it, the proportions of the paragraphs, each one neatly indented and just where it should be. Producing it had reminded him that writing was something that you could delight in. That it could be like a dance, a place where you could be nimble and fleet of foot.

Colin traced the shape of the final paragraph with his finger. He hadn't always been a football writer. It felt important to think this. To not forget it. For a few years he had written about all kinds of things. Music. Books. Travel. And before that, other wilder, freer things.

As he so often did when he was feeling self-aggrandisingly melancholic about his wasted potential, Colin found himself thinking of his *Sketches*, fifty or so pages of prose, written while he was at university, which more than ten years after the fact still occupied a totemic place in his sense of himself.

His had been a last-minute decision to do a history degree. Days, even hours, before the form had to be filled in and posted, he had been resolved to apply to read English. But when it came to it, it had just seemed too implausible to his seventeen-year-old self that someone like him would be allowed to study something so rarefied, something so obviously pointless. And so he had chosen history. Which had just felt realer. Earthier. Somehow more honest for someone like him.

And so for all that his university years were by a wide margin the sweetest of his life, they were not without a back note of regret, a sense of a better path not taken. It did mean, though, that when – just ahead of the final term of his first year – he had been encouraged, along with everyone else, to take a course from outside the department, he had unhesitatingly chosen creative writing.

His had been a small group, just ten of them in the seminar, none from his course or halls of residence. Ordinarily utterly at sea with the social codes and underlying dynamics of a given situation, he had found himself, for once in his life, able to read the room and from the first seminar onwards, he had understood what they all expected of him. Here, after all, was a boy from Peterdown, the backdrop for Arthur Toyle's *Riveted*, which so many of them had read for their GCSEs. He could tell from the moment he had first opened his mouth that they all had him nailed as another kitchen-sink realist whose work would just be an update on the 1950s original: stories about street racing in the suburbs, or taking drugs in Debenhams. And Colin could have done that. Indeed, Colin might have done that if they all hadn't assumed so blithely that he would. But he didn't. Instead, he produced what ended up being called *Sketches*. There were about twenty of them, some of them a paragraph long, some five pages. Each of them was written from the same perspective, a character that both was him and wasn't him, a kind of him without him, without all the stuff that weighed him down. There wasn't a narrative that connected them – one was about the feeling of swimming, another about the colour yellow – but apparently they shared a *sensibility*, and that had been enough to earn Colin a distinction.

It was only a couple of years after he had graduated – by which time the laptop the *Sketches* had been written on had broken down irreparably and he no longer had access to his university email account – that he had started to think about them in the way he now did. In part, obviously, the fact that his most decorated piece of work was irretrievably lost chimed perfectly with Colin's tragic sense of himself, and it helped too that the *Sketches* could be exalted in his mind without him having to confront the reality of a nineteen-year-old's idea of profundity. But he also thought of them as often as he did because they genuinely were a reminder that the page was a place where he might defy expectations. And find, perhaps, a liberation of sorts.

He scrolled through his piece again just to get a feel for the shape of the words and then looked over at Rick in his glass-walled corner office. He was at his desk, ashen-faced, his glasses on his forehead. Rick had worked for the *Post* for twenty-five years, fifteen as editor. He had endured the paper's demise stoically; optimistic that, however steep the decline in revenue, however dramatic the management overhaul, however hubristic the digital relaunch, he could continue to produce a local paper with integrity and heart.

All this had changed when Sinderby took over. Before then, the strategic changes of direction had all been commercial; his team may have been steadily decimated but he still had total control of the editorial output. The hedge-funders at Sinderby had other ideas. They wanted a paper that had an opinion, took sides: pro-business, tough on crime. The chief executive spoke openly of his admiration for Kirk.

Colin got up and walked across the office. The art team had printed off a series of alternative layouts for the proposed cover story, written by the paper's news editor Neil Henderson. Colin picked up one of the options.

ASBO CENTRAL
IS PETERDOWN SINK ESTATE WORST IN BRITAIN?
Larkspur Hill residents responsible for 62% of all town's crime
Brutalist style said to encourage antisocial behaviour
Rats outnumber residents

On the desk were prints of the images being considered to illustrate the article. One showed the Larkspur's main walkway at night, a figure lurking suspiciously in the shadows. Another featured four boys loitering, their caps pulled down, their collars turned up. There were close-ups of piles of rubbish, overgrown flower beds, water-damaged concrete.

Taken as a set they were about as different as you could get from Ellie's Instagram pictures of the estate shot at oblique, flattering angles against a bright blue sky.

Colin paused. Neither set of photos – these nor Ellie's – came close to capturing his own feelings about the estate, which were defiantly ambivalent. He could see obviously that it was a singular building and understood the argument against knocking it down but he struggled to appreciate what qualities it had other than its singularity. For all of Ellie's exhortations as to its sublimity and scale, it was, when it came down to it, a series of big blocks of flats, about which he found it hard to summon a passionate opinion one way or the other.

The photocopier churned. Two phones rang, one on the off-beat. It was 12.30 p.m. Colin looked up and noticed that Rick had emerged from his glass cube and was talking to Neil. He was destined for bigger things, Neil. The *Sun*, everyone felt, or maybe the *Mirror*. That was his thing. Being someone who was going somewhere. That and wearing ties the same colour as his shirt.

Colin sidled over and caught the end of the conversation between the two of them.

'There's been an application put in for land to be re-zoned around the airport. If they get it the developers will be able to build a mega-casino,' Rick was saying. 'I think we need to come out against it.'

'Why?' said Neil.

'It's our new national airport. Our gateway to the world. It's where all those first impressions will be formed. We don't want the world thinking we're some sort of knock-off Las Vegas.'

'I mean, why would we want to write about it?' said Neil, because he was going places and that gave him licence. 'It's in Kent. No one gives a shit about what we think about it. Let the nationals cover it.'

Rick shook his head, muttered under his breath, stomped back into his office.

'What's the word?' asked Colin.

'He's being a pussy. Doesn't like my piece, doesn't like yours. Says he's uncomfortable with unnamed sources. Which is a big barrel of cock and balls. We all know he doesn't like yours because he doesn't want to fuck off the board . . . which I can understand as Kirk is pretty much the only cunt that advertises in this paper . . . And he doesn't like mine because he thinks it's beneath him even though he knows it'll shift two thousand extra copies.'

Neil perched on the edge of his desk, right hand in his trouser pocket jangling his keys, both legs bouncing, head swaying slightly as if he were listening to a soundtrack that no one else could hear.

'You're laying it on a bit thick, aren't you?' said Colin limply. '*Asbo Central*?'

'The sooner they get rid of that dump the better. The world is coming to Peterdown, Col. Town's got to get its best face on.'

This was delivered in Neil's 'street' voice, which was Essex-y with an undercurrent of aggression, and could barely have been more different from his phone voice which was pretty much received pronunciation, and was, in turn, nothing at all like his 'local' voice, which sounded – even to Colin's well-trained ears – quite convincingly Peterdown-like, being soft and round and a little bit nasal.

Colin had never been able to work out which of these voices was closest to Neil's real voice, if indeed there was such a thing. He had heard a dozen different versions of Neil's back story, most of them, it seemed, as they were being invented – on the fly – to suit whatever situation he found himself in. After hearing him once say down the phone to a would-be source, 'My son is a similar age. But I can't even begin to imagine the sense of loss,' Colin had found himself staring open-mouthed, unable to hide his horror, until Neil ended the call, giving a little shrug as he did so and saying in an American accent: 'The game is the game is the game, Col. If you ain't playin', then you ain't stayin'.'

Of the many things that Colin hated about himself, wanting Neil to like him ranked high up near the top.

'Are you sure about the stats, though? They look pretty extreme to me.'

'I've got a source. It's all bona fide.'

'Come on, you know me. I'm all for taking a critical stance on things but ...'

'This is what it comes down to,' said Neil, 'he *wants* to publish yours but knows he shouldn't and *doesn't* want to publish mine but knows he should. And if we don't do something about it, he's going to spike mine to make himself feel better about spiking yours.'

Colin felt all the energy drain from his limbs.

'We've got to turn him round,' continued Neil. 'We need him to publish yours and then publish mine to make himself feel better about it. And it's going to take both of us. It's going to take a Ryder–Henderson one-two.'

On the most recent layout the headline to Neil's piece had been revised to **BUILT IN DELINQUENCY**.

Neil had pulled out his notebook and was writing down a list of phrases. Colin could see both *obligation to tell the truth* and *not in this business to be popular.*

'Which ones do you want?' asked Neil. 'I think I should have: *journalism can never be silent.*'

'I'll take *our duty as newspapermen,*' said Colin with a heavy heart. 'And *arbiters of local democracy.* You can have the rest.'

'Nice,' said Neil. 'Right, let's do this.'

Fifteen minutes later they emerged from Rick's office. Colin had the four/five spread and the whole of the back page. Neil had the front page and the two/three spread. He had also managed to force through his choice of title:

WELCOME TO HELL

They were upping the print run to 20,000 copies. It would be on the newsstand Friday morning.

9

Originally, the plan had been that they would simply meet at the estate, both of them driving their own cars. And then this original plan had – for environmental reasons, apparently – turned into him offering her a lift, which she had happily agreed to. But then his car had had to go in for a service and the plan had evolved into them cycling – the forecast was good and he had a new bike about which he was boyishly enthusiastic. With the geography as it was it made sense for him to stop by at hers to pick her up, which she had presumed would involve him waiting in the street while she retrieved her bike from the little shed in the front garden.

At no point had she imagined he would be ringing her doorbell a full fifteen minutes before he was due to arrive, and yet that was exactly what appeared to be happening, judging by the blurry shape she could see through the frosted glass of her front door.

Her rucksack already on her back, she answered the door as confidently as she could, only to find him standing on the doorstep, his arms up in surrender, his shirt sleeves rolled to the elbow, both hands black with oil.

'I am so sorry,' he said. 'I have made an absolute dog's dinner out of this.'

Ellie froze. Despite its many twists and turns, at no stage had the plan involved him coming into the house.

'I don't know if it's because it's a folding bike, but the chain kept coming off and getting stuck in this gap into which it is clearly not supposed to go and really it was an absolute nightmare getting it out. At one point I thought I was going to have to yank it out with my teeth.'

She stood there, unmoving, desperately trying to remember if there might be some ancient baby wipes that could be pulled from the back of a cupboard so that the whole thing might be dealt with on the doorstep.

'I want you to know that I rang the bell with my elbow,' he said with a smile. 'The only thing that I've managed to do at all competently this morning.'

The calculations whirred in her head. They didn't have a washing-up bowl but there was a fruit bowl that she could empty and fill with water ...

'I know it's incredibly bad form to come barging into your house uninvited, but if I promise not to touch anything could I possibly please come in and wash my hands?'

Ellie drew a sharp breath and bowed to the inevitable.

'Of course,' she said, forcing a smile. 'Of course. Please, please come in.'

She walked down the hall trying to regain her composure. It was totally ridiculous to be reacting in this way; people came to her house all the time.

'Oh my god,' said Pankaj, his hands still in the air like someone had a gun trained on him, 'look at this place. It's incredible.'

They were standing in the knocked-through living room, Ellie's homage to Cabanon, the Riviera holiday hut that Le Corbusier had built for his wife in the 1950s. She had pulled up the carpets and painted the floorboards white. One wall was covered in plywood panelling. The other was painted racing green. The base of the sofa was plywood, as were the box stools, the chest of drawers and the side table. The screws were counter-sunk, the joints dovetailed. The handles of each drawer had been custom-made from cherry dowel sourced from a specialist in Broadcastle. All of a sudden she felt deeply self-conscious about it all.

Pankaj was looking at the lampshade she had had covered in period-specific fabric. She waited, her breath held, for a reaction. Strange that she never looked at it through other people's eyes when the other people were less complicated. Colin's parents, say. Or Patrick. The guy that came to read the electricity meter.

'Did you do all this?'

'Yes, some of it. I mean I designed it all, but I didn't build most of it. A joiner did most of it.'

'It's a hymn to plywood.'

'It is. My closest friend here calls it the hurricane relief centre.'

Pankaj laughed, his hands still up in the air.

'We don't own the house,' said Ellie. 'And I didn't want to invest too much into something that I couldn't take away with me. So this all seemed like a neat solution. All the panelling will come with us when we go. And all the furniture of course.'

She led him through to the kitchen.

'And on it goes,' he said. 'Look at this!'

She had conceived of the space as an endlessly adaptable series of free-standing self-contained plywood units, each of them on wheels. There were six in total, not including the static sink. Some were doubles, others singles. They could be lined up to make a long counter or dotted about, as they were at the moment. Colin's dad, it had transpired, was handy with a jigsaw.

Ellie blushed as she reached to turn on the tap for him.

'I am sorry I've barged in on you like this. I am completely useless with machines of all kinds.'

'No, god, I'm sorry,' she said, as she pulled some hand soap out of a cupboard. 'I don't mean to be so rude. Of course you're welcome to come in and wash your hands.'

She opened a drawer looking for a fresh towel.

'It's odd to have you in here, that's all. Architects can be funny about their houses. It can all feel like a bit of a vanity project. This isn't at all representative of the kind of thing that I want to do. Looking at it with you it all feels terribly self-indulgent.'

She blushed again.

'Be that as it may,' he said, looking around him as he scrubbed his hands. 'I still think it's utterly brilliant. Can you move it all around?'

'The sink stays where it is for obvious reasons. And we don't really move the oven. Although it's electric and I did get the spark to put in an extra-long flex so in theory we can, but we tend not to. But everything else can go pretty much wherever you want it to. My daughter and I like to change things up when we need a fresh perspective. The current layout is her work. They've just started doing the Greek myths. Her head was full of minotaurs and labyrinths.'

Ellie looked at the kitchen arranged as it was, chaotically, in classic Daisy style. Inwardly, she felt the rare sensation of a small victory won. Her own childhood home had been a place where there was barely space to breathe, let alone plant a flag. The adult world had colonised its every corner. Her mother's stuff was everywhere. On every surface. In every room. Books by the hundred. Hats. Clothes. Trinkets. The expensively acquired accoutrements of passing fancies: Tibetan singing bowls, bread ovens, vintage sewing machines. It was not at all unusual to come home and find a euphonium and three huge boxes of hymn sheets dumped at the end of your bed because there was simply nowhere else to put them.

'The Daedalus of the Vale of Peter,' said Pankaj.

Ellie laughed through her nose.

'Something like that.'

'What does your landlord think about all this?'

'He hasn't been here for years. As long as the rent is paid he pretty much leaves us to get on with it.'

She passed him the towel, smiling sheepishly.

'That said, we probably won't be getting our deposit back. Most of the kitchen that was here originally is in the loft. Whether or not it could ever be reassembled is very much a live question.'

He laughed as he dried his hands.

'Oh wow,' he said, gesturing to the corner of the room. 'Look at those. Homemade Joseph Cornells.'

Ellie glanced over her shoulder at them.

'I took my daughter to the big retrospective last year. She's obsessed.'

'And she made these? How old is she?'

'She's nine.'

'She's nine and she made that?' he said, pointing to the box on the right.

Ellie blushed again.

'That one's mine, actually. The other two are hers.'

'OK,' said Pankaj, walking over to them. 'But hers are still wonderful. What a phenomenal kid. Imagine being into Joseph Cornell at nine years old. Incredible.'

He stopped at the box on the right. Hers. Dime-Store Alchemy.

'Look at the detail in this. It's beautiful.'

Ellie stood where she was, trying to appear calm. She had vowed only to use things she found in Peterdown's charity shops, its car boot sales and second-hand stalls. She and Daisy had gone out together four weekends in a row, planning their routes ahead of time, making sure they got in early, got access to the best stuff. And what a delight it had been. Scouring shelves, riffling through old boxes, unearthing hidden gems.

She looked at her box. It was, objectively, a pleasing composition. The lovely contrast to the textures. The wildly different scales. The muted colour palette. It was only now, though, looking at it with him, that it occurred to her how obviously revealing it was. Caged birds. Pinned butterflies. Extinguished candles. She hadn't written LIBERATE ME on the glass, but you didn't exactly have to be Carl Jung to read the subtext.

She stood motionless, staring at the box's centrepiece: a vintage padlock with a key which would clearly never fit it, waiting for him to say something flippant, or worse, something serious. But mercifully nothing came and he shuffled sideways to get a better look at the first of Daisy's boxes.

'The Big Apple in miniature. This is brilliant. And that cuddly little monkey does make for a very cute King Kong!'

Compared to her box with its measured use of objects and considered composition, Daisy's were exuberant and soulful, the contents thrown together with a gleeful abandon. Ellie looked at the Manhattan skyline, which had been cut wonkily from a magazine. It had taken every ounce of her reserve not to edit them. Not to declutter, nor to straighten. Not to correct the spelling, nor neaten the colouring. She let out a controlled breath. She had done none of these things. They were Daisy's boxes to name as she saw fit and fill as she saw fit. And that, if nothing else, was the point of the whole thing.

'Fascinating,' said Pankaj. 'But I've really intruded too long. Let's go to the Larkspur.'

'Yes,' said Ellie, finally relaxing. 'Let's.'

* * *

Half an hour later they were at the estate, standing in front of Europa House, the biggest and boldest of the Larkspur's five structures. Above them, carved into the concrete, was the original signage:

1.0 Europa House

'Marjorie designed that font. She called it Augustan, after him. It was a kind of love letter, a perfect unity of his European intellectual rigour and her pastoral English romanticism. The sans serif gives it a very modern feeling, but it's not austere. It's got a lovely warmth to it.'

They stopped and looked up beyond the sign to the external staircase, with its dramatic switchbacks and sculptural attention to detail.

'On his own Agosto couldn't have created work like this,' she said, looking up and shielding her eyes from the sun. 'You look at his buildings before they met – the theatre in Montpellier, the government buildings in Montevideo – they're outstripped by their own ambition. They promise more than they can deliver. It's only once he starts collaborating with Marjorie that he realises his full potential. It's not just that she humanises him, although she does, absolutely, she brings warmth to the buildings, and, of course, she was the one that brought the genuinely political dimension to the relationship. He was an aesthete really. It's only after they get together that he starts to take social housing seriously. But the assumption that that's all she brought to the table is totally false. He was the artist, but *she* was the great engineer of the two of them – the one chafing at the limits of the possible. She opened up his field of vision. She underpinned everything he did.'

She pointed up to the rooftop sky café raised on piloti. It was long derelict, but it didn't take much to imagine how its floor-to-ceiling windows would allow for amazing views over the Beagle Hills.

'The café is a case in point. She engineered it. He designed the windows. Everything was a conversation between the two of them. They were a creative partnership in the fullest sense of the word. They worked together, lived together, had children together.'

She climbed the stairs, a step ahead of Pankaj.

'There's this suggestion that she used him to get things built. That he was just a powerful man she could anchor herself to. It would be a lie to say she wasn't ambitious. She was and she never denied it. She was a grammar school girl trying to make it as an architect in the 1960s – of course she was ambitious. And clearly he was a lot older than her, but you read her diaries and it's obvious it was love. Sure, there was a bit of competition between them, but it was healthy, dialectical, it pushed them on and up. And really they complemented one another more than they competed.'

Behind them they heard the quick-fire cushioned thump of a bike being wheeled down concrete steps. From behind a wall emerged a man. He was in his early twenties, bleary-eyed, on his way to work. He looked them up and down and sniffed, before jumping on his bike and cycling down the walkway, his legs bowed and pumping furiously.

'He needs to change gear,' said Pankaj. 'He's on a horizontal path, not an Alpine stage of the Tour de France.' He shook his head, bemused. 'It's a thing, isn't it? Cycling like that. Half the kids do it. I don't understand why. It takes so much more effort …'

'Oh god,' said Ellie.

The door to number 1.17 was boarded up.

'There was someone in that flat last week. I have asked the council, I don't know, three, four, five times if they're decanting this estate and every time they say no, but I just do not bloody believe them.'

She walked over to the window and peered through a crack in the curtains. The room was empty and forlorn, but elegantly proportioned, substantial. Through an internal door you could see the kitchen, still with some of its original features, flooded with light.

'I know this looks shabby but every flat in this whole development is twice the size of the mandated minimum that everything is now built to.'

Ellie turned and headed along the walkway. Five of the six doors had door cages, and all the windows were similarly barred. Tellingly, though, four of the five cages were unlocked, evidence of the estate's relative calm since its nadir in the 1990s. The walkway was chaotic, lived in. They picked their way past a water-damaged sofa, patio furniture, abandoned toys, a pile of orange peel.

'Well, say what you like about the antisocial behaviour,' said Pankaj cheerily, 'at least someone's getting their five-a-day.'

Ahead of them the concrete was water-damaged, walls streaked black like cried-out mascara.

'I'm not going to pretend that the building isn't without its flaws,' she said. 'There are serious problems. I know there are issues with leaks on some of the flat roofs. But it could so easily be sorted. It just needs a bit of money. The problems with some of the rendering will take a bit more work but the technique was in its infancy when they built this – today we could easily recreate the panels as they intended them, and they would last forever.'

'I fear that Peterdown's council housing department might struggle to raise the kind of money you're talking about,' said Pankaj.

'I know, but it could be done over time. A bit of money and the long-term savings would be massive.'

They stopped on a high walkway and looked out over the estate.

'I couldn't work out what it was that's been bothering me and I've finally realised what it is,' said Pankaj, after a while. 'All the columns are uniform, decorated with that distinctive diagonal pattern – apart from that one,' he said pointing away to his right. 'The lines of that pattern go the other way.'

Ellie stopped cold. No one had ever noticed this before. Not in her years of proselytising, her dozen or so informal tours like this.

'It's funny, isn't it?' he said. 'I don't see how you could make a mistake like that. I can only imagine it was deliberate.'

'The wrong column *is* deliberate,' she said. 'Marjorie was born and brought up in Durham. It's an homage to the cathedral there. The architects of the day – in the twelfth century or whenever – had this thing that they couldn't make the building perfect. They had to acknowledge that only god is without fault.'

Pankaj laughed.

'Do you think if we asked Yvonne she'd say: "Yes, yes, the place would be perfect if it weren't for that column." Ha ha!'

'Yeah, well, no one ever said the Blofelds lacked confidence.'

For the next twenty minutes they walked the estate, and as they walked Ellie talked. And talked. All the thoughts, jokes, observations, anecdotes flooding out and apparently, for once, finding an appreciative audience. For a good while she had felt that becoming serious about something had made her less funny, less charming. She looked at Pankaj as he laughed at one of her jokes. How nice, for once, to like the sound of the things that came out of your mouth.

Eventually, they found themselves back at the car park.

'So where are you from?' he asked, leaning against the door of his car. 'You're obviously not a local.'

'I'm a Highgate girl,' she said. 'One of a long line of run-of-the-mill north London faux-bohemian narcissists.'

Pankaj smiled.

'Just the kind of people that my more-English-than-the-English parents found so baffling but wanted so much to gain the approval of. I was born just down the road in Belsize Park. Not that I remember it. We moved to Guildford when I was young. My parents prepared me well for a life surrounded by white people.'

Peterdown was coming to life, cars queued along the access roads, people walked the streets, school children shrieked, birds flew overhead.

'They pretend to be appalled at me not being married at forty, but seem very keen to broadcast the news to everyone they know. Secretly they're thinking to themselves: unmarried at forty, what could be more Western?'

Ellie stopped, thunderstruck.

'Fuck,' she said. 'Self-deprecating jokes. Oxford first. Human rights. Good teeth. Suits that fit you. It all makes sense. You're going to be prime minister, aren't you?'

'Ha! I don't know about that. I'm very definitely on the wrong side of the floor at the moment.'

'Seriously,' she said. 'Do you want it?'

'Do you have any recording devices on you?'

Ellie took her jacket lapel and pulled it in front of her mouth. 'Code Ten,' she whispered into it. 'Code Ten. Eagle Four is burned. I repeat Eagle Four is burned. Pull out. Pull out.'

Pankaj laughed.

There was a pause, a lull into which Ellie sensed a new kind of trust was being poured.

'I don't think anyone goes into this game unless they think they can do it,' he said.

'Shit,' she said. 'You're going to, aren't you?'

'If the mood of the country times itself right,' said Pankaj, smiling. 'Brexit goes wrong. The Scots come round somehow. We sort our shit out. It's not inconceivable that at some point in the future I'll have as good a shot as anyone.'

Ellie smiled, a little abashed. She had been harsh on him. A proper operator would never have admitted to this. Not to ambition and the self-regard it implied.

'I'll be all over the press when it happens ...'

'I hope so,' he said before she could finish what she was about to say. And it threw her. Ellie stopped, turned her head reflexively, felt a slight blush high on her cheeks.

He put on his helmet with a smile on his face.

'How did you know I went to Oxford?' he asked.

'The internet told me.'

'So you googled me?'

'Doesn't everyone google everyone now?'

'I suppose they do if they're interested.'

Ellie blushed again. There were two lines of communication in play. The literal one and the other one, which was physical, tonal, subtextual. He was using it, it seemed, to confer on her membership of some elite club, a place where, despite herself, she found she really wanted to be.

'My daughter's got a play date on Saturday,' she said impulsively, 'and I was thinking I might get a petition going in town. Try to drum up a bit of support.'

'That's a great idea. Where are you going to be?'

'I was thinking the corner of Richardson Road and Rothbury Way.'

'Perfect. I shall swing by if I get a chance.'

'Oh, and sorry if this a weird question, but you haven't heard of Total Solutions PR, have you?' she asked.

'No, I don't think I have. Who are they?'

'I don't know. They've been editing the Larkspur's Wikipedia page, putting in new paragraphs with made-up statistics about the crime rate, completely distorting the actual history of the estate. I correct it and they do it again using a different avatar. I don't know how to find out who they are. They're not online and not registered at Companies House.'

'Right,' said Pankaj. 'I shall start investigating on your behalf.'

He got on his bike and turned to face her.

'And what are you going to do for me in return?' he asked, twinkling.

'Well,' said Ellie, in a coquettish voice that she barely recognised as her own. 'That remains to be seen.'

10

There were eight pitches in total, clustered together under the A108 flyover. They were back-to-back, caged, artificially lit. Battery football, thought Colin, as he walked from the car park into the reception area.

It was Friday evening. 9 p.m. Kick-off time for the Night Leagues, five-a-side football for wayward teens, boys who had to be kept from the street. Colin was writing about it. Fifteen hundred words for the inside pages. The redemptive power of sport. It was a good-news story and that was exactly what was needed to keep him sweet with Rick, who was still angsty about his piece on the planning application and would be even more so, Colin predicted, when it hit the newsstands on Saturday morning.

The reception area was exposed brick and underlit. Street art on the walls. A bass-heavy soundtrack. Teenage boys milled about, texting, eating crisps. Almost uniformly they wore dark-coloured high performance sportswear, all of it discreetly branded, box fresh, the zips pulled up tight under their chins.

In among all this stood Brian, looking, it had to be said, every one of his fifty-three years. He was wearing a pair of lurid Hawaiian shorts, a black beanie hat and the 1992 Peterdown United away shirt rolled to his elbows, revealing old army tattoos, a good number of them clearly self-inked.

They walked past the reception desk, through the changing rooms and out on to the complex of pitches. It had been recently refitted, Brian explained, with government money. The funding model was intended to be self-sustaining: the after-work office leagues and weekend bookings would in the long term pay for the Night Leagues, which were free for the kids, staffed by outreach workers. Colin took his notebook from his bag and started to make notes.

Brian paused at the high fence that separated them from the first pitch, and stood, his fingers hooked into the wire, watching a game that was just kicking off. Colin had a vague sense that this was the kind of piece that required a liberal sprinkling of colour. He wrote: *light glittering raindrops wire fence.*

'They're not easy to reach, a lot of these boys,' said Brian. 'Their lives are tough. Really tough for some of them. You have to find the thing that they love and build from there. And this is what they love. They're desperate for the discipline, the order, the clear white lines they know not to cross and that they don't *want* to cross, that's the thing. This is where these boys find a set of rules that they buy into.'

A group of lads walked by in matching blue bibs. Brian addressed them all by name, cracked a gag, took the (funnier) comeback with good grace, pulled to one side a boy called Jerome and asked him a few questions that were ostensibly about his strapped knee but obviously really about how things were at home.

Colin watched the way that Brian's presence affected Jerome – a boy, he felt shamefully, he could easily imagine crossing the road to avoid – the way he responded to Brian's hand on his shoulder, the smile after the affectionate cuff that finished the conversation. Brian's was a kind of masculinity that would forever be foreclosed to him, he felt, however old and gnarled he got.

'They're clearly very comfortable with you,' he said, once the boys were gone. 'Every time I try to have a conversation with a sixteen-year-old I find my mind instantly empties.'

'I can relate to them,' said Brian. 'I know their lives. I was like a lot of them when I was sixteen. Directionless. Running with the Steam. Fighting all the time.'

On the pitch in front of them a little kid took the ball in his stride, rode a challenge, slipped it cheekily between the legs of the advancing keeper.

111

'Great finish, Ryan,' shouted Brian. 'Now get back into position. Pick up your man.'

Ryan looked over, smiled sheepishly. He ran back, picked up his man.

'He was a skeleton, that boy, when he first started coming. Wasn't getting much other than crisps at home. His school dinner was basically keeping him alive. He comes here every night we're open, and he gets fed. We take turns bringing him in something to eat.'

Colin watched Ryan running coltishly down the wing. He wrote *coltishly* in his notebook, crossed it out.

'No one is telling Ryan he's going to be the next Jordan Garry,' said Brian quietly. 'I don't sell this as a route out. I tell each of them when they come that they won't make it – that's not what this is about. It's about belonging somewhere and feeling wanted. Football can do that. The Chapel can do that. Kirk's new stadium? We all know what's going to happen. The prices will rocket. How many tickets will there be for lads like this?'

Brian walked off to check in on another game. Colin made a few colour notes in his book: *dominant smell once Deep Heat, now Red Bull.*

'You want a vision of the future? Look at City. I see it with our Kieron. My sister's boy. He grew up in Broadcastle, out Coldharbour way. He's a diehard fan but him and his mates can't afford tickets for the Broadcastle games. So they watch it in the pub beamed in from Turkey or Estonia or wherever else they can get a dodgy feed from. Everyone's on lager and lines of coke and there's no brake on their behaviour. Football was the one thing that dragged those guys into mainstream society. Now they're in their own bubble. And they're all white and they're all straight – or at least they pretend to be – and they're all men and they're all off their heads. The songs they sing. It breaks my heart. Songs about the fire, of course. Horrible, horrible songs about that fire. And that's not even the worst of it.'

Brian looked over his shoulder at a group of Asian boys to check that they were out of earshot.

'You should hear the racist stuff. Vile, it is. The kind of thing you just don't hear at the grounds any more. Or at least hardly ever.'

112

Colin was pretty sure that this wasn't what Rick had in mind for a Local Focus feature, but it would have been rude to stop taking notes so he carried on scribbling away. He wrote: *football as civilising force?! Don't tell Rod* ...

The eight pitches were all now full, matches under way on each of them, with plenty more kids waiting on the side lines for the next game to start.

'I shouldn't really be telling you this as the piece doesn't come out until tomorrow, but I managed to get my hands on some interesting information. About Grangeham. I've got a close source that says they're hiding something. Kirk and his inner circle. Something they don't want to come out or it'll ruin their chances of selling off the Chapel.'

'What is it?'

'I don't know for sure but I have a lead,' said Colin. He outlined the contents of the letter, the requirements of the planning committee.

'So you're saying we stop the move to Grangeham and we take away his only reason for wanting the club?'

'Yeah, basically.'

'Oh, man, it all makes sense now. I've found myself thinking a lot recently, about the club and what it could be. We need a vision for it, beyond saving the Chapel. What kind of future do we want once we've got rid of Kirk? Imagine it: a fan-owned club, right in the heart of the community. It could really be the start of something ...'

Overhead the traffic roared but you could still pick out the sound of the games: shrieked calls, the sound of the ball thudding into the hoardings.

'It's as obvious as a kipper what we've got to do. We've got to go after the Larkspur.'

'Um, yeah. No, I'm not sure that's a good idea.'

'Come on, Col. It's what everyone feels locally. It's the emblem of everything that's wrong here. Of everything that's been done to the place.'

'I mean, I'm not sure ...'

'I grew up surrounded by it, you know. Stories of the place as it was in the forties and fifties. Life was hard, for sure. But it was a romantic place, this town. The Peter was still a proper working river back then. My dad, my uncles, they used to talk about barges laden with so much coal it would cast you in its shadow on the riverbank. They all lived in Knoxley Heath, as it was then. It covered the whole area from Larkspur Hill right through to the Generator. Thousands of people lived in there. The tightest communities you could imagine. Kids in the street. Your auntie in the next house ... I never knew it. It was all gone by the time I was born. Ripped up. I grew up on the Ridgewater estate. Halfway to bloody Broadcastle.'

Brian stopped to watch one of the games.

'It was a tragic loss, you know,' he said, looking out on to the pitch. 'I was born into the loss. It was this thing that had been taken away from them. But also from me. My dad talked about the great warehouses that were tight against the river, huge great things. They would play there as boys, all of them up the poles, on the ladders, snitching what they could from the boats. And you should have seen the Yards in its heyday. The Assembly and Bolt shop was the longest free-standing single structure in Europe for decades. Everyone called it the Steam Shed. It was beautiful, the way the iron piers held up the glass roof. Fifteen hundred feet long, it was. You've never felt space like it. My friend, Jack, his uncle had the record for running it. You had to dodge between the piston parts and the engineering pits. Fifty-five seconds. There was none ever bettered it.' He laughed quietly to himself. 'I'm not saying it was perfect. Of course it wasn't. But it was a place with *pride*. Where you could live a whole life. You know what I mean.'

Here Brian interlaced his fingers to create a kind of ball.

'Integrated?' said Colin.

'Exactly. *Integrated*. There was something integrated about Peterdown and they ripped it up. They tore apart the fabric of this town and they put something else in its place.'

'Yeah, I don't know. I mean ...'

'My dad wouldn't let me work in the Yards. Not after the fire. Not after all kinds of other stuff and all.' He shrugged. 'Me joining the

Guards was my way of rebelling. It was a fuck you to him. A stupid seventeen-year-old's fuck you to his old man. And it got me out of here. But I came back. You know, I couldn't not.'

The night air was cold and thin, the afternoon's rain sat in puddles. Brian walked alongside the fence, Colin following, taking notes still although he wasn't quite sure for what.

'The worst of my drinking after I left the army, you know what got me through it? Reading Arthur Toyle. *Riveted*, obviously. But the other ones, too. And the poetry. He wrote beautifully about the Vale. About the landscape. And the wildlife. The birds. 'The Nuthatch', that's a beautiful poem. Have you read it?'

'No,' said Colin a little huffily. He had read a lot of Arthur Toyle novels as a teenager. Of course he had. But he had outgrown them, he felt, many years ago. Nonetheless, the completist in him was piqued: he had never read the poetry.

'The Chapel is one of the last places left of his Peterdown. Toyle himself stood on the Western Terrace when he was a boy and it wouldn't have been much different to how it is now. You know, not much, not really. And that's why it can reach across the generations. The Sheds, the unions, the working men's clubs – they were all places where lads who were sixteen could connect with blokes that were sixty. All gone. The Chapel's the only place left where you can build bridges, and it could be so much *more* besides.'

Shouts rang across the pitches. Two boys squared up, catching Brian's attention, and for a second it looked like there would be a fight, but quickly it calmed.

'I think about a future where we have the best bloody academy in the country,' he said, walking on. 'It would be like this but on a massive scale. Professional. Nurturing local talent. Local lads. With all the best will in the world. I look at Gunnarsson and I can't fault him. He's a great player. He's been a great player for the club. Works hard, great feet. But he's from Reykjavik. And I just don't have the same bond with him that I do with Jonny Ellis whose mum worked in the same factory as my aunt Sue. She's a lot younger than my Sue and they didn't know each other, didn't work together, I don't think. But our stories feel stitched together. Imagine how you'd feel if that team was mostly Jonny Ellises. Mostly Jordan Garrys. I'm not pretending we can turn back the clock and win the European Cup like Celtic with all the lads born a couple of miles from the stadium. That'll never happen again. But we can try to root this club in the place it's from. We can try our damnedest to fill the team with lads like Garry. Stacking shelves in the Eastfinche Road Asda until he was just shy of twenty-one. Don't tell me you don't feel it more when he scores.'

Colin demurred. The things he felt when Garry scored were deep and complex, freighted with an almost unbearable burden. It was, he thought with affectless nullity, the only time he really felt anything that was not instantly unsatisfying.

'I feel it,' said Brian. 'Every time he scores. Given the chance we could turn this club into a source of proper civic pride. Once we've got some civic pride there's nothing we can't do.'

'I think you might be asking a bit much of a football club. I don't think it's going to save us.'

'It won't save us, no, but we can save ourselves. That's what you've got to believe, Colin. I believe that this club can be turned around and I believe that this city can be turned around. The memory of the Yards run deep here. We just need to find some pride and when we do the jobs will come.'

'I mean, god, Brian. I'm on your side. I really am. But let's not get ahead of ourselves. The government just ordered a shitload of high-speed bullet trains and they didn't even *think* about building them here. Whatever happens to the club, however much civic pride it instils in people, the future of this town is not going to look anything like its past.'

'There are manufacturing jobs out there, skilled work that needs people who know how to build things. The work is there. We've just got to get it.'

'OK. Maybe. And I mean, outside chance, *maybe*, we could get some, I don't know, wind turbine manufacturing, that kind of thing. But what kind of investment would it take? And I don't mean just

116

the buildings, I mean the people. You're right, the memory of the trains does run deep, but the youngest of those guys are in their fifties, sixties. And, really, those jobs. How often do they come up? Hardly ever.'

Colin felt the familiar lethargy, the overwhelming sense that his life was one long steady deflation. He had stopped taking notes.

'And every time they do we'll be up against Pittsburgh and Bremen and Bilbao, not to mention half of Lancashire, Wales and the Clyde Valley. They're all in the same boat. It's not just Peterdown. What are all these other places *for*? I don't fucking know.'

'Come on, man. We're getting a station, high-speed—'

'Great. We'll need someone to sell the tickets and it'll have a McDonald's and a WH Smith and a branch of the Cornish Pasty Company, and there will be jobs in all of them, but it's not going to give us a role in the world, is it?'

A klaxon sounded across the complex to call time on the first round of games. Brian fixed Colin a look and then pushed open the door to the pitch nearest them and started to usher one set of boys off, and another on. Colin stayed grumplily outside, idling through his phone. The likelihood of anyone having sent him an important email at 10.30 p.m. was remote but he checked anyway. Nothing. Not even any spam. He logged on to Twitter, trawled through the conversations, the promos, a lot of very similar and not very funny jokes about an own goal in the Spurs game, until a short message caught his eye. It was Truther_78.

Oh dear, @Generator_Peterdown. Every week a record low. Don't drag us all down with you. 106 ain't no magic number.

He highlighted the words and copied them into a text which he sent to Ellie along with the message:

What the hell could this mean?

On the pitch Brian had finally corralled all the boys into the right places.

'Colin, get your arse in here,' he shouted. 'You're captain of the greens. Adil, Shaz, Omar, you're on Colin's team. And you, Callum.'

Colin looked at his charges. By his estimation Adil, Shaz and Omar were all about sixteen. They were lithe and tracksuited, each of them possessed of a single diamond earring.

'Shaz is up front,' said Omar in a voice that didn't exactly encourage dialogue. 'Me and Adil in midfield.'

'Callum's in nets,' added Shaz. 'Unless you want to go in.'

Colin looked over at Callum. He was wearing a wool jumper and very short shorts, his legs marbling in the cold. He looked like the kind of boy who mutilated cats in abandoned quarries.

'No,' said Colin. 'Callum can be keeper. I'll be a kind of ball-playing sweeper. Play the Beckenbauer role.'

The boys looked at him uncomprehendingly.

'Let's go,' shouted Brian, tossing a ball on to the floor and passing it to one of his teammates.

Colin jogged into position, waited, watched. Brian made a run down the wing, got the ball. Colin went to him but didn't commit himself to the tackle. He let Brian come on to him and showed him out, forcing him down the line. Suddenly and unexpectedly, Colin pounced, taking the ball off Brian's toe and in the same movement flicking it to Adil.

Brian looked at him, bewildered. The thing about Colin was that he wasn't shit. At football. Dancing. Singing. He wasn't *good*, and he himself was well aware of that, but he wasn't shit. And he was a lot better than he looked like he was going to be.

'So, it's like that, is it?' asked Brian.

'Looks like it,' said Colin.

For ten minutes they played without scoring, Colin's side pretty going forward, Brian's team staunch in defence. Brian was a solid footballer. He sat back, marshalling his troops, talking to them constantly, winning tackles, spreading the play. His side soaked up the pressure, running hard, harrying Shaz every time he got the ball.

Eventually, Omar broke the deadlock with a cute finish. Minutes later Brian hit a speculative shot that went through Callum's arms to make it one-all, which is how it stayed until half time.

Colin sat on the floor alongside his teammates, panting happily.

'Have you heard about the plans for Tuesday?' he asked. 'The game against Blackburn?'

'Who's playing Blackburn?' asked Omar suspiciously.

'United are. At the Chapel. On Tuesday night. There's a protest planned.'

'We don't go Chapel, bruv.'

'No? It's not always that easy to get a ticket, I suppose.'

'We don't support Peterdown.'

'Who do you support?'

'Me? I'm Chelsea. He's Man U.'

'What about you, Adil?'

'Me? Real Madrid.'

Just as Colin was about to interrogate whether a club that had won eleven European Cups really needed the distant support of sixteen-year-old boys from suburban Peterdown, Brian blew a whistle and they all jumped back to their feet for the second half.

Quickly, it was obvious that Brian's team's exertions in the first half were catching up with them. They dropped deeper and deeper, allowing Colin to come forward, join in the attacks. He picked up the ball, rolled it to Adil, got it back, rolled it to Shaz. It felt good to be running, moving, passing.

He took off his hoodie and tossed it behind the goal. Two minutes later he found himself struggling to suppress a smile when he heard Adil saying 'nice one' after his perfectly timed tackle had set up Omar to score. A sly give-and-go with Shaz earned him a waist-high hand slap. And then it just all started to click. He picked up the ball, went to pass to Omar but at the last second dropped his shoulder and ghosted past the defender. Without looking up he played a blind pass perfectly into Shaz's path. Three-one. And then four and then five. Colin was at the centre of it, giving and going, finding space, bringing the others into the play. Pass, move. Pass, move. Pass, move. It had a kind of hypnotic quality, a feeling of total synergy. It was as if the four of them had settled on a frequency, a direct communicative link that allowed them to pre-empt each other's movement, one, two, three passes down the line.

Not since he was a teenager had Colin been part of anything that was remotely like this. The football he had played at university had been thuddingly physical, the ball always in the air, the games uncontrolled and agricultural, dominated by the big men on either side. This felt like a return to something purer. The game played, as it should be, on the floor, a thrilling synthesis of maths and motion, of Euclidean space, instinctual trigonometry, form for form's sake.

Colin's experience of it momentarily bifurcated; he was somehow both totally enveloped in it, part of this thing that seemed to pulse and stretch and move, this collective entity, immeasurably greater than the sum of its parts, but he was also, somehow, watching it, almost having to suppress a giggle at its beauty, this lovely live and living thing, that would last only for a few short moments but while it lived it would lift all those involved, send them soaring on the swell of it, the kind of thing that when they looked back they would all realise was the culmination of many years of effort, a reward for years spent in parks and recs and playgrounds, a fitting celebration of years and years of love.

Adil picked up the ball, played a one-two with Shaz, cut it back into Colin's path. The ball bobbled a bit and then sat up invitingly. Colin set himself and without thinking about it he just leathered it. The ball didn't dip or swerve. It went arrow-straight, at pace, eight inches from the ground and crashed in off the inside of the post.

There was a brief pause, and then a kind of collective involuntary murmur. Colin tried to be cool about it, but it was impossible. The force of his grin overpowered all his efforts to contain it. He had scored a goal. And not just any goal. A goal for the ages. Brian was staring at him, open-mouthed.

'Fucking sweet,' said Omar, as he clapped Colin on the back. 'That was fucking sweet.'

11

Whatever she did, Ellie could not get the trestle table to open flat. She had thumped it and sat on it, kicked violently at its legs, but it was unyielding: it sat there symmetrically sloping from the centre like a shallow Palladian pediment.

Two pigeons landed near her, paused, flew off. She pulled a Toffee Crisp from her pocket. It was ridiculous, and she knew it, but she couldn't shake the feeling that this misshapen trestle had profoundly undermined her status as someone qualified to speak on architectural affairs. It was principally to blame, she felt with irrational certainty, for her only getting eight signatures on her petition despite spending three hours standing at the corner of Richardson Road and Rothbury Way on a busy Saturday morning.

The lights changed, traffic pulled away. She opened the Toffee Crisp, took a bite. The real kicker, she realised, was not that the trestle wouldn't open flat, but that she felt so beholden to it, standing there with its piles of leaflets and biros. As if it alone could confer legitimacy upon the whole production.

She looked down again at her petition. Eight signatures. It was embarrassing to be out here, in the drizzle, not knowing what you were doing.

'Look at you, Mother Fucking Teresa!'

Janey was pushing a buggy and pulling her isn't-this-totally-amazing face.

'She was a nun. What's that got to do ...'

'You know what I mean.'

'No, actually. I mean, I really ...'

121

Ellie gave up.

'Thanks for coming by,' she said.

'How's it going?'

'A bit slow.'

'I'd stay and help, but she's got to go to the doctor's,' said Janey, nodding down at Alexis in the buggy. 'Urine infection.'

'Oh, the poor thing, They're awful.'

'She was up half the night.'

'I can imagine.'

Janey picked up one of Ellie's flyers, turned it over in her hands.

'You know I love you and I don't want to be a dick about it, but the thing is, English people, they want to live in houses. It's just the way we are.'

'Have you seriously come here to tell me that you're not going to sign it?'

Janey rolled her eyes.

'Of course not, but I want you to know I'm only signing because it's you. Can I put that somewhere?'

'No.'

'Put an asterisk by it, or something?'

'No.'

'Janey Cole is only signing 'cos Ellie Ferguson is her mate.'

'No, you can't write that.'

'Even though it's true.'

'Yes, you've made that very clear.'

Janey finished filling in her address, added a heart on the 'i' in Edith Road.

'Course, the reality is I'd sign anything for you,' she said.

'No, you wouldn't.'

'Yeah, I would. And I still think it's amazing that you're doing this,' said Janey.

'That's nice of you to say so.'

'Even though it's bullshit.'

'Right.'

'It's heroic bullshit.'

'Thanks,' said Ellie.

Janey shut her eyes.

Where have all good women gone?

Even without a microphone, she could project enough to fill the street. Louder than the idling cars. Loud enough to catch the attention of the people in the square across the road.

And where are all the gods?

A couple walking past stopped and looked around bewildered, trying clearly to make a connection between the trestle table and the woman singing Bonnie Tyler.

'Oh god, please don't,' said Ellie, the blush rising in her cheeks.

Where's the streetwise Hercules to fight the rising odds?

A dozen people on either side of the road had stopped what they were doing and were standing still, staring. A cabbie was idling, staring at them too. Two office workers peered out of an open window.

'OK, well done. Everyone's looking now. You've done what you set out to do.'

Janey ignored her and carried on until she reached the end of the first verse. She opened her eyes and looked at Ellie.

'Come on,' she said, 'it's the chorus. Do it with me, this is your moment.'

'Stop now, please. Please. Oh god ...'

I need a hero.

Ellie shut her eyes. To use a phrase of Colin's, no one ever listened to Janey sing and felt like she'd done anything other than leave it all out on the pitch. This, though, was something else. She was hammering it, rinsing the emotion out of every syllable.

I'm holding out for a hero 'til the end of the night.

Janey emphasised this point with a clenched fist pull. And then it happened, as it always did; what Janey was doing went from being excruciating, not-knowing-where-to-look awful, to being suddenly hilarious and unutterably brilliant. Ellie shook her head and then did the only thing that you could in such situations, she closed her eyes and joined in.

And she's gotta be strong and she's gotta be fast and she's gotta be straight from the fight.

Seemingly simultaneously they both opened their eyes and looked at each other and smiled, and then at the absolute top of their voices they both hollered:

I need a hero.

Janey put a hand up in the air and Ellie high-fived it.

'I think that'll do us,' she said.

'Here's hoping,' said Ellie to her departing back.

For the next ten minutes she stood there, self-conscious but also happily proud. Janey's intervention had not led to a great outpouring of support but it had put her on the map.

She smiled to herself, newly emboldened. The 273 pulled up, wheezed to a stop, sighed open its rear doors. Six people got out, three of them kids. She scanned the faces of the three adults looking for clues, a spark of intelligence, the potential for sympathy.

A pensioner, her face set to. The mum of the kids, young, harried, hooped earrings. A guy. He was fortyish, nice-looking. Good hair.

She stepped lightly into his path, caught his eye, smiled, thrust a leaflet in his hand. The wording on it was uppercase, to the point:

YOU WOULDN'T BURN A PICASSO, WOULD YOU?

The man smiled, turned it over. On the back was a picture of the Larkspur, a few words on the architectural philistinism that had seen so many high Victorian masterpieces lost, the case for Grade II listing. He barely got past the picture.

'You've got to be kidding,' he said as he dropped the leaflet, pushed past her. 'Comparing that dump to Picasso? Jesus Christ. You're tapped, you are.'

Ellie went to say something, didn't. She swallowed hard and bent down to pick up the leaflet. Did it matter, she wondered, if your trestle wasn't flat? If your petition went unsigned? Did it matter if the whole thing was a pastiche as long as you were there? As long as you faced up to the indifference?

She raised her chin. The rain had not been forecast. It was light, the sort that coated your wool clothes in a fine film so that they shimmered slightly in the light. She rolled her shoulders down her back and stood stoically, waiting for more people to pass.

How silly of me not to realise that the animal rights movement depended entirely on you. There it was again. That voice. Unbidden. Its familiar clipped delivery. Its smugly ironic register. Her mother had made this observation at some point in the late 1990s, during an argument over a proposed family trip that clashed with a demonstration Ellie had organised.

Ellie felt a quiver of self-recognition, an abiding sense of shame. She had been thirteen, stridently vegetarian, the school organiser for PETA, her bedroom bedecked with images of fox carcasses ensnared in traps, models in blood-drenched mink coats.

Of course we'll change our plans so we can definitively make sure that the second years at Highgate Wood aren't wearing fur. I can hardly think of a more pressing political battle.

Ellie placed her clipboard on the trestle. Under extreme duress she had gone on the family trip (to her aunt's: an awful experience, obviously) and missed the meeting. The world had continued to turn. The animal rights movement had got along fine without her.

The church bell at St Benedict's started pealing twelve o'clock. She looked up. A familiar figure was shambling down the road.

'Christ,' he said. 'Are you not freezing?'

'I'm all right,' she said gamely. 'I brought a thermos.'

Colin looked down at the petition.

'Nine signatures.'

'Three hours I've been here. And I'd only have half that if it wasn't for four drunk guys who took pity.'

'Tough break,' said Colin, doing his best to sound sympathetic when it was pretty obvious, he felt, that she got off on the adversity. This, after all, was the woman who had insisted on hanging a giant blue and gold EU flag in their window in the lead-up to and for a long time after the referendum. Plenty of people had voted Remain in Peterdown, him included – although he had done so without enthusiasm and largely because the thought of staying felt so much less effortful than the prospect of leaving – but no one had campaigned for it as demonstratively as she had, or with such pietistic zeal.

'Anyway,' he continued, 'that tweet I forwarded you last night ...'

'Yeah.'

'It's been deleted.'

'Because it was total gibberish.'

'I mean, maybe ... but the guy who posted it ... I don't know if he's a guy, although I'm sure he is, in fact he just has to be ... Anyway, the guy that posted it. I don't know who he is, but he likes you to know that he knows stuff. Insider info. It's part of his online persona. He's boastful. Likes to talk himself up. Anyway, you can map the pattern with him pretty easily. He starts off pretty smart, pretty sharp, but over time he gets sloppier, his spelling goes, he starts saying things he ends up regretting.'

'You think he's a drinker.'

'Half his tweets are about Glenfiddich. He calls it Glenn like it's a person. He talks about Glenn like he's his best friend.'

'OK. So an alcoholic writes something meaningless and then deletes it, so what?'

'No, he only deletes the tweets that matter. He leaves all kinds of rubbish up there. He only deletes something if he wakes up in the morning and realises it's too near the knuckle. I don't think he took it down because it was wrong but because it revealed too much.'

'OK,' said Ellie, conceding the point, intrigued.

'So, he'd tweeted something like *don't drag us down with you, 106 isn't the magic number*. So you would think that the Generator's in trouble, right? But how bad is it? At first, I thought it might be that it's only getting 106 visitors a week, but they must be getting more than that, don't you think? That's like fifteen a day. Then I thought what if it's losing 106 grand a week? That would not be a very magic number, would it?'

'No,' said Ellie, doing the calculation quickly in her head. 'It would not. That's more than five million a year.'

'Not exactly financially viable.'

'Definitely not. We need to find out more about this. I'll ask around.' She paused and looked at him. 'Thanks,' she said.

Colin smiled, accepted the compliment. He picked up the clipboard and looked at it, smiled again, this time to himself.

'The four guys earlier. Big units, were they? Lots of spandex?'

Ellie looked at him quizzically.

'Jake Roberts. Randy Savage. Mr Fuji. Rick Rude. They're all WWF wrestlers from the late eighties, early nineties.' Colin didn't put much effort into trying to repress his smirk. 'Amazing that all four of them turned up here together. They really were a golden generation.'

She felt her mood drop like a heavy stone in thin air.

'This fucking town,' she said. 'And the fucking people that live here.'

'For pure spectacle,' said Colin, with a self-satisfied grin, 'I would put WrestleMania IV up there with the '81 Ashes and the 1970 World Cup.'

Ellie closed her eyes. She felt the cold, the pain in her lower back, the weariness in her limbs.

'You're no better than the rest of them. Fucking wrestling. I mean, what has that got to do with anything? I've half a mind to call them up and tell them to put the station wherever they bloody well want and we'll move the Larkspur panel by panel to somewhere where it might be appreciated. Somewhere that's not overrun with philistines.'

Colin looked away, his smirk gone.

'Yeah,' he said, conscious, even as he was saying it, that going down this road would be immediately self-defeating. 'I wonder where that would be?'

'I don't know, not anywhere in little bloody Brexitland, that's for sure.' Ellie paused. 'I imagine they could find a home for it in Marseille, though.'

Colin clenched his jaw, pyrrhically vindicated. He had a long and storied history when it came to seeking confirmation of the nobility of his victimhood. And nothing achieved this with greater efficiency than conversations about Marseille. The place was, famously, the home of the Cité Radieuse, as anyone who had lived with Ellie Ferguson for ten years could not escape knowing. It was also famously *dynamic and genuinely lived. Architecturally infinitely more interesting than pretty pretty Paris. Possessed of a unique vitality* ... All of which would have been enough for Colin to be fairly suspicious of it – from a distance, naturally, he had never actually been there – but Marseille was also the birthplace of Ellie's ex-boyfriend, the famously non-philistine Jean-Gabriel Bossis, and as such was out there, on its own, as his least favourite place on earth.

Colin stuffed his hands in his pockets and considered the direction the conversation would likely take were he to rise to the bait. He played the scenario out in his mind: him calling her out on it, her cutting rebuttal, his cornered counterpoint, her triumphant takedown. He pictured himself, emotionally bloodied, on his knees. Was it worth it, just to be right?

Colin looked down at the ground. No, it wasn't. It never was. In an act of almost inhuman will he looked up, forced a smile and said: 'Well it is probably the only building in town that might actually survive the journey. Although I'd like to see the ship that got it there.'

Ellie's reaction was not at all what he was expecting. She flinched, turned her head to one side and started to blush. Colin looked at her, bewildered. Had he shamed her into this reaction? He felt briefly elated. And then he noticed the direction of her gaze, which seemed skittishly fixed on something behind him. He turned round. Walking towards him was Pankaj Shastry, their local MP.

'Are you signing the petition?'

Shastry's voice was deep and resonant, and somehow instantly familiar. Colin looked him up and down. He wore a crisp navy suit, a grey roll-neck and the kind of shoes that people in Peterdown simply did not wear.

'I was just about to,' he said meekly.

'Excellent. We haven't met. I'm Pankaj Shastry.'

Colin faltered. The man's confidence was like a sonic boom, an invisible pulse that seemed to clear the ground around him, knocking you back on your heels.

'Yes,' said Colin, shaking his outstretched hand. And then, eventually, he added: 'I'm Colin.'

For what felt like an hour and a half but must have only been a few seconds they stood there, the three of them, exchanging glances, saying nothing. Colin had an acute sense that this was one of those moments where crucial information was being silently shared via feints and codes of the kind that invariably went over his head. He felt many things at once: hurt, fear, jealousy, but overridingly that he just had to get out of there.

'Well, nice to meet you,' he said to Pankaj, before leaning in to give Ellie a hamfistedly proprietorial kiss. 'I've got to go.'

'Are you not going to sign it?' she said.

'Do it for me,' said Colin. 'Put me down as The Ultimate Warrior, 19 Coopersale Road.'

Ellie scrunched her brow in incomprehension before she realised what he was talking about. She found herself blushing, on his behalf and hers.

'Actually, make that Brutus Beefcake,' he said as he picked up his bag from under the trestle.

She watched him go, his rucksack tossed over his shoulder, his jeans bagging round his arse like a bulldog's neck.

When she turned back Pankaj was standing there, a faint smile on his lips.

'Daisy's father?' he said.

'Yes,' she said.

'A wrestling fan, is he?'

'Apparently,' she said. 'Although it's the first I've heard of it.'

She picked up the clipboard, passed it to Pankaj.

'Ah,' he said on reading it. 'I see.'

'Yes,' she said.

'Nine names.

'Five, really.'

'Well, let's do something about that.' Pankaj put his briefcase under the trestle. 'I have a taxi coming to get me but I'll put it back. I don't think they'll mind if I'm a bit late for my next appointment.'

And just like that they did something about it. Pankaj took one clipboard, she the other. He approached and cajoled, wisecracked and charmed. Two more people signed up, then another three. He stood on a wall and without notes addressed a group of sixth formers, reeling off, almost verbatim, whole paragraphs that she had written. Ellie walked among them passing out pens, sheets for them to sign.

'How do you do it?' she said, returning to the table having ducked into a nearby Starbucks to buy them both coffees, just as two old ladies were walking away arm-in-arm, the pair of them still laughing at one of his jokes. 'You've been here five minutes and everyone likes you. I've been here for nine years and no one likes me. '

Pankaj laughed as he sat down on a nearby bench.

'I'm still in my honeymoon period,' he said, taking one of the coffees from her. 'And I don't believe for one second that people don't like you.'

'Oh my god, you've got to be kidding. I'm a disaster,' she said, sitting down next to him. 'I misjudge the mood. I rub people up the wrong way. My jokes fall flat.'

Ellie considered stopping here, but it was odd, these days, to find yourself in the presence of someone to whom you could talk naturally without all the usual checks and balances.

'Before I came here I used to fit,' she said. 'I used to work. People understood me, the things that make me *me*. They got the nuances and I made sense to them. I don't make sense to anyone up here.'

Here she paused for a second. There were, she felt, places where she might still make sense. The Upper West Side. The Third Arrondissement. Certain neighbourhoods in Berlin. All of which featured in heavy rotation as the backdrop to her fantastical parallel existence. And then of course there was London. Which was always there, too big and too real and too close to think about without sending yourself half mad in the process.

'Do you think about moving back?' he said, right on cue.

Ellie laughed a little half laugh.

'You can't be an architect and not have it there in the back of your mind. It's where everything happens. But there are things here that need to be finished,' she said, nodding at the table and its petition.

Pankaj leaned back into the bench and crossed his legs at the ankle.

'There was a time when I thought I might like to be an architect,' he said.

'Really?'

'It was a big part of my life growing up. My family and Chandigarh and all that. I even did work experience at a practice in Holborn. Two weeks in the summer between the lower and upper sixth.'

'And that put you off, did it?'

He shrugged.

'I think you've really got to love it,' he said.

'You do.'

'Did you always know?'

'Always. From when I was a teenager.'

He unclipped the lid from his coffee and took a sip.

'I'm always amazed at people who have such a keen sense of themselves when they're so young. *How* did you know?'

Ellie went to speak and then stopped and then she just found herself talking.

'My mum is a singer,' she said, her gaze fixed on a crow that had settled on top of a dustbin on the other side of the street.

'Mezzo-soprano. She doesn't do it so much any more but in her day she was good. She wasn't famous or anything, but she performed all over the country. And I would get dragged along. Particularly in the holidays. Christmas. Easter. When there was no one else to look after us. My brother and I would spend whole afternoons sitting in on rehearsals. My mum would be on stage with the rehearsal director and there would be musicians in the pit or whatever, but other than that it was often just me and my brother in a space that might seat two or even three thousand people. And we would sit there with our Marmite sandwiches and our cartons of orange juice, listening to her sing. Just the two of us, sitting there in these incredible spaces – Clifton Cathedral, Liverpool Metropolitan, the Royal Festival Hall. These great soaring places that were the backdrop to my early adolescence.'

She stopped to sip at her coffee. It was such an odd place to be having this conversation, on a city-centre bench, pigeons and buses and prams all around them.

'I've never really thought about it this way before,' she said, looking forward rather than at him. 'But I remember talking to a friend of mine, Patrick, when I first met him back in freshers' week, or whenever it was, back when it was still just about socially acceptable to ask someone when it was they first realised they were gay. I remember him saying that his first sexual fantasies – you know, when he was a young teenager – were about women. And then they were about a woman with a man. But it didn't take him long to realise that he didn't actually need the woman.'

She smiled in embarrassment at the memory of this, how sophisticated it had all felt at the time.

'And it was like that with me. I would sit there watching my mum and to begin with of course I wanted to be her. I wanted to be able to open my throat and sing like her. Handel. Rossini. *Agnus Dei. The Dream of Gerontius.* It was just amazing to look at her – my mum, this totally ordinary-looking woman, five foot six or whatever she is – it was amazing to look at her and hear it come out of her, all this incredible music. And so of course at the start, that's what I wanted. I wanted to be her.'

Ellie felt again the force of that feeling, how it still had the power to disassemble her all these years later.

'But the longer I spent sitting there in the stalls or on the pews or wherever it was, the less I found myself thinking about my mum and the more about the music in the space. The way the space made the sound so rich and deep and resonant. The interplay of the two forms. The way the one framed the other. The way the whole effect was kind of like a collaboration between the two.'

Ellie paused for a second; she had never articulated it like this before, never fully explored the through line, the way it all made such sense.

'And then eventually I stopped thinking about the music,' she said, still not really looking at Pankaj, 'which I knew to be a wonderful thing but one that had no mystery to me. It had been there all my life. And I started to think only of the buildings. Which seemed *so* mysterious. And so thrilling.'

Around them, the business of the day went on. Buggies were pushed, cigarettes were smoked, buses stopped and buses started.

Ellie talked on, over it all.

'And I suppose I have to admit that I was drawn to them because . . .'

Here she faltered a little.

'We . . .'

She sighed.

'We have a complex relationship, my mother and I. She's . . .'

Ellie paused, took a breath.

'Every time she sang it was always all about her. Even though the music was written by someone else and all these other musicians were involved, the way she performed, it was always so . . . *singular.* And these buildings weren't singular. They were built by hundreds of people. And that was something, I realised that even then. I used to sit there marvelling at the *work* that had gone into them. The intense effort. The incredible collaboration.'

Finally, she looked at him.

'My mind is neat and ordered. I like maths. I think calculus is beautiful. And I like the fact that you need it to make a building that will actually stand up. I *like* that architecture is a technical challenge as much as an aesthetic one. I don't think of that as some kind of failure. Like it's one step away from being an accountant, or whatever.'

She looked irritably away from him again.

'My mum's mind is a mess. A total mess. She's always late. She can barely remember her own birthday let alone anyone else's. She cooks with utter disdain for recipes. You know, sometimes I suspect that she can't really read music. She just knows it. Like baby mountain goats know how to climb mountains. It's just in her.'

She looked back at him again.

'I'm not like that. I want to make things that are monumental. But I want them to be real. I want them to stand up. And I want them to last for ever.'

At this, Pankaj started applauding.

'Hear, hear,' he said. 'To permanence and calculus and neat minds.'

'Oh god,' she said. 'That all came tumbling out. Sorry.'

'I became a lawyer because I liked the wigs and Rumpole of the Bailey.' He laughed. 'I feel completely insubstantial now.'

'I don't know where that came from. I'm sorry.'

'Don't be,' he said, standing up. 'It's left me wanting to know more.'

He tossed his empty coffee cup into a bin.

'But that will have to wait. I'm now more than an hour late and I really have to go.'

A taxi came round the corner with its light on. He stuck up his hand.

'Until the next time,' he said with a smile.

Ellie felt something rip through her. Something she hadn't felt for a long time. She went to speak but then didn't.

The taxi pulled away, the back of his head just about visible through the rear window. Suddenly, all she could think about was Colin. She felt a surge of warmth and tenderness. They were together for the reasons they were together and it would always be that way. But he never hurt her. Never hounded her. Staked no claim to know her absolutely, made no effort to subsume her, to bend her to his will.

And that was a form of respect. He had recognised in her the need to work and he had never encroached on that, never asked from her more than she had to give. But he had been there, unobtrusively. A calm and supportive presence throughout Daisy's early life when she had found herself overwhelmed and obsessive, forever convinced of imminent calamity. Throughout those years he had been there, uncomplainingly. It wasn't thrilling or vertiginous or spectacular but it was a form of love and it was authentic and enduring.

She folded up the trestle table, packed away the leaflets. She had not asked Pankaj to turn up and do this. She tossed her own coffee cup into the bin, abruptly aware of the chill in the air. She was about to come on, she could feel it, that massing in her womb. It was time to go home.

The folded trestle table had a strap so you could carry it on your shoulder. She stopped in at Patterson's to get herself some sanitary towels. And it was there she saw the front page of the Saturday *Post*.

* * *

Colin was in the kitchen when she got home. He was down on his hands and knees, filling the dishwasher with salt. He heard the front door close, the thump of her bag as it hit the ground.

'I've got the paper,' she called through from the hall.

'Isn't it great?' he called back. 'It's going mad on social media. I've never had a piece be shared so many times. I didn't think I'd ever say this about something I wrote for the *Post* but I'm really proud of it.'

'Proud of the *Post*?' she said as she came in the room, her face contorted in bewilderment. 'You're *proud* of it?'

'Ah, yes, I know what you're talking about. Sorry.'

'Well, I can see why it slipped your mind. It's only on the front page of your paper.'

'I fought that all the way. I really did. I did my best, Ellie. But I'm not the editor. I don't make those decisions.'

'Why didn't you tell me about it?'

'I was so preoccupied with my story. I'm sorry.'

Ellie threw her keys on to the kitchen counter, fixed him a look.

'Is there something I should know, Colin? Seriously, are we on the same side here?'

'No, and yes. As in, no, there's nothing you should know, and, yes, we're on the same side.'

'Because I look at this edition of the paper with this piece and your piece and you can forgive me for wondering if something sinister is going on.'

'It really isn't. Or at least if it is it hasn't got anything to do with me.'

'*Sources say*, that's all he keeps saying. What sources? These stats have got to be made up. I've never seen numbers anything like this before. Where's he getting them from?'

'I don't know.'

Colin felt a kind of trembling panic. He was just no good at this: raised voices, accusations, anger.

'What I can tell you is that Neil doesn't go out there and get things,' he said in a rush. 'When he said I've got these stats he meant someone had given them to him.'

'Yes, but who? What the fuck is going on?'

'I don't know but I can find out.'

'Do it, Colin. Find out. It's your bloody paper.'

12

Colin looked up at the stadium clock. It was old school, full of character, the minute hand always slightly shy of its target. 7.54 p.m. Nine minutes into the game, four minutes until it happened, or it didn't.

The Blackburn centre back hit the ball long but no one was really watching. The crowd was unusually quiet, with half an eye on the clock.

Colin had given up his spot in the press box and bought a ticket for the Radleigh Road end. The Radleigh was packed tight, bouncy with anticipation. Colin was in the middle towards the back where it was always liveliest. Rodbortzoon was next to him, drinking surreptitiously from a hipflask, his green and white striped hat pulled down over his ears.

'I feel good about this. There is a mood here. I know this mood.'

Colin rolled up on to the balls of his feet. He could feel it, too, the mood. It had shifted since the last game. His piece on the planning application had been shared two thousand times on social media and he'd had a dozen people approach him at the ground to talk about it, congratulate him on the scoop.

Despite this, he still felt deflated. Domestically, things were strained to the point of breaking. Ellie had banged about all weekend, hardly talking to him, still furious at the *Post*'s front page. And he was no closer to discovering Neil's source.

Even more depressingly, it had become obvious that for all his own article had been a useful recruitment tool rallying people to the campaign, it wasn't the thing, the secret Kirk and his cronies were harbouring. 'We have an excellent working relationship with Peterdown Council,' read their statement, 'and do not comment on their planning decisions.' It was not the response of a rattled man.

On the pitch, Guy Turner passed the ball out to United's winger, Amobi Okafor, who controlled it and knocked it into the space behind the Blackburn full back. There was a collective strangled shout as the crowd around Colin massed and moved, straining to see what was happening. Colin leaned into Rodbortzoon so that he could peer down as Okafor ran past the defender and sent a cross into the penalty box. In the stands there was a collective tightening, an inhalation of breath, followed by a stadium-wide groan as the ball shot hard and low along the six-yard line, beyond the reach of Per Gunnarsson's outstretched boot.

Colin looked over at the Blackburn fans at the far end of the ground. They had brought about twelve hundred, a good number for a midweek game. He could see a banner, hand-painted on a sheet:

BRFC. PUFC. LIONS LED BY CHICKENS.

The Blackburn fans had come through for them. He found himself swallowing, his lower lip no longer wholly under his command. This was an archetypal Colin response to a particular form of male solidarity – impersonal, blue collar, transcending divisions and overcoming odds – which he sentimentalised madly from a distance, having never himself been called upon to man a picket line, or fight in a war.

Eventually he managed to compose himself and raise a smile at how well it had all gone so far. There had been at least eight hundred marchers, if not a thousand. The police had been out in numbers but not intimidatingly so. Brian and his team of stewards had done a great job, taking them through the town, past people on their doorsteps shouting their support, cars honking, a bus full of waving kids.

He looked up. 19.57. A minute to go. He felt his skin prickle, his jaw clench. It had happened more than twenty-five years before he was born but, like everyone from the city, the events of 14 July 1958 were etched permanently in his consciousness. A hot, dry, windy day. A timber-framed building. An electrical failure. A locked door. Seventy-two men dead in the ten minutes it took to get it open. And then the years of obfuscation. The lies. The cover-up. The blame heaped on the men themselves ...

He was aware suddenly that the ground was already quiet. And then it started, an almighty shuffling, the sound of thousands of seats flapping shut as the whole Clock Stand seemed to rise as one and turn its back on the pitch. Around him, the thousands on the Radleigh, all of them cramped for space, were turning their own awkward pirouettes. The Blackburn end turned too. Rodbortzoon, next to him, was one of the last to go. Colin stayed, hanging on, staring at the dugout.

Christie was off the bench, patrolling his technical area. His face was riven, but also clearly a little haunted. He was making a great show of watching the game, tensely analysing its patterns, but Colin could see that he was distracted, evidently conflicted.

On the pitch, two players went up for a header and the ball ricocheted out for a throw. Christie watched the ball as it ran away behind a hoarding, and then slowly, deliberately, he turned round as if to talk to the rest of the coaching staff before pausing, his back square to the pitch, for two, three, four seconds, enough to make it clear what he was doing, but not long enough to prevent plausible deniability should Kirk call him out on it. Colin, who had long felt there was literally nothing that Paul Christie could do that would make him love him more, felt a tear welling in his eye.

The minute hand jerked forward. 19.58 p.m. Colin held his breath. He turned round, stood there, silent, his eyes shut, writing the experience in his head.

19.58 p.m. It is match night at the Chapel but all is quiet. The only noises that echo around the ground are thin, reedy: the shout of a player, the ref's whistle. A 23,000-strong crowd has turned its back on the action, turned its back on the club's owner, Andrew Kirk, and his business practices, but more profoundly, it has turned its back on football in its current state. For those of us made cynical by the game it is a rare moment, a witness to its power ...

The cheering that marked the end of the minute was joyous and exuberant, tinged with a sense of disbelief that it had gone so well. Colin stood, wobbly on his feet, flushed with pride. Then he heard it, over his shoulder, the familiar tune; and like everyone around him, he stood arms aloft and sang with full throat.

> *If you're coming to the Chapel then you're going to get*
> *   Ga-a-a-rried.*
> *Coming to the Chapel then you're going to get*
> *   Ga-a-a-rried*
> *G, we really love you and they're going to get*
> *   Ga-a-a-rried . . .*
> *Here at the Cha-pel of Steam*

There was a lull, a beat of silence, a collective pause, and then piercing through it came a lone voice. It was strong, powerfully projected. It picked up where the crowd had left off, continued the tune.

> *Be-lls will ring*

Their version of the chorus was a staple on the Peterdown terraces, but no one had ever taken it further. Almost every head in the stand, Colin's included, swung in the direction of the voice. It was Steve Wanless, Mick's sidekick on his podcast. He wasn't a big man, Steve, but he had some lungs on him and he could sing like a Welshman. The stand went silent, listening, willing him on.

> *The-e-e su-un will shine.*
> *I'll be Steam and the Steam'll be mine.*
> *We'll play here until the en-nd of time*
> *And we'll never go to Grangeham, I swear.*

The roar when he had finished was like nothing Colin had ever heard before. It fell from the stand like rolling thunder. It was a collective outpouring, a howl of rage and pride and face-first defiance.

140

Rodbortzoon was leaping about dementedly, hollering about Paul Robeson and Woody Guthrie. Colin stood with his scarf held high above his head, a fat tear rolling down his cheek.

For half an hour, the Radleigh roared. They ran through the full repertoire. All the players on the pitch were serenaded, as were heroes from the past: Gem McBride, Dave Burns, Jimmy Gleeson who stayed with the club after the relegation in '87 even when Sunderland had offered him all that money to leave.

While all of this was happening a game of football had carried on, largely without incident, and the teams left the field for half time with the score still nil-nil. Rodbortzoon sloped off for a pee, leaving Colin to queue for the stadium speciality: mushy chip butties, big fat wedges of potato covered with beef gravy and served in floury white baps.

The nearest food shack was deep in the concrete hollows of the Radleigh Stand next to the toilets with their intense smell of urine and industrial bleach. Colin stood in the queue feeling emotionally drained. Two fans walked towards him, guys from around the way. He didn't know their names but their faces were familiar to him from away games, long train journeys back from Plymouth, Yeovil, Crewe. They nodded as they passed him, their hands wedged firmly in their pockets. Colin experienced the exchange as if he were a spectator looking on. He felt at once deeply embedded in the evening's events but also at least a step removed from them.

He logged on to Twitter and looked through his feed. There had been more than three thousand tweets with the hashtag #ITurnedMyBack. He scrolled through them, astonished at the scale of it. On and on they went as he scrolled down. He flicked through them one after another, messages of solidarity, support, defiance. It was, he felt, as if he had been the midwife at the birth of something which had already outgrown him and moved on, started to dictate its own terms.

He paid for the butties and drinks and made his way back to the stand where he found Rodbortzoon and thirty or so other fans listening to Brian, who was sitting up on a crush barrier addressing the group as best he could.

Colin sidled up to Rodbortzoon and wordlessly held out the two hot chocolates so that he could add a shot of rum to each. Brian was talking about a fan-led buyout, elaborating on the case he had made to Colin at the Night Leagues. He talked about on-the-gate price freezes, cheap season tickets for teenagers, special deals for school kids.

'Make the club a mutual,' he was saying. 'And everyone in the ground can have a say in how it's run. Think about Kirk's vision. Unrealised commercial potential, that's all he cares about. We would do the opposite. Make it the most fan-friendly club in the country. I'm thinking a five-year commitment to the same shirts, one home, one away, so no one's pressured into forking out a hundred quid for new gear every Christmas.'

Colin looked around. At least eighty fans were listening and there were murmurs of recognition, nods of approval.

'He wants us to move out to Grangeham and have a whole tier of premium seats for corporate packages. You've seen them at Arsenal and the like. They're fairly full for the first forty-five minutes but they get in at half time for their bar and complimentary food and they never come for the second half. Best seats in the house, they get, and they're bloody stuck in the bar.'

'My favourite is the Wembley "family",' said Rodbortzoon to Colin, his mouth full of butty. 'Ha ha! The most dysfunctional on earth. But at least they're trying. You know the phrase: a family that eats together stays together? Maybe this is why they don't come out for the second half. Too busy with their noses in the trough working on their interpersonal dynamic.'

Colin wiped gravy spittle from his ear and turned his attention back to Brian. He was wearing a battered old pea coat, a thick fisherman's jumper, a simple, old-school green and white striped scarf.

'I don't want any of you to think I'm talking about turning it amateur. Garry would still be getting paid a decent wage. I've got no problem with working-class lads getting well rewarded for being good at what they do.'

He was a good public speaker, working the crowd, looking at them all, seeking out eye contact.

'But we'll also be reminding them that with a fat pay slip comes a fair bit of responsibility. For that kind of money we'd be looking at a fair bit of community work when their two of hours of training has finished for the day. The town's bookmakers might take a bit of a hit and it would free up a good few tee times at the Hawksworth but I think they'd all cope.'

The large group staring up at Brian was itself piquing the interest of more fans who stopped to listen as they made their way back to their spot.

'What I'm saying is: there's no reason we can't be fan-owned *and* successful. Look at Bayern Munich. Look at *Barcelona*. They're doing all right.'

Brian responded to the swelling numbers by raising his voice, talking faster, more forcefully.

'I know some of you have had your heads turned by people saying we couldn't get promoted, that the stadium won't meet Premier League standards, but it's not that simple. Everyone knows that the Prem is in trouble. I mean the very idea of it. The atmosphere is so sterile people don't even want to watch it on TV any more. All those kids in Singapore are starting to watch the Bundesliga for the noise and the colour. You look at Dortmund. Twenty-five thousand people in the yellow wall. All of them standing up. And it's safe as you like. The problem is overcrowding, not standing. Anyone here been to the Arsenal? They've got these state-of-the-art turnstiles that are activated by cards like the ones they have on the tube in London. Oysters. They're floor-to-ceiling, these turnstiles. Impossible to jump. For a fraction of the cost of relocating we could get them put in and I know if we went up the Prem would let us keep our terraces. They're already talking about it behind closed doors . . .'

Just as he was saying this the Peterdown players came out of the tunnel and on to the pitch. The cheering of the other fans turned the heads of Brian's audience, and quickly they started to spread out, making their way back to their places.

'Save the Chapel dot com,' shouted Brian, as a final salvo. 'Sign up when you get home.'

Colin watched as Brian pushed his way through to where he and Rodbortzoon were standing.

'What a night. Fucking hell. You just had fifteen thousand people turn their back on the pitch, Colin. I tell you what, something is catching fire. I can feel it. They want rid of Kirk and they don't just want some other bugger like him to take his place. I think we can do this. I mean, I really think we can. The *Post*'s doing its bit, eh? That piece on the Larkspur wasn't badly timed, was it? Good work, son.'

'That wasn't me,' said Colin urgently. 'Whatever you do, don't be putting it about that that was me.'

'And a bit of respect for the people of the estate would be nice,' said Rodbortzoon. 'They deserve our solidarity. If we are going to have a train station it will have to be on the site of the Generator.'

'It's haemorrhaging money,' said Colin. 'We can go after them on financial viability, can't we?'

'You're as daft as each other,' said Brian. 'They're no more going to knock down the Generator than they are Eastfinche Abbey. It's plain as day that it's going to be the Larkspur that gets chosen. And good fucking riddance. It's a disgrace. Was right from the start. My mam's sister and two of my dad's brothers had their houses flattened to make way for that dump. A whole community swept away like they were rubbish.'

'The Knoxley was a slum,' said Rodbortzoon. 'Don't tell me you're also nostalgic for Victorian working conditions, coal fires, cholera.'

'What do you know about it?' said Brian, pointing aggressively at Rodbortzoon. 'There was nothing wrong with those houses.'

'They were back-to-backs.'

'Bullshit. There was good in that neighbourhood.'

'They were demolished in 1966. Were you even born?'

'I have family members . . .'

Colin stood between them, having long before stopped listening. The players were back on the pitch. He scanned their faces looking for Garry but it was obvious he wasn't there. He had stayed on the bench, still not quite fit enough to play.

The ref brought the whistle to his lips and off they went again.

Two hours later he was sitting at his desk. The office was empty. He had written his match report, an eight-hundred-word celebration of the protest that barely mentioned the dreary goalless draw that had been played out on the pitch, and uploaded it to the website.

Overhead, the strip lighting buzzed. Colin sat in his seat, sipping at a cup of tea, his mind having already returned to more prosaic matters. He looked over at Neil's desk, full of foreboding, Ellie's words ringing round his head. It was time.

He got up, crossed the office and sat down in Neil's chair with no real sense of what he might be looking for. He pulled open a drawer, rifled through its contents. Ted Baker aftershave. A toothbrush.

He reached to turn on the desk light and in doing so brushed Neil's mouse with his sleeve. Unexpectedly, the computer monitor came noisily to life. Colin flinched. Not a tiny, appropriate flinch, but a heart-in-the-mouth, full-body spasm of fear. There was no one else in the room but he blushed anyway. Whenever he flinched like this, which he did often, it triggered a chain of thoughts in him which ended up always at an article he had once read about the Muslim Brotherhood's attempted assassination of President Nasser in Egypt in 1954. A gunman had shot at Nasser from twenty feet, the bullets barely missing their target. Standing at his lectern, Nasser hadn't flinched. Instead, he incorporated the attack into his speech. Colin tried to imagine himself reacting like this. A feather landed on a marshmallow and he flinched. A moth beat its wings in Nepal and he flinched. Dust motes clashed in the air and he flinched. He felt the hot shame burn inside him. He was, in every way, the anti-Nasser.

He sat morosely in Neil's chair and sprayed a little of the Ted Baker aftershave on to his left wrist. It was a strange and slightly creepy thing to do, he realised, as he rubbed his wrists together, but better probably than using another man's toothbrush.

He felt the thrum of his mobile phone vibrating in his pocket and pulled it out, looked at the caller ID.

It was Neil.

Colin sat in Neil's chair, his phone ringing insistently in his hand. How could Neil possibly have known what he was doing? He felt his breath shorten as his mind ran through an inventory of action movie surveillance equipment: laser trip-wires, heat-sensitive monitors, mobile phone tracking devices, internet cameras. Instinctively, he got up, flush with shame.

The mobile stopped ringing and the room was silent save for his own heavy breath and the sound of his heart thumping.

Abruptly, Neil's desk phone started ringing. Colin flinched. He looked down at its small digital screen. It said:

Neil Henderson (mobile)

Colin froze. The restriction in his chest was grip-like, almost debilitating. He scanned the room again, and felt with cold, paranoid certainty that he was being spied on. He took a deep breath, reached out and answered the phone.

'Col?'

'...'

'Colin, is that you?'

'Yes,' he managed finally, squeakily and without conviction.

'Fucking legend.'

'How did you know I was here?'

'I just tried Manu on reception and he said you were in. You're a fucking lifesaver.'

'I am?'

'Yeah. I've fucked up. I left my Fantasy Football open on a stalled transaction on my work computer and I can't log on at home because of it. I need you to do me a favour, mate. Can you log on and kill the page.'

'Umm.'

'It'll only take a minute. I've got an unused transfer for this week and I've got to schedule it by midnight tonight. Burnley are playing Spurs tomorrow and I need to get what's-his-face out of nets. He's going to ship a hatful.'

146

'Um ... OK.'

'You're the expert. Who should I put in? I'll have eight million. Kasper Schmeichel? Leicester have got Brighton.'

'Sounds smart.'

'Yeah, I thought so.'

Colin sat in Neil's seat, his fingers poised disbelievingly above the keyboard.

'So what is it?' he said.

'What?'

'Your password.'

'Oh, yeah,' said Neil. 'It's ...'

13

There was something centipedal about the columns in the Larkspur's community hall. It was the way they were laid out, two at a time, in neat rows, but also the way they were cantilevered like the legs of a massive concrete bug. Ellie stood at the far end of the room, staring through the five pairs of pillars, the perspective made more dramatic by the gentle curve of the room. The parquet floor was dull, the concrete water-stained, the wall of windows cloudy with condensation, but still it was inspiring to see it up close. Humbling, too.

For a while now, she had found herself circling round ideas for a new approach to social housing, one that synthesised the aesthetic cohesiveness of a planned environment with a kind of demotic DIY. And now finally she had found someone to talk to about it. Pankaj's mind was lawyerly and forensic, with a generalist's nimbleness. He didn't know much about the technical side of architecture but he was very good at asking questions. Which he did relentlessly, always arrowing in, with astonishing economy, until he had reached the crux of whatever it was she was talking about, compelling her to justify the assumptions that underpinned what she was doing, be more rigorous, think more clearly and productively. For the first time in months she had had her pencils out, had started sketching out ideas.

'Ellie love, you got any more tea bags?'

Pam Grealish. A woman who smelled intensely of cigarettes and had no concept of personal space. One who spoke at all times with the barking urgency of someone shouting a warning in high winds but who was full of such inexhaustible cheer that Ellie couldn't help but smile every time she looked at her. She was manning the trestle table. This time folded flat and ably supporting two kettles and a large metal teapot. They were at the first meeting of the Larkspur Residents Action Group. It was going well.

'I'll have a look,' she said.

Next to Pam's table, eight residents were sitting in a circle discussing the possibility of reopening the estate café. Behind the circle of chairs, a lawyer from a big practice in Broadcastle, whom Pankaj had roped in, was holding a kind of rolling seminar on housing law, explaining tenancy rights and reading through contracts.

It was 11 a.m. Even on this winter's day, the room was bathed in light. Agosto and Marjorie had angled the windows to maximise the sun at mid-morning for the mums-and-babies groups they had imagined using the hall, the pensioners, the Sunday watercolourists. Ellie took a moment. At least forty people had been in and out already. Nearly all of them had signed the petition and sixteen had written letters addressed to the secretary of state backing the listing. She looked over at Eileen Adams, mother of seven, grandmother to twenty-four, and as hard-looking a woman as you were ever likely to meet. Her letter was a masterpiece, directly stated and full of pathos. She had lived on the estate, in three different flats, since she was ten years old.

The door swung open and Pankaj walked in. He was wearing a long black coat and a showy green scarf. His shoes were immaculately polished and she could see a glimpse of yellow socks. She felt an electric charge, a hormonal rush. It was as much about the way he walked as it was the way he looked.

'Now we're talking,' he said, gesturing to the room around them.

He approached her and for a second there was an awkward pause as they collectively decided which set of norms to adhere to: those of their immediate locale, Peterdown, where nobody kissed; or those of their natural environment, London, where everybody did, at least twice. They settled on a single kiss and a sort of unintentionally intimate squeeze that caused Ellie's lips to brush against Pankaj's ear, which left her slightly flustered, and him with a broad grin on his face.

'I can't believe you've got this going at such short notice.'

Ellie shrugged. In effect, all she had done was give shape to something that was already there. All it had taken was an email to a few of the residents and quickly it had snowballed. After twenty-four hours she had seven founder members of the Larkspur Residents Action Committee. Between them they had covered the estate in posters, spread the word, got into the community hall, emptied it of rubbish and cleaned it up.

'I think it's probably worth telling you now that the methods by which we gained entry may not have been entirely legal.'

'Really?'

She looked over to the far corner of the room. Sellotaped to the table was a handwritten sign for the LARKSPUR HISTORICAL SOCIETY. Sitting behind it were the society's two founders, Ralph and Barry.

'I let the boys take care of it,' she said. 'I think a pair of bolt cutters might have been involved.'

They looked over at the pair of them. Barry was six foot two and weighed twenty stone. His hair was dyed a kind of burnt orange, and he shaved his beard along his jawline in what Ellie assumed was a bid to create the impression of angular definition but served only to heighten your awareness that he had a phenomenally thick neck.

In most situations he would be the person to whom your eye was drawn first. Not that day. Sitting to his left was Ralph Wilbraham. Thirty-two years old, boyish and whip-thin, Ralph had the quality of a keen intelligence misapplied. Ellie had known a few like him at university, the kind of boys who stop washing their hair, convinced that its natural oils will do the job. The kind whom you think nothing of for years until you see them on the news fighting extradition after they've gone and hacked the Pentagon.

Ralph was one of them and he was physically unremarkable; sandy hair, sallow skin. But you couldn't not look at him. He was wearing a belted orange tunic, ski boots and what looked for all the world like a cycling helmet that had been spray-painted white, but was – as Ellie had been told many times – an actual, as in from-the-set, *Danelaw*

150

Blizzard Corps helmet that he had bought from an authenticated memorabilia website.

Ellie smiled thinly. For thirty years *Danelaw* had been a cult concern, known only to art students and aficionados of low-fi avant-garde 1970s cinema. Its obscurity was hardly surprising: it was a three-hour, slow-moving, surrealist epic made by a bipolar Polish émigré that featured Danish-accented aliens invading a futuristic Britain, conquering half the country and making the Larkspur their headquarters. Even she had only watched it once. Then, in 2010, Quentin Tarantino had included it on a list of the films that had the greatest impact on his career and instantly it had been catapulted into the collective consciousness, honoured with a run at the BFI, reissued on DVD, and uploaded all over the internet. The infamous torture scene – a nightmarish sequence in which fascist aliens drown a whole family in the Larkspur's signature water feature – had been watched on YouTube more than 400,000 times, and had become, for many people, the defining image of the estate.

Ralph fiddled with his chinstrap. She had spent two hours the previous evening trying to dissuade him from wearing the costume but he had moved from a nearby village to live on the estate specifically because of the film, and was convinced that there might be others out there like him.

'Take me to your leader,' said Pankaj under his breath, as he walked over to them and introduced himself.

'I voted for you,' said Barry flatly.

'Thank you,' said Pankaj. 'Much appreciated.'

'I always vote Labour.'

'That's what I like to hear.'

'So it wasn't really a vote for *you*.'

'A vote for Labour is all I care about,' said Pankaj. 'Doesn't matter if it was for me or anyone else.'

'Have you seen *Danelaw*?' asked Ralph, looking half at Pankaj and half at the floor.

'Yes,' said Pankaj. 'I have. You're dressed like you're in the Blizzard Corps.'

Ralph paused for a moment, impressed.

'Was it the director's cut?' he asked with narrowed eyes.

'I'm not entirely sure which version it was,' said Pankaj, laughing. 'But it was certainly very long.'

Ralph looked at him intently, his left eye twitching.

'I've brought you this,' he said. 'It's Perkowski's preferred edit. Three hours fifty-eight minutes. Six deleted scenes restored.'

Here Ralph presented Pankaj with a home-copied DVD wrapped in a plastic bag.

'Goodness me, how lovely,' said Pankaj, the polished politician accepting a piece of cake at the WI. 'I will watch this when I get home.'

Ralph went to say something but Pankaj cut him off.

'If I'm going to say a few words it will have to be now as I've a train to catch.'

He walked to the corner of the room, cleared his throat.

'Just before I run off I'd like to say a few brief words . . . '

She stood at the back, watching as he addressed the room. It was warm and he had taken off his coat and suit jacket, rolled his shirt sleeves to the elbow. His forearms were closely muscled, like the hind legs of a big cat. His hands were similarly taut, possessed of a kind of snap, a kinetic energy. She felt very physical all of a sudden, aware of her clothes against her skin.

Pankaj praised the organisational skills of the group, their enthusiasm and energy. His delivery was natural and engaging, full of self-deprecating jokes and broad smiles. It felt strange being here with him, in this room. She looked again at the columns. Ten, fifteen years ahead of their time, they were only made possible thanks to Marjorie's engineering brilliance. But where would it have got her, that brilliance, without Agosto to open the doors, win the competitions, get them the work?

Ellie reached for a glass of water. What had always struck her about Marjorie, from reading her memoirs, was how unabashed she had been about marrying a powerful man in order to take command of her own life. She had gone into it knowing that it was freighted with risk, but she had done it anyway.

She stared over at Pankaj as he stood in the doorway, searching the room for her. He had finished his short speech, shaken a few hands, drunk a cup of Pam's lukewarm tea. For a second they locked eyes – the look he gave her was alive and laden with meaning. And just like that he was gone, his assistant ushering him off to the taxi that was taking him to the train and to London.

Ellie sat down on a spare seat and did her best to empty her mind of all thoughts. For a few minutes she sat in this semi-meditative state feeling oddly calm, too tired even to think.

Eventually she willed herself back into focus. Shelly and Jim McEwan had arrived; her in layers of wool, him dressed as he always was, like he had just got back from some epic hike across the Vale. They had both been councillors back in the day, when Peterdown council had been one of the most progressive legislatures in the country, introducing paternity leave, pioneering social care, commissioning buildings like this.

She rushed over and embraced Shelly first.

'Oh, my dear,' said Shelly as they hugged. 'This is a wonderful thing. Look how many people are here. You should be so proud.'

Ellie drew back. Shelly had become smaller and more frail since their first meeting seven years ago at the playground, the pair of them at either end of a seesaw, Daisy in one seat, Shelly's granddaughter in the other.

'How are you?' she asked.

'Oh, you know,' said Shelly. 'Old, but also not old at the same time.'

'Whereas I'm just old,' said Jim.

'Nonsense,' said Ellie. 'You look great.'

She made them tea, talked them through what they were doing, the legal advice, the plans for the listing application.

'I understand you've got our new MP on board,' said Shelly.

'I have. He's been amazing. You just missed him. He spoke. It was good. Funny, quite inspiring, actually.'

Shelly paused.

'I haven't got a fix on him yet,' she said. 'He's not another Kington, is he?'

'They're certainly not friends, if that's what you mean,' said Ellie. 'They seem to openly despise each other.'

'Well that's a good start.'

'Honestly,' said Jim. 'Stop making out Yvonne's some kind of ogre.'

'She cares about nothing but her own advancement.'

'Don't be so melodramatic. She's done a lot for this town. And you know she has.'

Shelly curled a lip, rolled her eyes at Ellie.

'Well she hasn't done much for this campaign,' said Ellie. 'I'm worried that she wants the station to be built here and so she's deliberately running the estate into the ground.'

'That would be madness. There are already thousands of people on the waiting list.'

'Have you seen how many flats are boarded up?'

'I did notice a couple on the way in,' said Jim. 'Could just be a budget thing. The central government cuts make it very hard to find money for maintenance.'

'Maybe.'

'I know there were problems with damp before.'

Ellie winced. It was the building's Achilles heel.

'Still,' she said. 'It would be awfully convenient for her, wouldn't it?'

'All this station business is after our time, I'm afraid,' said Jim. 'Not that we knew what she was thinking on most things by the end. She had got so secretive, always creating little sub-groups to work on things, making decisions away from the minuted meetings.'

'What about the Generator?' said Ellie, brightening. 'You were still there when it was being signed off, weren't you? Can you remember much about its operating costs? I've heard a rumour that it's losing over a hundred thousand pounds a week.'

'What!' said Shelly. 'That'll be a scandal if that's true. It's such a shame that it's been such a disaster. It did feel so exciting at the time. We were being told we were getting a Tate Modern. Here in Peterdown.'

'We got caught up in the excitement,' said Jim. 'They got all that money from central government and the lottery but I couldn't tell you the exact figures, it was so long ago. Yvonne cooked the whole thing up with that thug Philpott.'

'Philpott? Who's he?'

'James Philpott,' said Shelly. 'He's Kington's fixer. Does all her heavy lifting. He's not an elected councillor but his fingerprints are everywhere you look.'

'There's no point trying to get anything out of him,' added Jim. 'He'll never talk to you.'

'Although,' said Shelly. 'We actually *do* know someone who might be able to help.'

For a moment Jim looked puzzled. Then it dawned on him.

'Yes. Yes, you're right, we do,' he said, after he had checked that nobody was in earshot. 'She's an employee, so she'll only have limited access.'

'But she hears and she sees,' continued Shelly.

'Oh my god, that's amazing,' said Ellie. 'Someone on the inside. A source! I can't believe it. That's so exciting. What shall we call her?'

'Let's call her Ketchup,' said Shelley.

'Ha ha! Brilliant. She's our source.'

14

Daisy's fringe was plastered to her forehead in a series of looping whorls. If you had just looked at her hair you might have thought she was dressing up as a 1920s flapper in pearls and lace. The reality was more prosaic: she had hand, foot and mouth, and was sweat-soaked with fever.

Ellie shifted her weight trying to make herself more comfortable without waking Daisy who was lying, only half asleep, with her head in her mother's lap. Her own childhood had not been tactile and it thrilled her still that Daisy was capable of such intimacy with her, the way she would just melt into her when she was sick.

She looked over at the chest of drawers where, way beyond her reach, she could see her phone. She felt a slight agitation at the withdrawal, but also some relief from the compulsion to endlessly check for messages from Jim and Shelly. Or Pankaj. They had started sketching out ideas on how they might put together the listing application but for each message that contained something pertinent to it, they were exchanging half a dozen that weren't: silly puns, comic riffs, anecdotes about colleagues or constituents.

Colin came in, opening the door slowly and pulling it upwards so it didn't scrape on the floor, the way he did when he had been out drinking and knew he was back later than he had intended.

'How is she?' he whispered.

'Nearly there,' she mouthed back. 'The poor bunny. She's knackered.'

'Did you give her the paracetamol?'

'Yeah.'

Colin had with him the special thermometer they'd had since Daisy was a baby. He placed it lightly in her upturned ear, pressed the button. Her temperature was 37.9. On the way down.

'She'll be fine,' he said. 'Tomorrow morning she'll be a different girl. A good night's sleep will make all the difference.'

Ellie looked at the awful red welts around her daughter's mouth arranged in the shape of a goatee beard. Still, after all these years, after all these bouts, she had to repeat to herself the mantra: it looks much worse than it is.

Colin withdrew, quietly pulled the door to. This was Daisy's ninth bout of hand, foot and mouth, but it was the first for ages and it was a mild one. Nothing like the awful eighteen months when she'd got it five times. It had been different then, of course, with Daisy too young to understand what was going on. The nights had been awful; sleepless, vomit-flecked epics of uncertainty and melodrama. In that brutal year and a half, Ellie had read every book and every blog, had spent hours scanning comment threads, emailing other mums. They had tried exclusion diets, exercise regimens, probiotics, homeopathy and – in a last desperate act of near madness – a crystal ordered from Australia that had hung ridiculously at the end of Daisy's bed.

While she was doing this Colin had simply got on with it, stripping her sick-covered sheets in the middle of the night, searching out fresh pyjamas, cooling flannels under the tap for her forehead. He had an incredible capacity simply to endure, stoically and without comment.

She felt suddenly maudlin and full of recrimination at everything that was going on. They were a unit. Three sets of relationships. Two of which were good, one of which was problematic but not wholly a failure. She felt a stab of irritation. At herself, principally, but also at Pankaj for the way in which he was so blithely imperilling the cohesiveness of her family.

She stroked Daisy's hair again, leaned forward, kissed her brow. It was like she was a toddler again; clingy, needing to be close. She thought back to those days. Daisy had been beautiful, a golden child with her white-blonde ringlets. Ellie had been so proud of her, so proud that it hurt but also ... She blushed. It was a period of her life that she found difficult to look back at. Sharing the limelight had been something that she'd had to find accommodation with, and it had taken time. She blushed again. For the first few years, she had overdone it in the battle not to be her mother. She had talked about Daisy too much, too openly. Her devotion had been showy, performative. She blushed again to the tips of her ears. She had made her selflessness the only thing you could see.

She thought of all the vows she had made to Daisy then, the whispered promises of security, stability, love. What kind of person was she if she was willing to imperil all that so thoughtlessly?

It was five years ago probably since she had asked her mother why she had left. The conversation had gone how the conversations always went.

I don't see how me apologising for some offence I'm supposed to have caused twenty years ago makes any difference. I can say the words if you'd like. I can say I'm sorry. But I won't mean it. I no more feel guilty about that than I do about shitting in Aunt Grace's bath when I was five. I did what I did because I wanted to.

Stupid to have even brought it up. And stupider still to have continued the dialogue. What had she said? *Leaving dad was like shitting in a bath, was it?* Something like that.

If that's what you take from that, then yes, darling, leaving your father was a lot like shitting in a bath. Painless and something of relief in the moment but a bit messy afterwards.

Ellie could still picture her mother's face then, the look of exquisite delight at her own quickness, the virtue, in her moral universe, that trumped all others.

My leaving your father – and this may come as some surprise to you – was not some colour episode in the box set of your life. Our marriage had become an open wound. And it needed to be cauterised. It wasn't about you, Eleanor. Most things aren't. It was something that I had to do at the time. Have bad things happened as a consequence? Who knows? Things happen all the time. Untangling why they happened is impossible. And that's really the long and the short of it.

Ellie looked down. Daisy was deeply asleep. She wriggled out from under her, pulled the covers up to her chin.

Colin was downstairs. She could hear him in the kitchen. She walked in, stopped. The room was candlelit, the table set for two. He was wearing his suit jacket. With jeans. It was not, she thought immediately and irrevocably, that sort of suit jacket. Nor, really, were they those sort of jeans.

He was standing in the middle of the room looking at her beseechingly. On the stove top was a pot. The counter surface was strewn with utensils, empty packets, vegetable peelings.

'You cooked,' she said.

'Lebanese salmon skewers. I made it from the internet but I couldn't find pomegranate molasses so I used golden syrup,' said Colin, wincing. 'I think it might be a bit sweeter than it's meant to be.'

She looked at the table. On one of the place settings there was a cardboard box tied with ribbon.

'We were playing Darlington last week. I stopped in at Harvey Nichols in Leeds on the way home.'

'What is it?'

'Open it.'

Ellie pulled at the ribbon, lifted the lid of the box. Through the layers of crepe paper, she could see a lace edging. For an awful, gut-wrenching second she thought it was lingerie but when she pulled it out she realised it was a top. She felt first, but fleetingly, relief. And then a kind of essential sadness: it was so instantly and obviously wrong.

'Why did you buy me this?' she asked softly.

'I thought you'd like it,' said Colin, his confidence flying from him like birds from a tree. 'There was that one in the magazine. I thought you . . .'

'That's not what I meant,' she said. 'I meant, why did you buy me it now? It's not my birthday or anything.'

Colin stopped, took a deep breath.

'It was ten years ago today that you first spent the night in my bed. Or at least part of it.'

Even Colin understood instantly that this modifying second sentence was a mistake. Summoning everything he could he willed himself to stop talking but there was, as ever, a considerable disconnect between the thinking part of his brain and the speaking part. The words kept tumbling out, filling the air.

'The night, obviously. I mean, part of the night. Not part of my bed. When you were in it you were wholly in my bed.'

He stopped, startled at his own bumbling, tumbling inadequacy. He looked up at her.

'I just thought you'd like it,' he said.

Ellie stood rooted to the floor. She felt an awful wrench inside herself, a great welling sadness. Ten years. She felt instantly humbled. He was wearing his suit jacket. A thought appeared in her like a headline flashed across a screen. It was both staggeringly simple and immeasurably complex: his life was just as real as hers.

She felt momentarily overwhelmed. He was such a good person. So authentic, so kind. But she would never, in all of time, ever wear that top. He was standing in their kitchen, six feet from her. The distance felt wider than the sky.

'Thank you,' she said, her eyes wet with tears.

Colin walked over to the fridge and pulled out a bottle of Sancerre, bought from a specialist place in Broadcastle. In his best-case scenario for the evening, the gift opening would have been followed by wine and food and then sex. Already, things seemed to have veered calamitously off course. He stopped. It was the golden syrup that had led them here. None of this would have happened, he felt with unimpeachable certainty, if Morrisons had only had some pomegranate bloody molasses.

And then he remembered. He had a trump card.

'I've got Neil's password.'

Ellie opened her eyes.

'You have?'

'Yeah,' said Colin.

'How did you get it?'

Colin pulled the cork from the bottle, playing for time. The mood shift was instant, the tone of her voice, the set of her shoulders.

'You've seen *All the President's Men*?' he said.

'Yes.'

'You know the bit where Dustin Hoffman tricks the receptionist into leaving the room?'

Ellie narrowed her eyes, thought about it.

'I can't remember that scene.'

'It's a big scene. It's Hoffman's big scene.'

'Anyway ...'

'Anyway,' said Colin. 'It was a bit like that. It was good. It was *journalism*.'

'What is it?'

'What?'

'The password.'

'Oh, it's "password".'

Ellie stopped, laughed into her hand.

'Wow,' she said warmly, 'that must have taken some *journalism*.'

'I didn't *know* it was "password",' said Colin, pretending to feel wronged, as she ran upstairs. He opened the Sancerre and poured two glasses, his mood transformed. The skewers actually looked quite good, he thought, as he plated them up, with a dollop of yoghurt on the top. He tried a small piece. By any standards, it was really very sweet but by no means was it inedible. He put the plates on the table and repositioned the chairs so they could sit next to each other.

Ellie reappeared with his work laptop, sat down, sipped at her wine, ate some food, smiled. She put the laptop between their plates, opened it.

'I haven't had a chance to have a look yet,' said Colin as he turned on the machine, 'because he's been at work and if he's on his email I'm worried he'll know I'm accessing it.'

'But you know he's not now?'

'He's at a Kasabian gig in Broadcastle. He told me this afternoon.'

Colin paused, his fingers above the keyboard.

'Is it possible that he'll know anyway?'

'When he's not at the *Peterdown Evening Post*, is his other job writing code for the NSA?' asked Ellie incredulously. 'Of course he won't know. His password is "password".'

'What if he's emailing someone a photo of the gig?'

'*What?* Oh, for god's sake, just do it.'

Colin logged out from his email and wrote in Neil's username, his fingers trembling. He sensed that this was a reckless move that only imperilled further his already precarious position at the *Post* without in any way furthering the campaign to save the Chapel. He glanced to his left at Ellie. She was drinking the Sancerre, starting in on a second skewer. Her chair was close enough to his for him to feel the warmth of her, her breath.

Hesitatingly, he typed 'password' in the password box. You could get yourself out of most things by appealing to Rick's nobility, but get caught spying on one of your colleagues and you were just asking to be sacked. He looked again at Ellie. She was leaning over the laptop, expectant.

Colin felt his hands moving on autopilot. He was merely a pawn, she a queen. No, that wasn't right. He was merely a pawn, she was the person playing chess.

He sighed and hit return.

Neil's inbox filled the screen. It was a mess, a mountain of unread emails, clogged with junk. They scanned slowly through the subject lines looking for clues. Four pages back they found what they were looking for. The subject line read: The Larkspur: The Truth. The sender was info@totalsolutionspr.com.

'Shit the bed,' said Colin.

15

The park was unremarkable: two trees, some benches, a small, tired playground. Colin sat on a bench and ate the last bite of his sausage roll. Idly, he picked up the copy of the *New Statesman* that lay on the bench beside him and started reading, for the fourth time that day, a long piece on community-led protest movements that opened with a laudatory overview of the Save the Chapel campaign. The quotes were attributed to Brian, but he had written them, liaised with the journalist, sourced the images, made it happen.

He scrunched up the bag that had held the sausage roll and threw it in the bin. The publication of the piece had been the only bright spot in an otherwise bleak day. Despite his heroic investigative efforts, he and Ellie had not had sex the night before, nor that morning; instead, they had woken up, both slightly hungover and cranky, and managed to conjure an argument out of whether or not he was to blame for the fact that he snored.

He had then arrived at the office, irritated and deeply self-conscious about his sinuses, to a distinctly frosty welcome. Over the course of the morning, it had emerged that there was growing unease among his colleagues about the impact his 'Kirk-baiting', as Gail on the art desk had put it, was having on their job security. Much of this had been fuelled, it seemed, by his report of the protest at the Blackburn game, which he had uploaded, as he always did, on the night of the match without it being passed by the sub-editors, all of whom had gone home, as they always had. It was a system that had been in place for five years but was now, as Rick had declared later that morning, 'under review'.

All of which had made Kerry's urgent message summoning him to the park a welcome distraction. Not least because he got to see her wearing a trench coat, he thought to himself, as he watched her walk across the park towards him. It was a classic mackintosh, navy blue, belted at the waist. Colin couldn't quite put his finger on it but there was something about the way she wore it that made it especially easy to convince yourself she wasn't wearing anything underneath. Was it the heels, he wondered. Or the sunglasses?

She sat down on the end of the bench without acknowledging him.

'Stop looking at me,' she said without really moving her mouth. 'Pretend you don't know me.'

'What is this, *The Ipcress File*?'

'Stop looking at me.'

Colin did as instructed.

'Kirk's told us all you're barred from having access to the players or Christie.'

'*What?* He can't do that. How will I be able to do my job?'

'With difficulty. That's why he's done it.'

Colin felt a kind of fleeting joy, the thrill of noble martyrdom. This was followed by a couple of seconds of pure calm as he imagined a future devoid of player profiles, of never again having to interview a footballer, never having to transcribe their banalities, endure their clichés. And then, with crushing inevitability, the quotidian fears rushed in: the loss of status, the fear of joblessness, the prospect of life post-*Post*.

'I know I've said it before,' he said, 'but I really can't overstate how much I hate that man.'

Kerry was still sitting beside him, facing straight ahead, talking under her breath.

'Well, the feeling's evidently mutual,' she whispered. 'Seriously. Kirk is properly pissed off. All morning he's not stopped screaming. *The bloody Neanderthals* this. *The bloody Neanderthals* that.'

'And he means me, right?' he said. 'I mean, *us*. The campaign. The coverage we've had is getting to him.'

'Well something is. I heard him on the phone yesterday talking about getting someone to sort all the shit out. "Someone who can tell our story." That's what he said.'

'So we've got him rattled.'

'Honestly, I've never seen him so angry. It was actually pretty scary.'

'Do you think he knows about this? About us?'

'No. But things are already really tricky at work. I'm having to sneak about like you wouldn't believe.'

She paused, adjusted her sunglasses.

'It's only going to get worse when you write about this,' she said. 'He's going to go freak show.'

She put a folded copy of the *Post* on the bench between them. Tucked into it, Colin could see an envelope.

'What's that?'

'It's a memorandum on an email that was going round. It's a breakdown of the corporate structure of the Grangeham development. According to the plan the stadium is going to be owned by Peterdown United Football Club, but all the other buildings will be the property of Land Dominion. The stadium is obviously the most expensive bit to build and is going to come in at thirty to forty million, all of which will be loaded on to the club as debt. We all know he's been banging on about his substantial financial contribution. Twenty mil, he's been saying. But it's in exchange for twenty years of naming rights and it gets paid in instalments annually, not up front. And that million pound a year'll barely even cover the interest we'll be forking out on the forty mil debt. Not that he'll give a toss because by that point he can just let the club go bust. He'll still have his development. The whole thing's a stitch-up.'

Colin sat trembling in his seat.

'Oh my god,' he said.

* * *

Four hours later, Colin was sitting at his desk half-watching a Gem McBride highlights reel on YouTube, and half-watching Neil as he sat at his desk, texting furiously. The frosty atmosphere of the morning had developed into outright hostility; he was getting dark looks from all quarters, insults muttered as he passed.

Up until this point in his life, Colin had felt he had a pretty good sense of what it was like to be unpopular. His twelve years of schooling had given him plenty of practical experience. It was only now that he realised unpopularity had two forms: passive and active. In its passive form, unpopularity was simply the absence of popularity. This he knew well; the perma-anonymity, the generalised indifference, his always forgotten face. Active unpopularity was a new experience; nervier, more fraught. But it was one he felt at least partially prepared for. And it carried with it a kind of electric thrill: for once, he was unambiguously at the centre of the storm.

He looked over at Rick's office. He had raced back from the park and turned round his piece on Kerry's findings in less than two hours. The article was dispassionate and forensic. It laid everything out simply, just the facts as they were.

Neil cast him a filthy look and walked into Rick's office without knocking. Colin watched him through the glass partition wall, gesticulating at the piece on Rick's desk. Eventually, the pair of them emerged. Rick cleared his throat, addressed the group. He talked about the piece, its value to the public interest. He explained that he understood its potential impact and their understandable reservations.

'Being an editor is about making difficult decisions,' he said, 'but it's also about having faith in your team.' Rick paused. He looked off into the middle distance. 'And sometimes it's about doing both. Which is why I'm going to leave this to Colin. It's his story. He should decide if it runs.'

The room went silent. Colin could hear his own breath whistling through his nose. He looked at the managing editor, Anne McAllister. Her husband had left her with two kids and a mortgage she could barely afford. He wobbled. Mike Hardacre on the subs' desk looked after his mum who had Parkinson's. Hugh Trentwood was a recovering alcoholic whose confidence was so fragile that were he to lose his job he would break irreparably, Colin imagined, like a wishbone snapped in two.

But these were things outside of Colin's control. If the paper folded it would be for reasons that were complex and unknowable and well beyond his pay grade. He felt his nostrils ripple with tension. Now was the time to hold fast, stay true. He summoned all the strength he had, and nodded.

Neil stood up, strode out, and slammed the door behind him.

'Right then,' said Rick. 'It runs.'

16

Ellie worked half-days on Thursdays, which allowed her to pick Daisy up from school. That afternoon, though, Daisy was at her friend Isabelle's house, where they would be trying on makeup, drinking ludicrous amounts of Fanta and watching television programmes that were in no way age-appropriate, all with the explicit approval of Isabelle's mother. Ellie no longer felt capable of raising any objection, not least because, despite it being only 3.45 p.m., she was herself lying in bed with a mug of hot chocolate and a copy of *Concrete Plans*, Marjorie Blofeld's memoir.

She was rereading the chapter about Marjorie's years as an undergraduate. She had been twenty, down from Durham, lower middle class, fiercely ambitious, a wearer of mannish glasses and Oxford brogues, her fringe cut deliberately short. A scholarship girl making her way in the world. Agosto had been forty-six, divorced, semi-famous, on a sabbatical from Chicago. He had arrived in Cambridge at the start of her second year. They were lovers in a fortnight, husband and wife before the end of term.

Was it a calculating move on Marjorie's part? Or love? Ellie liked to think it was both. Letters to a cousin back in Durham showed her fondness for Agosto, the way she talked of him tenderly, romantically. But her world-view had been clear right from the start: make work or you don't exist. This from a girl whose mother had died when she was twelve, who had had to grow up quickly, the only child on hand to mop up after her fantasist of a father with his unrealised dreams and serial bankruptcies. All her adult life, Marjorie had carried with her the self-seriousness of a pre-teen: the need to build

168

had not been a constituent part of her selfhood. It had been her whole self.

Make work or you don't exist. When you thought about it in isolation, it wasn't exactly a statement that suggested equanimous mental health. And yet there it was, sitting squarely at the centre of her own sense of self like a granite megalith, not exactly unexamined but certainly unmovable.

There had been times in the long lonely years of Daisy's infancy when Ellie had considered becoming an academic. Even then though – when she was at her most desperate; chronically sleep-deprived and overwhelmed by self-doubt – the thought had terrified her. It would have meant a life spent in a world where architecture was just an abstraction. A thing that had been emptied out of perspiration and graft, until it was just a game for dilettantes, people happier conceptualising rainbows and exploring engineering through dance.

Even at her lowest, when she had felt furthest from it, she had always understood that the work was the point, that it was the thing that would save her, and that one day she would return to it, and that she would exist.

Ellie leaned back into the pillows. Her mother had prioritised making work above all other things, including her own child. She felt a pang of mawkish self-pity. Had it made her mother happy? It seemed such an absurd word to use about the woman. It hadn't even given her any peace. Much of her life had been lived in a kind of sardonic, uncontented fury. But her work had made her serious. Of that there was no doubt. When she sang she was alive, she existed.

Outside in the street, she could hear the shriek of kids, the thud of a ball against a wall. She pulled back the duvet and lay flat on the bed, thinking about Marjorie and her mother, when her phone rang, jolting her upright. She scrambled about her scrunched duvet until she found it.

'You haven't done something stupid, have you?' asked Leonie.

Ellie rolled her eyes. She had been a bit free and easy in a couple of texts earlier in the week.

'No,' she said, pretending to be petulant. 'Of course not.'

169

'Done something you already regret?'

And there had also been a WhatsApp message after a few glasses of wine that might have been misleadingly suggestive.

'Nothing. Honestly. Cross my heart.'

'Are you sure?'

'*Yes.* For god's sake.'

'Because I love Colin.'

'I know you do. Everyone does.'

'I love the way he makes you feel like a woman when he kisses you.'

They had snogged for five seconds during a freshers' week game of spin the bottle, a moment from which Leonie had got much mileage.

'Very good.'

'More than ten years ago and still it haunts me.'

'I'll happily swap if it means that much to you.'

Leonie's husband, Finn, was a six-foot-four rugby-playing cardiologist from New Zealand.

'And I love the way he wears his rucksack with both straps over his shoulders like he's an American teenager.'

'Really?'

'And I love him because he's the only person I've ever met who takes amphetamines and falls asleep.'

To Ellie's knowledge Colin had tried speed twice – once at university and once just after graduating – and on both occasions they had found him tucked away in the corner of the club, in the comfiest spot he could find, sleeping beatifically.

'And I love that he used to make sausage curry when we were at university.'

Ellie groaned.

'And sausage stir fry,' she said. 'With Uncle Ben's sauce.'

'Do you remember the sausages, the colour of them? What were they, two quid for twenty, or something? He'd always have a massive sack of them in the freezer. He called them "snags".'

'Everyone here calls them snags.'

Leonie yelped.

'Now that I think about it, he was basically the first outsider chef, wasn't he? All of it was a kind of unconscious avant-garde fusion food. Think about what he could have gone on to do. Sausage en papillote ... Sausage sushi.'

'Sausage ceviche.'

'A couple of snags and a squeeze of lime.'

Ellie laughed.

There was a pause. An ellipsis between friends, warm and full.

'But I also love him because he's funny and clever,' said Leonie.

'I know.'

'And he's kind.'

'I know. Point taken.'

'And that's important, being kind.'

'I know it is.'

'And I love him because he loves you and I love you.'

'I know you do. And I love you too.'

As they were saying their goodbyes, Ellie opened her laptop to discover an email from Shelly. Miss Ketchup had been in touch. She had stumbled across an email thread. The operating costs of the Generator were being channelled through a recently created quasi-autonomous disbursement vehicle called the Peterdown Regeneration Fund. It was not subject to full council oversight and the public knew nothing about it because it had written into it a commercial confidentiality clause, making it immune from proper scrutiny.

Ellie ran downstairs, heart beating, feeling existentially alert. Colin was in the living room, on his laptop.

'I've got a scoop for you.'

'God, really?' said Colin, without looking up. 'They're like London buses, these scoops. What is it?'

'The Peterdown Regeneration Fund.'

'What's that?'

'It's a shadowy off-book fund that the council are using to disguise the one hundred and six grand that the Generator loses every week.'

'Really? Christ. OK. What have you got?'

'What do you mean, what I have got? I've just told you.'

'That's it?'

'*That's it?* This is massive. It blows everything wide open.'

'OK. Let's start at the start. How do you know about the fund? Where are you getting this from?'

'I've got someone.'

'What do you mean you've got someone?'

'On the council. On the inside. They're telling me things.'

Colin stared at her in disbelief. He had vowed repeatedly to himself that he wouldn't tell her about Kerry but this changed the game. *He* was the journalist and there was no way that he was going to be out-moled.

'Well, I've got someone, too …' He hesitated, fatally. '*They're* telling me things.'

Ellie stopped, fixed him a look. Colin's horribly expressive face let him down once more.

'You said "they're", so it must be a woman.'

'I was disguising *their* gender,' said Colin with all the indignation he could muster.

'Nonsense. It's a woman and you didn't want me to know. Do you fancy her?' she said, amusedly, to disguise a disorienting slew of emotions: pique at the thought of *him* leaving *her*, a momentary thrill at the possibilities that this might open up, but mostly sadness that the life she had made for herself was so full of fault lines. 'Nothing's happening with her, is it?'

Colin blushed furiously.

'No. God, of course not.'

'So it *is* a woman.'

'Look, woman or man, it's none of your business. What matters is that I know the stuff *they* get me is bona fide. You're coming to me with a deleted tweet and a whisper about a fund and asking me to write an article based entirely on your guesswork. It's not going to happen.'

Ellie stood looking at him, tight-lipped.

'I'm hanging by a thread at that place as it is,' he said.

'I'll remember this,' said Ellie. 'Don't think that I won't.'

And with that, she picked up her laptop and went to the Crooked

Billet where she drank one large and then two small glasses of Pinot Grigio, as she wrote a long and wide-ranging blog post on the Generator, expounding lengthily on its architectural failings and curatorial haplessness, before moving on to its financial shortcomings, which she blamed squarely on Yvonne Kington, citing the Peterdown Regeneration Fund and its £106k a week shortfall.

Once she had uploaded it on to her website, she posted links to the piece in the comment threads of six of the most widely read architecture blogs, tweeted it, Instagrammed it and put it on Facebook. Finally, for good measure, she emailed a link to the producer of the Peterdown FM breakfast show, whom she had met once on a hen do.

When all this was done she sat back in her chair, slightly scandalised at herself, but certain that she existed in a way that felt full and deep and round.

17

The bus rumbled round the ring road. Colin sat up top, summoned to the office by a terse text from Rick. Outside, he could see a concrete wall, a slip road, a chain-link fence and in the middle of it all, a strip of grass upon which you couldn't imagine any human had ever set foot. When they were still in the old office his journey to work had been into town, heading for the heart of the matter. Now his was a non-journey, elliptical, circulatory, centrifugal. He went from nowhere to nowhere via nowhere.

Through his headphones he was listening to the Peterdown FM Breakfast Show. The song finished. 'Gold' by Spandau Ballet. The main DJ started talking. Had we heard the rumour? Was the Generator losing a hundred and six grand a week?

He urgently texted Ellie, entreating her to tune in.

The bus stopped. People got off. People got on. The DJ's sidekick was doing the thing that he did, which was to come up with a playlist for the story. 'Burning Down the House'. 'My Generation'. 'Money's Too Tight (To Mention)'.

The main DJ interjected, changed the tone. 'But seriously,' he said. 'The show producers have been doing some research. What does a hundred and six grand a week buy you? Two hundred and twenty-six care workers. A hundred and seventy-three classroom assistants. Housing benefit paid on nine hundred flats.'

Colin pulled his sleeve over his hand and wiped condensation from the window.

'Is it time to put it out of its misery?' asked the DJ. He cued into a record. The Style Council's 'Walls Come Tumbling Down'.

Colin sat up in his seat. It had been publicly stated, and as soon as something was articulated it was made possible. The Generator was now on the table, part of the equation in a way it hadn't been before. He felt a brief flicker of hope. There was, he thought for the first time, at least a small chance that it all might work out, that he and Ellie might both come away from it with a win, something they could celebrate together.

This fleeting rush of optimism was followed almost immediately by a sobering sense of reality. The events of the week just gone – the protest, the conflict at the office, the spat with Ellie – had occupied him so fully that he had been able to avoid thinking about his encounter with Pankaj Shastry. He had batted away the memory; the way Shastry and Ellie had looked at each other, the lines of communication that existed between them, their shared jokes. The way they looked so right together.

Two nights earlier, while he was doing the washing up, she had mentioned that Pankaj was part of the team that had convinced the Kenyan government to commute all its outstanding death sentences. Three thousand lives saved. The team had worked on it pro bono, Ellie had told him, in between their other cases. Colin had made some lame joke about U2, mostly to deflect from the fact that on the day she had shared this with him, he had spent his nine working hours ekeing out four hundred words on the state of the Peterdown left back's cruciate ligament.

In this sort of situation, Colin's traditional method of self-protection was to concentrate on his educational record. He'd gone to university, the first person in his family to do so. And it was a proper one, too. Leeds. Which was a thing when you'd gone to the school that he'd gone to. It was something you could stand behind, hang your personhood on.

Deep down, though, he had always known that there was something slightly off about this version of his past, and he found himself, as he so often had, thinking back to the congratulatory pint of bitter that he had been bought by his English teacher, Mr Williams, on the day he'd got his A level results. He'd had more than one, Mr Williams, and he was in the mood to talk.

175

Colin could picture it in perfect detail. Mr Williams had wiped the beer from his lips and told him that he, Colin, was the Chosen One. There was at least one, every year, he had said, at Ottercliffe High, sometimes as many as four or five. This year there had been two. Colin Ryder and Elaine Crowther. She was off to Manchester; he was celebrating getting into Leeds.

The chosen ones were picked early, by the second year at the latest, a couple of students to pump and prime, pupils the faculty could really *teach*. You needed to be bright to be chosen, but there were other criteria. They looked for kids with upper working-class parents, the sort which valued industry, obedience, propriety. The not-quite petit-bourgeois. Kids with something to lose and a lot to gain. And no one that was too cool, Mr Williams had said, patting Colin on the knee. No one that was going to have their head turned by boys, or girls, or guitars.

We tell ourselves we do it because it's essential to the smooth running of the school, he had said. *But the truth is: we do it for the system. To maintain the illusion of social mobility. We do it because we need to delude ourselves. We need to convince ourselves that things are just and the things we got – degrees, jobs as heads of department, cars, houses – we got on merit. And so we chose you, Colin. And you didn't let us down. You didn't let us down.*

Colin took stock of his reflection in the bus window. He had the posture of a lifelong hod carrier; shoulders slumped, back bent. He sat up, peered more closely, appraised his scalp. The hair at the front of his head was being isolated by a pincer movement, leaving it per-ilously detached from the rest of its corpus like an ice sheet before it collapses terminally into the water. He went to try to manage the thinning hairs but stopped before he started. There was nothing he could do. It was simply there for all to see, a mocking reminder of the limits of human agency: the onset of male pattern baldness.

The rain was coming down on the diagonal, people walked into it hunched, others ran, picking up their heels to avoid the puddles. The radio DJ faded out of the song mid-flow.

'I know it's sacrilegious to interrupt the mighty Weller before he's finished but we have breaking news. Peterdown Council supremo

Yvonne Kington is on the phone live and direct. Ready to scotch the rumours about the Generator.'

'Oh, Carl,' said Kington. Her voice was echoey, slightly delayed. 'I don't want anyone to be thinking that I've been demanding you interrupt the Style Council.'

'Of course not. That was all on me.'

'Because that would be a sacrilege. You know I'm a massive fan. I was there when they played the Sidings in 1988.'

'The man himself. In Peterdown. What a gig.'

'One of the best.'

'But that's not what you've called about.'

'No, Carl, it's not. I need to address this rumour before it gets out of hand. I want to say here and now that the claims made on a certain blog are wholly false. First off, her visitor numbers for the Generator are just fanciful. It's the first week in February, which isn't the busiest time of year obviously, but we have had hundreds of thousands of people through the doors since it opened. By any measure it is a success.'

'Surely the crucial question though is about how much money council tax payers are forking out to keep the thing going.'

'Absolutely, Carl. Of course it is. Are operating costs higher than receipts? Yes, they are. No one's pretending they're not. It's an arts venue and it needs to be subsidised. But a hundred and six grand a week? That's fantasy. I don't want to call her a liar but ...'

'OK, what is the right figure?'

'I couldn't tell you off the top of my head. But the real thing is that our friend the blogger makes it sound like us running the operating costs for the Generator through the Peterdown Regeneration Fund is part of some great conspiracy, but commercial confidentiality agreements are standard practice up and down the country. Local government is a partnership with the private sector. It has to be and we have to respect our partners' rights to privacy.'

'If you don't give access to the figures people will wonder ...'

'Which is exactly why, in this case, I'm prepared to put together an abbreviated set of accounts so people can see what's going on.'

There were, Colin had essentially always felt, two sets of people in the world. The first set were the people who used phrases like 'abbreviated accounts'. The kind of people who had pensions and working printers. And then there were people like him. People who talked about 'false consciousness', and who printed their airline tickets at the internet café on the high street. There was a reason the first set had been in charge for the full span of human history.

'When will we get to see these accounts?' asked the DJ.

'In the next couple of days. But I don't want that to become the focus of this conversation because it's about something much bigger. Look, I know the woman who has made these claims. She is a signed-up member of the Keep Peterdown Crap brigade.'

Colin shut his eyes wishing fervently that he hadn't sent that text message. He would be implicated in what was to follow. He may just have been the messenger, but they were the ones who always got shot first.

'They're stuck in the past. Always looking backwards. They don't want us to create jobs and opportunities for the people who live here. They don't want institutions that we can be proud of. They throw mud in spite, not having the faintest idea what they're talking about.'

'You're saying she's resorted to making things up.'

'I can't speak for her. All I can say is we're entering into the most exciting period in Peterdown's modern history,' she continued. 'The biggest infrastructure project in Europe is coming here. This is a once in a lifetime opportunity and we need to grasp it with both hands. We've set up the Peterdown Regeneration Fund as a vehicle for channelling funds into the modernising of the town . . .'

Colin took his earphones out from his ears. The bus had reached his stop. Outside, the rain had stopped but the smell of it was still in the air, and everything felt heavy, soaked through. He walked along the wide, empty pavements, down the sloping grass verges and through the Cluster's car park.

Inside, Heather on reception was idling, chewing gum. He nodded to her as he passed and stood waiting for the lift, aware that it might be the last time he did so. He felt immediately ridiculous about the things that he'd said about the *Post*. To the Toms. To Leonie. To Patrick. Complaining amusingly about their lot was the thing they did, their group-defining shtick. In person, via email, over the phone. It was the way they communicated, expressed their love. The riffs were comic, self-deprecating and unsparing; the topics wide-ranging: childlessness, penury, underemployment.

Colin had long understood that even though they were always couched in irony, for the rest of his university gang these rants were always semi-serious; a product of the endless upwardness of their lives and the despair they felt any time this process stalled. They were restless, expansive; constantly acquiring new skills, new experiences, new languages. Little Tom had changed career three times, retraining every time. By her thirtieth birthday Leonie had bought and sold four London properties, each time moving up the chain, extending and excavating, adding value, building her asset. Big Tom had completed marathons on six continents and was trying to raise funds to run one in Antarctica. They were like economies in miniature, on the hunt for opportunity, striving always for their 3 per cent personal growth.

When it was Colin's turn to rant his longstanding theme was the provincialism of the *Post*: its stories about scooter thefts and cats, his laughably retrograde colleagues, his cul-de-sac of a career. His monologues were despairing, operatic, made even more piquant by their context: he spoke not a word of Italian; couldn't make crème patissière; in all ways, wasn't growing.

The lift gently sighed to a stop, opened its doors. Colin stepped in, and thought reflexively of the boys he'd been to school with, the carpet fitters and plumber's mates, the call centre operators and long-term unemployed. Each of them would have killed for his job.

He pressed the button for his floor, heavy-hearted, thinking back to a long session with Tom and Suzie when, over several beers, he had had them crying uncontrollably as he itemised in unsparing pathos-laden detail the lunchtime habits of his colleague Kelly-Anne with her self-actualisation flow charts, enema cleanses, yoga-boxing and unyielding sixteen-stone bulk.

The lift slowed, stopped. Colin blushed, awash with self-loathing.

It had all been a lie and he knew it. You could get richer, sure, but you couldn't get *better*. It just didn't work like that. He was what he was. And he was where he was. Where he needed to be. With Kelly-Anne. At the *Post*. The only job he had ever wanted.

He walked into the office. Nobody looked at him. Not Hugh Trentwood. Not Anne McAllister. Not Kelly-Anne, who stared resolutely at her screen as he tried imploringly to catch her eye.

At his desk, he turned on his computer. There were eighty-six unread emails in his inbox. Some were messages of support congratulating him on the piece. Some were junk. The remainder were all part of a long email chain involving the whole office. They were about the extraordinary meeting called the night before by the Sinderby board to address 'the virulently anti-business agenda being pursued at the *Post*'. Rick had been summoned to it, warned that he was imperilling the future of the paper. He had been ordered to take a new editorial position, a humiliation that he appeared to have swallowed without a fight. Colin scanned down the emails until he came to one from Hazel in circulation. Early indicators were showing sales of the issue up by 34 per cent. Colin felt relief flooding through him. He looked up to see Rick looming above him.

'Am I being fired?' he said.

'No,' said Rick. 'But only bloody just.'

Walk II

The True Mystery of the World is the Visible: nowhere to somewhere

They say it doesn't matter now, where you are. Now that we're networked, our lives lived online. Place – the 'meat world' as they call it – is over. Made inconsequential by cyberspace.

But it doesn't feel like that, living here. We don't walk down the Ottercliffe Road thinking we might as well be in Seoul. Or even Solihull. Whichever way we look, we're always inescapably in Peterdown. Perhaps, we think cynically to ourselves, they might be telling us that place doesn't matter any more because they're in the process of selling it off. Forests. School playgrounds. A slice of this park. A sliver of that one. A bit here, a bit there. This ongoing, unrelenting privatisation of the realm. We can't seem to stop it but we can bear witness. Make the record. Mark the loss.

And so we drift. Nowhere to somewhere. Or sometimes the other way round.

Our rules are simple:

One, no Google. We have maps, but they're mental. Vertical as well as horizontal. Sensible only to those who understand that the legend updates in real time. That the symbolism isn't fixed. That we can keep reinterpreting this place for ever. Its signboards and street names, highways and byways, hidden alleys and blind corners.

And two, no photography. It's over as a medium, turned in on itself. It's been hijacked by the narcissists. Become an accelerator of aspiration. An enabler of lifestyles. We don't do life*style*. We only do life. And to see life, you need to see it unfiltered, unmediated. The lens may have once been a way of seeing but that flash has cracked. These days it's only walking that makes the world real.

Today, we pick a point, each one as arbitrary as the other, and we start. Here? we say. Why not? we say. And we're off, fallen scholars of the street, always and forever in pursuit of our present history, our illuminating moment.

Apt, then, that we find ourselves just a short hop from the Geoffrie Experience Centre. We bundle up the road towards it. Our top tourist spot, or so we're told. We laugh hollowly. They've taken our trickster and tamed him, trademarked him, turned him into the fat man on the pub sign that swings in the wind, his pint spilling, his belly half-exposed.

But that's not Geoffrie. Not *our* Geoffrie. To us, he will always be a provocateur. A truth-teller whose courtly chat prickled with political intent.

Nothing about him is certain. Some place him in the inner court of Edmund Ironside. Others, the Coeur de Lion. And plenty question his very existence. Does it matter? He is in our DNA whether he was real or not.

Not the way they have him here, though. We peer through the window and cringe at how they've neutered him. Made him gift-shop safe. Tea-towel friendly. A bumbling agony uncle to a kindly king, all accidental aphorisms and the wisdom of the fool.

When we think of him, we think of his *Spiels of Angeldrom*, the transcripts of the tales he told about his own imagined arcadia. Or at least the fragments that survive today. In Geoffrie's anarchic imagination, Angeldrom was a peaceful place. Harmonious and happily horizontal in its power structure. A place where everyone sang, all the time. Danced, all the time. Think medieval musical theatre, only so much stranger. Which made it dangerously satirical when read against the realities of the day: piety, hierarchy and unrestrained machismo.

We stare into the gift shop and lament this half-witted, half-cut court jester version of him. Where is his dream space of mind-altering mushrooms and rivers that run with wine? His aesthetic paradise of outrageous stylings and theatrical absurdity? The *Spiels* tell of total frivolity and utter fabulousness. Of men who are quick to laugh, extravagantly embroidered, forever combing their hair. Of women who cross-dress, talk in riddles, tell bawdy jokes. Read the *Spiels* closely and you realise Angeldrom is basically New York in the 1980s, only with a lot more lute.

We sigh and walk on. Down the Eastfinche Road, past the bus stop, over the traffic island and then down Richardson Road. A classic shopping promenade with all its English particularity: Boots, Burger King, Greggs, Ladbrokes, William Hill, Peacocks, Paddy Power, another Greggs. On they cling, the cynical survivors of the high street apocalypse. Baked goods and betting slips only. It didn't always use to be this way. Number forty-six is a Sports Direct these days, but it was once McEwan's, as grand a department store as any in the land. Sales girls in pillbox hats. Long leather gloves. A whole section of scarves. The window display as a work of art.

We look up, knowing that these are buildings with nobler pasts. Above the Vape Palace's temporary sign is a plaque that identifies this building as Glebe Hall, a one-time Chartist rallying point. The second of the two Greggs, number seventy-one with its Deco stylings, was home back in the sixties to Libris, the book binders. Employee-owned and radically minded, Libris was the first publisher of one of the town's most famous sons: prose stylist of the people, Arthur Toyle.

Halfway up the Ricky, we duck down Union Terrace and peer at the frontage above the minicab office. Our only work by Max Compeer, the Dutch draughtsman. Son of an émigré engineer brought to Peterdown for his canal-building knowhow. It's a minor piece in comparison to his later works – the town hall in Broadcastle, the Pinnacle Hotel marooned ridiculously in Hull – but even on this scale you can see evidence of his demented fabulism. The Guignol gargoyles, the funereal lilies, the crypt-like quality that can still summon a shudder.

Compeer wasn't the first to leave in search of something bigger and better. And he certainly wasn't the last. Every year we lose another lot. The go-getters go. Off elsewhere in search of something a bit spanglier. Which leaves us with a lot of left behind. And a serious generational gap; a glut of grey hairs. Golden-agers. Our streets don't exactly hustle and hum. We move at more of a shuffle.

It has its virtues, though. Trundling allows us to inhabit the street, sense its suppressed memories. We stand in the middle of Rothbury Way and shut our eyes. It might be somnolent now but in days long past it was occasionally the setting for Peterdown's annual 'foteball' match, Eastfinche Parish vs Ottercliffe. A free-form game, with few rules but plenty of drama. Not so much in terms of goals, which were notoriously hard to score, what with it being upwards of seventy-five-a-side, but more in terms of its orgiastic violence. Every match was the same. Windows were broken. Collarbones shattered. Onlookers attacked. Blood feuds started. But other, more serious stuff went on, too. Fayres and foteball games made great cover for seditious meetings. Whispered entreaties. Old-school muckraking. The authorities were forever trying to ban it, so every year they changed the date, announced the venue at the last second. And still the people came in caravans a hundred deep, proto-ravers, off to make their own entertainment outside the scope of the state.

A thunderplump rolls in and we take refuge in the Capricorn Shopping Centre. It's off-peach inside. Or once-peach. Forgotten peach. *Abandoned* peach. This is what we surrendered our centre for. These low ceilings, gloomy corners. These discount card shops. Second-hand jewellers. Bulk buy perfumers.

As soon as the weather breaks, we duck down Market Road looking for clues, keywords, anything that might help us unpick the puzzle of our predicament. Back in the day this was the commercial hub of the region, drawing people from right across the Vale to its monthly market. It would all come up the Peter on boats: yarn, wool, leather goods, a hundred varieties of cheese. Today, there's a market still on Thursdays. Some fruit. A bit of veg. But mostly stalls of last resort for capitalism's jetsam, its wash-ashore. Cheap Chinese toys. Bashed boxes of cereal. White-label toiletries. Dodgy DVDs.

From Market Road, we skip up the steps of Fanon House, Kington's Kingdom as it is now. It wasn't always like this – frantically modernising, souped-up with strategic partnerships. In recent memory it was a redoubt, a socialist barricade holding out against the Thatcherite tide. The Peterdown Commune, they called themselves, tongues only half in their cheeks. A self-declared autonomous zone. Leaders of the apartheid boycott and pioneers of paternity rights. A refuge for picketing miners. The only council to appoint an ambassador to the West Bank. They never saw a cause on which they couldn't hang a flag, lead the conversation. Not always brilliant, mind, when it came to collecting the bins.

From there, we take the circuitous route round St Jude's, its stone tower standing tall. The nave is Saxon, they say. Evidence that this place has deep roots. It gets a mention in Bede. He talked about the village of a thousand years, an ancient settlement out this way that must have been us.

We continue past St Jude's and on through residential Rothbury for a couple of minutes, until we approach it. Round the corner, hugging the hillside, all lean-tos and shanty sheds, sprouting broccoli and crowds of cabbages. A verdant slum in miniature. The Dilston Allotments.

In we go, through a latticed arch, heaving with honeysuckle. To our right stands a shed wrapped bunkerishly in black rubber. Beyond it, another, fashioned seemingly from a dozen old doors, is listing alarmingly like a ship destined for the ocean floor. Tarpaulins flap. Bunting flutters. Broad beans sprout. Cat's-cradles of green wire connect bamboo sticks in precise patterns. Green shoots appear at random. Jerry-built glasshouses are stuck with shells, grotto-like. Tabloid flags fly at half mast, lamenting a long-lost World Cup.

This site has been hacked and hoed at for the best part of a hundred years but it seems unlikely to see out its century. In all the hullabaloo about where the main station will go, the fate of the allotments has been a side note, filed away without fanfare. For this area has been earmarked as the site of the new railway's electricity substation, a big old box of capacitors and circuit breakers that will help propel Excalibur along its tracks. We look about forlornly, powerless in the face of it, knowing that it will continue on for ever. This great conveniencing. And everything that goes with it. The blast-cleaning. The scrub-clearing. The urban-titivating. The never-ending de-placing of England.

18

I f anything it was a bit much, this most super of Super Sundays.
Chelsea vs West Ham at 12 p.m., Spurs vs Arsenal at 2 p.m.,
and in an almost too perfect final flourish, Liverpool vs Man
United at 4 p.m.

In front of him, taken from their packets and plated up, stood the
massed ranks of Colin's provisions: a family-sized Melton Mowbray
Pork Pie, a sharing box of honey-glazed cocktail sausages, eight mini
Scotch eggs, and a Ginsters Deep-Filled Chicken and Mushroom
Slice. He was fairly confident that when she designed it Ellie had not
considered whether or not her one-off Corbusier-style coffee table
would be exactly the right size to accommodate just the right amount
of food for six hours of top-level, high-definition televised sport, but
unconsciously or otherwise, she had done an excellent job.

He settled into the sofa and let the soothing sounds of Gary
Neville's pre-match analysis lull him into a bovine calm. It was
exactly what he needed after the drama that had been playing out
at the office. Rick's spinelessness in the face of Sinderby's ridiculous
demands had forced him to accept for the first time the extent of
his own corruption and he had spent the rest of the day taking his
frustration out on Colin.

And then the weekend, which had offered little solace. Ellie had
spent the whole of Saturday morning raging at herself for being so
impulsive and at Yvonne for being so cruel and at Colin for just being
there. He had finally managed to get away at 2 p.m. to the sanctuary
of the Chapel, where he had watched United sneak a one-nil win over
Hull thanks to a dodgy penalty decision.

On the screen, the referee blew his whistle and the first game of the day kicked off. Colin edged his fingernail under the ring pull and cracked open his first can of Carlsberg. He felt immediately thankful to the game for the way it asked just the right amount of you, demanded attention but not attentiveness. Distraction without effort.

Five hours and four cans of lager later, he was sprawled on the sofa brushing pastry flakes from his lips. The Man United–Liverpool game was approaching its forty-minute mark and even the absurdly boosterish commentators had given up pretending that the first half had been anything other than abject. The north London derby had been similarly stale, the atmosphere dulled by the early kick-off. But at least it had been a contest until the end. Chelsea had gone three-nil up against West Ham in the first twenty minutes and the rest of the game had dragged on at half-pace.

Colin watched two players go up for a header, the ball break loose, a centre back hump it out for a throw. He closed his eyes, let his head sink into the cushion. Days like this reminded him, acutely and despairingly, that football was nothing more than men kicking a ball between sticks. It was a game in which people invested far too much. The narratives it engendered had no deeper meaning, no wider resonance. It taught you nothing about the universe.

He let the empty can of lager slide from his hand and land on the floor. He had dedicated his life to it, this meaningless game. Would have been one thing had he been playing it. But he didn't do that. He wrote about other people playing it.

The doorbell rang.

Kerry was on his doorstep, looking morose.

'I called twice but you didn't answer,' she said. 'And I texted.'

Colin had never seen her like this: scrubbed of makeup, flat shoes, a hooded top, jeans.

'I think my phone's in the kitchen.'

'I was passing. I thought I'd stop by.'

'You didn't get sacked, did you?'

'No, I'm fine. Well, you know, I'm not fine. But I've still got my job.'

'But it's not good news, is it?'

Kerry smiled thinly.

'Can I come in?' she said.

Colin tried gamely to recall the exact state of the living room. As he remembered it there were at least three empty lager cans on the floor and a half-eaten Ginsters that he had at some point lost track of.

'Of course,' he said, tentatively.

He led her inside and was relieved to discover it wasn't as bad as he had feared.

'Nil-nil?' said Kerry, reading the score from the screen.

'Yeah, it's been crap. United have parked the bus.'

'This place is something else,' said Kerry, looking around at the plywood panels, the massive modernist painting. 'Did your other half design it all?'

'Yeah, she did.'

'I can't imagine living in a place like this.'

'You get used to it after a while.'

It seemed to occur to Kerry that they might not be alone in the house and she tilted her head to one side and gestured upstairs with a nod.

'They're out horse riding,' said Colin. 'There's an open day every year at the Broadcastle stables. The kids get to ride on the horses and muck out the hay. It's pretty much the highlight of Daisy's year.' He stopped, heavy-limbed and awfully tired. 'I don't know why I'm not there.'

Kerry sat down on the sofa.

'Can I have a Scotch egg?'

Colin handed her the plate.

'Lager?'

'Are you having one?'

'I've had four already,' said Colin, as he muted the television. 'But I could probably squeeze in a fifth.'

They sat side by side, drinking lager, eating Scotch eggs.

'So,' said Kerry.

'So,' echoed Colin.

'He's released a statement. It's just what you'd expect. Unique development opportunity ... State-of-the-art stadium ... Massive corporate investment in the naming rights ... Debt-funded expansion model being the essence of capitalism ... A destination stadium at the heart of the region's most dynamic new neighbourhood ... Etc. etc.'

Kerry's voice was flat, devoid of its usual bounce and enthusiasm, her professional polish and unflappability.

'All of which was pretty predictable. What I didn't expect was for them to be so cool about it. Their attitude has been: people were going to find out at some point, nothing about it is illegal, it's ordinary business practice.'

Colin cut them both a slice of pork pie.

'So this isn't the thing?'

'I don't know. Maybe it is the thing. You know, maybe we were expecting too much of the thing ... Either way, I thought it was going to change everything, this. I thought it would shame them into shelving the whole idea. But they're not even that fussed. They're just going to ride it out. I actually heard one of them say: "What does it matter when the fans hate us anyway?"'

Colin looked down at his plate. His piece of pie comprised a bit of meat and some pastry but it was dominated overwhelmingly by a thick wedge of murkily transparent aspic jelly. Not without good reason, he felt, as he had many times before, that the universe had a habit of reminding him more than it did other people that life was, indeed, suffering.

'Doesn't really matter,' he said. 'I've been told I can't write any more about it anyway.'

'Really?'

'Our board wants the *Post* to help foster a pro-business environment.'

The pie had been out of the fridge for too long; the pastry was warm, the jelly sweaty. Colin ate it anyway.

'Do you ever sometimes think it would be a lot easier to just go with it?' he said as he chewed. 'I have this colleague, Neil. And Neil goes with it. He's bought into the now. Technology. Instagram. He's on board with the whole kit and caboodle. And you know what the thing about Neil is? Neil's content.'

He took a long pull of his lager, swilled the pie from between his teeth.

'There's nothing rewarding about swimming against the current,' he continued, 'it's exhausting and demoralising and the best you can hope for is stasis. Because everything that's coming at you is just relentless. I mean history, you know. The big shit, obviously, but also the incalculable number of things that just happen without me having any control over them whatsoever.'

On the television a United player turned his back as he went to block a shot and the ball hit his arm. Liverpool were awarded a penalty. Colin turned up the volume. A Spanish international who was ordinarily very good, very neat, ran up and smacked the penalty over the bar.

It had been that kind of game.

'I think everyone has something that they've known to be true about themselves since they were a small child,' said Colin as he turned off the television.

Kerry was sitting on the sofa with her head right back on the headrest so that she was looking up at the ceiling.

'I had a friend, Luke,' he continued. 'At school. He once told me about these two recurring dreams he had when he was a kid. He had one where he was ridiculously massive. He'd be lying on his bed, on his back, knowing he was dreaming but also sort of conscious of what was happening. It was why he could always remember them so well. He said when he was having this dream he could feel the blood pulsing at his extremities. He said it was like being Gulliver in Lilliput, everything else tiny in comparison. He said in those moments it was like he was everything in the world, dwarfing everything else.

'But he had these other dreams, too. Tiny dreams, he called them. The complete opposite. Dreams where he was minuscule, insignificant, totally powerless. He never had the two dreams on the same night but he talked about them as if they were complementary. He called them his clarity dreams. He said, and I remember this like it was yesterday, word for word, he said, *they weren't scary, they were true.*

'It broke my heart, that conversation. And I never told him. It broke my heart because I only ever had the second dream, the small one. I never had the big dream.'

Kerry rested her head on Colin's shoulder.

'You're not like other people,' she said.

'Whatever I do isn't going to make any difference, is it?'

'You don't know that.'

'It's going to happen or it's not going to happen with or without me. Everything I've tried to do so far has been a disaster. We've gained absolutely nothing and everyone at work hates me. I just don't see the point of carrying on.'

Kerry lifted her head from his shoulder.

'All right,' she said. 'Enough wallowing.'

Colin looked over at her. Accustomed as he was to spending his life with a woman who really did look more beautiful without makeup, it was a strange experience to encounter someone who didn't. Kerry's face and hair and clothes were essential to her mystique and seeing her without them was . . . Well, it was astonishingly intimate. It was a kind of nakedness, he realised, and it possessed a powerful erotic pull. He shut his eyes. He would have the hug first and then the kiss. Anything else would just be too much.

'It's up to me and you to do something about this and I need you to bloody well grow a pair.'

Colin reeled. She had just made a direct reference to *his* testicles. He sat up, drunk, full of a kind of lurching purpose.

'You know Kirk said he was getting someone on board to sort it out. Tell his story. Could it be a journalist?'

'It could be anyone. Why?'

'I think something might be going on at the *Post*,' he said.

He opened his laptop and logged in to Neil's inbox.

They sat scanning through the emails. None appeared to be from Kirk, or any of his employees. But there was one that caught Colin's eye. It was from Total Solutions PR. Its subject header was: More Lies from the Larkspur Listing Campaign.

Colin clicked on it. The first paragraphs rehashed all the statements that had already been released about the Generator's rude financial health. Colin's gaze danced down it to the second paragraph, which was a straight-up character assassination, each sentence more brutal than the last.

'Is this talking about your Ellie?'

He scrolled down through a series of suspect statistics, half-truths and outright smears until his eyes alighted on the last line of the email.

Word is she's sucking Shastry's cock just to get him on side.

'Oh,' said Kerry.

19

Colin sat shivering on the bonnet of the Astra looking at his phone. He had stupidly come down without his coat or his car keys, having had some vague notion that the cold air might cut through his hangover.

It wasn't working. He felt a wave of queasiness rise and then subside just as it started to lick at the bottom of his oesophagus. After Kerry had gone, he had sat on the sofa, increasingly maudlin and self-pitying, and had drunk a sixth and then a seventh can of lager, enough to see him flat out and snoring on the spare bed at 8.30 p.m., a full hour before Ellie and Daisy arrived home from their annual post-horse riding pizza.

Upon waking, he had then dragged himself through the usual fevered routine with its hastily grabbed slices of toast and rushed showers, never finding the right moment to enlighten Ellie as to the contents of the email from Total Solutions.

But it wasn't something that could be delayed for ever. He called. She answered.

'Where are you? It sounds like you're in a wind tunnel.'

'I'm in the car park at the Cluster.'

'Can't you call me from the office? I can barely hear you.'

'No, I can't. It's confidential stuff.'

'Really?'

'I was looking through Neil's inbox again. There's another email.'

'From Total Solutions?'

'Yes.'

'What does it say?'

'It says you're a Stalinist architecture student from London who is trying to impose Soviet housing developments on working people despite living yourself in what they call a "substantial semi-detached house".'

'I can't believe it,' she said.

'I know.'

'I am not a fucking *student*.'

'Yes,' said Colin after a pause.

'Who are these people?'

'I don't know, but they really go to town on you for that blog post about the Generator. Saying it shows you can't be trusted. Saying you made up all the numbers.'

'I didn't make the numbers up, I got the numbers from you.'

'And I told you not to use them,' he whispered urgently. 'You took it too far.'

Colin could hear her seething furiously down the line.

'Did it say anything else?'

He paused, the exact wording of the email's final sentence stuck fast in his mind.

'No,' he said gamely. 'That was it.'

Ellie hung up. Across the Larkspur concourse she could see Pankaj walking towards her. He had seen her too, which ruled out running home to bed and crawling under the covers. The last four days had been without doubt the most embarrassing of her life, and now she had to face him – the man to whom everything came effortlessly and flawlessly – just as her confidence had taken another knock.

Everyone she knew in the town seemed to have either heard Yvonne's call to the radio programme or listened to it after the fact, through the station's online playback service. From Friday morning onwards she had received non-stop texts and emails, most of them genuinely supportive, others transparently gleeful at her humiliation.

And now him.

He reached her, leaned in for a kiss on both cheeks.

She recoiled, shocked and perturbed.

'Have you been smoking?' she asked, slightly disbelievingly.

Pankaj looked at her sideways.

'Don't tell anyone,' he said.

Ellie scoffed, more aggressively than she'd intended.

'Smoking's just perfect for politicians, isn't it? It's legal, obviously, and it doesn't impair your judgement so no one can really call you out for doing it. But of course we all know it's bad for you and that you shouldn't do it.'

She paused, conscious that she was being unnecessarily confrontational but overwhelmed by her mood, which was spiteful and angry and driving her onwards.

'I mean don't you think it's a bit obvious? A bit of a cliché. Like you really want to be Obama. Or, even worse, what's his face from *The West Wing*? Charlie Sheen's dad.'

Pankaj winced.

'Bartlett,' he said. 'Martin Sheen's character was called President Bartlett. And, yes, he did smoke in the show.'

'I'm sorry, but whenever I see a politician having a fag I can't help but think that they're doing it because they think it will make them look more human, more approachable. It just looks false.'

'OK. Well, that's me told.'

'I'm sorry. I just think it's a bit studied.'

Pankaj was sort of grimacing and grinning at the same time.

'I feel like a little boy caught with his spoon in the jam,' he said. 'If it makes it any better, I hardly ever smoke. Just the odd one every now and then. And certainly not in front of anyone. It's a legacy of going into court. I dealt with some pretty full-on cases. Extraditions. Whole families depending on you. It was high-stakes stuff. And I found sneaking the odd fag was a way of managing the tension.'

'Oh god,' said Ellie, suddenly contrite. 'I'm sorry. That was so unnecessary.'

'And I really never do it in public. I really don't want you to think I'm one of those MPs who spends half his time drinking pints for photo ops.'

'Please ignore me,' she said. 'I'm knackered.'

Ellie looked at the ground, disgusted at herself. She had spent weeks trying to be her best self for him, and in a moment she had ruined it. She rubbed her face trying to bring some life back to it. She had hardly slept for three nights.

'I've had a difficult week,' she said.

'Yes, I heard Yvonne on the radio.'

'I feel like such a dick.'

'These things happen.'

'Everyone in Peterdown thinks I'm an idiot.'

She looked up at him. His smile was gentle, non-judgemental.

'While we're dealing with the not-so-great stuff, have you heard of the Generator Users Group?'

'No.'

'It's clearly a response to your campaign. A rival community group.'

'But nobody goes to the Generator.'

'Well. Somebody does, it seems. There are posters and flyers. Well designed. Someone's put some work into them.'

'Oh, Jesus.'

Ellie shut her eyes, pinched the bridge of her nose.

'I've got something that I hope might cheer you up.'

He had a large cotton tote bag over his shoulder from which he pulled a package wrapped in brown paper.

'This is for me?'

'It is.'

She took it from him, opened it, her breath held. It was a small A4-sized poster. From the 1960s by the look of things. And original, obviously, judging by the thick paper, the faded colour, the slight damage. It was a screen print. Le Corbusier's Open Hand sculpture that stood in Chandigarh.

Ellie looked at it, totally overwhelmed.

'Indian Railways produced a whole series of these in the sixties, to encourage tourism. They commissioned them for Kerala, Goa, Dharamshala, everywhere. They did four for the Chandigarh complex, which had just been finished. My grandfather kept hold of them and gave them to me. I have a duplicate of this one. It seems silly for me to have two.'

The print was four-colour, the ink saturated deep into the thick paper. It was the best thing she had ever been given.

'You had it framed.'

'Well ... Yes, I did. I thought it looked better that way. And, you know, it's an old poster.'

She had been given this object, this perfect object. For the first time in a long time she felt intimately known. She put her hand on a handrail and leaned on it, thinking that she might just burst into tears. A few seconds passed until she gathered herself, slowed her breath, her lips quivering.

She looked at him, a film of tears in her eyes.

'Thank you so much.'

She then tucked the framed poster under her arm and walked briskly up a flight of stairs, knowing that if she didn't quickly shift the focus, she would say something that she would not be able to take back.

Pankaj followed her up the stairs. At the top was a door. Its window was smashed. A piece of cardboard had been stuck over the hole. On the door just to the right of the handle was a sticker.

Red Arrow Maintenance (Broadcastle area)
Report a problem: 01632 242424

'This is getting ridiculous,' she said, pulling her mobile phone from her pocket. She dialled the number, spoke to a receptionist, then the maintenance man in charge of the area and then finally his manager.

'I'd have my boys out there in a flash, love. But I'm not a bloody charity. When it was the council housing department what paid us, we got paid on time, no problem. Since it's all been outsourced we've not had a penny and I've said we're not coming back until we get paid.'

'Who did it get outsourced to?'

'I'll tell you,' he said. 'It's on a piece of paper here.'

Ellie heard a rustle and a shuffling.

'Peterdown Regeneration Fund,' he said, eventually. 'Whatever the hell that is.'

STEAMING IN: A PODCAST WITH MICK CLARIDGE AND STEVE WANLESS PLUS SPECIAL GUEST GRAHAM COBB

ORIGINALLY AIRED 6 p.m.
TUESDAY, MARCH 8th

MICK

So, welcome to *Steaming In*. I'm Mick Claridge and I'm here with my old mucker Steve Wanless. Short-arse Steve. The Chapel's Charlotte Church.

STEVE

Afternoon.

MICK

He's become an unlikely celebrity since his little solo performance a couple of weeks ago. Bit of a sleeper hit it was, but it's going off now. Eleven thousand hits on YouTube.

STEVE

Although half of them were my mam.

MICK

Sadly, there's no time to get Steve on the karaoke today as this evening we've got a special guest. Graham Cobb. Terrace legend and editor of *Living the Steam*, the best bloody football fanzine in the

history of the world. 1985 to 2006 it ran. Twenty-
one years of glory before it moved online. And
then became a Facebook. But, in massive news for
nostalgic old fucks everywhere, it's back. Printed
and folded and stapled. Graham, welcome to the
show. It's a treat to have you here.

GRAHAM
Thanks Mick.

MICK
So tell us about the relaunch.

GRAHAM
We're going make them the way we used to make
them. You don't need to put it on a website, you
know? Who needs global? We're not Chelsea. No one
in Singapore gives a shit about Peterdown United
Football Club. It's local. It's meant to be local.
It's a local club. You need local knowledge for a
local club.

MICK
Everything's too everywhere.

GRAHAM
Exactly. Everything's too everywhere. I used to
like it when you had to find something, it weren't
just there instantly in your pocket.

MICK
Now you're talking my language.

GRAHAM
We're going back to paper because we wanted

200

something special. And it doesn't work on the
internet. Our kid tried to show Terry Mac how
to draw on an iPad. It was a joke. Looked like a
left-handed five-year-old had drawn it, do you know
what I mean? I was like, What the fuck is that?
And he was like, It's Jonny. And I was like, Jonny
Ellis? And he was like, Yeah. And I was like, It
looks like a fucking squid.

MICK
Terry Mac is old school.

GRAHAM
And that was part of the reason to go back to
paper. You know? Terry Mac *is* old school. He's not
iPad, is he? But it was also because we were bored
of website. Do you know what I mean? We wanted
something you could only get on match day and
you could only get it at a few pubs and like two
places outside the ground. I don't want *everyone* to
have it. I want it to be a thing that only a few
people have but those people really want it. Does
that make sense?

MICK
So much sense.

GRAHAM
And you know what. It's been magic. Our kid and
his mates love it. Normally, they'd rather be
watching videos of people playing FIFA.

MICK
What?

GRAHAM

I'm not shitting you. They go on YouTube and watch
other people playing video games. *Professionals*.
Professional computer game players. I've told him
it's the first sign of madness ... Anyway, they
loved it, him and his mates. They were helping
us all put it together last week. Eight of us in
my gaff and he was there with two of his boys.
Longest I've seen them off their phones since they
were bloody children. Cutting up and sticking down
and ripping it up and starting again. It's not like
we did it on typewriters like we once did. We used
computers but we were still printing and cutting
with scissors. You know, actually *making* something,
and that felt pretty good. And it is pretty good.
Do you know what I mean? That's the thing. Terry
Mac. He can't do iPad or owt, but he's still
funny as fuck.

MICK

Oh, he is. He makes me cry, that man.

STEVE

Nobody can rock a deerstalker like Terry Mac. Not
even Sherlock Holmes.

GRAHAM

I can't believe he's still wearing that hat. What
is it, nearly forty years since it was a thing?
Only Terry.

MICK

God, is it that long? That makes me feel old.

STEVE

Our younger listeners — all four of them — won't
know what we're talking about here.

MICK

True. Absolutely true. But who better to tell them
about it than Grazza? The man that was right in
the thick of it. Come on, Graham, tell the kids
what it used to be like before anyone even thought
about wearing a replica shirt to game.

GRAHAM

You want me to tell the story of the deerstalker?

MICK

Right from the start.

GRAHAM

OK, so everybody knows about Broadcastle and
their run in the '82 Fairs Cup. Worst time to be a
football lad in Peterdown. Absolute worst. I mean,
this is 1982, right? There's no EasyJet then. None
of us went on holiday to Spain or owt. Skeggie
maybe. And there's Broadcastle going all over the
place on coaches. Massively subsidised by the club,
they were. Massively. It were a quid or something
stupid to go. Anyway, they lasted three rounds of
the cup. Each round's two legs: home and away, and
they beat Genoa and Marseille before they lost to
Gothenburg.

MICK

We're at home playing Southend and Scunthorpe and
they're off to the south of bloody France . . .

GRAHAM

Exactly. And every time they go away their lot go
on the rampage. I mean, *rampage*. Like a plague of
locusts. Turning whole department stores. Diadora,
Kappa. All this Italian shit that none of us had
ever seen before. And I'm talking shirts, jackets,
shoes, these special coats what they wear in
Sweden cause it's so cold — Broadcastle came back
with the lot. Proper flash gear. You couldn't buy
any of it in England back then. There were none
of the shops like today. And even if there had
been we'd have never afforded it. It were proper
gear. To begin with we were jealous as all hell.
But you know what? It was the best thing that
ever happened to the lads in our end. It gave us
something to go up against, you know?

MICK

And that's how it started?

GRAHAM

It were a lad called Jim Marshall what started
it. He turned up at the Chapel — I'll never forget
this — it were 1983 and we were playing Carlisle
and he rocks up at the Radleigh in fucking
tweed. We were like, what the fuck? He's got this
jacket from a charity shop and he's taken it to
a tailor — now you've got to remember there were
still a few old-school tailors in them days,
cheap, you know, for ordinary folk — so he takes
it to this tailor and gets it lined in green. I
tell you, it looked magic. He says to everyone:
Broadcastle can wear what they want but I'm
English me, not some Eyetie. Next week everyone's
at it. Tweed jackets. Wax jackets. Wellington

boots one lad had. Tommy Quinn had got a van and
gone to some sale, a house clearance I think it
was. And he's filled it. Some of it were right
musty but there was a load of good gear in there.
And it was all proper English. I tell you what,
we got it pimped. Proper linings in the jackets.
Pocket squares. None of it were fashionable. Could
hardly have been less fashionable. But it was our
thing. Our look, you know. Six months or something
we did it before it just slowly died out. But,
man, we looked mint, a load of lads from plant
marching down the Western Way like we were going
to bloody Ascot.

          MICK
Everyone gave it up apart from Terry Mac.

          GRAHAM
Everyone but Terry. He still wears that bloody
deerstalker. You should smell the fucking thing.
Christ alive.

          MICK
It couldn't happen now, could it?

          GRAHAM
Nah. It wouldn't happen now. It couldn't.
Everything's too everywhere . . .

20

The thirty or so screens were bolted high up on the wall in clusters so that they roughly approximated the world map. South America was a big computer monitor and two smaller tablets. Australia was on an old-school television. None of the world's smaller islands had made the cut, apart from Britain which was represented quite cutely, Ellie had to admit, by an iPhone floating just off the coast of the Eurasian landmass. According to the wall text, the image on the screens was dictated by an algorithm that recorded changes in people's relationship status on Facebook. There was, by the looks of things, an awful lot of heartbreak in Kamchatka.

She sat on a bench watching the screens change colour. She was in the Generator having bought a full exhibition pass. She wasn't quite the only person to have done this. On the other side of the room an elderly couple were standing, nonplussed, in front of an interactive time capsule machine that made short videos of whoever was using it, which, as soon as they were made, went into a sort of digital cold storage, encrypted in such a way that they were rendered unwatchable until the 2070s.

In the time she'd been watching them, the couple in question had inadvertently made at least seven such films of themselves, all of which had seen them push the button and simply stand there, mutely staring at the screen. Given their age, which on both counts looked to be in the upper eighties, it seemed at once a poignant stab at immortality and a numbly brilliant critique of contemporary museum design.

Ellie felt a stab of sympathy. She, too, had had her fill of pushing buttons, pulling out drawers, turning handles, swiping screens; the full panoply of distraction techniques that were singularly failing to disguise the fact that there was remarkably little to see.

Apart, of course, from the building, which was there, everywhere you looked, making an exhibition of itself. The windows were globular, placed at odd, awkward heights; often too low to be comfortable to look out of, or too high to adequately light the space. Each staircase had a feature – one was held up by jaggedy chrome iceberg-like supports, another had a profusion of steam-bent struts – that meant they took up three, four, five times the volume necessary.

Ellie got up from the bench and started along the corridor. She knew that the idea for an arts space on the site had been kicking round since the eighties when it had been proposed as a smaller version of the South Bank with its own theatre troupe, an exhibition space for travelling shows, a concert hall and independent cinema. After four different proposals had been rejected it was finally green-lit as an arts centre 2.0; a home, it was proposed, for the hive mind and user-generated content.

Not that the users had much of a role in generating the building, she remembered noting at the time, which had been tendered out to the American architect Francis Spear, or at least his London office, which knocked out the 'iconic' building at such speed that you couldn't help but wonder if they already had the design waiting on the shelf.

By the time it had finally opened – predictably late and way over budget – this pioneering digital culture hub consisted mainly of a series of commissioned artworks about social media (all of which had proved too expensive to ever replace), and a wall-sized digital display networked into the web that was shut down on its second day when the organisers realised that if you allow people to anonymously upload material they will almost exclusively share libellous jokes about suspected paedophiles, racial epithets and hardcore pornography.

Ellie continued down the corridor to the performance hall. It had launched with a piece of digitally enhanced contemporary dance and the promise of immersive theatre and TED talks, but budget cuts meant that for the last six months it had been effectively a comedy club with 'Googling My C**k', as the posters demurely had it, only the latest of a series of lucrative stand-up tours that dominated its schedule.

Ellie stopped at a window and leaned her forehead flush against it, enjoying the cold chill of the glass. On the concourse below she could see a group of teenagers. They were carousing performatively, the exuberance of their yelps and squeals audible even through the thick glass. For a couple of minutes, she watched the interplay of two girls, the way they shadowed each other, their reactions in perfect concert, one of their hands always on the other's arm, the intensity of their friendship declarable only through a kind of elective siamesing. Ellie watched them react to something one of the boys said by turning to face each other and pausing comically, before bursting into irrepressible adoring laughter.

She felt an acute sense of her own loneliness, of how parenthood and living in Peterdown had allowed her to withdraw into herself, shrink her world.

She reached into her bag, picked out her phone, called Patrick.

'Fergie! Oh my god, tell me you're in London.'

'Afraid not. I'm in Peterdown in the circle of hell reserved for people who upload inspirational quotes on to social media.'

'Ha,' said Patrick. 'Tell me you're dancing like no one is watching.'

'No, but I totally could be. I'm at the Generator and I'm pretty much the only person here.'

'Aha. A reconnaissance mission.'

'Something like that. Honestly, I can't believe this place isn't haemorrhaging money. There's no one here.'

'What's it like? I thought it was supposed to be a Cedric Price sort of fun palace. I thought it sounded kind of amazing.'

'Oh god, Price's Fun Palace was going to have Joan Littlewood as its creative director. And it was conceived when people still had the quaint idea that a museum might have more to teach them than they had to teach it. This place makes you long for some old-fashioned Reithian paternalism.'

At the end of the line she could hear Patrick fiddling with his phone.

'Darling, I've got to go. I've got another call coming in. It's a work thing.'

'I wish you were here. You would be funny about this place.'

'And *I* wish you were *here*, darling. Which you could be. Easily. All you have to do is move. I'll pay for the train ticket.'

Ellie hung up and walked down an undulating ramp, feeling even lonelier than she had before she called him. Overhead the lights glowed pink. The walls were decorated so that they looked like circuit boards. Finally, at the end of it she could hear buzz and chatter, the sound of human life.

There had been much talk when it opened about the Generator's world food café, which had been touted as a kind of rolling pop-up with different parts of the community taking charge of the cooking on different days; but as far as Ellie could tell this had never actually happened and the catering contract had been outsourced to the same people that did the food in the swimming pool. She ordered a cheese and tomato panini and a cup of tea, and sat down in the far corner with her book.

She was only two pages in when she heard the voice.

'Oh my god, you're eating a panini.'

Ellie looked up. Janey was standing above her, mouth agape.

'In my head you eat carrot sticks and hummus, maybe a low-fat muffin, but not a whacking great panini. How can you have your body and eat paninis? I mean, where's the justice in that?' Ellie self-consciously pushed the plated panini to the corner of the table. It was the size of an oven glove and striated with fake black griddle markings on its top. Milky white mozzarella oozed from one side.

'I didn't know you came here.'

'Twice a week,' said Janey with a shrug. 'Sometimes three.'

'*Three times a week.*'

'Parking's free if you spend a fiver.'

Ellie nodded. She had never known anyone so devoted to their car.

It was a huge great thing, a four-by-four, black with tinted windows, and always polished to a high shine. She used it to ferry her brood in from their huge house in the Vale. Her husband, Steve, had made his money doing something only ever vaguely referred to, which Ellie strongly suspected was related to PPI claims.

'What do you do here?'

'Stay and Play Tuesdays,' said Janey. 'Zumba class on Thursdays at eleven o'clock.'

'They do Zumba here?'

'With. A. Free. Creche.' She swooned. 'A-mazing.'

'And?'

'Third time is normally just whatever. I'll take Alexis to look at the exhibitions. Get coffee and a cake. You know, whatever.'

'Oh god, you're not part of the GUG, are you?'

'GUG?'

'Generator Users Group. It's a thing. They're campaigning to save this place.'

'Sign me up,' said Janey, her eyes twinkling with provocative relish.

'I'm amazed they haven't already, what with you coming here three times a week.'

'Wait a sec. Last week I was here *four* times,' said Janey. 'Me and Steve got in a babysitter and went to "Googling My Cock". Have you been yet?'

'No.'

'I wet myself. I'm not joking. Just a little bit. Four kids, I tell you. Pelvic floor's like a bloody sieve. But, honestly, Ellie. Oh my god. He did this thing where he scanned his—'

'Don't tell me.'

'No, honestly it was hilarious. He's got a scanner on stage and—'

'Janey, if you tell me what you're about to tell me I will never be able to unknow it, and just knowing it will be some kind of tacit endorsement of it.'

'The night we were there, he trapped it.'

'*Janey.*'

'I'm not joking.'

'I've heard him on a couple of radio things and he is honestly the most self-satisfied prick . . . '

Janey snorted through her nose.

'What?'

'Well, you know, it might not be without good reason. I mean, you never actually see it, he makes sure of that. But you don't *not* see it.'

Here Janey exhaled showily.

'There's this silhouette . . . I tell you what, it had Steve squirming in his seat, bless him.'

Ellie found herself grinning despite her best intentions. 'Really,' she said, 'hosting that man's tour is reason enough to knock this place down.'

Janey pulled a so-appalled-I-might-die face.

'They can't knock it down. It's only five years old. It cost forty-five million quid.'

'These aren't reasons not to knock it down if it's terrible and the other buildings on the list are really good. Or at least one of them is really good and the other one is important to some people.'

Janey tilted her head to one side with impudent intent.

'This place is important to me,' she said.

Ellie raised a knowing eyebrow.

'OK,' she said. 'I'll accept that it's been useful to you at a particular stage of your life. But of course you could just as easily do Zumba in a church hall. This is not supposed to be that. It's supposed to be something else. You know, Janey, in places like Poland high culture is part of everyday life for everyone. It's not just a distraction for north London wankers.'

Janey smiled. This was a direct quote from her.

'A place like this could have done that. It could have been a real part of life here. Instead, it's *this*. It's worse than nothing at all because it tricks people into thinking that space has been filled.'

Ellie paused and went to take a bite of her panini, when she realised her phone was vibrating on the table top. It was Shelly. She looked at Janey, who nodded her assent.

'I have word,' said Shelly.

211

'What?'

'The figures Kington released, Miss Ketchup had to collate them for her. They seem to add up.'

Ellie felt a great deflation in her chest, a sense of her whole body sagging.

'Really? I can't get my head round that. I just can't see how this place isn't completely tanking . . .'

'But that's not all Miss Ketchup had to say.'

'No?'

'She got a rare glimpse into the books of the Peterdown Regeneration Fund. And you're right, they stopped the direct debit to that maintenance company a couple of months ago. But that wasn't what really caught her eye.'

'No?'

'There's a six grand a month retainer going out of the account. And guess who's getting it?'

'Who?'

'Total Solutions PR.'

21

The house was an old worker's cottage, part of a terrace. It was centrally located and had no front garden so the door opened up right on to the street. The perfect place to rent, all told, if you wanted to communicate that you were accessible, available, a man of the people.

Inside, the house was white-walled and uncluttered, a virtue made of its simplicity. Ellie sat on the sofa. On the opposite wall, framed and hung in a simple grid formation, were the four posters from Chandigarh.

'You've done a nice job of the house.'

'You should have seen the wallpaper when I moved in,' said Pankaj. 'God, it was like living in a 1970s fever dream. Poor old Aidan spent two days scraping it off. Probably the best work experience he'll get while he's with me.'

Under the window, a giant yucca sat in a faded terracotta pot. On a sideboard, there was a seventies turntable, a pile of records.

'I like this sofa,' she said, running her hand along its seam.

'It's from Ikea,' he whispered theatrically. 'We spend our allowances judiciously these days.'

Ellie smiled but she was tired already of the small talk. It was twenty-four hours since she had called him, immediately after she had spoken to Shelly. He had asked her to let him deal with it and she had agreed, conscious that he needed to maintain good relations with the local members of the party; but it had left her agonisingly out of the loop and she was desperate to know what was going on.

'So,' she said.

'So,' echoed Pankaj with a broad smile. 'Total Solutions PR is a front company used by James Philpott, Kington's problem solver.'

'I *knew* it.'

'He was being employed through the Peterdown Regeneration Fund to look for efficiencies across a number of their projects.'

'Was?'

'He got the sack this morning.'

'What about Yvonne?'

'She was the one who sacked him.'

'But she told him to do what he did.'

'She says she didn't.'

'That's bullshit.'

Pankaj was sitting on the arm of the sofa looking down at her. He smiled.

'It may be, but I'm not going to call the woman a liar. Particularly when we don't have a shred a proof that she is.'

'Why else would he have done it?'

'She says she told him that he needed to find efficiencies but claims she never authorised him to scrap the Larkspur's entire maintenance budget.'

'What about the Wikipedia stuff? And the emails to the *Post*?'

'She says he went rogue. That it was nothing to do with her. He went rogue and she sacked him for it.'

'But why would he have been doing that?'

'She says she got the sense that he thought that if the Larkspur got listed it would cost even more to maintain. She wasn't defending him – she said what he did was way out of line – but you've got to remember they'd had their central government funding slashed and they're all under incredible pressure. And she's sacked him. And he was close to her. He was her man. It's a big scalp.'

'I don't want a scalp. Christ, I obviously don't give a toss about this guy. She can sack him or not sack him. It doesn't matter. All that matters is that a guy who is, or was, working for her was preparing the ground so they could build the station on the site of the Larkspur.'

Pankaj smiled.

'Have a look at this,' he said.

He placed a piece of Peterdown Council headed paper on the coffee table.

For immediate release:
Having carefully considered the various options on the short-list we are now in a position to publicly declare that Peterdown Council's preference is for the new station to be built on the site of the Chapel football stadium and that Peterdown United FC be relocated to the proposed development at the old Grangeham forge.

Ellie looked up at him.

'Amazing, isn't it?' he said. 'I don't know how much sway it will have with central government but it can't do any harm.'

'Did you ask them to do this?' she asked guiltily, her head full of thoughts of Colin.

'No, it was totally their initiative. I had been pushing them for a commitment that they weren't decanting the Larkspur and this is what they produced.'

Pankaj walked through to the kitchen, opened the fridge.

'I know it's ludicrously early,' he said. 'But I got given this very nice-looking bottle of Saint-Véran a couple of months ago and I feel like celebrating.'

Ellie followed him into the kitchen and sat down at the table, the sound of her heart booming in her ears. She had made this happen. She felt a powerful surge of guilt, and disloyalty. But also, compellingly, purpose. Her years in Peterdown all finally made sense. The isolation. The dislocation. It had all been building up to this. At last, she had been called upon to act and was doing so, decisively and to great effect.

'I'm not pretending that this is in any way the end of it,' said Pankaj, raising a glass. 'We're a long way from getting it listed but it is a victory. And you win wars battle by battle.'

The wine was the colour of straw in the sunshine. Ellie picked up her glass and held it poised.

'To the Blofelds,' said Pankaj. 'A great creative partnership.'

'To the Blofelds,' replied Ellie, meeting his glass with hers.

Pankaj had a large piece of Gruyère that he'd brought up from Neal's Yard in Covent Garden. He put it out on a plate with some grapes and a knife. For twenty minutes they talked and ate cheese. The plan was two-fold: to build a high-profile, resident-led campaign and at the same time put together the greatest listing application ever presented to English Heritage. Ellie had commissioned a young architecture critic to write a short essay, which she planned to present alongside letters from a dozen or so experts in the field. Already, she had gathered statements of support from Richard Rogers, Adam Caruso and the Twentieth Century Society. Pankaj's sister worked for one of the Sunday supplements and she had called in a favour from a landscape photographer, who had shot the estate for them earlier that week. They were expecting the final photos that afternoon.

Ellie slipped out of her shoes and pulled her feet up on the chair. Pankaj had changed the record. Fleetwood Mac. She listened to the opening bars of the first song, feeling energised and full of a new kind of clarity. She could see where she was heading, how she could go about constructing the arc of a life. Starting with the listing, which was an end in itself, obviously, but also, potentially, something that might catapult her into an arena in which she could make her ideas concrete.

'My mother can't believe I'm devoting so much energy to this,' said Pankaj. 'She looked up the Larkspur. Saying she's not a fan would be something of an understatement.'

'Really? I thought your family were responsible for Chandigarh?'

'That was my dad's side. If my mum had her way everything would be stuccoed and Georgian.'

Ellie paused, aware that she was on the brink of a conversation that would be revelatory in ways she wasn't necessarily ready for.

'My mum likes the Larkspur,' she said eventually. 'It's difficult. She likes *difficult* things.'

The hard-edged emphasis she placed on the second 'difficult' left this statement hanging awkwardly in the air.

'Was she difficult?' asked Pankaj. 'Growing up?'

Ellie laughed hollowly through her nose.

'Was she difficult? *Is* she difficult? Christ. Everything about her is difficult.'

Ellie rubbed her hands down her face.

'And so she's made a virtue of difficulty,' she continued. 'The books she reads. The music she listens to. Her relationships. Her approach to motherhood.'

'Are you still in touch?' he asked after a respectful pause.

'In a manner of speaking. She keeps me at arm's length. And I mean that. She *keeps* me there, at arm's length, in her psychological vice, never really letting me in, but also never letting me go. Arm's length is perfect for her because it's within eyesight but not obscuringly close; the ideal distance from which to make withering judgements.'

Pankaj went to top up Ellie's wine, but she put her hand over it, conscious that the first two glasses had gone to her head and that already she was talking unguardedly, letting it pour out, the sentences coming out in whatever order the thoughts formed.

'I have a daughter,' she said. 'And being a mum when you have my mum as your mum. It's . . . It means you can't be my mum. To your kid. You can't.'

She stopped, said nothing for a second or two.

'I mean,' she took in a big deep breath. 'It *is* her fault. But it's not her fault, too. I mean, god, she was fucked up in her turn. Christ alive, my grandmother. She was a monster, emotionally. Narcissistic beyond words. Deep into her seventies she was still in the thick of it, on the attack, playing people off against each other, looking for any sign of weakness she could. She would talk me up but only in front of my mother, only when talking me up was a way of talking *her* down. At the time I thought it was all a kind of family joke. It was only when I got older that I realised how pitiful it was. My mother kind of knew it was happening but was powerless to stop herself. The thought of her with her mother is so painful. Her desperation. The way she competed with me . . . And the way my mum talks about her mum's mum . . . From the sound of it she was basically a sociopath.'

Pankaj took an ashtray from on top of the fridge, pulled some cigarettes from a drawer.

'And that's why I'm here,' said Ellie.

'What do you mean?'

'In Peterdown. That's why I'm here. My mum. And her mum. And her mum's mum. I'm here because of them. As soon as I saw that blue line, I mean from that *very* moment, I knew it was going to be a girl. I know it sounds ridiculous but honestly I knew, I just *knew*, and it made having an abortion impossible. The burden of it would have been too much. It would have been the ultimate expression of the whole fucked-up inheritance. Such is our contempt for our daughters that we've started terminating them in the womb.'

'Jesus,' said Pankaj. 'How old were you?'

'Twenty-three.'

'God.'

'It was oddly empowering actually. I think at some deep level I thought of it as an opportunity. A chance to nip it in the bud. To end the cycle.'

Ellie paused, took the cigarette from Pankaj. 'Of course in the same situation, at twenty-three, in a time with no social stigma, my mother would have aborted in a heartbeat. So it was another way of proving that I wasn't her.'

Pankaj exhaled sympathetically.

'And I've done it. Daisy and I are mother and daughter. We're not combatants. Or rivals. We love each other. *I* did that. It means that I'm here working on an Aldi for the Castleford bypass; but that's what needed to happen for me to take command of the situation.'

Ellie looked pointedly at him across the table.

'And now you're here imperilling all that I've done.'

Pankaj held her gaze.

Ellie dragged again on the cigarette. The orange butt was papery between her fingers. She was conscious that what she was about to do represented a moral failing that jeopardised her family but the thought appeared to her only smudgily, like she was perceiving it through frosted glass. In the front of her mind – totalising and absolute – there resided a single thought: you have just one chance at life.

'Let's go to bed,' she said.

22

Colin was standing on the Radleigh, doing his best to look pissed off about it. He had been banned from the press box indefinitely, the club's hierarchy having taken exception to his piece in the *Post*. Not being a man presented with many opportunities for self-aggrandisement, he had found himself gripped by a sense of righteousness so powerful that it had sent his heart soaring to the skies. At the local level at least, his name would be carved forever into the annals of the profession, a byword for the cost of speaking truth to power. But his thrill at martyrdom was not without its attendant anxieties: he was hanging on by a thread at the *Post* as it was and his enforced exile from the press box would surely further undermine his position there.

His pushed his hands into his pockets and surveyed the scene. It was a mild night for the time of year and the smells were the smells of football as it has always been: Polo mints and Mars bars, chips frying, beery breath, the drift of the odd sneakily smoked fag. But even before the game had started there was a charge to the air, an anticipatory crackle. He watched an accidental nudge escalate into an exchange of words, a squaring up. Some fans were talking fast and loud and swearily. Others were looking about, casting around, keeping their eye on the stewards. It had been like this, he remembered, in the nineties. Shifty. Heavy. Simmering.

At the back of the stand the Peterdown Partisans, as they called themselves, were in a raucous mood, even by their standards. There were about fifty of them, most of them lads in their twenties, their heads mostly shaved, a lot of them in bombers and keffiyeh scarves.

Along the back wall of the stand they had stuck up improvised banners, most of them hand-painted on bed sheets.

Colin watched as one of them clapped his hands above his head and quickly the others all joined in.

One man went to war, WAR!
Went to war on Kirky,
One man and his baseball bat,
Went to war on Kirky.
Two men went to war, WAR!
Went to war on Kirky . . .

'I don't know about the whole ultra thing,' he said. 'It's just not very us, is it? The whole thing makes me feel a bit embarrassed for them.'

Rodbortzoon rubbed the end of his nose.

'I like them. They are intense, very antifascist. They don't have a leader but Frankie Kerr is maybe their spokesman. I taught him. He is an interesting young man. An autodidact. Very internationalist.'

'I just don't know,' began Colin but he was interrupted by a thickset man who was walking past and put a hand on his shoulder.

'Good job, son,' he said. 'You've got people right riled up, you have.'

'Yeah,' said Colin warily. 'Thanks.'

He could feel it, roiling just below the surface. The anger and resentment that had been building for years. For the first time in a long time he felt genuinely scared at a football match.

'You know what this mood needs to really get it going?' said Rodbortzoon cheerily once the man had moved on.

'Dean Baker,' said Colin with a sigh.

'Exactly,' said Rodbortzoon. 'Ha ha! The spark for the tinderbox.'

Colin turned over his programme and looked at the team sheets on the back page. There he was in Blackpool's number four shirt. *Dean Baker*, the Broadcastle fans used to sing. *He's not a baker. He's not a candlestick-maker, he's a butcher, he's a butcher, he's a butcher . . .* Which was about right. Cleaving into players, slicing them up; this was Baker's modus operandi. For eight years he had been the fulcrum of Broadcastle's midfield, their brutal enforcer, revered on their terraces, despised everywhere else. In 2017, after years of winding up opponents, he had found himself on the wrong end of an elbow that shattered his eye socket, resulting in a strabismus, or deviating left eye. After a lengthy recovery period he had managed a couple more seasons in the Premier League with Broadcastle and was now playing out the last years of his career at Blackpool.

Colin thought back to Baker's previous visits to the Chapel.

'I'm really not sure if this is the right time . . .'

As he was speaking, the Peterdown players emerged from the tunnel and on to the pitch. First out, his socks pulled characteristically up over his knees making his short legs look even shorter, was Jordan Garry, finally match fit after six weeks out injured.

He's one of our own.
He's one of our own.
Jor-dan Garry,
He's one of our own.

The Peterdown players congregated at the Radleigh end of the pitch. Some were doing exercises, stretching out their hamstrings, touching their toes. Others were knocking a ball about. One of them hit it hard to Garry, about waist height. He flicked his leg up, killed the ball dead. Colin watched him drive his foot through it, the perfect geometry of his swing, the loose-limbed economy of movement, the precision, the power.

He was the Last of the Street Footballers. Colin felt a surge of sentimental pride. They had overlapped at school, but only just. Colin was finishing his A levels when Jordan was in his first year, a callow little eleven-year-old about whom he had known nothing at the time.

Colin watched him flick the ball up, catch it in his instep. It wasn't simply that he was from Peterdown. It was the quality of his talent; its unschooled, irrepressible exuberance. Garry rolled the ball out from under his feet, curled it effortlessly into the top corner. The crowd gave a half-cheer and started up again.

If you're coming to the Chapel then you're going to get
Ga-a-a-rried . . .

But before they got any further the Blackpool players emerged from the mouth of the tunnel. Dean Baker was captain and he came out first. As soon as they saw him the crowd surged forward like they were clamouring to touch him, claw at him, rip him apart. The noise that accompanied the movement was a kind of primal baying, a howl of rage and hate. Slowly, from the incoherent yawp a single chant began to emerge.

Freak. Freak. Freak.

It certainly wasn't being sung. It wasn't even being shouted. It was being intoned. Summoned up from somewhere deep. Colin felt the noise as if it were penetrating through him. It had a ravening quality, like a swarm of locusts, ready to devour everything in its path.

Freak. Freak. Freak. Freak.

The Blackpool players were now all out of the tunnel and had started warming up on the far half of the pitch, the other end of the ground from the Radleigh, the source of the most vociferous chanting. On it went.

Freak. Freak. Freak. Freak.

Colin watched, feeling profoundly unsettled, as Dean Baker approached the halfway line and gave an ironic round of applause in the direction of the Radleigh. The stand convulsed, enraged.

Freak. Freak. Freak. Freak.

Once the game started there was a bit more variation – anti-Kirk chants mixed in with pro-Garry songs – but still they howled it every time Baker touched the ball.

Midway through the first half, the Blackpool centre forward cushioned a header down to Baker's feet only for the ball to spin awkwardly and bounce off his shin. Twenty-five thousand people jeered deliriously. But before the noise had died down, Blackpool had won the ball back, worked it out wide. A cross came in and their centre forward reached it before Guy Turner.

As soon as the ball hit the back of the net, Dean Baker was off. Full pelt, he ran, past his celebrating teammates to the foot of the Radleigh where he stood with his arms raised above his head, a look of wounded defiance on his face.

The reaction in the Radleigh was instant and animalistic, like the snarl of a cornered cat. They surged towards him, held back only because the row of stewards held firm. Over the tumult, somebody screamed: *Do his other eye.*

Baker stood there for another second doing his best to maintain a front but it was obvious that even he was scared.

'Christ,' said Colin. 'This is too much.'

Rodbortzoon looked at him, shrugged.

'Without cruelty there can be no carnival,' he said.

'OK, whatever, but this is too much. It's pure hate.'

'Can you blame people for being angry? Don't they have plenty to be angry about? And I don't just mean about Kirk and where some stadium goes. I mean everything. The degradations heaped upon this town. The constant humiliations. Can you blame them for being angry about *everything*? You think it's unpleasant, this chanting, infra dig. I think given the circumstances it shows extreme restraint. I stand here every week and I think to myself, why are they *only* chanting?'

Ten minutes later, the half-time whistle sounded with the score still at one-nil and Colin made the halting trudge to the toilets. As he was queuing for a free sink to wash his hands, Kerry called.

'It's quite a mood out there, eh?'

'They're angry,' she replied. 'You've stirred them up.'

The light in the Chapel toilets was a kind of menacing yellow, like the light in films from the seventies. The urinals emptied into a single sluice piled high with faded blue deodorant blocks and the smell was sharp and astringent.

'What's it like behind the scenes?'

'Weird, kind of weirdly happy. I know you've been banned and everything but it's like they've forgotten about all that already. Kirk's people are bowling about saying they don't give a stuff about the Neanderthals. Now it's all football. You should hear them. Bitching and moaning that the transfer window's shut. It's proper weird. Two months ago Christie's banging on his door begging for some cash and he wouldn't have a bar of it.'

'Kirk's taking an interest in the results?'

'It's like he's just discovered the game,' said Kerry. 'He's talking about tactics, formations, what we all think about the games coming up. It's obvious he doesn't know shit about anything. He was looking at the fixture list and asking me about Leeds. Are they any good? And I was like, yeah, they're not bad, they're only ten points clear at the top of the table.'

A sink came free. Colin wedged his mobile phone against his ear with his shoulder.

'I told him I thought seventy-two points would get us into the playoffs. Honestly, it's the first time we've ever talked about the game. I don't know what's going on. It's night and day.'

Colin pushed down on the silver plunge tap and the water gushed into the basin.

'Where are you?' asked Kerry.

'Just washing my hands.'

'Oh, for god's sake, Colin.'

'Wait a sec, I wasn't ...'

But she had already hung up.

By the time he made it back and found Rodbortzoon, the second half had kicked off with Peterdown attacking the Radleigh end. Christie had made a couple of half-time substitutions and switched formation. Right from the whistle, they started playing a high press, disrupting Blackpool's passing game, harrying them out of possession.

Eventually, Garry picked up the ball and turned, sashayed, beat a man. In the first half you could tell he was just back from injury and struggling for rhythm. But he had been liberated by the formation change. He dropped his shoulder and then veered right, skipped past the Blackpool left back. Immediately, the crowd were up on the balls of their feet, urgent, expectant. Garry strode into the area and shaped to shoot. The tackle, when it came, was off-balance, ill-timed and sent him spinning in the air. The referee's response was immediate and self-preserving: he pointed to the spot.

Colin remembered that he had a match report to write. His laptop was in his rucksack but he could hardly get it out in the middle of the Radleigh. He started writing the copy in his head.

Garry stands, his hands on his hips, waiting to take the penalty. The capacity crowd is hushed, knowing that this is one of those moments when sport distils the totality of life. In this moment, Jordan Garry is surely more than just a footballer. He is a stand-in for everyone that has been knocked down and got back up again. More profoundly, he stands for a town that has been knocked down and might yet one day get back up again. The referee blows his whistle. Garry runs up. He shoots. There is a great collective gasp . . .

At first, Colin thought he had scuffed it, miskicked it completely. But he hadn't scuffed it, he'd chipped it. A Panenka it was called, after its Czech pioneer. You ran up as if to blast it, but instead of smashing it, you chipped it with a gossamer touch, like a dinky little golf shot. It was the ultimate in sporting impudence; a way of not just beating but also humiliating the keeper who, having already committed to his dive, finds himself on the floor, flapping pathetically as the ball arcs insouciantly over him.

For Colin, just for a second, it was as if the cosmic ordering had suddenly made itself clear, harsh realities made impossible to ignore. Eighteen thousand people were watching and Garry had had the self-belief to Panenka the penalty. Most days, Colin barely had the self-belief to pee standing up.

He watched Garry as he was engulfed by his teammates. How blessed he was to operate in an environment in which you could make decisions, take action, see the outcome. He had chosen to Panenka the shot and pulled it off. And now eighteen thousand people were singing his name. As he so often did, Colin found himself feeling enormously grateful for football. In the swamp of life, it was an arena of clarity. A place of clear-cut results, decipherable cause and effect.

For fifteen minutes, he stood on the terraces without a thought of his match report. The noise around him was intense and unyielding, the anger transformed into a kind of stadium-wide yearning, a desperate *willing*. On the pitch, the Peterdown players were responding, throwing themselves into tackles, streaking forward whenever they got the ball, creating chance after chance.

And then, in the last minute of the game, Jonny Ellis picked up the ball and smacked it into the space behind the defensive line. The centre back had a five-yard start on Garry but it wasn't going to be enough and they both knew it. He wasn't a glider, Garry, one of those players who cuts across the pitch like a boat in water. He was a scurrier, his compact thighs piston-like, all compressed energy and relentless forward momentum.

The crowd were all up on their feet, willing him on. Almost immediately, Garry pulled alongside the defender so that the two of them were shoulder to shoulder, leaning into each other, their chins slightly raised as they strained to find that last little bit of strength. But then, just as he seemed to be pulling clear, Garry fell, neither forward nor back, but down, like a horse at the National, his legs crumpling beneath him. The defender, who had been leaning into him, collapsed on top of him, leaving the two of them, lying prone and entangled, their chests heaving as they sucked in huge lungfuls of the cold night air.

The eruption that followed was guttural and beseeching. The stadium turned its attention to the referee who was looking over to his linesman. Time slowed. For a second or two there was a collective held breath as the two men shared between them a fortifying glance. Play on, waved the referee. No foul.

The reaction on the terraces was a kind of epic communal keening. Colin jumped in the air.

'How can he not give that? Is he blind? How can he not give it?'

Seconds later, the referee blew for the final whistle and sensibly made his way very quickly to the tunnel.

Colin stood in the stands, heart thumping, as the boos rang round the ground. He was spent, emotionally wrung out. His throat hurt. His feet hurt. It was the kind of draw that felt like a defeat.

Deflated, he started the slow trudge out of the ground, trying to ignore Rodbortzoon's attempts to convince him to write his match report at the Geoffrie. Then, from nowhere, Brian appeared.

'You two,' he said, grabbing them both by the arm. 'I need you to come with me.'

'What's going on?' said Colin as they followed Brian through the crowd.

'Word's got out that Kirk's actually bothered to turn up for once, and there's a load of lads standing outside Gate Five and they're pretty pissed off and they say they're not going anywhere.'

'What am I supposed to do about it?' said Colin.

'You're going to help keep things calm and you'll be there to be witness. I don't want Kirk controlling the story of what happens. You're a trusted voice.'

They rounded the corner. Gate Five was the access point for the stadium's back end; its offices, changing rooms and press box. Outside it, at least a hundred men were standing in a tight group. Many had their hands in the air and they were singing.

We'll steam in till we die.
We'll steam in till we die
We know we will, we're sure we will
We'll steam in till he dies.

Separating them from the doors was a line of twenty-odd policemen in their usual yellow jackets and black trousers.

'Interesting,' said Rodbortzoon, as he strode forward and pushed his way to the front of the group. Colin followed him with Brian alongside. He could see Mick and Steve at the heart of it, as well as a load of the Partisans in their keffiyeh scarves and bomber jackets.

Mick shouted something in Steve's ear. Steve took a deep breath, opened his lungs.

If you're coming to the Chapel then you're ...

The rest of the group joined in, Colin included. You didn't need to sing on the terraces, and Colin mostly didn't, but a small group like this had its own hierarchies and pressures. Conscious that everyone around him was singing, he picked up the tune, started bellowing out the words.

In big stands like the Radleigh, even if you were right at the front or right at the side, the mass of people still felt boundless, too large to confront. Here, in this tight little group, Colin had a sense of their power, but also their vulnerability. He looked nervously at the line of cops. They appeared calm but resolute, arms crossed, truncheons still attached to their belts.

He raised his hands above his head, conscious that by doing so he was compromising his ability to claim any kind of journalistic objectivity, but aware, too, that he didn't really give a shit.

Over the next five minutes, the crowd grew, guys joining in twos and threes, until it was closer to two hundred. Maybe more. To a man, and it was, as far as he could see, all men, they had started clapping their hands slowly and intimidatingly above their heads. Colin felt each clap like it was the heartbeat of some giant amorphous organic thing that he had been absorbed into, something that had taken on a life of its own and would be very difficult to stop.

'I've not willingly missed a home game in thirty-five years and I won't start now,' shouted Mick. 'Don't like it, he says, don't come. Well, he can fuck off.'

The lights on the stadium's exterior walls were bright and angled at the ground illuminating the concourse where they stood. For about ten minutes they stood there, singing, chanting, the group slowly growing until there were around three hundred of them. Over this period, the police presence had doubled, too. And across the concourse Colin could see a line of riot vans.

Then, just as it looked like the whole thing would peter out, one of the club's office windows opened about thirty feet above them. Kirk stuck out his head. Instantly, the crowd surged forward until those at the front were nose to nose with the police.

'Come down here,' someone shouted. 'Come down here, you fucking coward.'

Colin looked up at the window. Kirk's public persona was built on confrontation, his love of a scrap, and Colin could see that he was excited but also a little awed, like a surfer surprised by the size of a wave.

'I know you're angry,' he said. 'That's coming across loud and clear ...'

Someone threw a mushy chip buttie up at the window. As it flew through the air it dispersed, two gravy-covered chips just missing Kirk as he ducked back through the window.

'CUT IT OUT,' he shouted angrily as he stuck his head back out the window. 'You want to talk. And here I am, so stop messing about.'

The crowd calmed, started to police itself. A couple of big guys gesticulated for quiet, brought the teenagers to heel.

'Thank you,' continued Kirk. He was still talking at the top of his voice but the bark had gone. 'Look, I know why you're angry. You think I'm doing this for my own personal gain. But that's not what this is about. I'm doing it for the club because the club can't afford not to move. The finances are a mess. We've got huge debts and massive monthly outgoings.'

'Save us all your bullshit,' shouted Brian.

Kirk ignored him, continued where he left off.

'The club is on its knees. The gate we get at the Chapel isn't enough to sustain it going forward. The television money in the Championship is nothing like the cash you get in the Premier League.'

'So you're saying if we go up we'll be all right? We won't have to move.'

Kirk stopped, thought about it for a second.

'Yes . . . ' he said. 'Yes, that's exactly right. If we go up, Grangeham is off the table.'

Brian looked like he'd just been blindsided by a bus.

'What did you just say?'

'You're hearing this straight from the source,' said Kirk, newly full of confidence. 'If Peterdown United are promoted I promise you I will not pursue the Grangeham proposal. Whatever the conspiracy theorists may tell you I can't stop the government slapping a compulsory purchase order on the ground, but if we go up, from my perspective, Grangeham is off the table.'

'You're bullshitting us.'

'My word is my bond. My whole career has been built on it. All I want is what's best for the club.'

Kirk looked down at them all, evidently pleased at the reaction, which was stunned silence.

'OK,' he said. 'I think we're done here for the night, don't you? Goodnight, gentlemen.'

He pulled his head back through the window, fastened it shut behind him.

Down on the ground everyone stayed quiet for a second or two as they digested the news. Eventually, Mick turned round and faced the crowd.

'Well there it is, out and simple. We've got ten games to save the Chapel. They'd better start playing better than that.'

Part Two

Walk III

The Epic of Disbelief Blares Oftener: the Sidings pub to the Woodvale playground

Who are we? We're the trimmed fat. The discarded chaff. The unnatural wastage. The left behind. And what do we do? Well, we walk of course. What else is there to do when all you have is time? That's what you get when you've had your place in the world taken, been rendered redundant. Time to linger, lurk, drift, find obscure angles, see again, see better.

It's a serious endeavour. Today more than ever. We're on pilgrimage. A search for spiritual significance. A rambling elegy to everyday miracles. A hunt for some kind of healing.

We start at the Sidings. A riverside pub. Plastic furniture on the patios. Branded umbrellas. A palm tree, incongruously, in a pot. Posters announce its not-at-all-unique selling points. Quizzes on a Monday. Curry nights on Tuesdays. Big-screen sports.

No mention of its heritage of course. Of the fact that this is where the founding seven sat on June 2nd, 1895 and swore in the inaugural meeting of the United Brotherhood of Locomotive Beaters, the first union in Peterdown. No mention of what the members of that union did throughout the town's exceptional eighty: the years from 1880 to 1960. No mention of the 226 Stirling Sabres knocked out in 1898 alone. No mention of the twenty thousand wagons built across the entirety of the Yards in the ten years 1948–1958. No mention of The Regal Negal's *annus mirabilis*, 1885, when they produced the world's first batch of corridor coaches *and* the Negal Oceanic, the first locomotive to break 80 mph. No mention, even,

233

of the Type Four freight trains still coming out at a rate of three per week in the late 1960s. No mention of the ten million piston parts. The hundred thousand miles of track.

We feel it inside us, stirring. This is what we did. Our people. Over a hundred years we made it all possible, the modern world. Unimaginable movement. Revolutionary connectivity. Suck on that, Silicon Valley, we shout into the air. We built the network long before you did.

We turn down Ashfield Street and stifle a sob at its shuttered state. It used to be a thriving side street of specialists. The Far Flung travel agency. Floyd and Sons Mapmakers. The Head of Steam pub, pints for a pound on Mondays. The Vacuum Centre. An HSBC. And a TSB. But they're all gone. Victims of the smoking ban and search engines, GPRS and mass data. All of them discarded by a throwaway culture.

We pause outside number twenty. Many years ago, this was the home of William Gwent and his illegal printing press. Gwent was famed for his productivity, banging out pamphlets on matters of all kinds. Attacks on the episcopacy. Agitations for educational reform. Broadsides against the king. He was the chief propagandist for the Ringers, the Vale of Peter's homespun nonconformist group. In the hurly-burly of the 1640s, the Ringers stood out for their worldly ambitions. They wanted it all: total tolerance, direct democracy, a society-wide state of grace. Obsessed with the oppression of the Norman Yoke, they read Geoffrie literally, taking his lurid imaginings to be historical record. Somehow, who knows how or why, they took it as given that he was a courtier to the original Stormin' Norman, Will the Conq, and that his *Spiels* refer to the Anglo-Saxon arcadia destroyed by those usurpers from northern France. Being Puritans they didn't embrace the *Spiels* in their entirety – the cross-dressing and carousing got axed, the delirious dancing was ditched, the soundtrack turned to psalms; but they kept the politics. The land reform. The radical democracy. They were called Ringers because they wore big metal key rings attached to their belts. Key rings without keys to illustrate both their lack of property and their dedication to openness, communality. They wanted an end to enclosure. Free rights to fish and farm on public land. Access to ploughs and seed drills, wagons and wains.

We walk up the hill and look east. The metal roof of the Generator glints in the sun. It was on its site, in 1646, that the Ringmen first took a sod of earth and burned it ceremoniously. A symbolic act of turbary, the common right to peat. They did it, the rogues, to enrage a local landowner, Josiah Temple. But also to announce the second coming of the folkmoot. The dawn of a new Eden. A place of abundance for all. Freedom from drudgery. Day one of *la vita contemplativa.*

For six weeks they held out. Seeing off raids by organised gangs. A lived instantiation of something spectacular. An inspiration to the foot soldiers of the New Model Army. A disestablished, autonomous republic. The most advanced polity on earth.

Ironically, it was the regicide that brought them down. The generals tightened their grip on power. The dissenters got sidelined. The mood shifted. An opportunity slipped by – but not out of memory. It haunts us, still, that moment. A reminder of our potential. What can be done against all odds.

Across the park we scoot and on to Durley Road, past its carwash. There used to be another one, half a mile away on the Ottercliffe Road. It was an automatic, a 'Water Wizard', a thrillingly opaque tunnel-like design into which you drove your car when it opened to great fanfare in 1984. But it shut. The technology today is less whizzy: a hose, some rags and six Moldovans, all of them wondering, no doubt, how they found themselves here.

From Durley, it's a left and then a right to the ring road and all its aggro. Garage music thuds from the tyre shop. A sofa sits outside the place where Paul's Minicabs used to be. Men line up at the window of the Ladbrokes, looking in, flicking at their fags, pulling pensively, hoping hard.

It used to be grand round here. Big detached houses on a handsome boulevard. Large gardens. Staff quarters at the back.

Homes suitable for the Gaitskill top brass, the important boys at Grenadier.

But those days are gone. The forges foundered, the families moved on, the road was widened, the traffic redirected. The houses were divided up, the gardens tarmacked, turned into mechanics' yards, loading bays. The unlucky few got the flats above the light industry. Light as in not heavy. And thin on the ground.

Now, it's just another hostile thoroughfare for cars, not people. It's like this everywhere in the city. Walking is under attack, our old routes wronged by developments, ley lines interrupted by angry new energies, the rage of the road.

We head down cobbled Rothbury Passage and allow ourselves a moment to remember the sensation of the stones beneath our feet. The tactility. The joyous physicality of walking. The feeling of being connected to each other and to the earth, inescapably. For five minutes we appreciate the slow unfolding around us. The architectural array.

We lope along, remembering always that the whole point of drifting is that it's inefficient, time-occupying, a drag on productivity, a form of civic resistance.

Finally, we arrive on Baxendale Street, the grandest in Woodvale. Its Georgian geometry has a solidity to it, a feeling of establishment entitlement. We cower accordingly and scuttle up to number six, where we stare at the letter box, certain that it's the very one that received the first Wroth letter, sent to this address in 1829. Back then, it was the home of Sir Timothy Williams, principal investor in the locomotive-powered Houghton–Peterport railway line, then under construction to transport tin ore from the pit to the barges waiting on the river. Up to this point, the three-mile trip had been undertaken by wagoners, teams of young men who pulled the pushcarts on wooden tracks. It was hard work, wagoning, but that didn't mean it wasn't a plum gig. It was above ground for starters, which must have been a relief if you'd spent your teenage years as a hurrier, carting an ore drawer up a two-foot shaft with only a candle for company. And it wasn't seasonal, so you could be guaranteed a year-round income. Work worth protecting.

They've got a copy of the first letter up in the Peterdown public library, framed on the wall.

Dear Sir,

This is to acquaint you and your railway with a truth not to be ignored. Unless you desist in your plans our correspondence will continue in the form of a lighted pyre.

As will be visited upon ye,
Major Wroth.

Who was Major Wroth? He was a phantom. A spectre. A collective nom de guerre. A mantle that could be picked up by anyone with a pen, or indeed a match. A wave of arson followed the letters. Hot on their heels. First to go up was the Peterport, just after the wooden foundations had been laid. You could see the flames in Broadcastle, or so they say. After that, a factory making the piston parts. On both occasions the MO was the same: a smear of coal tar to get the thing going, give it some lick. Soon after, the pamphlets started to appear, stuck to doors with tar, plastered on to walls.

Oh, you gentlemen of the parish, this is a warning. Desist now or find yourself struck by the black mark. To take a man's work is to wickedly force him upon the Poor Law. We have suffered too much but now it is our moment and we will not be stopt. Cease now or natural justase shall come to you in the indignity of the tar.

As ye will feel
Major Wroth

Over the course of 1829 the riots spread all over the Vale, particularly around the collieries in the south. Then further afield to Nottinghamshire, Lincolnshire, the depths of the Riding. Defence of wagoning was often the catalyst but the demands were almost always broader: working conditions, price hikes, the right to an income. The right to work.

He lost of course, Wroth. Even after all that arson. All those riots. Six men swung. Six hundred were shipped off to Australia. And of course the railway got built. The wagoners went the way of all things. Wroth dissipated. But they were all right in the end, that generation. Lucky to have been born in the engine room of Europe. An age of double-digit growth.

Our cheeks aflame, we run through Woodvale to the playground. There we climb its castle, a fortress in pine and plastic. Atop a turret, we stand and stare out over the houses to the Aspire Centre: zero hours, zero prospects, zero point in being there.

How did it happen here? we cry, anguished, our arms aloft. In this city of Ringers and Wrothmen? How did it come to this? Four hundred thousand tonnes of trains. Modernity made possible. The contemporary created here. How did it happen to us? How did we fall so hard?

23

'I 've never seen Jordan play that badly,' said Colin, dejected. 'That backheel on the edge of our box? What was that about?'

They were in the car on the way back from London. Brian was in the passenger seat. Rodbortzoon was in the back, drinking cans of beer and eating pickled eggs. Outside, the rain was driving down on the diagonal.

'You could see it in his eyes,' said Brian. 'It was like he wasn't even there. They were all just completely overawed, the lot of them.'

'There's no chance of going up now,' said Colin shrilly. 'We might as well not bother turning up for the rest of the season.'

Rodbortzoon burped.

'Anyone who imagines he can control the tabloid hysteria to his own ends,' he said with enormously self-satisfied solemnity, 'should not be surprised when he himself ends up becoming a hysteric.'

Colin thought about responding to this but decided against it. He could smart about it all he liked but, in retrospect, it had clearly been a mistake to agitate so forcefully for a big splash with his contact at the *Mirror*. The piece that they had ended up running, the day after Kirk's dramatic announcement, had gone out as the lead story on the paper's back page under the banner headline '**GET PROMOTED OR GET OUT**'. As soon as it was published it had been picked up by talkSPORT and the BBC, and then CNN and *Le Monde*. To say that the team hadn't responded well to the world's scrutiny would be something of an understatement. In their first game afterwards, away to Charlton, they were three-nil down by half time.

'And you know the problem now,' said Brian. 'This takes it all off Kirk. All everyone's going to be talking about is how it's in our hands.

But the fact is that we're six points off the playoffs and there are only nine games left. Kirk knows we've got no chance.'

Outside, the rain continued to pour down. Inside, all you could smell was vinegar and pilsner yeast. They were only at Luton.

'We need a proper strategy,' continued Brian. 'I know you boys are against it but we've got to start going after the Larkspur, make the case for why it's got to be the chosen site.'

'No. That's exactly what the council want us to do, they want to make it an either/or, Larkspur or Chapel. We can't get sucked into that game.'

'Why not? The council have come out and said they want it here. We've got to build on that. The big story here is about the rebirth of this town. A place that's been knocked down but is rising again. Fourth division, nearly bust, the youth team coach playing left back because the squad was that thin. And eight years later we're up there challenging for a place in the Premier League. That's what people respond to, it's inspiring. The story of United is the story of the town, right? Never knows it's beaten. Overcomes extraordinary challenges. Rises again.'

'It might be a hard sell,' said Rodbortzoon dryly, from the back. 'Losing four-nil to Charlton as evidence of some kind of post-lapsarian rebirth.'

'The Larkspur is the total opposite,' said Brian, ignoring him. 'It's emblematic of the worst times of the place, our decades in the wilderness. Knocking it down would be part of the renewal.'

'Yes, very good,' said Rodbortzoon. 'Let's make as our enemy the only other point of resistance in the town ...'

Colin zoned out as the two of them started up again an argument that he had heard many times before. It wasn't that he was instinctively against Brian's line of reasoning, only that its domestic implications were too much to contemplate. And for the first time in a long time he felt like he had something to lose. The mood had shifted. Ellie had earnestly sworn that the council's decision to come out against the Chapel had had nothing to do with her but she clearly felt guilty about it. Over the last week the house had been a place of good humour and warmth. A family walk in the park. Pizzas in front of the telly. And even, on one occasion, intimacy.

'We've got to get over this idea that the Generator is out of the running,' he said. 'I don't think the finances at that place add up, whatever they've said. And when you stop and think about it, it's got to be the best site, hasn't it? It's got all that space around it. I've been talking to a mate of a mate. He's an urban planner. He's going to have a look and see what's what, see if there's a case to be made for the Generator being the logical choice.'

For forty minutes they drove, past Milton Keynes and Northampton. They were approaching Leicester when Brian fell asleep. Rodbortzoon opened a third can of lager and summoned from his seemingly bottomless bag a cold Findus crispy pancake which he preceded to eat noisily. Colin drove silently past Loughborough, trying to fathom the thought processes of a man who would cook a crispy pancake and then wait six hours before eating it cold. It was evidence, surely, of some kind of pathology.

'What are you reading at the moment?' asked Rodbortzoon between bites.

Colin thought about this. He had not that long ago finished Roy Keane's autobiography, which was very good as these things went but wasn't, he felt, exactly what Rodbortzoon was after. He tried to cast his mind back to the last novel he had read but he drew a blank. Had he read one last year? If he had it had not stayed with him. Not that that was unusual these days. He had lost his faith in fiction, its ordered plots and arbitrary details; the whole thing felt hilariously ill-equipped to deal with the vastness of life, its constant chaos. Football, on the other hand, never pretended to pull meaning from the madness, all it did was bound it, accept that life was random, chance-filled, unpredictable.

'I'm reading Coetzee,' continued Rodbortzoon, oblivious to his silence. '*Slow Man*. Also, Sebald for the fourth time, Vivian Gornick, and every day just one page of Renata Adler's *Speedboat*. I have it at the end of the night like a little truffle after a feast, a little mouthful, very intense, very rewarding.'

Colin rolled his eyes, pulled into the fast lane.

'What was it you said you are reading?' said Rodbortzoon.

'Nothing.'

'*Nothing?*'

'Yeah. I'm between books.'

Rodbortzoon, who obviously wasn't wearing a seatbelt, leapt up from his prone position on the back seat.

'Who reads only one book at once?!' he cried. 'Wankers, that's who!'

He sat back down into the seat with a whump.

'The Colin I first met had always four or five on the go all at one time,' he said. 'Remember that young pup? Such spunk.'

Colin pulled into the fast lane to avoid the queue for the Nottingham slip road and tried to cast his mind back to the person he had been then, nearly a decade earlier, when he had first met Rodbortzoon.

He had returned to Peterdown just a fortnight before and had taken the first job he was offered: a six-month contract as an administrator at the further education college that had kept him going until he got the job at the *Post*. He had supposedly been working in the admissions department but, finding himself chronically underemployed, had mostly sat around reading and smoking fags with Rodbortzoon.

What had he been like, that boy? He certainly had things then that he had long since lost. Hope. Ambition. A thick head of hair. And the time, he mused wryly, to read five books at once.

But what about the spunk? Well, it depended what you meant. The vigour and valour had surely long gone. But the other stuff? It flowed out of him still. Always had. Since his early teenage years. Although 'spunk' was a terrible name for it, wasn't it? They hadn't taken any courage or determination, had they, all those wet dreams?

Colin found himself thinking back to a hot night in May, the start of his first, his only, summer in London. He remembered the whole thing like it was yesterday. It was the day of the last game of the season. United had been away at Brighton. He'd listened to it on the radio. A two-one win in a meaningless match, memorable

242

only because it had nearly been abandoned after two players had passed out with sunstroke. It had still been stifling, that night, the kind of close, muggy heat that left your clothes stuck to your body, your brain half-scrambled. When Ellie had returned late from the pub and snuck into his room, she had opened the window before slipping into his bed, her high-functioning sinuses oblivious to the record pollen count.

As he often unconsciously did when he was thinking back to the dramatic moments of his life, Colin drew away, saw the scene from outside himself, like a third person looking on. Here, he could see himself lying on his back underneath her, the ends of her long hair brushing against his chest, her hands on his shoulder blades, her eyes shut tight. So tight in fact that she hadn't noticed that Colin had been rendered mute by the sudden urge to sneeze, his ability to time his withdrawal compromised entirely by five seconds of asphyxiated paralysis which was followed, always and inevitably, by an uncontrollable release. Or in this instance, two uncontrollable releases.

The morning-after pill turned out to be only 87 per cent effective. Nine months later, to the day, Daisy had been born.

He indicated and pulled into the slow lane for the turning on to the A648, heard the *tssh* and tear of another beer being opened on the back seat. For half an hour they drove according to the rhythm of the A road: slowing for roundabouts, stopping at red lights. They were in the Vale now and beyond the street lights lurked a deep and empty blackness that went on and on in either direction.

Fifteen minutes later, they took the second approach road for Peterdown and were driving through the outer suburbs when Brian's phone buzzed. It was sitting in among the pound coins reserved for supermarket trolleys in a tray next to the handbrake. The noise woke him with a start.

'Oh, Jesus,' he said, once he had stretched, rubbed his eyes and picked up the phone. 'It's from Mick.'

'What does it say?'

Dolefully Brian read out the message.

Walking through car park after the game I overheard Gus
Taylor on his mobile. He said something I couldn't hear and
then "are we really selling Garry". ???

'Fuck,' said Colin. 'Jesus, fuck.'

'Who is this Gus Taylor?' asked Rodbortzoon.

'He's Kirk's right-hand man.'

'I knew something weird was going on,' said Brian. 'No wonder
Garry's all over the place.'

'They can't sell him,' said Rodbortzoon through a mouthful of egg.
'The transfer window is shut.'

'It'll be one of those pre-arranged deals. I bet it's bloody Chelsea.
They'll be getting him in the summer.' Brian banged his fist against
his forehead. 'What kind of moron unsettles their best player with
this kind of crap when they're in the hunt for the playoffs?'

Colin pulled up to stop at the traffic lights.

'One that's trying to lose,' he said.

He let this hang in the air as he thought through its implications.
'What?' said Brian.

He pulled away and turned down the Eastfinche Road into town.
Groups of teenagers swayed on the pavement, leaning into each
other, shouting.

'Why not?' said Colin, increasingly convinced by his own thesis.
'Irrespective of what he has or hasn't promised, we go up then that
changes everything. Think about the TV money – we'd get millions.
We go up and the club is instantly solvent.'

'Exactly, *he'd* get millions.'

'No,' said Colin. 'It would be the club's money. He couldn't just
take it out. '

'OK,' said Brian suspiciously. 'But the club would be worth a load
of money. He could just sell it.'

'Would it, though? If we were in the Prem for like one season? 'Cos
if we went up it's not like we're going to stay up, are we? And that's
not going to turn us into Liverpool, is it? We'll still be a small-town
club worth small-town money. *But,* if we get promoted you can be

sure the government won't kick us out of the Chapel, will they? Of course he doesn't want us to get promoted.'

It had been a long journey without a break and Colin's body had sunk into the driver's slump, his vertebrae seemingly fused together, his shoulders stiff and his ankles cramped – but sudden clarity and insight sent a jolt coursing through him.

'You saw Garry today,' he said. 'Did he look focused on the task at hand? Remember, he'll be getting ten per cent of any fee. I reckon Kirk could get at least eight, if not ten mil for him. That'd be at least eight hundred grand in his pocket. You think that's not going to turn his head? *Jordan Garry?*'

Brian sat upright, looking wounded.

'Christie would know,' he said. 'He wouldn't stand for it.'

Colin felt this physically, a blow to the heart. The thought of Paul Christie being in on it was too much bear. There had always been something almost painful about the man's nobility, his seriousness and sportsmanship.

'*Would* he necessarily know? Kirk could be doing it behind his back.'

'I don't know,' said Brian.

'Conspiracy theorists are the elite squadron of neoliberalism's useful idiots,' said Rodbortzoon, who had finished his pickled eggs and started in on a huge bag of scampi bites.

'Only last week Kerry told me Kirk was suddenly – like out of nowhere – interested in the team, in the game,' said Colin, speaking now only to Brian. 'He was even talking about the transfer window. It must have been because he was gutted that he'd have to wait to sell him.'

'Conspiracy theories represent the acme of false consciousness,' continued Rodbortzoon. 'On the face of it they seem to strike an anti-establishment pose but actually they are concerned always with the actions of individuals, not the workings of the system *per se.*'

'It's the only explanation,' said Colin. 'He's systematically undermining the team.'

'The desire to imagine that there is one individual or maybe a small group who are behind all that is wrong in our lives, it is understandable – particularly for those who cannot be expected to grasp the socio-economic complexity of the situation – but mostly all they ultimately do is obscure the ur-conspiracy, the one that hides in plain sight. The conspiracy of capital.'

He burped.

'If it makes financial sense then Garry will be sold,' continued Rodbortzoon. 'On the face of it this is uncontroversial.'

'It wasn't just that he was bad today,' said Colin, replaying the game in his head. 'He was so distracted. It makes you wonder ... '

'You can't be saying Kirk's been paying him to lose,' said Brian. 'I can't believe that about the lad.'

'But it is always worth remembering that the existence of crazed conspiracy theories and the overriding logic of capital doesn't mean there aren't actual real-world conspiracies.'

'What's he talking about?'

'He's just very slowly getting to the same conclusion as I have.'

'You know what?' said Rodbortzoon. 'I think Kirk might be compromising the team.'

'How do you put up with him?'

'I just ignore him,' said Colin. 'It's what everyone does.'

Rodbortzoon burped again.

'Which is why we're here,' he said dryly. 'In the actually existing utopia that is Twenty-First Century Peterdown.'

It was late and the town centre was quiet. Colin cut left up Market Road, past the Generator, its shiny steel exterior reflecting the street lamps, the headlights of the cars. At the lights, he turned right down Richardson Road and then left on to the Radleigh Road. Ahead of them sat the Chapel. The gates were closed, the floodlights off.

'You want to see a stark illustration of the extent of the already rampant housing crisis in this town?' said Rodbortzoon. 'Look over there.'

The large concourse outside the main gate was quiet, empty of the crowds that filled it on match days. Beyond it, Colin could see the grass verge that separated the concourse from the road. Underneath the verge's lone tree, a neat dome glowed red in the dark like the end of ET's finger.

'Funny place to pitch a tent,' said Brian.

24

They went above and beyond. As well as filing the standard online form they had created a document, printed it on thick paper, bound it with a cloth edge. You could feel its heft, its seriousness. They had had twenty copies made. One for the secretary of state. One for English Heritage. A few to be passed around the residents. The rest for the press.

The photos had been shot by a professional landscape photographer on a brilliant, blue sky winter's day. A graphic designer had laid them out, an image per page; close-ups of fixtures and window details opposite wide-angle exteriors shot from the Beagle Hills. Ellie ran her finger along the spine. It looked like an exhibition catalogue from a blue-chip art gallery.

She turned to the opening essay. They had typeset it in Augustan, Marjorie's font. The mere fact of the letters committed to paper – the light, lovely, unfussy beauty of them – seemed to her to be sufficiently persuasive, an argument in and of itself.

She scanned the text. The critic was fiercely left wing but you wouldn't know it from the essay, which was tactical and very cunning. Knowing that the application's ultimate audience was a Conservative cabinet minister he had written extensively about Betjeman and the Victorian Society and the essentiality of conservation, meditating at length on art and endurance and the historical long game. You couldn't get to the final paragraph without thinking that this was exactly the building that should appeal to anyone who liked Britten and Auden and valued above all asserting Britain's cultural superiority to France.

'Where do you want these?'

Barry's six-foot-two-inch bulk dominated the doorway of the Larkspur community hall. He was wearing sunglasses and mono-chromatic camouflage fatigues of the kind that you could imagine being issued to members of an elite squadron operating in the Arctic Circle. Held reverently in front of him was a large polystyrene tray that contained twenty-four pink and purple cyclamen.

'Well, we're not going to plant them in here, are we?'

'I guess not.'

'So outside would probably be better, wouldn't it?'

Barry nodded and withdrew, leaving a trail of footprints behind him. Ellie followed them out on to the concourse where fifteen or so volunteers were milling about, drinking tea from takeaway cups, col-lecting trowels and spades from a large pile, trying on gloves for size. She had taken the day off because today they were guerrilla gardening.

And it was exactly the day for it, crisp and cold and clear. Ellie looked out over the large concourse. In its centre was the estate's famous pond, a multi-level constructivist masterpiece of curves and sharp corners that seemed to be forever on the verge of offering up a line of symmetry without ever quite delivering one. It was surrounded by raised flower beds pick-hammered to reveal the aggregate, bespoke benches, picnic tables in poured concrete.

Stacked by the far wall, Ellie could see a pile of bagged compost, thirty trays of flowers, a dozen sapling trees in plastic pots. It had taken Pankaj ten minutes to source it all. A couple of emails, a phone call, and that was it. He made things happen, generated momentum in a way she had never encountered before.

She walked across the concourse, upright and energised, her blood pumping. That morning, when she was dropping Daisy off at school, she had seen Yvonne, and Yvonne had seen her, and the look that had passed across Yvonne's face had been one of unbridled contempt. Ellie felt her breath shorten as she remembered it. It had been a vicious look, penetrating, but evidence also of a kind of twisted admiration; the acknowledgement of a worthy nemesis.

In among the familiar faces – Barry, Ralph, Pam – there were a few volunteers Ellie didn't recognise. Evidence of a growing movement.

She climbed up on to a bench.

'Morning everyone,' she said, addressing the crowd. 'So great to see you all here. We've got a lot to do, so gather round and we'll start to divide up the tasks.'

For two hours, they worked. They cleared beds of rubbish, dug out weeds, scraped away moss, turned over the earth. Ellie was tasked with clearing a large bed in which they planned to sow wildflower seeds: bluebells, cowslips, foxgloves.

Once she had picked the stones and turned it a bit, she realised that the soil was good; rich and loamy and fecund-feeling. She pushed her fingers into the earth, dropped seeds into the pockmarks, found herself thinking about Pankaj. It had been a week since they had slept together and he'd been in London for nearly all of it. They had put the planning application together via email with the designer and photographer copied in to every message, which had ensured that they stayed on topic. Over the week, they had exchanged a few text messages which had been warm but guarded, written not to raise suspicion when they appeared, as was the modern way, brazenly broadcast on the screen of the recipient's phone.

She picked a handful of the earth, let it sieve through her fingers. There was nothing that even suggested, let alone concretely established, that the afternoon in his bed was something he wanted to repeat.

'What kind of soil does an azalea need?'

Ralph was standing behind her with a small, dark-green bush in his hand.

'I don't know, the funny one, I think. Just google it.'

'Yeah, I think we might have used up all the ericaceous stuff on a bush that maybe didn't need it.'

'Well, we're not going to dig it up, are we?'

'We could buy some more soil.'

Ellie breathed out heavily, her mind elsewhere.

'OK,' she said, just to end the conversation. 'I'll buy some more. I don't have any cash on me but I'll buy it over the phone on my card and you can go round and pick it up.'

Pankaj arrived while she was on the phone to the garden centre, stepping out of a taxi at the far side of the concourse and straight into a conversation with Ralph and Barry. After that, he stopped and exchanged pleasantries with three women, nodding earnestly at whatever they were saying before huddling conspiratorially to listen to a joke.

It was a full five minutes after she had finished her call that he finally made his way to her. Ellie stood still, aware that Pam and two young mothers from the estate were directly behind her, all waiting to greet him.

'Hi,' she said in a soft voice, looking for a connection, however tenuous.

'Hello,' said Pankaj. 'What a gorgeous day for it, eh?'

Pam was immediately between them, offering Pankaj tea and biscuits.

'Did you hear anything on the application?' Pam asked, once it had been established beyond doubt that Pankaj didn't have room for a piece of shortcake.

'I got an email on the way here. It's been received and accepted. They've given us a decision date. Friday, May sixteenth.' Here he turned to Ellie. 'When's the announcement due on where they're putting the station?'

'May twenty-sixth.'

'Ten days to spare,' he said smiling. 'Well, let's not waste any more time. Let's make this place as pretty as we can.'

Ellie watched him as he walked over to collect some gloves and tools. She tried to focus on the soil but was constantly checking, as subtly as possible, to see if he was looking at her.

He wasn't.

He was talking to Ralph and Barry, who were passionately holding forth on the only thing that interested them as much as 1970s sci-fi: a computer game called Demos.

'The longer you play it the more you see the necessity of moral legitimacy,' said Ralph.

As Ellie had unavoidably gathered, Demos was a multi-user

world-building strategy game that, if you were of a certain political bent, might or might not have the potential to engender a generational upsurge in civic responsibility.

'Hard power will take you to level five but if you want to progress any further you basically have to start building a meaningful civil society,' said Ralph.

Pankaj was leaning on his spade, having not done any actual digging during the seemingly interminable time he had been quizzing Barry and Ralph about the game.

'You're telling me there are kids out there writing whole legal systems from scratch?'

'They start off pretty simple. You know, basic laws about murder and stuff, but they quickly get more and more complicated. People swap ideas on the boards. About property rights and stuff. The only thing you can't do is just copy like, you know, England's laws, or something. You would just get totally slammed on the boards. They'd hound you out.'

She glanced over enviously as Barry – ordinarily monosyllabic if not mute in other people's presence – went on to talk about his personal experience of the game, how it had allowed him to experiment with ideas, encouraged him to rethink his world-view.

She watched Pankaj, the way he controlled the conversation with his questions. He had a way of focusing on a person and soliciting from them their everything. She had noticed it, too, with the photographer who had shot the images of the estate. Apertures, depths of field, the death of film, the rise of Instagram, Diane Arbus, the ubiquity of image culture, the future of the medium; they had covered it all in two hours, the photographer responding to each of Pankaj's enquiries more animatedly than the last, clearly thrilled to be able to voice the things that mattered to him most.

Ellie sank her spade deep into the mud. She had thought Pankaj's questioning a sign of his genuine interest in the people he represented, their fundamental hopes and fears. But there was, she realised, something vampiric about it, like he was sucking knowledge from them for his own ends, until they were spent and he could move on.

'There's a guy – he's Swedish, a nice guy, we message a bit – he's

251

trialling a universal basic income using localised, time-stamped money in this society he's created.'

'This is all happening in a computer game?'

'To begin with he had problems with inflation, but I did some calculations for him and it's looking better. There is literally no one who plays Demos who thinks that a debt-based money supply is a good idea. Not even the trolls.'

'Barry,' said Pankaj. 'Who *is* this guy? What calculations did you do for him?'

Ellie turned the earth, pulling at her spade until her shoulders burned. It was pathetic to be so affected by it, but wounding nonetheless: the discovery that this rapt way of listening, this all-consuming attention, was not something that was particular to her.

Ten minutes later, they broke for tea. She stood at the edge of the group, as Pam handed out cups and slices of Battenberg cake. While they drank and ate, they talked about the estate's old café and the possibility of reopening it, running it as a community venture. The suggestion was put to a vote, which carried unanimously. Pankaj promised to call in some favours.

As they collected up the cups ready to start working again, two women walked across the concourse, pushing buggies, smoking fags. The taller of the two was bottle blonde, substantially built. Her neck sloped bullishly straight into her elbows and she seemed to carry with her the possibility of sudden arbitrary violence.

'Oh god,' said Barry.

'What's this then?' said the blonde.

'We're doing some tree planting,' said Pankaj. 'Do you want to join us?'

'I don't know why you're bothering,' said the smaller one. She wore the hood of her coat up so that its faux-fur trim framed her face. In place of her eyebrows were two thick smears of brown makeup. There was a gap between her teeth. 'They'll be gone by tonight. If the kids don't have 'em the dogs will.'

'They're doing it 'cos it's easier than doing anything proper about sorting out this dump.'

'Actually,' said Ellie. 'There's a lot we want to do—'

'Like some fucking flowers will make any difference.'

'You don't like flowers?' asked Pankaj breezily.

'Flowers are all right,' said the woman pointedly at him. 'I just don't like pansies.'

At this, a knowing smile appeared on Pankaj's face. Ellie could feel him deliberately not looking at her, but something surely was passing between them, a shared appreciation of the irony of the situation.

'Well, I suppose it is each to their own when it comes to gardening,' he said blithely. 'We've got some nice agapanthus if they're more to your liking.'

The larger woman snorted.

'I know this is a small thing but it's part of a bigger thing,' he continued, remarkably unaffected by their scorn, his smile unwavering. 'We're genuinely committed to making this a better place to live and that means talking to you, listening to you.'

'Your lot have been in charge round here my whole life and you've done fuck all for us.'

'You're right, this is a Labour city with a Labour council and there's so much that needs to be done, but it's all being done against the backdrop of a Conservative government and their cuts.' Pankaj was standing now, his shirt sleeves rolled to his elbows, wellies on his feet. He opened himself up to them. 'You're both mothers, right?'

Ellie watched him as he did his thing, asking questions, listening to the answers, letting the two women think they were leading the conversation while he steered it like a collie, marshalling it where he wanted it to go. By the time they left they weren't by any stretch convinced but they weren't angry, and that, to everyone there, carried with it the sheen of victory. Barry was up on his feet, practically bouncing with energy. Caught up in the fervour and without properly thinking it through, Ellie approached Pankaj and whispered in his ear.

'You don't need to prove you're not a pansy to me.'

She took two steps past him and looked coquettishly over her shoulder. His reaction seemed, for all the world, to be one of absolute, pathological indifference. Without even looking at her, he picked up a rhododendron and started a shouted conversation with Ralph about its suitability to a shaded spot.

Humiliated, Ellie returned to her flower bed, avoiding eye contact all the way. She looked over at the three women planting cyclamen at the base of a beleaguered silver birch. This was what happened when you didn't take control of your own narrative. When you indulged your capacity to be content, play safe and settle. This, she realised, was what happened when you allowed someone else to hijack the story of your own life.

She threw her trowel into the flower bed and leaned against the wall. Above her, the low sun produced long shadows, dramatic contrasts between the shade and the light. It was just the kind of light that helped these buildings appeal to nostalgics of the recent past. People – like her – whose lack of imagination forced them to take refuge in the now of the then, not the now of the now. People willing to be a support act in the story of their own generation.

She walked sullenly over to the group that had gathered around Pankaj.

'I have to go,' he was saying. 'It's a wonderful thing we've done today. I'm only sorry I can't stay to properly clean up.'

'Don't be silly,' fussed Pam. 'You've been amazing. It's really such an honour to have you here.'

The group's attention seemed to turn collectively to Ellie.

'Yes,' she said eventually. 'Thanks for coming.'

'My pleasure,' he said. 'It was another very productive day. You're doing great things here.'

With this he reached out and offered his hand for her to shake. It was a like a slap across the face – the end of whatever it had been between them codified with all the passion of a business transaction. She stared at him, too shocked to cry. She swallowed and in an act of automatic propriety took his outstretched hand. It was only then that she noticed an almost imperceptible upward curl at the corners of his mouth and felt what she recognised immediately to be the cold hard contours of a front door key being pressed into her palm.

25

The back end of the Radleigh Road stand was showing its age. The brown brickwork at its base was chipped, and its corrugated steel skin had worn to a dull grey. Around it, the landscaping was similarly lifeless: a large concrete concourse that on match days was home to burger vans, scarf sellers and ticket touts, but at all other times was an empty space bordered on one side by a steady flow of traffic and on the other by the back of an NCP car park. All of which made it an unlikely place to find five brightly coloured tents that had been erected overnight in the stadium's shadow.

Colin walked past an orange two-man with a large banner tied on to its guy ropes.

WE'RE NOT GOING ANYWHERE.

Over by a green A-frame tent of the kind popular with scout troops in the 1950s, he spotted Brian dressed in a thick plaid shirt and beanie hat. Brian was carrying a tray of takeaway teas that he was distributing to the six men and one woman currently crouched in the doorways of various tents.

'What's going on?'

'We're occupying. It's the Peterdown bloody Spring. It's all over social media. We've had two tents go up this morning.'

'Was this your idea?'

'No. This lad, Andy. He's nineteen. That tent we saw the other night,' Brian pointed to the red dome underneath the tree. 'That's him. He's a proper fanatic for United and he's dead against Kirk, so he's just gone and stuck a tent here to show how much he wants the club to stay. Anyways, yesterday a couple of season ticket holders I know from around the way are walking past and they ask him what he's doing and he tells them and they're like, "I'll have a bit of that." And they pitched tents last night.'

'So now it's a thing, is it?'

'We've already got a Facebook page and a Twitter handle. @PeterdownSpring. Check it out. It's going off.'

'Are you sleeping here?'

'Haven't yet, but I will be tonight.' Brian patted the A-frame. 'This tent was in my uncle Rodney's shed. It's for anyone that doesn't have their own. Waifs and strays welcome.'

He looked pointedly at Colin, who was watching the progress of a passing pigeon as it flapped towards them and landed with a skid on the tarmac.

'I think I'm better off contributing to the cause as a sympathetic member of the press.'

'A first-hand account always makes for a powerful read . . . '

Colin was saved by the sound of his phone ringing. He looked down at the number. It was a landline with a Birmingham code. He gestured to Brian that it was a call he had to take and answered it as he crossed the Radleigh Road heading for Gordon's Café.

'James?'

'Hi Colin, is this a good time to talk?'

'It is. Did you get a chance to look at the drawings I sent?'

'I did. Have you got them on you?'

'I'll call you back in two minutes.'

Gordon's Café was hot, its windows cloudy with condensation. The place smelled powerfully of cheap watery bacon frying on the hotplate. Colin liked it; the mosaic exterior, the sign's functional rectilinear font, the furniture finished in a blue leatherette. He settled at the corner table with a cup of tea and an annotated aerial shot of Peterdown town centre spread out in front of him.

James answered on the third ring.

'OK,' he said. 'Decisions like this are almost never made according to what actually works. In the end it almost always comes down to money but looking at this purely in terms of unbiased master-planning then it really should be site A.'

Colin looked down at the plans, his breath held. Site A was the Larkspur.

'Stations generate concentrated agglomerations of traffic at peak times of day. Site A has two A roads that flow very nicely into it and a nice pedestrian flow into the city centre. But most importantly you would only need to minimally reroute the old Goods Line. Both other sites would require more work.'

Colin felt a rush of elation, quickly followed by a settling unease.

'I've not written you a whole report on it, obviously,' continued James. 'But I have written the executive summary to the report I would have written, if you know what I mean.'

'What about site C?' asked Colin. Site C was the Generator.

'Traffic-wise? Site C would be the second best option.'

'So, you're telling me that site B would be the worst place for the station?'

'From a traffic point of view, and it's also the worst choice in terms of the existing rail line. It's in the summary.'

Colin thanked him and hung up, trying to imagine the reaction if he went public with the findings. Ellie was charged, full of energy and purpose. Her listing application looked good enough to be published as a coffee table book. By contrast, their website – savethechapel.com – looked like it had been built in 1998. He stirred another spoon of sugar into his half-drunk tea. Not that it was a fair comparison. She had the MP on her side with all his contacts and access to cash. Colin felt a familiar fear take hold of him. Was she sleeping with him? He hesitated. The thought was too large, too potentially devastating to look at whole, he could only glance at it before turning away. Did it really matter anyway, the physical act? The very fact of her closeness with him was a form of disloyalty. He found himself speculating bitterly about what she would have done with a report like this if the evidence was reversed. She would have leaked it, he felt with unimpeachable certainty.

He walked back across the road. Two people were sitting on fold-away camping chairs, drinking tea. A middle-aged man wearing a United replica shirt over a thick wool jumper was lying on an inflatable mattress smoking a cigarette.

'You OK?' asked Brian.

'I'm all right,' said Colin. 'I'm just a bit worried that my source might have been rumbled. They've gone quiet. I've been trying to get in touch with them to see if they know anything about Garry being sold but I can't get through on the phone. And when I tried the club I got told they were off sick.'

'Why don't you ask Jordan straight?'

'I can't. Kirk's cut my access to the players.'

'Can't you go through his agent or something?'

'I'm waiting to hear back from the agent. He's difficult to pin down if whatever you want doesn't involve him making loads of money.'

They walked through the tents to where the others were sitting. Andy, who had started the whole thing, was busy on his phone. A woman wearing a green and white scarf was warming a pan of beans on a small camping stove.

'Well, if he's getting sold, he's getting sold,' said Brian. 'I just don't want to hear any more of that guff about him chucking it.'

'Yeah, well. Whatever. But I don't know. You saw him the other night.'

'Ah, man, he was just nervous. He's a good lad.'

The bloke in the orange two-man nudged his wife.

'Tell him.'

'Tell me what?' said Colin.

'My Nathan lives round the corner from Jordan,' said the woman. 'And?'

'He told us yesterday. Jordan's driving a brand-new car. A Lexus.'

* * *

Two hours later Colin was sitting at his desk, reading through a yet to be published five-hundred-word blog post on his screen. It wasn't, he felt, the subtlest piece he'd ever written but it had undeniable forward momentum. He read the final declamatory sentences, in which he baldly accused Kirk of deliberately destabilising the team and finished by asking not only if he could still be considered sufficiently 'fit and proper' to own a football club, but whether or not he should stand trial for fraud.

It wasn't a press day so the office was empty. In a distant corner, a phone was ringing, unanswered. Colin read the piece one more time for typos. There was no way it would get past the subs, let alone the lawyers. He would have to publish it himself, take full responsibility for its content.

The file was ready for upload. All he had to do was hit the return key. Just once. Something he had done thousands of times before. A compulsive person would have done it without thinking, but Colin was not a compulsive person. His conservatism was innate and it dictated the limits of his behaviour like a shopping trolley whose wheels locked if it strayed too far from home.

Colin sat there, his finger hovering two inches above the key. He thought instinctively about his parents, their propriety, their heads-down aversion to risking anything, their lifetimes of never straying from their station. He came from a long line of people who had never had nothing, but had never had much; people who knew how to hold on to what they'd got.

He kept his finger hovering above the button and shut his eyes. He played out the scenario in his mind. Even if the piece proved to be impossible to substantiate it would focus attention on the club, bring extra scrutiny to the results. The mere fact of its existence would stop Kirk from compromising the team. But publishing it would be the end of his career. Everything he'd worked for.

In his situation someone else might have acted differently. But he wasn't someone else. He was Colin Ryder and he played it safe, kept his head down, ruffled no feathers. This was just him doing what he did, had always done, would always do. With depressing inevitability, Colin shifted his finger up an inch and hit delete.

26

With its boxy grey concrete exterior, large round-cornered windows and angular piloti that anchored it to the northernmost corner of the roof of Europa House, the Larkspur Hill Café had the quality of a small interplanetary craft landing temporarily on a larger space station. The Millennium Falcon docking on the Death Star, as Ellie had flippantly described it a few days earlier, a comparison that had been met with instant outraged derision from Ralph and Barry who then spent the rest of the subsequent morning gleefully deconstructing it.

Not that Ellie minded. Their six-hour Star Wars conversation might have been singularly exhausting to listen to, but as they talked they had somehow brought the café's wiring back to life and built her a countertop out of old scaffolding boards and some polished copper pipe.

Ellie stood at the counter looking out at the café, taking in its incredible panoramic views, its charmingly affectless collection of furniture, and its heartening number of customers: eight at the current count.

Of course, it was Pankaj who had made it all possible. He had called contacts from his days working with refugees: a film director and a stand-up comedian. *A pair of loaded luvvies*, as he put it, but they were always good for a grand or two as long as you promised not to mention their names. Between them they had stumped up £3000, which, along with all the volunteer labour, had been enough to transform the space, stock it with food, get the whole thing going in just a week.

And as a way of saying thank you she had cooked him the French toast. It was Leonie's thing from university. She would never tell you that she'd slept with a man, only that she'd made him the French toast, a speciality of hers, reserved only for lovers.

It was a little sneaky to have stolen Leonie's tradition but slipping out for the ingredients halfway through their long morning together had given her an excuse to use the key, which she had done with the practised insouciance of a veteran double agent, even as her heart pounded at the exhilarating transgressiveness of it all.

As soon as she was back in the house, they had fucked. And then again. How insanely wonderful it was to be so desired, to be with someone with such an unmasked appetite for life. The way he wanted her was so urgent, so focused. And then, when they were done, they had eaten the French toast in bed.

The kettle came to its thundering boil. She threw some chopped mint in a pot, filled it with water. Out the window she could see the planter she'd worked on. Kids had torn out most of the flowers, but by no means had the gardening been a total failure. In the main, the larger shrubs had been left alone and in many cases they seemed to be thriving. The same was true, too, of the estate as a whole. In the two weeks since Philpott's sacking, the maintenance contracts had clearly been reactivated. Light bulbs had been replaced. Cracked windowpanes repaired. A communal door rehung. But most encouraging of all was the sight of the security boards being taken down from derelict units, locks being refitted, curtains put in place, doors opened up, whole flats being made ready to take tenants once again. She had noticed at least four and there were probably more. It was all timed perfectly for the arrival, that week, of a sympathetic journalist from the *Guardian* and the design critic at *The Times*.

She put the mint tea on a tray and took it to a table on the far side. She had noticed recently that when she thought about the campaign her very posture changed, as if the configuration of her vertebrae had been recast, making her taller, sharper, more alert. On her way back to the counter she caught sight of her reflection in one of the east-facing windows. She studied the new set of her shoulders, her new

261

silhouette. The more she thought about it the more she realised that it was, in many ways, the ultimate creative act: to stand up tall and be willing to forge your own existence, create the reality around you. And anyone could do it – it was simply a question of will.

She could see now where everything slotted into the narrative of her life, why she had ended up in Peterdown, how she would leave.

After she had taken payment from two happy-seeming customers, she unclipped the lid from a box of square slices of flapjack and started to stack them on a large white plate. As she stacked, she felt, not for the first time, a great surge of guilt about Colin.

Did he suspect? It was impossible to tell. The contract they had settled on – the underpinning of their fragile coupling – was to pretend that everything was normal. Colin had never demanded that she be in love with him. He asked simply that she act like she was. They shared a bed. Went on holiday together. Ate meals. Had conversations. Behaved as if everything was OK.

What had she asked for in return? What had she demanded from him, for deigning to stay? Not much. Only absolute acquiescence, total surrender. She felt a blush rise to her cheeks as she returned the Tupperware to the shelf under the counter. Why had *he* stayed? The feeling that accompanied this thought was pinched and unsettling. He had stayed because he was in love with her. And had been, she knew, since the day they had met.

'First pansies and now cupcakes. You love to get involved, you, don't you?'

Ellie looked up. It was the woman from the other day. Her friend was with her again. Their names, Pam had subsequently informed her, were Danielle and Lindsey.

Ellie smiled. 'I know,' she said, dry and deadpan. 'Gardening and now baking, It's all getting a bit Stepford, isn't it?'

Lindsey smiled a little, revealing just for a second the endearing gap between her teeth.

'Anyway,' continued Ellie. 'Welcome to the Larkspur café. It's a work in progress, obviously, but cut us some slack, it is only day two.'

Danielle was unmoved, her arms folded across her chest.

'You have some funny ideas, you. First your little flowers and now this. I don't get it. It's like having a picnic in a fucking car park.'

Ellie struggled to disguise her disdain.

'Erm, no it's not, is it? It's like eating in a café. One with the best views of the city.'

'You know what I think?' said Danielle. 'I think it's funny you always being around here. It's a bit creepy.'

'It is a bit weird,' offered Lindsey.

'Why are you doing this?' continued Danielle. 'You don't live here. What's it got to do with you?'

Ellie stared back at her. I wrote my graduate thesis on this building, she wanted to say. The woman who designed it was a Grand Architect of the Universe. I'm the daughter she never had, the heir to her project. What the fuck's it got to do with *you*?

Instead, she smiled warmly and said in a way that she imagined to be self-effacing: 'I'm very keen to protect this building. A lot of places like it have been knocked down and the couple that designed it are heroes of mine. Particularly the woman. Marjorie Blofeld she was called.'

'I bet she didn't live here, neither.'

'Well, she did actually for the first month it was open. She and her husband took the top-floor flat in Europa House. I'm not sure how much time they actually spent here. They were away teaching a lot. In Los Angeles and Vienna.'

The look on Danielle's face was one of crumpled incredulity.

'But, yes, you're right, that was a bit of a stunt,' continued Ellie, 'she didn't really live here. She spent a lot of her life living in Berlin.'

'In a house, I'll bet,' said Lindsey.

'No, I don't think so. Berlin is—'

'But I bet you live in a house, don't you?' interjected Danielle. 'Up in Ottercliffe?'

'Well actually I don't live in Ottercliffe, but I take your point. I don't live here.'

'Exactly, you had the choice and you didn't want to live here. But we haven't got no choice and you want to keep us trapped here.'

'I *did* want to live here. My daughter's father didn't want to.'

Ellie stood tall as she said this. It was true. She had lobbied at various points, but Colin had always played the school catchment area card and she had had nothing in her hand that could compete.

Danielle looked down at the menu.

'Who's going to be paying you four pound fifty for a sandwich?'

'People have,' she said. 'They've been very popular. They're made fresh to order.'

'Fucking mugs. Four fifty for a sandwich.'

Ellie battled gamely on.

'The Blofelds imagined this as a communal space which people could use to entertain, celebrate birthdays. Things like that.'

Lindsey twisted a strand of hair round her finger and pushed it behind her ear.

'Can't imagine telling your Kieron that we're not going KFC for your birthday, we're doing a party in a concrete box on top of estate instead,' she said dryly to Danielle.

'Do Zinger Burgers, do you?' asked Danielle mockingly.

'No, we don't,' said Ellie. 'I'm afraid we don't even have a coffee machine yet. We've got these loose leaf teas but they're a bit ... Anyway, I can do you builder's tea for a quid.'

'Don't patronise me. I'll have the posh one.'

'I didn't mean to ...'

'I don't give a fuck what you meant or didn't mean to do,' said Danielle. 'I said I'll have the posh one.'

Ellie felt the eyes of the room upon her.

'Which one?' she said resolutely. 'Assam, Darjeeling or English Breakfast?'

'Assam,' said Danielle with an ironically raised eyebrow. 'A pot for two. And I'll have one of them cakes and all.'

Her cheeks aflame, Ellie prepared the tea and took it over to them before returning quickly to the counter. Danielle was vulgar and vindictive but she was possessed of a certain kind of smarts, a capacity to see things as they were. Exactly the kind of person Ellie had long suspected saw her for what she was: essentially unserious. Someone who talked too carelessly, too candidly, before she had actually achieved anything, a person whose vision for their life was simplistic, jejune, wholly out of step with reality. She thought instinctively of Suzie, as she always did when she felt assailed like this, overwhelmed once again by a sense of her own ridiculousness.

A beautiful book for a beautiful friend. That was what Ellie had written in the front of the novel she had bought Suzie for her twenty-first birthday. A week or two later Suzie had asked her opinion on a plot twist in the story, only to discover that Ellie's inscription referred to the cover, not its contents. She had never read it. The look on Suzie's face, on learning this, had been one of disappointment but also, undeniably, affirmation; the look of a long-held suspicion concretely confirmed.

Ellie's skin cooled at the thought. Suzie would have made a good Grand Architect of the Universe. She had the dark imagination for it, that touch of the monster about her. Since graduating, she had maintained the pure brilliance of her talent by never using it. She was currently the in-house advocate for an offshore oil company.

She tried not to think of what Suzie would make of this; of her, here, working her way through a stack of wet cups as if there could be some meaning to be found in drying crockery. She could feel herself entering the dialectic of her self-hatred when, sniffing the air, her senses dragged her from her thoughts.

It was so alien these days to encounter smoke inside. For an awful terrifying second she thought the building was on fire. Two beats later she realised what was going on: Danielle had lit a cigarette.

'What are you doing?'

'Drinking me Assam,' said Danielle. 'It's a bit weak for my tastes but it's all right if you stick a fuck load of sugar in it.'

'You can't smoke in here. This is a café.'

'This isn't a café, it's an estate. And you can smoke here if you live here.'

'No, you can't.'

'I live here. You don't. I know what I'm talking about. It's my right. I know my rights.'

'I'm sorry, you don't have the right to do this. Whatever you think. There are people here with children. Please put it out.'

'You haven't got the council's permission to do this, have you?'

Ellie bridled. Of course they hadn't. Gonzo catering they'd called it, which had seemed hilarious and daring at the time but now felt horribly exposing.

'You don't care about rules,' said Danielle, pointing at her. 'I don't care about rules, neither. Same, same.'

Ellie mustered everything she had.

'I'm sorry, you can't smoke here. You either put that out or you have to leave.'

'Leave this estate? I'd fucking love to. I've applied a hundred times.'

'OK. We get it. Your personal experience of living here has been difficult. But if you hated it so much you could just get a job and then you could move yourself.'

'How can I get a job? I've got four kids.'

You didn't have to have four kids, thought Ellie, setting her face in a way that she might communicate this without actually having to say it.

'And then the fucking refugees come and jump ahead of you on the list. I can't get a house because the Pakis keep getting them.'

'OK, that's it. Get out. Or I'm calling the police.'

The look in Danielle's eye was one of agitated glee, a kind of black jouissance. She knew precisely where the line was and was thrilled at having crossed it.

'Like you ever fucking would.'

She took a last drag on her cigarette and stubbed it out in the leftover cake on the plate in front of her.

'You know what? That cake, you know what it really needed? It needed some proper fucking gluten.'

She slung her coat over her shoulders and fixed Ellie with the mocking smile.

'You don't give a shit about us, do you?'

'You know what, Danielle, that's the whole thing in a nutshell,' she said. 'I really fucking don't.'

27

The tent was technical and exoskeletal; its vivid red fabric hung tautly from a pair of arched tensile poles. To Colin's eyes it looked like a professional piece of kit, something that might see you through an Arctic winter. He imagined the manufacturer's intended customer wasn't the kind of person who would gaffer tape to it an improvised flagpole bearing a black flag with a raised red fist. Nor did he imagine they had ever envisioned the guy ropes being rigged up to a lamp post. But these were minor points. All told, Rodbortzoon had done a pretty good job at his first attempt at camping.

'I think you're probably the only person here for whom this constitutes a step up in their living arrangements,' said Colin to the hulking mass straining the sides of the tent. 'At least you've got solid ground beneath your feet.'

Rodbortzoon stuck his head out of the front flap.

'Why have I never done this before? Urban camping! A great undiscovered pleasure. All the joys of a life under canvas without having to buy into the crazed fetishisation of the countryside.'

With his head poking out of the domed tent Rodbortzoon resembled some giant, bearded turtle of the kind that lived to one hundred and fifty on a remote island in the Pacific.

'The sound of the city at night has its own kind of poetry,' he continued. 'The distant chime of the reversing truck, the scamper of an urban fox.'

'What are you eating?' asked Colin. 'I imagine that thing doesn't come with a microwave.'

'Already, we have a secret benefactor. Someone comes early in the morning and leaves us hot porridge wrapped in foil. This morning's had cinnamon and banana with a sprinkling of burnt sugar.' Here he kissed the end of his fingers in appreciation. 'We are like the monks of Bhutan. Ha ha!'

'Where do you piss?'

'In Bhutan, the monks are highly esteemed. Every family sends their eldest son to the monastery. You are, I believe, the eldest son of your family. Will we one day see Colin Ryder here, taking alms?'

The camp was exactly the kind of political movement that Colin had always abstractly imagined he would one day throw himself into, a local cause that would supply the sense of solidarity he had always craved. But finding himself faced with such an opportunity his imagined capacity for sacrifice was coming up hard against the reality of the commitment required. The real-life privations. The prospect of sleeping in a tent.

'Where do you piss?' he asked again.

'Gordon at the café is doing us a special price and he allows us use of his bathroom. Fifty pee for a tea and a pee. Ha ha! It guarantees repeat trade.'

Colin walked on as Rodbortzoon pulled himself slowly and tentatively out of the tent. There were now twenty-odd of them arranged hotchpotch on the stadium concourse. Next to Brian's old-school canvas A-frame, someone had erected an open-sided mess tent. Brian was sitting outside it, warming a large stovetop kettle over a Calor gas fire. There were boxes of fruit, cereals, pints of milk in cool boxes.

It was classic Colin to walk through something like this – so full of promise and good cheer – and, before it had even really got started, already find it immiserating; so typical of him to intuit immediately the near-certainty of its noble failure, its futility in the face of global forces. But what could he do? In the last month, the mood had shifted. Only a few weeks earlier it had seemed unbelievable that the government would go against the wishes of tens of thousands of fans; now it felt eminently possible, even probable.

The bulk of the protesters were out enjoying the sun, sitting on the concourse in the gaps between the tents. Mick and Steve were lying on a sleeping bag, propped up on their elbows, eating supermarket sandwiches.

'What's going on, Col?' said Mick. 'The word round here is that he's nobbling the team and that you know but you still haven't written a word about it.'

'I haven't got any proof.'

'Four-nil at Charlton and then bloody two-nil at Leyton Orient?' said Mick.

Colin sighed. If anything the performance at Orient, who had been second from bottom going into the game, had been more suspicious than the one at Charlton. Garry had been particularly awful, missing two straightforward chances and making terrible decisions at every turn.

'I've got a lead I'm following,' he said. 'I've found a way straight to the source.'

'Well you better pull your finger out, son. We're bloody tenth, and there are only eight more games to go. We can't afford to lose any more, can we?'

'I'm doing everything I can,' said Colin. 'Why do you think I'm here? It's because I've convinced my editor to run a piece about the camp. Get your voices in the paper. There's a good chance it will be front page.'

'Well it better be a good write-up.'

'Get off my back and it will be.'

Colin walked over to two guys who were kneeling on the floor surrounded by scraps of material. One of them was cutting large letters from what he took to be a charity shop curtain. The other was crudely sewing them on to a white sheet. So far they had 'SAVE TH'.

'Right,' said Colin. 'Let's bloody do this then. Who wants to talk?'

'Andy was here first,' said the guy cutting an E from the curtain. 'You should probably speak to him.'

Colin looked at Andy, who was sitting cross-legged on the floor typing out what looked like a duty rota. His clothes were those of a boy that still lived at home: band T-shirt, embarrassingly practical coat, shoes that even Colin could see were at least five years wrong.

On Andy's laptop bag Colin could see the Ottercliffe High crest, which was odd if Andy *was* nineteen, too old to still be at sixth-form college. Perhaps, Colin mused, he was retaking his A levels. Maybe just one of them. Maybe the one that would get him into Oxford. Colin felt his breath slow as he looked down at Andy, at the pink skin in the parting of his hair. Andy was the chosen one. Like he had been. He just knew it.

'So,' he said falteringly, his voice choked. 'Andy, you're in charge, are you?'

'No one's in charge,' said Andy without looking up. 'If we want a club that's run for us, by us, then we need a camp that does the same.'

Colin heard in his voice the keenness of his intelligence, but also an unaffectedness, the clear presence of Peterdown's rounded vowels, ringingly provincial. Colin felt a great swell of connection and kinship. They were practically brothers. He had to stop himself from reaching down and giving the boy a hug.

'Why are you here?' he asked.

'We want to save the Chapel. Get rid of Kirk. Make sure Peterdown United Football Club is fan-owned and fan-run.'

Colin scribbled it down.

'A total end to corporate sponsorship,' said the guy with the scissors, who was now working on a C.

'And ten-quid tickets to all games, home and away at all clubs in all leagues,' said Andy, looking up at him at last. From simply the way Andy regarded him – defiantly, but not directly – Colin felt he could intuit the boy's likes and loves: John Fowles novels, shoegaze indie bands from the early nineties, Soviet-era Eastern European football strips.

'But for starters, we're concentrating on what we can achieve here,' said Brian, who had appeared at Colin's shoulder. 'That's our first goal. To save the Chapel and transform United into the club it could be.'

'And we want to dismantle the Premier League,' added Rodbortzoon, who had ambled up and was looking down at Andy like a father watching his firstborn ride a bike for the first time.

'That's right,' said Andy. 'We want the TV money to be equally distributed between all Football League clubs and those in the Conference.'

'Which is exactly the kind of thing we'll be talking about once we've saved the Chapel,' said Brian. 'It's our first priority.'

'Oh, and we want to sign Lionel Messi,' said the guy doing the sewing.

Andy looked up at Rodbortzoon, a smile spreading across his face.

'Those are our demands,' he said as he turned to Colin. 'All we want is the people's game to be returned to the people.' He paused for dramatic effect. 'And to see Lionel Messi in green and white. You can tell Kirk and his people that that's what we want and we'll be here till we get it.'

Andy closed his laptop and walked confidently back to his tent.

'I like that boy,' said Rodbortzoon. 'He has great potential.'

'Poor kid. Does he know he's the Eliza Doolittle of the radical fringe?'

'Ha!' said Rodbortzoon with a twinkle. 'There is nothing wrong with having a project.'

'That's what it is, is it? Fine. I'm off. Some of us have jobs that entail, you know, actual projects.'

'Yes, yes. Frontline report on the Vale of Peter under-fourteen judo championships.'

'Actually,' said Colin. 'I'm going to interview Jordan Garry. At his house.'

Rodbortzoon cocked his head, pursed his lips.

'I thought you were on the blacklist.'

'Yeah, well they didn't reckon with Colin Ryder, the bloodhound of Peterdown,' he said as he turned on his heel. 'The man who never gives up.'

Colin walked away feeling entirely unconflicted about his decision to avoid telling Rodbortzoon that the interview request had been granted not by the club but by the press office for the Huateng Ultraglide, a new-to-the-market razor which had recently added Garry to its stable of ambassadors. He also felt no shame at having chosen not to mention that the club, upon hearing of the interview, had insisted that Kirk's consigliere, Gus Taylor, sit in on the whole thing, that Colin use a list of pre-approved questions, and that the club get copy approval before anything was published. Because none of that really was relevant to the matter in hand. He had an in.

* * *

By footballers' standards Jordan Garry was not rich. He was part of a squad that had only recently been promoted to the Championship, which meant they were all basically on League One salaries, and Colin knew that even though he was the club's top earner he was still only getting £4,500 a week. Which may have been a pittance compared to what his peers were earning in the Premier League, but, in Peterdown, it was money to make Croesus blush.

On those earnings he could have easily afforded a big house in Edenvale or one of the two or three other charming villages out in the Vale, but Colin couldn't imagine wisteria and drystone walls being Jordan's bag and wasn't at all surprised to discover that he had recently moved to a six-bedroom new-build house just inside the Peterdown ring road.

It was the kind of place that Colin might have aspired to live in himself had he not met Ellie. In fact, the living room was just how Colin's would have almost certainly looked without the civilising presence of a woman and a child. A huge flat-screen television was attached to the far wall. Dangling down from it, like two high-tech spiders, were the controllers for an Xbox. In between the sofa and lazy boy there was a coffee table. And that, literally, was it.

Colin was sitting on the sofa, drinking a cup of tea, admiring the room's ascetic honesty. Standing in front of him, talking down to him, was Gus Taylor, a small man in a boxy suit, who carried with him two mobile phones and the sweaty, furtive air of someone who watches a phenomenal amount of pornography. Taylor was itemising conversational topics that were off limits. These included Kirk, the campaign to save the Chapel, Land Dominion, Jordan's private life, Moolah, any rival payday lending companies, the Grangeham development, the council, politics in general, religion, sex, and Jordan's physical, mental and emotional health. Once this had been established he forcefully thrust a list of Huateng-approved questions into Colin's hand. If he asked five about grooming, he would be allowed to ask three on football.

'Got it?'

'Yes,' said Colin. 'Got it.'

Taylor walked to the door and called Garry into the room.

Seen from the distance of the stands and in the context of their peers, professional sportsmen always appear much more normal than they are. On the pitch, among his teammates, Jordan always looked relatively small. In person, he looked like he could run through a wall.

'Hi Jordan,' said Colin. 'It's good to see you.'

'Yeah,' said Jordan tentatively, 'It's good to see you too. Thanks for coming'

There was something uncharacteristically cowed about him. Colin registered the way he kept looking nervously at Taylor. He seemed to be diminished by the presence of him, the hard power of his suit and tie.

'So,' Colin said. 'Tell me, Jordan. What is it you like so much about the Ultraglide?'

'Well, I'm simple. I got one focus: goals. And the Ultraglide's simple. One blade. Super sharp. I'm like that. One chance. One goal.'

And on it went like this. They talked shaving tips, mirror angles, the importance of properly hot water. After fifteen minutes, Colin was nearing the bottom of his approved list.

'How important should grooming be to the modern sportsman?'

'Well, when I'm running I've got to be fast, haven't I? Aerodynamic.'

'And getting rid of the stubble on your chin's essential to that, is it?' said Colin not quite sarcastically.

'Not just your chin, bruv. I'm talking all over.'

'Right, so you shave your chest as well?'

Garry pulled off his top to reveal his sculpted torso. Across one hip there was a tattoo:

273

'And the rest. That's the way it is these days. If a man wants a woman to be clean he gotta be clean, too, if you know what I mean?'

Involuntarily, Colin found himself thinking about his own pubic hair. It had never once occurred to him to trim it, let alone shave it off. He tried to imagine what his hairless groin would look like. And then it came to him, a mental image he would never be able to erase. Eerily white, pliably smooth, limply tentacled; his hairless groin would look like a squid. A dead squid.

'I'm telling you. You need a good, sharp blade. Because you don't want to be getting no nicks.'

Colin looked down again at his list of questions but couldn't bring himself to ask another.

'I couldn't use your loo, could I?'

'Course,' said Jordan, pointing to the corridor.

Colin shut himself into the small downstairs toilet, pulled out his phone. He needed a distraction. Something to get Taylor out of the room. Ellie knew nothing about football. Kerry? He would know her voice. Brian? Colin called him but it went straight to voicemail. With a heavy heart he threw his Hail Mary pass.

'You know you are literally the only person that calls me on this. Ha ha!'

'I need you to do me a favour,' Colin whispered urgently.

'I might as well have a two-way radio. Although I would miss playing Candy Crush.'

'For fuck's sake, just shut up and listen.'

'Ha ha! Yes, boss.'

'I've just texted you a mobile number. It's Gus Taylor's. Kirk's right-hand man or whatever he is. He's here at the interview and I need him out of the room. Call him and pretend you're a brand manager for something . . . anything, I don't know, sunglasses. No, football boots. A boot deal. That's it. You work for Adidas and you want to talk about a boot deal for Jordan Garry. Keep him on the phone for as long as possible.'

'Hello,' said Rodbortzoon, his voice drained of its usual antic. 'My name is Maarten De Vries. I am the head of influencer recruitment and upstream marketing for Adidas Europe.'

'Oh my god, that's amazing.'

'We are looking for leverage opportunities in the fast-paced brand ambassador athletic footwear market.'

'God, you're a genius. Call him now.'

'We think that an emerging talent like Jordan could be a disruptive presence across all our platforms ...'

'OK. Enough. Just call him now.'

Colin hung up and showily flushed before returning to the living room.

'So,' he said as he picked up the list of approved questions, his heart thumping. 'Talk me through where you are on the great gel versus foam debate.'

'Well,' said Garry tentatively. 'Gel is cool, you know ...'

Gus Taylor's ring tone filled the room. He looked at his phone and seemed to think about ignoring it but at the last second chose not to.

'Hello?'

Colin could hear the faint strains of a voice, disguised, but still clearly Rodbortzoon's. He watched a broad smile break across Taylor's face as he gestured to them both and disappeared out into the corridor.

As soon as he was gone, Jordan looked at Colin and put two fingers in his mouth as if they were a gun and pretended to blow the back of his head off.

'Fucking hell, Col. If they'd told me it was going to be this boring ...'

'It's not been much fun for me either.'

'Fucking media training. They've been at it all week.'

Colin snuck up to the door, put his ear to it. He could hear Taylor outside talking animatedly on his phone.

'What's going on?' he whispered urgently.

'What do you mean?'

'You were rubbish at Charlton and then even worse at Orient. What was that about?'

'Last week was rough. Women stuff. Pregnancy. All that stuff. It's all cool though. It was nothing in the end. False alarm. But I've been all over the place about it. I'm back now, though. Focused. I've got goals in me. I can feel it. I've got goals in me.'

'Tell me straight. Are you being sold to Chelsea?'

'No.' Jordan cocked his head. 'Well, I don't think so. What have you heard?'

'Someone I know overheard *him*,' said Colin, pointing towards the corridor, 'saying that they were *really selling Garry*.'

Momentarily, Jordan looked aghast but then a broad smile spread across his face.

'You got it all back to front, bruv. *Really selling me*. That's all the talk there at the moment. They ain't *selling* me. Last of the Street Footballers. I'm a brand and they ain't been selling me. There's bucks to be had. That's what this razor shit's about. Selling me to the world.'

'You're sure?'

'It's all lined up. Huateng. Samsung.' He nodded outside. 'Lexus.'

'The new car's a brand thing?'

'I'm the new face of Lexus in Malaysia. Did the photo shoot the other day.'

'For the Malaysian market?'

'I know,' he said, shrugging. 'But they love it, apparently.'

Through the wall they could hear Taylor yelping with pleasure.

'Jordan, tell me straight. Is Kirk offering you money to play badly? You know, to lose games?'

Jordan reared back, mortally offended.

'No way.'

'The performance last week looked a lot like that was what was happening.'

'I told you, last week was rough. And everyone was talking about ten games to save the Chapel. It was tough. We'll be back though.'

'But you can see how it's in Kirk's interests for you to lose . . .'

'Col, you ain't listening. It's not like that. Yesterday, he's gone and doubled our promotion bonus. The boys are humming about it.'

'*What?*'

'Serious. He wants us to go up. For real.'

'You promise me you're not going to Chelsea in the summer?'

Jordan glanced towards the corridor and then looked fixedly at Colin.

'You're Ottercliffe. I'm Ottercliffe. We aren't going to fuck each other, right?'

Although he struggled to see quite how a school from which Garry had been unceremoniously expelled, and at which he had been relentlessly tortured, might be the basis for some inviolate social bond between them, Colin was in no mood to quibble.

'You know you can trust me,' he said.

'This off the record?'

'Yes, if you want it to be.'

'I'm not going nowhere.'

'You're going to stay? I can't tell you how much that will mean to so many people. You're a hero to the whole—'

'I'm running down my contract. Two years left. And then I'll be like a bird. I'll fly. Free like a bird.'

Colin felt his mouth hang open in shock.

'You're running down your contract?'

'If we get promoted this season it'll be on me, won't it? I've scored more than half our goals. So, we get promoted. I do one year in the Prem and then I'll be gone. With no transfer fee I'll be looking at a hundred and fifty grand a week, easy.'

Colin sat back in his chair, appalled. The club had plucked Garry from obscurity, invested in him, given him a chance. He was its most valuable asset. And despite everything it had done for him he was willing to walk away, leave it with nothing.

'I'll go Milan or Madrid. Somewhere they don't care about all that street footballer shit.'

The thought of him playing for someone else felt unimaginable, like discovering Shakespeare was actually French.

'Spain would be nice. Or Germany. Anywhere I can get away from that fucking song.'

Colin felt a smile creeping up the corner of his lips. The thought of losing Garry was awful but it would all be worth it if it meant he

277

was focused for the promotion push, motivated, firing in the goals. The next eight games were all that really mattered.

'Right. Turn it on again,' said Jordan.

'What?'

'Your recorder.'

'To be honest with you, I'm only here so I could talk to you about the club. There's not going to be a piece.'

'Col, I ain't shitting you, you got to run the piece. Face time with the press, it's part of the contract. I need column inches.'

'I can't publish a piece on razors. I'm a sportswriter.'

Jordan picked the voice recorder up from the table, turned it on.

'I'm Jordan Garry,' he said, his voice all smooth. 'The great thing about the Huateng Ultraglide is its glide. We're talking smooth. Baby's bottom. Billiard ball. Smooth, man. Smooth, smooth, smooth ... In the groove, super smooth.'

'All right,' said Colin. 'I'll do it. But do me something in return. Come out and publicly say that you want the club to stay at the Chapel.'

'Too late, bruv. The MP talked to me already. Asian guy. Nice fellow. He was here with his missus.'

'What?'

'You know how it is. I'm Larkspur, aren't I? Last of the Street Footballers. He's signed me up. We wrote a thing for his whatever you call it.'

'The listing application.'

'That's the one.'

'Wait a sec, what do you mean he was here with his missus? He's single.'

'Not any more.'

'What did she look like?'

'White woman. Tall. Good-looking. Long brown hair.'

'That's not his missus.'

'Yeah, she is.'

'No, she's not.'

'Well, they was all over each other in his car. I saw them out the window.'

28

'Have you got everything?'
'I think so.'

It was Monday morning. Daisy was going on her first proper school trip. Five nights on the Isle of Wight.

'Here's an extra tenner,' said Colin. 'Buy yourself something nice.'

Daisy did the rumpled face thing that she did which she knew Colin found to be cute. He pulled her in for a hug.

'I'm going to go up and say goodbye to Mum.'

Colin watched her run down the corridor. Seventy-two hours had passed since he had walked, shell-shocked, from Jordan Garry's front door. He had spent the first couple of them sitting in his car, outside Garry's house, capable only of meta-thoughts, his mind too blasted for anything else. Eventually, recovering some cognitive cohesion, he had driven to the Holly Bush Inn, a large mock Tudor pub on the ring road, where he felt he was guaranteed anonymity. There, he had spent the next two hours nursing a single pint of cider, as he ran through the full gamut of things he imagined he might say to Ellie: the magnanimous monologues, the cutting dismissals, the ferocious insults.

By the time he had got up to order a second pint, his initial surge of hate and spite and sadness had crested and he was entering into the classic Colin middle period, during which he started to find a perverse vitality from the confirmation of his blameless victimhood. For half an hour he sat at the bar, drinking another two pints of cider, itemising in his head all the ways in which an external, dispassionate, omniscient observer would have found him to have been the better half of their relationship; more effortful, more compassionate, more patient, more kind.

Partly because this middle period always tended to be short-lived and partly because cider really wasn't his drink, he had quickly found himself entering the final stage of his evening's emotional journey: the long maudlin. This had involved some tears, much introspection and an awful lot of self-pity. The conclusion he reached, after all this reflection and two disastrously misjudged gin and tonics, was that just because his situation was terrible that didn't mean it couldn't get worse. After weighing up all the options he had decided on a course of action. He would do nothing. His plan was to keep shtum, swallow it up, ride it out.

Outside, a car honked its horn.

'Is that Lucy's mum?' said Daisy as she came clattering back down the stairs.

'Yes, it is,' said Colin. His own car was still in the Holly Bush car park.

'See you later, Dad.'

'Bye, darling.'

Colin kissed the top of her head and watched through the window as she ran out the front door and into the back of the waiting Audi Q3. She waved to him and he waved back, thankful that at least the sharp pain behind his eyes was finally easing.

The twenty-four hours following his bender at the Holly Bush had been surely the worst of his life. He had woken at 7 a.m., on the sofa, still dressed, a kebab in his hand, his tongue gummed firmly to the roof of his mouth and his trousers covered inexplicably in what looked like brick dust. Desperate to avoid Ellie, he had fled immediately, forsaking a shower, and hurried to the bus stop as the black paranoia of his hangover enveloped him in its grip.

Even though it was a Saturday, United weren't playing, their scheduled opponents, Sunderland, having made it, against the odds, to the quarter-final of the FA Cup. It meant an afternoon free from football, but not of work. Pitilessly, it was his turn to be on rotation, which meant a day at his desk, albeit in a relatively empty office.

On the 277 bus, gulping down an energy drink, he had started to see the pattern that was developing: endemic disloyalty, widespread deceit, people abandoning him in droves. Where, for starters, was Kerry? He had called her twice from the pub, without luck. Half a dozen texts had also gone unanswered, which made it five days since they had had any contact. How cosmically perfect for her to have gone quiet just when he needed her to be there, in his corner, the perfect rebuke to Ellie and Pankaj and Kirk and London and everything else that tried to make him feel shit about everything all the time.

The misery had continued at the office where he had arrived to find, spread out on his desk, the final dismaying proofs of Monday's paper. Rick had cut his piece on the camp almost in half, losing the three quotes most critical of Kirk and altering the headline to make his support sound hedged and grudgingly given. All of which would have been insult enough, but the space it had occupied at its original length had, in part, been taken up by one of Neil's ludicrous 'In Business' features on, of all companies, Land Dominion, which he lauded for its entrepreneurial energy and the progressiveness of its in-house environmental auditing.

Finding conspiracies everywhere, Colin had taken advantage of Rick's absence from the office and gone home, where he had spent the rest of the afternoon and evening squirrelled away in the attic, muttering blackly to himself and attempting to take his mind off things by running simulations of the rest of the season, searching for a plausible route by which United might reach the playoffs. He was trying to convince himself that Leyton Orient might sneak a point at Coventry when it occurred to him that, just because Jordan almost certainly wasn't being sold to Chelsea, it didn't mean he wasn't lying about accepting bribes to throw games. It was at this point that he started drinking again.

Colin watched until the Audi had turned the corner before he shut the front door. The previous night's wild speculation had left him emotionally drained. He walked down the hall and into the kitchen.

Ellie was standing at the stove with her back to him. Her hair was up, tied in a French knot. A few fine downy strands had escaped her clip and were curling softly at the top of her neck. She was wearing a white shirt that was cut architecturally short in the sleeve, showing the faint cluster of freckles just above her elbow. The lines of her arms were angular and balletic, her skin already olive after a few days' sun.

Colin smiled ruefully. While they were together nobody could say that his life had been a failure. Whatever else, he had her as his undeniable, the thing that made him count.

He placed both his hands on the back of a chair, held on to it for strength. The problem with his plan, he was discovering, was that you couldn't not say anything, could you? That just wasn't the way it worked. Everyone had within them their own most petulant self, the one that acted always against their own best interests. And it was in exactly these moments that Colin's most petulant self was irresistibly drawn to the stage.

'You're having an affair with our MP,' he said as surely and inevitably as the sun rose in the morning.

Ellie placed a glass on the drying rack, didn't turn round.

Colin registered this non-denial for what it was and felt something inside him burn and snap. It was the filament in his bulb, he thought, the thing that animated him; it had always been fragile and now it was gone.

'Of all the people in the world I found out from Jordan Garry,' he said quietly. 'How fantastically predictable that he should be the messenger of my greatest humiliation.'

Colin let his chin slump to his chest, newly aware of all the sadness inside him and how it weighed him down like water in a bucket.

'He saw you necking in the car like a couple of teenagers.'

Ellie still hadn't turned to face him.

'I'm sorry,' she said.

Colin felt his mind empty. His most petulant self had taken him into territory of the kind for which he had no map. What were you supposed to do in this situation? What were you supposed to feel? How were you supposed to act? He had a vague sense that this was the point when people howled, incredulously, *why? Why him? What does he have that I don't?* But these were not questions to which he felt he was lacking answers.

On the table in front of him he could see Rio Ferdinand's biography, a DVD of *Danny Dyer's Football Foul-Ups* and an official Peterdown United oven glove. Colin gathered them up and put them, shame-faced, into his bag. He felt a wave of self-disgust at the mere presence, in the adjoining room, of the television set on which he had watched so many meaningless matches. All those hours. Hundreds of them. *Thousands.* All that time he would never get back, time that they could have spent talking, drinking wine, having sex.

'You know,' he said. 'It's important to me that you know that throughout it all, I have loved you. Unwaveringly. Even if ...' He faltered.

Ellie turned finally to face him. Her eyes were filmed with tears.

'I'm so sorry,' she said. 'That was an awful way to find out.'

'I mean, yeah, it was, but actually the finding out about it was pretty immaterial at the end of the day. It's the thing itself that's the problem.'

Colin felt unsteady on his feet. Tempest-tossed. Like a plastic bag on the surface of the sea.

'What happens now?'

'I don't know.'

'Is that how it works? Do I just not get any say in the matter? Does it just happen?'

'Oh, Colin, I don't know.'

'Well I don't know, either. I mean, god. I have literally no idea.'

'We need some time apart,' she said. 'I'll leave. Obviously.'

'What about D?'

'We've got five days to think about it. We'll work it out.'

'Where will you go?'

'I don't know.'

'You're going to him, aren't you?'

'I don't know, Colin. I'm sorry.'

And then Colin said something which he fundamentally didn't believe.

'I can be better.'

Ellie put her hand on his arm, squeezed it gently, tenderly.

'I'm sorry I wasn't,' she said.

And with that she left.

And he watched her go.

* * *

Ellie knocked. It felt wrong to use the key, an unnecessary, compound betrayal. He opened the door, grinned broadly when he saw it was her.

'Colin knows.'

If Pankaj's brow furrowed it was only for a fraction of a second.

'Well, this is certainly rattling along,' he said. The look in his eye was mischievous, vitalised. 'I take it you're coming in.'

Half an hour later they were lying in bed, spent. Ellie was on her back, smoking, her heart still racing. Pankaj was lying on his side, propping himself up on his elbow. He ran his index finger down her forehead, over her nose, lips, chin, down her throat, between her breasts, over her stomach and down. Ellie felt her whole body contract and release.

'What a silhouette,' he said.

Ellie relaxed her shoulders and breathed into the mattress, let it take her weight. She had a vague sense that she should be feeling guiltier than she was, but overwhelmingly her emotions were relief and liberation. Like she'd been stalled for a decade and overnight her flow had returned.

'So,' he said, taking the cigarette from her. 'An interesting trip.'

He had been in London, in the House. Voting and things like that.

'Your endeavours have attracted attention in high places.'

She leaned up on her elbows, raised an eyebrow.

'The word is that Alice Campbell-Davys is on side.'

'Really?' said Ellie. Alice Campbell-Davys was a semi-famous jewellery designer whose work was much less formally interesting than she thought it was. She was also the prime minister's wife.

'I'm told she has friends in the art world who are leaning on her. Apparently, she's obsessed with getting their approval. My friend tells me all they care about in the fashion world is being taken seriously by artists.'

'She doesn't have any actual power though, does she?'

'God no,' said Pankaj. He had this way of using the side of the ashtray to obsessively sculpt the ash at the end of his cigarette. 'I really can't see the PM actually getting involved. He just doesn't give a shit about this kind of thing. But if there is the sense out there that the listing would go down well in his household then that'll certainly endear it to Harvey, he has aspirations beyond the DCMS.'

Ellie struggled to suppress her smile. It was too rarefied, this, not to be vaguely comic. She was the butterfly and she had flapped her wings and now, on the other side of the ocean, a storm was brewing.

Pankaj got up, turned the record over. The bedroom was a simple space: a stripped wood floor, Victorian chest of drawers, white curtains, white walls, white bed sheets. It was uncluttered, coherent, a place where you could think clearly, chart your course.

'Have I just left my partner of ten years?' said Ellie. 'Like *left him* left him?'

Pankaj turned round, evidently surprised at the change of topic.

'That's not something that I can tell you,' he said measuredly as he got back into bed.

'If I have left him, I haven't left him for you.'

'Good.'

'Although you've been a catalyst.'

Pankaj took a drag on the cigarette, exhaled.

'A catalyst increases the rate of chemical reaction without itself undergoing any permanent chemical change.'

Ellie looked at him quizzically.

'I had to learn that for chemistry A level,' he said.

He looked sort of at her, sort of past her.

'I'm not a catalyst. Because the catalyst doesn't undergo any permanent change. And I've changed. You've changed me.'

He looked at her, guardedly. And she looked back at him.

'Permanently?'

'Yes,' he said. 'I think so.'

29

If the experience of Ellie's departure had been one of bewildering disorientation, then at least the three-day melancholic wallow that followed represented familiar terrain.

About an hour after she had gone, Colin had pulled the single mattress and duvet from the spare room and positioned them in front of the sofa, turning the living room into a kind of improvised multi-level soft play centre in which he had languished, in various states of repose, for the best part of seventy-two hours, leaving only to use the toilet and answer the door to the various delivery drivers who were enabling his borderline suicidal comfort eating: two Licken' Chicken sharing buckets, three curries, a whole Peking duck, and, at the absolute nadir of his self-respect, a stuffed-crust pizza for breakfast.

For solace, he had turned to his eight-disc World Cup DVD collection, retrieved from its exile in the loft, but, wherever he looked, all he found was tragedy and injustice: the Hand of God, Schumacher on Battiston, the unfulfilled genius of Sócrates' Brazil.

By the time he had finally left the house, late on Wednesday afternoon ahead of that evening's game against Macclesfield Town, his epic self-imposed solitary confinement had only reinforced his certainty that, however paranoid it sounded, sometimes they (and by 'they' he meant Ellie, Pankaj, Kirk, Kerry, Neil, Rick and Jordan Garry, as well as his own genes and the cosmic forces that governed the universe) really were out to get you.

Being in no mood to stand for the duration of a football match (not least because of the tenderness in his lower back, the feeling of several organs in a state of near-collapse) and embarrassedly certain that he may as well have been wearing a pair of cuckold's horns, Colin skirted past the gates to the Radleigh, choosing instead to stump up the extra fiver for a spot in the West Stand with its tiered benches and family enclosure.

Compared to the Radleigh, with its roiling anger and constant plotting, the atmosphere in the West Stand was excitable and puppyish. Boys and girls shrieked and squealed while their dads chatted over their heads, and all niceties were observed: neighbours lent one another their programmes, everyone made way for passers-by, nobody pissed at your feet.

His seat was in a good spot, near the halfway line, between an old man swearing softly to himself and a family of four, all of them wearing replica shirts over the top of long-sleeve jumpers, giving them the appearance of fugitives from a precipitous tragedy who had had to throw on whatever they had, in whatever order they could. Colin found it easy to imagine the four of them sleeping on camp beds in a school hall while the flood waters rose outside.

He sat down, tucked his programme and his coat under his seat, opened a packet of crisps. The United players were already out warming up on the pitch, and Colin found himself flitting from one to the next searching for signs of nervousness; a tic or a tell that might reveal their corruption, a signal that they'd taken a kickback to throw the game.

Unsurprisingly, his gaze kept returning to Garry. He was warming up the United keeper, drilling balls for him to save. He placed one on the penalty spot and took a serious, studied run-up only to balloon it over the bar to ironic cheers from the crowd. The self-deprecating smile that followed was goofily theatrical, but was it, Colin wondered, also a little forced, almost pre-conceived? Wouldn't that be a fairly obvious play? To deliberately miss in order to lower expectations for the game to come?

All of a sudden everything about the man seemed artificial, stage-managed to achieve a particular effect. The way he characteristically wore his socks – scrunched halfway down his shin – seemed contrived, a clumsy announcement of his openness and transparency.

Colin watched him as he started his shuttle runs, tearing into them, as always, with his trademark enthusiasm, his famous abundance of energy. But isn't that exactly what you *would* do if you were planning on losing, show off your fervour?

Colin found himself looking at the other fans around him, sullenly conscious of his sense of isolation and otherness. Could they not see this? Did none of them have a sense of what was happening? Was it really just him?

Unease settled on his shoulders like a layer of dandruff. Where the fuck was Kerry? It struck him forcefully for the first time that nothing she had given him, none of the leads, none of her supposed inside gen, had actually led anywhere, changed anything. Was she in on it, too?

Colin sat in his seat, the world spinning around him. And then, just as he felt he was going to fall down a rabbit hole from which he might never emerge, the ref blew his whistle and the game started. United, in green and white, were kicking left to right.

* * *

Acute paranoia may be exhausting but at least it makes for a cohesive world-view. And so it was with a slight tinge of regret that Colin stood from his seat a couple of hours later, having witnessed not the listless display of suspiciously overhit passes and dubious unforced errors that he had been expecting, but a galloping four-nil victory inspired by a rampaging Jordan Garry, who had scored two brilliant goals before being substituted, late on in the game, to a standing ovation.

Of course, it was only a slight tinge of regret. Overwhelmingly, his emotional state was a mawkish soup of gratitude and schmaltz. Football had done what football did. It had come along, just when he had needed it, and it had saved him, as it always did, from torpor, listlessness and despair.

He walked up the staircase, heading for the exit. He had long known that at its worst, the sport as it was presently configured was venal, mercenary, ethically degraded, rampantly corrupt. And yet at the centre of it all was the game itself, which, whatever the

288

degradations visited upon it, remained pure and – when it was played as Garry had played it that evening – beautiful, something into which you could pour your trust.

The fans were still singing as they filed out of the stadium. Kids sat on their dads' shoulders, scarves hanging loosely around their necks. Old men scanned new phones, checking on the final scores from around the grounds. Colin, who no longer knew what to think about anything at all, allowed himself to drift with it and be swept up in the raucous free-flowing energy of the crowd.

He had just left the stadium when he felt a tap on his shoulder. Simply from the texture of it – light and lingering and placed play-fully close to the nape of his neck – he knew instantly it was her. He turned round. She was wearing a grey trouser suit and kitten heels with contrast caps at the toe. Her hair was up in a ponytail. Her earrings were gold and loopy. Her lipstick was a deep scarlet.

'Where have you been?' he whispered. And then immediately after: 'How did you know I was here?

'Erm,' she said, mockingly raising a finger to her lips. 'You're the football correspondent for the *Peterdown Evening Post* and I thought to myself where could he *possibly* be when there's a home game on?'

Colin leaned back, eyed her suspiciously.

'All right, but where have you been?'

Kerry took him by the crook of his elbow and steered him behind a pillar to a recess where they were out of sight and earshot.

'My bathroom, crouched over the toilet.'

'For a week?'

'I can't tell you, Colin. I've not stopped. There were times when it felt like I was going to throw up a kidney.'

Colin was struck by an awful thought.

'Christ. They're not poisoning you, are they?'

'No, Colin, of course they're not. *Jesus.*' The look on her face was one of utter incredulity. 'That doesn't mean it hasn't been awful. But I'm a lot better now. Thanks for asking.'

'Oh, yeah. Sorry.'

The crowds streaming past had started to thin.

'Today is the first day in like ten days that I've felt like an actual human . . . It did mean I only listened to your voicemail this morning.' Here Kerry winced in sympathy. 'I'm sorry.'

'What voicemail?'

'You were at the Holly Bush. Well, you were in the car park. It was one thirty in the morning according to my phone.'

Colin felt his stomach tilt and flip.

'What did I say?'

'You told me about your Ellie,' she said, screwing one eye shut in sympathy. 'I'll vote Lib Dem next time.'

Colin shifted his weight from one foot to the other.

'Did I say anything else?'

'You kept saying: anything else would be too much.'

'I did?'

'And then you said you'd have the hug first,' said Kerry as she spread wide her arms. 'So, come here.'

Colin allowed himself to be enveloped in her embrace, let his head rest on her shoulder, his body melt into the press of her flesh. Her perfume was heady, full of flowers and spice.

Ordinarily wide open and chronically suggestible, Colin let what little remained of his guard down. The realisations came flooding in. Ellie was the love of his life. And she had left him. And she wasn't coming back. And no amount of scarlet lipstick – however perfectly it had been applied, however suggestive its colour – would ever be able to fill that gap, or mend his broken heart.

From somewhere deep within him came a lowing, a deep and dulcet sound, full of hurt and pain and pity.

'You're a lovely person,' said Kerry, patting his back. 'Really, Colin. A lovely person.'

She pulled away from him, righted her hair.

'But don't forget, in the end, it all comes down to self-respect. And if she's cheating, she's got to go. You did the right thing, kicking her out.'

Colin stood there, his bottom lip gripped between his teeth to stop it trembling. He went to right this historical inaccuracy but then didn't.

'You'll be fine. You're doing the right thing, taking charge of the situation.'

'Thank you,' he said, for all kinds of things.

Kerry peered out of the recess, looked one way and then the other.

'Anyway, I got your other texts and all,' she said, once she was satisfied no one was listening.

'Yeah, so you can ignore them,' said Colin, gathering himself. 'I spoke to Garry. He's not going anywhere. And, obviously, it doesn't look like he's throwing matches.'

'I can't believe you ever thought he would. That's just so not him.'

'I thought Kirk might have had something on him. I don't know ...'

'There's nothing to be had,' said Kerry censoriously. 'And, anyway, Kirk's all over promotion. He's just gone and doubled their win bonuses again. If he doesn't want us to go up, he certainly isn't behaving that way.' She paused, ran her tongue across her front teeth. 'You know, for all that he's a prick – and he is a prick, *God* he's a prick – what can I say, it seems genuine: he wants us to go up.'

'Jesus, Kerry. Come on. It's a classic piece of misdirection. He knows it's not going to happen.'

'Portsmouth lost today. And Coventry.'

'This is exactly what he wants us to do. Focus on promotion. Take our eyes off the real story.'

'If we did, though, Grangeham could be as bent as it likes and it wouldn't matter. We'd be staying here.'

'You've got to stop thinking like that. Listen to me. We. Are. Not. Going. To. Get. Promoted.'

'You saw him today. He was on fire. If he plays like that for the rest of the season ... Just think about it. The Premier League.' She punched him playfully on the arm and started walking off before stopping and turning to him again. 'Seven games to go and we're still in with a chance.'

And then, despite himself, Colin did think about it. Even though he knew that this was exactly what Kirk wanted him to do. Even though he knew that the odds were still massively stacked against them, even though it would take the stars to align, he allowed a small flowering of hope to take root in his heart. Because the thing was that they did occasionally align, the stars, which was the whole point of sport. Anything could happen. And, if you thought about it, it already had: Coventry had lost three-one at home to York. Not even in his most optimistic moments had he ever imagined that that might happen.

He continued down the concourse, overcome at the prospect of it. *Match of the Day*. He felt teary. Nobody would be able to say that his life was a failure. Not when they were on *Match of the Day*.

Colin turned the corner and the concourse opened up in front of him. In the five days since he had last been there, the camp had doubled in size and had a whole new sense of permanence to it. There were at least ten new tents.

He walked on. Organisers stood behind trestle tables handing out flyers to the passing crowds and urging them to sign petitions. A man on stilts was dressed as a Grim Reaper-cum-referee, blowing a tin whistle and occasionally brandishing a giant red card with Kirk's name on it. Chants started, died, started again. People laughed, drank beer, revelled in the win.

Colin briefly considered getting involved with a penalty-taking contest that was being held using the side of Brian's tent as a goal (as ever, Rodbortzoon was illustrating his surprising nimbleness with a string of agile saves), but he had a match report to write and so he continued on, through the happy throng and down on to the Radleigh Road. From there he turned the corner on to Vale Street where he was confronted by the giant billboard that hung, cut off from pedestrians by the dual carriageway, on the huge south wall of the Aspire Centre. As always, it bore an advert for Moolah. Colin had walked past it a thousand times. He barely noticed it any more, but today it couldn't be ignored. On the billboard, in thick tar, the brushstrokes evident in the still-sticky bitumen, someone had written a single word:

WROTH

30

I t was the spring instalment of the quarterly Houghton-down-the-Vale car boot sale. Hundreds of cars were arranged in a grid formation big enough to cover four rugby pitches. Tarpaulins had been laid flat, trestle tables erected, boots opened. And everywhere you looked there was stuff. Out of garages it had come. Lofts. The backs of cupboards. The drawers under beds. Rusty saws and screw-driver sets. Medal collections and canteens of cutlery. Out-of-date annuals and mass-market paperbacks. Cartloads of cuddly toys. A staggering number of awful paintings.

All Ellie's favourites were there. The woman who sewed very convincing fake Dolce & Gabbana labels into wholly unconvincing knock-offs. The man in the flat cap with his dozens of bottles of half-used toiletries, each one individually priced. The couple who sold army fatigues and gas masks and tins of homemade biscuits.

'Look at this,' said Daisy, holding out a tiny paper plane made from a vintage airmail envelope, red and blue chevrons running down its wings.

'That is really cool.'

'It was 20p.'

'Bargain.'

'I thought it would be good in Out of the Woods.'

'Oh, darling, it totally would. *Paper aeroplanes flying.*'

'Yeah, and they're sort of free, aren't they? And it's also made out of the woods, you know, trees.'

'Darling, that's so good. You've really thought about it. And it's so pretty. It's going to look amazing.'

'I thought we could hang it from the top of the box on a piece of string.'

'Genius!' said Ellie, putting her hand up for a high-five.

She was aware that she was in danger of overdoing it but it was a case now of needs must. It was day six of the new reality. For the first four of them – while Daisy was still on her trip to the Isle of Wight – she had stayed with Pankaj at his house. It had been unseasonably warm and each evening, after they both got home from work, they had opened a bottle and taken it to his small courtyard garden with its period table, plants in terracotta pots and wisteria on the west wall. There they had sat, eating simple home-cooked meals, drinking wine and talking into the small hours. The four nights had seemed to both stretch out forever and disappear in an instant.

On Thursday – the eve of Daisy's return – it had been decided, over the course of one surprisingly short telephone conversation, that Colin would move out to his parents', and she would move back in, which she had done, a little ruefully, the following morning.

Arriving back at the house had been the first deflating reminder that there was a messy reality to be reckoned with beyond the bubble she had created for herself. But the full extent of her emotional entanglement had only really hit home the moment Daisy walked through the door that afternoon. Her reaction – to the guilt and self-loathing and acute sense of her own dereliction of duty – had been to smother Daisy with love and spoil her rotten. They had gone to the cinema and then out for pizza. And now they were here, early on Saturday morning at the car boot sale.

'Mum.'

Ellie turned round and there she was, her arms laden with what looked to be at least a dozen Fresno dolls, with their awful lurid nylon hair.

'Oh, wow.'

'I got thirteen,' said Daisy excitably, the words spilling out of her. 'The man had more but that's all I could afford. After I'd paid for them, another girl came and bought the rest but she only got three. I got thirteen.'

She leaned forward and let the dolls tumble from her arms gently on to the table.

'That's Princess Talia when she's in her riding gear. This is Lady Lucille. She's a personal shopper to the stars.'

Ellie looked down aghast at their outfits. One was in a sparkling bikini. Another in a school uniform and thigh-high socks.

'Did you spend all the rest of your money on these?'

'I only really had the money for twelve but he let me have thirteen.'

'But I thought we were here for stuff for our boxes.'

'He was selling them for a pound each.'

'I don't get it. Aren't these the hot thing at the moment?'

'The guy selling them totally didn't know what they were. He just had loads of stuff on his table. It was all a pound. Even a tennis racket.'

She picked up a doll wearing a tiara and what to all the world looked like a porn star's negligee.

'This is a night-time InstaQueen. Do you have any idea how rare they are?'

Ellie faltered. Even though she knew she was up against a vast marketing budget, a huge network of self-reinforcing peer pressure and an essentially misogynist culture, she couldn't help but feel that at a fundamental level she had failed. There had to be a way of mothering daughters that made them impervious to this crap but she had not hit upon it. Had she cocooned her too much? Or too little? Was it too much television? Too much internet? Or was it more profound than that? Not enough attention? Not enough time?

She stood where she was, trying to maintain an impassive face. Her desire to grab every last one of the dolls and throw them into the river was tempered by the knowledge that she had just done something wholly selfish that was going to impact on Daisy's life far more than these shitty little lumps of plastic ever would.

'I didn't know it was a rare one, no. I didn't know there *were* rare ones.'

'I thought you would understand.'

'Of course I do,' she said softly, overcome at the guilt and remorse.

'I hadn't realised they were only a pound. Aren't they normally at least a tenner in the shops?'

'Nine ninety-nine for the normal and twelve ninety-nine for the glitter elite.'

'And InstaQueen's in the glitter elite, is she?'

'You should see her Fresno palace. It's in the Hollywood Hills. It's got three swimming pools.'

'Three swimming pools,' said Ellie dryly. 'They must require an awful lot of maintenance. Is there a Fresno doll that takes on contract cleaning?'

Daisy looked at her, half-comprehendingly. It was as if she was aware of the irony but suspicious still of its motives. The look reminded Ellie that her daughter was at the age where she had to navigate effectively being two people at the same time: a proto-teenager, keen to engage with the adult world, and also essentially still a little kid, in need of certainties and security at all times.

'Do you want a waffle?' she said.

'Ohmygod, yes.'

'The guy that does the good ones is over there.'

'The hot chocolate man?'

'The very same.'

'Oh my god, Mum, this is the best day ever. You know I'm going to have to set up Fresno palaces for all of them.'

'OK. But I'm not paying for thirteen of them.'

'I'll save up, I promise.'

'If that's how you want to spend your money I won't stop you.'

Ellie queued while Daisy scoured the nearby stalls and then, once they had received their order of two waffles with salted caramel and a hot chocolate to share, they took the tray of food to the picnic tables where they sat for ten minutes eating and drinking companionably.

As they were finishing the last of Ellie's waffle, Daisy's school friend Samantha appeared, her father standing mutely in the middle distance, and Ellie agreed that the two of them could explore on their own as long as they promised to stay close by. As soon as they were gone, she picked up a discarded Saturday supplement, grabbed herself a hot black coffee and spent an enjoyable ten minutes reading with her face in the sun.

She had just finished a pleasingly awful money diary written by an absurdly overpaid twenty-three-year-old social media manager when she looked down at her phone and noticed she had a missed a call. Leonie.

For the most part it had been pretty obvious how their friends would divide over it. And so far they had duly delivered. As expected, Suzie had gone all-in for Colin with malign relish. He'd got Big Tom, too, with his keen sense of solidarity with downtrodden fatherhood. Having had so many affairs himself, Little Tom had predictably opted for Swiss-style neutrality. And she of course had got Patrick. Although his attempt at solidarity – a thirty-minute phone call the night before in which he never mentioned Colin, let alone enquired as to his wellbeing – had had the inverse of its intended effect, leaving her virtually immobilised by guilt for hours afterwards.

But the great imponderable was Leonie.

'Ellie.'

'Hi.'

'Why didn't you tell me?'

Ellie tried to muster a response to this. Embarrassment was a factor, obviously. Guilt. And also a weird lack of guilt. And then more guilt at that lack of guilt. And also the knowledge that had she called Leonie in those first few days it would have been very hard not to sound excited. There were other reasons, too. The desire to carve out a space that was all her own. The thrill at having secrets. Absentmindedness. None of which felt easily explicable and so she kept quiet, took the hit.

'I found out from *Suzie*. You should have heard the delight in her voice when she realised that I didn't know.'

'I'm sorry.'

'I spoke to Colin.'

Ellie felt a piercing sadness.

'Did you? How is he?'

'Haven't you spoken to him?'

'Once. On the phone. But it was mostly practical things. You know, who goes where, Daisy stuff.'

'Oh Christ, of course. How's *she*?'

'She doesn't know.'

'Oh god, Ellie, what a mess.'

Ellie felt this fully, the whole messy mess of it.

'How is Colin?' she asked in a quiet voice.

'He's gutted, obviously. How do you think he is?'

For ten minutes they talked. Or rather Leonie did a lot of talking and Ellie did a lot of listening. The topics covered were Colin's mental health (fragile), Daisy's life chances (imperilled), their friendship group (fractured), and Ellie's current situation (a total fucking mess).

Eventually, Leonie asked her a direct question.

'What are you going to do?'

Again, no meaningful response would cohere.

'I don't know,' she said.

Before Leonie could respond Ellie was forced to hastily end the call at the sight of Daisy walking towards her holding a large cardboard box.

'Look at these.'

Ellie did a double-take. In the cardboard box were two smaller period wooden boxes, each with a glass front. They were a similar size, both a little larger than a shoe box. One was a dark mahogany colour, the other had been painted white.

'The man wants twelve pounds for the pair,' said Daisy, nodding to a guy behind a fold-down who was mostly selling fishing tackle and superhero DVDs. 'I know I've spent my allowance, but can I borrow . . .'

'Oh my god, of course you can. I can't believe you found these, they're amazing.'

'They were at the end of the table in this box. I just got this feeling there was going to be something good in it.'

'You're like some kind of divining rod. I can't believe it. These are just *perfect*.'

A minute later they were walking away, the boxes in a carrier bag, the two of them barely able to suppress their smiles. You could say all you wanted about Peterdown, and she frequently did, but it was still a place where you could find stuff. Curios. Oddities. Things that anywhere else would be on eBay for silly prices.

'*Twelve pounds for the pair*,' she said, through her teeth.

'I know,' said Daisy. 'We are the best *ever* at this.'

Ellie felt her daughter's fingers interlace through hers, the slight strain in her still-small hands, the softness of her skin.

'We'll have to come up with two new themes,' said Daisy. 'One each.'

'We so will.'

'Any ideas?'

'I think I might call mine Blank Space,' said Ellie.

Daisy looked at her, her mouth wide open in delight.

'*Amazing*,' she said. 'Why don't I call mine: All You Had To Do Was Stay?'

Ellie felt her throat go instantly dry. She looked at her daughter, panic spreading through her. Daisy looked back at her innocently, happily squeezed her hand.

'Why not,' said Ellie eventually. 'I mean, what could possibly be wrong with that?'

* * *

Children's parties. For some reason she always went into them with hope in her heart. She could vividly imagine the ones that she would hold when she became the woman she was planning on becoming. Sun filtering through the trees. Hand-cut gingham bunting hanging from the low branches. A rustic picnic table. Home-baked treats. Drinks made from crushed raspberries and mint leaves. Innocent games. Infectious laughter.

All of which was a strange fantasy to carry in your head when you were going to what was basically a stainless steel shed on the Ottercliffe Road for an under-elevens roller disco.

She pushed open the door to the Peterside Leisure Centre and in they went. Daisy saw Erin and they both shrieked. And then Daisy saw Kirsten and *they* both shrieked. And then the three of them ran off to the machine that dispensed the slush puppies.

On the far side of the roller rink there was a dimly lit café area. At a corner table surrounded by party bags was Kirsten's mum, whom Ellie had met far too many times not to be sure of her name. She was a vast woman, red-faced, always seemingly just short of breath.

'Thanks for coming,' she said when she saw Ellie.

'Thanks for having us. Daisy has been so excited about it. The Isle of Wight and then a party – what a week.'

'The Isle of Wight.' She rolled her eyes. 'Kirsten came back shattered.'

Kirsten's mum put a candy cane in one of the bags and then took it out again.

'God, Daisy too.' Ellie dug her hands into her pockets. 'Is there anything I can do to help?'

'Oh, that's sweet of you, but no, really. It's all in my head. Who's allergic to what, all that stuff.'

'Are you sure?'

'Yeah, you go grab a tea. We're on the rink in twenty. The kids can play until ten to and then we need them to get their boots on.'

'You're sure I can't help?'

'Sure, sure. Get yourself a tea.'

Ellie settled at a table in the far corner next to one of those machines with the claws in them that you used, in theory, to grab one of the cuddly toys piled in the prize pit: the Smurfs and sea lions, the powder-pink unicorns with their spacey oversized eyes, the single stuffed monkey, its face squished up against the glass.

She logged on to the centre's WiFi and got to work. Alice Campbell-Davys had mentioned the listing campaign in an interview on Radio 4, for which she had been swiftly admonished by some hack on the *Daily Mail* website, a piece which in turn had been picked up by various fashion blogs. The whole brouhaha had driven hundreds of people to Ellie's Instagram and they needed to be cultivated, their posts liked and commented upon. All of them brought into the circle.

Five minutes later, Ellie heard a table being pulled declaratively across the floor and knew instantly who it was. She looked up. Janey was in the process of kicking a chair out of her way. She was carrying two large green plastic glasses, two miniature bottles of gin and two miniature cans of tonic. A bag of nuts was wedged between her chin and shoulder like it was the butt of a violin.

Ellie felt a sudden bloom of shame and a clench of self-reproach, because leaving Colin, if that's what she was doing, was also, ultimately, leaving Janey. Probably not immediately, but inexorably. And not just geographically, but spiritually, too.

'They insisted on giving me these fucking straws.'

She had the straws held fast in her armpit. Slowly, Janey started to release the various objects so that they fell gently on to the table, the bottles and cans, and then the plastic cups and then finally the nuts and the straws.

'I'm not even going to tell you what I have just paid for these.'

'I was having a cup of tea.'

'Don't be daft, we're not going to get through this without gin.'

Janey cracked open the various bottles and cans, dispensed their contents into the two cups, opened the nuts, plonked a straw in each cup, stirred them up.

'So,' she said, her eyes alight. 'Fucking hell.'

'What?' said Ellie.

Janey pulled a you-know-what-I'm-talking-about face.

Ellie exhaled incredulously.

'How do you already know? I was literally about to tell you. How can you already know?'

'I'm a shaman.'

'No you're not.'

'A seer.'

'How are you a seer?'

Janey took a huge gleeful suck on her straw.

'All right, I'm not a seer. But I'm a hearer. I've never told you this before but my Carol, Steve's Carol, my sister-in-law, her cleaner's his cleaner.'

'Why didn't you tell me that?'

'I thought you would think it was a bit stalkerish, you know. I don't know, like I was all up in your shit.'

Ellie shook her head and sighed.

'When it turns out you're all up in your own shit. I mean, god, neck deep in it.'

'Oh, Janey, what have I done?'

Janey hooted.

'You've only gone and banged the future prime minister. Look at you, Norma Major,' she said, immediately before she was struck by an obviously better thought. 'Oh my god, Jackie O. *Jackie O*. You're the fucking Jackie O of the Vale of Peter.'

Ellie was about to respond to this but had to still her tongue. Felicity's mum, Denise, had just pulled up a chair beside them.

'They're not going to make us bloody skate, are they?' said Denise.

'Oh god,' said Ellie. 'I hadn't even thought that was a possibility. It's under-elevens only, isn't it?'

'Yeah,' said Janey. 'All we have to do is sit here like it's an episode of *Strictly* and rip them all to shreds.'

And that's exactly what they did. For thirty wonderful minutes, Ellie didn't think about her life or her lover, or the mess she'd made of things. Instead, she sat there with Denise and Janey, drinking gin, the three of them quietly but mercilessly mocking the skating children, their own very much included. There was a lot of low chuckling and the occasional shriek. At the wipe-outs and crap conga lines. The abject pirouettes. The atrocious attempts at flirting. They were particularly savage about a try-hard ten-year-old in a neon-pink all-in-one.

'My round,' said Denise, tipping her glass at the two of them, to which she received two enthusiastic nods.

Janey waited until she was out of earshot and then she said:

'You remember what I was like after I'd had our Alexis?'

'Of course I do.'

'How I completely lost my fucking shit.'

'Darling, you had post-natal depression and I'm pretty sure PTSD, too. Forty-two hours for god's sake. It was inhuman.'

Janey bit her bottom lip.

'I'll never forget how you supported me through that,' she said. 'I thought I was losing my mind. I mean it, I really did.'

'It was what any friend would have done.'

'No it wasn't. It was a lot more than that.'

'I'd do it for you again. In a heartbeat. You know that.'

Janey's eyes were rimmed with red.

'Although, Christ,' said Ellie, 'please don't have any more bloody kids.'

They both laughed at this and then looked at each other meaningfully.

'Oh god, you're not, are you?'

'No. Bloody hell. Four's a fucking nightmare as it is.'

'Thank god for that.'

Janey had her hands together in her lap so she could worry her wedding ring with her forefinger and thumb.

'Anyway,' she said, 'you remember in the pit of it, how I was talking about leaving my Steve?'

'You talked about a lot of things then. Crazy stuff. It wasn't you, you were in the grip of something you just had to ride out.'

'This isn't that.'

Ellie stopped, as she grasped the true direction of the conversation. 'Really?'

'Yeah. I mean your Colin, bless his cotton socks, but he's not . . . I don't know, you and him . . . I mean, he's not that MP, is he?'

Ellie closed her eyes.

'No,' she said. 'He's not.'

31

Colin stood in the camp mess tent, looking out. The weather was old-school English: steady rain, grey clouds, drabness everywhere you looked. It was Monday morning, the bitter culmination of a disastrous few days.

The high from Wednesday night's four-nil win hadn't lasted long. He had woken up the next morning feeling strangely confident, somehow convinced that everything was going to be all right. This odd sense of invulnerability had stayed with him all day and it was probably why that afternoon, on the spur of the moment, just after he had completed a nine-hundred-word player profile on Peterdown United's reserve goalkeeper, he had elected – in what he had thought would be a blindsiding tactical swerve – to illustrate his magnanimity by agreeing eagerly, even forcefully, to everything Ellie suggested.

Of course, he hadn't expected that this would lead, three hours after he had adopted the strategy, to him packing his bags and moving in with his parents.

Once upon a time this might have meant a return to his old room in the family home with its reassuring familiarity, its rich memories, its deep roots, but that house had been sold years ago. His parents now lived in a bungalow down a cul-de-sac off the Broadcastle Road. Colin was shacked up in their spare room, in a single bed – hitherto used exclusively by Daisy – sleeping under a *My Little Pony: Friendship is Magic* duvet and pillow set.

Naïvely, he had assumed that his new sleeping arrangements had to represent an unsurpassable low, but he hadn't reckoned on the confidence-razing impact of spending so much time with his mother, who was struggling to contain her pride-tinged astonishment that he had been cuckolded by a member of parliament. *You know, Colin, I always thought she would leave you for a doctor*, she kept telling him disbelievingly, like she was apologising for having sold him short all these years.

After a couple of nights of this, he had managed to get away, at least temporarily, down to Plymouth and the comparative luxury of a night in a Travelodge, but United had been held to a nil-nil draw, which had seen them fall dispiritingly back to ninth in the table.

A result like this, which made promotion ever unlikelier, should have seen him redoubling his efforts to find out what was really happening at Grangeham but his investigations had stalled, buried under the punitive workload Rick was heaping upon him. Not to mention all the time he had spent texting Ellie.

Colin stared morosely out at the rain as it bounced rhythmically on the roof of the tents. He had sent the first message late on Saturday night from the corner table of the otherwise empty Travelodge restaurant. It was partly the wine that had encouraged him, but mostly it had been the growing sense that he had been the victim of an injustice that went beyond mere infidelity. The more he thought about it the more he realised he had not been dumped for reasons that other people were. Other people gave cause, they cheated or they were neglectful. But he hadn't. You could quibble about the details but when you got down to it, she had left him because he was a working-class boy from Peterdown. And that was a whole other level of wrong.

Colin felt a ripple of long-suppressed anger roll across his upper lip. He could say what he wanted about Peterdown – it was his right as a local – but she could take a running jump before she could start slagging off the place. Because there was nothing wrong with it. And there was nothing wrong with being from here.

This was what he had realised in his very core over the past two days. He was from Peterdown. This town of ten thousand trains. Of Johnnie Larkspur and Major Wroth. Of Gem McBride and the Radleigh Roar. A place that had been infinitely patronised but had infinite resolve. A place that was home to pound-for-pound the hardest, funniest, most fearless people you could ever hope to meet. And anyone who fancied themselves too good for it could fuck off.

Which is what he had told her, via text. And it had felt good. So he had gone on, expanded his critique – to her, obviously, and where she was from, north London and its fantastically misplaced sense of its own importance; to her family and their innocence to their mediocrity; and then, of course, back to her and her spectacular unoriginality.

'Colin, what the hell's the RPUFG?'

It was Brian, from behind him in the mess tent.

'I've got no idea.'

'The Real Peterdown United Fans' Group.'

'Never heard of them.'

'They've got a statement out. The official United Twitter account has just reposted a screen shot of it on their feed.'

Brian pulled his phone close to his face and read: '*The Real Peterdown United Fans' Group represents ordinary Peterdown United fans appalled at the behaviour of a group of left-wing extremists who are presenting themselves as if they speak for all the supporters. The RPUFG speaks for those who utterly condemn the camp, which although it may have had noble intentions, has been taken over by anarchists and vandals.*'

'Oh fuck off,' said Mick.

'*Furthermore, the RPUFG believes that success on the pitch should be the main aim for Peterdown United Football Club and as such supports the proposed move to a new stadium to fully maximise the club's earning potential . . .*'

'Jesus,' said Colin.

'Are there any names on it?'

'Jamie Daly and Luke Solomons.'

'Who are they?

'Buggered if I know. I can't think that they've ever been active before. But you know there's, what, twenty-five thousand fans. I don't know them all.'

'That's all we need,' said Colin. 'Kirk'll be all over it like a rash.'

'Weird, them calling us vandals. Are they blaming us for this Wroth stuff?', asked Mick.

Like every Peterdowner of his generation, Colin had had to put together a ten-page illustrated booklet on the wagoner riots of 1829 for his fourth-year local history project and so he, along with the rest of the town, had got the reference immediately when a second and then a third billboard had been daubed in tar. In both instances the message had been simple and to the point: WROTH, writ large.

Steve laughed through his nose and looked over at the Partisan section of the camp.

'Well, we all know it wasn't you, Micky,' he said dryly. 'The brush strokes were too neat and they spelled it right, all three times. But . . .'

He let this hang in the air.

'It wasn't Micky,' said Brian. 'And it wasn't us, and that's what we keep saying again and again. This isn't political. This is football. Our club. That's what this is about . . .'

Colin noticed a text appearing on his screen. Ellie's responses so far had been maddeningly measured, determinedly non-confrontational, and he was desperate for some evidence of hurt on her part, some sign that he had penetrated her defences.

But the message wasn't from her. It was Rick, with news of an urgent meeting at which Colin was required.

* * *

Forty minutes later, he was in Rick's office with the seven other members of the *Peterdown Evening Post* editorial team. Anne McAllister and Hugh Trentwood were perched on windowsills, Mike Hardacre was leaning against the wall. Neil was sitting on the small sofa, his legs extravagantly crossed.

'Thank you all for coming,' said Rick, once they had all settled. 'I have some exciting news which I want to tell you all at once. Neil and I have been working alongside the commercial team on negotiations with Land Dominion about the firm becoming the new sponsor of our property section. If it happens it could be a big deal. We're looking at something in the region of two hundred thousand pounds a year over the next couple of years.'

Colin groaned.

307

'Well, that makes sense, doesn't it?' he said, looking pointedly at Neil.

'What does that mean?'

'Well, we all know who your real paymaster is, don't we?'

Neil snorted.

'Who do you think yours is? The reader? At 65p a copy? God, you're even more naïve than I thought.'

'Your Land Dominion piece was an embarrassment.'

'The game is the game,' said Neil. 'That's just the way it is these days. And you heard him: two hundred thousand. What have you ever brought in?'

'It's not my job to *bring anything in.*'

'It's barely your job at all, if I've heard right.'

Colin looked enquiringly at Rick. He shook his head at the suggestion, but it was, to Colin's eyes at least, an unconvincing denial.

'We do all remember that this is the man who's banned me from the ground, don't we?'

'Actually, it was the club that banned you,' said Neil, 'not Land Dominion. They're two completely separate organisations.'

'They're both owned by the same person. And that person prevented a reporter from this paper from doing his job.'

'Way I heard it was they didn't ban the paper, they banned *you.*'

'OK you two. Calm down,' said Rick from his editor's chair. 'This is a potentially exciting partnership but I know that Mr Kirk and his various businesses are not to everyone's liking.' Here he looked pointedly at Colin. 'Which is why I've taken the unprecedented decision to put this to an editorial vote. What we're talking about is more than simply a commercial decision. We're envisioning a partnership. Land Dominion will benefit from our publishing know-how and we'll get the kind of sizeable cash support that will keep our jobs secure.'

'What does that mean, *they'll benefit from our publishing know-how?*'

'It means we'll help put together promotional material for them. There's talk of a magazine in the future . . .'

'Jesus, Rick. He's a loan shark. It's bad enough that we take his advertising.'

'He's not a loan shark. It's all totally legit. Loan sharks are—'

'One thousand, nine hundred and fifty-eight per cent.'

'You know, Colin. I've given it quite a lot of thought and really I'm not sure if the annual APR is actually a very useful way of assessing a loan which is only given for two weeks.'

'Oh, Rick.'

'And you know what else? They employ fifteen hundred people in a town that really needs those jobs.'

'On zero-hours contracts with the perpetual threat of the sack hanging over them.'

Colin looked around the room, desperate for some support from his colleagues. None came.

'Well, I'm glad we've had the opportunity for a robust exchange of views,' said Rick. 'Anyone opposed to the suggestion please raise their hand.'

'Isn't it normal to raise your hand if you're in favour of a motion?'

'When there are only two options it doesn't make any difference,' said Neil.

'Exactly,' said Rick. 'Now all those against please raise their hands.'

Colin stuck his hand miserably in the air. Nobody else moved.

'Well, I think that's fairly conclusive,' said Rick. 'Thanks for your support.'

'This is a joke,' said Colin as he barrelled out of the room, slamming the door on his way.

He walked through the office to the far window and stood staring out at the town below. So typical of Colin to be experiencing all at once righteous anger, pride that he had held the moral high ground – but also, and this was impossible to deny, no little relief. At the thought of greater job security, obviously, but also at something more nebulous. The sense of order re-establishing itself perhaps, or maybe affirmation for the part of him that expected, even welcomed, defeat.

Immediately to his right were the art desks. There, strewn across one of the communal tables, were the early mock-ups of the Land Dominion partnership material, including the latest renders of the proposed stadium.

He picked up a mock-up of the interior of one of the corporate boxes which were to be clustered round the halfway line, their private bars and kitchens sealed off from the rest of the stadium by thick glass walls. Why anyone would want to watch football like that was beyond him, but in terms of revenue generation he could see that they would be a step up from the top-tier hospitality at the Chapel, which was basically a cushion on your seat and some microwaved vol-au-vents at half time.

Inspecting the images, with their happy-looking crowds thronging the stadium, Colin felt a longing to be on the side of the shiny and modern and slick. There was, he conceded, an argument for the ground. If the team went up, the demand for tickets would be massive and it wasn't as if the steroidal crassness of the Premier League had exactly led to a great crisis in its popularity. He experienced again the familiar feeling of helplessness at having been left behind. That morning, it had been announced that the land near the airport had been rezoned, its use class changed, paving the way for them to build a massive casino less than half a mile from the departure gates. Everywhere he looked people were looking for angles, cashing in. Everyone but him.

'Unbelievable, the changes, aren't they?'

It was Rick.

'Neil and the others, they're out-of-towners, they haven't lived here all their lives. Not like us.'

Three years in Leeds, thought Colin. And then another one in London, fifteen months if he was going to be pedantic about it.

'They don't know how exciting all this progress is for us local boys who've lived here all our lives with bugger all happening for years at a time.'

'Progress, is it?' said Colin huffily.

'Yeah,' said Rick. 'It is. And you know it. We both know it. And that's why we're going to run an editorial in support of the stadium move.'

'*What?*'

'I'm no great fan of Larkspur Hill but it is vital housing stock. And there's no way they can take down the Generator, the loss of face for the city would be too much. I've thought about it and the Grangeham plan is such a neat solution. It makes sense to move.'

The noise that emerged from Colin's mouth came from deep within him. Rick looked at him, alarmed and a little disgusted.

'I understand if this is a resigning issue for you, Colin. You've always been very principled and I admire that.'

'You're asking *me* to resign in protest at *your* ethical degradation?'

'No, I would never ask you to resign. That would be constructive dismissal, as I explained to the board. All I'm saying is that if you did resign, I'd understand.'

Standing there, on the institutional carpets of the Enterprise Cluster's fourth floor, its strip lights buzzing overhead, the air conditioning whirring, Colin experienced something new. It was a feeling of unexpected farsightedness, existential certainty. The universe was chaotic, random, essentially unnavigable. But for the first time he could see clearly what he had always somehow known: in the absence of any route through it and any meaningful destination, all you could do, in any given situation, was own the moment, try to be good.

'No. Fucking. Way,' he said, his voice wavering. 'You're not getting rid of me that easily. I'm going to fight this into the ground. That's just the way it's going to be, Rick. I don't have any choice. It's just what I have to do. You. Kirk. Neil. Pankaj fucking Shastry. You're all just going to have to accept that I am in this now and, come what may, I will see it out.'

32

The chairs in the Eclipse were like thrones, oversized, ornately patterned, the wooden frames veneered in green rubber, the upholstery a lurid pink. Ellie sat in one of them, sipping her cup of tea, feeling more than a little ridiculous.

According to the promotional material that was plastered on the walls, the Eclipse was an all-day venue, but its aesthetic was slanted squarely at the night-time economy. The bar was wrapped in cushioned silver leather and topped with chrome. The floor was black and white chequerboard, the walls extensively mirrored. Even completely empty, at 11.45 a.m. on a Thursday morning, you felt that at any point a couple might emerge from the disabled toilet hastily rearranging their clothes and sniffing suspiciously.

Ellie looked up at the statement Swarovski chandelier. The place was basically Broadcastle in miniature with all its bling and powder, its bad money and fast taste.

But at least it was conveniently located, equidistant from Create:Space's offices and Broadcastle station with its main line London-bound train. She was taking an early lunch so they could grab half an hour together before Pankaj headed south to vote.

Ellie toyed with her teaspoon, filled it with sugar, emptied it again. Already the thought of not seeing him for two nights left her feeling anxious, full of foreboding and a kind of pre-emptive yearning.

Every night that week he had come round after Daisy had gone to bed, waiting in his car until he was sure the street was empty before sneaking up to her front door, and together they had lain in bed, eating takeaway food. Every now and then she would retreat to the bathroom where she would sit on the loo and read Colin's texts, answering them all, even the really nasty ones, as gently as she could. It had worked. After a few days his anger seemed to have exhausted itself to the point where they could talk on the phone without risk of him crying.

They had decided not to tell Daisy – not until they had worked out what they were going to do, how they were going to live – and she appeared to have bought the line that Colin had moved out temporarily to help his mum look after his genuinely fragile dad, a fiction they had managed to maintain by having him return for a couple of stage-managed family dinners.

It wasn't exactly the blank page she had been looking for but it felt nonetheless like the start of a new chapter, in which she could begin to draw together the various strands of her life, find some kind of harmony, maintain her forward momentum.

Which was exactly what she needed to do with things moving at the pace that they were. In the last week alone, a reporter from *The Culture Show* had come to film a segment on the campaign, Herzog and De Meuron had written an op-ed for the *Guardian* demanding that the Larkspur be listed, and six thousand, four hundred and thirty-two more people had signed her petition.

The combined effect was propulsive. Each item of media exposure or show of support was a small step towards the ultimate end. Or at least the immediate end. The ultimate end was further ahead in her future, something even more exciting and ambitious, something that changed the game.

She experienced the vertiginous feeling of being on the cusp of something, that surge of adrenaline you felt just before you jumped. The mood board on her wall was a mass of pictures: the plug-in city, ancient ziggurats, Greenwich Village, container pileups, Louise Bourgeois metal frames, Kowloon Walled City, geodesics, Venetian canals. In the middle of it all she had written a single word: *SYNSTRUCTURA*, because once you put a name to something it became a thing.

She was dreaming into being a new kind of social housing.

313

Something skeletal and modular. A framework for a ground-up, user-designed, self-made architecture. Adaptable to any existing site, they would make for dense, eclectic urban spaces, but ones that were still unified, harmonious and beautiful.

Which had made her call to Suzie, the evening before, all the weirder. This was the woman who had always smiled her contained little smile whenever Ellie talked about work, who always managed to be so silently patronising about how much time she had taken off to raise Daisy. The woman who was forever banging the drum about the sisterhood and female ambition and the responsibility to live a dramatically lived life.

And now, here Ellie was, doing exactly what Suzie had always seemed to be chiding her for not doing – thinking big, being bold, articulating a clear vision – and what was Suzie's reaction?

'I kind of get it, but it sounds – I don't know – less like architecture and more like social policy. It all sounds very policy-heavy, is this his thing or is it yours?'

Ellie smarted again at the thought of it. So typical of her to read the whole thing through the prism of her relationship, like that would always be the thing that defined her.

She picked up her pot of tea, refilled her cup. OK, perhaps she had allowed things to tumble out of her about that week with Pankaj. The wisteria on the walls. The Provençal rosé. The linguine in earthenware bowls.

'Well, it certainly all sounds very Instagrammable.'

Which was fine. Whatever. Suzie's version of her own life – free-spirited, full of love affairs and intensity of feeling – was, to anyone capable of anything approaching an objective perspective, wildly at odds with the reality of her existence, which was characterised by long periods of problem drinking and internet oversharing, punctuated by the odd calamitous one-night stand.

But that was by the by. Suzie could do her damnedest, as she always did, to make Ellie feel inconsequential, but on this she was wrong: Pankaj, and everything he represented, was not a retreat from ambition but an embrace of it.

Ellie added a little milk, stirred it in. The thing for her to do now was to forget about it. Reading her existence through Suzie's eyes was simply another way of relinquishing control.

She heard the door and looked up. There he was, his coat folded across his arm, his leather briefcase bashed a bit at the corners, a flash of red socks visible beneath the hem of his trousers.

'Nice choice of venue,' she said with a raised eyebrow as he approached her table.

'I found it on Google,' said Pankaj, smiling broadly. 'What do you make of it?'

'Having had a good look at it,' she said, keeping it deadpan, 'I would say it's a late flowering of the Discount Chingford Rococo.'

Pankaj's laugh was deep, from the belly.

'It's part of the underappreciated third wave of the style. Note the counter-curving in lime-green acrylic.'

Ellie ran her finger along the arm of the throne.

'Beautiful,' said Pankaj.

'Yes, but I'm not sure how much longer I can cope with the floor. If you look at it too long it starts to pulse.'

'Shall we get out of here?'

'How long have you got?'

'Longer than I thought. Forty-five minutes. I need to get the twelve forty train.'

'Come on then. Let's go for a walk.'

'I know it's on our doorstep and everything but I hardly know Broadcastle at all. I basically just change trains here.'

'Right then, I'll show you around. It's massively over-fond of itself but it's not completely without merit.'

For twenty minutes they walked. Through the city centre with its Gothic Revival churches and fashion boutiques. They picked up take-away coffees and continued on, looking in shop windows, stopped to admire the High Victorian town hall. Eventually, they reached the landscaped park high up on the hill. They stood on one of its terraces, leaning on a wall looking down over the city.

'What are we doing?' she asked.

Pankaj turned to look at her, trying to get a sense of her mood.

'I have a kid,' she said.

'Whom I like very much.'

They had met, twice now, and he had been brilliant with her both times, meeting her at her level, listening to what she said, showing an interest in her world, taking Fresno seriously.

'Being with a kid all the time is very different from being an adored uncle who swoops in every now and then and takes them to the zoo and buys them stuff. There's a lot of discipline and homework and tedium.'

Pankaj shrugged his shoulders.

'I've always imagined that there would be children in my life,' he said. 'A young person whom I could care about and be useful to.'

He was staring out over the city while he talked, not looking at her.

'But I've never imagined myself with a baby,' he continued, running his finger contemplatively over his Adam's apple. 'And the older I get the less I can. I'm forty-two, my job is demanding and I don't know if I could cope with the sleeplessness and nappies and all the other stuff.'

Finally, he turned to her.

'What I mean is I don't look at you and think to myself: wouldn't it be better if she didn't have a kid. I think: how great that she already has a kid.'

Ellie felt a hot fiery thing blaze inside her. It was the thing that allowed you to get burned but it was also the furnace that propelled you forward, gave you your thrust.

She felt the back of his hand brush against hers, allowed his fingers to curl round hers, pull her towards the path. For a few minutes they walked hand-in-hand through the park without talking, enjoying the sun on their faces. Eventually, Pankaj looked at his watch.

'We should head back,' he said. 'I haven't bought my ticket yet.'

'We can cut through here,' she said, guiding him out through the wrought-iron gates.

They walked down a set of stone steps and turned into Station Approach with its pavement cafés and people. Pankaj let go of her hand. Ellie stopped, let him walk a few steps ahead of her. She tried to quiet her mind, still her tongue, but the question had to be asked.

'Really,' she said, 'what are we doing?'

Pankaj shrugged the tiniest of little shrugs.

'I want to say we're together but I don't want to be presumptuous ... I don't know quite how adults handle this transition. I think I might be too old to ask you if you want to go out with me. Is there a language for it when you're the wrong side of forty? Even 'girlfriend' sounds ridiculous. If we were in a John Hughes film, I would say we were going steady.'

'Together is good.'

'Good. Let's consider ourselves together.'

'Publicly?'

'Personally, I think it would be judicious not to indulge in any heavy petting on the Richardson Road, but, yes, if it's important to you, *publicly.*'

They were standing on the concourse at Broadcastle train station, people everywhere around them. Without taking his eyes from hers he leaned in, kissed her.

'See you later,' he said, smiling.

Pankaj walked away across the concourse without looking back.

The sun was high in the sky, the streets full of shoppers, office workers out for their lunch. She walked from the station with her spine straight, her shoulder blades rolled down her back.

The only drag on her life now was Colin, or more specifically her sense of responsibility to him. The three family dinners they had shared since the split had been excruciating, him performing a version of himself – wearing a shirt, drinking wine – that he thought might win her back. The effort of it all had been hard to watch.

Unable, or at least unwilling, to give him what he really wanted she had determined to do the next best thing: she would save the Chapel. His obsession with the Grangeham site had caused him to miss the solution hiding in plain sight: the Generator. Something about Yvonne's balance sheet had been niggling away at her but she hadn't been able to work out what. And then, finally, it had dawned on her: the cleaners. They had been there, two of them, cleaning the Generator, when she was there. She had noticed them because of their distinctive orange polo shirts, worn by all employees of Rapid Clean, the contractor that also supplied cleaners for the Create:Space offices and the rest of the Landgate Plaza.

Back at her desk, she turned on her laptop and opened the balance sheet. The Generator's outgoings had seemed suspiciously low and now she knew why. On the evidence in front of her, no payments were being made to Rapid Clean. And if there was one omission from the costings, there was likely a whole lot more. Ellie smiled. This was how she could make it good. This was the way to wipe the slate clean.

33

The men from the council were going at it with pressure cleaners, the kind built to blast old chewing gum from paving slabs, but the smeary brown trace of the tar wouldn't shift and you could still read it easily from a hundred yards away: WROTH, written in letters as tall as a man on the side of the town hall.

Colin walked across New Square to join the handful of people who had stopped to watch the attempted clean-up. In just four days there had been at least another fifteen Wroth actions. Mostly it had been graffiti. All of it in tar, and – until the town hall had been hit – all of it aimed at Kirk and his various businesses. But there had been letters in the post, too. Three that had been made public, and surely more to people who were yet to admit it. The one Colin had seen had been put together like an old-school ransom note, the letters cut from newspaper pages. It had been sent to an executive at Moolah demanding that he cease all efforts to move the club from the Chapel and cancel all debts outstanding. The sign-off suggested that there was more to come:

As will be visited upon you,
Major Wroth

Colin watched the cleaners scrub at the tarred stonework with metal brushes and felt a shivery thrill at the thought of the night-time sortie the graffiti would have necessitated. Men in masks with buckets and brushes. Secret cells. A great underground network of dissenters, of which he couldn't help but feel, at least tangentially, a part.

He understood from conversations he had had with some of

319

the Partisans – all of whom were vociferous in their support of the movement without ever going so far as to admit to any actual involvement – that Wroth was a collective nom de guerre, as it had been in the nineteenth century. A mantle that could be taken up by anyone acting in the service of the cause, ensuring that the movement was leaderless and anonymous, with no centralised organisational structure and therefore impossible to infiltrate.

Colin took a photo of the graffiti with his phone and walked off towards the office. Thirty-five people were now sleeping in tents outside the Chapel and a guerrilla campaign had been launched against one of the town's most powerful companies. In *Peterdown* of all places, where nothing had happened for ever and now everything was happening all at once.

He set off across the square feeling oddly buoyant. By almost any metric, it had been an awful week. He had ended up sending Ellie at least twenty-five ever-crazier text messages, frothing himself up into a crescendo of rage, until he had woken up on Wednesday morning to find his anger had exhausted itself. Emotionally spent and deeply embarrassed, he finally put down his phone. Things at the *Post* had reached a new low. He was still living with his mum.

Despite all this, could it be possible, he wondered, that a certain skill set – literal-minded obduracy, Olympic-level fatalism, a form of epically resentful but nonetheless unyielding forbearance – might, after all, be exactly what was required, given the situation? If you had to pick a side to fight a doomed rearguard action on three fronts – romantically, professionally, politically – Colin Ryder would surely be the first name on the team sheet.

He reached the centre of the square and its blocky war memorial. A couple of drunks sat on its low plinth while three skateboarding teenagers clacked and clattered up and down its steps. Colin paused. It was an unlovely place. Red-brick and sharp-edged with an overabundance of once bright-yellow street furniture, it had been redesigned during the town's early nineties nadir and barely touched since. *Municipal eschatologism* was how Ellie had once described it, *designed to usher in the end times.*

Despite this low bar there was, Colin had noticed recently, something even more forlorn than usual about the place. The clock in the tower was stopped, the public toilets chained shut. It was almost as if the square itself was aware that the flowering of the Peterdown Spring one mile away, at some odd non-space outside the Chapel, was the ultimate confirmation of its own decline.

His phone rang. It was Kerry.

'You might want to check your email,' she said as soon as he answered.

Since she had reappeared there had been an extra bounce to their encounters, an uplift to the end of her sentences, a sort of playfulness. It wasn't exactly flirting, but it was definitely something worth noting, a thing to muse on in difficult moments.

'What is it?' he shouted awkwardly at the phone as he simultaneously pawed at its screen, opening first his inbox and then the email.

'It's a letter from Scott McKee, he's the head of sales at Land Dominion but in reality he works across all of Kirk's interests. I found it in a shared Dropbox that they don't seem to realise I've got access to.'

'What does it say?'

'It's to the Football Association asking them to waive their stipulation that the new stadium be no more than forty-five minutes on public transport from the old stadium.'

'You're kidding.'

'He says it would compromise the affordability matrix.'

The file finished downloading and Colin opened it. His first impression was that it was kosher. The headed paper, McKee's signature clearly visible at the bottom of the screen.

'All that talk about building a tram out there,' said Kerry. 'He must have had a reckoning about the cost.'

'So you're saying he wants to pull out of his commitment to help fund the public transport to his new development?'

'That's what it looks like.'

'Is there a response from the FA?'

'Not that I can see.'

'This is dynamite. There's no way the council can let that development go ahead if he's not going to stump up for the public transport. I mean, there's no way.'

'I'm your knight in shining armour, aren't I?'

The image that this involuntarily conjured in Colin's mind was one in which the Arthurian legend had become commingled with that of Lady Godiva and the kind of fancy dress that he imagined a certain kind of woman wore to American Halloween parties. He blushed. Not so much at the lewdness of the image but at its astonishing bad taste.

Two hours later, Colin was standing at Rick's desk watching him read his piece calling for a full council inquiry into the funding of the transport links to the Grangeham site. Through the glass walls of Rick's office he could see the rest of his colleagues glancing nervously at him, each one of them looking away as soon as he caught their eye.

Since the vote on the partnership with Land Dominion, his position in the office had been one of embattled isolation. Nobody offered him a cup of tea when they got up to make one (a snub which he showily reciprocated). He had been pointedly not invited to Hugh's after-work birthday drinks. Kelly-Anne had stopped following him on Twitter.

Rick looked up over his glasses.

'Where are you getting all these things?'

'A good source. Top level.'

'Yeah, *who*?'

'A protected source.'

'Oh, for god's sake, Colin. Don't be so suspicious. I'm not going to tell anyone who it is.'

'No, you're not.'

Rick sat back in his chair pressing the fingertips of one hand against the fingertips of the other.

'You know you're making it very difficult for me to be supportive of this.'

'This is big news. Locally, this is *big* news. The only question we need to ask is do we want to hold it for the paper, or run it online now?'

Colin knew that this was not a moment to overplay his hand, but he was aware too where Rick's weaknesses lay, where he might be needled.

'Don't forget, Rick, you ran that editorial based on your own dispassionate judgement, didn't you? Because you're not beholden to him.'

'No, I'm not.'

'Then let's just bloody publish it.'

Rick sat forward, fixed Colin a look.

'NEIL,' he shouted.

Instantly, he was in the doorway like some malign conjured spirit.

'Cast your eye over this.'

Neil took the piece of paper and leaned against the wall as he read it. Colin watched for a tell, a giveaway flash of recognition. Neil read on, dispiritingly impassive.

'We've got to go to them for right of reply,' he said when he was done. 'You can't print it before you do. It's standard practice. The *Sun*. *Mirror*. Everyone does it.'

Rick shrugged.

'Let's get in touch with him for comment.'

Colin felt his nostrils flare. He looked hard at Neil.

'Fine,' he said. 'They've got twenty-four hours.'

STEAMING IN: A PODCAST WITH MICK CLARIDGE AND STEVE WANLESS BROADCAST LIVE FROM THE PETERDOWN SPRING

ORIGINALLY AIRED 3 p.m.
FRIDAY, APRIL 4th

MICK

So, welcome to *Steaming In*. This is a special show today.

STEVE

An outside broadcast.

MICK

For any of you that don't know, me and Steve have been out camping for the last couple of weeks. Leading lights of the Peterdown Spring, we are. The Vale's answer to Fidel and Che. A couple of revolutionaries under canvas. You know the sort of thing. All the men wanted to be them. All the women wanted to be with them. It's a shame we've only got a two-man. Beating them off otherwise, we would be.

STEVE
(laughing)
There's been nowt being beaten off in our tent, not while I've been in there. Can't speak for you, mind.

MICK

Anyway, we're camping, which is why we've gone
quiet. For some reason it never occurred to us
that you could do this outside. But it turns out
you can. And it's exactly the same only with more
pigeons. So we thought we'd do something a bit
different. Because, you know, there's seventy of
us at the last count. Heroes, every one. And all
of them with something to say. So we thought we'd
set up a recording booth in the camp library so
as people can have a bit of a chat. A bit like the
Big Brother room. Say what they've got to say.

STEVE

So here they are, the people of Peterdown. The
vox populi.

TOMMY QUINN, 57, AND TERRY MAC, 59

My name is Tommy Quinn. I'm sitting here with
Terry Mac. I'd say he was going to chip in and
all, but he probably won't 'cos he's not exactly
talkative, our Terry. Anyways, we've both been
Steam since we were lads. I first went to Chapel
in 1971, Terry the year after, and we've had all
kinds of wonderful memories out of the place but
this is something else. The atmosphere. The way
people are chipping in together, getting things
done. You would think there's nowt to it but
seventy people need a lot of food and they produce
a lot of piss and that needs organising and we've
all chipped in — it's been amazing.

And we've got something big planned for
tomorrow. Can I say what it is?

(inaudible murmur in the background)

No, I can't apparently. But it's gonna be mint, I can tell you. People are going to go mad for it. Because what's happening here, it's already caught the imagination of football people everywhere. I've heard fans are seriously talking about doing something similar in Blackpool, Blackburn, down at Charlton. And we've had all kinds of support from all over. People sending cash to cover those that are missing shifts and the like. Local businesses sending us food and drink. People donating blankets. There's too many to thank them all but I would like to put in a mention here for Old Nick Hunter. He lives above the newsagent's on Radleigh Road. He's lived there forty years or something. Anyway, he's been letting us take showers in his bathroom. We've said we'll chuck in for his gas but he's not had a bar of it. He's even gone and bought more towels 'cos the ones he had were always sodden by the time the last people got in. Seventy-eight, he is, and not a young one either. Remembers standing on the terraces when Archie Floyd scored four against Wolves in 1956. What a bloke. Seventy-eight years old and having a load of lads troop through your bathroom three times a week.

But he's not the only one. Honestly, the work that's gone into this, it's incredible . . .

(inaudible murmur in the background)

What was that? Ha, ha. Talking of work, Terry wants it to be known that if anyone from the Department of Work and Pensions is listening that he's been actively seeking it.

(inaudible murmur in the background)

Three steps every week. Ha ha! He's been building his CV, working on developing his transferable skills. He says he's getting proper good at the crochet on the banners but they still don't want him at Dolce and Gabbana. Ha ha! What can you do, eh? What can you do?

LESLEY SHERIDAN, 32

Hiya, my name's Lesley Sheridan. I've been here since day five, camping with my sister, Helen. Twin sister. She's been telling me not to come on this because I won't be able to control my feelings. And I came in here with the idea that I'd be able to keep myself in check. But already I can tell that it's not going to work. What can I say? There comes a time when you just have to get it out there, get it off your chest.

(voice cracking)

'Cos we've fucked it, haven't we? OK, we beat Sunderland. But, Christ, they were *awful*. It's the performance against Plymouth that was the real disaster. I mean, we get one injury at the back and we have to bring on a midfielder to play in the heart of the defence because the squad's so thin.

I don't care about Moolah or any of that shit that everyone gets all worked up about here. I care about results. About promotion. Paul Christie's the best manager in the division. Everyone knows it. We don't go up and he'll have Premier League clubs crawling all over him for what he's done with us. With our squad, on our budget, he's worked bloody miracles. And of course he'll walk when he's getting no backing here. It's terrible to say it but it's true. This is a once in a lifetime opportunity for us to go up . . .

(voice cracking again)

. . . and he's fucked it. Kirk has. If he'd given Christie some support in the transfer market we'd be proper contenders but he's come in and he's fucked it. And now we're ninth. And Coventry are getting on a run and we've not got a hope in hell of catching QPR or Bolton.

(shouting)

He's just shafted us. Plain and simple, shafted us. Every man and his dog could see this was going to be our season. Our proper shot at it. And where all the problems were. We've got a League Two right back, no disrespect to him, he's an honest lad, but he's way out of his depth. And nowhere near enough creativity in midfield. And there's no cover for Jordan. And we've got Kirk there who's picked us up for a quid, that's all he's spent and all I want him to do is FUCK OFF. JUST FUCK OFF.

FRANKIE KERR, 26
Hello, my name is Frankie Kerr. I'm going to read out a prepared statement on behalf of the Peterdown Partisans.

The Peterdown Partisans are ultras and we make no apology for it. We take our inspiration from fellow ultras movements in Germany and

328

Italy, who help to create some of the most thrilling atmospheres in European football, a world away from the prawn sandwich brigades who dominate the Premier League. We stand against the corporate takeover of football and exist to battle the forces massing against ordinary football fans — the government, the Sun newspaper, Sky television — before they snuff out what is left of Britain's terrace culture.

Ignore the lies being spread about by the RPUFG. Being an ultra is not synonymous with being a hooligan. We are anti-hooligan. And anti-violence.

And anti-fascist. Always and forever anti-fascist. We have witnessed the poisonous influence of the EDL as they make inroads on the nation's terraces — any attempt to sow division among the United fans will be met by organised resistance.

We are anti-fascist but we are pro-noise. Pro-banners. Pro-drums. Pro-flares. We stand together at the heart of the Radleigh to ensure that Chapel remains the most intimidating ground to play at in the country. We don't want sanitised, sterile football. We want a cauldron.

Finally, we feel it necessary to address the speculation that the Major Wroth protests are the work of the Partisans. Nothing could be further from the truth. To imagine the Wroth actions as simply the work of a single group would be to grossly misread the situation. Wroth is so much more than that. It is a letter of intent from the wretched of the earth. A save-the-date for the coming insurrection. The poltergeist in the machine.

We're just a bunch of football fans, cheering it on from the sidelines.

JENNY SMITH, 40

Hello. My name's Jenny Smith. I'm here because I want to talk about my dad, Alfie Smith. He first took me to the Chapel when I was five. And it's because of him that I'm here, in my tent. It's not been easy. I've taken holiday that was owing to me and I've cut back on shifts, which isn't easy when you've got rent to pay, but I felt I had to be here. Because he would have loved this. He would have been here, for sure, camping. I know he would. The Chapel meant so much to him. It was where he was happiest. Walking around the stadium with him was like walking around with a celebrity, everyone would stop and say hello or share a joke with him, ask him what new chants he'd come up with. Because he was the first person to sing 'Going to the Chapel' on the Radleigh. His version was for Barry Burns, who played for United in the sixties, before I was born.

He had a terrible singing voice, my dad. Completely tone deaf, but he was very imaginative, very funny. He was always coming up with chants, jokes for the terraces. He used to write them up at home. Practise them while we were eating our tea. Swear words and all. My mum pretending to be appalled at it but she couldn't help but laugh along because he was a poet when it came to swearing, my dad, he just had an ear for it.

And I think it's why he was such a big presence on the terraces. He was so creative. Always wanting to be doing something, to be involved, have a sense of purpose.

(pause)

It was different after the plant shut. He never
recovered from it. He was so proud. He couldn't
be seen out. Stopped going to the Chapel. Stopped
everything.

(pause)

It's funny being in here and just talking to no
one. You find yourself saying all kind of things
that you didn't think you would.

(pause)

All I know is I miss him terribly. And I know
other people do, too. Because they come up to me
all the time. How chuffed he would have been that
we were singing his song for Jordan now. How much
Dad would have loved watching him play.

(falters)

I don't even think he meant to do it. I think it
was just a cry for help. Oh god, he should have
been here. He so should have been here. He was
only fifty-eight. He should have been here. He
would have loved it . . .

34

The Peterdown Marina sat on the south side of the River Peter, the local hub of a network of canals stretching in one direction out to Broadcastle and in the other to the old Grangeham forge and beyond. From where he was standing, Colin could see only the first of the marina's three basins, the one reserved for touring canal boaters. With its weeping willows at the water's edge and cute mooring shed, it had pretensions to pastoral idyll that were only partly thwarted by the tower blocks that loomed distantly over the tops of the trees. Still, its berths were full of period boats that had been immaculately restored, their polished brass fittings lustrous even in the last of the evening sun.

He walked along the side of the Peter, looking across the water at the retiree owners of these touring boats. Some of them sat on their decks, others on foldaway chairs by the water's edge. They were reading paperbacks, eating sandwiches; all of them exuding a fastidiously English form of propriety, the sort that takes its fullest expression in clipped Tupperware, beige leisurewear, sensibly small gin and tonics.

The particular kind of contempt that Colin felt for these people was the sort that can only be born out of a sense of deep identification and informed self-hatred and so he hurried past the first basin, doing his best not to have his head turned by the muted strains of Radio 2, the wordsearch puzzle books, the hush and the calm; the whole thing's exquisite mildness.

He reached the mouth of the Eastfinche Canal, crossed the footbridge and started up the towpath in the shadow of the old warehouses that lined the water. After a few hundred yards he turned right down a smaller tributary to the second basin, with its two large finger pontoons pointing out into the water. These were permanent moorings, home to dozens of boats in various states of repair. Some were smart, sleek and orderly. Others less so. Pot plants withered on their roofs, plumes of smoke rose from wood-burning stoves, paint peeled, plastic bags pressed against windows.

The sun completed its descent behind the treeline and the basin settled into a hazy, crepuscular calm. Colin reached its far corner where he saw Rodbortzoon ambling up the path. He had two packets of cigarettes in his hand and had dressed so that his gut spilled provocatively over the top of his trousers, an unapologetic declaration of his inexhaustible appetite for everything and all the world. Under his creased jacket, he was wearing a T-shirt that bore a single frame of a *Peanuts* strip. In the speech bubble coming from Charlie Brown's mouth it said: *My idols are dead and my enemies are in power.*

He knew Rodbortzoon's preferred greeting involved three cheek-to-cheek kisses, but even in the quiet of the marina, away from the macho expectations of the terraces or the back room of the Geoffrie, this was simply beyond him. As always, the thought of a handshake felt too formal and Rodbortzoon was a generation too old for the contemporary clinch, and so they settled, as they so often did, on a kind of ironic but affectionate nod.

'So which one is it?' asked Colin, looking out across the pontoons. They were attending the marina's monthly poker night, famed for its high stakes, home-brewed alcohol and frequent fist fights.

'This is the second basin,' said Rodbortzoon dismissively. 'A place for dilettantes. Part-timers. *Weekenders.* Nobody important lives here. We're going to the third basin.'

He hopped up on to the paddle beam of the nearby lock and sauntered across it without looking down at the water that rushed darkly below him.

'So I have told you before about the community,' said Rodbortzoon as he took two practised steps before swinging his considerable bulk over a low brick wall.

'Many times,' said Colin as he struggled over, 'but I don't think I've ever actually been listening.'

'It could be your epitaph: he lived in interesting times but he just wasn't paying attention.'

'Whatever.'

Rodbortzoon stopped, lowered his voice.

'So I have lived here for ten years. A long time, you think. But no. I am a tenderfoot. 1990 is the year zero. The year of riots and baton charges, running battles with the police. Back then, in the Vale of Peter there was no poll tax on a barge and so they came here. And they have never left.'

'They've all been here, living on a boat for nearly thirty years just to avoid paying council tax?'

'Everyone except the Admiral. He was here way before. Maybe his whole life. Who knows? The Admiral transcends biography.'

They emerged from a tree-lined stretch of the path into a clearing. Colin stopped. The thirty or so boats in the third basin existed in what looked to be a state of permanent agglomeration, the barges tied fast to each other so that they tessellated, or at least nearly tessellated. Jerry-built extensions, some two storeys tall, spanned two or three boats at a time, the walls thick with graffiti, lurid murals. Walkways had been fashioned from pallets and ropes. One deck was home to an open grill. Another, a fire burning in a brazier. Everywhere there were plants in pots, old oil drums, planting bags. The whole thing was lit by bulbs on strings that hung from poles nailed lopsidedly to the cabins. On the roof of one boat, a woman was playing a cello. People stood on their decks, drinking. The mood was tipsy, good-humoured, vaguely piratical.

'Bloody hell,' said Colin. 'I wasn't expecting white bread suburbia but this is . . .'

'Home,' said Rodbortzoon. 'Come. The game is about to begin.'

He led Colin on to the deck of the nearest boat, up a gangplank, under a stretched tarpaulin, past a man smoking a hookah pipe, down a rope ladder and into an open-plan barge. The room was scattered with large floor cushions. On the walls were Moroccan throws, and candle lanterns hung from the ceiling. Around a low wooden table, four people were sitting on cushions, shuffling cards, drinking and smoking cigarettes.

'Is this your place?' whispered Colin disbelievingly.

'No,' said Rodbortzoon. 'I am four barges along. The game moves about. Tonight, Seeta is hosting.'

Seeta was in her late forties. She had jet-black hair, heavily kohled eyes, rings on every finger.

'Texas hold 'em,' she said. 'Two in the pocket, five on the deck.'

'Right,' said Colin. 'I think I just about know how to play that.'

'Forty quid buy-in.'

He looked at Rodbortzoon, incredulous.

'Forty quid?' he mouthed.

Rodbortzoon looked back, unimpressed.

'You are new. You pay the new person buy-in.'

Colin groaned, but pulled two twenties from his wallet and chucked them on to the table.

'Right,' said Seeta, as she started dealing out the cards. 'Let's do this.'

Forty minutes and four hands later, Colin was enjoying himself. There were, he knew, effectively two games going on simultaneously. There was the one being played by his five opponents, which was full of bluffs and feints, card counting, close reading of tells and twitches. And then there was the one that he was playing, which was to fold at random, back bad hands, go all in on a whim. To everyone else's great irritation, Colin was up and they were all down.

Next to him sat Janine, a compact woman in her early fifties. She was an indecisive player, worrying at her pile of chips, only ever deciding whether or not to play at the very last second. To her left was Seeta, who had already made two trips to the bathroom, coming back each time a little janglier than she had left. Next to her was Pasquale, an Italo-Scot who, as far as Colin could tell, did a lot of the cooking for the community. He was wearing a shell suit in powder blue and pale pink, with a pair of two-tone leather wingtips, the shoes of a dapper villain from the 1920s, which he was evidently enormously proud of and cleaned constantly, licking his finger and wiping away imagined smudges. He seemed to be losing money he didn't have and was a muttering, frustrated presence.

Next to him was Rodbortzoon, and next to Rodbortzoon was Trench. Trench was forty-something, with long hair and a thick beard. He was missing part of his left ear. He spoke slowly but at great length and intimated long periods of absence from the community. Possibly because he had been in prison. But equally possibly because he had been in the Caucasus or somewhere, helping to establish a breakaway republic in exchange for a suitcase of cash.

Trench was wearing a singlet which revealed a tattoo that covered the whole of his right arm. It was abstract, boldly patterned, like the cover of a 1960s jazz record. It was the kind of tattoo that Colin would have had, he felt, if the idea of him having a tattoo wasn't so ridiculous.

Completing the circle, sitting on a low chair between Trench and Colin, was the Admiral, who wasn't at all what Colin had been expecting. From the way Rodbortzoon talked about him – as the community's founding father, its central charismatic force – he had been expecting a great big lump of a man, bald and sweating in the semi-darkness like Brando's Kurtz. But he was a neat little thing: clean shaven, sensible hair, a knitted tank top over a button-down shirt. His powerful pull came not from his appearance but from his muteness. He knocked the table to pass, chucked in chips, nodded. But he didn't speak. Not a word.

'Four to stay in,' said Pasquale.

'Fold,' said Trench, chucking his cards on the table in front of him.

The Admiral shook his head.

Colin took four chips and put them on the pile in the middle of the table.

'I'll see what you've got,' he said.

Seeta turned over her cards. Two pairs.

'Three of a kind,' said Colin, throwing his hand on to the table.

Rodbortzoon shook his head, disgusted.

'You had three of a kind and you didn't raise.'

Colin swept up the chips on the table. The record had stopped playing. Five columns of cigarette smoke rose in the still air.

'What do you lot *do*?' he said, emboldened by the booze and his winnings, which he was gleefully arranging into neat colour-coordinated stacks.

The Admiral exhaled. Seeta gathered together the discarded cards and started shuffling them back into the pack.

'What do we *do*?' she said archly, dealing out another hand. 'I'll tell you what we *do*. We choose not to define ourselves according to the dismal hierarchies of bourgeois culture.'

'We don't have occupations,' said Trench. 'We have preoccupations.'

'But how do you survive?'

'Bits and pieces,' said Trench. 'Odds and ends.'

'We grow food, cook communally, waste nothing,' said Pasquale.

'One of the moorings comes with estover rights to the Mawson Estate.'

'Estover?'

'We can collect wood from their forest. It's an ancient right and they can't take it away from us even though they'd love to. It means we have all the fuel we need.'

Colin picked his two cards from the table and looked at them. Ridiculously, he had a king and an ace for the second time that evening.

'And so what about you, Stakhanov?' said Trench. 'What is it you do that so declares you to the world?'

'I'm the sports correspondent for the *Peterdown Evening Post*,' said Colin, drunk on homebrew and remembering how he really did like the ring of it.

'You get paid to watch football?'

'Yeah, actually, I do.'

Trench turned over his hand to reveal four letters inked on the inside of his wrist:

P.U.F.C.

He smiled at Colin.

'And there's you making a big thing of none of us having a proper job.'

A few hours later Colin jerked awake. Rodbortzoon was standing above him.

'Good morning, Sailor.'

Colin looked at his watch. 4 a.m. He felt a sensation in his head like the cracking of an Arctic ice sheet.

'How long have I been asleep?'

'I don't know. You weren't missed. We were talking about our sexual encounters as teenagers. You would have had nothing to contribute.'

Colin rubbed the sleep from his eyes and looked about the room. At some point he must have made his way to what was clearly Rodbortzoon's barge. Every available surface had been used as a dumping ground: piles of clothes, stacks of books, scattered records, empty bottles. What carpet you could see appeared to be covered in blooms of algae. He had never seen so many ashtrays.

'I like what you've done with the place,' he said, letting his head sink back into the pillow.

'OK,' said Rodbortzoon, as he pulled a chair up to the bed, sat on it and poured himself a glass of wine. 'Time for deal-making. You want to see what I have to show you? I want a little something in return. A bit of commitment.'

'I'm already in a relationship. Sorry.'

'Ha. Ha. Ha,' laughed Rodbortzoon, wiping away a tear. 'It's funny 'cos it's not true.'

Colin shut his eyes. What was there to say? Rodbortzoon was right. He was no longer in a relationship. Which meant he was alone. But it also meant he was free. Or at least as free as he ever felt.

'I want you to move to the camp.'

Colin groaned. It had been coming.

'It is the perfect solution,' continued Rodbortzoon. 'How much longer can you stay at your parents' without Daisy realising? This solves all your problems. You move to the camp and your absence from the house is recast as a lion making a heroic stand, not a snake slithering off, accepting defeat.'

'OK,' said Colin.

'OK?'

'OK,' said Colin. 'I'll come.'

'Just like that?'

'Just like that.'

'Today?'

Colin shrugged.

'Today,' he said wearily.

'Very nice,' said Rodbortzoon, downing his wine. 'Right then, let's go.'

'Let's go where?'

'To see what we have to see.'

Colin levered himself off the sofa and followed Rodbortzoon up through the barge door. Behind them, Seeta's boat still glowed with life but ahead of them the towpath was silent and still, silhouettes of black on black.

'So Ferdinando, when he drinks a lot, he snores. And not just little snores. And so we agreed – as a group – that when he drinks more than one bottle of wine he must sleep away from the rest of us,' said Rodbortzoon, pulling back the branches so Colin could follow him between two giant buddleias.

Ahead of them he could just about make out the contours of a tent that had been pitched in a small clearing. Above the trees he could see the top floors of the Larkspur's towers.

'Ferdinando is not so much a young man any more and when he drinks he needs to pee in the night. And recently when he has been peeing in the night he has been seeing some funny things.'

Rodbortzoon took Colin to the edge of a bramble patch, and peered over in the direction of the estate.

'See the two men over there? With the tripod.'

'What are they doing? Taking photos?'

'That's not a camera. That's what you English call a dumpy level. They're surveyors. This is a little wasteland. You can't really see it from the estate. If you wanted to connect the site up to the Goods Line it's essential ground. Ferdinando saw them yesterday. That was the fourth time. This is the fifth. He says they come at three a.m. and are gone at five a.m.'

Colin shimmied round the bramble patch to a gap in the bushes which he squeezed through into a small clearing. From there, he could see the dark contours of the Larkspur's ancillary buildings, its electricity exchange, a run of garages, a shuttered-looking outhouse. And in front of them, running on the perfect horizontal, were two thin beams of green light that cut through the dark, precise and unbroken, like high-tech trip wires guarding an invaluable prize.

'They're not wearing high-vis or any uniform and they are working at night. Why? Because they are measuring up the Larkspur for a big project that they don't want anyone to know about,' said Rodbortzoon, his voice devoid of any triumphalism. 'Bad news for the fair Eleanor, I'm afraid, but good news for the Chapel.'

35

The Broadcastle Greenacre was Britain's fourth largest shopping mall, eclipsed only by the Greenacres in Salford, Solihull and London's Kensal Rise. Like all the others it was owned by a Canadian mining corporation, and like all the others it stood alone, a citadel in glass and steel, surrounded by expensively manicured gardens.

It was Saturday morning. Daisy was on a play date and Ellie had come in search of a new pair of trainers. She walked through the Greenacre gardens – past fruit trees and fountains, beds of tulips in yellow, purple and red – noting the unobtrusiveness of its fortifications: the moats to ward off ram raiders, the bollards built into bedding planters, the subtle struts on the benches to deter skaters and rough sleepers. She couldn't help but think that this kind of hyperdefensiveness, which was ubiquitous but also denied at every turn, represented, at least unconsciously, the shopping mall's cringing sense of its own fundamental culpability.

She walked through the towering entrance into the main concourse where the high-fashion stores were clustered in the best spots: a split-level Armani, a sprawling Dolce & Gabbana, and a Versace, its window display decked out in Swarovski crystals. The mall had been open for two years but still she found it remarkable that these shops were here, in the Vale of Peter. Who shopped in them she had no idea, but their very presence had become a source of civic pride, even to those who could never afford to buy anything, evidence of Broadcastle's elevation to international status.

With a kind of forlorn sympathy, she thought of Peterdown and its own mall, the Capricorn. It had a Ted Baker and a Primark. But the only Italian fashion available came from the Neapolitan Suit Company, which – according to the huge banners that dominated its windows – had been in the final weeks of its closing down sale for the entire time she had lived in the city.

Ahead of her a young mother paused, her bags resting on the ground, while her two kids took turns to slide down the back of a wooden tortoise. To her right, a family were sitting on two benches, talking idly, passing back and forth between them a large bag of sunflower seeds.

Ellie felt a sudden sense of unease, a pinch of anxiety. Everything about the Greenacre screamed *non-place*. The deliberate hyper-blandness of its design. The paranoiac and controlling layout. The pervasive sense of transience and affectlessness. It was, conceptually, the opposite of everything that was meaningful and good.

And yet.

She looked first left and then right at the two groups of teenage boys eyeing each other suspiciously. If all this had been taking place in a sixteenth-century Veronese piazza you would have identified it immediately as a lived environment, pulsing with authentic life.

She made her way distractedly to the back of the mall to a favourite shop of hers where she found herself buying the first pair of trainers she tried on, leaving her plenty of time to grab some lunch.

The Greenacre food hall was a vast circular space with a dozen different concessions spaced evenly around its perimeter and a huge pool of collective seating in the middle. Its aesthetic was Greco-Roman: vines creeping up columns, marble tops, faux ruins. She texted Pankaj as she waited in line for a falafel wrap.

Twenty minutes later, having eaten half the wrap and all but finished the *Guardian* quick crossword, she sipped the last of her carrot juice and allowed herself another look at her phone. Still no response.

She felt the unease between her vertebrae, a sense of things being misaligned that no amount of cracking could relieve. It was the first time that things had been difficult between them and it felt horrible to know that it was her fault.

She thought back awkwardly to the evening before. It had turned out that they had different lists of peoples about whom you were allowed to be xenophobic. Over their weeks together, disparaging generalisations about the Swiss (him), Canadians (her) and the French (both of them *ad nauseam*) had solicited delighted whoops of laughter; but the night before she had discovered that, flying in the face of all reason, his list didn't include *Australians*, and he had taken genuine umbrage at an admittedly tasteless joke about Michael Hutchence and Steve Irwin, derailing their whole evening.

She picked up her phone and looked at the archive of their text messages. The last in the thread, sent twenty-two minutes earlier, was from her:

At the food hall in the Broadcastle Greenacre. Ionic columns
+ pulled pork BBQ doughnuts = vision of the agora under
totalitarianism? Xx

Classical allusion. Absurd made-up fast food. Mordant social commentary. If ever there was a text that was going to be catnip to him, it was this. And yet. Twenty-two minutes on and still no response. This from a man who had FaceTimed her during a debate in the House of Commons.

Around her, the food hall carried on; children were scolded, orders were shouted, burgers sizzled on the grill. She pulled a piece of cucumber from the remains of her wrap and ate it pensively.

'They're better in your café.'

Ellie looked up. It was Lindsey from the estate. With the pound-coin gap between her front teeth. She was gesturing down at the wrap. The look on her face was hesitant and embarrassed.

'When have you had a sandwich in the Larkspur café?' asked Ellie softly. 'I thought they were for mugs.'

'I never said that,' said Lindsey, looking away as she said it. 'That was Danielle. That wasn't me.'

She was wearing the fur collar of her gold lamé coat up, over her head, even though they were inside. Her hair had been scraped violently back, her eyebrows pencilled high up her forehead.

'So you've been back?'

'Yeah, on me own. You wasn't there. The other girl was working. It was all right, you know.'

'Thanks.'

Lindsey paused, evidently uncertain if all this constituted enough of an apology.

'Do you want to join me?' asked Ellie. 'I've nearly finished this but I was planning on getting a coffee and a cinnamon bun. If you're not in a hurry I could get you one too.'

And so they sat together and talked, a little uneasily at first, then, when they moved to the topic of their children, with greater fluency and then, realising that they shared a deep well of despairing anecdotes about headstrong daughters, with something approaching genuine warmth.

'I can see why you're doing what you're doing but you're going to get people wound up having the MP involved,' said Lindsey, eventually.

'You think?'

'He's not from round here.'

Ellie smarted.

'What do you mean by that?' she asked irritably.

For a second their eyes locked.

'It's not racist,' said Lindsey forcefully.

Her way of engaging with the world seemed to involve hastily raising defensive barriers, which, in order to maintain dialogue, she then had to publicly and laboriously scale herself.

'Look at his clothes,' she continued, more softly, 'the way he talks. I bet he's never had someone come round and take his fridge 'cos they've had a loan and then couldn't pay it back.'

'Moolah?'

'Yeah.'

'The parasites.'

'It was for shoes.'

'Exactly. What do they expect? You to walk barefoot?'

'Not ones I needed.'

Ellie gave a shrug of solidarity that was designed to communicate that she too had, on more than one occasion, bought shoes that she couldn't afford.

Lindsey clenched her jaw.

'I mean, he's just so obviously not from here.'

Ellie felt the irritation blooming in her like ink in water. What was it with these people that they put such stock in being from round here?

'Oh, come on,' she said. 'That's rubbish and you know it. There are loads of people from Peterdown that look just like him. People that were born here. People whose parents were born here.'

'Are there fuck. There's loads of . . .' she looked pointedly at Ellie, '*Asians*. But they don't look like him. They work down cash and carry. They wear shit clothes. You look at him and you don't think he works down cash and carry, do you?'

Ellie blushed and looked away, disgusted at herself. She had seen it so many times in her mother, the rigidity of her assumptions, her iron faith in her own superiority. It had been a source of mortification throughout her childhood, listening to the woman dismiss people for nothing. For the way they held a fork. For watching ITV. For liking Puccini.

'His clothes look better than a woman's do,' continued Lindsey. 'Until I saw him with you, I thought he was a poof.'

Ellie sat back in her chair, assailed by the news that their relationship was a thing, out there in the world.

Lindsey laughed, a knowing laugh; it was through her nose, dismissive.

'Everyone knows you're together. Larkspur people might be scum but we're not stupid.'

'No one ever said you were scum,' said Ellie quietly, still reeling at having been outed.

'Yeah they did. A million times.'

She paused, tracing the outline of her teeth with the tip of her tongue. When she was with Danielle, Lindsey had seemed to possess a kind of existential impatience; her gaze never settling, her leg bouncing manically, her agitated exhalations and sighs evidence, seemingly, of her frustration at being held up from going wherever it was she imagined she was going. On her own, she had a stillness to her, the sense of a woman with the space and time to think for herself.

'And now all we're hearing is there's nothing wrong with the estate,' she continued decisively. 'You know, the building. Which means all the problems, they're because of us. I've heard it from you and your lot and all. *Housing policy* is what you say, but I listen, Ellie, and I know what that means: it means lumping together all the scum.'

'That's not what *I* mean,' said Ellie. 'It really isn't. All I was talking about was a high turnover of families and ...'

'Not that it's wrong. There's all kinds of shit living there. There's a guy, three floors above me, he pisses off his balcony. Right off the side.'

'I've never pretended that it's an easy place to live,' said Ellie quietly. 'For all kinds of reasons.'

Lindsey had cut her cinnamon bun into a dozen small pieces and was eating them delicately, one by one.

'My family, and I'm talking my grandad and my nan and everyone I've ever known – and it's not just me. It's Danielle and her lot, and Kieron and his lot, and everyone round the way – we've always been proud, you know. We look out for each other. Don't like strangers. Ready to drop one for our own. For nothing. For face.'

Lindsey faltered.

'It's a mentality. It's about looking out for people. For family. But it means we're always on top of each other and it's too much. It's always been too much. And then we got put in a great building where we all *were* on top of each other.'

She felt instinctively for the zip at her throat and tightened it.

'It was totally different from every other building in the town. You're talking about people who already feel they're different and then they're put in something that looks like a spaceship. And you wonder why everyone treats us like we're aliens.'

'God,' said Ellie apologetically. 'I've always liked it *because* it looked like a spaceship.'

'I didn't say I didn't like it.'

'Oh,' said Ellie, beaming.

'You left the lights on in your café the other night and it looked kind of magical up there against the black sky.'

'Oh, I'll leave them on again when I'm next in.'

'It's not going to make the damp go away though, is it?'

'No,' said Ellie. 'It's not.'

Lindsey ordered another coffee and told her about the reality of living there. The graffiti. The rubbish. The poorly lit walkways. The nightmare of trying to move about it with a buggy. The uninviting ground-level layout that added to its sense of isolation. Ellie listened and took notes.

'So much of what you're saying can be sorted out. I know it can,' she said. 'This is all great. You should be a spokeswoman.'

'What about painting some murals?'

'Yes, that's an idea.'

'And decent windows. Proper plastic ones that close tight.'

Ellie swallowed her reaction, shuddering inwardly at the thought of it. *Plastic windows.* She blushed at herself. At her own fundamental dishonesty. How much time had she spent banging on to Pankaj about her vision for a fully customisable social housing?

She felt again that sense of being adrift. It wasn't exactly ennobling but it had always been there and she couldn't deny it: one of the great draws of brutalism was that it was so despised by Little Englanders, retired majors, the petit bourgeoisie; that great grey-skinned group of people who were everything that she was not. It was a form of snobbery of course, but it had always been something she could rationalise away because of her abstract but keenly felt identification with the common man, the common woman. But the reality was, as she had discovered that morning looking at her Instagram account, that of the dozens and dozens of photos she had posted of the estate, not a single one of them contained a person.

'It's definitely worth thinking about,' she said. 'I'm sure they could be modernised.'

Beyond their table people walked past continuously. Their ice creams pimped, burgers loaded, pancakes stacked.

'I'm serious about you being a spokeswoman,' said Ellie. 'You could be the voice of the estate. You'd be amazing. You're so articulate. And direct. I could get you on camera.'

'Yeah, well I'm not going to do that, am I?'

'Why not?'

'Danielle would go spare, wouldn't she?'

'So?'

Lindsey scowled and rolled her eyes.

'I know it's really not my place to say this, but might it be worth considering how useful a person Danielle is in your life?'

'You don't know shit about her. Or her life.'

'No, I don't know her. But I've had some experience of her company. She's . . .'

'You've caught her on a bad day.'

'Well . . .'

'I don't know why I'm apologising for her. She'd hate it, to know it.'

'You don't have to apologise for her.'

'I know you think she's a twat.'

'Well . . . I don't know . . . That word . . . I—'

'She is a twat. I mean, can be. But honestly, the shit she's been through. I don't know. You'd be a twat and all.'

'I can only imagine,' said Ellie, who had hardly been through a thing in her whole life and thought herself to be enough of a twat as it was.

'And at the same time. You know I can't have a word said against her. When Kyle McAndrew was smacking me about the flat who do you think put the windows of his car in and had her uncle chase him out of Peterdown?'

Lindsey drummed her fingernails on the table top, agitated. She clearly didn't want to talk about it but also clearly couldn't not.

'She never met her old man. Not that that was necessarily a bad thing from what you hear.'

Lindsey sighed and out it came. The story of Danielle's life. Her dad and his reputation. Her mum and how she would just disappear for days at a time, and when she was there how she had encouraged Danielle to skip school, let her drink and smoke when she was twelve.

'She never got any change out of no one at school, neither. The teachers hated her. She was a gobshite but, I don't know, they treated her differently. Worse.'

Lindsey's jaw rippled.

'She's got four kids by three fellows. And they're all arseholes.'

'The dads?'

'No, the kids.'

Ellie felt her eyes involuntarily widen.

'Of course the dads. Although Jayden, her second, is like a wild animal. But that's his old man in him. Seventeen, she was, when she had her first one. She's daft. She goes in every time thinking it's going to save her. And then it messes her up when it doesn't. She used to be good-looking, you know. It was only with her last one that she got big.'

Lindsey sat with her hands in her lap.

'It's sad. 'Cos she's not going to meet anyone now. Not with all them kids and looking like she does.'

She looked up at Ellie.

'All that talk she was giving you about trying to leave the estate. It was bollocks. Where would she go? The Larkspur's all she knows. She hates it but she can't leave. She's got this block.'

Lindsey gestured at her forehead.

'Like she hasn't got the words for it.'

Ellie said nothing for a while, let this hang there.

'What about you?' she asked eventually.

'We've all got it. But I'm ... I don't know.'

'What?'

'My auntie. She lives in Liverpool. She's married to a teacher. He's always going on at me to do an access course.'

'You should.'

'I will one day. My Ryan'll be at school next year.'

'I could help.'

Lindsey seemed to welcome this offer and then instantly resent it.

349

'We're not all the same, you know.'

'I know.'

'I don't have any tattoos. Not one.'

'I've got a small one on my ankle,' said Ellie with a roll of her eyes.

'Really? *You've* got one? But I thought ...'

'I was nineteen. Ko Phangan back when it was still, you know ... Before it became ... Anyway, a load of us got them.'

'I can't believe that. You've got a tattoo.'

Ellie swung her legs out from under the table, pulled up the hem of her trousers to reveal, on her ankle, a series of letters from the Thai alphabet.

'It means tiger. Or at least I hope it does. Drugs were definitely a factor.'

'But I thought people like you ...'

Lindsey stopped before she got to the end of her sentence.

Ellie shrugged.

'I hardly think about it. Tattoos just don't mean anything any more, do they? Christ, Alice Campbell-Davys has like five or something, and she's the prime minister's wife.'

Had Ellie been more alive to Lindsey's body language she might have noticed how much this affected her, how cruelly it had punctured Lindsey's hard-won sense of her own exceptionalism. But she didn't. She was too busy experiencing her own sense of existential uncertainty. She couldn't put her finger on exactly why it was that the conversation had made her feel so odd, only that it had left her feeling essentially altered. And not in a good way.

36

The five-a-side pitch had appeared overnight, ready for match day. It had been created using a couple of dozen pieces of turf, a few of them lushly green, others piebald, some apparently on the verge of collapse. Taken together they just about tessellated into a grassy quilt twice the size of a tennis court.

Someone had fashioned goal posts from old wooden pallets. All the residents of the camp were out of their tents, up on their feet, watching a game being played.

'Did you know they were doing this?' asked Colin as they approached the pitch.

'It was a good time for us to go the marina, no?' said Rodbortzoon with a smirk. 'Saved us a lot of spadework! This English obsession with grass. It mystifies me.'

By the side of the pitch Brian was applying the finishing touches to a scale map that explained where all the turf had come from.

'Are you saying that is an actual piece of Old Trafford?' said Colin, pointing to a square of immaculate grass near the centre of the pitch.

Brian looked around, spoke out of the corner of his mouth.

'It's from one of their training pitches but it's near enough, you know. The rest are all bona fide, mind. There's a bit on the far side from Hillsborough and there's two or three big bits from Plough Lane that they were taking up to replace anyway. The groundsman there's a good lad and he put them aside for us. They might be a bit rough but they've got proper heritage. That's Sheffield United's actual penalty spot. Or at least their old one.'

'How did you get them all here?'

351

'Different folk have gone to get different bits. Graham. Lee. Mick's been up to the north-west and got us a few. But most of it's been fans of other clubs who've read about us on Facebook. We've had people driving up here all on their own accord. That bit over by the goal is from Parker's Piece in Cambridge where they wrote up the rules of the game for the first time. A student brought it up in a van. We've had a couple of people break in to lower league grounds where the security's not so tight and taken a shovel to the turf. They'll have got a bit of a shock when they opened Blundell Park this morning.'

On the pitch, Colin could see Adil and Shaz, one in a blue bib, the other in red, the pair of them playing alongside men in their fifties and six-year-old boys alike.

'The response has been something else,' said Brian, shaking his head. 'We've had journalists calling from *The Times*, the *Mail*, the *Mirror*. CNN. It's gone off the charts.'

Brian caught sight of the rucksack on Colin's shoulder.

'You're not joining us, are you?'

'It seems I am.'

'Well, well,' he said. 'Here we go. Colin Ryder does the full John Terry. Getting his kit on at the last minute to grab a bit of the glory.'

Colin smiled and took Brian's playful punch on the arm in good spirits. He resisted the temptation to tell Brian about the surveyors at the Larkspur. It was secret knowledge and the very fact of its secrecy was what gave it its power. He needed to be the guardian of it, shepherd it to its full potential. He was in no rush to tell Ellie, not until the time was right.

'I haven't got a tent yet. Can I crash in yours? I can't face the prospect of being in with Rodbortzoon.'

'There's plenty of space,' said Brian.

Colin threw his bag in through the heavy canvas flaps of the tent and checked his watch. 12.30 p.m. Two and a half hours until kick-off. Already the camp had swollen way beyond its eighty or so resident protesters. At least another two hundred fans had turned up early for the game and were milling about in small groups. Some were chanting, others ate mushy chip butties, a few managed both. The mood was bullyingly jovial, its tenor set by the needy intensity of large groups of men who had been drinking before lunch. It was the kind of atmosphere Colin had always found oppressive, one that wrapped you up and pressed you down, but it was also an atmosphere you could surf, if you came at it right.

Colin zipped the tent shut, ducked past two boys playing keepie-ups and walked through the camp. Sympathetic clubs all over Europe had sent expressions of their solidarity with the Partisans: scarves from St Pauli and Livorno, flags from Liverpool and a huge pennant of support from Celtic's Green Brigade. Dwarfing all of these, though, was the enormous banner put together by the Peterdown fans themselves. It told the history of the club from its formation to the present day. As well as images of great players and managers, it featured an homage to the club's roots in the railways, a huge tableau commemorating the sheet metal workers' strike in '78, and another celebrating the camp.

'Finally, folk art has its Guernica.'

It was Rodbortzoon, standing next to him.

'I particularly like the picture of Gem McBride,' said Colin. 'Although my sense is that it's unintentionally cubist.'

'All genuinely new forms are unintentional,' said Rodbortzoon blithely. 'They demand a monstrousness beyond the ego.'

Colin looked at him, an eyebrow raised.

'Do you think Andy knew what he was doing when he created this camp?' said Rodbortzoon. 'Do you think he realised he was bringing up the curtain on the stage of the street? Do you think it was his plan to rouse this sense of play? This capacity for spontaneous performance?'

Right on cue, on the far side of the camp a trumpeter started playing 'Going to the Chapel'.

'Andy is not the author of this,' continued Rodbortzoon. 'He was simply its conduit. An unknowing enabler of the *Geist*. You can't plan something like this. It emerges. Unconsciously. Extravagantly. Without a thought to the consequences.'

The trumpeter reached the chorus. People started singing. Couples danced. Rodbortzoon smiled broadly, his arms crossed across his chest with a fatherly kind of pride.

'Have the hearts of the people of Peterdown ever before been so spacious?'

Colin squinted in the morning sun.

'I really didn't see it coming,' he said. 'This and all the Wroth stuff. You can barely believe it, can you? In Peterdown.'

Rodbortzoon exhaled lengthily.

'Wroth,' he said in his kvetching, 'meh' voice.

Colin turned to him, aghast.

'*You* aren't into the whole Wroth thing? What the ...'

'Don't get me wrong. I am impressed that your generation is for once capable of overcoming its collective historical amnesia. It must be a shock for them to remember that they exist in history, not in some sublimated present, totally convinced of their own exceptionalism, but ... *Major Wroth*. Really? In this day and age ...'

'Christ alive, is there *anything* in the whole damn world that you can't find a way to be contrarian about?'

Rodbortzoon laughed, one hand on his belly.

'OK. OK,' he said in a conciliatory voice. 'I am not so interested in Wroth as a rallying point but, yes, you are right, broadly I admire their efforts. And the results have been nice, no? The town hall is not scrubbing up so well. Ha ha!'

Before Colin had an opportunity to respond, Rodbortzoon had caught sight of an old comrade and was off. Colin watched him go and then walked towards the café in search of a cup of tea. On his way, he rang the office.

Jill on reception put him straight through to Rick.

'What's the word?'

'The story's spiked. It was an administrative error. Land Dominion have supplied us with another letter retracting the first one. It's dated three weeks ago. Good thing we gave them right of reply.'

'What, you mean they wrote a new letter and put an old date on it? Christ, my nine-year-old could have thought that up.'

'We've been in touch with the FA. And they confirmed receipt of the letter the day after it was sent.'

Colin paused.

'You've found all this out already?' he said pointedly.

'Neil works fast.'

'It was *Neil* that was in touch with them, was it?'

'He has a contact from his business profile. He was happy to do it.'

'Yeah, I bet he was,' said Colin. He paused. 'I still don't understand why they sent the letter in the first place.'

'It was an administrative error. A mix-up. They realised they'd made a mistake and they righted it.'

'And you're just buying this line?'

'Colin, you've made an accusation and they've come out and said it was a simple mistake. Crossed wires. Colleagues not communicating properly.' Rick paused meaningfully. 'It's a non-story. Time to move on.'

'Are you not even a little bit interested in why they made that error in the first place? You don't just send a letter like that by mistake.'

'It's a non-story, Colin. Move on.'

'Rick, this is—'

'You're a sports reporter, Colin. There's a game on today. File your match report at the end of it. That's all I want from you. And let's not have eight hundred words on the fans and what songs they may or may not be singing. Your readers want to know who won and who scored the goals.'

Colin felt the blush rising up his throat.

'That's what I pay you to do. Write about the bloody game.'

* * *

The five hours that followed were one of the rare periods in Colin's life when he felt up close to experience. Having long stopped caring about his place in the press box, he watched the match from the heart of the Radleigh where he bounced and screamed and hugged and hollered as United hammered Bury five-one. After the game he dashed off his wilfully perfunctory copy – who had won and who had scored stretched to 800 words – before joining Rodbortzoon and Brian for his first evening at the camp. He arrived to find that a sympathetic landlord at a nearby pub had sent one of his staff over with two catering pans of hot stew and a couple of kegs of beer. The mood was buoyant. Statements of support were coming in from all over the country. There was talk of copycat camps being planned at Blackburn and Coventry. An appeal had been lodged against the rezoning of the land at the airport. It felt like a wave of resistance was sweeping the country and they were at the epicentre of it.

In the last of the evening light, a hundred or so people sat on upturned crates and foldaway chairs, listening to three invited speakers: a veteran from Zuccotti Park, a spokesman for Extinction Rebellion and an animal rights activist. Colin found a spot near the brazier, filled a bowl with stew and sat happily while Rodbortzoon poured him a beer.

'What the hell was that about?' said Brian once the last speaker had finished. 'The guy from New York had some interesting things to say, but the vegan? Liberating battery chickens? What's that got to do with the Chapel? And who invited her to start banging on about the police? They've been brilliant about this. It's been light touch all the way. We've had great lines of communication. Who would want to jeopardise that for something that's got bugger all to do with us?'

It was dark but the spring air was still warm and the low orange glow of the brazier and the distant streetlights gave the concourse a gentle, campfire quality.

'This was supposed to be about bringing people together. There's enough division in this town as it is. Football is supposed to be an escape from all that. The way this works is if it's a place where everyone is part of it. You're on the Radleigh you're one of us. That's the whole damn point. It's an *escape*.'

'Hmm,' said Colin noncommittally.

'It was Andy's idea to organise these talks. He's young and he was here first so we've all thought best to give him a chance. But he's clearly had someone in his ear,' said Brian, jerking a finger at

Rodbortzoon who was ambling back from the keg with an amused look on his face.

'We're losing sight of the reason we're doing this,' he continued. 'We're here to save our football ground, not to "dismantle the global capitalist order".'

'Tahrir Square started over the privatisation of a park,' said Rodbortzoon between mouthfuls of sauerkraut, which he was eating straight from the jar with an inappropriately small pink plastic fork. 'And it brought down a government.'

He raised the jar to his lips and took a large swig of the sour juice.

'You know why this is happening?' Rodbortzoon gestured at the camp. 'It is because your football club is the one thing you cannot change. The industry you work can be ground down, torn up, dispersed to the winds. You can walk away from your family. You can be catapulted from your class. You can, these days, change your gender as easily as your shirt.'

Rodbortzoon leaned in, poked Colin in the chest.

'But you can never change your football club. It is immutable. Permanent. Like a scar cut deep into your chest. That's what they don't realise. People have put up with so much. But this is different. You take a man's club from him and you radicalise him. You take his club from him and he knows that truly all that is solid melts into air. All that is holy is profaned. This is the moment when we see with sober senses the real conditions of life.'

He looked dismissively at Brian.

'This isn't just about the Chapel. This is replicable all over the world. Anywhere there is a club—'

Rodbortzoon stopped short, his attention caught by something on the far side of the concourse. Colin turned round. Five minivans had pulled up, all with tinted windows. Almost simultaneously the five side doors slid open and big bomber-jacketed men started pouring from them.

'Oh shit,' said Brian. 'That's Kyle Burrell.'

'Who's he?'

'He used to run the doors in Broadcastle. He's a proper gangster.'

'He's doing bits and pieces for Moolah now,' said Mick from the other side of the fire. 'Him and his boys. Working as bailiffs.'

Colin looked desperately around. The light-touch police presence constituted a fat middle-aged man and a five-foot-two WPC, both of whom were hurriedly shouting into their shoulder walkie-talkies.

'Oh god,' he said, 'this is not good.'

Everyone stayed sitting where they were. It seemed insane to do anything else. He watched as the line of men walked towards them. Twenty-five, he thought, maybe thirty. They were big guys. Bomber jackets. Black beanie hats. Leather boots.

'You're on private property,' shouted Kyle Burrell. 'You've got two minutes to clear off, or we'll be forced to remove you.'

Colin had long sensed that he didn't feel things as keenly as his peers. Love, pride, passion, rage; other people just seemed to experience them more deeply, inhabit them more wholly than he did. But not fear. Fear he felt with as much force as the next man. And nothing scared him like the prospect of immediate organised violence.

'I thought we weren't on private property,' he whispered urgently.

'We're not,' said Rodbortzoon with a wave of his hand. 'They can piss off.'

The line of men walked forward ten yards. Colin, who had many times in the past run away from situations far less threatening than this, found himself rooted to his chair, his feet impossibly heavy.

'It's actually disputed,' said Brian grudgingly.

'*What?*'

'No one seems to be totally sure who owns the bit we're on. It could be the council. It could be the club. We've been sort of exploiting the ambiguity.'

The line of men walked forward another ten yards.

'Jesus, Brian.'

'Ninety seconds,' shouted Kyle Burrell. 'We can do this whichever way you want.'

They were now so close that Colin could see their faces, their empty steroidal eyes. He had a long history of being justly petrified of guys like this. A dozen of the boys in his year at school had been the type; barely literate, quick to anger, devoid entirely of compassion.

'One minute,' shouted Kyle Burrell. 'I am not fucking joking.'

Colin's impulse was to run but no one had broken yet and he couldn't be the first. He sat in his chair looking despairingly around him. And that's when he heard it, cutting through the air.

When you walk through a storm.

It was Steve Wanless and his big, deep voice. Like anyone who had ever been to a football match, Colin's reaction to this line was preconscious: he felt the goose bumps rise, the hairs on his arms start to tingle.

'Thirty seconds,' shouted Kyle Burrell.

The line of men moved another ten yards closer. They were now just twenty yards from the tents. Colin could see all their faces, the anticipation, the bloodlust.

Hold your head up high.

Steve was standing up. He was a short man, but he was stocky and he could project. When he sang he placed his right hand on his chest. Colin felt his eyes dampen. He could have been a chorister with his voice. He hit all the notes, paced it perfectly.

And don't be afraid of the dark.

The line of men had stopped moving forward and all of them were looking at Steve. Apart from his voice and the crackle of the fire, the concourse was silent, heavy with the sense that something serious was about to happen. Colin felt his lip tremble. Every sinew in his body was screaming at him to stay seated. Keep his head down. Do his best to disappear, ride it out. But there was also something in him that was able to override these impulses, something in him that he was discovering was powerful enough to pull him, shaking, to his feet. He didn't have much of a voice but it was a song that could hide a multitude of sins as long as you went at it with gusto.

At the end of the storm.

Somehow Colin managed to keep his chin up, his gaze forward. He could see at least three of the bailiffs looking directly at him, like they were sizing him up, imagining already the shoeing they were going to give him. Never before had he experienced adrenaline like this. It was coursing through his body, shivering him and shaking him up. He opened his throat and sang louder.

There's a golden sky.

Next to him, Rodbortzoon stood up and threw his arm around Colin's shoulder. His voice was flat and loud, as much shouted as sung, but still there was something of the tenor about it, the way he conjured it up from the pit of his belly.

And the sweet silver song of a lark.

Next up was Brian. And then two women on the far side of the camp. And then Andy. And then dozens all at once. The bailiffs were all looking at each other, a seed of uncertainty planted in their minds.

Walk on through the wind.

Like the first pawn thrust out into the chessboard, one of the bailiffs broke ranks and took three paces forward, a long-handled torch hanging in his right hand. Immediately, Mick Claridge countered, taking a few paces forward himself so that the two of them were standing six feet from each other, Mick's long green hair splayed out behind him as he sang.

Walk on through the rain.

Colin looked at Kyle Burrell. He had clearly lost track of his count-down and looked utterly confounded by the whole thing, uncertain what to do or say.

Though your dreams be tossed and blown.

By the time they got to the chorus everyone was standing. And everyone was singing.

Walllll-k on. Walllll-k on.

Colin stood with his chest out, his hands raised high above his head, singing so loud his throat hurt. Kyle Burrell shouted some-thing inaudible above the cacophony. His men looked at each other, uncertain what to do. Colin caught the eye of one of them and held his gaze until the guy looked awkwardly away.

With hope in your heart.

Suddenly the dark square was filled with blue light. Colin glanced over his shoulder. Four squad cars had pulled up behind them. Burrell signalled to his men, directing them back to the vans.

And you'll ne-e-e-ver walk a-lone.

Colin felt his eyes film with tears. He wrapped his arm round Rodbortzoon's shoulder and together they threw back their heads and bawled at the top of their voices:

You'll ne-e-e-ver walk alone.

Walk IV

The Practice of Everyday Life: St Kilda's cemetery and back again

Well, haven't we got a spring in our step? It wouldn't be right to say we're drifting. Not today. If anything, we're skipping. Possessed, finally, of a feeling that it might be coming back, our sense of fun. Today, we're walking in a loop. Because what could be more gloriously pointless? Walking made pure, utterly devoid of utility. A journey denied a destination, turned into pure caper, and therefore pregnant, always, with possibility.

Of course, walking in a loop doubles nicely as an ambulatory homage to Johnnie Larkspur and his own circular narrative. *( )*, as it's come to be known. Or *Parentheses*, if you're saying it out loud. But it doesn't have a title, couldn't, not having a front page. *( )* was first published by a Parisian art gallery in 1953. Three metal rings and a hundred hole-punched sheets of paper. The booksellers were instructed to flick each copy so that its unnumbered pages fell open at random, the starting point irrelevant to a story that ranged and roamed back on itself, history's essential circularity rendered in miniature. So, having a laugh at his expense, we start where he ended, or at least ended up. St Kilda's cemetery on the Ottercliffe Road.

The older graves, nearest the church, are cruciform or crypt-like, many of them sinking into the earth. Blooms of lichen pattern the headstones. Slowly, though, as you walk through them, the aesthetic changes. There's more mauve marble. Polished black granite. The symbolism takes a more secular turn. Machine-cut motorbikes. Photo-realist football shirts. Tiny tombs engraved with a menagerie of passed-away pets.

It's over in the corner, unheralded, that you'll find him. All but forgotten. His books largely out of print. His readership reduced to a couple of tiny societies, the odd Facebook fan group.

We brush a couple of leaves from his headstone. Six books in his twelve productive years. None of them exactly book club fodder, but none of them nearly as difficult as his reputation suggests. He's thought of these days as austere but really he was a playful sort, all jokes and puns and shaggy-dog stories. And it wasn't like he didn't have a moment back in the day. The early Mods were drawn to his existentialist undertones and in 1962 there was nothing hipper than having a copy of *Are We Nearly There Yet?* poking out your pocket.

For some reason though he's never really been central to *our* sense of ourselves, poor old Johnnie, always eclipsed by Arthur Toyle. Which is ironic really as Johnnie's the one who stuck it out, lived and died in the Vale of Peter. You'd have to go down to Highgate Cemetery to find a headstone for old man Toyle. As soon as he'd pocketed the royalties for *Riveted* he bought himself a one-way ticket for the Smoke where he bunked up with a baroness and never came back. All the later works – the nature poetry, the maudlin memoir – were written from afar, through the long lens of memory with all its distortions and dreamed-up details.

We stroll out of St Kilda's and on to the Ottercliffe Road. Number twenty-seven's a Costa now, has been for years. But this was once Facchetti's, an old-school caff-cum-Italian delicatessen, replete with tea urn and espresso machine. The only fry in town that came with porcini and pancetta if you could muster a *ciao* for Enrico behind the bar. The cooler clerks from the Yards used to meet there, swapping paperbacks, trading vinyl. Thelonious Monk records on loop in the background. They were an interesting bunch. Something of a sleeper cell. Sure, they had a uniform like any unit of insurgents, but the boss can't exactly carp at a sharp-cut Italian suit, can he? The Mods railed against the drudgery of the day job by dressing better than the company directors. Looking back, it might have all been a shade too subtle.

We take a left down Union Terrace and then a right into Kingsland Court. The car park here is above ground, raised on columns. It's a drab building. Pebble-dashed for the most part. But the first eight feet up from the ground is covered in a thick band of graffiti, the high water mark of a stupidly exuberant sea.

We walk towards it. *Clack, clack, clack, clack, clack.* The sound of wheels on paving slabs. The scuff and scrape of attempted Eddies. The squeak of BMX tyres. They congregate here every day – always at least a dozen of them, sometimes double that – and away they go. No scorecards. No grades or goals. Here, they aspire to trickery as an end in itself. Freeform flow for the sake of it. We watch them for a bit and then walk on, infected by the rhythm, full of fellow feeling.

For half a mile, we skirt the River Peter, the water grey-green and stately. The setting is contemporary bucolic: barge moorings and waterside pubs, herons' nests and fly-tipped fridges. We cross at the Rothbury bridge. Our view is aerial, looking down. We catch glimpses of tented fishermen, their four-packs cooling in the water. On the benches lurk stubby-tied truants, weed smokers: a whole ecosystem of émigrés from the nine-to-five.

We stop for a half at the Printing Press. It used to be the offices of the *Post*. Now it's an epic pub. Famously cheap. Always busy. But also frighteningly quiet, at least during the day. It's the management's no music policy in part, but more than that it's the clientele. Society's superfluity. Average age in the upper fifties. The *Racing Post* folded in front of them. Eyes always forward. The conversation is occasional, directed rhetorically to the room, the subtext essentially always: *how did it come to this?*

We can only take it for so long. The sadness of the place. And so we head back into town. Up Rothbury Way. Mums with kids. Youths on bikes. The man in the plastic chair, who sits all day smoking spindly little cigarettes and drinking sweet tea. We pass the Ladbrokes and look up. For decades the first floor was offices.

Allied & Oakshott's headquarters until it closed in '86 and slowly went to seed. A couple of years later it got squatted. Not so much to live in. More a place to party. Back when we were all Baggies, in stupidly oversized T-shirts. XXXL trackies worn with the gusset at your knees. Chunky concept trainers. Dilated pupils to match. All night we went. Whoomp whoomp whoomp till sweat dripped from the ceiling and the bizzies bundled in to shut the whole thing down.

Muscle memory triggered, we bounce along the pavement, past a couple of lounging goths, and up the Radleigh Road until we see the camp. Eighty tents in all colours. A DIY football pitch cobbled together from fifty pieces of turf. Flags flying. A food station with a huge great pan on a couple of Calor gas canisters. People chopping carrots, onions. They're making the local hash. Fry up the veg – with a bit of garlic if you're feeling continental – then chuck in boiled potatoes, peas and black pudding. Ramp up the heat till it's crisping at the edges. And serve it with a fried egg on top. Heaven on a plate. We sniff the air, fill our lungs with it as we scamper into the site proper.

First up is an information post where a young woman is handing out leaflets, expounding the camp's purpose to passers-by, inviting them to lectures and organised debates, explaining to them how they can contribute, volunteer or, even better, move in.

Beyond her is a piano. A little bashed, not quite in tune, but still upright. Still a fine instrument. A young man is at it, playing slowly, but with some passion. 'When The Saints Go Marching In'. We hum along as we hurry over to the placards arranged in an awkward tessellation on the floor. The messages on the cardboard squares are anti-Kirk, but full of fun. We pause, smiling at the jokes. The bad puns. On we go, weaving through the tents. Around us, people are passing a ball back and forth, arguing urgently about the matters of the day.

The mood seems playful but deep down we can sense a steel-iness to the whole thing. We can't help but think of the spirit of the strikes in '78 and '86. Thousands of us out, pitching in, sharing food and fuel. The rallying round. The singing. The hours spent arm-in-arm. And the japes. When they were picketing, the men had to stay out of the Yards or they'd be sacked for trespass. But you couldn't sack their wives. Oh, the chaos we caused. A hundred women breaking ranks all at once. Slashing tyres. Chaining doors shut. Stealing spark plugs.

We walk away feeling that – just like our loop of a walk – history has come full circle. We've been waiting for this. We always knew they were there, these latent energies, ripe and ready to go, just waiting for a trigger.

We walk up the top end of the Ricky and can't help but feel that the things around us – the tattoo parlours, the nail bars, the tanning salons and giant gyms – are at odds with our essential character. Things imposed upon us. The idea of down time as 'me' time. Self-expression through personal marketing. Narcissism as relaxation.

We shudder as we pass the new gym, the town's third, and grab ourselves an oppositional iced bun from the bakers, all the time listening out, knowing that we'll hear it, coming out, canned, from one shop or another. And sure enough, a hundred yards on, halfway through our bun, there it is, piping out of Peacocks.

In the part of the Vale where we once all made trains
In a nothing town where it always seems it rains
There is a boy who brings with him the sun
Every time he gets the ball and starts to run . . .

How many times have we heard it? And yet still it stirs something in us. 'The Last of the Street Footballers'. The melody is mawkish and perhaps a little bit borrowed, but that doesn't mean it can't also be felt.

When he dribbles he dribbles like the little bird
An on-pitch dance of the kind that can't be learned
When you watch him with that ball at his feet
You know that he grew up on the street

No one's ever said the Panel Beaters rival Radiohead, but their naïve little song captures something about that untutored boy and the untutored town that made him. What can we say? It might be slightly syrupy but it speaks to us.

> *When you play like him*
> *You say something*
> *When you play like him*
> *You say something.*

Up the Ricky we go towards the cemetery. *When you play like him, you say something.* We smile. When you walk like us, you say something. You say *no*, obviously. No to prescribed paths. To skill sets. No to goal-oriented outcomes. But you also say *yes*, too. Yes to spontaneity. To cavorting and carousing. Yes to joyousness and rapture.

Yes, ultimately, to the revel.

37

'Hello,' said Ellie, determinedly unruffled. 'Can I get you anything?'

Yvonne Kington was standing in front of her in the Larkspur café. She was wearing her red coat, belted at the waist.

'I'll have a cup of tea, please,' she said like it was the most natural thing in the world.

'Sure,' said Ellie brightly.

She tossed a tea bag into a mug and put on the kettle, struggling to maintain a veneer of relaxed good humour. In the days since her conversation with Lindsey, she had lain low, feeling oddly vulnerable. She seemed to be constantly hijacked by her mood, making her skittish and sensitive, easily disappointed. She had become obsessed with the online petition, refreshing it constantly even though its once rapid growth had flatlined and she was getting no more than one or two new signatures a day. In the rare moments she had been able to motivate herself she made overtures to journalists, but they all seemed to have moved on. And to top it all, Pankaj was increasingly preoccupied with other things: constituency matters, the possibility of a place on a select committee.

Yvonne in her café was the last thing she needed.

'Sugar?'

Yvonne strolled from the counter to the low table with its handsome books and architecture magazines. She ran her finger along a sideboard, stopped to admire a succulent in a small concrete pot.

'No, thanks.'

She continued around the room – taking in the view, looking at the books – all the time maintaining a strange self-satisfied silence that called attention to itself as surely as shouting would have.

Ellie poured some milk into a tiny jug. This was a power play and she was determined not to be intimidated by it. In these situations, you needed to get on the front foot, dictate terms. She only had one card in her hand, and the moment demanded she play it now.

'Those figures you released about the Generator's finances,' she said. 'Why didn't you include the contract with Rapid Clean – the cleaning company? I saw their cleaners working at the site.'

Yvonne turned to look at her, held her gaze for a beat and then smiled.

'All the council cleaning contracts go through the same centralised account. We negotiate them as one. It saves us a fortune every year.'

The relish with which she said this gave Ellie pause. She held back from pushing for more details. She experienced an awful panicked sensation that she had initiated something, given licence for what was to come. Yvonne finally sat down at a table facing the counter.

'I used to be an activist.'

Ellie had no idea what to say to this. All that came to her was: *I used to be an architect.*

'Marches. Sit-ins. The whole nine yards. You might not believe me, but I have a lot of sympathy for what you're doing. I understand it.'

Yvonne poured some milk into the mug that Ellie had placed in front of her.

'It's one of the reasons I'm not going to close this place down – even though I could, in a heartbeat, if I wanted to. Another reason I'm not going to do it is because they're my people, the people that live here.'

Here she looked Ellie up and down, pausing sardonically at her trousers which were an eBay buy: vintage Comme des Garçons pantaloons that ballooned out at the thigh before tapering dramatically halfway up her shin.

'*My* people, who I have lived among and represented for many years.'

Yvonne took a sip of her tea.

'I know you care about them. It's obvious that you do. And I know that you'd never imperil them, would you? I mean, I'm sure the first thing you did was make sure you got all your fire certificates sorted.'

She nodded at the new coffee machine, a lovely Italian-made thing with a polished chrome finish.

'I bet that thing gets hot, doesn't it? Professionally installed, was it? All the wiring signed off by a certified electrician?'

Ellie blushed furiously. Ralph and Barry had rigged it up using a YouTube tutorial for a similar-looking model.

'And that'll be a fire door, of course,' said Yvonne. 'And I'm sure you've got emergency lights and all your alarms fitted.'

Ellie continued to stand dumb where she was, holding a tray. This was what it was like to be on the end of righteousness, to be blamed, shamed, punished.

'I *hate* that Tory attitude that health and safety is so much meaningless red tape, don't you?'

Yvonne took a last sip of the tea and stood up. She smiled threateningly as she collected her coat.

'But like I said, love. I'll not be shutting it.'

* * *

It was a lot bigger than she had expected. A tent city. Architecture without an architect. Master-planned in real time. Endlessly mutable. The ultimate form of participatory design. And at the centre of it all, a structure that seemed to be the HQ, a kind of mess tent and meeting point. It had been erected using a few pieces of two-by-four and some ply sheets. A blue tarp had been stretched over the frame, bricks holding it in place. At least three people in her year at university had written their graduate theses on exactly this kind of transitory vernacular architecture.

'Eleanor.'

She looked over to see Rodbortzoon walking towards her. He was, for once, not eating and appeared to have combed his hair. Still, his CCCP T-shirt was flecked with what looked like sweet chilli dipping sauce and his bootlaces were undone. She was here because of him, summoned to hear urgent news.

'Only my mother calls me Eleanor.'

'I am versed in European ways of address that I fear it is too late to unlearn,' he said, bowing theatrically.

'Yeah, yeah.'

'I would gladly start calling you by your diminutive,' he said, twinkling away, 'but for a man of my generation this is an intimacy reserved only for lovers.'

The thought had occurred to Ellie on more than one occasion that you might have electric sex with Rodbortzoon. He blew his nose noisily, returned a vast handkerchief to his pocket. Never before had she met a man who seemed so to delight in his animal physicality, his fleshy occupation of space, his appetites, his smell.

'Eleanor it is then,' she said.

Rodbortzoon led her through the camp, explaining their horizontal organisational structure, the increasingly sophisticated logistics they had in place for cooking, cleaning, managing waste.

'What was it you wanted to tell me?'

'Eleanor! All in good time. This is your first time here, no? There is so much I want to show you first.'

They walked through a cluster of tents where a bunch of boys were sitting around, smoking cigarettes, looking at their phones. They all wore black caps, the brims pulled low, and half of them had keffiyeh scarves wrapped round their necks. Above them, written on a sheet suspended between two poles, were two words:

DEBT STRIKE

It was all over town. On handbills. Tarred on to walls. Spray painted on every billboard and bridge. On one of the Wroth Facebook pages, someone had written an essay about machine-breaking in the digital age, messing with algorithms, disrupting capital pathways. It had gone viral with its hashtags: #massdefault and #dontpaybackthemoolah.

The response from Kirk had been immediate and aggressive. As well as sending letters to all Moolah debtors he had taken a full-page advert in the *Post* warning that anyone not making their repayments would have their details passed on to a collection agency.

Two days later, a team of sympathetic hackers – operating, it was suspected, out of Russia – created a bot that bombarded the Moolah website with fake loan applications until it crashed. *May our Wroth be visited upon you*, they wrote in an open email to Kirk.

'I am thinking of applying for a loan just so I can default,' said Rodbortzoon.

'Yeah, you could try that, although I think you'll probably need a more convincing address than your current one. I don't think they're going to lend much to Mr Rodbortzoon, Tent number four.'

'Ha ha!' roared Rodbortzoon. 'I will put up my sleeping bag as collateral!'

Seagulls wheeled overhead, looking for scraps. They walked past three people at a table making lunch. Beyond them, two men and two women were at laptops, updating social media accounts, fielding questions from the press, managing solidarity donations.

'We are the hub,' said Rodbortzoon, nodding at them. 'Spokes flying in all directions. Already there are three more camps. One in Wigan. One in Munich. One in Malaga. This is just the start. Every week, people are singing songs for us on the terraces. Manchester. Liverpool. Glasgow. Now, they are singing for us. How long until we see camps at every ground in the country?'

Three kids were kicking a ball back and forth over a tent. Others ran about, handing out flyers. Ellie imagined herself to be above petty one-upmanship, but it was obvious why she had avoided coming for so long. It was proving, as she feared, to be the last thing she had wanted it to be; somewhere packed with people, humming with energy. An authentic mass movement with a global audience.

Irritated, she followed Rodbortzoon as he ducked into a gazebo with a handwritten sign above the door.

Peterdown People's University: Department of Radical Football

As well as a dozen mismatched chairs there were floor cushions, and a battered-looking rug. A foosball table stood in one corner, a packed bookshelf in another.

'It is not the Bodleian but we have Gramsci's *Prison Diaries* and the *Rothmans Football Yearbook 1982*,' said Rodbortzoon. 'Essential works both.'

On the wall were quotes from Camus, Baudrillard, Bill Shankly. She peered at a schedule chalked out on a blackboard. Earlier that week there had been seminars titled 'Contra-Corinthians: Professionalisation and the Triumph of the Working Class' and 'Terrace Culture and National Self-Becoming in South America'.

Ellie looked at Rodbortzoon, rolled her eyes.

'Next week we are hosting a lecture on the revolutionary feminism of Iranian football. You should come.'

She laughed through her nose and left the tent.

'Are you coming to the game? We are playing Leeds. It will be a good one, I think.'

'No, I'm not.'

It was now only a couple of hours until kick-off and there were noticeably more people milling about. Behind her, one of the Partisan boys started up a chant to the tune of 'Feeling Hot, Hot, Hot':

Ole, ole, ole, ole,
Major Wroth, Wroth, Wroth
Major Wroth, Wroth, Wroth

Dozens and then seemingly hundreds more joined in, shouting at the tops of their voices. Although there was an unthinking blokishness to the way they bellowed the words, hearing it sung by so many people had its own pressing intensity. Ellie looked about at the swelling crowds. Three hours had passed since Yvonne had blasted into the café and she had managed to maintain a laboured equanimity about their encounter, not let it precipitate some great crisis of self-doubt. But in the context of the camp, it was impossible not to think about her empty café, the drop-off in media coverage, the waning enthusiasm of her volunteers, and wonder: who had the momentum now?

Ellie meandered through the camp. Ahead of her, the Chapel sat there, unobtrusive against the blue sky. The affection Colin had for it was surely nothing to do with its architecture. Its four stands were neither pleasingly harmonious nor interestingly arrhythmic; rather they appeared to have been fashioned in four different decades by four different architects, all of them motivated principally by their mutual contempt for each other's work.

At the mess tent she stopped and picked up a polystyrene cup of tea from a tray. A hundred yards to her right, a steady stream of fans walked past the tents towards the stadium. A couple stopped to join a large group of what appeared to be exclusively white men in early middle age standing with cans of lager in hand. A couple had their shirts off, revealing spidery blue tattoos across the span of their chests.

She had seen it before, all over the country, this awful sense of proprietorship. The way they took over pubs and station platforms, demanding that their particular form of freedom trumped all others.

Rodbortzoon ambled up.

'One of this lot delivering your seminar on feminism and Iranian football, are they?'

He laughed his barking laugh.

'Everyone contributes to the cause in their own way.'

'So,' she said, 'what is it that you had to tell me in person?'

'That can wait. First, for a minute, I want to talk about the Larkspur and the Chapel. We are on the cusp of something, no? For years, nothing. And now two flowerings of radical potential. We must resist the attempts of the capitalist class to pit us against each other. It is time we united. Football and housing. England's abiding preoccupations. If we work together we can radically transform Peterdown. And then, who knows, maybe the world.'

'With this lot? No, thanks.'

'We would be unstoppable. Let's get together, hold nothing back, share information, create a united front.'

'I just don't really see the connection. I'm sorry.'

'Come on! This is a demonstration of everything you are concerned with. We are literally re-territorialising the urban realm.'

And isn't it hateful, thought Ellie instinctively. Around her, black bin bags slumped sideways revealing their contents: stripped chicken thighs and tabloid newspapers. Pints of lager, she thought to herself. Bags of chips. Reebok trainers. Bald men in bad clothes. She felt the dark energy of her disgust, how it polluted and corroded.

Oh England, I carry a knife in my heart. Her mother, quoting John Osborne. A favourite line of hers that would be delivered out loud, never really at anyone in particular, more at whatever institution had most recently exemplified the decline: be it a supermarket or a swimming pool, a concert hall, her school.

Ellie felt a nasty taste appear in her mouth. Her mother had carried a knife in her heart, and it was there in her, too. A lovely inheritance; one that wounded no one but yourself.

She swallowed, longing for a glass of water. She had started to feel it more keenly, this awful sense that there were things that had been written into her, deep into the core of her being. And what could she do to overwrite them when so much of the early work had been done – carelessly and indelibly – by a woman with a poison pen?

'The uprisings are more potent every day,' said Rodbortzoon. 'Together the two campaigns would be irrepressible.'

Ellie looked at him, sullied by her own spite.

'I can't think why you think something as passive as being a football fan could ever be the springboard for political action. You are, by definition, a spectator not an actor.'

'Wrong, wrong, wrong,' said Rodbortzoon, punctuating the air with his finger. 'We are not spectators. We are not even fans. We are *fanatics*. It is a completely different thing.'

'Exactly,' said Ellie. 'It's ludicrous how important football is to this town. You know what Jim McEwan once said to me? He said: *If you'd told me back in the seventies that eighty per cent of men would talk about football eighty per cent of the time, well, I would have laughed in your face.* I mean, talk about bread and circuses. Can you think of a more ridiculous way to index the city's wellbeing than the performance of its bloody football team?'

Rodbortzoon had buttoned his jacket against the cold. He smiled at her.

'Eleanor, surely you see that it is the abstract quality of the club that makes the fanatical support so ripe with potential,' he said. 'What could be more threatening to the managerialist consensus than an illogical passion, fanatically pursued?'

The group of men chanting their chants had grown to about thirty. They were bellowing a song about Broadcastle and although she couldn't make out all the words the last line was clear: *and we'll kick his fucking head in when he comes.*

'There you go. There's your fanaticism right there. I don't even want to know what their version of utopia would look like.'

'Such squeamishness surprises me,' said Rodbortzoon. 'You are someone who admires the liberation of libidinal energies, as I understood it. Is not the Larkspur the product of an "imagination freed from pathological servility"? A building that "embraces the dark Dionysian depths"?'

Ellie shook her head. Another man quoting her back at herself.

'I can't believe you have the brass neck to compare that building with this thuggishness.'

'Ha! Perhaps we shouldn't be surprised that there is a place for brutalism in the *bien pensant* good taste for which you are so famous,' he said with an ironising smile. 'But there is not one for "In Your Broadcastle Hovel". Perhaps it is too far down in the Dionysian depths.'

'Oh, fuck off.'

Rodbortzoon shrugged.

'This song has nine verses. All iambic hexameter. What is *really* interesting though is that it starts off as a terza rima but switches structure halfway and the final verses are closer in form to a Petrarchan sonnet. What can I say? You want authentically demotic modernism then this is where you—'

'Christ,' she said. 'Enough. Why am I here? What is this information you had to tell me?'

Around them, the crowd were singing, hollering insults, whooping it up.

'Oh, that,' said Rodbortzoon pensively. 'You know what, it was nothing.'

38

The shirt had been designed on a computer. The entire chest area was puffed out, the six-pack prominent as if it was being worn by an extravagantly muscled invisible man. The badge on the breast was clearly that of Peterdown United Football Club but everything else about it was wrong.

'It's red,' said Colin. 'We've played in green and white since 1927.'

'I know,' said Andy. They were at the camp, staring at a laptop screen. He zoomed in on the image. 'It was leaked by someone who works at a design agency in London. Platinum, they're called. See, it's got their branding on it. And look in the corner. "Client: Land Dominion". I think it's kosher.'

Colin looked towards the stadium. At the periphery of the camp, he could see the newly bolstered police presence. It wasn't simply that there were more of them, they had a different feel; half of them in flak jackets, handcuffs and batons visible on their belts.

Twice already he had seen a couple of the Partisan boys hauled off for petty misdemeanours: lighting a flare, refusing to put out a fire. On both occasions they had been back at the camp a couple of hours later but what had previously felt like community liaison now felt like aggressive surveillance.

'Are those lines on the side of the shirt supposed to be steam?' said Andy.

'I thought so at first, but it looks more like fire, doesn't it?' said Colin.

He extended his neck and rolled his shoulders. Ten days or so he had been here, and the many hours spent lying on an inch-thick roll mat were starting to take a toll on both his back and his energy levels. He was barely getting five hours a night. But his mattress was only partially to blame. Their showdown with the bailiffs might have become instantly folkloric among the wider fan base, but the sense of threat lingered in the camp, keeping him up into the small hours.

Not that it had been all bad. Most evenings they gathered around a brazier to eat and drink and talk. Sometimes politics. A lot of the time football. Mick and Steve often held court and the Partisan boys loved listening to their anecdotes about away days to Millwall and West Ham in the seventies, the run to the semi-finals of the Littlewoods Cup, the joy of watching Gem McBride in the flesh.

On other evenings, Colin and Rodbortzoon would retire to the Department of Radical Football, where Colin would do wild and speculative online research about the RPUFG or Kirk's business interests, putting in freedom of information requests until his laptop ran out of power, after which he would charge his cocoa and settle down next to Rodbortzoon to read by the light of the battery-powered lamp. There was, he had to admit, a romance to it that he hadn't reckoned on.

'The fans are going to go spare,' he said.

'Oh man, they already have,' said Andy. 'You should see the message boards. It's going off. There's a Facebook group for people that are going to cancel their season tickets.'

Colin sniffed the air. He thought about going back to his tent to change his socks, but he knew he had worn all six pairs at least twice, some of them more. He tried to summon the will to drag his clothes to the launderette, all the while knowing that it wouldn't happen and that he would be turning his boxers inside out again the following morning. It had been three days since he had had a shower. At some level he knew he ought to be disgusted at his self-defilement, the dirt under his nails, his fetid socks. But he was finding a kind of nobility in it, like the dirt was an index of his determination, an essential part of his effort, an anti-Kirk statement in itself.

And it was sort of comfortable, too, once you got used to it. Something you could settle into, over time.

'Changing the kit colour?' he said eventually. 'It seems such a pointless way to wind people up.'

'I reckon it's just spite. You heard what Tory Rory said, didn't you?'

'Tory Rory' was Rory Kincaid, a solicitor who lived in a big country house in the Vale of Peter. He had been very vocal about Pankaj being parachuted into the seat and was rumoured to be considering standing against him at the next opportunity.

'I can tell you from the conversations that I've had with people in London that the Conservative Party will be listening to the people of Peterdown.'

'I know that's what he said,' said Colin, 'I do work for the paper.'

'So, should we be getting excited about this?' asked Andy irritably. 'He's talking about the central government, right? The people who are going to decide.'

'A few years of doing this and you learn to be pretty sceptical about people like Kincaid and their conversations.'

Andy clearly heard more of a rebuke in this than Colin had intended.

'Eight years,' he said pointedly. 'You've been at the *Post* for eight years. More than just a few.'

There was something thrilling about the certainty of Andy's contempt. It was ridiculous to be so proud that only he was worthy of it, but Colin couldn't help himself. It was a sign of respect.

He had been largely right in his assumptions about Andy. He was the chosen one. Head boy, too, with an offer from Cambridge he would have easily met had scarlet fever not knocked him out two days before his final chemistry exam. Andy had ended up sitting the paper in February, aced it, and was filling time until September when he would take his place at Christ's College.

'He means us, though, doesn't he, Tory Rory? Listening to the people means they're not going to put the station here.'

He crouched over the laptop, typing with his generation's light touch, their ease around the keyboard. Colin looked at his bowl-cut hair. It was strange to desperately want someone to get out there in the world and prove themselves, and simultaneously desire nothing more than for them to stay in Peterdown forever.

He looked around, checked no one was listening.

'What I'm about to tell you, you can't tell anyone, you get that?'

Andy looked at him, nodded eventually.

'They've already picked the Larkspur for the station.'

'*What?*'

'That's all I can tell you and, Christ, you mustn't say anything to anyone but, rest assured, we're good on that front.'

'How do you know?'

'I can't tell you, but I know.'

'If it's true, that's brilliant.'

'Well, it *is*, but it doesn't stop him moving the club to Grangeham. He wanted to do it before anyone had even written up the damn shortlist and he's going to carry on wanting to do it whatever happens.'

Andy sucked his teeth. 'If only we'd beaten Leeds.'

Colin assented with a shrug of the shoulders. Ordinarily, he would have been thrilled at getting a point out of the runaway league leaders, but Coventry and Hull had both won their games which meant United were stuck fast in eighth.

'We're not going to get promoted, Andy. It's just not going to happen. The only way to guarantee that we're at the Chapel next season is to find out what's wrong with the development. You know, the thing Kirk is trying to cover up.'

Colin opened a screenshot he'd taken the night before. It was a tweet posted at 11.54 p.m.

@Truther_78 · 10m
Shite town. Shite club. Even your future has problems with its past.

'That's the guy that's always mouthing off on the boards,' said Andy. 'He's a gobshite.'

'Yeah, he is, but he knows things. I don't know how but he does. He deleted this tweet this morning and he only does *that* when he's got pissed and written something he shouldn't have.'

'Our future has problems with its past. You reckon he means Grangeham?'

'I think that's exactly what he means.'

'Could it be the site? You know, the land?'

'What do you mean?'

'My grandad's brother worked at the forge. He was a line worker, chrome-plating components for the carriages. It makes the steel harder, longer lasting. Back then, they didn't know about chromium six. He died when he was young. Fifty-something.'

'Because of the chromium?'

'Because of everything – the conditions, the chemicals, the lack of ventilation. Who knows? But chromium-six is an absolute bastard. Have you seen the film *Erin Brockovich*? That whole story was about chromium pollution.'

Colin looked up, his ears pricked.

'You think the land is contaminated?'

'The land'll certainly be contaminated. Flashing. Clinker. All kinds of stuff from the work that was going on there. But you can clean most heavy metals fairly easily. It's chromium-six that's the nightmare. I know there have been sites that have been abandoned because it was just too expensive to get it out. I had to do a simulated case study on it for my geography A level.'

'Oh my god,' said Colin, feeling the crackle, the exquisite experience of two things connecting in his head. 'That piece Neil wrote for the *Post*. On Land Dominion. He kept going on about the in-house environmental auditing team. They know about it and they're covering it up.'

Colin was up on his feet, already pulling his phone from his pocket. 'Andy, you're a prince among men. I'll see you later and I'll be buying you a pint.'

He found the number he was looking for and called it as he walked away.

'Hi, James. It's Colin Ryder. Tom's mate. You did that master-planning analysis of Peterdown for me. About where the new station might go. I've got one more favour to ask. Do you know anyone that knows anything about contaminated land?'

In 2004, the Peterdown College of Further Education was moved from its original Victorian home on the Ottercliffe Road to a new, lavishly financed campus on the outskirts of town. Set back from the road, the central curving atrium was clad in orange and purple panels. Its two wings were plate glass. A lone tree stood gamely at the front. Colin had never been east of Greece, but he was happy to accept that the college was, as Ellie had once put it, designed in the style of a South Korean airport hotel.

Rodbortzoon's contract with the college, signed when he joined the institution in the late 1980s, was a product of a different era of industrial relations, when loyalty went rewarded. Held in place by a stupefyingly expensive break clause, it stipulated that with every passing year the division of his time between research and teaching would be more slanted in favour of the former. His pedagogical commitments now amounted to a four-week course in the autumn term and a single public lecture, delivered annually, in the spring.

Colin pushed open the door of the lecture hall and chuckled to himself in disbelief. Every desk was taken. Both aisles were thick with people standing, leaning against the wall. At the front, people were sitting on the floor. He quickly scanned the crowd, identifying faces from the camp, lots of veterans of the Peterdown left. But there were young people, too, many of them.

He was ten minutes late. Up on the stage, Rodbortzoon was already deep into it.

'Moolah has stopped hiring. From now on it is natural wastage, as they say. The only area they are taking on new staff is in *recovery*, i.e. the goons who tried to attack us the other night. Is this productive work? No, it is guard labour in its purest form.'

He had a heavy cold. But he always had a heavy cold. His handkerchief lived in his breast pocket. Colin marvelled once more at the fluency of the movement that transported it from the pocket to the nose and back again, a single circular movement achieved, it appeared, without disrupting the main thrust of his thought, which was about robots and the coming automation.

'Very soon the robots will make the robots. I know it sounds scary. Makes people think of Skynet. And Arnie is too old now to save us. Ha ha! Too busy in California dreaming that he could still one day be the robo-president. But this is dystopian. And we in this room are utopians. We can dream of a future in which people are liberated. Oh great, we say, the robots can now drive the cars and the lorries and the trains. All the drivers – taxi drivers, lorry drivers, limousine drivers, school bus drivers, big truck drivers, little golf buggy drivers – all of you are now free to go about your lives. You have been freed. We will pay your wages but the robots will take up the slack. Thank you for your hard work. Enjoy!

'The productive capacity of the economy remains unchanged. So no one will lose out. People will not feel negative solidarity at their liberation but collective ecstasy. I will be next, they say. God willing.'

Colin was accustomed to Rodbortzoon's oratory style, which featured face rubbing, ear tweaking, collar flicking and nose wiping with such frequency that it might, to the untrained eye, have appeared that as well as delivering the lecture in the conventional sense he was simultaneously signing it for a deaf student at the back of the room.

'How do we get there, you ask. From actually exiting neoliberalism to the future of our best imagination?'

Here Rodbortzoon started to expound at length on the intellectual left's long-standing over-reliance on the possibility of the 'Event', much of which Colin had endured in different forms on a dozen different car journeys. As Rodbortzoon restated his familiar discourse on the left's failure to seize the moment after the 2008 crash, Colin's attention drifted to his phone. After checking his email, he opened the *Post*'s website to see if there were any new comments under his piece on the camp, only to discover, trailed prominently on the homepage, a new piece by Neil under the headline:

IS PETERDOWN HOME TO BRITAIN'S BRAVEST ARTS VENUE?

While Rodbortzoon talked about the need for the immediate introduction of a universal basic income, the creation of a department of socialist robotics, and the possibility of a cross-class alliance to demand a phased reduction in the working week, Colin ploughed through the piece, just about resisting the temptation to hurl his phone at the wall as he read paragraph after paragraph lauding the Generator for having the foresight to host the 'controversial but courageous and important "Googling My Cock"'.

'People always say to me: yes, but the people who own these robots, they will be the Masters of the Universe,' continued Rodbortzoon. 'To which I always say: in the past, to nationalise industries you had to seize coal mines, steel works, factories. To nationalise an algorithm all you need to do is cut and paste. Ha ha!'

Not that Colin heard any of this. He was furiously texting Kerry.

Did you read Neil's latest piece on the Generator?! He's got to be working for Kirk! Can we get access to payroll for Land Dominion?

'But, the naysayers cry, our work is the source of our self-identity, our purpose, the infrastructure for our socialisation. To which I say: and look where it has got us! Mental health crises. A planet on the brink. Intellectual and spiritual torpor. Perhaps if we stop configuring our self-actualisation in terms of our productive capacity then we will also stop understanding our self-worth in terms of our consumptive capacity.'

Payroll details are on a server you can connect to from our office but I don't have access. I could jump on someone else's machine but I'll need some time ...

'We have to remember,' said Rodbortzoon, leaning on his lectern, his chin in his hands, 'that these days our problem is no longer simply alienated labour but also alienated *leisure*. Terrible movies. Shopping malls. Televised football. Instagram. All of it submissive. Anti-libidinal. Inert. Dead.'

He stood upright again, agitated, waving his arms theatrically.

'In addition to an end to meaningless work we need an end to meaningless leisure. In their place we will demand the society of play. A universe fit for *Homo Ludens*. A place of intellectual openness, spontaneity, sensual pleasure. A place where we might remember that the central task of play is *self-becoming*.

'To play is not only to create the individual self, but also to expand the possibility of selfhood. It is a teleological unknown! The activity of walking down the path creates the path. You know the scene in *The Last Crusade*. Indiana Jones must cross the invisible bridge which is not there until he stands on it. This is like that. Not blind faith, some hokey Spielbergian parallel; self-becoming is a process that contains within it a propulsion to its telos but no idea of its location. The pursuit is the act of creation.'

Colin wouldn't have bothered trying to unpick this even if he had been listening, which he wasn't. He was typing urgently. Two thumbs.

We're running out of time. What about an environmental audit? Have you seen one? Heard anyone talking about one?

'Mr Rodbortzoon, I can hear you saying, what has all this got to do with the Chapel and the camp we have created to protect it? And to that I say: we wanted at the very least to save a space suitable to the unlimited deployment of our passions. But of course this was not easy so we found ourselves forced to do so much more. Ha ha!'

No but I'll have a dig around xo

Colin read this and leaned into the wall, staring vacantly at the stage. Rodbortzoon was talking about how the residents of the camp had realised – through some great collective revelation, the details of which went unexplored – that their historical calling was more than simply to save the stadium. They had assumed responsibility for creating the template for the city of play; a model polity in miniature, one that encouraged extemporaneity, inclusivity and the revel.

To Colin it was simply noise. He was too busy thinking about Kerry's XO.

He felt the familiar stirring, the slightly dry mouth, the shallow breath. They had seen each other three times in the past week and each time their encounter had felt freighted with something unsaid. It was, surely, undeniable that something had changed between them since he had split with Ellie. She was different around him. Her cheeks pinked in his presence and she was unusually self-conscious about her body.

He looked again at her message.

Rodbortzoon was nearing the end of his lecture. Colin let his head rest on the wall behind him. The mood in the hall was exultant but impatient. It had been going on now for more than an hour. They had all done very well, but now, really, it was time for a drink.

'As is so often the case our overlords are keen to present us with the choice between two terrible outcomes: lose the Larkspur or the Chapel. On the face of it, the radical response would appear to be to demand that we choose the Generator – a building that so succinctly expresses the cultural logic of our late-stage seppuku capitalism. But is not the truly radical solution to say, actually, when it comes to it, we would prefer not to have a station at all? Take the Bartleby position. Ha ha! Who wants to go to Singapore anyway? Dubai? Why the haste to fly to the capitals of authoritarian neoliberalism, the worst of all possible worlds?'

Rodbortzoon picked his notes from the lectern and folded them into his pocket.

'I say to you, the people of Peterdown, it is time to declare that we have had enough. We will have no more trains and no more stations. No more growth. And thank you, anyway, but no more jobs.'

He wiped his nose one last time and looked up at the hushed audience, a big smile on his face.

'The time has come for us to produce ourselves rather than the things that enslave us. And this will be work enough for us.'

39

Ellie looked again in disbelief at the letter. The lease had come up on their house and instead of rolling it on for another twelve months as she had done every year for the best part of a decade, she had let it slip, and had instead applied for a flat at the Larkspur. Not simply a council flat *per se*, but very explicitly one at the Larkspur.

A single mother, as she now was, earning barely enough to get by from her three and a half days a week at Create:Space, she should, she felt, have been installed instantly at the top of the list, certain to get one of the empty units that the council claimed so adamantly that no one wanted.

And yet here it was, in black and white, an official letter telling her that her application had been turned down. The news had been so unexpected that she had had to scan the letter a second time to make sure she hadn't misread it. This was not what was supposed to happen. The whole thing had been so perfectly plotted in her mind. The way she would move triumphantly on to the estate just ahead of the listing. It would have stopped her critics in their tracks, made for a perfect story.

She placed the letter on the table and sat, dazed, in her chair. It was her second body blow of the week, coming as it did two days after she had been forced to close the café. Pankaj had freaked out about the fire safety, ignoring her entreaties that the space was made entirely of concrete and was absolutely free of cladding of any kind. Round and round they had gone, arguing the same points until she, tearfully, had relented.

She had looked into the possibility of getting the space certified but doing so required the consent of the owner and that, obviously, was never going to happen.

And so, on Tuesday night, she had bolted the doors knowing she would not be opening them again the next morning, feeling angrier at Pankaj than she was at Yvonne. It wasn't so much his reasoning that had disappointed her, more the way he existed so comfortably in the certainty of its logic.

Ellie sat silently in her kitchen, listening to the churn of her fridge. First the café. Now this letter. She had mapped out a narrative in her head and none of it had come to pass. In the past this kind of minor setback wouldn't have knocked her so hard. The old Ellie would have absorbed it or ignored it, seen these little sub-plots for what they were, tiny distractions in the context of the main arc of her life. But that was the old her.

Pankaj walked into the room, buttoning his cuffs.

'I'm doing a radio interview this afternoon.'

'Right,' she said limply.

He had his back to her as he tied his tie in the mirror.

'I'm not going to call for the Generator to be chosen.'

Ellie looked up at him, bewildered.

'But we talked about it.'

'I know, but it would humiliate the council and my relationship with them is strained enough as it is.' He pulled the end of his tie down through the knot. 'And it would be an embarrassment to the town. It would look like a backward step, like culture came here and it didn't work.'

'It came here and it didn't work because it was crap culture.'

He tucked his tie into his waistcoat and turned to look at her.

'That's not what the perception will be. It would be a step back and we need to look forward. The stadium relocation looks forward. It means growth. It means jobs. And the station needs to go *somewhere*.'

'You're going to come out in favour of moving the *Chapel*?'

'No, of course I'm not, because it would be insane electorally. But that doesn't mean I don't think it's a good idea. I'm going to have to give a tactful non-answer.'

'Really?'

'Sitting on the fence is not as daft as it might sound. Colin's lot are only a subset of the actual fan base. The rest of them might hate Kirk and would love to see the back of him but fundamentally they don't want anything to change.'

He hooped his watch over his wrist and clipped the band shut.

'The Premier League, whether Colin likes it or not, is an absolutely fantastic product. Fairy-tale outsiders winning the league. Charismatic managers. Wonderful players. Great drama. It's world-beating for a reason.'

Ellie looked at him, perplexed.

'Where did *that* come from?'

'I know enough about it to hold my own.'

'You've literally never mentioned it before.'

'I've never been particularly drawn to it. Tennis is just so much more complete as a sport.'

Here, he tossed an imaginary ball high up into the air and hit it with an imaginary racket.

'It's just more aesthetic. So much more complete and contained. One-on-one. Five sets. Power. Precision. Grace. Endurance. It's the ultimate test for an athlete.'

He shrugged.

'But football is football and I'm a bloke, and it's just so much easier to know than to not know. University. Bar school. Here. The House. It's a lubricant. It starts conversations, breaks down barriers.'

Ellie raised a sympathetic shoulder.

'Anyway, the thing that Colin and all his lot don't get is that it's good because of the money. They talk about it like the money is the problem. Get rid of the money and everything would be pure and perfect again. But you think the Dutch or the Swedes or whoever else wouldn't bite your hand off for it to be *their* league that was so corrupted by the money that's attracted Mo Salah and Thierry Henry and all the rest?

'The reality is that this is what triumphant working-class British culture looks like. It's a bit gauche and there's too much money going to too few people, but it's bloody glamorous and exciting. It was the same with the Beatles and, you know, Oasis, or whatever. It's high-class showbiz with all the bells and whistles that come with it and people lap it up all over the world.'

He picked up his jacket and pulled it on with a practised flourish.

'Fine,' said Ellie. 'I obviously don't care either way, but Colin's expecting you to come out for them. I told him . . .'

'Well, Colin is going to be disappointed.'

'*I'm* disappointed.'

He turned to face her. He looked primed to pounce, like a cat. Or a lawyer.

'Some perspective here would be a good thing, I think,' he said coldly. 'I've stuck my neck out for you and that estate. And it is not exactly a massive vote winner. There are plenty of people down in London who are asking me why I'm spending so much time on it. So I really don't need to hear my motives being questioned. I've got a lot riding on this. If it doesn't get listed I'm going to look like an idiot.'

Ellie winced. Obviously, she wanted it to happen as an end in itself, but she had felt for a while now that she also needed it for them as a couple. The achievement of it would cocoon them in its embrace, locking them into history, the flush of their love held fast in its amber.

'There's a space coming up on the Joint Committee for Human Rights and my name's being bandied about. If I get it, I'll be the first member of parliament to be on a committee within two years of joining the House.' He looked skywards in irritation. 'Which, of course, is totally irrelevant to anything but it would be noticed. It would be a forward step.'

She felt her nostrils flare. Hard to hear it so boldly declared: the running was all with him. He was simply too propulsive, his ambition too intense, not to find yourself dragged – she hedged here – *half* willingly into his path.

'It's ridiculous that perception matters so much but it does. The whole thing is a game and you can rail against its rules, but ultimately you have to play if you want to get anything done.'

She watched him smooth his jacket pocket. She had anticipated some let-up in their desire for each other, a waning of the intensity the longer they spent together. But no. They wanted what they wanted.

'Where are we with the petition?'

Ellie rubbed her face. What duty did you have to yourself, as a woman, other than to own your own soul?

'We've got thirty-seven thousand names,' she said.

'OK. Not bad. Not brilliant, but at least it clears the Klingon test.'

Ellie looked at him quizzically.

'They got twenty-eight thousand signatures to make Klingon an official language.'

She smiled. And then he did, too.

'God, I hope I don't get any questions about all this Wroth stuff,' he said. 'I won't have any choice but to come out against it. It's gone too far. Somebody set fire to a billboard yesterday. It was put out before it damaged anything else but they can't expect to always be that lucky. If they carry on like this someone's going to get hurt.'

Ellie turned a spoon over in her hands.

'I got turned down for a flat at the Larkspur.'

'Oh,' he said, evidently surprised at the news that she had applied and not told him. He steadied himself, looked at her again, smiled.

'You should talk to your MP about that.'

40

The internet café in the back of the Houghton-down-the-Vale village shop was a charming relic of a bygone age; two battered old PCs that could be rented for 50p an hour. The back room of the shop didn't have any CCTV and it was cash only, which, if you were of a particularly paranoid bent, made it the perfect place for anonymous online subterfuge.

Colin was at a machine, getting down to it. Pankaj had been on the radio a couple of days earlier and had been explicitly asked to come out in favour of the Chapel, which was, frankly, the very least he could have done. But he hadn't. He'd equivocated. Sat on the fence. And that, well, that opened the door for Colin to make use of the master planner's report. It didn't equivocate. It stated boldly and unambiguously that in terms of traffic management, pedestrian safety and emergency access, the Larkspur made the best site for the station. It was information you didn't need to sneak around with. You could be upfront with it. Look your opponent straight in the eyes and stab him in the chest.

Colin, however, was not that kind of man, which was why he was in an internet café, five miles outside of Peterdown, setting up a new email account: general_wroth@gmail.com. It was, he thought with a slightly sneaky pride, his second covert action of the day.

In a parcel, recently deposited in the post box, were six soil samples that he had collected early that morning from six different parts of the Grangeham site using a hand auger – basically a giant corkscrew – which he had bought online. The samples were bound for Liverpool, addressed to a specialist in contaminated land who, on hearing that

Colin could blag him two away tickets to see Everton play Feyenoord in the Europa League, had agreed to do a fast-track, off-book analysis in his lab. Colin could expect the results in five days.

Sitting in his cubicle at the back of the village shop, with its handwritten signs prohibiting file-sharing and porn watching, Colin contemplated what he was about to do. The Larkspur had already been chosen. That he knew. Making the report public would make no material difference to the outcome. But some things had to be done just because they had to be done.

He put his pen drive into the USB port, uploaded the summary of the report and emailed it, anonymously, to Neil.

Dark clouds were gathering as he drove up Houghton-down-the-Vale's high street, past its petrol station, its shuttered pub. Colin drove up the approach road to the A108 and found his thoughts turning, as they did with increasing frequency, to Kerry.

He pictured her as she had been yesterday afternoon, just after the game against Doncaster, the two of them still buzzing at the result. Her hair up in a casual ponytail, a simple polo-neck jumper, less makeup than normal.

He had brought her up to date on the possibility of the land being contaminated, explained the link with *Erin Brockovich*, made a bad joke about who would play him in the film.

Honestly, Col, she had said warmly, *you're not like anyone else I've ever met.*

The traffic was moving again and as he drove through the open fields of the Vale of Peter with its rolling hills, ancient stone walls, clusters of sheep, Colin felt a lump rise in his throat. The clouds were low in the sky, heavy and bruised, but a small bud of hope had flowered in his heart. Whatever else happened in his life he would always be, at least fleetingly, the man who was not like anyone else she had ever met.

He followed the A108 for a couple of miles until it took him down through the M13 underpass and into the Peterdown hinterlands. Abruptly the landscape changed. For half a minute he drove alongside the vast edifice of the windowless Ottercliffe depot and its unchanging stainless-steel façade. He glanced at the loading bay where dozens of sixteen-wheelers lined up greedily like a litter of piglets feeding on a sow.

He pulled up at the crossroads and peered down Talacre Street. It was still there as it had been that morning, cordoned off with police incident tape: the remains of a burned-out van, its windows blown out, the rubber from its tyres pooling at its wheels. The charring had given it a marbled look; whorls of black and grey with just the odd streak of purple showing through by which you could identify it as one of Land Dominion's fleet. According to the news bulletin it was one of three that had been torched overnight. At each scene a message had been spray-painted on the tarmac:

SIGNED ON BEHALF OF THE WHOLE, WROTH

The lights turned green and Colin followed the traffic up towards the centre of town. The stickers were everywhere, on every bus stop, lamp post, bike stand and bin. *The Face of Wroth*. Although the illustration owed a lot to the *V for Vendetta* mask – the striking monochromatic lines and anonymous black eyes – it was recognisably its own thing. Unlike the playful *V* mask with its knowing smile and Van Dyke beard, the Face of Wroth was strictly business: big mutton-chop sideburns and a glaring muscularity.

Despite, or because of, this unsmiling seriousness, fans all over the country were using it as their profile picture on the internet and he had seen pictures of it on T-shirts on the terraces from Plymouth to Sunderland. A Wroth cell was operating in London, defacing Moolah advertising and plastering the Face of Wroth stickers on buses and tube station platforms.

He turned on to the Radleigh Road. Even from a distance, he could sense the agitation. No one at the camp seemed to sit around any more, they were all constantly up on their feet, milling about, sniffing the air for danger. And with good reason. The police presence had doubled. Three riot vans were now positioned permanently at the side of the concourse, and everyone speculated endlessly on whether or not a raid was imminent.

All of which was hardening opinion against the Partisan boys, who had clustered together on the stadium side of the camp and were now openly and identifiably pro-Wroth. They seemed to come and go, but Colin thought there were about thirty of them all told. They were genuine Peterdown fans, all of them, but they were only committed to saving the Chapel in the context of their wider aims: bringing down Moolah, Land Dominion and then the council. After that, the Premier League. Then the government. And finally, the global market economy.

Colin found them intimidating and exhilarating in just about equal measure and they still had a lot of support among the camp's veteran activists – Rodbortzoon among them – who ran the Department of Radical Football and seemed most interested in the protest as an end in itself. But beyond this old guard, there was growing resentment at their presence; partly for their late-night chanting and drumming, but mostly for the attention they brought with them. As far as Colin could tell, this increasingly was the majority opinion among ordinary Peterdowners, men and women, all of them long-standing season ticket holders, who made up the bulk of the camp and kept it going: they cooked the food, sorted the rubbish, maintained relations with the police, administered the first aid.

Colin arrived at the roadside edge of the camp and walked between two tents, both electric blue and box fresh. They were occupied by four young self-styled 'footy lads'. They were affable enough, but they all had a streak of the pillage in them. He recognised two of them to be sons of Terry Palmer, who was still in prison for puncturing a Broadcastle fan's lung in a pub car park.

He made his way through the camp to where Brian was talking with three policemen.

'Officer, I understand that it's all gone too far. I'm with you. But what evidence have you got that any of those lads was involved?'

'No one's being arrested. We're just taking them in for questioning so we can eliminate them from our enquiries.'

Through the still-open door of one of the raid vans he could see three of the Partisan boys, at least one of them in cuffs.

'That looked like a pretty rough way to take someone in for questioning.'

'What do you want me to do, Brian? Throw the book at him for resisting arrest?'

A policeman slammed the van door shut.

'Of course not, but he was only struggling because your man had him in a headlock.'

'Three vans got burned out last night. This isn't a few stickers any more. This is serious public disorder. If they didn't do anything then they've got nothing to worry about.'

Colin and Brian watched the van drive away and then walked over to the mess tent to where a dozen or so people were preparing the evening meal.

In the background the twenty-odd Partisan boys who hadn't been arrested had started drumming, punctuating the rhythm with breaks to shout abuse at the police.

Colin picked up a peeler and started in on a pile of carrots.

'I'm all for solidarity,' said Graham Cobb, who had been there from the start. 'But only for what we're doing here. Not anything else.'

'Kirk's made himself a target,' said Mick as he scrubbed a potato. 'I don't have any problem with a couple of his vans getting torched if it convinces him to walk away.'

From where Colin was standing, he could see the four footy lads who were now up out of their tents. They were hovering on the fringes of the camp, looking shifty. Two of them were on their phones.

'Fine,' said Graham, looking over at the Partisans. 'I've got no problem with that. I can see how that's got something to do with the Chapel. What I can't see is how any of this is connected with Palestine.'

'I wouldn't read too much into it,' said Colin.

'Yeah?'

'Yeah,' said Colin with a distracted air. 'I don't think we're going to get dragged into the Arab–Israeli conflict, are we?'

All four of the footy lads were talking to a couple of older guys Colin hadn't seen before, one of them bald, the other in a flat cap, both of them wearing technical jackets drawn up under their chins.

'Aye, you're probably right,' said Steve Wanless, who was frying sausages in a huge pan over a Calor gas ring. 'Anyway, we'd be too busy building extensions for all the refugees we're going to be taking in.'

This was met by a round of low chuckles.

'Imagine getting out of Syria and finding yourself in Steve's garden shed.'

'Don't mind the pigeons. He's a fancier.'

On it went like this, mordant, deadpan, knowingly fogeyish.

The footy lads had been joined by another six blokes, all of them deep into middle age. Anonymous clothes. Hard bellies. Colin couldn't name any of them, but he was fairly sure at least two of them were faces from the Railway Boys, back when they had been a serious firm in the eighties.

'Haven't seen that lot here much before, have you?' he said.

They all looked over.

'Phil Cooke,' said Mick. 'Tony Holmes. Dale Hill. Old faces. But they're all right. Don't worry about them. We're all Steam, aren't we?'

'Yeah,' said Colin tentatively. 'I guess so.'

For the next few minutes, Colin kept his eye on the group. They were all drinking cans of lager and he could see a bottle of vodka being passed about. The police had noted their presence but were keeping their distance. Eventually, over the sound of drumming a chant started. It was call and response, led by a thick-set bald guy in his early fifties.

Whose club?
Our *club*

They were standing by the road on the far side of the camp facing the stadium and, at least abstractly, its owner and management team.

But they were also facing the Partisan boys with their rainbow flags and banners supporting the camps at Calais and Lesvos.

> *Whose club?*
> Our *club*
> *Whose club?*
> Our *club*

All the men in the group were standing with both their arms raised in a V-shape above their heads. The Partisan boys put down their drums and were up on their feet, uncertain how to react.

The police were less tentative. They were all up, out of their cars, lined up, waiting.

Colin looked at Brian and then Mick, trying to work out whether they, too, had noticed that they were standing squarely between the two groups. He put down his peeler and started inching slowly away, only to bump into Rodbortzoon who was blearily walking between two tents, having clearly just woken from one of his many naps.

'We have new arrivals,' he said approvingly. 'You know you are on the cusp of something when you start radicalising the whole spectrum of the working class.'

He was steadily making his way through a packet of those lurid yellow cheese slices designed to be eaten in burgers, delicately peeling each slice from the pile before folding it into a triangle and popping it into his mouth.

'That's what's happening, is it?' said Colin.

'Football is the only arena in which this is possible,' he said, offering Colin a square of cheese, 'it's the only place we can redirect the populist energies the politicians create but can't control.'

Colin declined the cheese, looking uneasily over his shoulder. On the other side of the camp, the chant had changed.

> *We'd rather be dead than red*
> *Oi!*
> *We'd rather be dead than red*

Oi!
We are, we are, we are, we are
We are green and WHITE
Oi!

He looked at Rodbortzoon sceptically.

'They don't like the new kit design,' said Rodbortzoon with a shrug. 'That's common ground we share. I'm sure we can build on it.'

Seemingly in response to this latest chant, one of the Partisan boys had lit a flare, which he was holding high above his head, the thick pink smoke hanging in the thick air. Another had picked up a drum and started their own counter-chant. At least fifty yards separated the two groups but from where Colin was standing they appeared to be inching towards one another.

The police remained on the sidelines, watching on. Their body language – arms folded across their chests, eyes staring impassively forward – seemed to suggest that should anything start they might be very much inclined to stand back and let it play out.

'This is exactly what they want, isn't it?' he said. 'Fans fighting among themselves. It would be the perfect excuse to shut us down.'

'We could keep a lid on all this while the camp's focus was saving the Chapel,' said Brian. 'As soon as all these other things came into it – the end of capitalism, solidarity with the Gaza Strip, the bloody Gaza Strip, what the fuck's that got to do with us? – you've opened it up to all this.'

Brian was hissing now, struggling to keep his voice down.

'Oh god,' said Colin. 'It's going to kick off, isn't it? And it's going to be on the front page of every newspaper tomorrow morning.'

'Nothing's going to happen,' said Brian. 'I'll talk to them. I used to run with lads like them. They know me, they trust me. I can relate to them. I'll talk to them.'

Colin watched Brian walk towards them. He looked around at the rest of the camp, all of whom were standing in among the tents watching nervously. If it did kick off which side would they be on?

The casuals had gone back to their original chant and he could see a couple of people he knew and liked echoing the response.

Whose club?
Our *club*
Whose club?
Our *club*

Colin had only properly started attending football matches in the mid-nineties after the Pavarotti World Cup and Nick Hornby and Sky Television had supposedly brought an abrupt end to the seventies and eighties and all the bad things that had happened then. Which might have been true at Fulham, maybe, or Arsenal, with their all-seater stadiums and celebrity fans. But it hadn't felt like that at Turf Moor in 1999 when he found himself sitting in a seat ten yards away from Burnley fans who had spent half the game pelting them with lighters and pound coins. And it hadn't felt like that two years later when the carriage he was travelling in had been mobbed by a load of Walsall fans as it stopped at Crewe train station. And it hadn't felt like that when he was nineteen and he had found himself in the Ottercliffe Road underpass wearing his replica shirt while around him the Railway Boys fought a load of Newcastle fans armed with bottles and a hockey stick.

He looked over at Tony Holmes and Phil Cooke with their pinched little faces and bald heads. Once, researching a piece, he had spent a whole weekend sifting through the dregs of Netflix, watching football hooligan films: *Spilling the Claret*, *The Minority*, *Cockney Firestarters*, *Kicker Conspiracy*. By the end, all he could think about was how much the whole thing stank of failure. They were the hunting pack that came home every time empty-handed, the unit rejected by the Territorial Army, the men who couldn't mask their loneliness, their shame.

He watched two of the younger casuals bowl forward on bow legs, faces contorted, beckoning with their arms and screaming provocations.

Then it started to rain. It wasn't one of those downpours that starts softly and builds. It was instantly biblical. A single thunder crack and immediately it came down in sheets.

For a while it looked like the casuals and the Partisan boys might ride it out, neither side wanting to be seen to be backing down. They continued chanting, squared off against each other, their drenched clothes pressed to their bodies.

A combination of journalistic impulse and morbid fascination kept Colin outside too, even as all the other campers were scrambling into their tents. He flicked the hood up on his cagoule, glad for the wellington boots he was still wearing from his morning collecting soil samples.

And then, the mud started to leach out from underneath the improvised five-a-side pitch. At first it came in rivulets of brown water, but as the pitch began to disintegrate the slurry got thicker, heavier, deeper. The slope of the concourse was gentle but it was enough to send it all down into the camp.

Colin watched the casuals run for it, picking their feet up exaggeratedly, avoiding the puddles, trying to preserve their pristine white trainers.

Fifteen seconds later, he was alone in the deluge. Even the police had retreated to the cover of their vans. He leaned his head back as far as he could and stood there with his eyes shut, letting the rain thud on to his upturned face, exhausted.

41

There wasn't much on the kitchen countertop but what was there was just right. Six red apples in a Moroccan bowl. Wooden spoons in a terracotta pot. A vintage chopping board that had warped over time.

'In the end, the vote wasn't as close as we thought it might be. We thought we'd take more Tories with us than we did. Still, it was symbolically important.'

Ellie was laying the table: stone-coloured linen napkins, an earthenware water jug, pewter-style cutlery. She picked up a fork and felt its weight in her hand. Daisy and Colin were at the cinema. Thursday night movies, a tradition of theirs. Colin's version of parenting. Until recently, she had used the time to go to Pilates. Now she did this.

Pankaj was grinding coriander seeds with a pestle.

'But we've had a poll bounce off the back of it, which is something at least.'

Ellie put two wine glasses on the table, at least half-listening. She had spent the afternoon trying and failing to convince Lindsey to be the estate's representative at the 'stakeholder sessions' being run by some civil servants who were coming up from the Department of Transport to talk to them as well as some football fans and the Generator Users Group. Instead they were going to have to send Pam, which was far from ideal, but in the end it had been a straight choice between her and Ralph.

She filled two tumblers with water. At least it had been something to think about. The rest of the week had simply been a case of grinding through the days at work and doing her best to be as supportive as possible to Daisy as she gently introduced the idea that they were moving, even if they didn't as yet know where to. The whole thing stank of *waiting*. And it wasn't something she was good at.

'The one that came out this morning had us plus four.'

'That's good, right?'

'It's OK. At this stage in the electoral cycle we should really be up at eight, nine if we're going to have a realistic chance of getting in.'

He had knives. Six of them in a block. Japanese steel. Samurai-sharp. The tip of the blade barely left the board as he chopped. Bam, bam, bam, bam, bam. A dozen crescent moons of red onion.

He had a tea towel tossed over his left shoulder on which he would periodically rub his fingers, dry a utensil, wipe clean a plate. It put her in mind of someone who had picked up the affectation at some kind of Cordon Bleu summer school.

Here he comes, straight from central casting: the boyfriend. Just look at those teeth.

Her mother on Jean-Gab, the first time she met him. Delivered straight to his face in that awful oily voice of hers, which meant nothing to him – what with him being French and not versed in the nuances of the English contempt system – and so he had assumed it was a compliment and smiled.

Aren't you just exactly the leading man she was looking for? The pair of you will look so perfect on the poster.

And he had smiled again at this, that creased, rather thoughtless smile of his that looked so good on the back of a horse or the deck of a yacht.

Onwards and upwards, darling. This obviously had been directed at her. *Onwards and upwards.*

She had never come out and actually said it. Couldn't. For her mother to have accused her of social climbing would have meant acknowledging that there were people above her in the social hierarchy and that was anathema to someone who considered them-selves a kind of natural aristocrat, part of an imagined artist class of philosopher-kings. But it had always been there, unsaid, in the background.

Of course, by contrast she loved Colin. Or at least made great play of pretending she did. *We share a sense of humour, darling.* Always delivered with that tone. That *you don't* tone. But it was true. They did. And whatever other reasons there might have been for her to be so delighted that Colin of all people had ended up as her daughter's partner, she did genuinely seem to like him. And he could talk to her about cricket, which no one else could.

Onwards and upwards, darling.

Ellie sat down at the table. One day she would have to tell her mother that she was dating an MP. But that day could wait.

'After the vote, I bumped into Angie Duncan.'

'She's the head of the select committee.'

'The very one. It was a weird conversation. She's normally very partisan, quite standoffish. But she would barely let me get away. God knows if it means anything but Aidan's very excited. He thinks it's in the bag. Anyway, we'll find out soon enough.'

He checked the oven and sat down next to her.

'So, while I was down there I had conversations.'

'Right.'

'From what I can gather it sounds like there's a split in the transport tsar's office. Some of them are keen to put the station on the site of the Chapel because plans for a new stadium are already in place. But there are others who think it would be a massive misstep politically.'

The wine they were drinking was orange, bought from a specialist shop in Blackheath. Ellie sipped at it tentatively. It wasn't the sort of thing you could buy in Peterdown and she was still developing a taste for it.

'OK,' she said. 'Sounds about right.'

'I don't think you should underestimate how well the campaign to save the Chapel is playing around the country. Football fans everywhere are behind it. And the Tories want to show that they're in touch with working-class people from this part of the world.'

'But that won't affect the listing, will it? You said Harvey hates Eddington. He'll list it just to make things difficult for him.'

'He does hate him, for sure. But the campaign has changed the political weather. If it gets to a cabinet-level discussion they're going to want all the options for the station on the table. Harvey won't want to have been seen to be screwing Eddington for sport.'

'Shit.'

'Yes,' he said with a concessionary shrug. 'But also, no. There's just as good a chance that Harvey has hardly had a moment to think about the station or the Chapel or any of that, and he'll just assess the listing on its merits. They're all so busy and there are so few lines of communication between the departments I wouldn't be at all surprised if that's the case.'

He was back up on his feet, pulling together the meal.

'There's no need to panic.'

She watched him scatter fine-chopped parsley. He raised his hand two feet above the plate so that it fell prettily on its large white rim. It didn't really add anything to the dish but it looked nice.

'Are you happy?' she said.

He looked at her, raised an eyebrow.

'With us?' he ventured tentatively.

'No ... Or at least not just us. I don't know.'

She paused, winced. Shut her eyes.

'Do you feel you're achieving some kind of self-realisation?'

Pankaj laughed, relieved.

'Where did that come from?' he said.

I don't know, the experience of being human, she thought to herself. But that wasn't quite it.

'Colin's friend, Rodbortzoon. The crazy old one with the beard who I was telling you about. He did this lecture at the college last week. I watched it online. He talks a lot about self-realisation. I don't know ... It made me think.'

Pankaj placed the plates on the table. Roasted vegetables. Cauliflower rice. Chopped nuts. Pomegranate seeds. The herbs contrasting prettily with the purple of the onion. *Well, it all sounds very Instagrammable*, said Suzie's voice, in her head.

'Ever since I was fourteen I've wanted to be a Grand Architect of the Universe,' said Ellie, out loud, for the first time in her life.

Pankaj smiled.

'When they invented Google I realised that's what the Freemasons call their version of God. Either way, I'm a long way off.'

He laughed.

She had poured all her hopes and desires into this dream of herself, a crucible in which she might realise her potential. What if, all along, it had had a hole in it?

'So?' she said. 'What about you?'

Pankaj swallowed his mouthful.

'I don't know,' he said. 'I thought I would be more excited about becoming an MP. It's great at the start. Walking the corridors. Drinking in the bar. Learning all the codes. But quickly you realise how insignificant most MPs are. It doesn't mean anything unless you're in government. Really, you need to be a cabinet minister to get anything done.'

Ellie watched the way he swirled the wine in his glass. It was all so breezy and blithe. So frictionless and easily assumed. She put down her own glass. The thing about orange wine, she was discovering, was that it tasted like shit.

'I don't know if I really know what it is that you want to get done.'

'Oh god,' he said with a wave of the hand. 'So many things. Legal aid reform. Mental health provision. All the things you've talked about, land and housing. But all of that is completely irrelevant when you're in opposition. You need to be in government. That's the first step. Everything else follows from that.'

She got up and went to the fridge looking for some tonic that might go with the gin she could see on the shelf above the sink.

'It's the same with you. You need a career plan. A back of the envelope sort of thing.'

'Christ. Do I? Really?'

Pankaj leaned back in his chair.

'If I get on this select committee I'm going to need to be in London a lot more than I am now.'

Ellie pulled the tonic from the fridge and turned around to look at him. It had always been a possibility but neither of them had articulated it before.

'It's been eighteen months once you add in all the campaigning. I don't think anyone could say that I haven't done my time up here. I'd keep this place on of course. I'd still have to be up here now and again, but the bulk of my week would be spent in London. If we were based down there, there would be a lot more job options.'

Ellie could hear what he was saying and all that it implied – a set of thoughts that were both thrilling, and totally and utterly beside the point.

'It's not about just getting a job at a better practice.'

'Maybe not, but getting a job at a better practice would be a step in the right direction wouldn't it?'

'I don't want just to have another bloody *career*. God, there are enough careerists in the world.'

Pankaj shrugged resignedly.

'Well I don't know. What do you want me to say? You hardly stop talking about how awful it is at Create:Space.'

'It is awful. But I hardly think I'm going to start feeling less existentially empty just by getting a job at a slightly less shit firm.'

'Jesus,' he said, getting up. 'What do you want me to do?'

'I don't want *you* to *do* anything.'

'Well what's the point of this conversation then?'

Ellie was about to launch into a thoroughgoing explanation of the point of the conversation when she noticed her phone was ringing.

'It's Shelly McEwan,' she said, looking at the screen.

'Answer it.'

For two minutes, Shelly talked. And Ellie listened. Variously she said things like *wow*, and *oh my god*, and on one occasion, *you are fucking kidding*. Pankaj sat patiently, straining to hear both sides of the conversation, until he eventually gave up and went to make the gin and tonics.

'So?' he said, when she hung up.

'Ketchup found a memo from Yvonne Kington to someone else. Not sure who. It's about the Generator. You know I was telling you about the cleaners and how it didn't add up and how Yvonne totally cut me down when I asked her about it? Well, it turns out I *was* on to something. The Generator's not paying any of the cleaning because it's all rolled into this massive PFI contract. The whole thing was paid for on tick. And I mean *the whole thing*. They've had a three-year repayment holiday but it ends in September. Then they have to start paying for it: the ongoing maintenance cost and the repayments on the capital costs. They must have bargained on it bringing in ticket money, but it's obviously not. It's going to be *haemorrhaging* cash.'

'How did they keep all this quiet?'

'Commercial confidentiality agreements. But that's not all. According to Ketchup, on this memo it says that the first year is sorted, covered by 106. Apparently they've got eight million confirmed. Remember Colin's dude? The guy on Twitter. He was going on about 106 being a magic number or not being a magic number and we thought he meant it was losing a hundred and six thousand a week.'

'I mean, they might be,' said Pankaj, 'but this is almost certainly talking about Section 106 money.'

'What's that?'

'Bribes, basically. Developers don't want to include any affordable housing in their projects, so they bribe the council with a cash payment to get their buildings through planning.'

'Oh my god.'

'Eight million would be a lot even in central London but up here that would have to be a really massive development . . . '

'Like Grangeham,' said Ellie.

'Yes.'

'And the memo says it's confirmed.'

They exchanged a long, loaded look.

'The temptation in this situation is obviously to go public. Make a big fuss,' said Pankaj. 'But we need to be strategic. This is potentially very good news for the Larkspur.'

He picked up the ice tray again, cracked three cubes into a glass.

'It's not at all impossible that someone in Eddington's office is having back channel conversations with the council. I wouldn't be at all surprised if they've basically made the decision and they're preparing the ground ahead of the announcement.'

Ellie pushed her plate to one side. It was easy to be riled by his confidence, but it was what you needed if you were going to operate at this level.

She felt her lungs expanding, the exaggerated movement of her ribs. Accustomed as she was to thinking herself coolly in control, she hadn't been prepared for how exciting she would find this. Being on the inside. Being a grown-up.

'You really think that might be what's happened?'

'From the sound of that memo it sounds like they're already mentally spending the money. I can't see them doing that without . . .'

He exhaled lengthily.

'It doesn't look good for the Chapel, I'm afraid.'

She felt a pang. But just a little one.

'No,' she said.

'You know if this gets out they're going to go nuts. They'll ramp up the protest. There will be a national outcry. Think about it, while the season's still on they'll be able to call on sympathetic fans from other teams. There could be protests all over the country.'

Ellie took a long pull of her gin and tonic to hide the smile that was spreading involuntarily across her lips. Suzie could think what she liked. What did she know about them and the decisions that they had to make?

'If we go public with this,' continued Pankaj, 'it's only going to inflame an already volatile situation.'

'You're saying we don't even tell Colin.'

'Yes,' he said soberly. 'That's what I'm saying.'

It was what you did in these situations. You looked at things strategically. Played the long game.

'OK,' she said. 'We'll keep it to ourselves for now.'

42

Colin stood proprietorially at the mouth of his tent, watching the police as they made their way through the camp. There were about twenty of them, working in pairs. To begin with they had concentrated on the Partisan boys, but their efforts had quickly spread to the whole camp. They were unzipping each tent without asking, pulling the contents out on to the concourse, emptying sleeping bags and riffling through rucksacks. He wasn't entirely sure what they were looking for, but it was pretty obvious why they were doing it.

That morning the residents of Edenvale, a pretty village five miles downriver, with its famous granite-fronted shops and Michelin-starred pub, had woken up to find two dozen police officers milling about the high street. The village green was cordoned off with incident tape, and sitting right in the middle of it was the still smouldering remains of a burnt-out Mercedes S Class.

It had quickly transpired that the personal details of all eight members of the Wintercrest management team had recently been posted on the main Wroth message board. As well as their names and addresses (three of them were conveniently close neighbours in Edenvale), it outlined exactly how much each of them had earned the year they signed off on the relocation of the Crackerjack factory from the outskirts of Ottercliffe to the Wałbrzych special economic zone in south-west Poland. Oliver Farrell had taken home £1.5 million in pay and shares; David Firth, £1.2 million; Andrea Powell, £960,000.

The perpetrators had left an unambiguous sign-off on David Firth's pristine whitewashed garden wall.

Colin felt giddy just thinking about it. First Peterdown and now Edenvale. He could hardly keep up.

In front of him, a young callow-looking copper was pulling Mick's clothes from his bag and tossing them over his shoulder like a magician pulling handkerchiefs from a hat. Pants, shirts, socks, up in the air for all to see. Mick was standing his ground a couple of feet away, looking on with murderous intent.

When it came to his turn, Colin felt strangely elated as he watched two latex-gloved officers pull apart his bag, feeling at its lining, searching through its pockets, running their fingers along its seams. It felt good to be mistreated so publicly, it put lead in your pencil, stoked the fires of your righteousness.

When the police were finally done, Colin took stock of the camp. The five-a-side pitch was now a much diminished and misshapen lump of earth and brown grass, with a single despondent corner flag poking out in capitulation. The tents were still mud-streaked and wilted. And everywhere in between was strewn with torn rubbish bags, discarded clothes, scattered wash kits, empty rucksacks. It looked like the aftermath of a natural disaster.

Eventually, Rodbortzoon, who had missed the raid itself, strode into the camp looking uncharacteristically irritated.

'This is a nightmare,' he shouted.

'Finally, some bloody sense from the man,' said Brian. 'It *is* a nightmare. All this Wroth bullshit. It's out of control. It's just criminality now.'

'Not that,' said Rodbortzoon scornfully. 'Some payback for what those pigs did was long overdue. I'm talking about *this*.' He threw the morning's copy of the *Post* at their feet. The headline dominated the front page.

THE GREAT SCHISM
- Lefties at war as Wroth takes aim at Larkspur

- Report leaked by rival protesters shows estate to be best site for station

Colin read the subheadings, swallowed quietly.

'It can only have been a saboteur,' said Rodbortzoon.

Colin looked away, did his best not to blush.

'It must be the work of a fifth column,' shouted Rodbortzoon, gesticulating wildly. 'No one in the movement would have done anything so obviously self-defeating.'

The piece had been published with Neil's headshot at the top of the page, like they did with pundits on the nationals. Colin's first, not very noble thought was that this was a honour that had never been extended to him. He skimmed through the copy. The tone was caustic, full of acid aspersions and a couple of frustratingly good jokes. He shut his eyes. What *was* it with him and the initiative? How was it that *it* seemed always to take *him*?

'The opportunity now for a united front is sundered. We have been riven in two.'

'What bloody planet are you on?' said Brian. 'Look what's happening here.'

Rodbortzoon looked at him witheringly.

'You think this is rough? I was in Bucharest in '89. Genoa in 2003. This isn't even a shakedown. It's a gentle pat.'

'You weren't even bloody here. It wasn't a pat, it was a raid. And it was too much for Johnny and Deborah. They've had enough and gone home. We're losing our good people because your lot are off burning cars.'

Rodbortzoon shrugged phlegmatically.

'In the context of the damage done when they closed the Crackerjack plant, one chargrilled Mercedes is neither here nor there.'

'Be that as it may, it's got nowt to do with the Chapel. And it's got nowt to do with us but we're the ones bearing the brunt of it all. And there's a lot of people getting seriously fucked off with that lot,' he said, pointing at the Partisans. 'We need to start again. I'm not joking. This is not what was supposed to happen.'

'Aw, Jesus,' said Graham Cobb, looking up from his phone. 'That's all we need.'

'What?'

'The presentation this afternoon. There's four groups. The housing committee from the estate, some people from the Generator and then us. But they're also seeing the RPUFG and all.'

'What?' said Colin. 'But no one even knows who they are.'

'Kirk'll have been agitating for it.'

'Jesus. I can't believe this.'

'S'all right,' said Mick. 'Graham'll do a job for us. The RPUFG's bullshit. The government people will see right through them.'

'You reckon?'

'All right,' said Steve Wanless. 'Enough now. Focus. York City. That's what this afternoon's about. We've only got two and a half hours until kick-off. Let's get this place sorted out before thousands of people start arriving.'

Sullenly, they started sorting through the mess. After Colin tidied his gear back into his tent, he picked up a dustbin bag and started collecting the rubbish. Soon after, Andy joined him with a recycling sack and together they moved through the tents gathering bottles, cans, chip wrappers, rolled-up toothpaste tubes, days-old papers; the damp and muddy detritus of eighty-odd urban campers.

'So,' said Colin as he picked up a cob that had been stripped of its corn. 'What do you know about land held in common?'

Andy looked at him, squinted.

'Not much,' he said.

'This guy down at the marina told me about this right that they've got to take wood from the Mawson Estate. It's a right of common, apparently.'

'You think Grangeham might be land held in common? Like we have the right to graze cows there, or something.'

'The right to graze cows, fish in its streams, collect dead wood. But you know what you can't do on land held in common? Build a stadium.'

As soon as they'd finished the clear-up, they got to it, Colin on his laptop trying to arrange for access to the National Archives, Andy on his phone trying to decipher the Commons Registrations Act of 1965. By the time they reached their seats in the Chapel, ten minutes before kick-off, Colin was scrolling through Wikipedia's history of the Inclosure Acts, while Andy read out sections of the DEFRA website.

By the time the players went in at half time, with Peterdown one-nil up, Colin had successfully applied for a press pass to the Commons Register, and Andy had discovered, after twenty minutes on the phone to Her Majesty's Land Registry, that Kirk had bought the Grangeham site in a single deal, but that it had been parcelled together by the previous owner from five different pieces of land.

They barely noticed the restart, both of them glued to their screens, looking up only to catch Garry wheeling away, having scored Peterdown's second goal. Ordinarily this would have been thrilling of course, but while Hull were winning at Darlington and Coventry were one up against Sunderland, it barely mattered what happened at the Chapel. And so, they were urgently cross-referencing the parcels of land against the Commons Register.

On they went deep into the second half, plugging away at the database, hardly watching the action on the pitch, until their attention was caught by a half-cheer that had begun to spread haltingly round the stadium. And then the information reached them: the Coventry keeper had been sent off for handling the ball outside the box and Sunderland had equalised from the resulting free kick.

Colin closed his laptop.

'What's going on at Darlington?'

Andy flicked to the BBC website.

'Bloody hell,' he said. 'They've just equalised.'

'Oh god,' said Colin as he watched the York City winger running at Ash Connelly. The winger streaked past Connelly and hit a low hard cross into the Peterdown box.

'Please,' said Colin. 'Just for once.'

The York centre forward reached the ball before Gavin Parsons and calmly side-footed it into the bottom corner.

'Why?' said Colin plaintively, looking up at the sky.

Andy was looking down at his phone.

'Calm down,' he said. 'We're still one up and it sounds like Sunderland are all over Coventry.'

Colin watched as one of the York midfielders won the ball from Per Gunnarsson and worked it out wide. He felt an involuntary twitching in his thigh, a kind of all-body contraction towards his groin.

'It would be the most us thing ever if we fuck this up from here. It's York, for god's sake. They've got nothing to play for. *Nothing.*'

The next ten minutes went much the same way – Colin howling profanities, agonising over every tackle, every clearance, the whole lower half of his body engulfed by an epically slow-moving sphincter-tightening spasm.

And then, with three minutes to go, Andy screamed.

'Sunderland have scored!'

News spread around the stadium. Colin shut his eyes. If it stayed like this – Hull and Coventry held to a draw, them winning – then it would be mathematically possible. Promotion. Not likely. But not lost. If it stayed like this, they would go into the last game with a chance.

Colin felt the blood drain from his head. The tension was too much. He leaned forward, eyes closed, and held his head in his hands.

He stayed like this for a full minute and then, seemingly from nowhere, he heard it. The ref's whistle. Unexpected and oddly serene.

Then came the cheer, which was neither.

Colin opened his eyes and looked up.

Around him the whole stadium was writhing in delirium.

'God,' he said to no one in particular. 'I don't know if I can take much more of this.'

* * *

'We need to find out everything we can about this fifth parcel of land,' said Andy. They were in the Department of Radical Football, sitting at a trestle table. He had Google Maps open on his laptop and was tracing an area of land around a brook. It was scrubland, adjacent to the old forge buildings but undeveloped by comparison, just a couple of sheds and an outhouse. It seemed that the registration of common land was an ongoing project, based on close reading of manorial transcripts and seventeenth-century legal documents.

'No one seems to know much about it. I think it could be the key to the whole thing.'

It was about an hour after the game. Colin had filed his copy and bought them a six-pack of lager and a large bag of chips, which they had covered in vinegar and curry sauce and were eating with tiny wooden forks.

'From what I can tell the site is at the meeting point of three other areas of land that were enclosed at different times. There's a chance that our little parcel wasn't included in any of the three acts. If that's the case, it could still be held in common.'

'But somebody owns it though.'

'It doesn't matter who owns it. It's common so you can't build on it in a way that would prevent people from exercising their right to pasture or whatever.'

Andy had picked up all this in a day. Colin took a pull on his can of lager and looked sideways at him, trying to remember how he had been at the same age. A blunt tool by comparison. Gauche. Desperate for the affirmation of adults. Shy. Sad. Lonely.

Colin experienced these thoughts dispassionately. When he thought about his youthful self it was with a sense of detachment not dissimilar to the way he thought about complete strangers, or figures from the newspaper or television. The nineteen-year-old Colin Ryder came to him as an abstraction, no more essential to the *him* of today than his ashes would be in seventy years' time.

Nineteen. He had been so impressionable then, instantly persuaded by any show of certainty which might anchor his insubstantial self. He thought back to the blustering faux confidence that he had developed in sixth form after the student body had dramatically thinned and his peer group's definition of cool had shifted at least some way from the criminal to the cerebral. Christ, he had been a blowhard with his clumsy contrarianism. His intellectual grandstanding. His tendency to exaggeration and elision.

He speared a chip with his fork and ran it through a smear of sauce. He was simply another person, that boy ...

And yet, he thought, surprising himself, that didn't mean he was someone you couldn't feel affection for.

Colin ate the chip, blindsided by a swell of pride. He had been gauche for sure, and yes, entirely lacking in self-awareness. Nowhere near as clever as he had thought he was. But.

He swallowed the chip and with it the lump that was rising in his throat.

But it had been him and no one else who had written the essay that had won the Vale of Peter prize for English, beating all the kids from St Margaret's Day School and Broadcastle Grammar. And it had been him that had a piece published in the *Post* before he had finished his A levels. And it had been him who, against the odds, had gone to university and made friends and become someone.

Slightly drunk and deeply maudlin, he looked at Andy and thought seriously about pulling him into a great big bear hug.

'I'm going for a pee,' he said, before he did something stupid.

Outside, the camp was busy, the numbers swollen by fans who had hung around after the game. It was a mild evening. The smell of burgers frying drifted on the breeze. The sounds were of kids playing, idle chat, tipsy laughter. He walked through the tents, past people sitting around drinking tea, smoking fags, talking in twos and threes.

Everywhere, the conversation was the same.

'If Coventry drop points at QPR ...'

'If the Orient can just get a draw against Hull ...'

'If Garry stays fit ...'

'If our prayers are answered ...'

Walking back into the low sun he found a group of five teenagers standing in a circle juggling a football between them. He joined them, controlling the ball with his thigh when it came to him, before knocking it up to one of the boys on the other side of the group, who caught it on his head. The boys were good. Full of tricks. The ball stayed up for fifteen, twenty touches at a time. Heads, chests, thighs, feet, popped up in the air off a shoulder.

He was so caught up in the game that he barely registered the three or four guys that had congregated outside Gordon's café. When there were ten of them he started glancing worriedly over. It wasn't until there were at least twenty that he stopped playing. And then just like that there were forty. All men. A lot of them in their thirties. Some older.

'Are they Broadies?' said Mick, shielding his eyes against the sun.

Colin couldn't tell. They weren't the type to be wearing scarves or replica shirts.

'Who were they playing today?'

'Sheffield United,' said someone. 'Away.'

The men were standing in one big group, separated from the first tents by about forty yards of empty concourse. There was something particularly sinister about the anonymity of their clothes. The jeans, the windcheaters zipped up tight under the chin, the way they seemed to be one great undifferentiated washed-out blue mass.

'Jesus,' said Mick. 'Tell me they haven't had the brass neck to turn up here.'

And then it came, arcing through the air, the answer to his question. A can of lager, spraying its contents like a Catherine wheel. It landed well short of them, skidded along the ground. Then they started to sing.

The Yard's a bonfire
The Yard's a bonfire,
We'll close the door on all you lot
Chuck some water on the wiring
And watch the Steam come out the top

Mick was up on his feet, walking towards them.

'Not here,' he was saying. 'Not that song. Not here.'

Steve Wanless was alongside him, trying to pull him back, but Steve was half his size and Mick was powering on.

'There's fifty of them. They'll kill you.'

'I don't care. No one sings that song and gets away with it. Not here. Not on our patch. Not that song.'

'Let it go.'

'If they kill me, they kill me. But no one sings that song without getting Mick Claridge in their fucking face.'

The Broadcastle fans were on to the second verse, the one about the smell of the burning bodies and how you could taste it in the air. Mick kept going, walking steadily on, his head up in defiance.

Colin watched. They exhausted him, these shows of strength that so loudly announced themselves as weaknesses. This obsession with front, face, imagined honour codes. It was an open admission that your reputation was all you had. The only thing worth defending. He remembered when it had first dawned on him, this. It was the moment when he realised that he had become middle class, or at least middle class-ish.

'It's only a song, Mick,' he shouted. 'Just let it go.'

'No,' said Mick. 'It's not only a song. And I won't let it go.'

One of the Broadies had picked up the plastic chair that Gordon kept outside his café for smokers. It spun oddly, lurching in the air and landing not far from Mick's feet. He stopped, Steve still by his side.

For a few seconds there was a lull, just Mick and Steve facing the mob. Then from nowhere Dale Hill was alongside them. And so was Phil Cooke. And Tony Holmes. And ten or twelve others.

They stood in a line, facing off. All of them, apart from Phil Cooke. He had his back to the Broadies and was addressing the dumbstruck Peterdown fans like a lieutenant rallying his troops, shouting at each of them in turn.

'STAND YOUR GROUND.'

The ferocity of his delivery caused the skin to tighten whitely around his mouth. He was pointing at Graham Cobb, staring at him with a crazed intensity.

'AND YOU, YOU'RE PETERDOWN. STAND YOUR GROUND.'

He pointed at Colin. Looked him squarely in the eyes.

'AND YOU,' he shouted with even greater urgency. 'YOU WILL STAND YOUR FUCKING GROUND.'

Colin, obviously, did what he was told. More literally, in all probability, than was intended. He stood his ground. Unmoving. As motionless as a statue.

Around him, people were running, scrambling to get away from the imminent violence. But he had been singled out, directly addressed, *identified*. And so he stood there, his breath held, incapable of coherent thought, totally immobilised.

Or at least he did until he realised his phone was ringing in his hand. It was the soil specialist.

Phil Cooke had turned his attention to Andy and was bellowing at him NOT TO GIVE AN INCH. A volley of beer cans was launched by both sides.

Impulsively, he answered his phone.

'So, I've got the results,' said the soil specialist.

'Tell me,' he whispered.

'They're clear. Nowhere near dangerous chromium levels.'

Colin sighed, oddly unmoved.

'That's the thing with historical plating work,' continued the soil specialist. 'It all depends on what metals they used. If it was tin plating, it's not a problem. Tin's non-toxic. Doesn't matter how much there is down there.'

On someone's call they charged. Twenty Broadies pouring forward as one, raining blows on the front line of Peterdown fans, who fought them off, chased them back. It was chaos, obviously. Totally headless and instinctual at the level of the individual. But the way the groups moved had a kind of massing, mercury-like choreography to it.

Colin watched it with detachment, the scattering and resettling, sort of, somehow, like schools of fish. It was an odd sensation to be in it but not of it; at its centre, but also adjacent to it. It meant he could see it coolly, at a weird half-pace, and also that, just for once, he was not scared.

'What if I didn't do the sampling properly?' he said unhurriedly. 'I might not have dug deep enough.'

A couple of Broadie youths ran across the concourse and aimed a couple of Cossack-style high kicks at Mick, which he batted away, hardly flinching.

'If the land was seriously contaminated, I'd have found substantial traces anyway, but there was nothing there. I ran it for lead, nickel, zinc, mercury. It came up well within the range for all of them.'

A roar went up as Tony Holmes led a counter-charge of Peterdowners, 'Steam ... Steam ... Steam ...' they shouted as they ran.

'What's all the noise?' asked the soil scientist.

'Nothing,' said Colin, as he watched Dale Hill fix a vast Broadie in a headlock, his stubbly double chin bulging like a puffer fish. 'Match day.'

As always in these situations, someone had found a long pole which they launched through the air like a javelin. Colin watched as it crashed ineffectually on to the ground. To his right, two middle-aged men were windmilling each other with straight-arm punches.

'Could it have been the jars? I just used normal jars.'

'You think a bit of bit of leftover jam might have neutralised the chromium?'

A trestle table had been upturned and a pile of Save the Chapel flyers blew away in the wind.

'OK, yeah. Probably not.'

Phil Cooke dispatched a fleeing Broadie with a kick up the arse before turning back to Colin, who remained where he had always been, rooted to the spot. The look on Cooke's face was blackly euphoric. He stared wide-eyed at Colin for a second or two before picking up an empty Calor gas canister and running at the Broadies, hollering.

'Sorry I don't have better news,' said the soil scientist.

Outside Gordon's café, Dale Hill had a man on the floor and was kicking him in the ribs. A big fat bloke who could have been from either side was walking around in a daze, blood seeping from a cut in his head. In the distance, the first sirens sounded.

'Me too,' said Colin.

Two of the younger Broadcastle fans were running away from Mick, who lumbered after them violently, his green hair blowing in the wind.

'Anyway, it was interesting soil. More alkaline than the stuff I normally see. Bit of a wasteland, is it?'

'Yeah,' said Colin as the police swarmed across the concourse, sending the fans running, dozens at a time, through the tents, skipping over the guy ropes and away down the road.

'Sounds like a site ripe for development to me.'

'Right.'

'Sorry.'

'Don't worry,' said Colin, strangely relieved. Chromium (VI) would surely have been only a passing headache for Kirk. Even if the site had been riddled with it, it would still surely have made sense to clean the land, such were the sums involved.

'Now, about those Everton tickets ...'

The Broadies had scattered. The police were everywhere. Pinning individual fans to the ground, corralling groups back to the camp. Colin watched it all whirl on around him. Throughout, he had stood his ground.

'I'll stick them in the post,' he said.

He hung up, looked out across the chaos of the concourse. Contaminated earth could always be cleaned but land held in common could not have its history so easily erased. He and Andy may have failed in their efforts to make sense of the archaic statutes but that was no matter. He knew exactly the man he needed.

And where to find him.

43

'What I don't understand is why you don't use a napkin. You drop food on your clothes more than anyone I have ever met and still you don't use a napkin.'

Ellie flicked the offending piece of spinach from her lap. Too late. There was a stain on her trousers, halfway up her right thigh. Hollandaise.

'You're either an incredibly elegant clumsy person or an incredibly clumsy elegant person,' said Pankaj. 'I can never work out which one it is.'

They were at the second-best place in Broadcastle for brunch. The best place was full.

'It only happens because you've made a thing about it.'

'No, that's definitely *not* why it happens.'

'Observing a phenomenon necessarily changes that phenomenon,' she said. 'It's actual physics.'

Around her, people sat at wooden tables eating avocado on toast, eggs Benedict, granola out of enamel mugs. The walls were white tile. The grout was black. The bright copper fittings had been polished until they gleamed.

Revivalist Urinal Bling is what she would have named it, on his behalf, if she was sharing that kind of thing with him.

Which she wasn't. Because he had returned to his copy of the *Atlantic* and was doing the thing he did by way of declaring that he was not interested in small talk. Shoulders up. Gaze fixed on the page. Jaw clenched. It was his way of saying, not while I'm *reading*.

There was a last smear of hollandaise on her plate. She ran her finger through it, scooping it all up. How funny, right now, to be missing Colin, she thought. He wasn't a great bruncher, as they went, but he could listen. They all could, Colin and his long line of small-talkers. A whole family tree's worth of people who – if her experience was anything to go by – had no big talk. No inclination to really dig down deep into something, put the world to rights, *philosophise*. But they were never short of something to say, the Ryders. Would always happily lend an ear. The whole lot of them could chitchat for England.

She licked her finger and looked at Pankaj, at his arrow-like concentration, his intensely communicated seriousness. You could say what you wanted about football but at least it was accommodating. Colin could be watching it – as he so often had been – and still be listening to her, semi-engaged in both. Which most of the time was all that you ever wanted in such situations. To be at least half-heard.

Ellie looked down at her plate and felt a great flood of feeling for him. Never once had he tried to solve her, assumed that the thing she needed from him was fixing.

Even if she did. Need fixing. She looked down at her nails. She had painted them black a while ago and they were chipped enough now at the tips to look like ten little pints of Guinness.

Pankaj reached for his coffee without taking his eyes from the page.

They were a young couple out for brunch in a nice place.

Or at least young-ish.

Or at least young-looking.

And yet.

* * *

A couple of hours later, she was on her own, at the Larkspur café. It had been shut for two weeks, but only now – going back to clear the fridge of its food: a near-liquid bag of salad and an almost solid bottle of milk – did she feel fully her disappointment at its wasted potential. When they got the estate listed, the café could of course be revisited as part of a wider renovation, but she felt a pang at the prospect that she might not be around to be a part of it. Pankaj had been called in for an interview by the chair of the select committee. London seemed to be their unstoppable destiny.

She picked up a bin bag, feeling an odd, thin kind of sadness. By all accounts, Pam had done well with the civil servants. She had been authentic, open and personable. Even charming. Particularly when compared to the football fans, two of whom had got into an argument as they had waited for their turn, which had descended into a slanging match so ferocious that they had to be physically separated by a security guard.

All of which had come on top of the Sunday papers' coverage of the fight at the camp. She felt a pang for Colin, regret that there wasn't more that she could do for him, a sense of deflation at the direction things seemed inevitably to be heading for him.

After an hour of cleaning and tidying, she found, in a jar behind the counter, a surprisingly edible brownie, which she took along with a cup of mint tea to the best table by the window with its view right out to the Beagle Hills and beyond.

Beneath her, Peterdown spread out incoherently like a jigsaw jammed together from four different sets. Cramped where you wanted room and open when you wanted intimacy, it was a town of dead space, roads to nowhere, twilight zones.

Yet looked at aslant, it had its own crooked charm.

She pulled out her laptop and absentmindedly opened Facebook.

Ellie looked disbelievingly at her feed. She felt the blood rushing from her head as she read the top post. Two months after he had launched it, Benjamin Willis's practice had its first commission. Not a restaurant redesign or a house extension. No. He had won the competition to masterplan Terminal City North, the two-hundred-home neighbourhood that would make up part of the £4 billion redevelopment of the old Gatwick site.

She stared out of the window, blankly. Two seagulls wheeled in the breeze. It was pointless now trying to pretend otherwise when it was obvious to all: if anyone from her year was going to be a Grand Architect of Anything, it was Benjamin Willis.

The brownie sat squarely on its plate. She picked up her knife and cut it into twelve small pieces, as Lindsey had. She ate a piece, licked crumbs from her lips. Had he been the best of them? He had been up there, for sure. But in terms of raw talent Elaine Thompson had been better. And so had Roshini Kumar. But neither of them had been to Bryanston School, and nor had they had an uncle who was an arts correspondent at the BBC, who had taught them exactly the right opinions to hold on Aalto and Venturi and Kenzo Tange. And crucially, *definingly*, neither of them had been born with a dick.

Her phone was ringing in her bag but she ignored it. Ellie had identified a rare opportunity to position herself as the victim of a structural injustice and there was no way she was going to give up the opportunity to start driving a wedge into the hairline crack between the levels of privilege that differentiated Benjamin's upbringing from her own.

She put another morsel of brownie in her mouth and let it sit there without chewing it. Her school had been OK, a north London comp. Full of bright kids, but no one had left it assuming it was their natural right to be a cabinet minister or a diplomat. In fact, Kieran, who had been seated next to her for fifth year biology, had, as she remembered it, been told by the careers advisors that the computer program had decided, based on his answers to the questionnaire and predicted grades, that he, a lifelong resident of Kentish Town housing estate, was best suited to being a shepherd.

She thought about Benjamin, how he'd walked into the lecture hall on the first day of their first year: his trousers worn voguishly short, his screamingly ironic NHS glasses, his quietly expensive bag. No one had ever told Benjamin Willis or anyone from his school that they ought to think about being a shepherd.

Finally, she looked at her phone. The missed call was Ralph. Summoning her to the Beagle Hills. Something she simply had to see.

When she arrived, ten minutes later, he was up on the top of the highest hill, wearing a white balaclava, a white polo neck with black chevrons and white cargo pants. He looked like a Bridget Riley painting that was about to go skiing. She sighed. It was a costume from *Danelaw*. The Blizzard Corps officer class or something like that. A detail that she refused to remember.

'Now I want you to come at this with an open mind,' said Ralph.

'When you see what I'm about to show you, I want you to think about it without prejudice.'

'What are you talking about?'

'Zone Eight?'

'*What?*'

'It's out there. The truth-teller on the internet talks about it. He has inside information, prior warnings, occult knowledge. It's a secret but he can't contain it, it's too much for one man. Imagine it, Ellie. Zone Eight.'

Ellie furrowed her brow.

'I thought there were four zones in the film?'

'Yes.'

'So what happened to zones five, six and seven?'

'Finally, you're asking the right questions.'

'Oh Jesus, Ralph.'

'Flat five point two, Ganymede,' he said, pointing in its direction without looking up from his watch. 'Five, four, three, two, one,' he counted, and snapped his fingers.

The lights all came on.

'Ralph, is that even meant to be impressive? You've got Barry to switch the lights on in his flat at 5 p.m. Seriously, I walked all the way up here.'

'OK,' said Ralph. 'Flat six, Europa.'

He snapped his fingers. The lights came on.

'You think Barry could run from Ganymede to Europa in anything like thirty seconds? I've seen him take that long to stand up.'

'You've got someone else in that flat!'

'I don't have three friends,' said Ralph in a voice that was plainly matter-of-fact, entirely absent of self-pity. 'Barry and you. That's it.'

Ellie stopped and looked at him in a way that was supposed to communicate admiration and warmth but not pity.

'I don't like drinking,' he said with a shrug. 'I don't speak with a proper Peterdown accent. I don't like football.'

'I can't pretend I don't like drinking,' said Ellie. 'But I'm with you on the other two.'

'Barry's worried,' he said. 'He's worried he's going to get behind on his rent and get kicked out. You used to get a bit of leeway, you know, if you got behind, but now they're kicking people out for nothing. For sub-letting and stuff. Things they never used to care about. He's worried they're going after him because he's been helping you.'

'They can't do that. I won't let them. Our MP will rain all kinds of shit down on them if they try anything like that.'

Ralph looked down at his watch.

'Flat seventeen, Ganymede,' he said.

Ralph clicked his fingers. Another light came on.

'It's a code. But who's issuing it? And who to?'

'You're not serious, Ralph.'

'I'm not saying *Danelaw* was a prophecy, Ellie. I just want you to think for yourself. I'll ask you again: *Where is Zone Eight?*'

'Oh god, Ralph. You are the cleverest idiot I've ever met.'

Ten minutes later she was walking back to the café when she passed Ganymede House. She stopped and then went to walk on, but hers wasn't the kind of mind that easily let things go. She sighed and walked to flat 5.2.

The lights were on. All of them. The curtains were a heavy net, drawn tight to the frame. She peered through them, trying to make out shapes in the room. But there was nothing. No furniture. No signs of life. Just below her nose, though, she could see three shiny new screw heads. The window wasn't simply locked. It had been screwed shut.

She felt her heart quicken.

She walked over to the door and felt at its edges, pressed it for give. Looked at from a distance, it seemed normal. But when you got up close and felt it, you could tell that it had been welded.

The lights were on a timer.

She stood looking in puzzlement at the door. If it was just a security thing they would simply have boarded it up. Somebody had gone to an awful lot of effort to make it look like people were living there.

But they weren't.

44

The Geoffrie Experience Centre was housed in a red-brick building at the south end of the Eastfinche Road. The only things
to indicate that it wasn't another unremarkable office block were the
portcullis that hovered above the door and the window decals of a
drunken monk raising a pint of ale. They hadn't been changed since
the centre opened in 1988. Which was true of much else about it.
Although they did now have a website.

Colin followed Rodbortzoon in through the door. The reception
area was as it had always been: an institutional carpet, a vending
machine, tills topped with grey plastic ramparts.

It was early on Tuesday morning and the space was empty of customers. The man at the till was wearing a light-brown tunic tied at
the waist and a dark-brown hood that came down over his shoulders.

'Well, well, well,' he said, recognising Colin. 'Serf number three.
It's been a long time.'

Rodbortzoon snorted gleefully.

'You told me you were a knight!'

'I was serf number three for like four days,' said Colin huffily. 'I
was a freeman for, I don't know, a week. And then a squire for no
time at all. I was the second fastest person to be promoted into the
nobility in the centre's history.'

Rodbortzoon roared with joy.

'Who was fastest?'

'Me,' said the man at the till.

Colin looked up, allowed their eyes to meet. Evan Havers.
Master mead-maker. Simulation jouster extraordinaire. The only

man trusted to play the eponymous monk. Colin felt the thing pass between them that had always passed between them. It would be wrong to call it erotic, but it had a charge. And it made him feel quiveringly alive. From 2005 to 2009 they had been the Borg and McEnroe of the Geoffrie Experience Centre, their intense rivalry pushing each other to ever greater heights of medieval one-upmanship. During his first stint working there, in the summer before he took his A levels, Colin had learned verbatim whole sections of *Gawain and the Green Knight*, which he would recite at length in what he imagined to be a period-specific accent. In response, Evan spent a whole week only eating pottage. Colin went on a falconry course. Evan took up lute playing. Colin insisted on going to work with an actual mace. Evan designed his own heraldic shield and had it tattooed on his arm.

'Ten years ago, you vowed you would never set foot in this building again,' said Evan.

Colin bridled. There had been something of a declamation the summer of his graduation year, on the eve of his move to London. A need to end one life in order to start another. Doors had been slammed. He may or may not have thrown a replica cudgel. It may or may not have hit the then manager.

He looked around instinctively.

'Don't worry,' said Evan. 'Samuels isn't here no more. Got the big job at Jorvik, didn't he?'

'God, did he?'

'Asked me to go along and be his number two.' Evan pursed his lips. 'I didn't fancy it. What's there to do in York?'

'You didn't get his job here?' said Colin, surprised to find himself so deeply wounded at the injustice.

'They brought the new guy in from Chessington World of Adventures,' said Evan stoically. 'He's got qualifications. Tourism and leisure.'

'It should have been you.'

The beat or two of silence that followed seemed to contain reservoirs of regret and longing.

430

'So,' said Evan. 'Ten years since we've seen you. What's brought you back?'

'I need you,' said Colin, unguardedly. 'No one else would do.'

Evan tried to be implacable in the face of this but Colin knew his tell: a twitch of the left cheek, echoed soon after by a similar movement in the right shoulder.

'No one knows this town's history like you do,' he continued. 'I need to know about Grangeham. About the enclosures. Is it possible that part of the land out there is still held in common?'

Evan smiled the involuntary smile of the clever boy who always knows the answer.

'Historically, that is an interesting part of the Vale,' he said. 'Not a lot of people know that the—'

The back office door opened and a man – whom Colin clocked immediately to be the guy brought in from Chessington World of Adventures – walked into the reception. Evan stopped talking and started staring awkwardly at the wall.

'Buy tour tickets,' he said, under his breath. 'There's no one else in there. We can talk on the cart.'

The Geoffrie Experience Centre tour carts were oversized golf buggies with room enough for eight people. Rodbortzoon sat up front alongside Evan with Colin in the second row, leaning forward into the gap between the two of them.

'Keep your arms and legs inside the buggy. Please don't touch anything. And no flash photography.'

'OK. Thanks Evan.'

'You know I'm not covered if I don't read you it.'

'For god's sake, we're not going to sue you,' said Colin.

But he was not to be placated and so they sat through the whole spiel. The location of the fire exits. The different kinds of alarm. The emergency lighting protocol. What to do in the event of a flood.

Finally, they were off. Evan drove them down a tunnel and out into the experience proper. Ahead of them, illuminated by a spotlight, was a waxwork of a woman stirring a large bowl of soup.

'So we start with food,' said Evan, slowing the buggy to a crawl.

'Of course, the aristocracy would have been eating mostly meat. All the usual ones: beef, pork, chicken and lamb. But these were beyond the peasantry, who had to make do—'

'Jesus,' said Colin. 'We don't need the bloody lecture.'

'Yes, we do!' shouted Rodbortzoon. 'That woman is cutting up a hedgehog!'

'Well spotted,' said Evan. 'The peasants were also very fond of squirrel.'

'Enough,' said Colin. 'What's interesting about that part of the Vale?'

Evan steered the buggy on to the next set of waxworks, which centred on a metalworker, his hammer raised high above a chest plate. He drove right up to it, stopped.

'The Grangeham forge is on the site of the old Temple Estate. There used to be a house there but it burned down in, I think, the 1880s. An insurance job. The guy that owned it was broke and it had run completely to disrepair. The gardens were all gone to seed, the house was falling down. A farmer picked it up for nothing and never rebuilt the house. Over the years, the farmer and his son ended up selling the land in pieces to the Gaitskill family and a load of others who built the works out there, that we ended up thinking of as the forge.'

The metalworker's hammer fell animatronically on the shield, sending a loud clang echoing round the hall.

'But back in the day, when it was the Temple Estate, it was all one piece of land. And it was pretty grand. It was all built in the 1630s by Josiah Temple. A total headcase. Mad drinker. Was accused of beating one guy half to death and loads of other stuff but he kept getting pardoned by the king, because he was a rock-solid monarchist. Whenever Charles I needed some muscle in the locality, he called on Temple to get together a mob.'

Evan glanced up at the CCTV camera and restarted the engine. He piloted the buggy round a corner and into the interior of a medieval keep. A couple of knights were on horseback in chain mail. Various scruffy peasants were frozen mid-scuttle, carrying and fetching firewood, chickens, an urn of beer.

'Before Temple owned it, it was a royal forest. There were loads of them all round the country. Charles I couldn't raise money through parliament so he had to sell them off to his pals for cash. Like all the royal forests, lots of local people were surviving off it. Some ran pigs in it. People used the timber for housing and everything. A lot of them even lived in it. All of this was informal, but it was tolerated and had been for decades.'

Evan drove them on to a life-size diorama of the royal court. The medieval king sat on his throne, various cronies whispering entreaties in his ear. Stuffed dogs sat at his feet. Standards hung from the ceiling. And there he was, the monk himself, grandstanding.

A mechanised laugh went up and the king stiffly slapped his thigh. Geoffrie had spilled his mead. Again.

'Temple cleared them off, the lot of them, and there was nothing they could do about it. It wasn't even enclosure because they hadn't had no rights. That was what precipitated the Rising of the Vale, it's how the Ringmen emerged.'

'So this Temple guy scrapped all their common rights to the land.'

'Not even. There was none there to begin with. People were tolerated but never had any proper rights.'

'You're sure?' asked Colin morosely, knowing that he was.

'Hundred per cent. The common land round here is all over in the Mawson estate. Now that's interesting because—'

Without warning bright orange flames were projected on to the side of the Abbey. Smoke started pouring into the room from all four walls.

'What the fuck is going on?' said Rodbortzoon, pulling out his handkerchief and covering his mouth.

'It's the dissolution,' said Evan. 'The Abbey's on fire.'

'But that doesn't happen for another four hundred years!'

'1538 it happened. They booted out all the monks and then burned it down to get the lead from the roof.'

The smoke had filled the room, great dry blooms of it, glowing orange and yellow in the projected light.

'Five minutes ago, it was the middle of the twelfth century,' cried Rodbortzoon despairingly.

'We had to significantly compress the historical process.'

Colin sat in the back of the cart, remembering the smell of the smoke, its horrible taste. In the brief period of his life that he had occasionally frequented nightclubs the smell of smoke machines had always transported him back here, to the moment of dissolution and the feel of it in your mouth, matt and acrid.

'This is totally crazy. I can't see anything.'

'It's our thing. At Jorvik, they've got the smell. Here, we have the smoke.'

'What is he talking about?' shouted Rodbortzoon.

'Jorvik Viking Centre smells of shit,' said Colin to a background of screaming monks, the crackle of a burning cassock. 'It's the only thing that anyone remembers about it. When they were building this place, they wanted something memorable. Hence the smoke. No one forgets the smoke.'

The roof of the Abbey fell mechanically to the floor. Rodbortzoon was on his feet now, transfixed, his handkerchief tied across his face like a rioter dodging tear gas.

'Why didn't you take the job as Samuels's number two?' asked Colin.

Evan looked at the wall, twitched a little.

A monk's cry pierced the air.

'I don't know,' he said. 'I'm from Peterdown. What do I know about York?'

'What does anyone know about anything until they've been there?'

Evan stopped the cart, turned the key in the ignition.

'I'm on to a good thing here.'

Colin didn't say anything. For some people, leaving was something that existed outside their imagination. And he got that. But the bounding of your universe wasn't something that could happen independently. You had to connive with it, enforce its border lines, wilfully reject its expansion. Sitting there, in the buggy, he realised that he, Colin, hadn't done that. He had made a decision, opened himself up, welcomed in the world.

'I'm on my lunch break in five minutes,' said Evan, as the smoke thinned and the lights went up. 'Fancy a pint?'

'Yes,' said Rodbortzoon. 'Always.'

Colin looked at Evan. There was something animated about his eyes, the look of a man who had been starved for a long time and was ready to feast; on companionship, conversation with equals. He felt a great surge of sadness at all those wasted years.

'I can't. Sorry, mate,' he said. 'I've got to go and meet this guy Brian who runs the Chapel campaign. He's been on at me all morning. I've got to go and see what he wants. But you two should go get a jar.'

'I will buy the drinks if you take me backstage,' said Rodbortzoon to Evan. 'I want to see the costumes. The swords. All that stuff.'

Evan looked over one shoulder and then the other.

'Come on then.'

* * *

Brian was in the corner booth at Gordon's eating fried eggs on toast. Colin slipped in opposite him and signalled to Gordon for a plate of the same.

'Thanks for coming,' said Brian as he chewed.

Colin shrugged.

'The Grangeham land's not contaminated and it's not held in common,' he said. 'If there *is* anything wrong with the site, I don't know what it is. It looks like we'll just have to hope that results go our way on Saturday.'

It was Brian's turn to shrug.

'Anyway,' said Colin. 'What was it that was so urgent?'

'I wanted to tell you first. Not least because you'll need to find somewhere else to sleep.'

Colin looked down at the rucksack at Brian's feet.

'You're leaving the camp?'

'Your stuff's in with Rodbortzoon.'

'Oh come on, Brian. I know things have been a bit ... I don't know ... complicated recently, but this isn't the time to leave.'

Brian smiled gently.

435

'The irony of the whole thing is it's the camp that's been the inspiration,' he said. 'The camaraderie. The working together. Building something from scratch. I don't want you thinking I'm going because there's been moments where it's been tricky. I mean, Jesus, I can handle a bit of bother. All the bullshit in the *Post*. It's not that. These last few weeks have been incredible.'

Brian fixed Colin one of his meaningful looks.

'I'm not going to fuck about with you, son. I'm starting a new club.'

'*What?*'

'I've been in touch with Northern Counties Second Division. They've got a slot for us but I've needed to move fast, which is why I'm only telling you now. I've scraped together the registration fee and we've been told we can use that pitch on the rec by the Eastfinche Road. It's only got a tiny stand but it's a start.'

Colin felt himself sinking into the hot leatherette. He closed his eyes. There was one game of the season left. Unquestionably the most important game in the club's history. The kind of game that cleared the decks, made it impossible to think about anything else. The kind of game that you could organise a life around, remember forever. And now this.

'Oh, Brian.'

'I'm talking to a fellow I know about taking charge of the team. He's had a bit of experience managing non-league and he's willing to do it for nowt to get himself back in the shop window. He's got contacts and he reckons we'll be able to pull in five or six young lads. Squad players from the Conference looking for a regular run in the first team. For the rest of them we'll be holding trials on the marshes in a couple of weeks. We want local kids, you know.'

'Don't do it, Brian. We could be just four games away from the Premier League. Think what it'll do for this place if we go up. We'd be able to stay at the Chapel. Think about the money the club'll get. God, even if Kirk is still in charge next season, things will have to change. Look at what's happening. He's going to have to reckon with a whole new kind of fan base. We'll be able to wring all kinds of concessions from him. Get the outreach stuff going again ...'

'Staying at the Chapel isn't a victory, Col, even if we go up. If anything it'll be worse. This club gets into the Prem and he's going to go mad with it. Commercial revenues? Fucking hell. That club goes up and that's it, you'll never get rid of him.'

In his head Colin began totting up those that Brian would be taking with him. Ten minimum. Maybe twenty. All of the moderating influences.

'You walk away and he wins.'

'We need to start again, Colin. The whole of football. We just need to start again.'

'This is exactly what he'd want us to do. We get divided and he wins. The Chapel's gone, flattened. A hundred years of heritage destroyed.'

'What does it matter where the club plays when the players have got *Moolah* written on their shirts?'

'You're giving up too easily. We stop the Grangeham move and he'll walk away. He's only interested in the club if it gets him his development. We stop it happening and he'll offload it in a heartbeat. Then there'll be a club that can be completely remade.'

'It's too late, Col. It's all started. We've registered with the FA. We talked about calling it Lokomotiv Peterdown but there's enough looking back in this town as it is, so we've gone for AFC United of Peterdown. We've been talking a lot with the lads in Wimbledon and Manchester and it's a tribute to them both. A statement of solidarity.'

Brian stood up, pulled his rucksack over his shoulder.

'Sometimes the only way to keep something alive is to split away from its main body. The more I think about it the more I've come to realise I'm not sure I want to support a club in the Premier League. Yeah, you get to play against Liverpool and the like, but you have to put up with the endless bullshit. I just don't know if it would be worth it.'

Colin watched as Brian pulled a fiver from his wallet and tucked it under the bottle of brown sauce at the end of their table. He felt a sharp panic in his chest.

'Is Andy going with you?' he asked.

Brian grimaced tenderly.

'I won't pretend I didn't try,' he said. 'But no dice. He's sticking with you.'

* * *

Forty minutes later, Colin was on the Ottercliffe Road, ignoring the light rain. He was experiencing the heightened perception of the acutely disappointed, a kind of romantic alertness, a sense of portent. Alongside him, cars rolled and stopped in the traffic. A street cleaner pushed his cart. A crow cawed. All of it seemed to tremble with meaning.

He had decided to walk to the office. Over the Drewdale bridge, its old stone balustrades whelked with chewing gum. Through the Uppervale Rec, the swings long removed from their rusted frames. Up the long Ottercliffe Road, with its shops set back from the street: the glass merchants, the Topps Tiles, Diamond Minicabs, the cars idling in its forecourt.

This was the place that Evan had never left. Colin looked over the road at a café called The Sandwich House, which had been operating under that name for nearly two years but which everybody still called the Grapes, as it had been known under its previous owners.

He crossed the road to a Tesco Metro. It wasn't that nothing changed in Peterdown. That at least would have been a situation pregnant with the possibility of its own overcoming. It was worse than that: even when things did change they still stayed stubbornly the same.

He grabbed a bottle of Lucozade from a fridge and went to pay for it. There, in a cardboard stand by the tills, he found himself looking for the first time at the front page of that day's *Post*. They had led with a piece about the camp. The headline was sensational. The copy was savage. The byline was Neil's.

Colin threw the copy of the paper back where he'd found it.

Enough was enough.

* * *

438

The office was quiet when he arrived, all of them sunk still in the post-lunch lull. Anne McAllister was on the phone, nodding. Hugh Trentwood was eating crisps.

Colin strode to the middle of the room and cleared his throat. It was a fool's errand to imagine that you could swim against the current of your time, but that didn't mean that, at the very least, you shouldn't go down kicking.

'Can I have your attention please, everyone,' he said, sombre, like an actor.

Eight heads swivelled in his direction. Rick got up from his desk and leaned against the frame of his door.

'I'm sure I'm not the only person aware of the strange things going on at this newspaper. The way that lines of investigation are being closed down and diverted. The way that when we start to ask challenging questions about Land Dominion or Andrew Kirk they always seem to end up being "handled" by the same person.'

Here he paused for dramatic effect.

'Neil Henderson.'

Neil snorted through his nose. The look on his face was a mix of incredulity and amusement. Which, Colin rationalised, was exactly the look you'd go for if you were attempting to disguise your guilt.

'And I can't be the only person,' he continued, 'who is increasingly alarmed at the way many of his recent pieces have taken on the hysteria of the right-wing tabloid press, flying in the face of the fine traditions of this newspaper. And whose interests does it serve, this agenda?' Here he stabbed the air like Lenin on the cover of *What is to be Done?* 'Corporations like Moolah. And Land Dominion. The very behemoths that a local newspaper is obliged to keep in check.'

'OK, Colin,' said Rick. 'I think we've heard enough.'

'No, I won't be silenced on this. The blame lies squarely at your door, Rick. I'm sorry but it's true. As soon as you agreed to let Land Dominion sponsor the property section, you opened the door to this sort of thing.'

Colin faltered, derailed by the overabundance of doors, unsure which of them to go through.

'I have evidence,' he continued without great conviction, 'that Kirk has employed someone to – and here I quote – "tell his story".'

The room around him was silent. Kelly-Anne hadn't moved since he started. She sat, mouth open, her fingers still hovering above her keyboard.

'You've all experienced it, haven't you? The way he's on his mobile out in the car park or the corridor.'

Colin paced the floor, each stride serving as a punctuation mark, a way of underlining his point. It was an attempt at gravitas. Atticus Finch was his model. Henry Fonda in *Twelve Angry Men*.

'Whispering, his hand over his mouth, and then he shuts up whenever you get near.'

He paused. And then he hit them with it, his devastating conclusion.

'There's no way to sugar-coat it so I'll just come out and say it: all the evidence points to Neil being bribed by Andrew Kirk.'

Finally, Kelly-Anne gasped. Neil, perched against the photocopier, started to applaud sarcastically.

Rick shook his head.

'I don't even know what to say to that.'

'Just tell us the truth,' said Colin, unsure whether collective pronouns were exactly called for. 'That's all we're asking for.'

Rick looked at Neil. Neil shrugged, assented with a nod.

'I had been waiting until the end of the day to tell you this, but I guess we'll have to do it now even though the champagne won't be cold yet,' said Rick. 'I'm proud to say that Neil has been offered a job on the news desk at the *Mail on Sunday*. With my blessing he's been in conversation with them for a couple of weeks, but he didn't want anyone else in the office to know, which is why he's been on his mobile. He didn't want it to be a distraction.'

Colin looked morosely at the floor. At the periphery of his consciousness he was aware that he had profoundly humiliated himself in front of the whole office. But that was a secondary matter. Right now, a single thought sat front and centre in his mind: Neil was going to the nationals.

'I spoke to the news editor at the *Mail* this morning,' continued Rick. 'Neil's piece in today's paper convinced him to offer him the role.'

Without looking up, Colin could feel Kelly-Anne looking at him with her unblinking animal stillness.

'Anyway,' said Rick with a sigh, 'now you all know. Not quite the grand announcement we'd imagined. But hey ho. Let's get on with getting this paper together and we'll come together again at 5 p.m. for some bubbles.'

Slowly the team returned to their desks. Someone put the radio back on. A fax came noisily through the machine.

Colin perched on the edge of the art table. He looked up. Rick was staring at him. He was no longer angry. The look on his face was worse. It was pity.

'You know, I always thought it would be you, Colin.'

Colin kept his mouth clamped shut, pursed his trembling lip.

'And look at you now. My god.'

STEAMING IN: A PODCAST WITH MICK CLARIDGE AND STEVE WANLESS PLUS SPECIAL GUEST COLIN RYDER

ORIGINALLY AIRED 7 p.m.
SATURDAY, MAY 3rd

MICK
(incoherent guttural roar)

STEVE
(similarly incoherent crazed yodelling noise)

MICK
(another incoherent guttural roar similar
in pitch and tone to the first, only three
times louder)

STEVE
Unbelievable. Unbelievable. UNBELIEVABLE.

MICK
What were the odds? Hull only getting a draw at
Orient. Coventry going down two-nil to QPR. And
Per Gunnarsson — Per bloody Gunnarsson — scoring a
hat-trick away at Bolton?

STEVE
(singing)

442

Six-th place. Six-th place. We've only got sixth place. Six-th place.

    MICK

It's been emotional, as you can probably tell.

    COLIN
    (dryly)

I think 'tired and emotional' is the phrase they use in the media.

    MICK

Oh, yeah. In the excitement, we've gone and forgotten to introduce our special guest, Colin Ryder, sports correspondent for the *Peterdown Evening Post*. Sorry, Col.

    COLIN

Quite an occasion to be making my debut. Particularly as I had to stay sober in order to write my match report. Whereas you two — well ...

    MICK

What a fucking game! What an occasion. Three-one away at Bolton. Per Gunnarsson should be given the keys to the city.

    COLIN

Per, or maybe Paul Christie. Because that was a tactical masterclass. Using Gunnarsson at the tip of a diamond was brilliant. It freed up Jordan and Amobi Okafor to run in the channels between their centre backs and full backs. And playing that high a press was risky but it totally—

443

MICK

(interrupting)

Colin, son, sorry but we don't do that kind of
chat on this podcast. That sounds dangerously like
analysis. And we don't do that. We do hyperbole
and invective. We do ranting and we do raving ...

STEVE

And all-time elevens ...

MICK

And all-time elevens. We do a lot of all-time
elevens. And I'll tell you what. Per bloody
Gunnarsson has just played himself into mine this
afternoon.

STEVE

Oh, that third goal. He is officially my favourite
ever Viking.

MICK

Because the thing is, Colin, proper football fans
don't give a fuck about tactics. They like sliding
tackles and diving saves and thunderfuckers
smacked in from thirty yards. That sort of stuff.

COLIN

Right. So I might be allowed to say that we
won with a couple of Viking thunderfuckers from
outside the box and because we wanted it more.

MICK

That was *exactly* what I was going to say.

STEVE

Just in case any of you have been on Mars or
something. This is what's happened. Nottingham
Forest have finished third. QPR are fourth, Bolton
are fifth, and we're sixth. It means we play Forest
home and away and then the winner goes to Wembley
to play the winner of Bolton—QPR.

MICK

WEM-BER-LEE, WEM-BER-LEE. We're just two games from
going to WEM-BER-LEE.

COLIN

Yeah, but two pretty difficult games, no? Forest beat
us home and away. They've won five of their last
six. They're easily the best team in the playoffs and
we're, well, we're obviously not. I know it is very
exciting and just finishing sixth is a monumental
achievement on the lowest wage bill in the division,
but the reality is that we're still rank outsiders
and all this is just a massive distraction.

STEVE

Oh, Col, let us have an afternoon to dream.

COLIN

Sure. But let's not forget that this is exactly
what Kirk wants. It's like he's scripted it.
If we'd finished tenth or whatever, this camp
would be rammed. But this way we bow out with a
noble defeat against a big club like Forest and
everyone'll think we gave it a fair crack and we'll
go home talking about what a ride we had while he
ships us off to some dump in the middle of nowhere
so he can build himself a massive B&Q.

                MICK

Not if we get promoted, though.

                COLIN

We're not going to win. We're playing Nottingham
Forest. *Over two legs*. They've beaten us home and
away already this season!

            STEVE

Garry was crocked.

            MICK

At ours, you're right. Jordan had just done his
hamstring. And still we only lost one-nil. And,
god, didn't their keeper have a game that day?
I remember him saving a header from Amobi,
point blank.

            STEVE

And when we went to their place it was early in
the season and we hadn't clicked yet. They were
still getting used to the new formation.

            MICK

Oh god, I think we can do it. Their centre halves
are big lads but they're not exactly quick. And
with the tip of Colin's diamond I think we might
be able to just stick it up 'em.

            COLIN

I give up.

            STEVE

Admit it, son. You're a little excited. Just a
little bit.

        MICK

Two games from Wembley, Colin. Two games from
Wembley.

        STEVE

Wouldn't it be something if we did, eh? Two
fingers to Kirk for starters.

        MICK

And the Broadies. And the BBC. The London lot.
The fucking EU. Everyone who thinks we're shit and
we don't count for squat. It'll be two fingers to
all of them.

        STEVE

Come on, Col. The bloody playoffs. I mean, you'd
have taken it at the start of the season, wouldn't
you? We're so bloody close.

        COLIN

        . . .

        STEVE

Just for the record, the sports correspondent
is smiling.

        MICK

Hey, I'll tell you what, if you'd just gone and set
up your own club you'd be a bit gutted about this,
wouldn't you? Ha ha ha!

45

'She said they were doing it to stop the estate feeling deserted. Boarded-up flats make people depressed.'

Pankaj was in London. He was fresh off the phone from Yvonne.

'So she's *still* claiming they're not decanting it?'

Ellie was standing on the platform at Peterdown station having just got off the trundly little train that shuttled backwards and forwards to Broadcastle. It had been a long, deeply dull day.

'She said it was part of their investment in the site.'

'Did you tell her about me, about how I didn't get a flat?'

'She said she couldn't comment on any individual application.'

'Right.'

Ellie pushed her train ticket into the slot and walked through the gates.

'She said people get turned down for social housing for all kinds of reasons.'

She snorted.

'It is possible that she's telling the truth.'

'Yeah, right.'

'Either way, I really don't think this is the time to start making a fuss about it.'

'Why not?'

'My relationship with the council is fractious enough already. I have to work with them on dozens of different things and I don't want to completely poison the relationship over this one thing.'

'They're up to something.'

'Yes, we know that. But it's the Chapel that's going to suffer because of it, so let's just keep quiet.'

'I don't trust her, Pankaj.'

'Be that as it may, we don't have any actual proof they're decanting the residents.'

'I got turned down!'

'Yes, you got turned down. You're a bloody architect. Did you really think you were going to be top of the list?'

'I'm a single mother,' she said. She nearly added *thanks to you*.

'There's nothing else I can do right now,' he said. 'My meeting's about to start. I'll call later.'

Ellie walked out of the station, passed the street florist with his depleted buckets of flowers you never wanted: three-foot lilies wrapped in plastic, lurid blue carnations, pastel pink gerberas browning at the tips. She looked up and saw the back end of her bus disappearing round the corner. Which was fine. It was a mild evening. She could walk home through the park.

King Edward's Green was a handsome park and its horse chestnuts were glorious things, especially in early May when they were budding, their young leaves joyously light and lovely and full of life. Ellie walked underneath them, awed, as ever, at their grandeur and scale. It had been a funny couple of days. The more she had discovered about Benjamin's commission the better she had felt. It was a nice gig, obviously, but one that would have to be articulated in the vernacular of its context. All boxy bricky newness. He'd do it with good grace, of course; tastefully, demurely, exactly the right amount of just-so detailing. But it would no more announce him as a Grand Architect of the Universe than her Aldi on the Castleford bypass. It wouldn't matter. Wouldn't change anything.

On the grass, schoolboys played football, their coats and bags tossed in a pile. She paused for a second to watch, as Colin always did. They were probably eleven. First years at Rothbury Manor where Daisy would be going if they had been staying put. Which they weren't. With no flat to be had at the Larkspur they seemed to be moving in with Pankaj by default. It had been mooted but never concretely decided upon and then it had got lost in the talk of London and now it just seemed to be happening. Without fanfare. Or initiative.

By the bandstand, three teenagers idled on a bench, texting and smoking fags. Ellie walked past them, jealous of their indifference. Would she not be happier, she wondered, if she just surrendered to it?

He was an incredible man, handsome, clever, kind. And being with him meant London with its bustle, its bounteous opportunities.

And yet, she thought.

And yet.

* * *

'I wasn't expecting you to be here.'

Colin was standing in the kitchen doorway, conscious that he was leaning more than a little wanly into the frame. It had been a week of daily abasement and humiliation punctuated by the one vertiginous high of securing sixth place.

He screwed an eye half-shut, looked at the floor. His position at the *Post* had reached an all-time nadir. Despite Neil's departure, the paper's editorial line had, if anything, hardened against Wroth and, as one damning piece came out after another, he had found himself ever more isolated and embattled.

At the camp, things were similarly fractured and depleted. Brian had taken two dozen protesters with him, all converts to his new club. And in the days since the win over Bolton, another ten had packed up, Mick and Steve among them, claiming with a resigned air that it was promotion or bust.

He allowed himself to slump, looking even more dejected. Pankaj had started posting pictures of Ellie on Instagram with indecent frequency. Kerry seemed to be constantly distracted. And when it came to scuppering the Grangeham development he had completely run out of ideas.

In the circumstances, he could, he felt, stand exactly as he pleased.

'I thought you were going to be out,' he said eventually. 'Daisy's at my mum's, right?'

'Yeah, she is. I was going to be out but now I'm not. I can go if you want.'

'Don't. I won't be long. I was going to make a start on some packing. That's all.'

'You carry on. I'll busy myself somewhere.'

She took off her coat and hung it up on the rack. He hadn't moved. Barely looked like he even had the energy.

'Look at you,' she said softly. 'How many days a week are you eating takeaway pizza?'

Colin looked away in a manner he imagined to be inscrutable. The more penetrating question would have been: how many *meals a day* are you eating takeaway pizza?

'It varies,' he said.

'Processed food gives you cancer.'

'Divorce gives you cancer.'

'We were never married!'

'OK, the breakdown of long periods of cohabitation gives you cancer.'

She laughed dryly, through her nose. Just as she went to speak, the doorbell rang. It was Rodbortzoon.

'Oh God,' she said. 'Just what the situation needs. Tweedledee.'

'Eleanor,' he said, bowing theatrically.

'I didn't invite him,' said Colin. 'He just turns up. He does that.'

The three of them filed into the kitchen. She started going through the drawers, sorting through their contents. On the countertop were a handful of pens, a ball of string, a pocket torch, two lipsticks, an assortment of Allen keys, a single glove. The little things that always just survived the cull. The things marginally too precious to jettison.

Colin looked enviously at the glove and then beyond it to a second pile. Chargers for a decade's worth of mobile phones. Nokia, Samsung, iPhone fat, iPhone thin. Together they had witnessed four technological leaps forward. And all the time they had been going backwards.

451

'There's some wine in the fridge,' said Ellie.

'Don't worry,' said Rodbortzoon. 'I have come prepared.'

He pulled from his bag a flagon of something that really should have been confiscated at customs. The liquid in it was murkily opaque, full of cut herbs and sticks.

'Christ alive,' said Ellie. 'What's that?'

'Slivovitz,' said Rodbortzoon. 'Homemade. The best kind.'

'How many people has it blinded?'

'This batch?' said Rodbortzoon. 'So far, zero.'

On the table in front of them he had placed three glasses.

'You drink it in shots. It's not really for sipping. After each shot you wait five minutes before you have a cigarette. It's advisable.'

'Go on then,' she said. 'I'm game.'

They had a shot each. It was like drinking semi-set jelly made from pine disinfectant. Even Rodbortzoon winced as the first one went down.

'I'm supposed to be packing,' said Colin.

'I had come to help,' said Rodbortzoon as he placed his own glass back on the table and refilled it. 'But I am too depressed to be much use. This new club. It is madness. A withdrawal from the arena. Totally insane. We are three games away from the world stage and he does this.'

'What new club?' said Ellie.

'I can't talk about it,' said Rodbortzoon. He poured them both another shot and then ambled upstairs, taking the bottle with him.

'Where's he going?'

'I think he's going to have a bath.'

'He has *baths*?'

'Every now and again.'

'So what's this new club?'

Colin felt for his temples. The impact of the Slivovitz was immediate, a malign gripping on the brain.

'Brian's setting it up,' he said. 'They're going to start in – I don't know what it is – the ninth division or something. He's calling it AFC United of Peterdown.'

He downed the shot in front of him.

'Well that's perfect. Why don't you all go and support that one? It can be totally . . . I don't know . . . *uncommercial* or whatever it is you want it to be and you'll all be in control of it and the one that Kirk has will become valueless because no one supports it. There you go. Problem solved.'

'It doesn't work like that,' said Colin. 'I can't just start supporting a new club like it was my old club. I mean, what is it? Gem McBride didn't play for it. Archie Davison didn't cry the day it got relegated. It hasn't been the constant backdrop to my life. I don't love it.'

'Couldn't you learn to love it?'

'Not like I do United. You don't just support the team on the pitch. You support all the teams there have ever been. Decades and decades of them. You take it all on. All the injustices. The rivalries. The tragedies. It's like there's this great story being played out and it started before you were born and it will carry on after you die. And it will contain all of life. Incredible heroism. Abject failure. Moments of beauty. Moments of despair. And anyone can be part of it. All you have to do is decide to care. And then you're a fan. And you belong. And you are not no one. I can't get that from anything else. It has to be United. I'm in too deep.'

Ellie fetched the wine from the fridge. She had for so long despaired at his bloodlessness, and yet there had been this thing in his life that aroused great passion in him and she had never made any effort to comprehend it.

She poured them a glass each.

'It's not just because we're in the playoff semi-finals. I mean, we're not going to go up. We've got Forest for god's sake. They beat us home and away. It's not about success. It's about continuity. Brian's club doesn't have any history. How can I dream about it?' Colin held his wine glass in his lap like it was a wounded bird. 'When the bad thoughts come how can I fight them off by thinking about its all-time greatest eleven?'

'Is *that* what you do?' said Ellie.

'Yes,' said Colin, his chin on his chest. 'Mostly the line-up just picks itself but I can never decide between Kimble or Fensome at left back. The head says Kimble of course, but the heart will never forget Andy Fensome's goal against Everton in the Rumbelows Cup.'

'So that's what sport's for,' said Ellie, downing her shot.

'What do you do?' he said. 'You know, when you're sad. What do you do to stop yourself thinking the bad thoughts? What do you do to drown them out?'

Ellie placed her shot glass delicately on the table.

'I don't stop myself from thinking the bad thoughts, Colin. I try to do something about them. I confront them.'

He slumped down on the table.

'Now I see what the problem was between us,' he said with a crooked, defeated look on his face. 'You think problems can be solved. I know otherwise. I know things will never get better. That's why it never worked with us. We were all mixed up.'

Ellie smiled. She had never really loved him, but she had never not liked him. In fact, she had always intensely liked him, right from the day they had met.

'Look,' she said. 'I've got something to tell you.'

Colin sat up like a marionette jerked back urgently to life.

'Is there literally *any* thunder of mine you can't steal?' he cried. '*I've* got something to tell *you*.'

'OK. What is it?'

'No,' he said grumpily, 'you first.'

And so she told him about the 106 money, about where it was coming from and what the council planned to do with it.

'Oh El. I'm sorry,' he said. 'That money, it isn't coming from Grangeham.' He looked at her tenderly, full of remorse and guilt at his silence. 'It's coming from the Larkspur. Rodbortzoon took me down to the marina the other night. You can see across to the estate. There were surveyors there, measuring it up. At four a.m. They didn't want to be seen, but they've already started work. It's a done deal.'

Ellie heard this and for a second her heart stilled; then she remembered.

'But it doesn't work like that. The government doesn't pay 106 money. That only gets paid by developers. If the station was going to

454

replace the Larkspur there wouldn't be *any* 106 money coming in and Yvonne Kington's talking about it like it's a done deal.'

She tried to take some succour from this, but there were lights on a timer to make it look like there were people in the flats when there weren't and now she was hearing that there were surveyors secretly visiting the site.

'Come on,' said Colin. 'Think about all the stuff she had that Philpott bloke doing. She's desperate to get shot of Larkspur Hill.'

'The council have explicitly come out and said they want you to move stadium.'

For a second or two they both worked through the permutations.

'Oh god,' she said eventually.

'Yeah. Fuck,' said Colin, who was arriving at the same conclusion as she was. 'They want to . . .'

'. . . knock them both down,' they said in unison.

'Yours for the station,' he said. 'Mine for the money.'

They sat in silence for a while. Colin picked up his wine, drained it.

'You know, the stakes might feel higher and everything,' he said, 'but the reality is: you get the building listed and it doesn't happen.'

Ellie looked up at him warmly.

'And you find a reason they can't build on the Grangeham site and that doesn't happen either,' she said.

'And if the Larkspur gets listed and they can't build on Grangeham then the Generator's finances will be really properly shafted, what with the council not getting any 106 money to pay for it.'

Ellie's right eye crinkled a little as she smiled at him.

'So they might as well build the station there.'

For a few seconds, neither one of them spoke. It couldn't be faked, Colin thought, this kind of silence. It had its own texture. It could only be achieved by two people who knew each other deeply, had put in the time. Pankaj might be all the things that he was but, at least for now, he couldn't compete with Colin's hours on the clock. It would be years before they would be able to do this, sit in this kind of comradely silence.

Colin let himself sink into the golden glow of this tiny victory, this long glorious moment of being there with her, while Pankaj wasn't; not looking at her, but not *not* looking at her, and her doing the same with him.

His phone started to ring.

He looked at it and blushed.

'It's her, right?'

'Yeah.'

'So it *is* a her.'

He blushed again.

'Answer it.'

Colin picked up the phone, turned away from Ellie.

'Oh my god, Col. I did it. Gus Taylor's mobile rang and he went outside to take the call and left his laptop open so I just went for it. I'm not joking, it was proper CIA. The whole time I thought he was going to come back and catch me but he didn't and I got on to the server and *I found the payroll*.'

'Was Neil Henderson on it?' he whispered plaintively, the offer of redemption opening up unexpectedly in front of him.

'Oh yeah, no. He wasn't.'

Colin crumpled inwardly.

'But Col, listen, it's better. There was all the usual above-board stuff but I found another file, called "contractor". There were just two names in it. Some bloke called Douglas Dublin, whoever he is. And you'll never guess who else .. James Philpott!'

'Shit the bed,' said Colin.

Ellie looked at him beseechingly, desperate to know what was going on.

'The payments to him start right after he got sacked from the council.'

'Wow.'

'I'm buzzing, Colin. I can't tell you, I am *flying*.'

'You're amazing,' he said.

Colin placed the phone back on the table. He reached for his wine. The washing machine was in the final churning stages of its spin cycle. Around him, the contents of their life were piled up, ready to be portioned out. For a second he sat there, looking at Ellie, having just put down the phone to Kerry. His feelings were reflex guilt, mild titillation and total confusion. How, he wondered, did anyone ever have any certainty about what it was they wanted?

'So come on then, what makes her so amazing?' said Ellie with an eyebrow suggestively raised.

He explained. Not what made her amazing. Or who she was. Or where she worked. But the information she had shared with him: James Philpott and his new job.

'The whole thing is so corrupt,' said Ellie, once he was done. 'The council and the developers, the revolving door between the two of them. It's the same all up and down the country. It's time we blew the whole thing open.'

'Let's do that,' said Colin, who at an existential level didn't really know what it was he wanted, but knew, concretely, that he didn't want the evening to end.

'Yeah?'

'Yeah, let's write the piece. The definitive piece. You and me. Let's blow it open. Let's do it now. Let's get it all out there: the Generator, the PFI stuff, the massive debts, the 106 money, the sneaky shit that's going on with Kirk and the council, the surveyors at the Larkspur. The way they're trying to stitch this whole thing up without anyone knowing about it. Let's hit them with everything we've got.'

Ellie bit her bottom lip.

'I'll get some more wine,' she said.

Colin sat at his laptop with Ellie on his shoulder. Together they hashed out a structure. He transcribed her ideas, editing as he typed. She suggested topics, lines of argument, and he turned them into paragraphs.

They ordered pizzas. And on they worked. And while they worked, they drank. The rest of the wine. And then two Belgian strawberry beers that had been in the fridge since a holiday in Ghent three years earlier. And then finally a glass of Baileys each, because that really was all that was left.

'So, is she beautiful?' asked Ellie. She was swirling the Bailey's in the glass, enjoying the way it clung to the sides in a fine viscous layer.

Colin didn't look up from the draft he was reading.

'I don't think you would think she was,' he said in a measured tone. 'But you do.'

'I'm not sure if beautiful is the right word. She has something though. A quality.'

He put down his red pen and looked up at her.

'But no one is beautiful like you,' he said. 'Really, no one I've ever met. No one I've ever seen.'

Ellie looked back down at the page she was reading, a hint of a blush across the top of her cheeks. She tucked a lock of hair behind her ear.

'There's a typo at the start of paragraph four,' she said. 'You've missed out an "of" in the second sentence.'

Colin scrolled through the document, added the missing word. As he did so he stole a glance at her. She was leaning forward, so that her hair fell over most of her face. But, still, it was obvious: she was smiling.

Twenty minutes later it was done. All fifteen hundred words of it. Colin read it over one last time. It was forensic and unsparing: it named names, didn't shirk the big calls. Apart from Daisy, it was the best thing they had ever done together.

'This is what you should be doing,' Ellie said as she finished the final paragraph. 'No more bloody match reports. More of this. Get it out there.'

Colin sat at his table, his finger hovering above the mouse. This was it. The point of no return. It would mean no more match reports, possibly ever again. He toyed with the idea of hitting delete, but it was nothing more than a thought experiment. He was going to do this. In fact, from the perspective of his future self, he already had. History had swept him up.

The software was set up so that posts written on his laptop auto-filled with his byline, but he knew how to override it. He considered putting 'Eleanor Ferguson and Colin Ryder'. But instead he deleted his name and in its place, he typed a single word:

WROTH

He looked at Ellie. She looked at him. He took one long final breath and clicked.

'And off it goes,' said Ellie.

'Off it goes.'

Suddenly her face drained of all colour.

'What?' he said, instantly panicked. 'What have we done?'

'Rodbortzoon!' she said. 'Oh my god, has he fucking drowned in the bath?'

Colin was up on his feet first, Ellie only just behind him. They scrambled upstairs and burst into the bathroom. The bath was empty. No Rodbortzoon. No water. Everything had been left neatly, the towels folded over the rail, the various unguents lined up, their lids on.

'Oh,' said Ellie from the hall. 'I've found him.' She was standing in the doorframe to what had been their bedroom. He was asleep in what had been their bed, his hair combed into a side parting. Even his beard looked like it had been brushed. Colin went and stood next to her like a proud co-parent.

'He looks like the Raymond Briggs Father Christmas after he's got pissed in Vegas.'

Ellie laughed and looked over Rodbortzoon's snoring bulk at the clock radio.

'Christ,' she said. 'It's three in the morning.'

'I can't face going back to the camp now. Why don't you sleep in Daisy's bed? I'll go in with him.'

'I'm too pumped to sleep.'

'I know what you mean,' said Colin. 'Fancy another Baileys?'

'I want to see these surveyors.'

'Yeah, you really should. They have these really cool lasers. You can see them in the dark, these little beams. There's something lightsabre-ish about them.'

'Let's go now.'

'*Now?*' said Colin. 'I can't drive. I'm absolutely hammered.'

Ellie paused for a second.

'My bike's in the shed,' she said.

'But I can't ride Daisy's, can I?' said Colin.

'I think he cycled here,' she said, gesturing at the bed.

'Sod it,' said Colin.

Together, they lifted up the dead weight of the sleeping man's arm and pulled a set of keys from his jacket pocket.

Rodbortzoon's bike was an old-school Dutch model, with a black frame and sit-up-and-beg handlebars. Your dream bike, basically, if you were ever to find yourself out riding with the most beautiful woman you had ever known, through deserted moonlit streets on a lovely spring night.

'Direct and a bit grim, or long and scenic?' he shouted over his shoulder as they neared the turning for Woodvale Street.

'Long and scenic,' she shouted back as she raced past him on the outside and turned down Woodvale. Her bike was second-hand, its green paint peeling from the frame, the wicker basket unravelling a little at the edges. She rode it standing up, her back straight. Like a ballerina would have done, he had always thought.

The tall trees on Woodvale Street threw dramatic shadows on the road. They rode alongside each other, pedalling in sync, the only sound the cushioned tread of their tyres on the tarmac.

'When was the last time you did this?'

'Too long ago,' shouted Ellie. 'I love it.'

Colin stood high on the pedals and leaned into the corner, let the weight of his body roll him down the hill. He had forgotten what a different order of movement it was, how free it felt, but also how high-wire, especially when you were going downhill fast. How it was a kind of letting go, a sort of surrender.

'Do you remember when we rode right out into the Vale of Peter? You had Daisy on the crossbar in that little seat.'

'That was lovely.'

'It was so lovely. She had those darling little wellington boots.'

'The yellow ones?'

'Yes, exactly. She used to wear them with that hilarious waterproof all-in-one.'

'God, she was cute then.'

'She was *so* cute then.'

They were in the middle of the road, weaving in and out of the markings, a convoy of two. Her first and then him. In and out they went.

'I can't believe those seats are even legal now. They can't be safe.'

'I know. But she loved it, didn't she?'

'She did. And so did I. She was like a little joey in my pouch.'

They reached the start of the ascent of Church Hill, both of them pushing hard, in the highest gears they had. Colin could feel the crud in the bottom of his lungs unsettle and shift, a burning in his thighs, his face starting to redden. He would do this more, he vowed. Cycling, or anything that would get him fit. He would do it for her, because of her. She was just like that: despite yourself she made you want to be the best you could be.

They passed the church at the top of the hill and soon they were soaring, not headlong down a steep incline, but gently, gorgeously, along an almost imperceptible gradient that went on and on so you could coast effortlessly. The lights were red at the junction of Rothbury Terrace but they didn't stop, didn't even slow.

'Take the right fork,' he called to her from behind as they reached the marina. 'We need to go to the third basin. It's the one furthest from the river but it's the only place you get a clear view of the estate.'

When they arrived, the basin was quiet, the lights off in almost all the barges. They leaned their bikes against a tree and Colin led her to a space between the bushes. Ellie pushed back a branch and gazed over at the Larkspur. It was lit the way you might light an opera house, or a grand cathedral. It gave the estate a kinetic quality, made it look like at any moment it might activate its engines and take off like a rocket.

She looked down to the funny scrubland between the marina and the Larkspur and saw them: lasers. Three beams, all on the perfect horizontal. Soon enough, she could just pick out the figures of three men crouched over tripods. She felt pained, undeniably, but also, perversely, a great thrill. It would make victory all the sweeter when she won. And she would win. She had to. No one, in a sane world, could look at this building at night, lit as it was, and not think that it deserved preserving for eternity.

Colin was just behind her, watching her gaze at the Larkspur. Even in the poor light he could see that it provoked in her a kind of rapture. It was almost, and he had thought this before, as if through it she could intuit the order of things, make sense of the world.

He didn't delude himself. He had never had access to this kind of insight, certainly not from a housing estate. But it was heartening nonetheless to see her so rapt. Colin looked out at the Larkspur himself, at its bulky mass, its missing lightbulbs, its defiant awkwardness, and felt for the first time a genuine warmth for the building. It was far from conventionally good-looking, but still Ellie loved it. Which in a weird way meant there might be hope for him, too.

The moon was low in the sky and there was a light breeze. All was mild and calm and quiet. Then, on the other side of the bush, maybe fifteen yards from them, someone stepped on a stick and it cracked noisily.

Ellie gasped and turned into him, feeling for his arm but missing it, so that she stumbled a little into him and he had to hold her steady. For the few beats that followed they crouched, practically in each other's arms, faces inches apart, breath held, straining for stillness and silence while their hearts pumped at the absurdity of the situation. Colin held tight to her arm, overwhelmed by the feeling that if he kissed her she wouldn't object.

For a few more seconds there was silence and then the sound of footsteps, the crackle of static from a two-way radio. Colin felt Ellie stiffen in his arms and instinctively, protectively he pulled her into a clumsy embrace. She seemed to be mostly excited and a little bit scared and it really had to be the case that this was a hinge moment in his life and whatever happened would dictate everything else from here on in.

The footsteps, whoever they belonged to, were receding, but the pair stayed where they were, locked in their tangled clinch. To kiss her, all he had to do was lean forward six inches. Colin shut his eyes. Six inches. It was nothing. He felt his nostrils flare. All he had to

462

do was lean forward. He swallowed the lump rising in his throat. It was a hinge moment in a literal, material, quotidian way in that it would dictate, or at least shape, who lived where and with whom and in what bed. But it also had the potential to be more than that. It had the potential to be the moment that something was definitively banished, the feelings that had multiplied in him over time: the inadequacy, the fear of failure, the sense that the mantle had eluded him his whole damn life.

Six inches. How ridiculous that it was an unbridgeable gap.

'I'm sorry it took me so long to tell you about these guys,' he said, because he had to say something and saying this felt tender and intimate and sort of analogous to kissing her.

'That's all right. I'm sorry it took me so long to tell you about the 106 money.'

He shook his head gently, to communicate she had no reason to apologise.

'And I should never have leaked that master planner's report,' he said. 'Sorry.'

Ellie recoiled, confused. She blinked a couple of times and seemed to be shaking her head like she was trying to shake the booze out of it.

'You what?'

'Oh shit. You didn't know about that.'

'No, I didn't.'

She pushed her way out of the bush.

'Not telling someone something is one thing but going out of your way to leak – *anonymously* leak – stuff to the press? That's something else.'

She picked up her bike and righted it.

'I cannot believe you did that, that's just so fucking sneaky.'

Colin tried to push his way out of the bush but his jumper was caught in some branches and he was finding it difficult to turn around so he could free himself.

'Wait a sec,' he shouted, still in the bush, as she cycled away. 'Rodbortzoon's in your bed.'

'I'll stay at Pankaj's,' she shouted without looking back at him. 'I've got a key. But seriously, Colin. I'm not joking. You'd both better be gone in the morning.'

He watched her red tail light until it disappeared into the trees. The bush still had him ensnared. He gave up fighting it and let his body flop to the floor, defeated. All he had had to do was kiss her. And he hadn't. He let his head sink into the matted weeds. At a certain age you had to start to wonder if your inability to make a mark on your own life was less to do with the unnavigable chaos of the cosmos and more to do with the fact that you were, by almost every metric, a total fuckwit.

He lay on his back for another couple of minutes, sunk in a sea of self-loathing, when he felt the distinctive vibration of his phone in his pocket. He grabbed at it urgently, desperate for it to be a message from Ellie, an expression of regret, a statement of solidarity, anything that might suggest that the door was still ajar.

But when he looked at the screen he was instantly aware that it wasn't from Ellie. It was from Rick, fresh, Colin imagined, from having read their piece.

It was succinct and to the point. Just two words.

You're fired.

46

Daisy had managed to shed her bag and then her jacket with the minimum of fuss, just a few barely observable shifts of the shoulder. Ellie looked at the discarded things, crumpled on the floor between the front door and the kitchen. Hardly the behaviour of someone intimidated by their new habitat. She felt a mixture of relief and regret. They were at Pankaj's house for the night, acclimatising.

'Can I have a snack?'

'Yeah, what do you want?' said Ellie as she picked up the jacket and hung it on the back of a chair. Her laptop was on the table, the online petition open in the web browser. She refreshed the page and the new total appeared: 112,435 signatures. Ninety-eight added in the last hour.

She grinned. Two days had passed since she and Colin had uploaded their article and even though it had been quickly taken down, a screenshot had been shared on Facebook. In the forty-eight hours since, six thousand people had signed her petition, a feature had run in the *Telegraph* favourably comparing the Chapel to the soulless corporate stadiums in the Premier League, and an editorial had been published on the *Independent* website citing the Generator as the emblem of Britain's disastrous experiment with PFI and calling for it to be pulled down and replaced with the station.

Daisy picked an apple from the bowl and then pulled open the fridge door so she could assess its contents.

'Dad got fired,' she said, as matter-as-fact as you liked.

'*What?*'

'From his job. He got fired.'

'Are you sure? How do you know?'

'Evie McAllister told me. Her mum told her.'

'Oh god, that's terrible.'

'Evie said it doesn't matter. She doesn't live with her dad and he doesn't have a job either.'

'Oh darling, don't say that.'

Daisy turned and looked at her.

'Do you think Evie McAllister's dad lives in a tent, too?'

'Your dad doesn't live in a tent.'

'Yes, he does. James Kirklee says he sometimes goes to his house for showers.'

'Right. OK, he's in a tent at the moment, but he doesn't *live* there. He's protesting. It's actually a really noble thing to do,' said Ellie, aware that this was the first time that she had acknowledged that it *was* a noble thing to do.

'Well where does he live?' asked Daisy.

'I ... He's ... He'll find somewhere proper soon.'

She watched Daisy pour herself a glass of orange juice and retreat to the sofa with Pankaj's iPad. Ellie's mind was doing that thing that Ellie's mind did when she wanted it to concentrate on someone else's sadness but all it would do was think about the possibilities that said sadness opened up for her. Colin had been fired and jobs for sacked sports correspondents weren't exactly two a penny in Peterdown. He would have to move. London was surely the best bet – and that would mean she needn't feel guilty about moving his daughter there too.

She heard the key in the door and walked instinctively into the hall.

'Turn the radio on,' said Pankaj, waving his phone at her. 'She's being interviewed right now.'

Ellie turned on her heel and ran to the kitchen. She frantically twisted the dial until Yvonne's voice came booming out of the radio.

'Before you go any further,' she said, 'I'm aware of the speculation and half-truths in this piece, but I think it's worth pointing out that the *Post* has taken it down and sacked the person responsible.'

Pankaj looked at her, perturbed.

'I literally found out five minutes ago,' said Ellie heavily.

'We've had a written apology from the editor and so I believe has Andrew Kirk,' continued Yvonne, 'but I'm aware that issues have been raised by the article that have got people talking and I want to address some of them now.'

'How bad is the situation at the Generator?' asked the interviewer. 'Is it really going to cost us millions of pounds a year?'

'First off, I want to get past this knee-jerk reaction to the Private Finance Initiative. It's allowed us to make capital investments of the kind we would never have been able to afford from public funds alone. The Generator is a case in point. We have this beautiful new arts centre, which we wouldn't have otherwise. I know people want to dig down into its finances, but the reality is that we have to respect the right of our private sector partners to protect the details of their pricing structure with commercial confidentiality agreements.'

'People are calling it a secret slush fund.'

'It's totally unremarkable to have a commercial wing which is beyond the scope of freedom of information requests. All councils need them because the private sector is such a vital part of what we do.'

'Are you pushing through developments to keep the Generator afloat?'

'We're pushing through developments to keep this *town* afloat. New jobs. New houses. New shops. All the things that we so desperately need.'

'Yes, but are you diverting money to the Generator to stop it going bust?'

'The suggestion that money is being taken from one place to pay for something else is both a gross simplification of the reality and a commonplace truism of life running a unitary authority. Like our colleagues in local government across the country, ours is a complex series of accounts and we choose to think holistically about the way this money comes and goes. We know that in certain years, different parts of our portfolio will require more direct investment than others. But we're working on some very exciting potential partnerships. New revenue streams for the Generator that will help it become self-sustaining. Until then, all we care about is that the overall budget balances, which we've every confidence it will do.'

'What do you say to the residents of the Larkspur who are worried that you're decanting it because you already know it's going to be the station?'

'As I've said a dozen times already, the council's preferred outcome is for the station to be built on the site of the Chapel and for the club to be moved to the new state-of-the-art facility that its owner has planned.'

'So you're not decanting it?'

'We're investing in its future. Our commitment is to high-quality housing for the people of Peterdown.'

A message buzzed through on her WhatsApp. It was Shelly.

> Are you listening to this?

> > With gritted teeth

> She's lying!

> > ??

> All new applications for flats at Larkspur are being automatically turned down. Ketchup showed me the template letter.

> > Knew it!

> She sounds confident but it's all front. Lots of people in that council very angry with her over all this!!

The radio interviewer was thanking Yvonne for her time. Ellie showed Pankaj the thread on the screen of her phone.

'I've heard much the same,' he said. 'Even allies of hers are apparently pissed off that process hasn't been followed.'

Pankaj sat in the chair at the end of the table and unknotted his tie.

'Council politics can be very fickle. She's been a great vote-winning

468

machine around here but she relies on a small coterie for everything and a lot of people feel excluded. You can get away with it when everything's going well but as soon as the wind changes it can leave you horribly exposed.'

He pushed the cuff links out of his buttonholes.

'I've heard that at least two very senior council people are fuming,' he said as he rolled his shirt sleeves to the elbow. 'One of them is a young guy, very dynamic, Alan Daish. He's probably too young to replace her but the other one, Janine Chapple, she could certainly take over. She's got experience. A good speaker. No real enemies.'

He took an apple from the bowl and twisted its stalk, weighing up a thought.

'I promised I wouldn't say anything,' he said, 'and I really don't want to lose my good faith with Alan, so if I tell you this you have to absolutely promise that you're going to keep it to yourself.'

'Of course.'

'She's in trouble. People keep using the word *irregularities*.'

'What kind of irregularities?'

'I don't know. They're keeping things in-house at the moment, but there's no doubt about it, she's lost a lot of friends.'

'Oh my god, can you imagine if we get it listed and she gets the boot in the same week. That would be just too much,' said Ellie, as she got up to check on the potato she was baking for Daisy's dinner.

Pankaj rubbed the apple against his trouser leg like he was shining a cricket ball.

'I know she's difficult but . . . I don't know,' he said, 'there's something kind of tragic about it all.'

Ellie snorted through her nose.

'She's not gone about it the right way but all she's been trying to do is keep the Generator open. She fought tooth and nail to get it built.'

'Well then she should own it. The whole damn disaster of it. Debts and all!'

Pankaj was spinning the apple out the back of one hand and catching it with the other.

'I know it cost a lot of money and I appreciate that it hasn't quite found its feet yet, but isn't there something honourable about wanting to build these things where you wouldn't expect them?'

'You're making it sound like it's the Musée d'Orsay! My problem has never been the building of it *here*; it's the building of *it*. It aspires to the condition of social media, for god's sake.'

'I don't know,' said Pankaj. 'You talk about social media like it's the end of civilisation, but your great vision is for a framework that people can use to create their own space.'

He finally took a bite from the apple.

'Doesn't that sound exactly like, I don't know, Facebook or whatever?'

Ellie lost control of the tray she was holding and the baked potato slid off it on to the countertop. She couldn't speak. It was like someone was sitting on her chest.

He shrugged, took another bite of his apple.

'As far as I can tell the Generator was supposed to be a bit like that, a space that allowed people to create their own culture. OK, it hasn't worked yet. But with some investment it could. I don't know. I just think it would be a shame to lose it. I mean, I know you hate it, but I quite like the building. It's vibrant.'

She didn't respond.

'Anyway, I thought I'd make chermoula aubergine tonight. Any idea where the lemons are? I was sure we had a couple in the bowl.'

She walked to the fridge and found two half-lemons on the top shelf, the leftovers from that week's gin and tonics.

'Here you go,' she said quietly as she placed them on the table in front of him.

The next hour passed much like this. Pankaj made his chermoula while he and Daisy engaged in a long and spirited debate about whether or not the films of his childhood – *The Jungle Book*, *101 Dalmatians* – were superior to the films of hers: *Toy Story*, *Madagascar* and their sequels. The whole thing seemed to boil down to whether or not you considered *Frozen* the zenith of all human endeavours, on which matter they were both unmovable.

Throughout, Ellie stayed quiet. When it was ready she wordlessly placed Daisy's jacket potato with tuna mayonnaise on the table in front of her and then withdrew to the kitchen counter, her back to the room, where she silently blanched green beans and made the salad.

Her anger was following the classic Ellie arc: first outwards in all directions and then quickly inward with a white-hot intensity.

Doesn't that sound exactly like Facebook? So typically glib of him to find some superficial similarity between two things and run with it, even when one was about corporate surveillance and the other was about open democracy. Participatory design. Freedom.

She smarted.

And yet.

He had, as ever, hit on something essentially true. Something she had been too blind to see. There were no new ideas in the world.

All her sketches, her notepads, all her imagined buildings. None of them were going to make her the Marjorie Blofeld of her generation. Nothing would. The historical conditions no longer existed to do what Marjorie had done. And this was a fact that you could not simply will yourself past, however hard you tried.

Ellie put the knife back down on the chopping board. A thought plummeted through her like a lift cut from its cable: she was an ordinary person with ordinary ideas who would lead an ordinary life.

She took Daisy upstairs and put her to bed. When she came down, Pankaj had laid the table properly and opened a bottle of wine.

'We should talk about Monday,' he said, pouring her a glass.

'Yeah, we should,' she said numbly, taking a seat.

'You need to go in hard on its aesthetic significance. Harvey's not a philistine. There were loads of photos of him at Bayreuth last year. And he's always at Glyndebourne. If you can sell him its virtues, he'll listen.'

'OK.'

'He's ambitious and he's always got one eye on what's in it for him, but he's always looking for opportunities to show that he's capable of making unpopular decisions. It's a big thing with the Tories, the historical long game. How will this decision be judged in a hundred years? You need to convince him that history will remember him as the man that saved the Parthenon from the wrecking ball.'

'OK, I can do that.'

'Just whatever you do, don't talk about municipal socialism ...'

The doorbell rang.

'Expecting anyone?'

'No.'

She answered it. On the doorstep was Colin. He was wearing his smartest white shirt, unironed and untucked, over tracksuit bottoms and a pair of those blue and white plastic slippers that Frenchmen wear to the shower at camp sites. A plastic bag dangled apologetically from his right hand. In it was what looked like the bulky outlines of a box of detergent.

'Hi,' she said.

Colin watched her take in his outfit.

'I was at the launderette,' he said, realising that it was an embarrassment to her. Not only because it was objectively embarrassing, but also because being embarrassed about someone's outfit was itself a source of embarrassment to the sort of people who imagined themselves to be above such things. He let his carrier bag fall to the floor.

'These were the only things that were clean,' he said. 'I ...'

It had been a mistake arriving like this. At no point had he really planned on it; he had been local and found himself walking this way with no kind of strategy or meaningful aim, just an overwhelming desire to see inside the house.

'I heard about your job,' she said. 'I'm sorry.'

Colin winced.

'Is Daisy still awake?' he asked calculatedly.

'I don't think so. Do you want me to check?'

'Yes.'

'Come in.'

He picked up his carrier bag and climbed the two steps up into the house. As soon as he was in the hallway he sensed that it was a calamitous idea, but that it was too late to do anything other than keep going into the open-plan living space, where the scene that greeted him was one of such stylised refinement that it could only be interpreted as an all-out attack on him and everything he held dear.

Pankaj was sitting at the wooden table, laid for two. Music was playing. Classical. Not something he knew, obviously. A pair of large glass goblets contained an inch of honey-coloured wine. Half a dozen candles flickered on various surfaces. A bunch of meadow flowers stood in a vase. A piece of fabric ran down the middle of the table. On it was a large shallow serving dish piled with rice, and on top of the rice squeaking green vegetables, and on top of them, aubergines cooked black with spices and then heaped with yoghurt, herbs and nuts.

A bit different then from his dinner. He had had a takeaway pizza. Only he hadn't really taken it away. He had eaten it, the box balanced on his lap, in Domino's waiting area, a tiny space with a single seat, designed without tables to explicitly discourage food consumption, where you found yourself jostled constantly by delivery drivers shouting order numbers through their helmet grilles. The only positive thing that could be said about it was that it was better than eating in the rain.

'Hello,' he said coldly to Pankaj, as Ellie disappeared upstairs.

'Hello,' said Pankaj warily in return.

On the kitchen countertop were five bowls; one of them, earthenware, was full of plums, the other four, all Moroccan in various shades of blue, were piled with avocados, bananas, pears and some kind of niche-looking apples, each one misshapen and orangey-green. Next to them, loose on the surface, were three of those small pumpkins or squashes that you saw sometimes at farmers' markets in Broadcastle that no one – surely *no one* – actually ate.

'I've just come to say goodnight to Daisy,' he said.

'Of course,' said Pankaj.

On the table, at his elbow, was a copy of *The Brothers Karamazov*, a bookmark sticking from it, maddeningly near the end. Colin's first thought was: you're not actually reading that, you pretentious prick. But this was closely followed by a far more insidious realisation: you *are* actually reading that, you terrifying monster.

'Can I get you a glass of wine?'

'Sure.'

'Please sit down.'

Colin faltered as he pulled out the chair, something gnawing at him. What was it that was so disquieting about the place? It wasn't the Dostoevsky, or the dim light, which were devastating but not existentially fatal. He scanned the room. A shelf of books. A vintage record player. Records. Plants in pots. And then it struck him.

No television.

It was then that he knew. Like the apple falling from the tree. The water being displaced from the bath. The thing that had always been there hazily in view was finally crystal sharp. She wasn't coming back. Whatever had or had not nearly happened in that bush. Whatever outfit he wore.

He sat down with a thump.

Ellie appeared again at the bottom of the stairs.

'Sorry,' she said. 'She's asleep. I don't think we should wake her.'

'No, don't. It's OK. I won't stay,' he said with a sigh. 'I have to get my washing.'

The look on Ellie's face was the one she adopted when she was talking to people she knew to be drinking too much or eating too little. It was open and soft and concerned and deeply, profoundly patronising.

'Are you OK?' she said.

'Yes,' said Colin, his voice measured. 'I am OK.'

'OK.'

'I'll see her tomorrow. It's not a big thing.'

'OK.'

'Right.'

'Before you go, I wanted to ask you something about Grangeham,' she said. 'Just quickly, what's the budget for it?'

'A hundred and ten million,' said Colin, because at least it meant thinking about something else. 'Fifty-five for the stadium. The rest on all the shops and flats and stuff that he's planning to put up.'

'Only a hundred and ten?'

She turned to Pankaj.

'Are they really paying out eight million quid in 106 money on a hundred and ten million build? That seems like a lot.'

'It wouldn't be anything like that. I would have thought it would be half that at the most.'

'It said eight on the thing Ketchup saw. So where's the rest coming from?'

Colin took a long measured breath. Had he any self-respect, he thought to himself, this would be the moment that he kept his counsel, held his secrets tight to his chest. But it had never worked like that for him. When you were in possession of information that other people weren't, the only way to prove it was to tell them.

'I think I know,' he said. He paused. It was his last card and he was playing it on an unwinnable hand. On he went, regardless. 'The other night, after you left, I was just getting ready to go when a guy walked past talking on a two-way radio.'

'Right.'

'The person on the other end was James Philpott,' he said. 'I heard a snatch of their conversation.'

'*What*? Why? He works for Kirk now.'

'Exactly.'

'I don't get it. Why would *they* be measuring it up? It can't be worth anything much at all if they're lining it up to be the station. If the government want it, they'll just slap a compulsory purchase order on it.'

Colin paused. He could stop here, hold something back, maintain some kind of dignity.

'What if the government don't want it, though?' he said dolefully. 'What if the station's not going there? If you wanted to knock down a lot of social housing to build something else – say new flats that would appeal to commuters who like the sound of being a five-minute walk from the world's fastest train – you would have to pay a load of 106 money, right?'

'There's your irregularity,' said Pankaj.

'Oh god,' said Ellie.

'It's the only thing that makes sense,' said Colin. 'It's why they're emptying it. They don't want the station there. They're selling the Larkspur to Kirk.'

47

It was 3.15 p.m. Saturday, May 10th. Fifteen minutes into the most important game ever to be played at the Chapel: the first leg of the playoff semi-final. A representative of the *Peterdown Evening Post* was at the game, sitting in the press box, though of course it wasn't Colin. Colin was outside the stadium, at the camp, guarding the tents, listening to the game on the radio.

And the ball is up in the air, Beck and Connelly contest it and it bounces loose. Ellis mis-controls and it's picked up by the Forest number seven. Leadbitter. Leadbitter drives forward but he's tackled by Turner ...

Colin took a deep breath. He was sitting in the doorway of the mess tent, a D-lock half-heartedly shackling his ankle to one of its exterior poles, trying to decide if this was more or less humiliating than his appearance the evening before at Pankaj's house.

Less, he decided, given the audience. Or rather the lack of it. At the height of the camp's popularity, it took at least ten people to guard the site when it emptied during games. Now, the camp had been reduced to a rump and so had its defences. Colin made up half of the bulwark; the other half sat thirty yards away, shackled to the media tent via his neck rather than his ankle, eating luncheon meat straight from the tin.

'I love this commentator,' Rodbortzoon shouted jovially, his mouth full. 'Ten minutes in and it's already all Sturm und Drang.'

As was always the case with the games broadcast on Peterdown FM, the commentator in question was Richard Joyce. Colin knew him vaguely from press conferences and club functions but having been present at every Peterdown game, home and away, for nearly ten years, he had rarely heard him at work. His default style was frenzied mock-heroic.

He's hit the bar. The Nottingham Forest number nine. Pérez. Twenty-five yards out and he's hit it. Off the top of the bar. Oh this terrible and beautiful game. How it plays on your nerves.

'I would take nil-nil,' shouted Rodbortzoon. 'At the moment I would take it. Nil-nil. Go to theirs without conceding.'

Colin nodded in agreement as he felt his stomach pitch and tilt. He had not been able to eat anything all morning. It was basically everything now, this game, their only hope.

He looked out through the flap of the tent. Where there had once been forty tents there were now six. Brian and his lot were said to be boycotting the playoffs, concentrating instead on the creation of their new club. A constitution had been written establishing it as a fan-owned collective run along mutual lines. They were designing the kit and the crest collaboratively, reaching out to various bodies for funding, sending delegates to Wimbledon and Manchester to get tips and build alliances. Colin, confusingly, found himself simultaneously rooting for them and hoping bitterly that the whole thing was a complete disaster.

He stared up at the vast tapestry, which, despite the rain damage, still hung proudly over the camp. The ultras were keen to maintain a connection to the protest, even if their numbers had been decimated. Frankie and a load of his mates were at the Ottercliffe Road police station, in for questioning on suspicion of criminal damage, their arrests apparently deliberately timed so they would miss the game. Others had just had enough of the camp, its endless meetings and tedious logistics, but there were at least four or five whom Colin suspected had left so they could focus on Wroth without making themselves an easy target.

He sighed. It wouldn't be long before it was just him and

Rodbortzoon. Did it matter? Probably not. They had already achieved more than he could have ever hoped possible. Articles in newspapers from Australia to Brazil. An outpouring of support from fans around the country. They had become, undeniably, a cause célèbre.

But did it *matter*? Yes, it did. An awful lot. It had been tongue-in-cheek, calling it the Peterdown Spring, but that didn't mean it hadn't been the most vivid thing to happen in the town in his whole damn life. And it didn't mean that it hadn't been an authentic flowering of sorts, however quickly it had faded.

Colin looked despondently out at the concourse. There was still a slight discolouration where the pitch had been, the feeling of a memory that had not quite faded. He shut his eyes. All his life he had never really been at the centre of anything: his gang of university friends, the paper he had served his whole career, his own goddamn family. And now the thing that he had been irrefutably vital to, essential to its very existence, was coming to an end.

The ball breaks to Beck and he's put through Pérez down the right. Pérez is on the ball, he's broken free on the right. Oh. Oh no. Calamity. He can't have meant that. He's scored. But it was a fluke. Disaster for Peterdown. Surely he was trying to cross it. But it's gone in. Forest have scored.

'Shitting fuck,' shouted Rodbortzoon.

'Yeah,' said Colin flatly. 'Shitting fuck.'

He had known this moment was coming. This reckoning. The deflated departure. Nobody ever remembered the team that lost in the semis. They limped off, out of history. Forgotten.

His phone rang.

Ellie.

Someone he both did, and profoundly did not, want to talk to. He turned the phone over so it was face down on the floor.

They were one-nil down in the home leg.

You could try all you liked to imagine that the world wasn't divided between winners and losers but over time patterns emerged that became impossible to ignore.

The vibration of the ring tone was moving his phone rightwards across the concrete in tiny increments. Colin watched it creeping away from him. He witnessed his mind doing that thing that it did when it wanted an excuse to act: it conjured the apocalypse. What if something's happened to Daisy? it asked.

'Are you OK?'

'Yes.'

'Everything's fine? Daisy's fine?'

'Yeah, Daisy's fine. She's watching a film. I just wanted to call to say thanks.'

Colin felt relief and gratitude and irritation at the sound of her voice.

'Not listening to the game then?'

'Oh, is it on now?'

'Yeah, it's on now. We're losing.'

'Oh, that's a shame, but there's another game, right?'

'Yeah, but it's not looking good.'

'Well, I'll be rooting for you.'

'Thanks.'

Corner to Forest. On the far side. Beck to take. He's got his arm in the air. And here he goes. In it swings. And. Oh no. It hasn't, has it? It has. The Forest players are mobbing Beck. No one got a touch. It's gone straight in. This is a catastrophe for Peterdown. Total catastrophe. Two-nil down in the first half.

'Double shitting fuck,' shouted Rodbortzoon.

That really is a cruel way to concede a goal. Really. Straight from the corner. Another fluke. Two-nil to Forest. This really is the nightmare scenario for Peterdown.

'Well, that's that,' said Colin. 'It's over. We're not coming back from that.'

'I'm sorry,' said Ellie.

'Yeah, me too.'

'Anyway, I was just calling to say thanks for coming round last night to tell me about Philpott. It was nice of you. And you were right. My source at the council basically confirmed it. It looks like some kind of deal has been struck.'

'Yeah. Well, I'd say we should write another piece about it, but I don't know who would publish it.'

This hung in the air for a bit. Eventually Ellie said:

'We're actually going to keep quiet about it, save it for the minister. Pankaj thinks going to him with privileged information will make him feel special. The plan is that I tell him about Kirk and make it clear no one else knows so he can list the building and screw over a Labour council, and still claim he didn't know at the time.'

'And Pankaj is on board with that?'

'Not officially, obviously. But it's a good plan, I think.'

'You're going down on Monday?'

'Yeah.'

'OK. Well, good luck.'

'You too.'

He hung up, resentment bubbling in him volcanically. Obviously, she would get the damn thing listed. Nothing about his life so far suggested that the universe was going to be content with simply ensuring that he lost. She would also have to win.

Colin lay down on the concrete. He had watched enough sport to know all about winning. It was never just about talent or tactics or the rightness of your cause. Winning was a psychological trait, a thing which some people could do and some people could not.

On the radio, Richard Joyce announced the end of the first half and the Peterdown players trooped off, still two-nil down.

For ten minutes Colin sat there, watching Rodbortzoon eat a family-sized pot of fromage frais and smoke two cigarettes.

'Hi.'

He looked up. It was Kerry. She was carrying a mushy chip buttie wrapped in white paper, patches of it translucent from the grease.

'I brought you something to eat.'

480

He sat up.

'That's very nice of you.'

She was wearing a jumper, jeans, fur-lined slipper boots. For once, Colin didn't feel radically underdressed in her company.

'It's good of you to be out here. Doing this.'

'Doesn't sound like I'm missing much.'

'They're all so nervous. No one can get their foot on the ball. We're getting hemmed into our own half.'

'I don't know why we're all so surprised. Forest beat us home and away. They're better than us.'

'I know, but you just . . . ' Kerry shrugged. 'Don't you?'

'Yeah, you do,' said Colin, unwrapping his buttie. 'And you know, we get one back in the second half and we're not out of it.'

'Yeah.'

'And really, thanks for this.'

'To be honest, I was looking for an excuse to get out. I was finding the crowd a bit oppressive. I needed, you know, a bit of space.'

Colin pulled out a gravy-covered chip, trying to imagine a scenario in which Ellie would have, unprompted, bought him a mushy chip buttie.

'I might just listen to the rest of it out here with you, if that's all right?'

'Of course it is.'

The whistle blew for the start of the second half.

'Do you mind if I sit down?' she said, gesturing to the plastic garden chair in the corner of the tent. 'I feel a bit guilty with you on the floor but I could do with a seat.'

'Go for it,' he said, gesturing to his ankle. 'I can't get on it anyway.'

Kerry dragged the chair across the floor until it was next to him. She sat down and picked a chip from his wrapper.

'Sorry,' she said. 'I'm suddenly starving.'

Colin opened up the buttie and offered it to her. They may have wanted for a bottle of Chablis, candles, expensive cutlery; and Richard Joyce didn't create quite the same mood as some Chopin. But that didn't mean that the quarter of an hour they sat there, sharing the chips and listening to the game, wasn't the most romantic of Colin's life.

'Jordan's totally isolated,' said Kerry after another hurried Peterdown clearance gave the ball straight back to Forest. 'Christie's got to hook Gunnarsson and get Sean Davis on. Flood the midfield.'

Colin looked up admiringly only to see Kerry pinching the bridge of her nose, a tear rolling down her cheek.

'Hey, it's not over yet.'

She sipped from a bottle of water.

'I'm sorry,' she said. 'I've felt so emotional these last few days.'

'Me too.'

She paused for a second to gather herself.

'You know, I really thought we were going to do it. Me and you.'

'So did I.'

'I thought we'd find out what was wrong with it, with Grangeham.'

'So did I,' said Colin. 'I really thought we'd do it. I thought we'd take him down and I would get to be the hero.'

He ate the last-but-one chip.

'Normally, people called Colin don't get to be the hero,' he continued, wistfully. 'But I was going to be the exception to the rule. It would have made me unique. It would have made me feel *real*.'

He ate the last chip.

'Didn't happen that way.'

Garry gets the ball, he beats one. On the outside, he's gone round him on the outside and he's in space. He's bearing down on goal. It's a foot race now. Here comes Varga, the Forest centre half. ARGH. He's cleaned him up. That's got to be a foul. Garry's on the floor. In a heap. Crumpled. No foul. No foul?! The ref waves play on. And Garry is on the floor. He doesn't seem to be moving.

Colin felt Kerry's hand on his shoulder.

OK. It's OK. He's up. He's up on his feet. He doesn't look to be limping. He seems to be OK. Meanwhile, up the other end Forest are attacking.

'God,' she said. 'If anything happens to him ...'

'I know. If we lose him, we might as well not bother turning up for the second leg.'

Kerry breathed out steadily through her nose.

'The whole Philpott thing never went anywhere, did it?' she said. 'I thought it would lead to something.'

'Well, not for us ...' He stopped, aware for the first time that his sense of loyalty had shifted. It felt newly important that he kept quiet about Ellie in her presence, not the other way round. 'Not for us it didn't. It didn't go anywhere.'

'What about the other guy on that list. Douglas Dublin?'

'I don't know. You checked him out, right?'

'No, I just assumed you would.'

Colin got out his phone and typed the name into Google. There were lots of hits for an American basketball player. He ploughed his way through the pages.

The game entered its last five minutes. Paul Christie took Gunnarsson off and put on Sean Davis.

Colin limited his search to British websites. The basketball player disappeared. A new person now dominated the results. He was a scientist. A PhD from Brunel University. A member of the Institute of Environmental Auditors. Colin clicked on a link.

And here's Sean Davis finding space. He's made a real difference. Oh, and that's brutal. A terrible tackle. Straight through the back of him. It's a free kick to Peterdown, twenty-five yards out. Just to the left.

'He's an environmental auditor,' said Colin in disbelief.

'You think he worked on Grangeham?'

Colin returned to the search results. He clicked a link that took him to a page within Brunel University's Department of Life Sciences. He steadied himself. Douglas Dublin had written his PhD on brownfield site pollution and the great crested newt.

Colin mouthed a silent prayer. And then he was struck forcefully

483

by the memory of another conversation. *Interesting soil. More alkaline than I'm used to.*

He held his breath as he typed 'great crested newt soil preference' into Google. The answer came back.

Alkaline.

Two minutes left. A miracle is needed. What can the prodigal son do? Come on, Jordan. Come on, Jordan.

The wall of noise came to him in stereo, booming out simultaneously from the stadium and the radio:

GOOOOOOOAAAAAAAALLLLLLLLLLLLLLLLLL Jordan Garry. Jordan Garry. Joooor-daaaaan Gaaaaa-ryyyyy. Our saviour. Our saviour. He's handed us a lifeline. We are not out of this yet. We are down but we are not out. Joooordaaaan Gaaaaarrry. Oh my days. Oh my days. What a game. What a game it is . . .

Kerry and Rodbortzoon were yelling crazily. Colin lay back on the floor and let loose a delirious howl. The whole thing had slotted magnificently into place. The Grangeham forge was home to Britain's only endangered amphibian.

All he had to do now was find one.

48

S t James's Park was basking in the full glory of an English spring day. Families ambled. Tourists posed for pictures on their way to Buckingham Palace. The willows at the water's edge cast shadows on the grass.

Ellie was sitting on a park bench, fresh from her meeting at the DCMS. It had gone well. In person, Miles Harvey had been just as she had expected: erudite, extravagantly charming, lizard-quick with his questions. She got the sense that he had barely been aware of the application until that morning but prided himself on being able to get instantly up to speed.

It was obvious that he had liked her, and not because she had dressed for the meeting (a sleeveless top, vintage Margiela trousers, proper heels). She had seen it in the smile on his face when she told him about the council's plan to sell the building to Kirk. It contained a flash of recognition.

Had Ellie been the kind of character that she imagined herself to be, she would probably have felt more conflicted about this kind of collusion; as it was she sat there smiling at her worldliness, musing on the fact that although Harvey had made no promises, he had nodded in all the right places and on three separate occasions told her that the application was the best he had ever received.

She pulled a copy of the presentation from her bag. The photo on the cover was her favourite of the estate. More than any other it captured the building's weirdness, the way it seemed to occupy space according to its own inimitable geometry.

She threw her bag over her shoulder and walked through the park into St James's. The neighbourhood had always been moneyed but in the last few years it had gone into overdrive; everywhere around her were new black marble buildings that discreetly whispered their uber-wealth.

She stopped in front of a half-built block of flats. The cladding around the site was decorated with expensively rendered images of the building as it would be: large windows, generous balconies, open-plan interiors. Ellie looked achingly at the development's name.

STRUCTURA.

She blushed, then she laughed. It really was a shit name. She reached into her bag for her phone to take a photo to show Pankaj and it was only then that she realised she had left it at the DCMS. She could visualise exactly where she had put it down, on a coffee table in the waiting area while she had gathered her things.

It took her ten minutes to walk back through the park and up past Parliament Square. The man on the desk recognised her and sympathetically waved her through.

The departmental waiting area was a large room with two sets of sofas, two coffee tables. Her phone was on one of the tables, just as she had known it would be. As she retrieved it, she glanced through a half-open door and saw the secretary of state warmly greeting his next visitor.

The visitor was Andrew Kirk.

* * *

Half an hour later she was on the train, powering north through the Hertfordshire countryside, as wired as she had ever been. She had run straight from the DCMS to the tube and jumped on to the first train she could, panicked. Everyone she had tried to call had either rung out or gone straight to voicemail: Pankaj, Shelly, Colin, Leonie, Patrick.

Her copy of their presentation was on the table in front of her, the photograph on the cover as familiar to her as any image had ever been. The historical conditions no longer existed to make a building like this. And they might never come again. She felt her skin prickle.

The realisation came to her with total clarity. This was her encounter with greatness.

Ellie stared out the window of the speeding train, her mouth dry. She simply could not allow him to do what it was he planned to do. It just could not be allowed to happen. She had no choice.

She walked to the vestibule between the carriages. Sometimes you just had to do whatever it was you had to do.

'Hi Jim,' she said, when he answered.

'Ellie,' he said. 'Were you after Shelly? I'm afraid she's out but she'll have her mobile ...'

'It was you I wanted to talk to.' Ellie's voice was honey-coated, barely a whisper.

'Right,' said Jim.

'You've been so good to me. You've been there for me so many times.'

How many times had she caught him looking at her, only for him to blush and look away? It was never leering, never lecherous, but it was an infatuation of some sort.

'Well ... Of course, we're very fond of you ... I'm very fond of you.'

Ellie felt a stab of recrimination, but some paths, once you'd started down them, you just had to keep on going.

'I'm in trouble, Jim. I need to talk to Miss Ketchup.'

'I don't think Shelly would think that was a good idea. She – I mean "Miss Ketchup" – is someone who needs to be protected.'

'I need to be protected, too, Jim.'

'I know you do.'

'I called you because I knew I couldn't call Shelly. I knew you were the person I had to turn to. I would never have done it if it wasn't urgent.'

'Are you OK, Ellie? Just tell me you're OK.'

'I'm fine. But I need to talk to her today. I mean, I need to talk to her right now.'

The end of the line was silent.

'Jim,' she said. 'I need you to come through for me.'

'Oh, Ellie.'

'Don't tell me her name. Just tell me where she works. Which building. And I'll go and I'll know her when I see her, won't I?'

Jim said nothing.

'Just the building she works at. I wouldn't be asking if it wasn't absolutely essential.'

'Fanon House,' said Jim, flatly. 'She works at Fanon House.'

'Thank you,' she said.

But the line was already dead.

* * *

And she did. As soon as she saw her, she knew. Small. Skittish. A drawn and pinched little face. And the air, inescapably, of someone who had, in her time, been a drunk in a way that had damaged her forever.

The Fanon House car park was underground with spaces for maybe fifty cars and plenty of pillars to hide behind.

Ellie watched as the woman walked, head bowed, past the spots reserved for the top executives to the far side of the space. Hers was an old car. The sort that still required a key inserted in the door. Ellie was alongside her the second she went to open it.

'You're Miss Ketchup, aren't you?'

Her reaction was an instant confirmation. A turning of the head. A widening of the eyes. A consuming look of total horror.

'I thought so,' said Ellie.

Ketchup's face betrayed an instinctual animal calculus. Where she might run. How she might hide.

'Don't worry. I'm your friend. They tell me the stuff you tell them.'

'I don't know what you're talking about,' she said, fumbling with the lock.

'What she's doing is illegal. Yvonne. Your boss. And there are going to be serious irreversible consequences unless we do something about it now.'

Ketchup couldn't get a grip on her keys. She started welling up.

'If I tell you, they'll know it's me. And I was involved, I wrote the documents. I would be an accomplice.'

'So it *is* illegal?'

'I don't know. Is it?'

'Tell me what it was and I'll tell you if it was illegal.'

Miss Ketchup had the door open and she turned away from Ellie.

She was crying softly now; she made a whimper, an actual whimper. Ellie felt a flash of self-disgust.

'I'm sorry,' she said. She raised a hand apologetically. 'I didn't come here to put you in an awkward position. I know you've taken risks.'

Ellie paused. She could feel her nose running in the dank underground air.

'I'm going to go now.'

She turned and started to walk away. The light in the car park was comically bright, nothing like the filmic chiaroscuro of her imagination.

'I write them all dozens of letters a day.'

Ketchup's voice was thin and urgent. Ellie turned.

'But they never get signed. And if they don't sign them I can't send them and I get behind and I miss my targets.'

She leaned her head plaintively to one side.

'I learned their signatures. The council cabinet. All of them.'

'And?'

'If I tell you, you promise never to come near me again.'

'I promise.'

'And Yvonne knew I could do it.' She closed her eyes. 'She got me to forge the other councillors' signatures on documents they hadn't seen. So she could push things through behind their backs ...'

A large metal door opened with a great clang and through it came a cleaner with his cart, catching Ellie's attention. In the time it took her to register what was going on Ketchup was in her car with the key already in the ignition.

Ellie didn't try to stop her. She had enough.

For fifteen minutes she hovered by the keycard-operated access door that led from the car park up into the building proper, until she saw a man approaching the doors from the other side. She timed it perfectly, smiling at him as she held the door so he could walk through, like she had done it a hundred times before.

She took the lift to the second floor. The corridor was quiet, boxes of documents sat in piles. On the walls, pinboards carried messages about fire officers, best practice.

'Oh god, I'm such a klutz,' she said to the first person she saw. 'I've got a meeting with Yvonne and I was sure the receptionist said the second floor but now I'm not so confident.'

'Fourth floor,' said the woman unsmilingly. 'Last office on the right.'

'Thank you so much.'

Ellie got back in the lift and pressed the button for the fourth floor. When she was young she had believed in romantic love with the doctrinal rigidity of a Vatican hardliner. It had to be everything. No concessions. No compromise.

The lift doors opened and she walked into the corridor, heading for the last office on the right. She would *never* have betrayed Jean-Gabriel. Not for anything. She would have gone to the gallows for him, for the tiniest slight on him, which made what she was about to do all the harder to get her head around.

She didn't knock. She just walked straight in.

'You're faking your colleagues' signatures and I know all about it.'

Yvonne looked up at Ellie uncomprehendingly and then a crack of anger flashed across her face.

'That little bitch. She's finished.'

Ellie bit her lip, sensed a possible future galloping away from her like a startled deer.

'*She?*' she said. 'Whoever *she* is, she's got nothing to do with this. I got it from Pankaj. That's how I know it's kosher.'

Yvonne was up on her feet now, her glasses hanging round her neck on a lanyard. She was wearing a fluffy red jumper.

'That stuck-up prick,' she said, jabbing a finger in Ellie's direction. 'I'll crucify him. Doing one on a party member? McNichol will have him on toast for this. He'll be deselected. Fucking British Obama. Fuck off.'

The office was chaotic. Marketing material for council initiatives.

490

Two large yuccas. An empty dog basket. Family photos in frames.

Ellie stood her ground.

'You're selling the Larkspur to Kirk,' she said.

Yvonne went to say something but seemed to get stuck with her mouth open. It was the first time Ellie had seen her rattled.

'You've been illegally signing off whatever he's got planned for the estate.'

Yvonne's eyes narrowed, calculations whirring in her head.

'Say that again,' she said.

'You're selling the Larkspur and you've been falsifying signatures on the paperwork.'

'I don't know what you think's going on at the Larkspur but I'll say this in front of anyone you want – your boyfriend, a judge, whoever. I swear on my mother's life I've never had her sign a damn thing about the Larkspur and I'll sue anyone who says otherwise. Now get out of my office.'

Ellie stood in the middle of the room, gobsmacked. This was not what she had anticipated happening.

'But Pankaj ...' she said, without the conviction to finish the sentence.

'Believe me, I'll sue him first. The bastard.'

Ellie swallowed.

'Kirk was at the DCMS today. I saw him.'

'I bet he was. And I'm sure he put across a convincing case why it needs to be knocked down and something decent put up in its place.'

'Anything he had to say to the minister is irrelevant. The sale is illegal.'

'The decision to sell the Larkspur had full council backing. It's happening.'

Ellie's heart was hammering. She felt suddenly dizzy. Totally out of her depth.

'Tell Pankaj he'll be hearing from me. No, tell him his lawyer will be hearing from my lawyer.'

* * *

491

Back in the car park, Ellie was busy on her phone. Her first call had been to Jim. It had been tear-streaked, beseeching and eventually successful. It had yielded a number.

'Hello?' Ketchup's voice was tentative, enquiring.

'It's Ellie.'

'How did you get this number? You said you wouldn't contact me again. I don't want to talk to you.'

'Wait, please just … I confronted her. Yvonne. Just now. She denied it of course but, I don't know, it felt quite convincing.'

'No,' she said. 'No. You promised.'

'Are you listening to me? She denied it all.'

'I'm going to lose my job, my pension.'

'No, you're not. I told her I got it from someone she hates far more than she could ever hate you. And she believed me. She wanted to believe me. You're fine. Your job's fine. But she denied everything you told me and, as I said, it was pretty convincing. She said she would sue anyone that accused her of signing off the plans for the Larkspur.'

'The estate?'

'Yes, of course the estate!'

There followed a long pause during which bad thoughts flooded into Ellie's mind like water pouring through an open sluice.

'They weren't anything to do with Larkspur Hill,' said Miss Ketchup eventually. 'I never signed anything about Larkspur Hill.'

She paused again.

'The Grangeham development,' she said barely audibly, her voice cracking. 'It was for that. A report.'

'Oh god.'

'I don't know anything about the Larkspur.'

'Oh god.'

'I'm going now,' she said. 'Don't call me again. I mean it. Don't call me ever again.'

'Oh god,' said Ellie again. But this time there was no one to hear.

49

'Can it be any kind of lizard?'

'They're not lizards,' said Colin, looking over at his daughter as she pushed back some long grass with a stick. 'Lizards are reptiles. We need newts. They're amphibians. Completely different thing. I can't believe you don't know that. You know how to spell pterodactyl but you don't know what a newt is. The syllabus is totally out of whack.'

Although the old Grangeham forge was technically Andrew Kirk's private property it had always been an open site and there was nothing to stop you walking through it. Not that anyone ever did. It was served only by one access road, which led nowhere else, and it wasn't the kind of place that attracted day trippers: the few buildings that still stood were crumbling and overgrown, the waterways were muddily overflowing, electricity pylons loomed over its tarmac plains.

'You've got to look in the water. The one we're looking for has a ridge on its back.' He looked down at his phone. 'And a tail that looks a bit like a feather. And we've got to find that one, not just any old newt. It's called the great crested newt.'

The forge had historically been served by a small network of canals, but about half the banks had collapsed creating a muddy wetland full of reeds and strange pieces of concrete jutting out irregularly.

'Spot test,' shouted Rodbortzoon, who had borrowed a pair of waders and was waist-deep in the water. 'Name a fourth amphibian.'

Daisy rolled her eyes.

'This is getting way too like school.'

'Frogs, toads, newts – easy,' continued Rodbortzoon, ignoring her. 'But can you name a fourth?'

'Iguana?' said Colin.

'Reptile, obviously.'

'Chameleon?' said Daisy.

'Reptile!'

They were standing, father and daughter, looking down at Rodbortzoon from a large concrete slab that looked like it might have once been the foundations for a corrugated steel shed. Big buddleia bushes had grown through the cracks.

'I can't make the thing go on the thing.'

The mesh part of Daisy's net had become detached from its pole and she was struggling to fix it back on. Colin took both parts from her.

'How did your mum's meeting in London go?' he asked innocently.

'I don't know,' she said, gladly giving the pieces up. 'I don't think it went well. She tried to hide it from me but I could tell she'd been crying.'

'I'm sure you gave her a hug and made it better. Pankaj too, I imagine.'

'We were at ours.'

'Really?'

'Yeah,' she said, reaching down to adjust one of her boots. They were special Fresno wellingtons which were designed so you could clip Fresno key ring dolls round the top of each boot so that they hung down and rattled as you walked. Colin found all aspects of Fresno culture profoundly disturbing but it was these boots that freaked him out the most: every time he looked at them they put him instantly in mind of a rogue recon marine wading through the Mekong Delta wearing a necklace of human ears.

'Were you packing?' he said as he clipped the net back on to the pole.

'No, just doing stuff. Watching TV, you know.'

'So he came round, did he?' said Colin as he handed her back the mended net.

'No, not on Monday. Or last night.'

'Right,' he said, distracted. It was interesting information, this. But really it was too little, too late.

Overhead, two crows cawed. The pylons crackled. Making sure that Daisy stayed where she was, up on the relative safety of the slab, Colin jumped down on to a plateau of crumbling tarmac where he crouched by the water's edge and pulled back some reeds.

'Gecko?' said Daisy from up on the slab.

'Reptile!' roared Rodbortzoon.

Colin stared into the water. He could see minnows darting in the shallows. He watched them flick and flitter, always, it seemed, on high alert, the possibility of imminent predation never absent from their minds. It was a pitiable existence in many ways. But there was something heroic about that urge to live on, even if it only meant a few more days in a muddy canal on the old Grangeham forge.

As well as the minnows, he could see water boatmen catamaraning across the surface. A dragonfly buzzing in the reeds. A cormorant sat up high on a metal pole, surveying the scene. Everywhere you looked there was life. But there were no newts. No newt spawn. No tell-tale folded-over leaves with eggs on the underside.

'Let's try over there,' said Colin, pointing to the second canal.

Rodbortzoon waded out of the water and the three of them walked down an old road, the tarmac fraying at the sides with yellow ragwort, cow parsley, more buddleia.

'I hear your father is taking you to Nottingham for the all-important game,' said Rodbortzoon, waddling squelchily in his waders.

'I won't get home until eleven o'clock,' said Daisy. 'At the *earliest*.'

At the edge of a moss-streaked patch of tarmac stood the remains of a concrete lamp post which had snapped, its top half sagging on to the floor, the two pieces connected still by the rusted steel reinforcing bars which spilled from the wound like the entrails of a pig. Colin guided Daisy past it, avoiding its sharp edges.

'So,' said Rodbortzoon. 'What do you think our chances are? You know one-nil is not enough. We need to win by two.'

'I think we're going to do it.'

'So do I!'

'Yeah,' said Colin in full parental expectation-management mode, 'but we've got to remember it's a long shot. The bookmakers are offering three to one on us doing it, which they really wouldn't if they thought we had a chance in hell of winning.'

'I still think we'll do it if we try hard enough,' said Daisy.

'Ha ha,' said Rodbortzoon. 'Ordinarily, I am against trying too hard on ideological grounds but on this occasion I am with you. Come on you Steam!'

They reached the second canal and got to work with their nets. Rodbortzoon in the deeper water, Colin and Daisy in the shallows.

'Is it turtles?' said Daisy. 'They live in water and on land.'

'At last, a reasonable guess,' shouted Rodbortzoon, 'but no, they too are reptiles. The scales are the giveaway.'

It was a clear day, just a few hazy clouds high in the sky. The light breeze disturbed the leaves on the saplings that had sprung up around the site.

'Andy Willis's dad says that if they put the stadium here they'll build a Jumping Jungle as well,' said Daisy. She had given up looking for newts and was throwing stones at a fly-tipped washing machine, enjoying the ping each time she hit it.

'A Jumping Jungle?' said Rodbortzoon. 'Enlighten me.'

'They're indoor adventure playgrounds with loads of trampolines in them,' said Colin. 'We went to one in Manchester when we were visiting auntie Kath, didn't we? It was actually quite good, as I remember.'

'Dad did a slam dunk.'

'They have a basketball ring above a trampoline,' said Colin, trying not to sound too impressed with himself. 'It's obviously not the same as sinking a dunk on a normal court but it still takes a fair bit of—'

'Why would anyone want to build an adventure playground here, of all places,' said Rodbortzoon, talking over him. 'It is already a playground!'

'You what?' said Daisy.

Rodbortzoon had waded out of the water and was sitting on an old lump of stone with his face in the sun. From somewhere, he had pulled out a massive bag of biltong.

'Your place is a jumping jungle. A wannabe jungle. It aspires to the condition of the wilds but knows it will always be only ersatz. Why build that here on the site of the actually existing wilds?'

Daisy looked one way and then the other.

'Like, how is *this* a jungle?'

'OK. It isn't a *jungle* jungle, but it is the modern wilderness.'

'Wilderness?' said Colin. 'I can literally see the road over there.'

'You are mistaking wilderness for remoteness. Category error.'

Daisy rolled her eyes but stayed where she was, listening.

'There are places that are remote still. Sure. Alaska. Siberia. Australian interior, etc. etc. But they are not wild. Not with GPS. Satellite phones. Not now they are already indexed – the monitor on the eagle's talon, helicopter surveillance footage, butterfly migration data, acoustic imaging of underground oil supplies, and on and on. The grid has outgrown the globe. We have been everywhere already. All of it is mapped, known, indexed. These places no longer give us the shiver.'

'Is it an eel?' said Colin, who wasn't really listening.

'Good god,' said Rodbortzoon. 'When did you ever see an eel on land? An eel is a fish!' He pulled a huge piece of biltong from his bag and tore a chunk from it with his back teeth. 'But this place,' he said, gesturing around him. 'This place definitely gives you the shiver. This place is *unheimlich*.'

Daisy's face was an uncomprehending grimace.

'Uncanny,' said Rodbortzoon. 'Familiar but unnavigable.'

Colin watched Daisy recoil in horror as Rodbortzoon offered her a piece of the biltong. In the near future when she announced that she was becoming a vegetarian he would be able to trace the decision back to this moment.

'However much we might want to suppress the urge we can't help but look at this and wonder if it is a portent.'

Daisy looked over at Colin, bewildered but not bored.

'He means: is this place what the future will be like?'

'How we will have to adapt to live here? This is the thought that gives us the shiver.'

Daisy raised an eyebrow.

'I don't care what happens. I am *so* not living here.'

Rodbortzoon laughed, spraying biltong juice into the ether.

'Not yet,' he shouted merrily. 'But embracing this kind of place is the first step towards the abandonment of the aesthetic of denial. Virgin forest. Pristine countryside. Perfect anything. It doesn't exist. The plastic is everywhere and it will survive for four centuries. Plutonium-239 has a half-life of twenty-four thousand years. We need a new way of relating to the world that accepts this. We will call it, maybe, the aesthetic of the *as is*.'

Rodbortzoon waded out of the river and sat down on the bank.

'We can then perhaps learn to stop *working* towards an unattainable perfectibility and realise that we might find joy *playing* amid the ruins of the recent past.'

Daisy stood where she was, her eyes narrowed. She seemed to be mulling over something, giving it serious consideration.

'Duck-billed platypus?' she said eventually.

'*Mammal*,' shouted Rodbortzoon, incredulous. 'A bloody weird mammal, but a mammal nonetheless.'

* * *

On the way home they stopped at the Eastfinche services. Colin filled the tank and then parked up at the Little Chef where he ordered teas for him and Rodbortzoon, and a Coke for Daisy. They sat at a plastic table on moulded plastic chairs.

'Time to give up?' said Rodbortzoon.

Colin bridled. It was self-evident that you were, in the grand scheme of things, a minnow. A tiny little thing in terms of the universe. Insignificant. The cosmos didn't give a fig whether or not you fought hard for some dignity in your crappy little puddle. But from the standpoint of your minnow-sized subjectivity it mattered a great deal. Whatever you did, you probably wouldn't save the world. But you might just save yourself.

'No way,' he said. 'It's too important. I can't just give up. I can't just let him win.'

'Not on the Chapel, you idiot,' shouted Rodbortzoon, thumping the table with his fist. 'We will never give up on the Chapel. I mean the amphibian!'

'Oh yeah. The amphibian. I give up.'

'Me too,' said Daisy.

'Salamander!' shouted Rodbortzoon. 'A fine and noble creature. Or you could have had caecilians but they are just glorified worms.'

Colin sighed and went off for a pee. When he arrived back at the table he looked down at his wallet. It wasn't where he had left it and the zip was slightly open. On the other side of the room, he could see Rodbortzoon standing at the fruit machine, chugging pound coins into the slot.

'He didn't take any money from my wallet, did he?'

Daisy blushed.

'No,' she said guiltily. 'He didn't.'

'I was only joking,' said Colin ruefully, as he picked it up. 'Do you want anything else?'

'No. I'm good.'

'OK. I'm going to get a bottle of water for the way home. You wait here and I'll be back in a minute.'

Colin walked to the till, aggrieved that what had been a day of pretty successful father–daughter bonding was being soured by the nagging suspicion that Daisy had been stealing from him. Ordinarily, he had no idea of what was in his wallet but when he had paid for the petrol on his card he had noticed that he had exactly twenty-five quid. Two notes. No coins. He pulled the water from the shelf of the fridge and walked to the till, his whole perspective on the day turned on its head.

For all that it had been fun, searching for newts, it had been fruitless. He couldn't help but feel that from start to finish Kirk had played a blinder. He had set the whole thing up to be a heroic English failure of the sort that everyone expected and secretly desired.

'That'll be ninety pence, love,' said the cashier.

Colin stood in front of her, not moving, his hand clamped round his wallet. He felt awfully, achingly sad. They weren't going to save the Chapel. He wasn't getting his job back. Ellie wasn't coming home. Daisy was all he had.

'Ninety pee, love, when you get a chance. There's a queue.'

Slowly Colin drew back the zip on his wallet. The feelings came crashing in, piled up on top of each other. Relief first, at the sight of an old gnarled twenty and the sharp edge of the new plastic fiver; then guilt, obviously, at the false accusation, and then finally hope that all was not lost.

50

It was a lovely May evening. A cloudless sky. The sun low and warm. People rode bikes. The trees sang greenly with their darling buds. Ellie walked along the street oblivious, trying, but failing, to shake the sense that she was unspooling.

It was 5.30 p.m. on Wednesday, two full days since she had run sobbing from the council car park. In the forty-eight hours since, she had lain low, her phone barely out of her hand as she waited for Pankaj to call, desperate to hear from him but utterly incapable of calling him herself.

It had become a fixation, the waiting, and it had rendered her virtually catatonic, incapable of raising herself to read or do yoga, let alone get out and engage with the world. And so she had moped about, feeling increasingly disassociated with each passing hour, ever more aware that the thread of her life had frayed to near nothingness and she was no longer who she had always understood herself to be.

Prior to these two depressive days, Ellie had always imagined that the absolute, unmediated her – the one with whom she had the whispered self-relationship, the one from whom she had always drawn her sense of fixity – was essentially unchanging. She had fundamental, enduring characteristics. Believed in certain things, like throwing yourself into the fire in the service of love.

Ellie walked along the pavement avoiding the cracks, each paving slab an island on to which she had to hop. For stability. She breathed in through her mouth. Forty-eight hours she had had of this – thoughts careering round her head like birds in a locked room.

He had not called her. She had not called him.

Enough was, eventually, enough.

Five minutes later, she arrived on his doorstep and took a breath. She reached into her coat pocket, felt the hard metal edges of the key. *His* key. It was stupid to think of it as hers, she had surely squandered that privilege. She felt distraught at everything she had thrown away. The jokes. The conversation. She winced. *London*. She could forget about that now, too.

She left the key where it was and rang the doorbell.

'So,' he said when he opened it. 'She lives.'

He stood his ground, one hand on the doorframe, one hand on the door. Which meant she had to stand hers, two steps down from him, looking up.

'Hello,' she said softly.

'Hello,' he said, not softly.

'Kirk was there. At the DCMS. Talking to Harvey.'

'I heard.'

'I left my phone and I went back and that's when I saw him. And that's why I had to . . . I panicked. I'm sorry.'

He stood where he was in the doorway, saying nothing.

'Did she call you? Yvonne?'

'Yes, she did.'

Ellie stopped herself from imagining what it must have been like, that conversation.

'I'm sorry,' she said. 'I saw him there and . . . He's a Tory party donor. And I knew he'd be going in there and banging on about jobs and investment and I just had to do something. I called you three times, four times. I don't know. You were in the House. It was that debate. And so of course you didn't answer, but I did call. And I couldn't get through to you, and I just had to do something. I'm sorry.'

Finally, Pankaj let go of the doorframe and took a step back so that she could come into the house. He walked through to the kitchen and put the kettle on.

'There was a question on the floor of the House yesterday. About PFI. It was a Lib Dem. She used the Generator as her example of all that is wrong with the system. She was asking for an inquiry.'

502

He shrugged.

'It won't happen. The inquiry. But Yvonne is fatally wounded,' he said, his back to her. 'For all sorts of reasons. She'll be gone by the end of the week.'

'Is she going to sue you?'

'She's in no position to be suing anyone.'

He placed tea bags in two mugs before turning to her.

'But you didn't know that.'

'No,' she said. 'I didn't. I'm sorry.'

She saw the corners of his mouth turning up in that familiar knowing way. He shrugged an almost imperceptible little shrug.

'You did what you had to do,' he said.

Ellie looked at him, utterly perplexed.

'You're not angry?'

'I was pissed off for a bit when she first called me, but it didn't last long. You did what you had to do. That's what marks out people who aren't ordinary from people who are ordinary.'

She felt the physical presence of him in the room. But also more than that. It was like there was a sixth set of data that came rushing in. It was abstract. Hormonal. And it bypassed the usual checks and balances and went straight to the seat of her.

She could see now that there was something hard and unknowable about him, a part of him from which she would always be excluded. She had absolutely no idea why but it was the thing that made her want him.

'There will be times in the future when I also have to do what I have to do. And I think I know now that you'll understand.'

Was there part of Ellie that listened to this and wondered how it fitted with the relationship as she had always conceived it would be: nurturing, open, honest, kind? A part of her that might stop and ask how she squared it with the future she had mapped out? If so, it was overwhelmed by the part of her that was finally free to want what it wanted, when it wanted it, which was now.

She was kicking off her shoes when his phone rang. Which was a shock because it was ordinarily on silent. They both stopped and looked down to where it sat on the table. Together they read the name on the screen.

Robert Cooper.

He was one of the deputy directors to the permanent secretary and had been at Oxford at the same time as Pankaj.

'Already?' said Pankaj. 'God, I wasn't expecting this for a couple of hours yet.'

'What?'

'The decision.'

'But it's not being announced until Friday.'

'It's not being *announced* until Friday, but the decision is being made today. And Bob will know what it is.'

'Oh my god, answer it.'

Pankaj touched the screen; once and then again.

'Shas?'

His voice was echoey, distant.

'Yes, Bob. You're on speakerphone.'

'Ah right. I suppose that means there are a few of you listening. Well, you'll all know why I'm calling and I'm sorry ...'

Bob paused, exhaled sadly.

Ellie felt instantly drained like a shop awning tipped empty of rainwater. She leaned into the table, held it for ballast.

Bob held the silence for another beat.

'... that I'm not there to tell you this in person,' he roared, 'as I'd love to see your bloody face. Somehow that great lump has just been awarded Grade two listing. They're going to announce it Friday morning.'

She gripped on to the table as the room dissolved around her.

'I don't know how you did it but you can pop the fizz, old boy. You've got a brutalist bloody council estate forever associated with your name. Hopefully it won't completely ruin your career.'

'Christ, Bob,' shouted Pankaj at the phone, 'you nearly gave me a heart attack.'

'Seriously, Shas, congratulations. People are impressed. Everyone keeps going on about how dynamic you are. I'm doing my best to disabuse them ...'

Ellie sat down. On the floor. Right where she had been standing. She sat on the floor and filled her lungs like someone freed from a too-tight corset and able finally to breathe again.

* * *

A few hours later, they were in bed, an empty bottle of champagne on the floor beside them. Pankaj had lit a cigarette. Ellie watched him smoke. It was so strange to be there, with so much of what it was you wanted and to feel that you hadn't really earned it. That it had just landed in your lap.

'Incredible to think it'll be there forever now,' he said, as he exhaled. 'You've made something permanent. That's a thing to have done. Almost as significant as having built it in the first place.'

Ellie watched the blue curls of smoke wind their way upwards, wondering why it was that she felt so empty.

'And the station won't be there now. Which means it'll have to be somewhere else. Very probably on the site of the Chapel.'

He took another drag.

'And none of it would have happened if it wasn't for you.'

She took the cigarette and took a drag, listening to him but not really hearing him. It was a state of profound disbelief.

'Am I all right to smoke inside?' he asked. 'Daisy's not coming back tonight, is she?'

'She's in Nottingham with Colin. They're going to stay at his mum's.'

'Of course. Christ. What time is it?'

Ellie leaned over so she could see the radio.

'Coming up for ten.'

'Quick, put it on, the radio.'

Ellie found the right station, turned up the volume.

And that's it. The final whistle. The final whistle!!

The commentator's voice was squeaky and emotional. Any higher and it would have been outside a human adult's audible range. He sounded drained and disbelieving and like he was all but ready to die. From somewhere he summoned one last surge of adrenaline.

Robin Hood, can you hear me? David Pleat, can you hear me? Two-nil in your own back yard. Nottingham, birthplace of giants. Robin Hood. Alan Sillitoe. D. H. Lawrence. Su Pollard. Your boys took one hell of a beating! Your boys took one hell of a beating!

'Does that mean what I think it means?' said Ellie.

'Yes, it bloody does. Peterdown United are going to Wembley. One more win and they're in the Premier League.'

Part Three

Monday, May 19th

C olin sat at his desk, weighing up his options. It turned out that trading in great crested newts was illegal in Europe but there were people in America who seemed willing to sell him one. The issue was shipping. Which at the best estimate was looking like six to eight weeks, customs issues notwithstanding. He had seven days before the announcement was made, which meant if he was going to plant a newt in the Grangeham waterways he was going to have to fly to Dayton, Ohio and smuggle the damn thing back on his person. The question which even Google couldn't seem to answer was: would a newt survive a fourteen-hour flight in 100 ml of water?

Colin leaned back in his chair trying to imagine how it would show up on the X-ray, a great crested newt in a miniature bottle of shampoo.

He was sitting in what had been their living room, a trestle table rigged up as his desk. Ellie and Daisy had all but moved out, which pretty much gave him the run of the place. And that was a relief after so long under canvas, even if it was strange and sad to be back in the half-disassembled house. He had the radio on in the background to give the place some life, but you could still hear the larger silence behind the babble, a silence that wouldn't be filled again. Or at least not for another fortnight when the new tenants moved in.

Around him were mostly bare walls, all of them covered in a fine layer of dust and full of holes, fragments of red Rawlplugs poking out from them. The plywood panels had been taken down and put in storage. A temporary structure that he had always imagined would be there forever. The kitchen. The boxes. The paintings. All gone. He would never again live in a house like it.

He chewed the end of his pen. Where would he go? It was an ever more pressing concern. The camp was all but over. The Portaloo people had come and collected their toilet, citing unpaid debts. The council had blast-cleaned the graffiti. And the Department of Radical Football had collapsed in on itself and no one had the wherewithal to right it again. Only three tents and the mess remained. It was obvious that the police had been holding off from doing anything, hoping that it would wind up naturally on its own, but they were getting impatient again and it was surely just days before the last occupants were forcibly evicted.

Colin closed his laptop with a sigh.

The boxes were lined up against the far wall, some sealed with brown tape, others still flapping open expectantly. Each box had a letter written on it in thick marker pen. There were plenty of Es, even more Ds. In the corner, on its own, sat a lone C.

He walked over to it and looked inside. Sitting on top of the DVDs and books was the half-size replica of the FA Cup that he had won at the 2011 Regional Football Writers' Gala Dinner and Quiz.

He picked it up and turned it over in his hands. It had been his greatest triumph. After eight rounds of questions he had found himself in a three-way playoff. To settle it, they had asked for, in descending order of size, an eight-bird roast comprised entirely of club mascots.

Involuntarily, Colin rattled it off in his head. A swan (Swansea), then inside that an eagle (Palace), then a seagull (Brighton), after that an owl (Wednesday), then a bantam (Bradford), then a magpie (Newcastle), and inside that a robin (Charlton), stuffed with a canary (Norwich). He could picture it still, written out like that on a piece of paper. Him handing it to the compère. The compère reading it out, confirming he had won, the dull groan from the audience, the begrudging applause.

It was the bantam that had won him it. It wasn't that no one else had known that Bradford City were nicknamed the Bantams. They all knew that. It was just that none of them had known a bantam was a chicken. Which was ironic, he'd always thought, as it was the one bird in the roast that you would actually consider eating. Unless you were the Queen, of course. Who, he had some vague sense, ate swans.

He tossed the trophy back into the box. For years it had been his prized possession. The thing he had always said, only half-joking, that he would rescue first from the fire. It was only recently that he had come to realise what it had cost him. The books he hadn't read. The languages he didn't speak.

Colin closed the flaps on the box and shoved it back in its corner. On the wall in front of him was a pin board. He had imagined that it would be his mind map, like the ones detectives had in TV shows, all pathways and potential suspects, routes out of the mire. But it hadn't worked out like that. He hadn't got any further than putting up a single picture of a great crested newt, which sat there in the middle of the board with its stupidly disproportionate tail looking, with the best will in the world, like some awful misjudged evolutionary cul-de-sac that really wasn't worth saving at all.

He pulled it down and threw it in the bin. All that was left now on the board was a ticket, down in the corner. He pulled out the drawing pin that held it in place and took a proper look at it. The sponsor's logo in the corner. The shiny counterfeit-proof hologram in the other. And there, printed in the middle, the scarcely credible words:

Championship Play-Off Final
Wembley Stadium, Saturday May 24th
Kick Off: 3:00pm

A part of him found it hard to believe that it wasn't part of some enormously elaborate windup. Peterdown United were a game away from promotion. To the Premier League. It was ridiculous. Absurd. And yet here it was, in black and white. With a hologram. The ultimate authenticator of the real.

Holding the ticket, Colin felt something in him give. It was the defences he had built up against expectation. They cracked a little and then a lot. And then down they came. And in it poured. The thing that triumphed over experience. The thing that slowly killed you. The last thing lost.

Hope.

He sat down in his chair with a thump and shut his eyes. All they had to do was win one game and it would happen. The thing he had ached for since he was a boy. The thing that would salve his wounds, make him whole.

Promotion to the top flight.

One goal. One swing of the boot and all that yearning and wishing and wanting and needing would be over.

One swing of the boot and everything would be all right.

For five minutes he sat in his chair dreaming goals. Garry smashing it in from twenty-five yards. Garry slaloming through the QPR defence. Garry chipping the keeper. Garry squeezing it in from a tight angle. Garry with the outside of his boot. Garry with the inside of his boot. Garry with an overhead kick. Halfway through a whole-team passing move that was about to culminate in Garry nutmegging the QPR keeper with a no-look backheel, Colin was disturbed from his reverie by the sound of his phone ringing.

It was Ellie. Instantly, the thought reared in his head: it wasn't going to be the Larkspur. Not now that it was listed. He felt a wave of nausea. It was basically them versus the Generator. And really, who'd fancy them in that fight?

'Hi,' he said.

'Hi.'

'Congratulations.'

'Thanks.'

'You did it.'

'We did.'

Colin exhaled another resigned sigh.

'There have been points in the last three months when I tried to convince myself otherwise,' he said, 'but really I always knew you would. You know, I just *knew* you would.'

Ellie listened to this, hearing the words but feeling entirely unaffected by them. She understood what he was saying. She, too, had spent the last three months feeling, at some deep level, that it would be the thing that would happen, the listing. That it was in some way ordained, the only outcome that the presentation deserved. Now that it had happened, though, it felt weirdly like just a thing that had happened. Not *her* thing. Just *a* thing.

'I know it makes things even more difficult for you,' she said.

'Does it?' said Colin. 'I always wanted them to choose the Generator. That's the only outcome I've ever wanted.'

Ellie felt a lump half-rise in her throat. She had only ever wanted it to be the Generator in a public, declared sort of way; but had anyone, at any time, told her she could save the Larkspur at the expense of the Chapel she would have taken it in a heartbeat. Not that this mattered. The choice had never been hers to make.

'You know they still might,' she said. 'The finances of the place are doubly screwed now. The listing means Kirk's not going to buy the Larkspur so the council won't be getting any money for it. I just don't see how they can possibly afford to keep it open.'

'But it's so new, Ellie.'

'And they'd be replacing it with something even newer.'

'I suppose that has its own twisted kind of logic.'

'Anyway, there's something you need to know.'

'What?'

'You know my source at the council? Basically, Kington has been faking other councillors' signatures, approving certain projects. I *thought* she was fast-tracking selling the Larkspur to Kirk. But it turns out it was nothing to do with the Larkspur. It was about the Grangeham forge.'

'Shit. Really? Was it something to do with newts?'

'Daisy told me about you and your newts.'

'Not just any old newt. The great crested newt. They're super protected and I think they might be breeding at Grangeham. I think they're trying to cover it up.'

'I don't know about it in any detail, but I could try to find out more.'

'That would be great. A biodiversity report. Anything like that.'

'OK,' she said. 'I'm on it.'

Ellie hung up, feeling only marginally less guilty than she had at the start of the conversation. Because there were two things he needed to know and telling him about the first didn't really make up for the fact that she hadn't mentioned the second.

Benjamin Willis had offered her a job.

In London.

Starting in ten days' time.

The call had come at the weekend. He had congratulated her on the listing and then got straight to the point. His practice was expanding at such a pace that he didn't have time to interview people he didn't know. He needed people he could trust. People with known talent. She had smiled at that – *known talent* – almost laughed with glee, but as soon as she put the phone down she had found herself feeling mysteriously hollow.

Ellie leaned back into the headboard. It was a far more senior role than anyone with her experience could reasonably have hoped for. Not quite where she might have expected to be had it not been for Daisy, but not far off.

Which made it all the more remarkable that it was only the week's second most exciting piece of employment news in the household.

Pankaj walked into the bedroom where she was sitting cross-legged, her phone on the pillow beside her. He paused at the mirror to knot his tie.

'How do I look?'

'Like someone in the shadow cabinet,' she said in a tone of voice that made it deliberately unclear whether this was supposed to be an insult or a compliment.

Pankaj smiled his practised self-effacing smile. It was, she had realised over their time together, the smile of someone so accustomed to getting compliments that they had had to develop a pro-forma response.

'Shadow front bench,' he said. 'Not shadow cabinet. Shadow Minister for Steel, Postal Affairs and Consumer Protection. One of the great offices of state.'

Ellie barked out an instinctive little laugh.

It had happened on the Friday, the day after the listing had been announced, the previous holder of the post having had to resign over some mistake in their campaign expenses.

'You know Colin's dad works at the sorting office, don't you?' she said idly.

'I do. Although, for obvious reasons, I don't think I'll be going to him for policy suggestions.'

Ellie felt first a little stab of recrimination at this and all that it implied, and then quickly afterwards a flash of anger that he, of all people, was bringing up the betrayal. It only reinforced her sense that the fact that she hadn't told Colin about the job offer was somehow evened up by the fact that she hadn't told Pankaj either.

She lay on the bed, watching him look at himself in the mirror as he pinched and shaped the knot of his tie. She had convinced herself that she hadn't told him because elevation to the shadow front bench was a big thing and he deserved his moment in the sun without her intruding on it, and also because delaying bought her a bit of time before he started insisting that she accept it.

Of course, had Ellie drilled down a little deeper into the reasons for this reticence, beyond the things that she was telling herself, she might have found that there lurked a more haunting explanation. The certainty that this 'good' job would no more scratch the existential itch than her current 'bad' job. That it would be there, gnawing away at her, whomever she was sleeping with and however she was employed, until the day she died.

Pankaj pulled on his jacket. It was his special one, made for him on Savile Row. They were going to an event in Broadcastle. The Chambers of Commerce. Some celebration of local entrepreneurship.

'Why is this thing on a Monday night?' asked Ellie in an irritated voice, even though she was secretly in exactly the right mood to go to an event at which she had licence to gleefully hate everyone there.

'All these things are on Mondays and Tuesdays. They're the only nights that no one is doing anything else. It means they get a full house.'

He looked over at her, at the white slip dress she had laid out on the bed.

'They're normally awful, these things. But this one's not bad, as they go. The champagne flows all night. I didn't feel right for about three days after the last one.'

'Is Yvonne going to be there?'

'She might be. I don't know. I was expecting her to have gone into hiding but she does seem to be tenaciously clinging on.'

This was the other thing making Ellie irritable. Yvonne had been on the radio, lamenting the listing, and had been tweeting away bullishly about the future of the Generator.

'Are the other councillors really rallying round her?'

Pankaj had a shoe horn which he was using to slide himself into his monk straps.

'Yeah, they are,' he said in a wearily disappointed voice. 'I forgot to tell you. It turns out quite a few of them have had rather a lot of meetings with Land Dominion that it seems had to take place at some of Broadcastle's most expensive restaurants. Quaranta. The Merchant. The River Grill.'

'You're kidding.'

'If what I've heard is true, a couple of them have pretty expensive tastes when it comes to wine.'

'And she's reminded them of this, has she?'

'They do all appear to have lined up behind her on the Generator. Everyone's all gung-ho again about keeping it open.'

'I don't understand how the hell she thinks she's going to finance it.'

'She claims that she's got something lined up.'

'Has she got anything left to sell?'

Pankaj laughed as he grabbed his keys from the top of the dresser.

'Look, if she's there, she's there. What does it matter? You won. The building's listed. And there's nothing she can do about it.'

He leaned down and kissed her.

'If my meeting finishes early I'll call and we can a grab a drink by the river before the thing starts. Otherwise, I'll just see you there.'

'Sure,' she said.

After he had gone she busied herself with all kinds of things that didn't urgently need doing. A couple of emails. Some dishes that needed washing. The days since the listing had all been like this. Hyper-aware of the passage of time and the fact that it needed to be filled. It reminded her of Daisy's birth. A momentous thing had happened and she should have been ecstatic, but instead the hours had dragged and all she could think about was how the momentous thing hadn't made her feel remotely like she had imagined it would.

She dumped the laundry on the bed and started sorting through the clothes, pairing Daisy's socks, piling Pankaj's shirts for the cleaner to iron. But nothing could be put off forever. When she finally summoned herself to do it, she did it in a rush so there was no time to reconsider. Once you had dialled you couldn't just hang up.

She stood there, phone pressed to her ear, listening to the ring tone. And then just as she was thinking she might get away with it and the call would go through to voicemail, Shelly answered.

'Hello, Ellie,' she said in a voice that communicated a disappointment that had hardened into something dispassionate and terrifyingly calm. It was a voice that would brook no dissent, had punishments in mind.

She swallowed stoically.

'I'm sorry,' she said.

'I can't believe you went behind my back. Did you not stop to think I was protecting her for a reason?'

'I'm sorry.'

'And to drag Jim into it.'

'I'm so sorry, Shelly.'

'Do you want me to tell you a bit about her life?'

No, thought Ellie. I really don't.

'Yes,' she said. 'I think you probably should.'

* * *

The event was at an old church, long deconsecrated. The ancient arches curved up into a colossal ceiling, lit now with pink light. On each circular dining table was a centrepiece of branches painted white, crystals hanging from them. Every chair was shrouded in a white cotton cover.

The guests were yet to be seated and had congregated round the bar at the end of the room. Pankaj emerged from the throng as she walked in.

'What do you think?' he said with a knowing smile.

Ellie shifted her weight on to one hip. It was fine, all this. Up to a point. Even if it was just a version of herself that she was playing. It wouldn't be long until it was something she did for his friends, a vaudeville turn.

She looked around.

'Bulgarian Wedding Baroque,' she said acidly, aware even as she was saying it that the corrosion was indiscriminate.

Pankaj laughed and pulled her into an embrace.

'Don't look,' he said, sotto voce, in her ear. 'But she's over there.'

Ellie looked over to the far side of the room where, away from the crowd, Yvonne Kington had Andrew Kirk cornered.

'She's totally colonising him. Everyone here wants a bit of him but she's had him on her own for ten minutes, ripping strips off him.'

Yvonne was talking in a violent whisper and jabbing the air as she spoke. Kirk had his arms crossed and was leaning forward penitently but he had the look on his face of a schoolboy conspirator, enormously amused at his own joke.

'Oh my god, you know what's happening, don't you? He's pulling out of the deal for the Larkspur. We're witnessing it in real time.'

Twice Kirk tried to put a placatory hand on Yvonne's shoulder and twice she batted him away. Ellie peered harder. Yvonne was talking and Kirk was giggling at her. There was no other word for it. He was giggling. From nowhere Ellie felt overwhelmed with sympathy for Yvonne. He was giggling at her. Giggling with its air of self-satisfaction, its infantile knowingness. Laughter was open, giggling was closed. It was about power and exclusion, and he was giggling at her in front of all these people.

Ellie found herself overcome with a desire for Yvonne to hit him. In the mouth. With a closed fist. Properly leather him. She wanted something that would detonate. Blow the whole thing up.

Kirk looked over Yvonne's shoulder at Ellie. Their eyes met. Kirk's face didn't fall as she had hoped it would. Instead, she felt herself on the end of an instant appraisal, followed by sustained eye contact.

Yvonne followed the direction of Kirk's gaze until she was also staring squarely at Ellie. The look on her face when she saw her was one of utter contempt, but it was also weirdly dismissive. Exasperated rather than angry. And it left Ellie feeling awkward and unsettled and also dissatisfied. It felt endemic, this fraying of her life. Nothing could be tied up any more.

Ellie walked over to where a waiter was standing, holding a tray of champagne flutes. She took one with the closest thing to an authentic smile that she had managed all day and deliberately lost herself in the throng.

She talked to someone whose name she didn't catch, about something she didn't really understand. After five minutes he seemed to clock that she was utterly lost and, pointing tentatively at someone on the other side of the room, he made his excuses and moved on. She then grabbed another glass of champagne and enjoyed herself, moaning about motherhood with an overdressed and already deeply drunk woman who was holding two drinks and had the slightly crazed quality of a domestic dog let loose in an open field. After enduring a ten-minute monologue by the marketing manager of the Broadcastle tech incubator, she scanned the room. They were gone. Kington. And Kirk, too.

'He does that,' said Pankaj, who had appeared at her elbow. 'He only ever stays at these things for half an hour and then he's off. Maintains the mystique.'

Two hours later the dinner was over. Empty bottles of wine sat upturned in ice buckets, puddings lay about half-finished. Ellie was in her seat, detached from it all, watching people dance badly to Sister Sledge.

She saw Pankaj walking towards her, a tube under his arm. He had been working the room.

'Done enough gladhanding?'

'Always,' he said. 'But also, unfortunately, never.'

He sat down beside her.

'I'm a bit worried what you're going to think about this,' he said.

'About what?'

'Zone Eight.'

Instantly, the image of Ralph in his Blizzard Corps outfit appeared in her head.

'The lights were on a timer,' she said.

Pankaj looked at her uncomprehendingly. Ellie felt suddenly the full force of the booze.

'Wait a sec,' she said, 'what are you talking about?'

He moved some glasses so he could unroll an A3 poster on the table in front of her. It was a composite of images. The largest was an exterior shot of the Larkspur, or at least what looked like the Larkspur in disguise, half of it hidden behind pastel cladding. It was like it had been shat on with kitsch.

'What the hell is this?' she said.

'A party donor who works in the building trade just gave me it. It's Kirk's presentation to the minister. It was the basis of his bid to get the building listed.'

Ellie heard this but also didn't hear it.

'He was in with the minister lobbying to get it listed. It was part of his pitch. He's now using it as early marketing material.'

In the render in front of her, the community hall had been fitted out as a gym.

'Wait a sec, I don't understand. He's still *buying* it? What did we . . .'

This idea was too big for her to see it whole and she was still feeling for its edges.

'Already has.'

'But it's been listed.'

'He got it for three million.'

The cladding on Europa House was pink and yellow and sky blue.

'He got the whole thing for *three* million?'

Pankaj nodded again.

'The original plan had been for him to provide twenty-five per cent affordable housing and then use his 106 contribution to buy himself out of the social housing obligation.'

'That was the original plan? You're telling me that there's a *worse* suggestion than that?'

She looked down again at the image. There was a shot of the café. As it was. Her café. *As it was.* In somebody's mind it was of a piece with this imagined exterior.

'He's now saying that conversion is more expensive than levelling it and starting again so he won't be providing any affordable housing or paying any 106 money. It has compromised the affordability matrix.'

Ellie looked down again at the plans. There was a concierge with a fish tank.

'Did I hear you right? The basis of *his* listing application.'

Pankaj exhaled sympathetically.

'There are a lot more where these came from. It hasn't been cobbled together since last Wednesday. He's been planning it for some time.'

Ellie shut her eyes.

'Zone Eight?'

'The assumption is that the Chapel will be the site of the new station, only forty minutes into London. So, Zone Eight. Welcome to the commuter belt.'

'But why eight?' she said, aware that in the grand scheme of things it really didn't matter but unable, for some reason, to let it go. 'There are six zones in London, right?'

'Eight's a lucky number in the far east. It seems he's hoping for off-plan sales.'

'Wait a sec, this was the basis of *his* listing application.'

'Yes.'

'He wanted to get it listed.'

'He did.'

'So it was nothing to do with us?'

'The building is saved, Ellie. Forever. And you did that.'

'No,' she said, and she found that was all she could manage.

Tuesday, May 20th

'I got doughnuts.'

Kerry opened the top of the bag so that Colin could peer in. The doughnuts were the English sort: engorged, sugar-coated, oozing with jam.

'We're on stakeout,' she said. 'You've got to have doughnuts if you're on stakeout.'

They were in the Astra, parked over the road from the Land Dominion offices with an uninterrupted view of the front door. The evening before, Ellie had emailed him with big news: her contact at the council had confirmed that the document being illegally signed off was a forged environmental impact form.

His eyes darted to the dashboard. Sitting on it was a picture of the Brunel University Department of Life Sciences circa 2009. On his personal website Douglas Dublin had just announced that he had secured funding for a newt reservation in Shropshire. The plan was to snare him on his lunch break.

'So who's Riggs and who's Murtaugh?' he said, picking out a doughnut.

Kerry looked at him, her nose wrinkled.

'You know, in *Lethal Weapon*. Which one of us is the by-the-book one and which one of us is the loose cannon?'

Kerry was eating her doughnut with her teeth bared to keep the sugar off her immaculately made-up lips. She took a bite, mulled it over for a bit.

'Don't they kind of hate each other?'

'Yeah. I mean they do, at least at the start anyway, but cops always start off hating their partner in films. It's the first law of Hollywood.'

'Turner didn't hate Hooch,' she said.

'Didn't he at the start, a little bit? Or actually quite a lot.'

'I don't think so.'

'God, are you about to tell me I'm Hooch?' said Colin. 'I thought I was going to be Riggs.'

'I just think we like each other too much for *Lethal Weapon*,' said Kerry.

Colin looked at her, doing his best not to blush. There was a single white crystal of sugar at the corner of her mouth. Sometimes, it was just all too much.

'Cagney and Lacey didn't hate each other,' she said.

'When have you ever watched *Cagney and Lacey*?'

'It's always being repeated during the day. My mum loves it.'

'Right,' said Colin dryly. 'Let me guess, which one of us is the ridiculously glamorous career woman and which one is the frumpy one raising the kids?'

Now it was Kerry's turn to blush. She looked away, changed the subject.

'Have you seen Kirk's latest thing?' she said. 'Zone Eight?'

'No. What's that?'

'He's launching it this morning. He's basically turning the Larkspur into a load of yuppie flats. Reckons people are going to commute into London. I suppose they could do. I mean, the train'll be quick enough.'

'He's not buying the Larkspur,' said Colin, licking the jam from his fingers. 'It got listed.'

'Damn right, it was him that got it listed.'

'*What?*'

'That's what everyone's saying. He went down there and convinced the minister himself.'

'*He* got it listed?'

'I know. Weird, eh? I thought he'd be buying it to pull it down. But it looks like he's converting it. God knows how much that'll cost.'

Colin processed the implications of what he had just heard.

'Am I getting this right?' he said. 'Kirk just bought a

523

four-hundred-flat council estate and then got it listed just to get it off the shortlist. Are you telling me that's what we're up against?'

'Yeah, something like that.'

'Fuck.'

Kerry grabbed the print from the dashboard and held it up in front of them.

'That's him,' she said, pointing out the window. 'There, in the grey jacket. The newt man. He's heading for Greggs. Go on. Collar him.'

Colin scrambled open the door and made his way between the cars in a sort of running half-squat of the kind he felt was employed in such situations by members of SWAT teams. Using a passing bus as cover, he ran across the road to the opposite pavement where he continued his pursuit, flush to a wall, his eyes on his target, his heart thumping at the thrill of the chase.

By the time he reached Greggs, Douglas Dublin was already inside, standing at the open-fronted sandwich fridge. It was 11.55 a.m., well before the lunch rush, and they had the shop to themselves apart from a lone woman behind the counter. Colin stayed by the crisp rack, ostentatiously deliberating between a packet of Frazzles and some salt and vinegar Hula Hoops. He watched Douglas Dublin choose a tuna crunch baguette, finding it hard to shake the sense that this had to be in some way significant.

After he had picked up a carton of Ribena and then decided against it, Douglas Dublin walked over to the main counter where he stood perusing its trays of bakes, cheesy bacon croissants and sausage rolls in three sizes. Colin took his place behind him in the queue and waited.

Eventually, Dublin asked about the availability of a Nacho Chilli Cheese Bake.

'I can do you one,' said the woman behind the counter with a sigh, 'but it'll be a couple of minutes.'

Dublin nodded his assent and the woman retreated into the kitchen. Colin took this as his moment. He leaned forward.

'I know about the newts,' he hissed.

Dublin turned around. He was bespectacled, with a kind,

teacherly face. His hair was starting to grey at the temples. For a second or two, he appeared to be a little put out at the blatant invasion of his personal space, but this quickly dissipated and, even though Colin was standing ridiculously close to him, he broke out a broad smile.

'Do we know each other?' he said disarmingly. 'From a conference or something? I'm sorry I didn't recognise you. I thought I knew most people in the newt world.'

He followed this with a self-deprecating laugh.

Colin was flustered. Douglas Dublin seemed nice, which confused things.

'I know about the newts at Grangeham forge,' he said. 'And the forged document. And that you've been bought off.'

At this, Dublin paled. For a second he looked like he might be sick. And then he bolted.

* * *

Forty minutes later, Colin and Kerry were at Grangeham. Colin parked the Astra on an access road and after they had retrieved what they needed from the boot, the two of them walked through the buddleia bushes and on to the site of the old forge. Grey clouds were massing low in the sky and the air felt heavy with the prospect of a storm.

'I would have had him if it wasn't for the bus,' said Colin for the fourth or fifth time. 'Honestly, I ...'

'Stop beating yourself up about it. It doesn't matter. His reaction's told us all we need to know.'

'I just don't want you to think I was outrun by some dweeb who likes newts,' said Colin. 'He just got the right side of that bus and by the time I was round it I couldn't tell which way he'd gone.'

Above them, wires sagged from long-dormant pylons. Behind them stood a building with empty spaces where its windows and door had once been, a tree growing through the roof. They walked across a large foundation slab, the concrete rippled and water-stained.

'Whatever happens, he's in trouble. He did a runner with that tuna crunch baguette,' said Colin as he walked round a pile of discarded plastic piping, enmeshed in the weeds. 'At the very least he can expect a lifetime ban from Greggs.'

Kerry laughed.

'What kind of prick has the tuna crunch?' she said.

'I just don't understand how anyone can go to Greggs without ordering a steak bake.'

'It should be illegal to do anything else.'

'All right,' said Colin as he sat on an old concrete pillar and started to pull on Rodbortzoon's waders. 'Ideal Greggs lunch?'

'Easy,' said Kerry, counting out the items on her fingers. 'Ham and cheese toastie, steak bake, Frazzles, chocolate éclair. I mean, I don't have it much because I'd be a whale if I did, but my thinking is: when you do Greggs, do *Greggs*, right?'

Colin looked at her, open-mouthed. He felt a rush of blood and lust and wholly illogical certainty.

'Eight pounds forty-six,' he said.

Kerry gasped.

'Oh my god, how did you know that? What are you, Rain Man?'

'No,' said Colin. 'I know it's eight forty-six because that's literally my order. Every time. Sometimes I add a tea for a quid if I'm in the mood, but ham and cheese toastie, steak bake, Frazzles, chocolate éclair, that's my order.'

Kerry clapped with delight.

'I can't believe it.'

'I sometimes open up the toastie and chuck in a few Frazzles,' said Colin.

'For extra crunch.'

'*Exactly!*'

'Oh my god, you're like my Greggs soul mate.'

Here, for a second or two, their eyes met, but for once it wasn't Colin who looked away in embarrassment. An opportunity had been presented to him when he was in the bush with Ellie and he hadn't taken it. He wasn't going to make that mistake again.

He jumped over a two-foot-wide brook that ran between two

larger bodies of water, turned round and offered his hand to Kerry to help her across. She screwed up her face cutely.

'Do you really want to be Riggs?'

'More than I do Hooch.'

Kerry shifted her shoulder, a sort of half-shrug.

'I've been out with a couple of Riggses in my time. Reckless bastards. You're not a Riggs, Colin.'

Colin looked down at the waders, which flapped around him, two sizes too big. It was difficult, he conceded, to imagine how a man who was defeated by oversized wellington boots might be able to overpower his kidnappers or survive a drive-by shooting.

'Yeah well, I guess that's probably true,' he said.

'I meant that in a good way,' said Kerry softly.

Colin turned to look at her but she was already down at the water's edge poking at the long grass with a stick. She had her designer trousers tucked into a pair of Ellie's old wellies and was wearing his too-big fleece. Her hair was up in a headband and she had on washing-up gloves, but still all he had to do was look at her and every atom in his body seemed to pivot.

Colin clipped the last of the waders' buckles into place and picked up his net. Keen to prove something or another, he walked to the side of the canal. The gun-metal water was forbidding, unyielding. You couldn't know what lay beneath its surface but you could speculate: splintered poles, disguised shafts, broken bottles. Colin wavered but then he picked up the end of an old chain-link fence and, using it as ballast, lowered himself into the water, his net between his teeth.

Even at its deepest, the water was only waist-high, but still each step felt like a small act of courage. He took a breath and walked on, his lip trembling at his own nobility. He had never been the kind of man who took on the major challenges: the fire-building, the wheel-changing, the leap from the high rock. He had always been the guy standing at the side, holding the matches, the tyre iron, the towel.

But every now and again you were called upon to stand up. And if it meant doing something that lost you your job, then that was what you did. And if it meant sleeping in a tent, then that's what you did.

And if it meant wading into treacherous waters in search of a four-inch amphibian then you did that, too. And you just got on with it without making a fuss.

For ten minutes they searched in companionable silence, Kerry in the reeds, Colin in the water, the straps of his waders crisscrossed over his shoulders, the cuffs of his sweatshirt soaked through.

'Right,' said Kerry, once she had exhausted the bank, 'where haven't we done?'

The tops of the trees were bending in the wind. Seagulls flew overhead. Colin scanned the forge.

'Rodbortzoon had a pretty good look over there,' he said pointing, 'and Daisy and I did a decent hunt of that bit by those trees. So we could try over there.'

Side by side – Colin in his waders, Kerry in her wellies – they walked back across the concrete plateau, leaving a trail of footprints as they went.

'It's a big old site and a newt's a slip of a thing.'

'I know,' said Colin. 'I looked into buying one. From America, to, you know, plant here.'

'Why *don't* we just buy one?'

'It's illegal in Europe.'

'All right then, why don't we borrow one? We could just go and get one from, I don't know, Scotland or wherever.'

'We don't have time to be scouring every pond in Britain for a newt.'

'No, but we could easily narrow it down. I'm googling it.'

Kerry sat down on an old wall with her phone, and while she researched the national distribution of great crested newts, Colin continued his search, sticking to the shallows, trying to move as little as possible so as not to disturb any animals that might be there. He pulled back leaves and pushed apart the long grass. He turned over rocks and peered into crevices. After about half an hour of this, he sat on a rock and for the first time it occurred to him that he might not find one. That there might not even be one to find.

He lay down, felt the warmth of the stone on his back. When you were a football fan you were the twelfth man, roaring the team on from the sidelines, geeing them up, giving them hope. The degree to which you wanted something *did* impact on the result. Or at least it was easy to convince yourself it did. But life wasn't like that. You could want and want and want but all the ardour in the world wasn't going to magic you a result. The reality was that somebody always had to lose. Somebody always had to fail. He shut his eyes and thought about all that he had lost. Ellie. And also, in a different way, Daisy. And his job. And his house. And what had he got for it? Nothing. Not even a newt.

In the far distance he could hear the rumble of lorries. Resigned, he sat up and opened his eyes. And it was then that he saw her, across the water, the one person he hadn't lost, sitting on the wall, wearing wellies and a shapeless fleece, and yet still in possession of a silhouette to fell a man.

* * *

The year sixes were doing their annual play. Their teacher, Miss Dunn, was, as she had it herself, a dramaturge manqué. She wore colourful scarves and blue eye shadow and was always in a state of low-level fluster. It had been her choice to do *Mother Courage and Her Children*, which she was restaging as a musical with gender-blind casting. Daisy was Swiss Cheese. And Ellie was late. The lights were already down when she arrived but through the gloom she could see Colin in the middle near the back, waving to her.

'You saved me a seat,' she whispered, once she had bashed her way past seven sets of knees, apologising all the way.

'Of course I did.'

'That was nice of you.'

'I figured you could do with someone looking out for you,' he said. 'I saw the thing, Zone Eight.'

To this Ellie could muster nothing more than a weak smile. The argument with Pankaj had started at the venue and continued in the taxi and had kept going until they had both fallen sullenly and drunkenly asleep. They had then picked it up again – with greater clarity but no less ferocity – when they had woken up that morning.

For the first half hour of the play she sat in her seat rehashing their positions. 'You're talking as if the choice is between this and them being brilliantly maintained social housing stock,' he had said. 'That isn't the choice. It's between this and them being knocked down.' Which she had tried to explain over and over again hadn't been the case as recently as a week ago, and anyway he was unthinkingly buying into the kind of false binary that the 'modernisers' employed all the time.

On stage, principal characters seemed to be being dispatched with astonishing rapidity, but Ellie had given up trying to follow the plot. At 9 a.m., after half an hour of increasingly tetchy back and forth, she had made the impulsive decision to tell him about the job offer simply so she could then pointedly declare that she wasn't going to take it, in what had felt hazily like an unarticulated stand against the state of contemporary architecture, the current government, and philistinism in general. Of course, this had spectacularly backfired – from that point on, it was all Pankaj could think or talk about. Eventually, she had snapped, said something stupid, something mean. And that's when he had said it, the kicker: 'It was you that convinced him of its worth. You made it aspirational. All those pictures on Instagram.'

It was this that had silenced her. Kirk's marketing materials were basically her presentation to the DCMS. He was keeping her café.

She had wanted to reply but couldn't. All she could hear was her mother.

Things happen all the time. And that's really the long and the short of it.

Just when she thought she had been on the cusp of definitively banishing it, when she had seemed to be on the verge of taking genuine ownership of her life, when all the pieces felt like they were coming brilliantly together, the through-line had snapped and everything had started to unravel.

Ellie felt the rage in every vein in her body.

The one thing that she had wanted least in the all the world had come to pass. Her mother had been proved right.

The chorus assembled at the front of the stage and broke into hesitant song. Daisy was at the back, obviously mouthing the words but not actually singing. Colin smiled. He had long understood that at some essential level he had become middle class. But he understood too that on a similarly essential level he hadn't. Nothing reminded him of this more than trips to the theatre. He had been forced to sit through Brecht once before, an experience that had all but made him start voting for UKIP. This time, though, he was quite enjoying it.

'Our girl,' he said under the cover of the chorus. 'I'm so proud of her.'

'I know, she's amazing, isn't she?'

Colin glanced at her and she glanced back at him.

'I saw the drawings.'

Ellie grimaced.

On stage the singing stopped, a small child started in on a halting monologue.

Colin dropped his shoulder and leaned towards his ex.

'I'm guessing you're not that into the candy-coloured Fresno brutalism?'

Ellie snorted.

'If that's what they want to do,' he continued in a contained whisper that was intended only for her, 'they might as well knock the damn thing down.'

'*Thank you*,' said Ellie with the involuntary emphasis of someone celebrating clarity after hours of obfuscation.

'Shh,' said someone from behind them.

'At least if she'd done it, it would have the courage of its convictions,' continued Colin, nodding at the stage. 'If you're going to infantilise a building then do it bloody properly. Daisy would've decked it out with lipstick kisses.'

'Shh,' said someone else.

'And she would have made sure there was a nail bar.'

Ellie laughed.

'And where are the unicorn stables?'

Ellie laughed harder.

A woman in front of them turned around and fixed them with a death stare. Colin held up his hand. Ellie smiled an apology.

'I'm pretty sure Daisy's bit is over,' whispered Ellie. 'I mean, she is dead, isn't she?'

'I kind of lost track because they kept changing costumes, but I'm pretty sure she is.'

'Shall we?'

'Yes, let's.'

They bashed their way along the line, doing their damnedest not to look at anyone, but aware all the same of the murderous glares coming at them from all sides. Near the end of the row, Colin tripped on someone's bag and had to steady himself with a hand on the deputy head's knee.

'I know I famously don't have an intuitive sense for these things,' he said, once they were out in the corridor, 'but I'm pretty sure that leaving the school play halfway through isn't the done thing.'

'Everybody here hates me anyway,' said Ellie with a wave of the hand. 'Sorry if I've finally dragged you down with me.'

Now it was Colin's turn to snort.

'What?'

'The idea that *you* have ever dragged *me* down.'

The corridor was echoey, the floor polished. Along one wall were drawings on a nautical theme. Ellie ran her finger along a papier mâché sculpture of an octopus and found herself reappraising the weight of their years together. It was possible, she realised, that when something anchored you somewhere it didn't only have the effect of stopping you sailing, it also might save you in a storm.

'Did you mean it? What you said in there?'

'*Modernism is an ethic rather than an aesthetic*,' said Colin, with a self-deprecating shrug. 'I *was* listening, you know. I might have been watching television at the same time, but I was always listening.'

Ellie was overcome by the sense that she had no idea which way her life was going. Why anything was happening. What was what.

'Although I'm not sure if I really understand what all this is about,' continued Colin. 'I thought if it was listed you had to leave it as it was.'

'You can't knock it down but you can modernise and update it. All you need is permission. He made it clear to the minister what he was planning to do. The plans will be waved through.'

'Is there nothing you can do?'

'I've been in touch with campaign groups. People that have fought planning decisions. A couple of journalists in London, people that specialise in this sort of thing. But I don't know ... It's not like getting it listed. That, you just need to do once. This would mean fighting and fighting. Constant appeals.'

'I can imagine.'

'I don't know if I've got it in me. It's just so disappointing.'

'I know it is.'

Colin looked at his watch.

'There's at least another half an hour until she's out,' he said. 'Let's walk the halls.'

The school was a single-storey building designed in a square around a central courtyard. Through the window, they could see sandpits, water features and planting beds, neat rows of tomato plants poking up through the soil. It was early evening and the cutouts of animals stuck to the windows cast hazy silhouettes on the floor.

'This place is just so much *nicer* than it was when I was here,' said Colin, as he jumped from the shadow of a lion to the shadow of a hippo. 'There was never anything on the walls back then, and everything was beige, brown or orange: carpets, curtains, furniture. It was like an old people's home.'

They rounded the corner and peered into an empty classroom, a vast watery science experiment spread across five jammed-together tables.

'This was my room for year six. So I suppose I was ten. Ryan Watkins and I used to sit at the back madly rubbing at our heads until we'd covered the whole of his red ringbinder in dandruff. We'd then write in it with our fingers. We called it druffiti.'

Ellie laughed.

'If I rubbed my head like that now I'd lose half my hair.'

She laughed again.

That was the thing about Colin Ryder. He wasn't conventionally attractive. In fact, if anything, he was fairly conventionally unattractive. He wore crap clothes and he ate crap food. He was socially awkward and pathologically unambitious and not exactly brilliant in bed.

533

And yet.

Ellie leaned into the wall. She felt like a snow globe violently shaken, her emotional glitter swirling here and there and everywhere.

'I've been offered a job,' she said, because he deserved to know.

'Oh, right.'

'Do you remember Benjamin Willis from university?'

'Yeah, I think so. He was on your course. Blond hair. Bit of a wanker.'

Ellie laughed.

'Yeah, that's him. Well, he's set up his own firm and it's taking off and he wants me to go down and join the team.'

'To London?'

'Yeah, to London. I spoke to him again this afternoon. I'd be working on a football stadium of all things.'

Colin looked at her sideways.

'Not *your* one. All I know is it's in Asia somewhere. It's all happened at the last minute and I need to tell them by Thursday.'

'So are you going to take it?'

'I don't know. There's a lot to think about. Daisy, obviously.'

'She'd be fine,' said Colin. Despite all that had happened he still found that his first instinct with her was to be helpful.

'Would she though? She's used to tiny little Peterdown. London would be such a shift.'

Colin looked at her, the shape of her fingers, the way she tucked her hair behind her ear. Pankaj could be all the things that he was, but no one – *no one* – could match Colin Ryder when it came to munificence. He was simply the crown prince of self-sacrificing generosity of spirit.

'She's tough,' he said softly. 'And smart. She'd be fine.'

'Do you really think so?'

'I think it could be the making of her.'

Colin folded his arms across his chest, looked at the floor. The thing about Ellie and Daisy going to London was that it meant he would have to go, too. Which was a terrifying prospect of course. Ruinously expensive. A cold and hard place. But also a place where a life might be turned around. And if he went, it would be all on her, without him having to take any responsibility for the move. Which was pretty much the dream combination. Particularly if he could take Kerry with him.

'That's really nice of you to say, Colin. You're so lovely. Thank you.'

'That's OK,' he said, smiling humbly.

Half an hour later, they were outside with Daisy, taking shelter from the spitting rain under a large tree.

'I'll give you a lift,' said Colin.

'It's OK.'

'Don't be silly,' he said. 'You'll get soaked.'

'No, I mean ...'

'Oh,' said Colin.

'He's already on his way.'

'OK.'

'Colin ...'

'It's all right,' he said. 'I understand.'

He kissed Daisy and congratulated her again, before departing with a shy little smile for Ellie that had just the right level of meekness, he thought, a feeling which was confirmed as he registered the look on her face.

On the way home in the Astra, Colin found himself occupying what was, for him, an unusual position: the moral high ground. Or at least some version of it. It was harder than it sounded. It took grace, humility and a kind of nobility, if you were to do it right. And he was owning it; front and back and side to side. He smiled as he turned off the Ottercliffe Road. He hadn't found any newts but whichever way you looked at it, the day could not be described wholly as a failure.

The rain had stopped and the air had a springy freshness to it. Colin had the window rolled down and as he drew near to the house, he saw there was a car parked outside it. And in it he saw two men, both in matching black bomber jackets. With his breath held and his eyes fixed on the road ahead, he carried on driving. Because it was obvious as you like that the two of them were waiting for him.

Wednesday, May 21st

Colin opened one eye and then the other. Every morning, from the moment the dawn broke, the inside of the tent glowed pink with a light that was enveloping and womb-like. Just for a second, he felt a kind of sunk-in stillness, like he was five minutes into a hot bath. And then he remembered why he was there, back in the tent, next to the snoring Rodbortzoon, and not in his actual real-life bed. He felt a spreading panic as he recalled the paucity of his defences: the lightweight canvas covering, the unlocked zip, the exposed concourse.

Still in his sleeping bag, he wriggled caterpillar-like to the entrance of the tent.

Since the start of the week, the police presence had been scaled down to a single cop during the day and no one at night. And the prospect of protection from his fellow protesters was similarly slim. The camp was down to three tents: theirs, the mess, and a final one, occupied by Eddie and Ron, two middle-aged veterans of the Peterdown left who Colin suspected were possibly the only two people ever to have attended a football match who would be less use in a fight than he was.

He unzipped the door and peered out. Around him, the concourse was empty, which was an immediate relief but did little to calm his anxious mind. He slipped out of his sleeping bag and dressed hurriedly, in urgent need of food and water and the sanctuary of people.

On the other side of the concourse, Gordon's Café was already half-full of labourers in hard hats, eating breakfast and reading the paper. Comforted by their muscular presence, Colin took a corner booth and ordered a plate of eggs on toast.

Getting to sleep the night before had required most of a half-bottle of rum lifted from the sleeping Rodbortzoon's bag, and he urgently gulped his tea as he surmised the chain of events. What had happened was surely obvious: Douglas Dublin had reported back to Kirk and moves were being made to silence him. The question was, how to react? He considered writing up what he had, but beyond the echoing ravine of social media, he had no outlet to publish what was at best a sketch of an outline of a theory.

His food arrived and he ate it quickly and without pleasure, flicking from app to app on his phone. He was scrolling aimlessly through Twitter when he saw something that stilled his blood: Truther_78 had mentioned him.

> @colinryderwrites doesn't know what he's up against.
> Poor kid. He's going to do himself a mischief. Cut
> himself off at the knees. And he can't even see it.
> #steamersareidiots

Colin felt his insides contract. It was 7.30 a.m. If this was one of Truther's drunken truths, he knew what would happen next. For ten minutes, Colin sat where he was, his eggs cooling in front of him, repeatedly refreshing his feed until, in confirmation of everything he had feared, the tweet disappeared.

Around him, the café continued its morning routine. Orders were shouted. The tea urn hissed. Colin felt beads of sweat pricking on his brow. He was facing premeditated violence, or at least the threat of it, and the expectation was that he would buckle. Indeed, his overwhelming instinct was to do just that: to walk away and accept the inevitable triumph of the strong over the weak.

Colin felt his nostrils flare involuntarily. Everything about him – who he was and how he had lived – suggested that this was what would happen. But that didn't account for his capacity to imagine an alternative version. And if you had the power to *imagine* yourself differently, then you had the power to *be* different. All you had to do was act.

First, he needed internet know-how and so he emailed Patrick with a request: who is this guy and how can I find him? Then he looked at his list of recent calls. Two names stood out: Ellie and Kerry. But who to call, in this, his hour of need? To go to Ellie now would be evidence of his vulnerability, which was catnip to her, and it would remind her of their shared history. Tactically, it made sense, but instinctually it felt wrong. He shut his eyes, a line rattling inescapably round his head: *you're not like anyone else I've ever met.*

'Col?' said Kerry, answering on the third ring.

'I got home last night to find two of Kirk's goons outside my house. They're trying to frighten me,' he said. 'But I'm not going to let them.'

'I'm coming,' she said. 'Where are you?'

Twenty minutes later, she was sitting opposite him, her fingers wrapped round a cup of tea. She had stopped dyeing her hair and its true colour was showing at the roots; an unremarkable light brown, much like his. And her earrings weren't in, their absence revealing a tiny red dash on either lobe.

'Word is that Douglas Dublin's not turned up to work today. And the webpage for his newts thing has been taken down.'

She cocked her head to the side for emphasis.

'They know we're on to them. We've got to go back out to Grangeham,' he said. 'The announcement is being made on Monday. We need something now.'

'Is it safe, though? If they're looking for you?'

Colin thought about the prospect of being out at the forge, totally isolated, with the two goons haring after him.

'I don't want to let them intimidate me.'

'Have you told the police?'

'What could I tell them? The guys outside my house didn't do anything. And I forgot to take a screen shot of the tweet before he deleted it. I've got nothing.'

'You could still tell them.'

'What are they going to do, take me into protective custody?'

'Yeah, OK. Probably not.'

Colin sat in his seat, various scenarios playing out in his head. They could get him on the ground and give him a shoeing. Or they could come at him with a blackjack. Or a snooker ball in a sock.

He stopped and looked up. Kerry was finishing off his uneaten toast. He didn't feel particularly brave. But no one had to know that as long as he pretended otherwise.

'Right,' he said, draining his tea. 'I hope you've got your boots.'

Kerry brushed a crumb from her lip and smiled.

'Come on then,' she said.

They were just about to get up when, from behind the counter, there was a voice:

'Oi, Col, have you heard this?'

It was Gordon, his tea towel tucked into the fold of his apron.

'What's her face from the council's on the radio.'

Gordon reached over to his old-school transistor and turned up the volume. Yvonne was mid-sentence.

'... incredible work of my colleagues and the brilliant management team at the Generator. The deal is a five-year full package sponsorship deal worth ten million pounds in the first year alone. It involves naming rights so we'll be calling it the Selamat Generator from now on. Which I think has a great ring. Of course we'll have people yagging and moaning about it but it was always the plan to have a corporate partner. That's just the way of the world these days.'

'Oh my god,' said Colin, 'tell me I am not hearing this.'

'Obviously a lot of people won't have heard of Selamat,' continued Yvonne, 'but it's huge in the Far East and apparently it's already a thing in London. There's talk that it's going to be the next bubble tea.'

'Right,' said the host.

'You know the bubble tea.'

'With the balls in it.'

'Exactly.'

'This isn't that, though.'

'No, Selamat make a range of carbonated soya milk smoothies.'

'Jesus wept,' said Colin.

'It comes in five flavours,' continued Yvonne.

'One for each year of the deal,' said the host dryly.

'That's right,' said Yvonne pointedly. 'Five years. Financial security for five years. Which should see off any daft chat about pulling it down.'

Colin slumped forward, head in his hands.

'And it's because I know that the Generator is safe,' continued Yvonne, 'that I am able to make a second announcement. The signing of this deal will be my last act as leader of the council.'

'Whoa,' said the host. 'You're leaving?'

'After thirteen happy years of public service, I'm ready for a new challenge. Knowing that the financial security of our world-class arts centre is guaranteed, I feel ready in my heart to move on.'

'What are you going to do?'

'From next week I will be taking up my new role of director of business development at Land Dominion, where I hope to make the city's most dynamic business even more competitive than it already is . . .'

'Cover-up,' shouted Colin. 'Cover-up! They're going to bury it. Fuck. Fuck. Fuck. This is all about burying the report.'

The elderly woman in the booth by the door looked up in alarm.

Colin was on his feet.

'They're covering their tracks. She's got too much on the other councillors and too much on Kirk and they're all going to wrap it up neatly without any of it getting out. We can't just let this happen.'

He banged the table with his fist.

'We need to get that report from the council offices. We have to get in somehow.'

'Into Fanon House? You've got to be kidding. Security's way too tight.'

Kerry paused, ran her tongue over the tips of her teeth.

'We *could* get into Land Dominion, though, or at least try,' she said. 'The alarm code showed up on an internal memo. All we'd have to do is jam the lock.'

Colin slid back into the booth.

'I think I know someone who could help us with that,' he whispered.

Kerry shrugged.

'We've either got to find a newt or we've got to find that report,' she said. 'And I can't face another afternoon at that bloody forge.'

Colin sat up straight. Objectively you were powerless in the face of history. A dust mote in its grand sweep. But it couldn't have felt like that for Napoleon, could it, or Nasser, when they were bending events to their will. He felt his chest expand. They hadn't simply been born like that. At some point, they must have had to take a leap at destiny. Colin stood up. They had probably felt like frauds then, too, before they crossed the Alps or whatever. He gripped the edges of the table. If history taught you anything, it was that all you had to do was fake it 'til you make it.

'OK then,' he said in a powerful whisper. 'Let's do it. Tonight. It's now or never.'

* * *

'And they had this black rice sushi cone thing that had like a whole monkfish tail in it. It was incredible. And it's right round the corner from my place. Honestly, you're going to love it.'

Pankaj was cooking with his back to her. He took a sip of his wine.

'I'll book it when we've got our dates finalised. We can celebrate there.'

This was the way things were now. Presented to her, fait accompli. It had been like this since she had gone to Yvonne behind his back. She had ceded something to him, handed him the running, and now she was supposed to tag along. All the way to London, it seemed. It was all he could think about.

Ellie was laying the table, putting out the cutlery, filling the water jug.

'I'm staying,' she said impulsively. 'To fight it. I'm going to turn down the job.'

She placed the knife she was carrying down with a thud to emphasise the point. Pankaj sighed.

'I'm serious. I'm staying. I'm not taking the job.'

She had spent the afternoon at a three-hour emergency residents' meeting; a hundred desperate people in a room. Pam was being offered a flat on the Ridgewater estate, which was halfway to Broadcastle and grim beyond words, but at least it was local. Ralph and Barry were both considered low priority, which meant they were being offered housing as far away as Rotherham and Hull.

Ellie straightened the knife, felt a rush of emotion. Half of them had been in tears. All of them had looked at her like it was her fault – the queen irony of the whole thing, when it wasn't her doing in the end. She had simply been a patsy, a useful idiot.

'I'm going to fight it.'

'No, you're not.'

'Oh, I'm not, am I?'

'No, because you're not insane. That ship has sailed. The estate has been sold. Even if they did still own it, the council can't afford to maintain it, not with their current funding. It was an unintended consequence of the listing but it's the unavoidable reality and it's not going to change.'

'I can't believe you're being so defeatist. There's loads that can be done.'

'Like what?'

'We can demand a judicial review.'

Pankaj turned around with a sceptical look on his face.

'Into what?' he said.

'The way they sold the estate,' said Ellie sarcastically, because she did, actually, as of that morning, know what a judicial review was for and so he could piss off.

'It got full cabinet backing. There was nothing wrong with the process,' said Pankaj, turning round again. He picked up his tongs and started to flip the frying slices of courgette. 'Most people would jump at a chance like this. It's a great job with a dynamic firm.'

Ellie rolled her eyes at his back. In the story of her life that she had always told herself, she had never really paid much attention to how her fantastical structures might be actually commissioned, let alone created. But the reality was that you couldn't just go off and be an architect in splendid uncorrupted isolation. She needed a job. To pay the bills obviously, but also to get better at it, learn all the necessary stuff before she could start to do things that might be useful. Slowly, she was starting to appreciate that all this was something that had to be reckoned with, but disentangling it from Pankaj's careerism was a complicated business and the two had become poisonously intertwined in her head.

'I don't understand why you're not outraged about what's happening to the people on that estate,' she said impulsively, changing the subject.

'I am outraged, and I will be making every effort to make sure all of them are housed as near to Peterdown as possible. That's what our efforts need to be focused on, not buying back the estate. It's Kirk's now. Accept it.'

For a second or two this hung in the air while Ellie seethed.

'No,' she said. 'I won't.'

The thing that was stuck in her head, and wouldn't go away, was the café. Which Kirk, or at least his people, wanted to keep. As it was. Because it fitted right in with their vision for Zone Eight.

It was a stupid thing to be fixated on in the context, nothing compared to what the residents were going through. But her whole life she had understood that your taste was who you were and that good taste was more than simply a set of preferences; that it was somehow moral, a form of virtue. And for all that this was looking pretty thin now, as a way of putting yourself together in the world, it was still there burning away in her and she couldn't just let it go.

'I don't know why we're even bothering to have this conversation,' said Pankaj as he ground some salt into the pan. 'We both know whose benefit it's for.'

'Oh, we do, do we?'

'You need to feel you've at least considered doing the thing you feel you *should* do before you can do what we both know you're going to do, which is to take the job.'

Ellie felt a flash of cold rage. She kept her eyes fixed steadily on the door, refusing to look at him. It wasn't so much the content of what he said, which had, she grudgingly conceded, a maddening kernel of truth to it. It was the tone. And the presumption that what she needed was for someone to come and explain her to herself.

She picked up her glass of wine and took a large gulp. Nothing about her life was working out the way she had planned it. Things were moving in the wrong direction, with a momentum all of their own. Out of nowhere, it was obvious to her that they needed to be torpedoed.

'I can't take the job because it's Colin's bloody stadium.'

'What?'

She had heard from Benjamin that morning with a clarification: it was *for* an Asian client, but not *in* Asia. A massive Malay conglomerate. The Mun Sen Corporation. A quick online search told her that they owned dozens of companies including Global Build, the construction firm that was partnering Kirk on the conversion of the Larkspur. They also owned a certain brand of carbonated soymilk smoothies.

'The people building the stadium work with Kirk. They own Selamat,' she said. 'They sponsored the bloody Generator so it's financially viable and the Chapel will be chosen as the station. The Moolah stadium drawings you've seen are just sketches. I'd be helping to draw up the actual plans.'

'Are you sure?'

'It's a football stadium in England being built by a company that has just spent millions sponsoring the Generator!'

Pankaj pursed his lips. He started to take the slices of courgette out of the pan and pile them on to the plate with the quinoa.

'How can I know this and still take the job?'

'Just pretend you don't know.'

'I do know, though.'

'Yeah, but only I know you know, so pretend you don't and that'll be that.'

'I need to tell Colin.'

'What difference will it make at this point?'

'Of course I fucking need to tell Colin.'

'Do you though? He leaked that master planner's report.'

'Only because we didn't tell him about the 106 money.'

'Don't tell him.'

Ellie felt a smile spread across her lips.

'I'm telling him.'

* * *

'What's that buzzing?'

Colin felt the vibration in the pocket of his jeans. They were at the back door of the building that housed the Land Dominion offices, crouching behind a large refuse trolley.

'For fuck's sake, I said phones *off*.'

Colin looked at the screen. It was Ellie. For a second, he found himself thinking how brilliant it would be if he could stop time and answer the call so he could tell her that he had enlisted the help of a man called Trench, who had part of his ear missing and who lived on a barge and was to all intents and purposes an *actual pirate*, and how they were currently breaking and entering into the Land Dominion offices using what looked like an ice pick, and how everything she had ever thought about him, Colin, was just so obviously wrong.

But, of course, he couldn't.

'Sorry,' he said. 'It's off now. Like off, off.'

Trench had the pick-like object in one hand and what looked like an unfolded hair grip in the other and he was using both to probe the keyhole. Colin was next to him. And next to Colin was Kerry, who was leaning into him for ballast.

Colin listened to the clicks and scratches as Trench worked. He could hear the call of a pigeon nearby, the holler of the high street and its pubs in the distance. He was experiencing a kind of alertness he had never imagined possible. Even in the low yellow light from the one distant street lamp, everything around him – the industrial bins, the parked van, the grilled windows, the ventilation shafts – pressed upon him in perfect definition. He would be able to recall it all, he felt, in exact detail for the rest of his life.

Trench had his eyes closed, feeling into the lock, tracing the contours of its interior like he was creating a mental map of its construction. There was something painterly about the way he manipulated the hair grip, gently but always precisely.

Then it clicked. And the handle came down. And the door swung open. And Kerry was inside and at the key pad putting in a six-digit code. For a long second Colin watched the red light on the key pad and listened to its beeps, his heart stilled.

And then the light went out and it fell silent.

'Come on you Steam,' said Trench with a wink. And then he was gone, off into the night.

Colin looked at Kerry, and Kerry looked at Colin. If she hadn't been there, he would have turned and run and not stopped until he was home. He felt that the same was true for her, too. But they couldn't do that, not while the other one was there.

Looking at her, Colin felt that there passed between them a shared sense of the thing that they were about to do. Its inviolability. And how it would bond them together for ever.

'Let's do this,' he said.

Kerry led the way, up the stairs to the first floor, which was open plan and empty of people. The lights were off, just a few monitors blinking in the dark. There were fifteen, maybe twenty desks. Half a dozen filing cabinets.

'Where do we start?'

'That side,' said Kerry. 'And we'll work our way across.'

Colin went to the far desk, in the corner, Kerry to the one next to it. Before they could start, something behind them made a noise. The two of them stood completely still where they were, neither of them moving a muscle, as they listened intently.

Eventually, Kerry pointed to a spot between a desk and the wall. They tiptoed to it and sat down with their backs against a cold radiator.

After a while, they allowed themselves to breathe normally again and then when they hadn't heard anything for at least a minute, Colin leaned forward and whispered:

'It's like the bloody *Da Vinci Code*, this.'

'Colin, it's nothing like *The Da Vinci Code*.'

Colin could see something enflamed and alive in her eyes.

Kerry held a hand up while they listened, ears cocked like prairie dogs. 'All right, it was nothing.'

'Let's give it another two minutes,' he whispered.

Colin shifted his weight off his coccyx. Around him were Ethernet cables, power plugs, a pen that had fallen on the floor and not been picked up.

'*The Da Vinci Code*,' said Kerry dismissively.

'I mean, I haven't actually read it so I was just kind of ...'

'*You* haven't read it.'

'No. I mean, not in the way I haven't read *War and Peace*, but ...'

'Ha! A book I've read that Colin Ryder hasn't!'

She looked at him triumphantly and something passed between the two of them, he just knew it did.

'So what else do you read,' he whispered, 'apart from *The Da Vinci Code*?'

Kerry screwed up her nose.

'*Cosmopolitan*,' she said ruefully. '*Livingetc*, *Grazia*, now and again.'

'No books.'

'Not really.'

'I didn't for a while either but we didn't have a TV at the camp and I started again. And they were better than I'd remembered. I could do you a list.'

Kerry laughed through her nose.

'Colin Ryder,' she said, 'talking about books halfway through a break-in.'

'Sorry.'

'Don't be. It's sweet.'

Colin blushed and for a few seconds they sat, listening to the hum of an extractor fan.

'All right,' said Kerry. 'Let's do this.'

For twenty minutes, they searched methodically. They opened cabinets and riffled through papers. They leafed through document holders on the floor and scanned every page for a mention of newts.

'Where are the Grangeham files?' said Colin. 'I'm hardly finding a thing about it.'

'Me neither,' said Kerry. 'It's all Zone Eight.'

Colin pulled the drawers from a desk and emptied everything on to the floor. And then he went through it. The lot of it. Presentations and Post-it notes. Receipts, reports, email print-offs. He scanned every page.

Nothing.

And then something.

'I bloody knew it,' he said. 'They're financing the Generator Users Group and the RPUFG. They set the whole thing up. The websites and everything.'

'At least we've got something.'

'Yeah, but it's not newts, is it?'

Kerry looked despondently at the files scattered across the floor.

'Are you done?' she asked.

'Looking? Yeah, I'm done looking. There's nothing here. You?'

'I've got one drawer left.'

Colin pulled a tall aerosol from his backpack.

'What are you doing?'

'Throwing them off the scent.'

He shook the can and started writing on the wall, tentatively at first and then with greater confidence and flow. Once he was done he stood back to take stock of his work. The five letters were amateurishly rendered, fuzzy at the edges and uneven where the paint had dripped. Still, they didn't lack impact, being bright red and four feet high.

WROTH

'What do you think?' he said. But Kerry wasn't listening. She was holding a single piece of paper.

'Oh god, Colin. Look at this.'

It was a list of names. All of them journalists; some local, others on the nationals. One name was ringed in red.

And that name was his.

Thursday, May 22nd

The Signalman Inn was on the corner of Coopersale Road and Dilston Terrace. If you stood, as Colin did, on the Dilston Terrace side, you could peek your head round the corner for a good view of his house without anyone seeing you. Which was what he was about to do. When he plucked up the courage.

He had been awake all night, lying in his sleeping bag, listening. For footsteps or voices, the sound of a car slowing, the slam of a door. Anything that might suggest they were coming. Whoever *they* were. It had been exhausting and unimaginably stressful but ultimately uneventful: no hitmen had appeared.

He stood tight against the wall. His hours awake in the tent had given him ample time to process the voicemail that Ellie had left for him about Mun Sen and Benjamin Willis's commission for the stadium. He now saw how Kirk had engineered the whole thing. Listing the Larkspur, getting his cronies to balance the books at the Generator. But the real masterstroke had been to distract the fans. Make it all about events on the pitch. Kirk was setting it up for them to be beaten at Wembley so the whole thing could tumble neatly into place. Colin blinked back tears. The only thing Kirk hadn't been able to control, until now, was him. He was the bulwark. The defiant last man. And he still had forty-eight hours to do something remarkable.

Colin swallowed and inched his head round the corner. Immediately, he knew. The position of the car. The silhouettes in the window. He leaned into the wall, his breath reduced to near nothing, feeling faint at the drama of it. He wanted to be safe, of course he did. He wanted to sleep soundly in his bed. He wanted to know that he was secure in his own damn house. But really, more than any of that, he wanted to matter. And the pleasure at discovering that he was worthy of such attention writhed in him like an eel.

The walk back into town passed in a blur of fevered thoughts. The end game was coming and it was time to abandon any pretence of subtlety or sleight of hand. Now was the moment to throw on four strikers and just go for it. He stopped at a café on the Eastfinche Road and got to work. He put together everything he had and uploaded the lot on to Facebook: Yvonne's dodgy dossier; Kirk's funding of the Generator Users Group and the RPUFG, his ties to Selamat and the Mun Sen corporation; Douglas Dublin and his newts. He then linked it all into the Wroth Instagram and Twitter accounts and, because there would surely be safety in numbers, he finished with a call for every fan of Peterdown United to meet at the Grangeham forge armed with the nets and buckets that might just save football from itself.

He then walked back to the camp, buoyed at his bravado, only to discover, when he rounded the corner on to the concourse, that it was no longer there.

Over by Gordon's, he could see Rodbortzoon, sitting on the pavement with Eddie, the two of them surrounded with stuff: a couple of flattened tents splayed on the pavement like dead jellyfish, heaps of clothes, plastic bags with food spilling from them, books bent open backwards and a toothbrush which Colin recognised as his.

'What happened?'

'We have been evicted.'

'Yeah, I can see that. Was it the police? Did you put up a fight?'

Rodbortzoon shrugged phlegmatically.

'The timing was not so good,' he said. 'I was in the café, having a shit. Apparently, Eddie put up quite a struggle and Ron, it seems, has been arrested, accused of biting a policeman, but they were outnumbered ten to one.'

'So that's it?' said Colin.

'Yes, it would seem that it is.'

'There's no way we can stay here tonight.'

'They have issued the four of us with an exclusion order that says if any of us set foot on the concourse we will be arrested.'

'You realise this means I'm homeless,' said Colin.

Rodbortzoon shrugged again.

'The true radical is always homeless,' he said. 'And I mean that in a more profound sense than some literal description of his living arrangements. I mean that in terms of his . . .'

Colin wasn't listening. He was texting Kerry.

There are two thugs outside my house waiting for me and the camp has been cleared by the police. Any chance I could crash on your sofa tonight?

* * *

In the hard sun of the spring day, the windows of Europa House were brilliant squares of white light, giving it an impenetrable icy calm.

Ellie was sitting on a bench at the far end of the estate thinking about Marjorie and everything she owed her.

It had been that kind of day, loopy and introspective. Pankaj had left for London early in the morning and Daisy had got a lift to school with a neighbour, leaving her alone in the house, free to lie on the bed, spread out on top of the duvet, watch the dust motes and think about her life with a kind of teenage solemnity.

She kept coming back to the realisation that whatever future she tried to claim for herself would be fudged and ill thought-through, overwritten with addenda and caveats. By the time she got round to living it, it would be unrecognisable from what she'd planned, a whole life dictated by its imperatives and restraints. All these things that had just happened to her. Getting pregnant. Needing to keep the baby. Needing to come here. Being compelled to stay. Needing to go.

'So, you got the damn thing listed.'

It was Janey, behind her.

'Now we'll all have to live with it while you fuck off down to London.'

551

Ellie laughed quietly through her nose.

'I heard about the job in the shadow cabinet,' said Janey, sitting down beside her. 'Minister for posties, by all accounts.'

Janey got out a pack of chewing gum and offered her a piece.

'Doesn't Colin's dad ...'

'Yeah, he does,' said Ellie, declining.

'Funny how these things work out.'

'How did you know about London?'

'He's already talked to his cleaner about how he won't be needing her so much. She told Carol.'

Ellie felt odd about being talked about in this way but it wasn't something she cared particularly to get hung up on.

'I got offered a job, too,' she said.

'No way. You and him, you're incredible.'

'It's a new firm. One that's really going places. I know the guy from university.'

'You're amazing. I'm totally in awe of you, you know that.'

Ellie did know it and she stopped herself making the usual play of humility.

'So, when are you going?'

'I don't know if I am going,' she said.

'*What?*'

'Have you seen the plans for what they want to do here? It's a total horror show. If I don't stay to fight then ...'

'What are you *like*? It's a bit of colour to liven the world's greyest fucking building. It'll give all the folk who live there something to smile about. And they're keeping your café. I thought you'd be chuffed ...'

Ellie leaned her head back against the bench. There were times in your life when you had the energy and times when you didn't.

'Can you ever imagine leaving here?' she said. 'Living somewhere else?'

Janey leaned back so she too was lying half-slumped into the bench, the pair of them sort of looking over at the estate and sort of up at the sky.

'Not really. I mean, Spain's nice, obviously. But I wouldn't want to *live* there, I don't think. And I've always liked Norfolk when we've been there, but it's a bit, you know, *Norfolk*.'

She took the chewing gum from her mouth and wrapped it in a tissue.

'My mum's here. My sister's here. Steve's sister's here. We're all here. And that's my life, isn't it? If I went anywhere else, I'd just spend my whole time on the phone to them.'

She put a fresh piece of gum into her mouth.

'It might be a dump but this is where everything happens for me. I know other stuff happens in, I don't know, Wales or whatever, but I don't care about it. I want to know if Claire Kerr will ever get round to leaving her shithead of a husband and if Mandy Pike's still banging her way round the school gates.'

'She's not shagging someone else now, is she?'

'Tommy Dodd.'

'Felicity's dad?'

Janey nodded, her mouth open as far as it would go, her eyes full of gleeful faux outrage.

'Oh god, what is she *thinking*?'

'He better be insane in the sack, right? I mean, it's like he was born without a chin.'

Ellie reached out and took Janey's hand in hers. They interlaced fingers.

'God, I'd miss you if I went.'

Janey squeezed her hand and stood up, righted her jacket.

'I've got to go get Alexis,' she said. She fixed Ellie a look. 'I'll never meet another person like you as long as I live. And I'll miss you like crazy. But really, pet, you'd be fucking mad if you stayed.'

Ellie listened to Janey's footsteps as she walked to her car, the door slamming shut, the sound of the engine. For a while afterwards she stayed there, her eyes closed. Eventually, she looked up at the building, brutally conflicted. She couldn't take the job but nor could she turn it down. She needed someone else to make the decision for her.

He answered on the third ring.

'Hi.'

'Hi,' she said tentatively.

'The signal's not great. I'm at the Grangeham forge.'

'Oh, right.'

'Yeah, there's about twenty of us here, all looking for newts.'

'That's good, no?'

'Out of twenty thousand fans. It's not exactly overwhelming.'

'Still, for a Thursday afternoon.'

Colin sat on the bank at the side of the canal, looking out over the forge. Bright light. Blue sky. Hardly a hint of wind. It was one of those days that made everything pretty, even a decrepit outbuilding with a tree growing through its collapsed roof. And still he could feel his mood souring at the edges. It wasn't enough. Taking part wasn't what counted. Winning was what counted. And they weren't winning. And he had no plan B.

'The rest of them are pinning everything on Saturday,' he said. 'Which is just madness.'

'Is there no chance they'll win?'

'Yeah, I mean they *might*, but they almost certainly won't. QPR finished fourth but they could easily have got one of the top two spots. We scraped sixth.'

Colin got up and walked away from the water so he wouldn't be heard.

'I've got all these people out here looking for bloody newts but I don't know what else to do. I've been on the phone to the council. They've completely closed ranks. Everyone's pleading ignorance. I've put in a freedom of information request but it's going to be six weeks before I hear anything. And I've tried to go with what I've got but no one at the *Post* will even return my calls and none of the nationals will touch it until I've got some proof.'

'I'm sorry.'

'All afternoon I've been going over the same things in my head. Was the contaminated land test bona fide? Is there any chance the site could still be held in common? I just don't know what to do any more. I can't prove that he's done anything illegal.'

Colin stood up on a raised concrete bed, looking over the site.

'The Chapel is the last remnant of any kind of meaningful heritage in this town,' he said, his voice breaking a little. 'You look back over the years, there's pretty much always been someone on the pitch who was born in the streets literally alongside the stadium. It's not just a building, Ellie.'

All around him was brownfield nothing. And then, in the distance, warehouses and the A115.

'We leave there and come here, to some awful sterile island of massive shops and bowling alleys and a fucking Ikea, and I don't know how you'll be able to meaningfully say it'll still be football. There'll be a ball and goals and everything but it won't be football. It'll be something else. And there'll be no reason to give a shit about it any more.'

'I know,' said Ellie. 'I understand.'

Colin breathed out slowly and deliberately.

'I got your voicemail,' he said. 'Thank you for telling me. You didn't have to.'

'I can't take it, can I?'

Colin sat down on the stump of an old breezeblock wall and let his chin drop to his chest. He could see his exit strategy closing ahead of him. London only made sense if she led the way. Then, if it all went wrong, it wouldn't be his fault. But at the same time, the thought of her working on the Moolah arena felt like a terrible aggravated humiliation.

'I can't answer that for you,' he said.

Eventually, Ellie plucked something straight from leftfield.

'Colin, I was thinking of coming home.'

Colin, who was shielding his eyes from the sun, looking down at what might or might not have been movement in the water, heard only 'home' and said abruptly:

'You can't.'

'Are you sure? That seems very—'

'Do not go to the house,' said Colin, enunciating every word. 'Not you, not Daisy.'

'OK.'

'Promise me you won't.'

'OK. That's just ... Are you ... I mean, is there someone ...'

On the far side of the canal there was a commotion. He looked up. A couple of people were jumping down a bank to join someone else.

'I can't talk now, I'm sorry. Just don't go home, Ellie. I mean it. I'm sorry, but it's just not an option at the moment.'

'I mean, if there is ...'

But Colin wasn't listening, he thought he'd heard someone say *spawn*.

'Sorry,' he said. 'I've got to go.'

Ellie was stunned. He had rung off. Just like that. She was left with one single thought: Marjorie would have walked away. She would have taken the job and gone to London. In a heartbeat.

Ellie felt the clarity of the blue sky overhead. The future would come to her in whatever way it came. She stood up and looked one last time at the Larkspur, perfect as it was on this most perfect of days. Finally, it all made sense. You had one obligation as a woman and that was to live your own life.

* * *

Kerry lived on the fifth floor of the Granary, an old grain depot which had been converted, three years earlier, into flats. Hers was a corner unit with floor-to-ceiling windows on two sides. The central living space was dominated by a white L-shaped sofa and a glass coffee table. A breakfast bar jutted out from one wall. Everywhere, there seemed to be an impractical overabundance of regimentally ordered throw cushions. It reminded Colin of the time they had visited Ellie's cousin, Mark, who made a lot of money in the City and lived in a similar sort of flat in Canary Wharf, which Ellie had described, under her breath, as a *show home for aspirational hairdressers*. Colin remembered at the time murmuring his assent but was struggling now to see what the problem was.

'Nice place,' he said, putting his bag down by the side of the sofa.

He had packed light. His laptop, a change of clothes and the toothbrush, which he'd retrieved from the pavement.

'Thanks,' said Kerry from the kitchenette, where she was filling a bright pink kettle. 'Tea?'

'Yeah, that would be nice. Thanks.'

'How was the pub?'

'There was a kind of gallows solidarity to it,' he said, determined to salvage something from the wreckage of the day. The thing that had caused the commotion hadn't been spawn, just a bloom of algae. They had hunted until it was dark, until there was nothing to do but head to the pub where he had had a couple of pints and what he was realising now was a fatally misjudged Tex-Mex platter.

'We talked about going back again tomorrow,' he said with his hand on his chest, 'but I don't know if it's the best use of the day ...'

Colin caught himself, arrested his mood. The disappointment was familiar to him, something he knew how to inhabit, wring out for all it was worth. But for the first time in his life he felt he had a way out of its grip.

'We've got one last day,' he said. 'And we've got people who'll help us. We just have to keep going and not let up.'

'Damn straight,' she said, placing his tea on the table in front of him.

On the way back from the pub he had stopped into another pub where he had changed into his best available outfit: his smartest jeans, his cleanest trainers, and a shirt that didn't look too crinkly when it was tucked in. Kerry, maddeningly, seemed not to have noticed.

'How are you? How was your evening?'

'Fine, I had a load of work to catch up on, paperwork.'

On the dining table there was a large glass pot full of what looked like moss with an orchid growing out of it, two scented candles, a bowl of polished silver stones.

'What was the reaction to last night?'

'To the break-in? Total madness.'

Colin swallowed hard, but he could feel a tightening in his chest, acid in his stomach. It was the hickory-smoked onion rings.

'But they don't suspect you?' he said.

'No. I was worried that they'd know I'd put in the alarm codes, but whatever your mate did made them think we manually overrode it. With that, and the graffiti, they all think it's another Wroth thing.'

'No mention of me?'

'Not that I heard.'

'They were there waiting for me outside the house again, so we must be close.'

Kerry cocked her head and smiled sympathetically.

'I'm sorry you're having to sleep on the sofa.'

Colin looked at her, yearning for her to suggest a solution to this predicament.

She yawned.

'I'm normally such a night owl, but I'm knackered at the moment. Sorry, Col, I'm going to go to bed,' she said.

Colin found himself unable to decipher whether or not this might have been an invitation, partly because he was always crap at reading these things but mostly because he was battling an enormous burp that was building at the bottom of his oesophagus.

'Good night.'

Colin tried to speak but couldn't. He clamped his mouth shut and nodded.

'All right,' she said. 'I'll see you in the morning.'

The door to her bedroom swung shut with a cushioned whump. Colin waited a beat or two until he allowed himself to finally burp, into his cupped hands, which contained the sound but intensified the smell.

Disgusted at himself, he ran to the bathroom. He had, he reasoned, five minutes in which he could knock on her door before it would be really weird to do so and he needed urgently to get himself in order.

The bathroom was compact and extravagantly stocked. In a glass-fronted cupboard mounted on the wall were her perfumes; a dozen or so of them, arranged like trophies in a cabinet: cut-glass, gold tops, a different abstract noun on every label. On silver shelves by the shower were the shampoos, conditioners, gels and foams. Colin rifled through them, and then he spotted the cabinet under the sink. He pulled open the doors and started reading the labels: paracetamol, ibuprofen, vitamin C, folic acid.

Then he spotted a wash bag, small and pink and tucked away at the back. Colin paused, his fingers already on its zip. It wasn't unreasonable to assume that it might contain antacids. He pulled the zip. Colin felt the blood rushing from his head. Inside was an ovulation thermometer. He steadied himself with a hand on the sink and sat down on the loo.

She practised the rhythm method.

He let out a steady breath. Kerry believed that everything happened for a reason. Who was he – sitting in her bathroom, with her ovulation thermometer in his hands – to question this perfectly plausible explanation of the evolution of the cosmos?

Above the basin there was a vanity light. He switched it on and looked at himself in the mirror. His stomach was churning like a washing machine but he was just going to have to ride it out. He closed his eyes and practised a visualisation technique he had picked up from a sports psychologist. He would knock on her door. And she would open it. And their eyes would lock. He would have the hug first and then the kiss.

He undid the top button of his shirt and walked purposefully into the living room. His phone was on the arm of the sofa. As he walked past it, a message appeared on the screen. He thought about ignoring it but curiosity got the better of him. It was an email from 'Major Wroth' and its subject matter was The Truth about Grangeham Forge.

Colin grabbed the phone and opened it. There were no words, just an attachment. A PDF claiming to be the 'Grangeham Forge Initial Environmental Impact Assessment'. For a second he feared that it might be a virus, part of an attempt to compromise his phone. He considered deleting it, unopened. But, really, what did he have to compromise?

He opened the attachment. On the cover was the name of the

author: Douglas Dublin. Colin skimmed through the first two pages: a dry analysis of the site's water drainage, lots of indexed paragraphs and tables that he didn't understand.

Then he came to Illustration 1.2.1. It was a photo of a slab of rock very much like the one Rodbortzoon had sat on while he was eating his biltong. Underneath it was a short caption:

Illustration 1.2.1 Probable hearth. Appears to have been exposed by recent collapse of the 20th century canal banks. Difficult to accurately date without carbon analysis. But early indications suggest likely to be evidence of Neolithic settlement.

Friday, May 23rd

Colin clicked refresh. There were now 1,522 comments underneath his piece. Two dozen more than there had been five minutes earlier. He reeled, exhausted and elated. He had been up all night, first exchanging a flurry of emails with the duty editor on the *Guardian* sports desk and then writing up the article.

Illustration 1.2.1 was just the start. Douglas Dublin had also found three flint heads and what looked like it might be a perimeter wall suggesting a substantial settlement. He had managed, after a couple of false starts, to get through to an academic on secondment to a university in California who was still at her desk and was happy to answer his emails. If the early indications were right, she was confident that it would be one of the biggest European archaeological discoveries in decades and pretty much guaranteed UNESCO world heritage listing.

Colin stared in disbelief at the screen of his laptop. His piece was prominently placed at the top of the front page of the *Guardian* website. The article itself was accompanied by a picture of his face, taken that morning by Kerry up against her kitchen wall.

'Another cuppa, Col?'

He was in Gordon's, where he had been all morning, receiving visitors. Word had got out that he was there and half of his old camp-mates had dropped by to congratulate him. Mick and Steve. Tommy Quinn and his lot. Even Brian had been in to wish him well. For a good part of the morning, Rodbortzoon had been sitting next to him puncturing his swelling ego with a serious of deflationary jokes, but as he was leaving he had enveloped Colin in a bear hug and slipped a big fat cigar into his breast pocket to be smoked later that night when they were – as they planned to be – absolutely smashed.

'Another cuppa would be lovely. Thanks, Gordon.'

It was another sunny day and the light in the café was lovely, soft and warm and full of promise. Bacon was frying on the grill. Toast toasted. The tea urn whistled its morning tune.

'What about you, Kerry?'

'I'll have an orange juice,' she said from her seat in the booth opposite him. 'The good stuff, not that crap in the cartons.'

'Only the best for you, my dear,' said Gordon with a bow. 'It's all on the house this morning.'

'I'll have another bacon sandwich then.'

'Right you will. Good lass!'

Colin looked at her and smiled broadly. She had finally gone to bed, exhausted, at three in the morning and then was up again at six to proofread his piece, which he had filed at 7.30 a.m.; too late for the Friday print edition, but he had been promised a spot on the Saturday cover. He giggled. The front page. Not the sports section. The paper proper.

He leaned back into the leatherette and savoured the alien but ambrosial taste of success. The move to Grangeham had been torpedoed. There was simply no way that the government could opt for the Chapel.

On the table, his phone buzzed. Another text. It was from his cousin Alan who lived in Florida. He was getting messages from people he hadn't seen for years, old university friends, kids from school, former colleagues, football people. And there were too many voicemails to listen to: Little Tom, Big Tom, Patrick, Leonie, two of his uncles. Even Rick had left a message.

He picked a chip off his plate. An hour or so earlier, a representative from the British Archaeological Society had been quoted on the *Today* programme claiming that they'd have people at the site as early as that afternoon. Even if it wasn't a hearth or a perimeter wall, the initial report meant at the very least there had to be a full archaeological survey, which would set back any building work by two years at the absolute minimum.

Colin closed his eyes and breathed in through his nose. He was exhausted and elated and emotional.

'*There* you are.'

Colin opened his eyes. It was Ellie, her sunglasses on top of her head, her sleeves rolled to the elbow, dragging Daisy behind her.

'Somebody has something to tell you.'

Daisy was still behind her, head bowed, her eyes red from crying.

'I'm sorry, Dad.'

She wiped her eyes with the heel of her hand.

'So are you going to tell him? How is it that your Fresno castles are so much better than the other girls'?'

Daisy mumbled some further apology.

Ellie barely let her finish.

'It's because they've been furnished with in-game credits bought with a Moolah loan that was taken out against your credit card. And, obviously, not paid back.'

Colin looked disbelievingly at Daisy. That time, in the services, she hadn't been in his wallet for his cash, it was for his card.

And then he realised.

'The guys outside the house . . .'

'So you *did* know about them. I can't believe you didn't tell me.'

'I thought they were . . .'

'They're bailiffs.'

Colin blinked, still struggling to take this in.

'So they were nothing to do with Grangeham or our investigation?'

'No, it's about the loan that hasn't been paid back. I was over there this morning picking something up and I saw them outside and asked them who they were and that's how the whole story came to light. You, or rather your daughter, were twelve hundred quid in debt.'

'*Twelve hundred quid.*'

'Don't worry, it's dealt with.'

'You paid it?'

'No, I got Pankaj to call the head of their public relations team and ask her if she wanted him to start asking questions in the House about their child protection policies. She's wiped the debt.'

'OK,' said Colin uncertainly.

'Not that any of that makes Daisy's behaviour any less awful.'

At this, Daisy moaned again and wiped away snotty tears with the sleeve of her jumper.

'So they've gone have they, the bailiffs?' asked Colin.

'Yes, they've gone.'

'And it's safe to go back to the house?' he added, a little forlornly.

'Of course it is, yes.'

Colin smiled a sad little smile.

Kerry took advantage of this lull in the conversation to return from the counter and place in front of Colin the cup of tea that Gordon had made for him.

'Hi,' said Ellie.

'Hello,' she replied.

'You're ...'

'Yes,' said Colin quickly. 'My contact.'

'Wow,' said Ellie in a manner that could have been interpreted, Colin felt, in probably a dozen different ways, at least half of which made him feel momentarily good about himself. And half of which he didn't really care to think about.

For a second or two they stood there, the two women, at the end of the table, looking at each other. Eventually, Colin summoned the power to speak.

'Kerry,' he said. 'Would you mind taking Daisy over to get a drink so me and her mum might be able to have a quick chat?'

'Sure,' she said.

'Yes,' added Ellie, 'that would be great. Thank you.'

'Come on, Daisy,' said Kerry, steering the girl away from the table over to the fridge. 'Let's get you a drink.'

'No Coke for her,' said Ellie. 'And actually no juice, either. She can have water. *Tap* water.'

Colin winced a little, in the way he did when he was asking Ellie to go easy on her.

564

'I know,' she said, once Daisy was out of earshot. 'I *know*.'

Throughout the whole conversation Ellie had stayed standing at the end of the table. Only now did she flop down into the seat opposite him.

'But what I can I do? Half of me wants to gather her up in my arms and tell her that everything's going to be all right and it's not her fault and that she's acting out because her terrible mother has put her through all this bloody upheaval. But the other half of me is very conscious that we can't let her get away with this. *She took a loan out in your name.*'

'Yeah, that probably isn't something we can just let pass.'

'No shit.'

Colin blew out through his mouth.

'So,' he said. 'An eventful twenty-four hours.'

'Oh my god,' she said, her mood shifting abruptly from hard to soft. 'I'm so sorry. I read your piece.'

'You did?'

'Yeah, me and everyone else in the world.'

'It's done OK, I think.'

'Yeah, it's done OK, Colin.'

Colin smiled.

'I don't know what it means for you and your job,' he said.

'What do you mean?'

'Well there's not going to be a stadium now, is there?'

'Oh,' said Ellie. 'I see what you mean. But no, the offer's still there. I spoke to them this morning.'

'Oh, right. I guess we were wrong then. Must be a different stadium, after all.'

'In fact, I spoke to them to tell them I'm taking it.'

'Oh. OK.'

'You know that parable about the drowning man? The Christian one. I was always being told it at primary school. This guy is in the sea or a lake or whatever, and he's half-drowning, and a dude comes past on a raft and tells him to get in but he's like: "It's cool, God will save me". And then, I don't know, someone else comes by in a boat. And he's the same. Well, it's a bit like that. These things come along

565

and you just have to take them. You just have to. You kind of don't have a choice in the matter. That's just the way it is.'

'Right.'

'Without the god stuff, obviously.'

Colin felt a faint smile creep up at the corners of his mouth. He had saved Peterdown and now he had to go to London. Even if Rick offered him his old job back. He would have to turn it down to be near his daughter.

'He has a place down there, right? Daisy said it was south of the river.'

Ellie went to bat this away but then stopped. She found herself intently picking at one thumbnail with the other. The night before she had called her mother. For the first time in months. She was the only person Ellie knew would understand. They had talked, or rather she had talked and her mother, for once, had listened. And she had been understanding. And then she had been useful.

'He does,' she said to Colin. 'But we're not going there. Although he doesn't know that yet.'

'Oh.'

'My uncle has a place. We can have it for a few months until we find our feet.'

'Oh, right.'

Ellie wasn't looking at him, she was addressing him but looking past him.

'I'm not going to be a Grand Architect of the Universe,' she said, wincing a little. 'I'm not going to be the Marjorie Blofeld of my generation.'

Colin smiled at this.

'I'm not going to be the Hemingway of mine,' he said. 'Although literally nobody ever thought I would be. Not even me. I could do the terse prose but I'm just not the kind of person who could ever catch a marlin. I mean, have you seen how big they are?'

Ellie laughed an instinctive, impulsive laugh, high and sharp. Everybody's dreams were just as ridiculous as everybody else's. She felt a flood of warmth and affection for him.

'I didn't get the Larkspur listed,' she said looking past him, her eyes fixed on a blank bit of the wall. 'I thought I did, but I didn't. There are all these things that I thought I understood about myself that I just don't feel confident about any more. Things about me that I realise ... I don't know. I feel like I don't have any certainty left.'

Finally, she looked at him, in the eye.

'You can't just will yourself to be a Grand Architect of the Universe,' she said, filling her lungs with air before she exhaled. 'But you can ... I don't know ... own your own soul.'

Colin's eyes were filmed with tears, partly because it was all very emotional but mostly because he was just so damned tired.

'For once, I think I actually know what you're talking about,' he said.

'And I can't do that with him.'

'Right.'

'I'm discovering that it might be possible to be in love with someone and be not at all sure if you actually like them.'

'I could see how that might be the case,' said Colin, looking down at the Formica tabletop, its whorls and cracks and patina.

'I've never not liked you,' she said.

Colin was aware that this was the point at which he was probably supposed to say, *but you've never loved me*, but it just didn't seem worth it.

'I've always loved you,' he said, 'and I liked you most of the time.'

He looked up.

'Or at least some of the time.'

Ellie smiled. She looked over her shoulder at Kerry and then back at him.

'You deserve someone who you can love and like in equal measure,' she said.

Colin blushed and looked to make sure Kerry hadn't heard.

Ellie laughed.

'Right,' she said, putting both hands on the table. 'I need to have a very awkward conversation with our MP, but first I'm going to drop Daisy off at your mum's, where I may or may not summon the courage

to tell her that I'm moving her beloved granddaughter to London.'
She smiled a crooked smile. 'Want to come?'

It was Colin's turn to smile.

'I would have loved to,' he said. 'But I haven't been to bed yet and
I am literally about to fall over.'

* * *

Colin experienced the walk home at one remove from his usual
experience of reality. It reminded him of the booming stillness he felt
when his ears were full of water. That way everything was heightened
and loomingly close, but also unintelligible and weirdly distant. The
Ottercliffe Road and its buses, King George Park and its joggers,
the shopping streets of Eastfinche; all of them intensely detailed but
also weirdly wrong, like the rest of the world hadn't caught up with
the new reality.

For six hours he slept, his head deep in the pillow. Six hours of
blissful, dreamless sleep. But when he awoke, he did so in a flapping
panic, completely disorientated.

His phone was ringing.

'Patrick,' he said.

'I called you this morning. Did you get my voicemail?'

He looked at his watch. It was 10 p.m.

'No.'

'So you don't know?'

'What? I don't know what you're talking about.'

'Shit. All right. First, though, tell me, what is it with you two and
this guy?'

'What do you mean?' said Colin. '*What* guy?'

'This Philpott guy. What is he? Some kind of avenging angel?'

Colin sat instantly upright.

'*James Philpott* is Truther_78? Are you sure?'

'Darling, by the time I'd finished with him he was telling me
everything. And I mean *everything*.'

'Did you get his phone number?'

'Natch.'

'Oh my god, Patrick, you are amazing.'

'I know. I know. Well done on your thing by the way. The story was on the news. The TV news.'

'Thanks.'

'Right, have you got a pen?'

After he had splashed his face with water and brushed his teeth, Colin sat at the dining room table and dialled.

'James Philpott?'

'Yeah, who's asking?'

'Colin Ryder, *Peterdown Evening Post*. No, sorry. Colin Ryder, the *Guardian*.'

'How did you get this number?'

'That doesn't matter.'

'Aw, shit ... Last night. That bird on the internet.'

'You were quite voluble by all accounts.'

'I knew that opening a second bottle was a mistake. Fuck.'

'You tweeted at me implying something was going to cause me pain. What did you mean, James?'

'What are you talking about?'

'You're Truther_78. You posted a tweet that said I was going to do myself a mischief.'

'Oh yeah, that.'

'What does it mean?'

'Well, it's a bit late now, isn't it? You've already written the piece.'

Colin heard the suck and sizzle of his cigarette. There was a pause and then a heavy exhalation.

'You know I quite liked it at the start, getting a job with Kirk. Being properly on the inside. I enjoyed causing you lot a bit of bother, you know? Pissing off a load of Peterdown fans, that was all right. And it was good to be giving Kington the runaround. She hung me out to dry, the bitch. And I knew about it and she didn't.'

'Knew about what?'

'The Neanderthals. We've known for months.'

'You mean the Neolithic village.'

'Yeah, that.'

'Neolithic villages weren't populated by Neanderthals,' said Colin incredulously. 'You're out by like tens of thousands of years.'

'Fucking hell. Do you want to know, or what?'

'Sorry. Yes.'

'So we knew about the Neo-whatever stuff. That gimp Dublin found it.'

'And he didn't say anything? Why? It would have made his name. It's a Neolithic village for god's sake.'

'He's a freak. He doesn't give a fuck about anything but newts. Kirk kept him quiet by giving him money to set up that pond thing in Shropshire. He's looking like a right cunt now, isn't he? Now that we've leaked you the report.'

Colin's heart stilled.

'*You* leaked me the report,' he whispered hollowly.

'It was easy. You can set up a Major Wroth email address in five minutes. Bob's your uncle.'

'But why would you do that?'

'No idea,' said Philpott. 'Kirk told me to.'

Saturday, May 24th

Out the window, the view flashed past. It was exhausting to look at, just a blur of green. Colin rubbed his eyes and glanced across the table at Kerry. They were just past Newark, on the London train.

He took a sip of his coffee, trying to rouse himself. He had been up all night again, going over everything in his head, and still none of it made any sense. Why had Kirk leaked him the report? He couldn't think of a single plausible reason and it had nagged away at him so that by morning he was filled with a dread so deadening that he couldn't summon the will to tell Kerry about the conversation.

'They've just announced that the appeal failed and they've got that land rezoned for that casino,' she said, not looking up from the newspaper. 'At the Avalon. Fucking great, I say. Have you ever been to Vegas? I saw Celine Dion at Caesar's Palace. Unbelievable. Love that place.'

'No,' said Colin. 'Never made it.'

'Oh, you've got to go to Vegas at least once in your life. It's wild. I won nine hundred dollars once, playing craps.'

'I've never really been into gambling.'

'No? I've got a tenner on us to win two-nil, Garry to score both,' she said. 'Fourteen to one I got.'

'Well you got those odds because they really don't think that's going to happen.'

'Jesus, Col. Cheer up. We're going to bloody Wembley.'

Colin looked out the window.

'I really reckon we can do it, you know. All we've got to do is believe.'

'Or be fitter and better coached and better resourced,' he said. 'You know, be better at football.'

Kerry half-stood up out of her chair and pulled her top up a fraction and her jeans down a touch, revealing a flash of cursive script that ran along her hipbone.

Never let your fear decide your fate

Colin read it and tried to remember where he'd seen it before. And then he read it again. And then he remembered. Jordan Garry. And then he felt humiliated with an intensity that he hadn't felt since the time Jonny Raine had pulled his chair out from underneath him just as he was sitting down and he had to be carried out of GCSE geography.

'When did you get that?' he asked.

'A few months ago,' she said, sitting down again. 'I was going through something and it was just what we both needed in the moment.'

Kerry kept chatting but Colin wasn't listening. The horror of it kept him quiet all the way to King's Cross. Jordan Garry and Kerry. Just thinking about it brought a sullied blush to his cheeks and he managed the rest of the way from Peterborough to London without looking at her.

At King's Cross they changed on to the tube, Colin still morose and basically mute. He trailed behind her, up the escalators and through the tunnels, listening to her excited small talk, nodding occasionally. The Metropolitan line train was hot and heavy with people and he had a premonition of being in London and being poor and single and overwhelmed by it all. Just like he had been the first time.

They got off at Wembley Park and shuffled out of the station with the crowds. Round the corner and then up the street until there it was ahead of him, with its giant dental brace arcing redundantly over it.

Wembley Stadium.

'Oh my god, Colin,' said Kerry, grabbing him and pulling him along. 'There it is. Amazing. I can't believe this is actually happening.'

Colin allowed himself to be dragged up Wembley Way. Around him, the fans mingled with each other, exchanging jokes, bursting into short-lived song, pausing for photos. Touts offered to buy or sell tickets. Street vendors hawked half-and-half scarves. The smell of cheap burgers drifted on the air.

They reached the stadium steps where they were to part company; Kerry heading off to the VIP entrance, Colin for the stands.

She threw her arms round him and pulled him into a hug.

'You've just got to believe,' she said, flashing him a smile as she went.

Colin stood where he was, watching her go.

'It doesn't work like that,' he shouted helplessly at her departing back. 'If you'd lived my life, you would understand it really doesn't work like that.'

She continued on, oblivious. He sighed and made his way eventually to the right turnstile and then once he was through it, past two merchandise shops and up three flights of stairs and past another shop and two food outlets, and finally out a tunnel and into the stadium itself, which was nearly full; the QPR end decked out in blue and white hoops, theirs a sea of green and white stripes. Colin found himself momentarily arrested by the sight and just for a second he remembered Peterdown United were playing at Wembley, and for all that this new stadium wasn't the old stadium with its towers and storied history just being there was the realisation of a dream he had nurtured since he was a boy.

He stopped where he was on the walkway and let the fans stream past him on either side. Overhead, the sky was blue and both sets of supporters were bouncing with expectation, every one of them holding the same hopes, hanging on to the same promise of happiness.

For the first time that day, the clamour in his mind momentarily quietened and he found himself awash with joy at the theatre of it, eighty thousand people in a single space, all of them imagining that they might be the decisive factor, that if they just cared enough their team might be carried to victory. Colin felt a tear form at the edge of his eye. Maybe she was right. Maybe all he had to do was believe.

'There you are!'

Colin looked over. Rodbortzoon was standing on his seat and waving. He was wearing his green and white scarf and was holding a hot dog in each hand.

Colin picked his way through three rows of fans and sat down next to him.

'Is one of those for me?'

'Don't be ridiculous,' said Rodbortzoon. 'Do you have any idea how much they cost? I could have bought a three-bedroom house in Peterdown.'

'I'm too nervous to eat anyway.'

He picked up Rodbortzoon's match programme from the floor between his feet and scanned it, looking for a team sheet.

'Do you know if Ellis passed his fitness test?'

'He was out warming up. He looked his usual self. I think he's fine.'

'Any idea what the line-up is?'

'It was just announced. Three at the back: Parsons, Ellis, West.'

'OK, that seems smart. We have to hold them and try to grab one on the break. Has he got Turner in centre mid?'

'Him and Connolly.'

For five minutes they talked tactics. How to contain the QPR full backs, whether or not Gunnarsson should be man-marking their playmaker. Colin studiedly avoided mentioning Garry's name but found himself cheering along with the rest of the crowd as he ran on to the pitch with his teammates.

The first twenty minutes of the game dragged by, all stops and starts and misplaced passes. Both sets of players were clearly overawed by the occasion and they were cancelling each other out with their incompetence and niggly fouls. As it wore on, each passage of play coming to nothing, neither team capable of carving out a chance, the atmosphere in the stadium grew tetchy. The fans stopped chanting and a stressed hush fell over the stadium, punctuated by groans and hollered obscenities.

Colin fidgeted in his seat, trying to make himself comfortable. The agitation of the crowd had started to get to him, but it was more than that. He took his coat off and stashed it underneath his chair, sipped at his water bottle, stretched his shoulders.

Rodbortzoon was sitting hunched, having long ago finished his hot dogs, staring out intently at the pitch. He wasn't exactly a classic role model but he had a thing about him. Something undefinable. And Colin had always wanted to make him proud.

On the pitch a QPR player went down clutching his knee. The referee waved on the medical team and everyone stopped for a second.

'Kirk leaked me the report.'

Rodbortzoon looked at him.

'Why?' he said. And then: 'Are you sure?'

'Yeah, I think so. Philpott told me. And I don't know why he would have lied about it.'

'Why would he do that?'

'Oh my god,' said Colin, something suddenly occurring to him. 'Have you got any signal?'

Rodbortzoon looked down at his phone, nodded.

'The rezoned land at the airport. Everyone thinks it's going to be a casino. What use class does the land need to be for a casino?'

Rodbortzoon tapped away at the screen.

'D2,' he said.

'But you can also build other things on D2 land, right?'

'Cinemas, concert halls, casinos,' said Rodbortzoon, reading from his phone, 'dance halls, swimming baths or any other indoor or out-door sports or recreation not involving motorised vehicles or firearms.'

Colin's lungs felt like they were tied with belts.

'It's not a casino,' he whispered.

'What?'

'It was forty-five minutes, right? That letter he sent and then retracted. The new stadium had to be no more than forty-five minutes on public transport. From the Chapel.'

'I think so. Sounds right.'

'Google the distance to the airport,' he said. 'Peterdown to the Avalon.'

Rodbortzoon tapped away at the screen.

'A hundred and eighty-two miles,' he said.

'The train does two hundred and eighty-six miles an hour. How do we work it out?'

'A hundred and eighty-two divided by two hundred and eighty-six times sixty,' said Rodbortzoon, incredulous. 'So-called best higher education system . . .'

'Do it!'

'Thirty-eight point two.'

'Is that minutes? You'll be able to do the Chapel to the airport in thirty-eight minutes once it's built?'

'Yes.'

'OH MY FUCKING GOD,' shouted Colin. Around him, a dozen or so fans turned to look. He continued, hushed. 'He's moving the club to the airport.'

'What?' said Rodbortzoon.

'He leaked the report so everyone knows we can't go to Grangeham. But that means if they choose the Chapel as the site of the station we'll have nowhere to go.'

'Oh god,' said Rodbortzoon.

'They just won their appeal to get that land by the airport rezoned. Everyone thought it was going to be a casino but what if it was going to be a stadium? That would explain why Ellie's still got a job working on it.'

'Oh god,' said Rodbortzoon. 'What the fuck are we going to do?'

Colin didn't have an answer, but he knew that there were people in the stadium who would. He had his phone out and he was writing a text.

Emergency. I'm going to need your access all areas pass

The corporate entertainment suite at Wembley looked like the function room of a hotel: high ceilings, patterned carpets, huge quantities of identical furniture. By the time Kerry had seen his message and got him the wristband, it was half time and four hundred or so grey-suited dignitaries had left their stadium seats and filed back into the large open space, where they talked in small groups as young waiters moved between them with platters of canapés and trays of champagne. This was good news for Colin, as it provided cover. All he had to do was keep out of the way of Kirk and Gus Taylor, whom he could see on the far side of the room, and he would be fine.

He took a glass of champagne from a waiter and started working the space, reading the name tags of the people he passed. The director of programming at Sky Sports. BT's head of consumer relations. What seemed to be Coca Cola's entire UK marketing team.

Through the vast floor-to-ceiling window that ran along one wall, he could see the players trooping back out on to the pitch. It had been a dire first half, cagey and goalless, and he was unsurprised to see how few of the VIPs seemed bothered about returning to their seats in time for kick-off, particularly when they would be able to watch the game on the many televisions fixed around the room.

He kept going, reading the name tags as he went. The deputy editor of the *Sun*. Barclays' sponsorship partnerships manager. Bet365's head of marketing.

A strangled shout went up around the room as QPR created a half chance that came to nothing, and for a few minutes Colin found himself absorbed in the game as Peterdown found themselves under a period of sustained pressure.

Eventually, a QPR player went down with cramp and the game stopped, breaking the tension. He kept moving about the room. As he paused to survey the contents of a large silver platter offered to him by a waiter, he heard a man behind him talking boisterously, like he'd had a few drinks.

'It's going to be the first club that's marketed principally to Asia. It's genius. The stadium's going to be less than half a mile from the arrival gate. We're talking special flights coming into the airport, private jet parking, limousine shuttles to the ground, on-site hotels and casinos, a retail park. The retail is going to be insane. That shop's going to be taking a million pounds every match day.'

Colin reeled. He turned around and took a sly glance at the man's nametag.

'They're savvy, the Malaysians. They're going Asia all-in. China, Indonesia, Hong Kong, Singapore, Thailand. They're going to be marketing it to the whole lot of them.'

Colin remembered where he had heard the name: Platinum was the agency that had done the kit redesign. He stayed in earshot, his back to them as Lee Cline talked co-branding opportunities and sponsorship deals, targeted marketing and corporate hospitality. As he listened, he watched the nearest screen. Peterdown were defending stoutly, repelling wave after wave of QPR attacks. The fans had started to take a perverse pride in this defensive rearguard, cheering every clearance, even those that went straight out of play.

'There was a lot of back and forth over the name but they've settled on the Knights, what with it being at Avalon airport. Bloody genius. Think about the branding, the swords and the shields and the pageantry. They'll lap it up. And think about the *merch*. What would I do for points on the merch. It's going to go off the hook.'

As he listened to all this Colin stared morosely at the screen. QPR were camped in the Peterdown half, pressing forward, creating half chance after half chance. Eventually, the room hushed, everyone absorbed in the action. QPR won a corner and then another. The entire Peterdown team was back defending. Big Jonny Ellis blocked a shot with his face. Gavin Parsons threw himself into a tackle and had to be stretchered off. But somehow they held on and the Peterdown stands erupted with glee when the referee blew for the end of normal time. There would be a five-minute pause before they played half an hour of extra time to decide it.

'It's got to happen,' continued Lee Cline. 'You think the kids in Hanoi and Singapore aren't starting to notice that the football's better in Spain and the atmosphere's better in Germany? The PL have got to protect their asset and they know it. They don't want to see boys walking around Guangdo Province in Bayern Munich shirts. This stops that in its tracks. The plan is to host at least one league game over there every year. They'll move it around season to season: KL and then Shanghai and then Singapore or whatever. The American footballers already play a game here every season, don't they? You've got to go to your markets. Everyone knows that. The potential is limitless. A club like that would be worth a billion quid before they'd even kicked a ball.'

Colin felt an overwhelming urge to scream, but getting himself embroiled with this blowhard marketing man would do him no good. He needed urgently to talk to someone from the FA. They surely couldn't have sanctioned this. He started walking forcefully about the room, no longer bothered if Kirk saw him.

On the pitch, the match was restarting, Peterdown kicking left to right, towards their own fans. Colin stormed out of the corporate suite and into the bank of prime seats alongside it. Unlike the hard plastic seats in the rest of the ground, these were fold-down, cushioned cinema-style chairs, right on the halfway line and at the perfect viewing height. Still, they were sparsely populated, with more than half the dignitaries having chosen to stay inside the suite, chugging down champagne while they half-watched the game on television. Colin walked to the bottom of the bank and sat down, his attention momentarily caught by a rare Peterdown attack. The game had got stretched. Spaces were opening up. Gunnarsson had the ball and was haring down the right but he was obviously knackered and his attempt at a cross was wild and ragged.

Colin turned in his seat and scanned the rows behind him. Grant Greaves was sitting on his own. The FA's head of media relations. They had met a couple of times, at a fundraiser and then at the unveiling of some sponsorship deal. They had got on pretty well, both of them relieved for once to find someone else who didn't conform to football's bantering blokey archetype.

The look on Grant's face when he saw Colin approach him cleared up instantly any doubts there might have been as to whether or not he knew about the plans.

'Tell me the FA haven't sanctioned this,' said Colin, as he sat down next to him.

Grant looked down sheepishly at the ground.

'Oh my god, Grant.'

Grant wore his hair swept back from the front of his head and was forever running his fingers through it to keep it in place, which gave him the appearance of a harassed house master at a minor public school, driven to distraction by the behaviour of his boys. He looked up.

'Nobody thought it would get this far.'

'Jesus, Grant.'

'It's going to be a media disaster. They're going to crucify us.'

'Of course they are. You're supposed to be the custodians of the game. I can't believe you agreed to it.'

Peterdown managed to string three passes together and the crowd started to chant ironically. Grant looked despondently out at the pitch.

'The Malay consortium made a ten-million-pound donation to our grassroots fund so we humoured them. There were so many ways in which it could go wrong, Colin. Nobody thought it would get this far.'

'Well, just give them the money back and tell them you can't sanction it because the club's been based in Peterdown for a hundred years and it's the lifeblood of the community and you've just realised that moving it is a fucking terrible idea.'

'We can't. We've already given half of it away. Most of it to this new community club. The one set up by your lot.'

Colin bounced up and down in his seat, his fingers tensed into claws of frustration.

'You've got to be kidding,' he said, banging his hands against his head. 'They're in like the ninth division or something. What do they need with all that money!'

'It's grassroots football, Colin. It's inclusive. And it ticked all the boxes. They've got some great ideas.'

'I don't give a fuck about their great ideas. We already have a football club in Peterdown. We don't need another one.'

The referee blew his whistle signalling the end of the first period of extra time. Wearily, the players changed ends, ready to go again.

Colin hunched over, head on his lap.

'Why us?'

'Well they couldn't do it with Spurs, could they? It had to be a club that nobody would care about.'

'*We* care about us.'

'Yeah, all right. But you know what I mean.'

Colin's attention was caught by a QPR break, Gunnarsson losing a fifty-fifty challenge in the middle of the park. Grant was up on his feet, hollering at the players. The QPR winger swapped passes with his centre forward and was shaping to shoot when a last-ditch sliding tackle sent him and the ball into touch. The two of them stayed on their feet for the resultant corner, but the ball into the box failed to beat the first man and had Grant slumping, dejected, back into his seat.

'I don't think I can take much more of this.'

'*You* can't take much more of this. God, Grant. What about me?'

'Honestly, we didn't think it would happen. We started worrying when that bloody housing estate got listed but I still never thought it would get this far. And then we heard about the government decision.'

'What government decision?'

Grant turned finally to look at him.

'You don't know?'

'No!'

'They're going to build the station on the site of the Chapel. Kirk's giving them the land. Totally free.'

Colin flopped in his chair, drained of energy.

'The deal's done. The demolition's going to start in a couple of weeks. They're going to immediately designate it a traffic hub, which will mean it'll get special protection under anti-terrorism legislation. They're not messing about. Anyone trespassing on it will be arrested immediately.'

The Peterdown fans were chanting 'Olé' every time one of their players touched the ball. The whole end was up on its feet, bouncing away. The QPR full back hit the ball long and high into the

Peterdown box. The ball broke to the edge of the area and the QPR number seven shaped to shoot, but Jonny Ellis was there again, throwing himself in front of the ball.

'How can they possibly build the stadium in time? Their next game will be in August. It's like three months away.'

Grant looked away, doubly pained.

'They've lined up this place for the first season,' he said, resigned, 'with an option on it for a second season if the build runs over.'

'You're going to let them play *here*? At *Wembley*?'

'We'd been staking everything on selling this place and when the deal fell through, a lot of people got bloody scared. We're still a hundred and twenty mil in the hole from the build and they're talking about giving us two million a game to play here.'

'Oh Jesus, Grant.'

'Nobody thought it was actually going to happen. You were tenth when we agreed to it . . .'

The referee blew for the end of extra time and pointed with both hands to the centre circle. They had played one hundred and twenty minutes of football and no one had scored. The game would be decided by a penalty shoot-out.

Colin looked out at the pitch. It should have been the most thrilling and agonising and tense ten minutes of his life and it was being ruined by a—

'Wait a sec,' he said. 'What do you mean, we were tenth? What's that got to do with it?'

Grant looked at him.

'It'll only happen if you go up,' he said like this was the most obvious thing in the world. 'The Malaysians only want a Premier League team.'

Colin's mouth hung open.

'You mean if we lose they'll walk away?'

'They've got a contingency in place with the directors of West Ham. Their fans will doubtlessly kick off about it, but, really, would it be any worse than Stratford . . .'

Colin was up on his feet and running. He knew exactly what

he had to do. He ran past the media table and grabbed a beach ball advertising a tabloid newspaper. He was still scampering out of the corporate suite when he heard the first penalty go in and Gunnarsson's name echoing round the stands.

QPR made it one each as he flew down the stairs. He got the commentary up on his phone and listened as he ran around the base of the stadium, crying out in anguish when he heard the QPR number nine ballooning his penalty over the bar.

When he finally reached his seat, Peterdown were leading four-three, with Garry lined up to take the deciding kick.

'So?' said Rodbortzoon.

Colin summoned all his seriousness, looked deep into Rodbortzoon's eyes.

'I need you to buy me five minutes,' he said, panting heavily. 'Before he takes that penalty. There's not time to explain but you know I wouldn't ask if it wasn't fucking important.'

Rodbortzoon fixed him a look.

'I understand,' he said, slipping off his jacket.

'You're a hero.'

He pulled Colin's scarf from his neck and tied it to the end of his, slung them both round his neck.

'One condition: this action, it is not Wroth, it is Geoffrie.'

'Sure, whatever.'

'No, no, no. It's important. This cannot be done in the name of boredom and immiseration. It can only be done if we are fighting for freedom and play.'

'OK.'

'It's important,' he said as he pulled his T-shirt over his head.

'I know. I understand. Be Geoffrie. Channel him.'

Rodbortzoon reached into his pocket and pulled out a rubber bald patch.

'I liberated it from your friend Evan at the place with the smoke,' he said as he placed it reverently on the crown of his skull. 'You know when you have a sense that one day you will urgently need something.'

Colin placed his hand on Rodbortzoon's shoulder.

'You're going to go down in the history of this club. Up there with Jordan Garry and Gem McBride. People will sing songs about you.'

'You bet they will,' said Rodbortzoon as he started unbuckling his belt.

Colin turned and ran down the steps, scanning the crowd. She was fairly near the front in the middle of the row. He clambered over six people to get to her.

'Oh my god, Col, we've nearly done it!'

Colin looked at her. She had taken off her jacket and was standing there in a T-shirt, a Peterdown flag draped across her shoulders. He felt his eyes rim with tears. She was the sexiest woman he had ever met and she loved Peterdown United Football Club. Never again would he meet anyone that combined these two qualities. And you could search all four corners of the earth but you surely only ever found one Greggs soul mate.

A huge roar went up around the ground. From a distance it looked like a giant garden gnome had come miraculously to life and was running across the pitch, its unfeasibly large penis flapping between its legs.

Colin took a deep breath.

He looked out on to the pitch. Somehow Rodbortzoon had got hold of the match ball and was dribbling at full speed, scarves flapping madly behind him, three security guards and two policemen trailing in his wake.

'You're with Garry, aren't you?' said Colin.

Kerry bit her lip.

'I would have told you,' she said. 'I should have told you. But we had to keep it secret. Kirk would have had me out the door in no time.'

'I know everything,' he said. 'The pregnancy stuff . . . that was what derailed him, wasn't it?'

Kerry blushed. Colin sighed a heavy sigh.

Rodbortzoon knocked the ball past a steward, evaded his despairing dive. There was simply no other way to put it: he had good feet for a big man.

'I need you to do something for me.'

'OK.'

'But first I need you to tell me something.'

'What?'

'Was there ever at any point the possibility that something might have, you know, happened, with us?'

Kerry bit her lip again.

'Oh, Colin,' she said.

'You never loved me, did you?'

'Oh, Colin.'

'I thought I knew what was going to happen, how all this was going to end. I always knew we'd fail and the stadium would be moved because that's just what happens, doesn't it? The relentless march of capital that I hear so much about from—' he pointed out to the pitch at Rodbortzoon, who had just dropped his shoulder and swerved past three stewards. Colin felt a lump rise in his throat. '— from that *hero*.'

He swallowed hard.

'But even when I knew we were going to fail, I imagined I would at least get some solace, you know. Something that made it bearable. I thought the lesson I learned would be something about solidarity, about the honest depth of feeling between two working-class heroes defiant in the face of it.'

An enormous collective wince rang round the ground as two stewards converged on Rodbortzoon, taking him down with coordinated pincer-style rugby tackles.

'And I thought I would find some kind of peace, you know. Some sort of maturity. A way of coming to terms with Peterdown. And I don't mean the football club, I mean the town, all it represents. I thought I'd found that in you, Kerry. That the outcome of my journey was going to be you.'

'Oh Colin. I'm from Nottingham. I only moved to Peterdown when I was seventeen.'

'I know you did.'

'And life isn't a journey.'

'I know it's fucking not,' he said, his voice straining as he raged against the sky. 'I mean, of all people, *I* know it's not. That's pretty much the *only* thing I know. That's me.'

Colin looked out on to the pitch, a tear in his eye. Rodbortzoon had been strapped on to a gurney and was being carried from the pitch, a grande cardboard coffee cup upturned on his groin.

Garry was standing over the penalty spot, looking right at them. Kerry waved at him, a cute little wave.

Colin gathered himself.

'OK, you never loved me,' he said. 'But you do love Peterdown United Football Club, don't you?'

'Yes,' said Kerry. 'You know I do.'

'Then I need you to do this for me.'

He produced the now semi-inflated beach ball. Of all people Colin understood the power of an unplanned pregnancy, how it could upend a life.

'Put this underneath your top.'

Kerry stood there for a second, thinking about it.

'It's a risk,' she said.

'I know. But it's a risk we've got to take.'

'OK,' she said, taking the ball. 'I'll do it.'

The police and stewards had left the pitch. Garry was placing the ball on the spot, positioning it to his liking.

'He knows where you're standing. Get his attention again. Do your whistle.'

'OK.'

Kerry put her two index figures into her mouth so they rested on the top of her teeth. Colin had never heard anyone who could whistle like her. She was like a human bullhorn.

The noise cut through the noise of the crowd, silencing it for a second. Garry looked up, recognising the sound, to see Kerry, who was jumping up and down pointing at the bump under her top.

Colin waited for the look of horror to spread across Garry's face, the discombobulating fear, the instant terrifying knowledge that nothing would ever be the same again. The awful burden of unwanted fatherhood.

586

But it didn't come. In its place there was a broad full-wattage smile.

'Why is he smiling?'

Kerry paused.

'I promised I wouldn't tell anyone until the season's over but you're like a little brother to me.'

'I'm four years older than you are,' said Colin in a squeaky voice.

'I'm sure it's the boy he's always wanted,' said Kerry. 'How did you know? We've only just had the twelve-week scan. I mean, I've felt awful but I'm not showing, am I?'

'Wait a sec ... You *are* pregnant. I thought you'd had a scare but it was a false alarm. He told me. Pregnancy stuff. It had scrambled his head.'

'It *did* scramble his head. But it was a mix-up at the clinic. It's incredible to think we ever thought he might be infertile, really. It knocked him sideways, just the idea, but you'd never know it now. Look at him, I've never seen him so focused.'

Colin stood, mouth open, incapable of speech.

'So he wants the kid?'

'It's all he's ever wanted.'

'Oh god.'

'Go on, darling,' hollered Kerry. 'Do it for your boy.'

Garry stepped back five paces. He took a deep breath and pointed explicitly at Kerry before he ran forward and hammered the ball into the top right-hand corner of the net.

The stand exploded. A great demented caterwauling. Colin slumped to the floor. Around him, people jumped, hugged, shouted for joy. For thirty seconds it was bedlam but soon they were all singing, all of them but Colin, their throats open, their faces turned towards the sky.

We're STAYING at the Chapel and you're going to get
    Ga-a-a-a-aried ...

Walk V

Demand the Future: Snaky Path to the Rothbury Recreation Ground

Why do we do it? Walk like we do? To begin with it was an elegy. The crosstown tramp as funeral march. A ramble in a minor key. An ambulatory lament for all that's lost. But more and more it's also been an expression of exuberance. A form of freedom asserted, and, although we didn't always know it, a form of ongoing protest as well. A taking to the streets. A declaration of sovereignty. Every step stirring something up, freeing us of false consciousness.

And it's in this spirit that we start, ceremoniously, back at the beginning. On Snaky Path, where we once bent back the boards for access to the Goods Line. The secret entrance to our under-the-counter High Line, anarchically planted with its buddleia and ragwort, its flowering bindweed.

Of course there's no sneak-through any more. The Goods Line is now sheathed from end to end, hundreds of hard-hatters hammering away inside, ripping up the old track and laying the new magnetic coil.

We stand outside it, looking at the hoardings. The images upon them are exotic: Sydney Harbour Bridge, the Taj Mahal, Machu Picchu. Reminders, as if they were needed, that this train is about passing through, getting out, going places other than here.

Peterdown International, they're calling it, without a hint of irony. Which is all well and good, but doesn't do much for the stay-at-homes, does it? Those of us happy here. What will we see other than departures, capital flight?

Riled, we wrap our scarves around our necks and button up against the day. The November light is thin, a grey wash. Ahead of us is a funny little structure. A hide hoisted on stilts, accessible by ladder, a pair of binoculars hanging by its horizontal window. They're a thing, apparently, these viewing platforms. Pioneered at the Olympic Park. The building site as visitor attraction. A way of keeping the locals on side – make them feel involved with the omnipresent overhaul, the imposed improvements.

We climb up the steps and down we look, over the tops of the hoardings, into the great nothing. The epic excavation. The haunted hole, stalked forever by the ghost of Gem McBride. For one hundred years, the Chapel stood here, our place of pilgrimage. Our dream space. And now it's gone.

It was only a week after the Wembley win that the wrecking ball got to work, taking our terraces in a way that no rival firm ever could. In just three days, they pulled up the pitch. Demolished the dressing rooms. Reduced the whole thing to rubble.

There was talk at the time of a challenge in the courts but it never went anywhere. In the days before the demolition team moved in, a handful of diehards attempted some direct action. A sit-in. Some shenanigans with superglue. But the clampdown was instant and iron-fisted. The site's designation as a strategic transport hub gave the government access to all kinds of off-book contingencies, summary sentences, express injustice.

We look out again at the great hole. Being here has us welling up, as always. This time they're funny tears. Sadness mostly. At the defeat. The crushing loss. But they're tinged with awe, too. Because it stirs something in us, all this weight. All this freight. These I-beams and A-frames. These giant girders and heaps of heavy gauge. Rivets as big as your fist. They transport us back to better days. It's impossible to wholly hate something that's shaping up to be one of the ultimate expressions of the kind of epic engineering that made us who we are. We stand there, conflicted. Does it soften the blow? Or do we feel it twice as hard? The sucker punch that can't help but haunt us: the knowledge that this railway was conceived elsewhere, imagined in ways that are now infinitely beyond us.

We pause at the top of the ladder and look out over the town towards Grangeham. We can't see the site from here, of course. It's eight miles away. And there's not much to look at anyway. Turns out the Neolithic settlement is bona fide but pretty boring. A fifteen-foot foundation wall. And another one. And that's kind of it. Archaeologically significant, no doubt. A find to rewrite the record book, launch a hundred PhDs. But still some way short of Skara Brae. A place for purists, not tourists.

We climb down the ladder, ever angrier. Word is, Kirk got £200 million for the club. And he got to keep an 8 per cent share of the new one. Which may not sound much but it could be 8 per cent of an awful lot, if early indications are anything to go by. Already, the Knights are looking like they might be building an all-conquering empire, at least on the commercial front. The marketing blitz has had a blockbuster budget. Television commercials shot by Hollywood directors. Social media saturation. A pre-season tour that took in Kuala Lumpur, Shanghai, Bangkok and Beijing. At each stadium they visited, the players made their way on to the pitch on horseback, in full sets of armour, each of them having been given his own coat of arms. There's already a bespoke video game. Plastic figurines have been pressed. Partnerships launched with airlines, hotels, tour operators, sports brands, cereal conglomerates, tyre manufacturers, insurance brokers, mobile phone makers, content creators of all stripes.

Twelve games into the season, they might only be sixteenth in the Premier League, but slowly the team's starting to gel. The Colombian who killed it at the World Cup is starting to come good. As is the big-name Brazilian, out of contract in China. The latest scion of the Maldini clan. They're all part of what's pretty much a completely new team. Poor old Ash Connelly and his journeyman huff and puff didn't quite synergise with the new brand identity. Neither did Jonny Ellis with his big head and his agricultural left foot. They wanted to keep Jordan of course, and he's still there in a manner of speaking. Only he's refusing to play, training with the reserves, running down his contract. The most principled player in football, according to the papers.

We allow ourselves a wry smile at the thought as we turn left on to Baxendale Street, shielding our eyes as we pass the Generator, trying not to look at it. It's not bitterness, it's regret at the opportunity wasted. A yearning for the Fun Palace that it could have been had it been born in a different time, under different conditions.

Six months into its shiny new era and already the lustre is long gone. The sponsorship deal simply served the debt – no new money was available for the programming. And it turns out no one had noticed the break clause in the contract, the one that allowed Selamat to walk away after twelve months. Which is what they're almost certain to do. Mun Sen are citing flat sales, but we all know that this must have always been their plan once its purpose had been served, the wider war won. Rumours abound that the panicked council are already in conversation with a sixth-form college about taking on the lease.

Our backs up, we head down Ashfield Street. Across the square we go, through the funny little park with its solitary swing, its always engorged rubbish bins. And then we're there. In front of it. Awestruck, as ever. And not just at its monumentality but also at its steadfast sameness. Because it's clear of cladding, the Larkspur. There's no sign of scaffolding, not a builder in sight.

Rather, an abundance of life. Washing hangs like celebratory bunting. Bike parts abound on balconies. Babies cry. Music blares. Business goes on, some of it shonky, most of it not. The Larkspur lives another day.

Turns out that its residents weren't to be so easily shifted. Sure, there's been a lot to leave but more have stayed to fight. Hunkered down for the long haul. Court orders are flying about. Writs have been issued. Funds set up. Eviction notices ignored. Pro bono lawyers brought on board. The MP's involved, but really it's been a resident-led insurgency.

Residents old and new. On a banner, fluttering from a window, we see the double P, the symbol of the Peterdown Partisans, who moved in en masse in one coordinated swoop. For them, the continuum is clear: debt strike runs into rent strike runs into general strike runs into *eternal* strike. Squatting is necessarily the start of it. The prerequisite to the definitive downing of tools. The one that lasts for ever.

We stride along the concourse and stare out across the city. There are still Wroth stickers everywhere. On bus stops. Lamp posts. The shutters of abandoned shops. But they're peeling, washing away with the rain. And there's not been any new tar for months. It's not so much that Wroth is over, more that it's mutated. Matured. Got much sillier. And at the same time more serious. The rage now is for monks' tonsures worn out in the open. Pranks. Provocations. Flying above the Larkspur concourse there's a huge flag adorned with the silhouette of a man skipping across the turf, scarves flowing out behind him, a great schlong dangling between his legs. All the talk now is of Angeldrom and how we might build it here.

Fizzing and full of it, we walk from the Larkspur up Rothbury Way, heads up, shoulders back, to the Rec. We hear it first. The chants. The cheers. The whoops and shouts. The laughter. And then we smell it. The singed sulphur of the flares. The yeasty belch of homebrew. It's only when we round the corner that we finally see it. Rothbury Recreation Ground with its recently erected stand. The new home for AFC United of Peterdown, currently thirteenth in the Northern Premier League, Division One South East. The eighth tier of English football.

We're late, as always, and the game is already going. The mood is antic, almost unhinged. There are maybe three thousand here. Twenty or so away fans, the rest home support. There are scarves everywhere, the classic colours of the town: green and white. Someone's on someone else's shoulders. Another person bangs a drum. Banners hang from every surface. Drifts of pink smoke float across the air. The mushy chip butty stand does brisk trade. Everyone is drinking.

We toss tenners into the donations pot and take a spot on the sidelines, leaning up against a railing. A perfect place for eavesdropping.

To our right stands a woman. She is London-beautiful, with a neck like a swan. Upper-bourgeois eyebrows. Interesting, technical clothes. An alien among the alienated.

She is talking to an extravagantly bearded older man. He is eating a giant garlic sausage, biting it at the end, like it's a banana. We keep our eyes on the game, but listen in.

'I've been thinking about your city of play,' she says.

'Yes,' he replies, his eyes on the pitch.

'Even if what you're talking about only half happens it's going to dramatically change the lived environment. All that retail. All those offices. We're talking millions of square feet that'll be standing empty.'

'Here, in the UK, last year alone, six thousand shops shut. It's not *going* to happen. It is happening right now.'

The swan leans against the railing. She has her back to the game, is sipping pensively at a bottle of pale ale.

'Has anyone started to seriously imagine what the city will look like after we stop working? How we'll inhabit it. What public space will look like.'

The man takes another bite of his garlic sausage, winces at another misplaced pass.

'Not that I know about it,' he says, distracted.

'We're talking about the opportunity to create a whole new architecture.'

'Of course,' he says.

She smiles self-deprecatingly.

'Because, you know, that sounds like a potentially interesting set of historical conditions.'

He laughs.

'Nobody ever thinks that they live in interesting times until—'

But he never gets to the end of this thought. On the pitch, the ball breaks to a man in green and he bundles it into the net. The stand erupts. Drinks are thrown in the air. Someone sets off a fire-cracker. Boys in keffiyeh scarves hurl themselves about, demented as punks in a mosh pit.

We stand at a distance, watching, until eventually a man emerges from the melee. He is a little older than most of the boys, and he staggers out, righting what's left of his hair. Holding on to his hand, her face flush with triumph, her eyes alive from the authentic danger, is a ten-year-old girl. They look at each other, the pair of them rumpled and rucked up, still smarting from the scrum. And then uncontrollably they start to hoot with laughter.

'I wish I'd taken you to the Chapel more,' he says, eventually. 'You would have loved it.'

'Was it as good as this?'

'Yes,' he says, 'But also, no.'

'Can we go in London?'

He looks away, a little forlorn, perhaps, at the mention of the capital.

'I looked on a map,' she continues, 'and there are loads of clubs that are sort of halfway between our house and your flat.'

'Yeah, there are. Dulwich Hamlet could be good.'

'I liked the look of Millwall.'

'Really?'

'You could practically walk there from your flat.'

'I know, but . . . '

'Their crest has a lion. It's going *rrrar.*'

Here, the girl bares her teeth and mimes the pose of a pouncing cat.

'Yeah, it does, doesn't it?'

'I think we should support them.'

For a second he looks apprehensive, but quickly he starts to smile.

'OK,' he says. 'I mean, it is a really cool lion. And that's as good a reason as any to support a club.'

'It can be our thing,' she says.

'Yeah,' he says, 'it can. It can be our thing.'

We watch them wander off, in search of a can of Coke, a bottle of beer. But we leave them to it.

Because while it's been their story, when it comes down to it, it's really been *ours* – we who have walked Peterdown from the beginning and will do so until the end. We're the ones with the all-important arc, the ones that went through the big change. The way we think. The way we feel. The way we *move*.

Our days of lumbering are over. These days, we scamper. Caper. Frolic. The events of the last few months have shifted something, got us going again. We can see now what we want and how we might get it.

We take a last look out over the pitch and set off. Irrepressible agitators for a joyous New Jerusalem, we cross the line, our hearts full of mischief, our eyes wide open all the time.

Acknowledgements

Writing a novel like this one that is so very long and covers so much ground requires a lot of research. I am indebted to the work of Alex Williams, Nick Srnicek, Peter Frase, Anna Minton, Lynsey Hanley, Rebecca Solnit, Marshall Berman, Slavoj Žižek, David Graeber, Eric Hobsbawm and George Rudé, Vivian Gornick, Alex Niven, Joe Kennedy, Iain Sinclair, Marc Augé, Patrick Keiller, Michael Sorkin, Jane Jacobs, Jonathan Meades, Douglas Murphy, John Grindrod, Barnaby Calder, John Boughton, Joanne Parker, Ian Nairn, Jedediah Purdy, Mark Gubbs, David Conn, Michael Calvin, Tom Bower, Arthur Hopcraft, David Goldblatt, Philippe Auclair, Barney Ronay, Jonathan Wilson and the many contributors to the *Guardian* Football Weekly Podcast. (Rodbortzoon only deigns to misquote thinkers from the top rank: Marx, Nietzsche, Guy Debord, Barry Glendenning.)

Particular thanks go to Owen Hatherley, who more than anyone else has made me rethink my relationship with the built environment, and the much-missed Mark Fisher whose writing on football's lost utopias and so much more besides has done so much to shape the way I understand the world.

I also want to thank my wonderful group of first readers: Paul Summers, Amy Grey, Will King, Hugh King, Camilla Cullen, Lily Jencks, Max Rushden, Matt Gibberd and Jonathan Stern. The book is better for all your input. As it is for the insights of my dear friend André Douglas who died in 2019 but is never far from my thoughts.

Thanks to my family and friends for all their amazing support, particularly my parents, Duncan and Lesley, and my children, Amelia and Gideon.

And thanks to the wonderful team of people behind the scenes who put the whole thing together, particularly Grace Vincent, Celeste Ward-Best, Steve Gove and Gesche Ipsen. Thanks to Nico Taylor and Jamie Keenan for making it look so nice. And a special nod must go to Martin Poyner for his brilliant drawing of Major Wroth.

Huge thanks to Luke Ingram, truly the best agent anyone could ever hope for. And Sarah Castleton, editor extraordinaire and great friend.

Finally, extra special thanks go to two very important people.

First, to my great friend, Tom Morton, who has been a constant source of inspiration and enlightenment throughout my adult life. It would be impossible to overstate how much he contributed to this book and how much I value his friendship.

And then of course there is Naomi, the better half of what has been a creative partnership in the fullest sense of the word. None of it would have been possible without you.